Praise for *The*

"We have the first great Americ[...]
Harrigan has given us a story[...]
grounding in history, fictional c[...]
help them blend perfectly with r[...]
Bowie, and yet with the latter presented as human beings, too, not glossy
caricatures. This is storytelling at its finest, and an opportunity to learn
and be royally entertained at the same time."

—Jeff Guinn, *Fort Worth Star-Tribune*

"Wonderfully well-written . . . Harrigan's historical Alamo is a version
for all readers, not merely historians and others fascinated by the heroics
of the story. It deserves a place among the best books ever written about
this legendary battle."

—Ken Wisneski, *Minneapolis Star-Tribune*

"Let's begin with the adjectives. Magnificent. Fabulous. Stephen Harrigan's robust novel about the siege and fall of San Antonio's fabled mission fortress merits every superlative. . . . This is a quest novel having
affinity with Charles Frazier's *Cold Mountain,* but with a character entirely its own. Masterful both as pulsating tale and provocative history,
The Gates of the Alamo is a fine book."

—Larry Swindell, *The Philadelphia Inquirer*

"A classic. *The Gates of the Alamo* tells the epic story of the legendary
battle from both the Mexican and American perspectives. Although wide
in scope it never loses its focus on the human characters. It belongs on the
shelf of anyone who cares about American history—or just appreciates a
riveting story."

—Margaret George, bestselling author of *The Autobiography of King
Henry VIII* and *Mary, Queen of Scotland and the Isles*

"*The Gates of the Alamo* races like a wild mustang . . . It's become faint
praise to call something a page-turner; it implies something with too little substance and skill to be literature. Okay, then call this one a page-
whirlwind, a vast and vicious tale told in unobtrusive style, and prepare to
be swept along."

—Marta Salij, *Detroit Free Press*

"In a sprawling narrative reminiscent of Larry McMurtry's tales of the
real west . . . It is the novel's successful, central strategy that none of
[the] three main characters begin with much investment in the struggle

for Texas independence, yet find themselves caught up in the fight. By focusing on these three, rather than on one of the zealots who instigated the movement, Harrigan captures how the Alamo transformed a scattered series of frontier conflicts into a legitimate revolution. . . . It is a tribute to Harrigan's careful blending of fiction and fact that in the end I was disappointed to learn that Terrell, Mary and Edmund never existed."

—Mark Bowden, bestselling author of *Black Hawk Down,* for *The Baltimore Sun*

"Riveting . . . The strength of Harrigan's extraordinarily authentic novel is its superior storytelling, no small accomplishment when a writer is looking down the hot barrel of history"

—Ron Franscell, *The Washington Post Book World*

"A crackerjack good read . . . A moving story of ordinary human beings caught up in extraordinary events."

—*Texas Observer*

"*The Gates of the Alamo* is a picaresque historical saga comparable to *Lonesome Dove* and *The Killer Angels.* This book is a new masterpiece in the literature of fact. . . . The characters, real and fictional, are enfolded so deftly in richly authentic detail that it's easy to forget this is a deeply imagined yarn. And that is the goal of the historical novelist, even with a myth-enshrouded event such as the Alamo: to blend fact and fancy until they are indiscernible."

—Ron Franscell, *The Christian Science Monitor*

"*The Gates of the Alamo* wildly succeeds in reinventing a tired American icon. Harrigan makes the Alamo worth remembering one more time."

—Dorman T. Shindler, *The Denver Post*

"Stephen Harrigan's gift to us is an artful, intelligent novel that makes the hard work of memory terrifically worthwhile. . . . Harrigan writes beautifully of the Texas landscape and beautifully of the failures of the human heart. While the amiable Crockett, the restless Travis, and the dissolute Bowie all play central roles in the taut, well-crafted narrative, it is Harrigan's focus on the travails of the Motts and Edmund McGowan that buoy the novel. His vivid portrayals of his minor characters . . . also elevate the novel to high status. Harrigan's knowledge of the military campaigns surrounding events of the Alamo is encyclopedic, but . . . he never allows the hastiness of events to impinge upon his devotion to storytelling."

—Alyson Hagy, *The Boston Sunday Globe*

PENGUIN BOOKS

THE GATES OF THE ALAMO

Stephen Harrigan, a longtime writer for *Texas Monthly* and many other magazines, is the author of the novels *Aransas* and *Jacob's Well*. His other books include *Water and Light: A Diver's Journey to a Coral Reef* and the essay collections *A Natural State* and *Comanche Midnight*. He lives in Austin, Texas.

THE GATES OF
THE ALAMO

A NOVEL BY

STEPHEN HARRIGAN

PENGUIN BOOKS

PENGUIN BOOKS

Penguin Group (USA) Inc., 375 Hudson Street,
New York, New York 10014, U.S.A.
Penguin Books Ltd, 80 Strand, London WC2R 0RL, England
Penguin Books Australia Ltd, 250 Camberwell Road,
Camberwell, Victoria 3124, Australia
Penguin Books Canada Ltd, 10 Alcorn Avenue,
Toronto, Ontario, Canada M4V 3B2
Penguin Books India (P) Ltd, 11 Community Centre,
Panchsheel Park, New Delhi – 110 017, India
Penguin Books (N.Z.) Ltd, Cnr Rosedale and Airborne Roads,
Albany, Auckland, New Zealand
Penguin Books (South Africa) (Pty) Ltd, 24 Sturdee Avenue,
Rosebank, Johannesburg 2196, South Africa

Penguin Books Ltd, Registered Offices:
80 Strand, London WC2R 0RL, England

First published in the United States of America by
Alfred A. Knopf, a member of Random House, Inc. 2000
Reprinted by arrangement with Random House, Inc.
Published in Penguin Books 2001
This edition published 2003

1 3 5 7 9 10 8 6 4 2

PUBLISHER'S NOTE
This is a work of fiction. Names, characters, places, and incidents either
are the product of the author's imagination or are used fictitiously, and any
resemblance to actual persons, living or dead, business establishments,
events, or locales is entirely coincidental.

THE LIBRARY OF CONGRESS HAS CATALOGED
THE HARDCOVER EDITION AS FOLLOWS:
The gates of the Alamo: a novel/by Stephen Harrigan.—1st ed.
p. cm.
ISBN 0-679-44717-2 (hc.)
ISBN 0 14 20.0429 4 (pbk.)
I. Alamo (San Antonio, Tex.)—Siege, 1836—Fiction. I. Title.
PS 3558.A626G38 2000
813'.54—dc21   99–33437

Printed in the United States of America
Set in Times Roman

In memory of
James E. McLaughlin
1918–1948

El Florón está en la mano, en la mano.
Vamos a ver los talleres de la vida.

(The flower is in the hand, in the hand.
Let us go see the occupations of life.)

—"El Florón," *a children's song of Mexico*

THE GATES OF
THE ALAMO

THE BATTLE OF FLOWERS

APRIL 21, 1911

TERRELL MOTT rode to the Alamo in a Buick touring car, creeping along behind a procession of horse-drawn victorias and tallyhos. Like the carriages, the big gasoline car had been covered with flowers, barely leaving space on the door panels for a sign identifying the white-whiskered relic who rode inside:

Mr. Mott
Messenger of the Alamo
Last Surviving Hero of San Jacinto
Former Mayor of San Antonio

He was so wondrously old. He waved stiffly at the crowds with his almost useless right arm—his shoulder socket still frozen from a fall a decade ago in a barbershop, his hand broken and fused into a claw ever since that night at the Cibolo Crossing when a Mexican musket ball had snapped the leg of his mare and he and the horse had hit the road with a velocity he still found unsettling to think about seventy-five years later. In the polished wooden dashboard of the Buick, in the gleaming brass of the passenger-side lamp, Terrell could see tenuous reflections of his ancient face, the bushy white chin beard cut square across the bottom like a paintbrush. He was perfectly toothless now, having surrendered the last of his venerable molars to a Mexican dentist in Laredito. His empty mouth, along with the consummate baldness of his head beneath his gray stockman's hat, filled him with a certain grim satisfaction.

Nature was almost finished with him. He had, at the age of ninety-one, no notion or need or anything further. For a few years after he had been saved from death at the Alamo, he had felt God's fierce, protective providence, but it had passed like a fever, and spiritual concerns had never troubled him again. Ponder it as he might, he could not see his approaching death as a mystery. It was just a shape on the horizon, a recognizable thing that had not yet come into focus.

"Old Sol has seen fit to shine after all," he announced politely to Parthenia and the driver, a young man from the Buick dealership whose already froggish face was comically accentuated by his bulging goggles.

"I suppose he didn't have the heart to disappoint all these people," the driver said, just as Terrell experienced a gentle swell of nausea. The streets of San Antonio were a sea of feathered women's hats, of spring boaters, and still the occasional sombrero. Terrell saw the crowd imperfectly through the distorting lenses of his spectacles and the cataracts that were slowly sealing his eyes into an opaque blindness. He waved his rigid arm in the vicinity of the onlookers and received negligent waves in return. The music of the mounted band up ahead reached him as a series of brassy tremors whose rhythm he could not locate, and the odor of flowers saturated the streets with a ripeness he could not distinguish from decay.

"Did you take your bitters?" Parthenia asked Terrell. "You look dyspeptic."

He patted his granddaughter's hand reassuringly and gave her a close-mouthed smile he had recently perfected. (He still had some vanity about his missing teeth and did not like to display his gums in an open grin.) A faint breeze rippled through his beard and helped take his mind off the reeking blossoms.

"I took my bitters," he said. "You worry about your carnival."

Parthenia was president this year of the Battle of Flowers Association. She had also taken over the role of Mistress of the Queen's Household when the original mistress, a dim but high-spirited young woman, had resigned after embarrassing the Order of the Alamo by getting drunk and appearing in public in harem pants. And Parthenia's daughter rode today in the lead carriage, seated on a throne garlanded by lilies of the valley, with attendants and pages at her feet and the Third Field Artillery clearing the way—Her Gracious Majesty Queen Julia, of the House of Toepperwein.

Terrell glimpsed Julia's carriage up ahead when the procession turned a sharp corner and began to follow the river downtown. He saw his great-granddaughter's gloved arm saluting the crowd, her chestnut hair flaring in the sun. He had been close to her when she was a child, an old man determined to show her all the latest marvels. They had sipped dolly vardens together and attended the kinetoscope parlors and gone boating on the swan boats at San Pedro Springs. But she was such a distant generation ahead of him he had already begun to feel spectral, a ghost who could not grasp her in his immaterial arms.

When Julia and her carriage disappeared behind a wall of stone buildings, he looked down into the green water, watching a hoary old snapping turtle paddle along beneath the surface. The ridges on the turtle's shell were worn almost flat with age, and its diamond-shaped head was as big as Terrell's fist.

"That one'll go forty pounds," he told Parthenia.

"What?"

"That snapper."

"Shall we stop and catch it, Opa?" She smiled at him. Her eyes were still bright and young, but below them her face was crosshatched with deepening lines. Terrell's granddaughter was forty-two, a widow. Her energetic German husband had been kicked in the face by an unshod horse

five years ago, and Parthenia had found him lying dead in
the yard with the front of his skull shattered and the skin of
his forehead sheared away by the sharp edge of the horse's
hoof. Grief had filled her with a vague, urgent resolve. The
Order of the Alamo—this "secret society" of prosperous
young men who met every year to anoint the most eligible
girls of San Antonio as duchesses and princesses and
queens—owed much to her cheerful efficiency.

Parthenia's duties struck Terrell as trivial. She was responsible for the color of the bunting for the coronation in
Beethoven Hall, the prepared outbursts for the Lord High
Chamberlain, the selection of music for the pages' gavotte,
the ordering of the engraved card cases as gifts for the
court attendants. But she brought a gravity to these tasks
that made him obscurely uneasy. There was something sinister, he thought, about the whole affair. The men of the Order of the Alamo, in, their secret balloting to decide which
girls would be elevated to royalty, reminded him of heathen
potentates reserving for themselves that year's crop of ripe
young virgins.

But something in Parthenia responded to all this hollow
medieval pageantry, this hearkening back to imaginary
gilded times. Terrell's own past was gilded that way in her
mind, as it was in the mind of Texas itself. She had written
a poem once—a society woman's poem; he'd seen dozens
just like it over the years—about the sacred walls of the
Alamo stained with martyrs' blood, about the ghostly tread
of the defenders' feet heard at midnight in the church.
About sacrifice, tryanny, undying selflessness. Last year
they had made a moving picture down at Hot Wells—*The
Immortal Alamo*—and Terrell guessed that when it was presented to the public it would be more of the same. A man
from the picture company who called himself a "scenarist"
had briefly consulted him about historical accuracy—"The
last time you saw Davy Crockett, what sort of hat was he
wearing?"—but Terrell knew that this was just a courtesy.

Accuracy did not matter to them, and increasingly, as his memory continued to dissolve like one of his nightly antacid tablets in its glass of water, it would matter less and less to him. For now, he clung to odd fragments of remembrance: the way the skin on his knuckles began to peel in the dry, cold air of that winter seventy-five years ago; the bats streaming out of the cracks and joints of the old mission during Santa Anna's first bombardment; how he had lost control of his bowels when the first of those shells exploded in the air above him, and how the scalp of the New Orleans Grey standing next to him had loosened in panic and the man's hair had fallen out and covered the shoulders of his linsey-woolsey shirt.

They passed a succession of saloons and restaurants— Beowulf Dreizehn, Schlagen & Vertragen's Bier Halle, Der Blaue Donner. The Germans called this part of the river the Little Rhein. Maybe one of these days they would change the name of the whole city to Little Berlin or Little Munich. Back in the forties, the first German colonists had lost no time in transforming Terrell's indolent little river village, throwing up their stone edifices, organizing themselves into singing clubs and gymnastic societies, sending their children to waltzing lessons conducted by stern old baton-waving professors. Terrell's late wife, Hannah—dead forty years—had been the daughter of a colonist who had come to Texas with Prince Solms. Hannah's father and her four brothers had industriously befriended Terrell, enrolling him in the new schuetzen verein in Alamo Heights, with its fancy clubhouse and shooting range. They had been determined to train him to shoot left-handed, since his ruined right hand had been unable to hold a gun since 1836. Hannah's brother Augustus was convinced it could be done because he himself was utterly ambidextrous. Using either hand, he could shoot the ashes off a cigar held in the mouth of one of his optimistic brothers at a distance of thirty feet.

But Terrell never learned to shoot with his left hand with any degree of accuracy. Perhaps he had steeped too long in Mexican fatalism to make himself believe the attempt could be truly worthwhile. And San Antonio de Béxar—"Bear," they had called it in the old days—would never be Little Berlin or any such place to him. It would always be a Mexican city, in its heart and his. As mayor, he had been perhaps overly tolerant of cockfights and monte games and the endless feast days that were celebrated with fandangos and rockets and games of gallo corriendo, in which young men thundered dangerously through the streets on horseback grappling for possession of a live rooster. He liked the feel of San Antonio the morning after a feast day, the clinging smells of candle wax and trampled flower blossoms and gunpowder from the previous night's fireworks, the tamale shucks as thick as fallen leaves on the streets, the vendedores quietly setting up their atole stands, their displays of feather work and ornamental birdcages and silver jewelry from Guanajuato.

"Do you remember that old candyman we used to visit when you were a girl?" Terrell asked Parthenia now as they headed toward the plaza.

"Of course I do, Opa," she said.

"He was always standing on this corner right here, swatting the flies off his tray with a sow's tail. He was fond of you because you liked those candied pumpkins that only Mexican children would eat."

"Calabazate," Parthenia remembered, looking amused and revolted. "I'm sure if I tried to eat one now I would have to borrow your stomach bitters."

He waved at the chili queens on Military Plaza. They all knew him. Until a few years ago he had eaten in the plaza three or four nights a week, walking there from his home in King William in the humid summer twilight, taking a seat at the long wooden tables just like any other citizen. But his legs and his stomach had begun to give out at about the same time. His knees were elastic and undependable now, and spicy food turned his insides into a gastric cauldron. One by one, his routines had been taken away: no more dining with the chili queens, no more tarpon fishing in Aransas, no more aimless strolling through the streets of old Bear. He spent his days now in his roomy cow-horn chair, trying to follow the jumping print in the newspaper.

The automobile travelled east on Commerce Street at hardly more than a lurching idle, following the balky horse-drawn conveyances up ahead. Terrell watched Parthenia as her eyes swept up and down the parade route. She was no longer a young woman, but she still had never quite over-come her girl's nervousness that something, somewhere, was happening without her. This high-strung alertness was a trait he had bequeathed her. They were both jumpy and impatient. Even now, with his aged heart slowed to the rhythm of an oyster, he still felt something in him racing, searching.

He heard a noise from the crowd up ahead—a collective gasp with an amused undercurrent. At the sound of it, Parthenia leapt to her feet in the open car and covered her mouth with her hand for a second.

But Terrell, still seated, could see the catastrophe up ahead as well as she could. The carriage conveying the Duchess of Bluebonnets had overturned while negotiating a sharp left turn. The duchess was lying on her back in a nest of chiffon while several young men—dukes who had sprung gallantly to her aid from the other floats—surveyed her for broken bones. The frightened horses were still drag-ging the capsized carriage down the street, scraping off its veneer of bluebonnets and sowing confusion throughout the whole parade.

"Dear God in heaven," Parthenia blasphemed, her eyes sparkling. "See that my grandfather doesn't escape," she said to the driver, and then climbed out of the Buick and strode toward the scene of the wreck, a slender, resolute

woman in a great flowered hat. Terrell watched her shoo
away the self-important young men who were advising the
supine duchess. Parthenia simply drew the devastated girl
to her feet, straightened out her dress, and spoke to her in a
brisk, casual fashion, as if nothing out of the ordinary had
happened. She then began directing, with simple efficiency,
the righting of the carriage.

"Mrs. Toepperwein seems to have things well in hand,"
the driver said.

"She loves a crisis," Terrell proudly agreed. "She'll have
this parade under way again in a whistle."

He sat back in his seat, feeling an elderly man's satisfying weariness—his body exhausted but his mind suddenly
as keen and taut as a fiddle string. He thought, with dreamlike clarity, about tarpon milling in the warm water of the
coastal bays, the way they leapt clear of the surface as he
fought them, the sun flashing on those enormous scales that
reminded him of a knight's plated armor. And spoonbills in
the sky overhead, their pink feathers as lush and ripe as
some exotic fruit. He wanted one more trip to the coast before he died.

"What's your favorite eating fish?" Terrell asked the driver.

"Well, sir," he said, turning in his seat and pushing his
goggles up onto his sweaty brow, "I'd have to say catfish."

"Salt water, I mean."

"Salt water? Flounder, I guess."

"Redfish," Terrell said. "Or king mackerel, cooked over
mesquite wood."

"Well, I can't improve on that," the young man said. Now
that the parade was going nowhere, the crowds along the
street were no longer waving or applauding. They just stood
about uncertainly, regarding Terrell and the other fixtures of
the procession with the kind of embarrassment reserved for
those who have been on exhibit for too long.

"A slow-burning mesquite fire," Terrell went on. They

had unhitched the team from the bluebonnet carriage, and now a dozen dukes and policemen were trying to right it.

"One thing I wanted to ask you, sir, if you don't mind," the driver ventured, after a moment of fretful concentration.

"You bet," Terrell said.

"Were you there when Colonel Travis drew that line in the dirt with his sword?"

"Travis never did draw any line," he answered. "That's for your private information."

"Well, I thought he drew it." The young man looked sadly disillusioned. "I thought he gave y'all a choice to leave or to stay and fight to the death."

"Well, I know what I'd choose, don't you?"

The driver pondered this in silence, the sweat running down the pouches of his cheeks. Terrell regarded him as a boy but realized he was probably in his late twenties, older than Travis was when he led them into the inferno.

They could not see the Alamo from here, though it was only a block or so away. The sprawling, ravaged old mission had been reduced over the years to only a scrap of itself, only a portion of the convent remaining, and the grim little church that the Army had patched up in the fifties for use as a warehouse. The city had grown up around the site, the buildings of downtown dwarfing it and cutting it off from view. The streets of San Antonio were haphazard and meandering. They created a maze that even Terrell Mott, the former mayor, had not always been able to navigate with certainty. And at the heart of the maze, like some charged object in a fairy tale, resided the Alamo.

On this stretch of Commerce Street where they were now stalled, just south and east of the unseen Alamo, there had once been a promenade lined with cottonwoods. Terrell had courted Hannah here, hiding his warped hand in the pocket of his coat, the girl beside him demandingly curious in spite of her slim command of English. "Dass iss snow?"

she had exclaimed in perplexity as the white cottonwood down drifted through the Alameda in the summer stillness.

"This was where they burned the bodies," Terrell said now to the driver.

"Sir?"

"Right here was where they burned the bodies. They put them in two big piles. A layer of bodies, then a layer of wood, then a layer of some kind of grease—tallow, I think. Then another layer of bodies and wood on up like that till it was ten feet high."

"You saw that?"

"Hell, no. If I'd stayed around long enough to see that, I would have been in the fire myself. I heard about it, though."

The fire had burned for two days and nights, a smoldering, blackened stew. Since there was no more space in the campo santo, Santa Anna's dead soldados lay in rows until a place could be found for them to be buried. The corpses swelled up like balloons, and for days the sky was black with buzzards. The stench of those dead Mexican soldiers was oppressive, but it was nothing, said the Bexareños, like the smell of basting flesh and tallow from the great pyres in the Alameda.

At his age Terrell could now see fire as just another neutral natural force. The incineration of a dead organism held no more horror or mystery for him than the evaporation of water or the slow ripening of a cactus fruit. But when he had first heard about the burning of his friends at the Alamo his mind could not let it go. For a decade or more the image had flared in his imagination like a fever. He saw their faces staring out at him open-eyed from the tangle of fuel branches that enclosed them like a bower. He saw their side-whiskers erupting in flame, their eyes melting in their heads. He saw the final cold slurry of ash and bone and rendered fat.

Sitting in the car, he tried to reclaim the wonder and horror of the image that had once haunted him so, but his calloused old imagination would not do the job for him. Instead, he thought again of that buoyant snapping turtle in the river, that school of tarpon in the warm waters of Aransas Bay. For a quarter of an hour more, while Parthenia saw to the salvation of the parade, while the young driver pondered in silence the thought of his ancestral heroes burning in that greasy fire, Terrell dreamed of himself as a hulking, contented beast, paddling about just below the surface of a placid sea, the sun on his back as he gently lifted his head for a breath of moist Gulf air.

"I believe that poor girl's elbow is broken," Parthenia said when at last she climbed back into the car. "She won't think of dropping out, though; she says she'll wave with her other hand."

"Tough as a nut," Terrell said absently. The parade was moving once more, though the long delay had taken the spirit out of the thing. The duchesses gamely resumed waving to the indifferent crowd, and the band started up again, playing "Come to the Bower" now, that inconsequential ditty from long ago that had fortified Terrell and the rest of the Texian army as they marched across the plain of San Jacinto with terror and vengeance in their hearts.

To his surprise, Terrell now heard himself croaking out in song. Seventy-five years to the day, and he still remembered the words:

Will you come to the bow'r I have shaded for you?
Our bed shall be roses all spangled with dew.
There under the bow'r on roses you'll lie
With a blush on your cheek but a smile in your eye.

"It's funny," Parthenia said, delighted at her grandfather's sudden animation. "The words are really very suggestive. It's not the song I would have picked to march into battle."

"Nobody really picked it, as I recall," Terrell answered.

"Houston only had a drummer and a few fifers, and none of them could play worth spit. They had to find a song they all knew."

"Well, you're in fine voice, Opa."

"A blush on your cheek but a smile in your eye," he repeated, this time in a distracted speaking voice, as the parade turned onto Alamo Street and headed toward the plaza.

And there was the old church of the Alamo, standing there in its strange solemn primacy, the holiest spot in all Texas. Most of the rest of the mission had been gone for many decades, the walls torn down to make room for meat markets and saloons. The site of the north wall, the weak point they had all fretted about so much, and that Travis had been killed trying to defend, was now occupied by a post office building. Except for the church, the only building that remained was the old convent, and the Catholic Church had sold that more than thirty years ago to a Frenchman named Grenet, who had turned it into a grocery store and famous monstrosity. Grenet had covered the austere lime-stone facade of the convent with wooden arcades and balconies, and had crowned its summit with turrets from which fake cannon protruded. The Grenet store was itself gone now, and so was the liquor store that had replaced it, but some of the "improvements" still remained, so that the venerable old convent continued to be an eyesore. Some of Parthenia's friends wanted to tear it down altogether, in order to clear a reverent space in which to showcase the church, which they claimed was the "real" Alamo.

It was an argument that Terrell stayed out of. As far as he was concerned, the "real" Alamo resided only in his memory. The church itself, which the Army had crowned with a curving parapet that reminded Terrell of the headboard of a bed, bore no real resemblance anymore to the broken, roofless, weedy ruin of the siege. They could tear it down too, as far as he was concerned. Everything passes from the earth, why not the sacred Alamo?

Remember the Alamo! Ah, but there was no one left but him to remember it, and his mind was already crowded with thoughts of silvery tarpon.

The plaza in front of the Alamo was paved now, but back when Terrell was mayor it had been a muddy expanse, filled with chugholes and prone to floods. He remembered the sight of horses trapped up to their bellies in the mud, thrashing in panic as if they were being swallowed by quicksand. Once a tearful German schoolteacher had appeared at the city council meeting to report that his beloved St. Bernard dog had been swept away by fast water in front of the Alamo and washed into the river.

And even those days, only the eighties, were impossibly long ago. He settled back into his seat, ready to reflect upon the passage of time, wanting it to be again the tormenting mystery it had been in his youth. But he could not move himself to agitation. He was just an old man contentedly divesting himself, minute by minute, of life and awareness. He would pass out of this world on a warm Gulf tide, heading out from the shallow bays into the blue offshore waters.

Then he saw something that filled him with terror. In front of the Menger Hotel, a man stood with chillingly correct posture, his hands at his sides, his feet evenly spaced. He wore a straw hat, a trim mustache, and a suit of clothes made from the skin of a jaguar. The man was short, with a sharp face. His mouth was pulled back in a half-smile, and he looked out over the parade with the glassy eyes of a snake.

Terrell's eyes jerked away from this apparition as if from the sight of something obscene. He didn't know why. But all at once his peaceful reveries of death had been blasted out of his mind, and his body seemed to fill up with a strange, intimate horror. Parthenia wiped the sudden sweat off his brow with a handkerchief, and he felt prickles of fright rising on the skin of his bald head.

"What is the matter?" his granddaughter asked anxiously.

"Nothing," he said. "The heat, maybe. But I'm fine now."

She watched him with intensity. Terrell, for his part, kept his eyes forward, away from the man in the jaguar suit and toward the Alamo, where the parade was coming to an end. The various dignitaries were filing onto the reviewing stand, and behind them the duchesses' carriages wheeled into position for the mock battle.

"I can have the driver take you home, Opa," Parthenia was saying as their car approached the reviewing stand.

"It was just a little spell," Terrell told her.

"What kind of spell?"

A spell of fear, he wanted to say. Once when he was a boy he had snuck off to a Karankawa mitote. The Kronks had given him yaupon tea to drink, so hot it scalded his throat, and he had watched them dancing all through the humid night. It was summer, and their bodies were coated with rank alligator grease to repel mosquitoes. The grease made them glisten like fairies in the firelight. The Kronks' songs were high-pitched and feverishly redundant, and they had a gnawing insistence that he began to believe was hostile. He caught the Indians' manic eyes, boring into him, judging him. The tea did something strange to his mind. He imagined his heart lying within his chest like a flat rock, then felt it lift and fall slightly as a rattlesnake stirred beneath it, trying to escape. But it was not just one snake, it was a whole writhing den, trapped in the center of his body, pushing against the rock.

The man in the jaguar suit had suddenly reacquainted him with that sort of odious alarm. But it was a boy's hysterical fear; why was he feeling it now, when he was an old man almost shorn of consciousness?

"Just an ordinary sinking spell," he explained to Parthenia. "I bet when you get to be a thousand years old, you'll have one too every now and then."

She said nothing, but kept regarding him with silent scrutiny as their car stopped in front of the reviewing stand and the driver got out and helped them down. With Parthenia at his arm, Terrell ambled stiffly to his seat, feeling the papery skin of his thin legs brushing against the fabric of his pants. His feet felt wobbly in his boots and he was desperately afraid of a fall, but his granddaughter guided him briskly to safety as a group of schoolchildren, bearing garlands of flowers in their tiny hands, filed out in front of the Alamo and began to sing:

> *We lay the crown of memory*
> *Upon the place of rest,*
> *Where noble heroes lie asleep*
> *Within earth's icy breast . . .*

Settled into his seat, shaded by Parthenia's broad feathered hat, Terrell allowed his attention to come and go. A woman in a hat overflowing with artificial flowers—"Can you imagine?" Parthenia whispered indignantly in his ear, "wearing artificial flowers to the Battle of Flowers parade?"—went on for quite some time in the usual vein: "This altar consecrated by Anglo-Saxon blood to the God of Liberty, where brave men chose glorious death rather than surrender to the tyranny of a despot."

And then the governor gave his own sober address, and bade Terrell stand so that the people could have a look at this curiosity—the lingering human vestige who had known Travis and Crockett and Bowie, who had stood within the walls of the Alamo during the siege; who had helped win Texas her freedom on the storied plain of San Jacinto. He stood and squinted into the midmorning sun hovering above the parapet of the Alamo. He waved yet again, and saw Julia and the flowery duchesses applauding him proudly from their carriages.

It was Queen Julia, a few moments later, who commanded that the battle begin, and then the duchesses' carriages began to circle in front of the Alamo as the girls pelted each other with broadsides of flower blossoms. For a long moment the facade of the Alamo was obscured by a continuous flurry of flowers, the blossoms wafting to the ground like heavy flakes of snow. The duchesses in their carriages were giddy. The governor smiled indulgently, and the onlookers in the streets cheered the battle on. Terrell could not get over the softness and silence with which the flowers drifted to the pavement in front of the Alamo. The old church, he realized for the first time, looked like a tormented face, with its gaping mouth of a doorway and the shaded niches above, which had once held statues of saints, now as dark and empty as the eye sockets of a skull. The face looked on as the flowers fell, onto ground that had once been covered with thick pools of black blood, the dead lying in stupefied silence with their vitals coiling out of their bodies, steaming with warmth in the cold air of that March morning. All it had taken was one terrible hour.

Through the falling petals he saw the man in the jaguar-skin suit, standing in front of the Alamo sweeping the crowd with his vacant eyes and his strange rictus of a smile. His gaze settled on Terrell, and then Terrell remembered what his own eyes had long ago confirmed, that death was not a gentle melding, not an easy passage from shallow to deep water, but a moment of savage oblivion. You would scream for the loss of your self, your awareness, as you would scream if a cannonball ripped off your arm.

The man took a step toward him, and Terrell's body made a spastic defense of itself, jerking like a hermit crab withdrawing into its shell. The movement caused him to tumble backward onto the benches of the reviewing stand. Falling was the thing he feared most, and here it was, as

Parthenia screamed, as the skin of his forehead compressed and expanded in alarm. From the corner of his eye, as he was falling, he saw Julia's horrified face, visible through a rain of blossoms. As he landed on his back, he felt a prolonged sting as the dry skin behind his ear scraped against a metal bench support, and then his thin scapular bones came crashing onto the wood. He took a few rapid, disbelieving breaths, and then managed to calm himself a bit. Whatever would come now, at least the falling itself was over.

"I'm all right," he said to Parthenia. "Couldn't be better." But he was in no hurry to begin the laborious process of standing up, in no hurry to discover whether in fact he would ever stand on his own two feet again. Lying there sprawled on the reviewing stand, with anxious faces peering down at him, he did not feel conspicuous at all. He put the man in the jaguar suit out of his mind and concentrated on the thick smell of commingled flowers. He thought he would just stay here awhile, like a torpid old dog, like a dreamy boy lying on a spring hillside, and remember what needed remembering, and bid the rest good-bye.

PART ONE

CHAPTER ONE

✳

IN THE EARLY spring of 1835 an American botanist
named Edmund McGowan travelled southeast from Béxar
on the La Bahía road, following the course of the San
Antonio River as it made its unhurried way through the
oak mottes and prairies of Mexican Texas. He rode a big-
headed mustang mare named Cabezon and led an elegant
henny mule loaded down with his scant baggage. Professor,
a quizzical-looking mongrel, scouted ahead of the little
caravan, sniffing out the road when it grew obscure and
threatened to disappear from sight.

Edmund McGowan was forty-four years of age that
spring, very much the confident, solitary man he aspired to
be. He was of medium height but heavy-boned, his hands
blunted and scarred by decades of hostile weather and various misadventures involving thorns and briars, snakebite,
and the claws of a jaguarundi cat. His features were pleasingly bland, but there was a keenness and luminosity in his
eyes. He possessed all his teeth but one, and most of his
hair as well, though his side-whiskers had lately broken out
in polecat streaks of gray. He wore a once-fine hat of brown
felt, a frock coat, and pantaloons that he protected from the
brush with leather botas that covered his legs from his
knees to his brogans. His saddle, bit, and round wooden
stirrups were Spanish, and like a vaquero he carried a loop
of rope on the pommel. It was his ambition to use the rope
to lasso a turkey.

Though the weather was mild, winter still lingered
across the landscape. The great live oaks, always in leaf,

formed intermittent glades along the road, but the limbs of
the hardwoods lining the river were bare, and few wildflowers had yet emerged from the brittle grass. No matter.
Edmund had packed a modest amount of drying paper, his
press, magnifying glass, a dozen vascula, and a few essential books like Drummond's *Musci Americani* and Nuttall's
Genera, but this was not a trip for botanizing. He was on
his way to pay a visit to his employer, the government of
Mexico, or at any rate the entity that was currently being
promoted as the government. No doubt by the time he arrived in the City of Mexico, another junta would have
arisen and taken its place. As far as he knew, his commission—to provide an ongoing botanical survey of the sub-
province of Texas—was still in effect, though in the last
year his payment vouchers had not been honored in Béxar
when he presented them at the comandante's office on the
Plaza de Armas.

He had no great hopes for this mission to the City of
Mexico; indeed, he feared that his continued employment
had less to do with a keen governmental interest in undescribed flora than with bureaucratic oversight. After the
completion of the Boundary Survey of 1828, he had expected his services to be courteously terminated, and yet
year after year, as Mexico suffered from an endless pageant
of civil insurrection and foreign intrigue, his quaint little
job on its far frontier had remained secure. But he had come
to depend on those 2,400 pesos a year. Without them, he
would soon be reduced to selling seeds to Kew Gardens, or
to hawking ferns to the London gentry like some common
Botany Ben. He considered himself to be a scientist, not a
scavenger and purveyor of ornamental plants. His little
house in La Villita overflowed with books and notes, with
dried specimens and drawings and Wardian boxes filled
with carefully nurtured living plants—all of the materials
that were waiting to be compacted into his *Flora Texana.*
He saw the *Flora* as a great, solid book as thick and incon-

trovertible as the Bible, a book that would justify a life of cruel endurance. ("What labor is more severe," he had been gratified to read in Linnaeus, "what science more wearisome, than botany?") But now, because no doubt of some fastidious clerk in a government palace, his work was in jeopardy. The only hope he had of restoring his commission was to present himself and make his case to whichever bureaucrat might listen.

The road out of Béxar led past a series of crumbling, desanctified missions, their old irrigation ditches clogged with leaves and their apartments inhabited by ragged Indian laborers who huddled within the broken walls at night in fear of Comanche raids. The Spanish friars had left behind mouldering aqueducts as well, and here and there Edmund spotted the crosses they had carved in the trees a century ago to mark the route of the Camino Real. Age had blurred and weathered the crosses, but at the place where the La Bahía road took leave of the old imperial highway the markers were fresh—a series of pointing hands sharply chiseled into the bark of the live oaks.

He followed the hands urging him southeast, toward the Gulf of Mexico a hundred and fifty miles distant. After a while the hands disappeared and the road itself grew faint, as if deferring to the greater authority of the river. Edmund retained an animal alertness as he rode along, but a part of his mind was lulled into hypnotic contentment. He watched kingfishers and herons sweeping along the bright river, the hawks perched with brooding detachment in the bare trees. He sighted the terrain ahead through the markers of Cabezon's bristly ears, and found himself entranced by the powerful sweep of her neck, the cascading hair of her cinnamon mane. He had bought the mare a year ago from a Lipan who had captured her in the Wild Horse Desert. The creasing scar still showed, a deep furrow in her neck that marked where the mustanger had expertly disabled her by tickling her spinal column with a rifle ball. Edmund rubbed the furrow idly now with his thumb, feeling the taut, vigilant muscle in which it was buried. Cabezon's scar saddened him whenever he considered it. It was the mark of her servitude, the sign that he would always be her master and never, as he strangely craved to be, her comrade.

Her left eye was bluish and weak, and her left ear in compensation was always nervously erect. The fact that she was nearly blind on that side made Edmund a bit uneasy in a country known for Comanches and dangerous brigands from the States. He imagined all sorts of hazards skulking in the field of her sightlessness. It would have made more sense to ride Snorter, the little mule, who had two good eyes and, it pained Edmund to realize, a finer mind than Cabezon. But, perhaps even more than most norteamericanos, he required the scale and grandeur of a horse. It was his habit to be aware of the figure he presented to the world.

Cabezon was prone to dainty, sputtering farts, and for a moment that's what he thought he was listening to. But then he realized the sounds came from above, from far away in the bright vault of the sky. It was a guttural, whirring chorus, a primeval sound that made his skin tingle. Uncertain, he slipped the leather hammer stall off the frizzen of his shotgun and waited to learn more. Professor, hearing the sound as well, came running back and looked up to Edmund for an answer.

The cries grew louder, and then he finally caught sight of the birds—hundreds and hundreds of lush gray cranes flying north, flying with such conservative grace that each wingbeat seemed a product of rigorous deliberation. They spanned the sky almost from horizon to horizon, and the whole procession moved with the quiet, ordained manner in which events unfold in a dream.

Professor woofed at the great birds as their chattering voices rained down upon the earth. Then, in confusion, he began to howl, his usual response to anything beyond his knowing.

The cranes were beyond Edmund's knowing too—he felt it acutely—but he watched their cloudlike passage in silence. The spectacle made him light-headed, but after the birds were gone the sensation lingered—a prickly, empty feeling in the top of his cranium. He feared that what he was experiencing was not the rhapsody of nature but an onset of the ague. After a few more miles, subtle pains began to seep up out of his joints, and he noticed with apprehension that his energy and good spirits were starting to trickle away.

In an hour or so Professor came running back again on his short legs, his eyes sparkling with new information about the road ahead. Edmund peered out over the grasslands and saw, a half-mile distant, the dark blue coats of presidial cavalry travelling toward him in a thin cloud of dust.

Professor growled at the horsemen as they approached, and danced about in indignation at Cabezon's feet.

"Shush," Edmund said distractedly, more a suggestion than a command. The dog, in his usual manner, seemed to think about it before complying, and he kept up a low, suspicious growl as the patrol rode up to greet them.

"Don Edmundo, it's good to meet you."

"Cómo está, Teniente," Edmund said, smiling. The lieutenant's name was Lacho Gutiérrez. He was a young man with one good eye and one leaky socket, whom Edmund had often seen promenading with his wife and three young children on the plaza in Béxar. He had lost the eye fighting the Tonkawas.

"You saw the birds?" Lieutenant Gutiérrez asked, showing off his English for the weary lancers behind him. "They were grullas, I think. I am sorry to have forgotten the English word."

"Cranes."

"Ah, yes. Cranes. Are you going all the way to La Bahía?"

"Más lejos," he answered, forgetting for a moment that they were speaking in English. "All the way to El Copano,

where I board a supply ship for Vera Cruz, and then on to
the City of Mexico."

The lieutenant cocked the eyebrow over his good eye,
impressed with the magnitude of this journey. He himself,
Edmund suspected, had never been out of the Provincias
Internas, and the capital of his country was as fabled and
hopelessly remote a place as it might have seemed to Cortés three hundred years before.

"How is the road ahead?" Edmund asked.

"Safe enough for a group of men, but I do not like to see
you travelling alone, Don Edmundo. Four days ago Comanches attacked a village on Las Animas Creek and killed
six people and stole a child."

"Which Comanches?"

"Those with the bald-headed chief. Bull Pizzle."

"I know Bull Pizzle."

"Ask him not to kill you, then," Gutiérrez said, smiling.
"And tell him we're looking for him."

Edmund bowed and reined Cabezon to the side of the
road to make room for the patrol to pass. The lancers' uniforms were faded, patched, and covered with dust, but their
horses and tack were well cared for and the men all pride-
fully wore a white crossbelt that identified them as belonging to the flying company of Alamo de Parras. The company
was garrisoned in the sprawling old Valero mission—better
known as the Alamo—that commanded a low rise several
hundred yards away from Edmund's house. The Alamo was
as decrepit as all the other missions, but it was the closest
thing Béxar had to a real fort.

"You look pale, Don Edmundo," Gutiérrez whispered,
with innate discretion, when the last of the presidials had
ridden by. "Are you well?"

"Well enough for the present, and no doubt better tomorrow."

"You are welcome to ride with us back to Béxar," the
lieutenant said, "and start your journey on a better day."

"Thank you, Teniente, but the day is good enough."

"As you wish. We have four men stationed on the Cibolo. It would be wise to stay there tonight rather than in the open. The Comanches know where all the usual parajes are. They might come up to you while you are camping and steal your horse and mule and scalp you and your dog."

Edmund smiled courteously at what he thought was a witticism, but the lieutenant's face was set.

"I have seen it, señor. A scalped dog."

They rode off with their lance points gleaming, their escopetas jouncing on their carbine sockets. The men of Alamo de Parras were seasoned frontier fighters, and Edmund watched them go with a vague unease, wondering to what use those lances and muskets would be put in the months ahead. Nothing was certain in Texas, except that some ugly event was brewing. Edmund expected war within the year, though he could not predict the nature of this war or who exactly its protagonists would be. Perhaps the radicals among the American colonists would be the ones to spark it. They were restless and aggrieved, always meeting in conventions and forming committees of safety, petitioning the distant Mexican government to make Texas a separate state, to grant it special concessions on slavery, on taxes, on tariffs—all the while harboring in their hearts the conviction that Texas should not belong to Mexico at all. The colonists had all sworn loyalty to Mexico and, sometimes with winks of disdain, had allowed themselves to be baptized as Catholics, as the colonization laws required. But Edmund knew that Mexico had come to perceive his countrymen as a nightmarishly avid race, a race of parasite worms that would eventually eat out the heart of the shaky republic.

But if a revolt came, he suspected it would not be limited to Texas. It might be a massive civil war in which the inhabitants of Texas, both Anglo and Mexican, would join with the citizens of Zacatecas and Coahuila and Yucatán to overthrow President Santa Anna and replace him with another just like himself, another tyrant stalking his way to power in the guise of a republican reformer.

Either way, the war would be one more wave in a forever turbulent sea. Seven years before, travelling with the Boundary Commission on the Medina River, Edmund had stopped to sketch a frostweed flower and had noticed a whitened oval buried at the base of the plant. It was a skull, and when he stood up and inspected the nearby ground he discovered he had come upon an ossuary, a field of bleached human bones—skulls and jawbones with loose, rattling teeth, scattered vertebrae, splintered femurs, and pelvic cradles. The bones marked the spot where another wave had passed back in 1813, when an alliance of Mexican and American adventurers had come charging into Texas, determined to pry it loose from Spain. Eight hundred of them had died here, their bodies left for the wolves.

He rode another five miles, his mind slowly twisting itself in thought, reaching for some connection between the scattered bones and the gray cranes spanning the sky. He felt an increasingly urgent need to find this linkage, to bind these images into a reassuring whole. But the world would not come together; it kept splintering apart. Professor looked up at him with deep concern.

"As I suspected," the dog said. "You have the ague."

Edmund could feel the warmth of the fever spreading through him.

"Have you seen these before?" Professor asked, standing in a sudden field of yellow flowers—small star-shaped flowers, notched at the tips, the blossoms completely evolved though it was still only March. "One of the *Compositae,* of course, though previously undescribed."

Edmund peered at the flowers with fleeting interest. His morale was sinking, and a glimmer of rational thought told him he was in danger. He remembered his last attack of the ague, several years ago, as an almost pleasant experience.

He had been collecting on the San Marcos River when he fell ill near the homestead of a family named Kenner. Hugh Kenner had claimed not to be a doctor—at least not anymore; like practically every other American in Texas he was in flight from an obscurely troubled past—but he had doctored Edmund all the same, binding him in tight bandages like a mummy to keep the shakes from rattling him to death, and then dosing him with Peruvian bark until the fever had gone off. Because of his skill, both the fever and the chills had been mild, and Edmund and Kenner had carried on a three-day conversation touching on everything from the treatment of hydrocephalic infants to their mutual distaste for the poetry of Byron, whose martyrdom in Greece had further annoyed them both.

But now Edmund had no Peruvian bark, and the fever was steadily enveloping him. In his delirium, Cabezon's ears assumed vast importance. He imagined that the ears, with their ceaseless twitching, were trying to communicate with him, the way Indians sometimes spoke in signs. It bothered him greatly that he could not decipher the message.

"What is she saying?" he asked Professor, possibly out loud.

But the dog had resumed being a dog and had no opinion.

Edmund McGowan had sought out a life of solitude and privation. It was a way of holding himself apart from other men. By nature, he was more gregarious, more tempted by comforts of all sorts than he was willing to admit. But he had always regarded these normal human yearnings as a deep threat, something that would pull him down into the undifferentiated ranks of humanity. He wanted greatness, and he wanted the cost of greatness.

Gruesome images out of that life of endurance, or out of his rampaging imagination, rose up now like a series of tableaux. He saw a fire in the Great Dismal Swamp, pine-tops exploding in flames, panicked shinglegetters falling through the crust of the earth into pits of flaming peat; a man impaled on a cypress knee; a crucified bear; two boys skinning a rabbit alive, just to watch it twitch. With unnatural precision he remembered almost starving to death in the Arkansas wilderness, and how finally he and the rest of his party had saved themselves by eating the dried mammal specimens meant for the Zoological Society of London.

The recent death of David Douglas haunted him as well. The renowned botanist had fallen into a cattle trap in the Sandwich Islands. A wild bull was already in the pit, and in its fright and rage it had gored and trampled the discoverer of *Pseudotsuga taxifolia* into a bloody paste. In Edmund's feverish meditations, it seemed natural that the discovery of a flower could lead to death by a maddened bull, as if the search for knowledge were an unforgivable provocation of nature.

He took a small diary out of his waistcoat pocket—"The Ladies' and Gentlemen's Pocket Souvenir for 1835"—and sketched the various positions of Cabezon's ears, so that he might decode the message at his leisure when he felt better and less frightened. And yet he was sure the message was a warning of some kind, apprising him of some immediate danger. He studied the ears with growing intensity, and slowly felt his mind and the mind of the horse beginning to merge in silent communication.

But then it broke off, and he was alone again in his human bubble.

"Help me," he whispered, forgetting his pride. The road was growing dark. A nightjar sliced across his field of vision like a knife stroke. He could feel the chill of evening in his bones at the same time he felt the raging heat of the fever.

Cabezon stopped without consulting him, pulled the reins out of his hands and began feeding on the wild grass that had grown up around the ruins of an old mission rancho. He knew this place: Las Cabras. The goats that gave the rancho its name were long gone, gone with the old Spanish dream of a civilized Texas, of wild Indians transformed into tranquil farmers worshipping the bloody Christ.

He made a dreamlike effort to unburden Cabezon and Snorter, leaving the saddle, pack frame, tack, and most of his baggage in the grass. He glimpsed himself hobbling the animals as well, though whether this had been accomplished in reality he could not say. Professor danced around a small rattlesnake at the door of the church. Edmund swiped it away with the butt of his shotgun and staggered inside. There was still a roof of sorts over the crumbling building. Edmund collapsed against a wall, his cheek pressed to the cool stone. The church was very small, no more than a chapel to service the vaqueros and herdsmen who had once worked the rancho in the days when it supplied meat to the padres and the Indians of the great missions upriver. But it was capacious enough for his purposes: a dark enclosed place to den up and pray for survival.

He closed his eyes and settled into his ordeal. The fever burned away not only his awareness but, it seemed, his body as well, leaving only a smoldering shell. He wept aloud in his discomfort and despair, and grabbed his dog, mistaking Professor for an angel of deliverance. But the alarmed animal wriggled out of Edmund's grasp and curled up a few paces away with a look of reproof, or perhaps pity, in his eyes.

Edmund emerged from this feverish turbulence into something worse. The chills came. He began to tremble violently from the marrow outward. He was lucid now, but that was no blessing, because his exhausted body could not defend itself against the shaking that now beset it. He felt as if someone had gathered up his bones in a canvas sack and begun pounding them with a hammer. If only he could slip away once more, even if it meant surrendering to the horrible fever dreams.

And so he did. The fever came, and then the chills again. And then the fever once more, roaring like a furnace and searing his mind into oblivion. He was aware, as the ague endlessly wore on, of cycles of daylight and new darkness, of soft footfalls coming and going into the church, of a fire crackling outside and the stamping and sputtering of horses. Someone spoke to him in good but lugubrious Spanish. He tried to open his eyes, but the effort to do so was too painful.

THERE WAS a fire in the church itself now. A good deal of time had passed and the sky had changed, at least as much of it as he could see through the gaps in the dried stalks that were all that was left of the church's roof. Lovely gray clouds cruised above him—a late norther that might have been brewed from the stormy turbulence within his own body. He was weaker than he had ever been in his life, ravaged and happy beyond comprehension. He fell asleep again like a child.

"Are you better, Tabby-boo?" said the man in the church with him. He spoke in the same pondering Spanish Edmund had heard in his fever, the natural rhythm of the language adjusted to the judicious pace of Comanche thought. It was night now. The man sat behind a fastidious little oak fire, his moccasins off, his medicine bag dangling from his scrotum. The spaces between the toes of his bare feet were painted red, a sign that he possessed wolf medicine. Bull Pizzle's broad face had an amused look, verging on an outright smile. His distinctive bare head—Edmund could not remember having ever met another bald Indian—shone neatly in the firelight.

"Much better," Edmund replied in his own Spanish, after

a fascinating five minutes or so of staring at the flames. "I'm glad to see my friend."

Edmund assumed his friend did not plan to kill him. Professor apparently assumed this as well, since the dog was asleep with his head on Bull Pizzle's knee.

"How long have I been here?" he asked.

"I don't know. We found you two days ago."

"Did I hobble my horse?"

"Yes. She's still here, Tabby-boo. Also the mule."

The word for white man was "tahbay-boh," but Bull Pizzle had been so amused by Edmund's clumsy rendering of it years before that he had applied it to him as a nickname. They had met back in the Boundary Commission days. The latest attempt by American filibusters to steal Texas had just been suppressed, and for once the province was full of Mexican troops. General Bustamente had seized the opportunity to call for a war of extermination against all the tribes, and Bull Pizzle—always as inclined to diplomacy as to war—had led his band into Béxar to establish a peace before the threat was carried out. As a gesture of friendship, the Comanches had invited the members of the Boundary Commission on a great festive buffalo hunt far to the west, beyond the cedar breaks and honeycombed limestone hills to an endless tableland of grass. Edmund remembered bounding on horseback over those plains as if in a dream, feeling the consent and complicity of the buffalo as he shot them down. He had never known bloodlust before, never considered that it might be a binding emotion. He had eaten of the buffalo's raw livers, startlingly flavored with their bile. He had watched the guarded Comanche faces collapse into giggling fits under a swirling dome of stars.

Bull Pizzle had waited until the Mexican forces had been withdrawn from the Provincias Internas to start raiding again, confident that the undersupplied presidial troops posed not much of a threat. The chief looked close to sixty now, his stomach slack and paunchy but his forearms still tightly muscled. His old eyes were as brown and moist as a cow's; there was savagery in them but no cruelty.

"You've been here two days?" Edmund asked, trying to grab hold of reality before it slipped away again.

Bull Pizzle slowly blinked his eyes in confirmation. Edmund could hear a good deal of talk and activity going on outside the church.

"Who is with you?"

"Fourteen warriors. Are you hungry?"

Edmund said no, and then yes. The thought of food made him feel suddenly hollow-boned and ravenous. Bull Pizzle stood up, dislodging Professor, and disappeared for an incalculable length of time. When he returned, after minutes or days, he brought pemmican and a battered tin cup filled with soup. Edmund crumbled the pemmican into the thin broth, stirring the grainy meat and dried hackberries with his finger, then stared for a long time into the cup, transfixed by the smooth, glistening buffalo fat floating on the surface.

"Drink it," Bull Pizzle said.

"I'm too tired."

Bull Pizzle took the cup out of Edmund's listless hands and held it to his lips. Edmund managed a sip or two and then grew distracted again, and Bull Pizzle had to take the cup away and ease his patient back down onto a fresh bed of moss.

He slept for another day, awaking to the sound of angry voices. He had once had a primitive grasp of the Comanche language, but it had vanished in the years since the buffalo hunt, and the argument outside the church was incomprehensible to him, except for the occasional spiteful use of the word "tahbay-boh." Edmund was alone with Professor, who looked at him as if expecting an explanation of the events of the last few days. The dog's right ear was drooping with the weight of a half-dozen swollen ticks. Edmund pulled them out, and the look of judgment in Professor's eyes softened a bit. Edmund stood, teetering with weakness. It was strange to be on his feet again, surveying the world from a forgotten pinnacle.

He walked outside. It was nearly dusk. The storm that had arrived during his illness had gone, and the evening sky was clear, with only a few radiant tufts of cloud. His sudden presence stopped all the talk. The warriors of the raiding party were clustered around a cooking fire. A group of them were playing hide-the-bullet on a spread-out deerskin; the rest looked bored and contentious.

Only a few of the party were familiar to him. Half of them were teenaged boys, too young to have been on the buffalo hunt back in the late twenties. But Edmund did exchange a mute greeting with a warrior named Quehtenet, whom he remembered as a brilliant and heedless horseman who even as a very young man had acquired a herd of more than two hundred horses. Quehtenet was in his thirties now, his face broader than Edmund remembered it, broad as a toad's, but strangely handsome. He had a ridge of scar tissue that ran across his left cheekbone all the way to a tattered earlobe—a musket ball, Edmund guessed, fired from one of the escopetas of the flying company back at the Alamo. Quehtenet had highlighted the scar with tattoos. He wore a vaquero's cotton shirt with the sleeves ripped off, exposing two arms that had once, at the beginning of the raid, been painted a bright solid yellow, but were now ocher with dust. His right thumb was gone, the stump freshly cauterized but still seeping blood. Quehtenet dabbed at the blood with a ball of cobwebs.

Edmund cut his eyes to Bull Pizzle, who directed him to take a seat near him at the edge of the fire. The Indians who had been playing hide-the-bullet went back to their gambling. Quehtenet, in pain, continued to glower at him. Quehtenet had never cared for tahbay-bohs, Texian or American. He had treated the Mexicans on the Boundary Commission with tolerance, even respect in some cases, but he had borne a grudge against Edmund from the start for his coarse American identity.

Edmund now noticed for the first time a little Mexican girl, four or five years old, seated at Quehtenet's side, staring into the fire and sucking her thumb, rubbing the bloody hem of her dress against her cheek.

"Cómo te llamas, niña?" he asked.

"She won't speak," Bull Pizzle said.

"Where are her parents?"

"Quehtenet killed them."

Bull Pizzle handed him a strip of strange-tasting meat. It was painful to chew it, has jaws still sore from clacking together during two days of violent chills.

"My friends aren't happy with me," Bull Pizzle said. "We've been here for three days, and they want to get home. It's dangerous for us to stay out for so long."

"You should go. I'm better."

"In a little while. Do you like that meat? It's skunk."

"What will you do with the child?"

"Why are you so curious about the child? Quehtenet will keep her. His daughter died, and he wants another one."

"What happened to his thumb?"

Quehtenet said something to Bull Pizzle in angry Comanche.

"He does not like to be spoken about, as if he were a child."

"Tell him I'm sorry."

"It's his own fault. I've told him for years I would teach him Spanish, but he's too proud to learn."

Edmund glanced at Quehtenet and noticed that his broad face registered a kind of gloating disgust.

"When we raided the village," Bull Pizzle went on, "Quehtenet got his thumb caught while he was roping a horse. It was a very bad rope burn, and it grew full of poison while we waited for you to get well. This morning we chopped it off with an ax. So he's not happy with you, and he's not happy with me."

Quehtenet spoke up again, demanding a translation of what Bull Pizzle had just said. As the old chief spoke to him in Comanche, Quehtenet gently squeezed the absorbent cobweb with the fingers of his opposite hand, his face tightening as he did so. Edmund could see the blood seeping up into the filaments.

"To lose a thumb is very painful," Bull Pizzle said to Edmund. "Probably the most painful thing you can lose except for your prick."

Edmund let his eyes drift over again to the little girl. She had not been harmed physically, but her dress was still stained with blood—her mother's blood, Edmund guessed—and her eyes, glazed with shock, had no more expression than a possum's.

"Is it true that Terán killed himself?" Bull Pizzle asked him.

"Yes, it's true."

"How?"

"He stabbed himself in the heart with his sword."

Bull Pizzle relayed this news in Comanche to the rest of the raiding party. The silence that followed might have been appreciative or horrified—Edmund did not know what Indians thought of taking one's own life. The Comanches had known and liked Manuel de Mier y Terán, the young Mexican general who had led the Boundary Commission and who had been horrified at the relentless encroachment of norteamericanos into the Mexican frontier. Terán had realized that the colonists—with their demands for ports and tariff concessions and relaxed slavery laws—were merely preparing the ground for a full-scale invasion.

He had been an emotional and strangely fragile man. One early morning during their survey travels Edmund had found him sitting on a rock terrace that shelved into a clear,

shallow river. Terán was holding a cup of chocolate, looking up at a towering limestone bluff on the other side of the
river. At that hour of the morning the bluff was still in deep
shade, but a band of sunlight illuminated the topmost stra-
tum of rock with an intoxicating brightness. Bats were
streaming back to their homes in the pockmarked bluff,
millions of them in a long, sinuous column that moved
across the sky like smoke. Swallows flew among the bats,
darting in and out of their mud nests below the overhangs.
Edmund could hear the hollow, fluting calls of doves, the
sound of water trickling into the river from springs hidden
behind thick mats of maidenhair fern.

Edmund had joined Terán on the rock shelf, and did not
notice for some minutes that the general was in tears.

"Texas is lost," Terán said finally, his soft voice echoing
off the sculpted rock. "You norteamericanos will take it. It
is only a matter of a few years. Texas is lost, and so am I."

Something had happened to Terán in Texas, something
Edmund understood only vaguely. During the course of the
survey he had watched the general's robust health begin to
deteriorate, though precisely what fevers or miasmas had
invaded his body was impossible to tell. Texas had been like
a shimmering vision to him, and he had withered ecstati-
cally in its sight. He had wanted to keep this brilliant country for Mexico, for himself, and he could not. His pleas to
the government to populate this country with more Mexican settlers, with Germans, with Swiss, with convicts—
with anyone but the rapacious Americans—had not been
answered, and he had begun to feel that heaven itself was
out of reach. The land's wondrous melancholy had settled
into his heart and would kill him.

"If a war comes," Bull Fizzle asked Edmund now, "who
should we fight against? The Mexicans or the Texians?"

"You fight against both of them already," Edmund said.
"That's true."

Quehtenet spoke up again, in his angry put-upon voice.

Edmund found that he was beginning to remember a few scraps of the language, but not enough to understand what Quehtenet was saying.

"He says we'll have plenty of fighting after the war is over," Bull Pizzle translated. "No matter who wins. Mexicans are no different from Texians, and Texians are no different from Americans. They all want what belongs to the People.

"Myself," Bull Pizzle went on, "I like the Americans. I'm willing to travel to Washington to meet the president."

He turned his eye to Edmund.

"Who will you fight for?"

"No one. I'm not a soldier."

Quehtenet evidently knew enough Spanish to understand this simple statement, for he emitted a disgusted laugh without the benefit of a translation from Bull Pizzle. Then he spoke in Comanche. Edmund couldn't follow it, but from the look of shock on Bull Pizzle's face he gathered it was an amazing insult. The other Comanches broke into an affirmative muttering that alarmed him. He had the feeling that his safety was no longer guaranteed.

"What did he say?" he asked Bull Pizzle.

"It was very rude. He said you would make a poor soldier anyway. Your medicine is weak, and the longer we stay here with you the weaker our medicine becomes."

Edmund thought for a moment, struggling against the lassitude of his mind and body. He needed to make a strong showing. Bull Pizzle's sponsorship was no longer enough to keep him alive. The Comanche words he needed came floating into his mind as if borne on the wind.

"Do you want to fight?" Edmund said to Quehtenet. "I'll fight you for the little girl."

Quehtenet's eyes widened with amusement or rage. In all his years of frontier travel, Edmund had never shot at a man or used his green river knife for any purpose more dangerous than trimming his nails. And he was so weak

with the ague he could barely keep his head tottering upright on his shoulders. His only real weapon was bravado.

Quehtenet countered with a dismissive laugh and a
statement in Comanche that Edmund couldn't catch.

"He says what's the point of fighting you?" Bull Pizzle
said. "You can hardly stand up."

"He has only one thumb. That makes us even."

Far from even, Edmund knew. Quehtenet would have
him down and scalped in an eye blink.

"If the point is the girl," Bull Pizzle said, "it would be
foolish to fight over her when you can barter." He repeated
this in Comanche to Quehtenet, who responded in a bitter
torrent of unintelligible words.

"He says he didn't take her to barter with. He took her to
be his daughter. He has no interest in selling her the way the
Americans sell their negro slaves. He wants to know what
you plan to do with her. Sell her back to the Mexicans?"

Edmund said that he planned to give her back.

Quehtenet wanted to know why the Mexicans were better for her than the Numinuh.

This word—the Comanches' term for themselves—
came explosively from Quehtenet's mouth. He made the
sign for it as well—a wiggling motion of the fingers that
meant Snake Travelling Backward.

"She is a Mexican," Edmund said. "If she were a Comanche and the Mexicans had taken her, I would say the
same thing. She belongs with her people."

Bull Pizzle relayed this to Quehtenet, and then Quehtenet's answer to Edmund.

"He won't fight you for her. He won't sell her to you. He
won't give her to you. But I think he is ready to kill you,
Tabby-boo, whether you're sick or not."

Edmund drew himself to his feet, reaching what seemed
like a dizzying height. His head wobbled on a body that felt
as light as a cane stalk. But in this ethereal state he was
somehow strong and charged with confidence.

"The girl will come with me," he announced, once again finding the Comanche words.

Quehtenet's face darkened, and so did Bull Pizzle's. Edmund walked over to the front of the church and bent down to retrieve his saddle. He grabbed the broad wooden horn and, knowing better than to try to lift the saddle, dragged it across the dirt to where Cabezon was grazing in her rawhide hobbles some distance away from the captured Mexican herd. He could feel the Indians' eyes on him as he slipped the bit into the mare's mouth and settled the bridle on her head. Professor stood guard at his feet, facing the cluster of Comanches by the fire, glancing up periodically at Edmund with agitated jerks of his head.

Edmund set his blanket on Cabezon's back and then bent down to the saddle. He thought if he marshalled his strength carefully he might be able to lift it and swing it onto the horse. But he managed to heft it only a few inches off the ground, and he stood there gasping after the attempt, his frail muscles twitching, his head filled with a sloshing sea of blood.

Bull Pizzle stood, walked over to him, and placed the saddle on the horse in one easy motion.

"Thank you," Edmund said as Bull Pizzle tied the cinch.

"Can you make it into the saddle?" Bull Pizzle asked.

"I think so."

Bull Pizzle took off the hobbles, and Edmund launched himself onto Cabezon's back, his muscles weak but his bones as light as porcelain. He sat atop the mare while Bull Pizzle unhobbled Snorter and loaded him with the packsaddle.

"Forget about the Mexican girl," Bull Pizzle whispered to him as he handed him the mule's reins. "You are being very foolish about her. This sickness is keeping you from thinking clearly. If you insist, what choice will he have but to kill you?"

Edmund touched his heels to Cabezon's flanks and rode

over to face Quehtenet. He felt giddy and unconcerned, flush with some strange authority he could not name.

"Niña," he said to the girl, "ven acá. Voy a llevarte a tu casa."

She looked up at him, and he could see the hope struggling to surface in her eyes, a hope he could not encourage or guarantee.

Quehtenet looked at Bull Pizzle and spoke to the older man in Comanche. Quehtenet's tone was now more exasperated than angry. Bull Pizzle, Edmund gathered, was pleading for toleration. He clearly considered Edmund's mind to be addled, and in a sudden flash of reason Edmund realized he was right. Why was he taking this girl? Her parents were dead, and the Comanche life, he knew, was as full of richness as any—a never-ending procession through buffalo plains and verdant hills, a dangerous and primitive life that was probably no more dangerous or primitive than the one from which the girl had just been stolen. He began to sense that this rescue was nothing more than a grand gesture whose only purpose was to satisfy his own vanity.

"Quehtenet is very annoyed with you, Tabby-boo," Bull Pizzle said. "So am I. Leave the girl here and go."

"Ven acá," Edmund said again to the girl. She started to move, but Quehtenet gripped her arm with his good hand.

He spoke angrily to Bull Pizzle again in Comanche, and the older man's exasperation was plain enough.

Quehtenet stepped forward, grabbed a horsehide blanket, and flapped it in front of Cabezon's face, shouting in a high, piercing voice. The startled horse leapt backward and then reared, throwing Edmund hard onto the trampled grass, his left leg landing in a nest of prickly pear.

He expected laughter but heard none. The looks on the Comanches' faces were pitying. It was almost dark now. In silence one of the warriors placed a moss-covered oak branch onto the fire, causing a vivid eruption of flame. Edmund pulled himself to his feet. The innumerable cactus needles had been driven in deep, and they stood up in a bristly line from his thigh to his ankle.

But Edmund could see that Quehtenet was in pain as well. The effort of spooking Cabezon had caused the stump of his thumb to throb anew, and he sat by the fire looking stonily into the flames.

Edmund hobbled toward him, his shoulder sore where he had fallen on it, the cactus needles rooted painfully in the meat of his leg.

Quehtenet glared at him. He produced a rawhide quirt. Professor growled, and one of the other Indians kicked the little dog a yard into the air.

"Don't kick my dog," Edmund said.

Professor ran over to Edmund and huddled at his feet. Quehtenet was striding forward with the quirt, ready to strike Edmund across the face, when they heard a raspy, high-pitched screech, a disapproving hiss that erupted from the roof of the ruined church. And then the owl came gliding between Edmund and Quehtenet. It flew low, at chest level, as white as a spirit, its heart-shaped face eerily blank. Edmund could hear the angry clicking of its bill, but otherwise it was silent, and in a moment its pure form had disappeared into the evening sky.

Quehtenet said nothing. He stopped, put down the quirt, and fell into a demoralized silence. The other men behind him murmured in Comanche. Some of them began to kick out the fire while others went for the horses.

Quehtenet spat a few words at him, and then stormed over to the horses.

"He says to keep the girl," Bull Pizzle said. "Keep the girl and your evil spirits. Did you know you had owl medicine, Tabby-boo?"

"No, I wasn't aware of it."

"We Numinuh do not like owls. A long time ago the People suffered badly because of Great Cannibal Owl. He would fly down out of the sky at night and pick up children like mice. He's gone now, but his bones are still around. I've never seen them, but my father did, in a cave in the mountains. He said the owl's skull was twice the size of a bison bull's."

Edmund looked at the girl. She was sitting alone by the fire now, still clutching the hem of her dress.

"So Quehtenet is going to let me take her?"

"Oh, yes. He doesn't like owls any better than the rest of us."

Bull Pizzle put out his hand awkwardly for a white man's handshake, a gesture Edmund knew he disliked. The old man's grip was tentative and limp.

"I don't really have owl medicine," Edmund said. "It was just an accident."

"You may have it or you may not. Your opinion about it doesn't matter."

The old Indian stood in silence for a moment more.

"Dark days are coming to this country, Tabby-boo."

He walked over to his horses on bandy legs. In a moment more they were all gone, off into the twilit brasada. Quehtenet made a point of not looking back at him. Edmund walked over to the fire and stopped a discreet distance from the girl. He begin pulling the needles out of his leg, working by the firelight as if engaged in a handicraft. Professor, sore from being kicked, curled up against his foot. The girl never spoke, but finally turned her dark eyes in his direction and watched him work.

CHAPTER TWO

✹

MARY MOTT was two years a widow. The first six months after Andrew's death had been wasted in grief and fretfulness, but now she kept a prosperous inn on Purísima Street in Refugio, on a mild rise that gave her clients a view of the Mission River and the rich coastal savannahs. Her clients were principally schooner captains and merchants and Mexican customs officials. They tended to come by sea, usually after a harrowing voyage whose trials did not end with their arrival at the Aransas Pass, since this pass between the open Gulf and the inland bays was notorious for the submerged bar that was as likely to destroy a vessel as not. By the time the voyagers had wended their way through the oyster reefs in the bay, made landfall at Copano, and then bounced inland for twelve miles by horse or oxcart to Refugio, the sight of Mrs. Mott's public house with its steaming coffee urns, its clean bed linens, its center table laden with redfish and fowl and cornbread, was almost enough to restore their shattered nerves.

Mary Mott was thirty-six, no longer as lithe as she had been but still strong in body, with a forceful, complicated face. Her eyes were hazel. Her nose was as straight as a blade. In her youth these features had helped create a doleful beauty, but her youth was long over, and whatever beauty remained to her seemed increasingly beside the point in this bracingly brutal wilderness.

She managed the inn with the help of her sixteen-year-old son, Terrell, and a middle-aged Karankawa huntsman named Fresada. The colony that contained Refugio had been settled by Irish tenant farmers, by families who for generations had had no hope of owning land in their own country but who now found themselves the proprietors of thousands of acres of coastal prairie. The Mexican government had granted them the land for almost nothing, since neither Spain nor Mexico had ever been able to settle the frontier of Texas and wrest it away from the Indians.

The Irish were not nearly as discontented about living under Mexican law as the Americans who had settled the other colonies. They were already deeply papist, and the dark and baroque rituals of Mexican Catholicism only made them feel more secure. The land was strange to them, to be sure—there were no rattlesnakes or prickly pear in Ballygarrett—but it was theirs, and the joy of owning it shone in their faces. More than once, Mary had seen an Irish colonist weep when his name was entered into the *Libro Becerro,* the great book, bound in calfskin, that declared to posterity the unbelievable fact that the land belonged forevermore to him and to his heirs.

In four days Dionysio O'Docharty, a sixty-year-old widower, was to marry poor Edna Foley, a vacant girl of eighteen. Few people in Refugio approved of the match, but there was to be a wedding just the same and a feast to be held at the inn. Mary, Terrell, and Fresada had brought an oxcart down to the bayshore—Mary to gather oysters, Terrell and Fresada to hunt doughbirds and perhaps kill an alligator if any of the superstitious Irishmen could be persuaded to eat it. (Mary, a brisk and pragmatic Protestant, had been amused when it was pointed out to her that the alligator was a messenger of the devil.)

She was fifty yards from shore, wading along a shell reef in a pair of old, stout shoes, prying out oysters with the blade of a bowie knife. It was a bounteous spring day, the sky clear after the passage of a late norther and thick with voyaging flocks of birds; the water so still that she could clearly see the faint ripples made by schools of redfish as they finned about below the surface. She was alone. Terrell and Fresada had wandered up the creek, Terrell carrying an old fowling piece that had belonged to her father, Fresada with the fine Kentucky rifle that had been given to Andrew by the faculty of Transylvania College when he ventured off to become an empresario in Texas. Her own weapon, a sturdy Spanish musket that she had taken in trade for a month's lodging, remained in the cart on shore.

She levered up the oysters and set them in a bucket, her mind happily engaged with a dozen challenges peculiar to life in the colonies. There were few candle molds in this part of Texas, so she would have to manufacture her own out of cane if she was to have enough illumination for the wedding feast. There was no axle grease to silence the screeching wheels of her oxcart, but she had been told by Mrs. Fagan that pulverized cactus root answered well enough for a lubricant. And she needed salt, which she would have to boil herself, and lye to make both soap and hominy. The thought of these tasks soothed rather than intimidated her. Her mind was otherwise too active, full of unfounded worries about Terrell, too keenly attuned to the deteriorating political situation in the colonies. Texas was a country full of blustering, posturing men—like that drunken peacock Sam Houston—and they were sure to make a mess of things sooner or later.

She heard a moan and turned to see Daniel, her old Durham ox, wandering along the narrow bayshore, bellowing to her in disbelief. A long cane arrow protruded from his neck, and his hide was already stained with a bright stream of blood.

The life seemed to fall out of her for a moment. She had not known a moment of hollow terror like this since her daughter Susie had died. An arrow sailed by her, close enough for her to feel its breath on her cheek, as a dugout filled with Karankawa Indians emerged from behind a spit of land fifty yards away. There were six of them, brilliantly naked. She could smell the shark oil on their bodies. They had been poling their craft stealthily along the margins of the bay, but now they put the pole away and produced paddles, stroking toward her with frightening velocity.

Mary was still standing there, beholding them as if in a trance, when another arrow struck her in the chest and knocked her backward onto the oyster reef. She could hear the Kronks' ululating cries of triumph as she struggled to climb back to her feet, lacerating her hands and the backs of her legs on the sharp shells.

The arrow had not penetrated; the point had been brittle and had shattered against her breastbone. But she felt as if she had been kicked in the chest all the same, and her skin was torn and stinging with salt water. She stumbled off the reef and tried to run to shore in the knee-deep water. Her feet sank in mud, causing it to bloom upward in a pestilential cloud. Once or twice she slipped, and when she tried to catch herself her hands tore through the gossamer bodies of jellyfish that lay open on the bottom like flowers.

No more arrows came; perhaps they were saving them.

The mud sucked off her tightly laced shoes. The water pulled at the hem of her linsey dress. She tried to cry out for Terrell and Fresada but produced only a gurgling mumble, the sort of lockjawed note of distress she had heard Susie emit during the long nights she had lain in agony waiting to die.

When she reached the shore she did not believe she could keep her trembling hands still enough to grab the musket and cartridge box. But she did, and she ran on with them toward the summit of a coarse, shell-covered dune. The pulverized shell dug into her bare feet, and before she reached the summit she fell, knocking the butt of the musket against a piece of driftwood. The accidental discharge exploded against her ear and caught her hair on fire. She ran on, patting out the fire and uttering something over and over, that same nameless grunt of terror—"Hnnhh! Hnnhh!"

At the crest of the dune she turned around and saw the dugout gliding onto shore. The Kronks came on. With her hands shaking violently she began to reload. From years in Texas, years as a widow, the action came as naturally to her as the burping of a baby: cock the hammer, open the pan, tear open the paper cartridge, prime, close the frizzen. Then powder, buck-and-ball, wadding . . .

They were on her. Karankawas were famously tall, and the Indian who charged out now in front of the others was a giant, his limbs powerful and sleek. He raised his war club, and in a strange suspension of time she studied him as if he were a subject sitting for a portrait: the shell gorget at his beautiful neck, the blue circles tattooed over his cheekbones, the rattlesnake rattles whirring at the end of his braid.

She had just set the ball, and there was no more time. She shot him with the ramrod still in the muzzle. She heard a horrible clattering sound as the kick knocked her backward again. When she looked at what she had done she saw the Indian sitting upright with his legs splayed uselessly in front of him, his torn guts seeping into his hands and the ramrod poking strangely out of his back, dangling like a reed.

The other Kronks, stunned, looked down at him and then at her. Mary stood, holding the empty musket, the smell of gunpowder still rank in her nostrils. One of the Indians grabbed the war club that the leader had dropped, walked up to her, and struck her full in the face. She felt the blow splinter her nose. She fell once more onto the carpet of broken shell, choking on the blood in her nasal chambers, blinking her eyes against the sun. Out on the bay she saw a porpoise fin rise and subside, a gleaming black shape that hinted of glorious unseen worlds.

She could hear them arguing and mourning. The wounded Indian was trying to sing, but he was as scared as she was to die, and his voice had a ragged, panicky edge that did not excite triumph in her but an odd, binding pity.

He sat in a growing circle of his own blood and filth while she gazed seaward, wondering what would come next. All the Karankawas she had known had been peaceable, either mission Indians like Fresada or beaten-down scavenging remnants of a once-proud warrior tribe. Stephen Austin and his militia had destroyed most of them back in the twenties. The Kronks, the wild ones at least, were supposed to be cannibals. Is that what they would do now? Drag her back to their camp and strip off her flesh and roast it before her eyes?

She tried to stand but could not, so she began to crawl away on the oyster shell. She had gone perhaps a yard when she felt them grab her feet and pull her back, as casually as they would jerk a dog on a leash. Through the bloody curtain in front of her eyes she saw them gathered around the wounded man.

He was still singing. His eyes, wide with shock, were staring at her. No one seemed to be able to decide anything—what to do with her, how to carry the gutshot man back to the canoe without spilling his insides onto the ground.

The Indian with the war club stood over her. There were tears in his eyes. His face was rigid with hate.

"Very bad for you," he said in English, and then struck her again with the war club across the ribs.

FROM BEHIND a tangle of mesquite at the mouth of the creek Terrell saw the Indian strike his mother. The rage he felt made him wild, and Fresada had to grab him by the hair and pull him back before he ran screaming out into the open.

"Wait!" Fresada whispered harshly. He took aim with the rifle, moving the barrel from one distant figure to the next.

"Hurry!" Terrell said. He knew the Kronks were out of range of his shotgun, and his inability to do anything, combined with Fresada's patience, was unendurable. His mother was lying on the ground, her face gleaming with blood. Perhaps she was already dead. It meant nothing to Terrell now whether he himself lived or died. He had to do something, to go to her.

But Fresada only compressed his lips, studying the Indians along the barrel of the gun.

Then the teary-eyed Kronk raised the war club again, and Fresada fired.

Terrell saw the ball strike the man's shoulder. A chip of white bone spun high into the air. The rest of them stood, arrows already fitted to their long bows, and scanned the trees at the mouth of the creek. They looked very nervous.

During the tense silence, Fresada reloaded, then shouted to the Indians in Karankawa.

"What'd you say?" Terrell asked.

"I told them to go away. Are both barrels loaded?"

"Yes."

"If they come, I'll shoot with the rifle. Then we trade. I shoot with the shotgun, and you reload the rifle."

"How bad is my mother hurt?"

"I don't know. She's moving."

The Karankawas stood their ground. Terrell saw the Indian whom Fresada had shot talking to the dying leader. Then holding his broken shoulder, he walked forward toward the trees. The front of his body was covered with a sheet of blood, and it stained the shell crust beneath his feet. After a few yards, he stopped, and shouted into the trees.

"What?" Terrell asked Fresada.

"They want a rosary. For the one who's dying."

Fresada took his rosary out of his pantaloon pocket, wrapped it around his trigger hand, and raised the rifle to his shoulder.

"Come on," he said to Terrell. "Be ready to shoot."

Terrell followed Fresada as he advanced out of the brush

onto the exposed ground. The wounded Kronk looked at them and said nothing. Then the three of them walked without speaking to where his mother and the dying Indian lay.

Mary pulled herself up into a sitting position. Terrell did not recognize her face. There was a hideous knot on her forehead the size of a peach, and the bridge of her nose was shattered and bent. The blood on her face and in her hair made her look savage.

"I'm all right, Terrell," she said when he ran to her. Her voice sounded strange and guttural. "I'm all right. You keep your attention on these Indians."

Fresada and the dying Indian looked at each other. The Kronk's skin was gray, and he trembled as if from the cold. The buck-and-ball had not only torn open his body but had broken his spinal column and paralyzed his legs. The ramrod, still dangling from his back, had punctured his lung, and a spume of blood hovered on his lips.

"He die now," the Kronk with the broken shoulder said, without bitterness, just as a simple, sad observation. Terrell kept his gun on him, and Fresada kept the Kentucky rifle pointed at the others. Two of them were ready to shoot with their bows, the strings taut. Terrell noticed that the arrow point aimed at his own heart was glass, chipped from a blue bottle. Of the other two Kronks, one had a club and the other a long lance. A useless old pocket pistol hung from his neck by a leather thong.

Fresada handed the rosary to the Kronk. He held it in his bloody hand and slipped the beads through his fingers without seeming to pray on them. He lay on his side, looking with shame at his exposed entrails. He sang a Karankawa song as he worked the beads, a dirge with long, sustained notes that kept expanding the blood bubbles on his mouth.

"Do you know him?" Mary asked Fresada.

"Yes. He was at the mission when he was a child. We called him El Pinto, because he had a white spot on his forehead. See? It's still there."

No one moved while they watched El Pinto die. He kept praying to his savage Karankawa gods as he moved the rosary beads rapidly through his fingers. Mary thought it odd that she felt such rage for the man who had struck her with the war club and yet such tenderness for this man whom she had killed. His eyes met hers as he died. Suddenly they had an opaque, lustrous sheen. The beads stopped moving through his fingers, and the bloody bubbles on his mouth stopped expanding and contracting and simply hovered there, waiting for the breeze to blow them away.

"Take him and go," Fresada said after a little while.

"Give us cow," the Kronk with the shoulder wound said, gesturing with a movement of his lips toward poor Daniel, who stood nearby, still looking bewilderingly toward them for help or explanation.

"No!" Mary shouted. She tried to stand, but the pain from her broken ribs forced her back down. "We won't give you anything! Go away!"

The wounded Indian looked at her hatefully, then his legs began to tremble and he fainted. For a long moment they all stood there, weapons pointed at one another, not knowing what move to make next. Then the Kronk with the pocket pistol, a young man whose loose black hair reached almost to the small of his back, carefully bent down to the body of El Pinto, removed the rosary from his hands, and handed it to Fresada.

Fresada and the Indian then fell into a conversation in Karankawa, a conversation that sounded almost shockingly civil to Terrell for men with guns and arrows pointed at one another. There were grunts of agreement, of accommodation.

"Leave your gun cocked," Fresada told him in a moment, "but lower the barrel."

He did as he was told. The Indians with the bows did the same.

"Can you shoot, Mrs. Mott?" Fresada asked.

Mary wiped the blood from her eyes. "Yes."

"Take my rifle. I'm going to help them carry El Pinto to the canoe."

Mary painfully brought herself to a sitting position, and Fresada handed her the heavy rifle.

"I think it will be all right," Fresada said. "They have had bad luck today, and I don't think they want to fight anymore. They want me with them so you won't shoot them on the way to the canoe."

"Be careful."

One of the Indians pulled the ramrod out of El Pinto's back and tossed it down to Mary without a glance. Then Fresada and two of the Kronks lifted El Pinto and carried him to the canoe while the other two stayed near Terrell and his mother.

Terrell kept the gun pointed at the ground. One of the Indians slapped a fly on his neck and looked up at the clouds as if he were planning to comment on the weather.

"Wouldn't your father like to see us here holding off these wild Indians?" Mary said.

"Are you going to be all right?"

Terrell's lower lip trembled when he asked this, but he kept his eyes steady on the Kronks.

"I believe so, darling. My nose is broken and a few of my ribs as well. I don't know about the blow to my head. I'm feeling disordered in my stomach, and that's not good. My brain might be swelling up. I may pass out."

"What do I do?"

"Calomel and jalap, once you get me home. Keep feeling me for fever. I might need a clyster; that shouldn't do any harm. But I don't want to be bled."

She glanced at him, seeing how heavily these instructions registered on his face. Terrell's features were as delicate as hers were insistent, his hair fine and already thinning a little at the temples. (He would grow bald early, like her father had.) Last spring she had watched a pair of egrets build a nest on top of a prickly pear by the river, flying in day after day with sticks in their beaks and setting them into place with elaborate, ritualized movements, tilting their heads inquisitively this way and that as if they were in a perpetual state of mild puzzlement about their own activities. The chick that finally emerged from the nest had looked so much like Terrell—so downy and awkward and solemn—that it tore at her heart.

Fresada returned by himself to the top of the dune and helped the two Indians remaining there to carry their unconscious friend down to the dugout. Terrell and Mary watched them carefully, their guns cocked and ready, but the violent mood had subsided, and it even seemed that Fresada and the Kronks were talking amiably. In a moment the Indians were gone, paddling the canoe out past the oyster reef and around the small headland that had obscured their approach from Mary's view.

As much as she hated to do it to the poor beast, Mary allowed Fresada to chain Daniel up to the oxcart. The arrow was still lodged in the taut muscles of his neck, but it had not penetrated deeply, and in fact the familiar routine of hauling the cart seemed to calm him.

Terrell and Fresada set her into the cart, next to the discharged musket and the half-filled oyster bucket. She closed her eyes against the savage brightness of the sun overhead. She longed for a dark, cool room, for rest and stillness. Terrell walked behind the cart, holding the loaded shotgun, never taking his worried eyes from her. With each jarring revolution of the wheels the pain inside her head howled against the confines of her skull, begging for release. She was in agony as well from the fractured ribs, from the shell cuts on the bottoms of her feet, and from the burns on her neck where her hair had caught on fire. She breathed through her mouth, trying to leave her poor fragmented nose in peace. But even with the movement of the cart she was no longer sick to her stomach, and she began to feel confident that her brain had not swollen so much as to crowd the cranium.

"Don't let me fall asleep," she told Terrell. "Not until we're home. Splash water in my face if you have to."

The boy nodded; his vigilance would be absolute.

"Oh, the poor Foley girl's wedding party!" she moaned.

"Me and Fresada can do it," Terrell said.

His mother began to weep. The only times Terrell had ever seen her cry had been in disappointment at herself, at chores she couldn't finish, at impossible things she couldn't accomplish. When his sister died, and then later his father, she had wept not out of grief, like normal people, but out of rage—rage at herself because she had not been wary or strong enough to keep death from sneaking in on them.

"Me and Fresada can do it," Terrell repeated. "There's no cause for tears, Mother."

He wiped the tears from his own eyes. Mary braced herself in the cart as the road grew rougher and violent waves of pain passed through her body. She would use the pain to stay awake. Birds called down from high overhead. She kept her eyes closed against the searing sunlight, but she listened gratefully to the birds. They were cranes, drifting along with velvety smoothness at the top of the sky.

CHAPTER THREE

✳

IT TOOK Edmund two days to travel the twenty miles from Las Cabras to the presidial substation on the Cibolo. He was still very weak, and he needed to rest and sleep with a frequency that alarmed the little girl, who seemed to fear that she would be taken again if he let go of his vigilance for even a moment.

When riding, the girl sat in front of him on the skeleton-rigged saddle, requiring him to inch backward in a new position that neither he nor Cabezon found agreeable. Edmund rode with one hand holding the reins and the other spanning the child's rounded stomach. The warmth of her little body against his hand soothed him in some novel way. Now and again, feeling safe there, she would drop off to sleep, leaning her head back against his chest, and then would start awake and begin to cry.

He would stroke her black hair then and sing to her. He was self-conscious about his dreadful singing voice, which neither rose nor fell in pitch but droned on in a pedestrian mumble. But the girl did not seem to mind, and Edmund had a good memory for verses. He sang hymns and parlor songs. He sang "The Lawyer Outwitted" and "Shocking Earthquakes at Charleston." He sang pro-Jack songs and anti-Jack songs, and love songs and corridos in her own language.

She never spoke to him and never slept except for those fretful dozings in the saddle. When he stretched out to sleep at night she lay with her head on his chest as casually and directly as if he were her own father. But she never closed her eyes and held on to his trunk with an ever-tightening grip that woke him at frequent intervals. During one of the brief periods when he managed to sleep he heard the girl crying and Professor barking and woke up to see a coyote bounding off into the darkness with his hat in its teeth. Edmund tried to run after the coyote, but his leg was still fiery and stiff from the cactus needles, and he was so weak he could barely run twenty yards. The girl screamed when he left her, and ran up to him and clung to him like a baby monkey. Edmund looked crossly at Professor, who sat there staring at the departing coyote without interest. A more spirited dog would have given chase, if not from outrage at the theft of his master's hat, at least from simple canine excitement. But Professor simply trotted back to their camp and curled up into sleep.

Without his hat, Edmund felt exposed and conspicuous. But there were few people on the road to notice. He passed only a group of heavily armed arrieros bearing a cartload of Chinese porcelain to Béxar, and a crazy old metatero whose occupation was to wander throughout Mexico repecking grinding stones with a little hammer.

At the substation on the Cibolo, an ancient Spanish fort that was now no more than a jumble of mouldering palisado buildings, Edmund encountered not only the four soldiers from the flying company who were stationed there but the remnants of the girl's family as well, a collection of uncles and aunts and cousins who had gathered there in the hope that they might eventually hear some sort of news.

When he rode into the fort he was greeted, to his secret satisfaction, like an angel from God. The girl's relatives rushed up to him with their arms outstretched, shouting "Mi gordita preciosa!" and wailing with happiness and astonishment. Their joy was so powerful it scared her at first, and she twisted in the saddle so that she could put her arms around Edmund and bury her face against his shirt. She still clung to him as he dismounted, and he did not know which pair of arms to give her to. Finally the woman he took to be her grandmother coaxed her away from him and carried her across the weedy parade ground to a solitary stone building. The girl held tight to the old woman but kept her eyes on Edmund as she was led away.

The child's name, he learned, was Lupita. Both her parents were dead, and two uncles, plus another man and woman, all killed and scalped in front of her eyes as they worked in the fields. The surviving members of the family had thought she was dead too, that the Comanches had either bashed her head against a tree or carried her far off to the buffalo country, never to be seen again. But now God had led Edmund to her, and Edmund had brought her back.

They wanted to take him to the village at Las Animas, to feed him cabrito and nurse him back to health. Hearing about how the coyote had stolen his hat, all the men tried to give him their own sombreros, but their heads were too small, and in any case he was too choosy about his headgear to accept them even if they had fit. No, he said, all he wanted was to sleep, and for someone to take care of his horse and mule and dog while he did so. So the soldiers led Cabezon and Snorter away to the corrals, and the children tried to entertain Professor. Edmund ate a meal of tortillas and beans and stringy guisado, and then followed a corporal to a tumbledown jacal, where he lay down on a shapeless mat and slept for three days.

EDMUND HAD REGAINED most of his strength by the time he reached Refugio, but he was ten pounds lighter than when he had left Béxar, and the loss of his hat made him feel lighter still. Refugio was hardly more than a collection of jacales and adobe huts, though a few houses were more substantial, built with scavenged stones from the walls of the abandoned mission, or from timber carried overland from the wooded colonies to the east.

It was midmorning when he arrived. Most of Refugio's population appeared to be gathered in the campo santo in front of the mission church, watching a group of men as they attempted to insert an upraised coffin vertically into the ground like a fence post. Edmund dismounted and stood watching from a discreet distance, next to a man in an old tricorn hat and blacksmith's apron who was angrily drunk, by the smell of him, on corn juice.

"I've never seen anybody buried standing up," Edmund remarked to him.

"And so you haven't," the blacksmith replied, in a blast of rank fermented breath. "I won't take no part in it myself. I'm sorry for the poor man, but I won't approve of blasphemy."

The poor man, the blacksmith went on to explain, had died on what was to have been his wedding day. He was sixty and his bride not even twenty, and simple as a child into the bargain. She had wandered off in fright and confusion two days before the ceremony, and when she came back her hair was as tangled as a bird's nest and her legs covered with festering cactus sores. She told her uncles, before locking herself into the barn, that the Blessed Mother had appeared to her and told her not to marry Dionysio O'Docharty.

"Dionysio took it hard," the blacksmith said. "Let out a great caoine like a banshee. Set everything on fire—house, barn, outhouse—then shot himself in the head. Left a note pinned to his body that he wanted to be buried standing up like Cuchellen himself, with his face toward Ireland. Well, bury him standing up, I say, but not on holy ground. His soul has already flown straight to hell. God does not forgive the sin of despair, as you know."

Edmund nodded without agreeing. Hard gods thrived in hard lands, and the Romish deity had a pitiless streak that made Him a not-too-distant cousin of the predatory Aztec gods He had supplanted. Maybe God would not forgive despair, but these people gathered in the campo santo, hundreds of miles away from any prelate qualified to enforce His will, clearly could not bring themselves to be so heartless on their own. Only the drunken blacksmith stood apart, looking on with an Old Testament glower.

They watched the coffin sink into the earth, and heard it land with a thump as it got away at the last moment from the struggling pallbearers. With no priest to officiate, the mourners began to mumble the rosary.

"They can say all the Hail Marys they want," the blacksmith said. "But there never was a soul raised out of hell yet. The poor lovesick fool's gone to everlasting fire and that's the hard truth of the matter."

He looked at Edmund, inspecting him with a drunken thoroughness.

"Have you no hat?"

"A coyote took it."

"And what would a coyote want with a hat?" the blacksmith almost shouted in amazement, his voice so loud that several of the mourners turned and looked at him sternly. "Why would a coyote steal a man's hat?"

"There's salt in the brim, I guess," Edmund said wearily. "Is there a public house in the town?"

"Mrs. Mott keeps it. The tigress herself."

He registered Edmund's blank look. "Have you not heard? The Kronks jumped her last week while she was out oystering on the bay. She killed one of them with her own hand. It was Jim Bowie that called her the tigress."

"Bowie's here?"

"Certain. Staying at the inn."

THE INN was a simple but oversized dogtrot cabin, a single public room connected to the owner's dwelling house by means of a shaded breezeway. When Edmund rode up no one was visible, though he could hear the sound of heroic snoring from within the public room. That would be Bowie, he surmised, no doubt sleeping off a drunk.

A teenaged boy appeared, carrying water up from the river, and invited Edmund to light and tie. The boy looked tired, done in by work and worry.

"Mr. Bowie and Mr. Despalier are asleep," he said, taking the reins to Cabezon and Snorter, "but you'll have your own bed. I'll see to your horse and mule and get you some supper."

The boy led the two animals away to the stable with the slow tread of a sleepwalker. Edmund carried his baggage into the inn, leaving Professor outside. The shutters of the room's one window were closed, and the chinking was daubed tight. A half-dozen shooting holes let in bolts of sunlight, but Edmund still had to grope through the darkness, feeling his way across the rough floor to one of the vacant mattresses. He set his things down and then began to creep out, not wanting to wake Bowie or the other man. Surprising Jim Bowie in the dark was a dangerous proposition.

Careful as Edmund tried to be, Bowie snorted himself out of sleep for a brief reconnaissance.

"Who the goddam hell is that?" he demanded.

"It's Edmund McGowan, Jim. Go back to sleep."

"They bring the alligator yet?"

"You're dreaming."

"You wake me when they bring the goddam alligator, Edmund."

Bowie rolled over and went immediately back to sleep, bringing down the pitch of his snoring an octave or two.

When Edmund walked outside onto the breezeway a woman was standing there, sitting out a plate and cutlery on a rough wooden table.

"I am Mrs. Mott," she said to Edmund, with a formality that, given her desperate appearance, seemed almost comical.

He introduced himself and managed not to stare, but that first unanticipated glance at Mrs. Mott had startled him. Her dark brown hair had apparently been burned on one side of her head, and then shorn on the other side for balance. A bandage covered what he assumed were the burn marks on her neck, and another bandage spanned and concealed the middle of her face. There were livid bruises around her eyes, but the eyes themselves were remarkably clear and somehow detached from the wreckage surrounding them. Edmund, habituated by his profession to a precise awareness of color—the starchy pink of *Palafoxia texana,* the calm, saturated blue of *Hydrolea spinosa*—had always been strangely uncertain when it came to recognizing or recalling the color of human eyes. Mrs. Mott's eyes had the brilliance and subtle tincture of glacial ice, though he would not have known whether to call them blue or green or hazel. They were, perhaps, a shining nacreous gray.

She moved in obvious pain, and when she tried to pick up a crock of buttermilk he had to rush to her aid and take it from her.

"Thank you," she said. "Several of my ribs are cracked. It's a great annoyance."

"You appear to be in no condition to play the hostess, Mrs. Mott."

"I'm not 'playing' the hostess," she said, "any more than you're playing the weary traveller. Please sit down to your meal."

Edmund did as instructed. Moving cautiously, she set down a bowl of cold turkey hash, a platter of cornbread.

"The cornbread is stale," she announced. "There'll be a new batch for supper."

"I'm not overly particular about food," Edmund said.

"Men always say that." She fixed him with a friendly, perturbed look. "But in my experience they never mean it. Do you mean to tell me, Mr. McGowan, that you don't care whether you're eating horse cracklings or ice cream?"

"I meant to try ice cream the last time I was in New Orleans, but it slipped my mind."

"At least Jim Bowie—" She winced, stood silently for a moment and breathed the pain away. "—at least Jim Bowie is an honest eater."

From her tone, he gathered she was aware of the general opinion that Bowie was not honest at a great deal else.

She commanded Edmund to eat, and he did so, as famished as a newborn.

"Won't you sit?" he asked.

"It pains me less to stand."

"I'm sorry to see you so knocked about," he said. "I understand you had a battle with the Indians."

"Yes," she said vaguely, not eager to speak of it, "a sort of battle, I suppose."

"I think your mare has sidebone," the boy said, coming up from the stable. "It ain't bad yet, but we'd better soak it."

"This is my son, Terrell, Mr. McGowan," Mary Mott said.

Edmund stood to shake hands. The boy's grip was secure, though his eyes were paler and less distinct than his mother's, and his manner more grave. He had the look of somebody who thought he had to hold the world together.

"She may be chafed, too," Edmund told him, remembering the last few days in which he had burdened Cabezon with unaccustomed weight and shifting saddle positions.

"She is, a bit," Terrell answered. "I can make a poultice." He bent down to Professor and scratched his ears. The dog rolled over onto his back, arrogantly bidding the boy to scratch his belly as well.

"What's his name?" he asked Edmund.

"Professor."

Terrell smiled as he regarded the dog's imperious face. He grabbed a piece of cornbread off the table and held it out to him, but Professor merely touched his nose to it.

"I'll get him some scraps," Terrell said, then looked up

crossly at his mother. "You shouldn't be moving around like that, not with your ribs the way they are."

"They're mending just fine, darling." She appealed to Edmund: "He'd strap me to a cradling board if he could, just to make sure I didn't move at all."

"One of those ribs might poke a hole in your liver."

"For heaven's sake, Terrell. They're not broken, just cracked."

With an exasperated shrug he stood and led Professor toward the cookhouse. Mrs. Mott continued standing at the opposite side of the table, apologizing once again for the stale cornbread.

"Real bread is what I miss most about the States," she said. "Texas would be a much better place if people would stop talking about revolution and start thinking about some way to grow wheat."

"You're not a War Dog, then, Mrs. Mott?"

"I would be if I were a land speculator with reams of worthless scrip to sell. Or if I were Sam Houston looking for a country to be emperor of. Would you care for more buttermilk?"

She poured him some, refusing his aid this time.

"Have you been ill, Mr. McGowan? You don't look much stronger than I do."

"The ague caught up with me, coming down from Béxar."

She studied him frankly for a moment, then put a hand to his forehead, a gesture that startled him in its unannounced intimacy. Mrs. Mott made him uneasy in general. Her movements were stiff just now, but he could sense the natural grace in her carriage, the distracting melodiousness with which, after a considerable moment, she pulled her hand away. And her face—bruised, swollen, burned, and bandaged though it was—stirred up a familiar longing in him, an unwelcome reminder of his own coarse humanity.

"You don't have a fever."

"No, the spell is over, but I was a long time in getting here, and I'm afraid I missed my passage."

"You did if you were planning to take the supply ship. It sailed a few days ago. Where are you going?"

"The City of Mexico."

"There's a packet calling next week, bound for Vera Cruz. I'll send word to the customs officer in Copano and find out if there's an empty berth."

He thanked her, then gestured toward the public room. The sound of snoring continued to roll forth like ocean breakers.

"Where's Bowie headed?"

"He and Mr. Despalier are returning from a business trip in Matamoros. They're on their way to Nacogdoches, if they ever wake up."

Edmund did not bother to inquire what sort of business had taken Bowie to Matamoros. No doubt it was another shady land transaction like the one that had gotten him run out of Arkansas. Or perhaps it was war business. Bowie was a loud War Dog these days. When he had first come to Texas he had carefully married himself into the Veramendi family, the most powerful Tejano family in Béxar. But his new wife and his influential in-laws had all died in the cholera of '32, leaving him their house in Béxar but little else. Ever since, he had been suing his late wife's estate. Like most of the men Edmund had known in Texas, Bowie had no real means, but he had a head bursting with schemes. The chaos of a war would suit him fine.

"Mrs. Mott!" cried a voice from up the road. "We have the dragon! Where is our Saint George?"

Mary turned and saw that the voice belonged to John Dunn, one of Refugio's two regidores, who was driving a cart down Purísima Street, followed by a procession of curious citizens. Fresada walked behind the cart, holding a massive scaly tail like a trainbearer to keep it from dragging on the ground.

"I doubt that Mr. Bowie was counting on such a big alligator," Mary said distractedly.

"Why would Mr. Bowie be counting on any kind of alligator at all?" Edmund asked as they walked to meet the cart. He could not see anything but the tail, but he judged the creature must be at least nine feet long.

"Bowie and John Dunn were quite drunk last night," Mary explained. "Jim was boasting about all the alligators he'd wrestled in Louisiana, and John decided to put him to the test."

Dunn had hired Fresada to find an alligator for him, and Fresada had set out early that morning to scout along the riverbanks. It was a simple errand, Fresada had assured her, since most alligators were still denned up at this time of year and so groggy from their winter's sleep that it was only necessary to dig them out and hog-tie them. Even so, Mary could not imagine anyone but Fresada having the courage to dig into an alligator's den in the first place, let alone pull out a monster like this one.

"Saint George!" Dunn yelled, pounding on the door of the public house. "Come on out, by God! The beast awaits ye!"

Bowie opened the door a few moments later, unshaven and squinting in the noonday light but otherwise respectably put together, wearing a tailcoat and a neatly tied cravat.

"Wake up, Despalier!" he called over his shoulder into the darkness. "I don't plan to do this twice!"

He noticed Edmund and silently coasted forward to shake his hand, squeezing it a little harder and longer than their casual relationship strictly warranted.

"Looks like they've picked a monster for me," he said, peering into Edmund's eyes with a gaze as steady and confiding as that of the reptile in the cart. "Of course, I'd rather have a monster like this than one of those feisty six-footers. Despalier! Are you coming?"

A short, sallow man came to the door, squinted at the

crowd of onlookers, and then promptly made his embarrassed way to the outhouse while Dunn, Fresada, and four other men dragged the alligator out of the cart and laid it on its back on the cleared ground in front of the inn. With its jaws roped shut and legs trussed up over its belly, the creature rested there utterly motionless, in an attitude of grave contentment. Edmund knew Bowie would kill the alligator when he was through with it—what else would you do with an alligator?—but its serene stillness made it appear to be already dead.

"Have you ever wrestled an alligator, Mr. McGowan?" Mary Mott said, taking the trouble to stand next to Edmund as Bowie made a great show of inspecting the creature, pacing off its length, and fingering the great teeth that hung comically over its closed jaws.

"The necessity never arose."

"Mrs. Mott is the one who should be doing the wrestling!" Bowie roared as he hung his coat on a peg. "I very much doubt there's a fiercer woman in all of Coahuila and Texas."

He led the Irish colonists in a huzzah or two for Mrs. Mott, during which time Despalier returned. He had a bit more color in his face than he'd had when he ran off, but he was still not a hardy man. Edmund guessed he was an agent from one of the big land syndicates, travelling with Bowie to buy up claims that could be turned over for vast sums once Texas was won from Mexico.

"Now, sir!" Bowie said to Dunn. "Shall I wrestle him in the water or on dry ground?"

"Do it here," Dunn answered. "He might get away in the water, and I want the hide after you've vanquished him."

Professor raced in circles around the alligator, barking furiously, and Edmund had to tie him up with a piece of rope, worried that when the reptile was righted and untied it might simply ingest the little dog.

While Professor howled in outrage at the end of his tether, Bowie and the other men tilted the alligator over onto its stomach. Bowie then ordered everyone back twenty paces, took his famous knife out of its fancy scabbard, and began to cut the ropes binding the creature's legs. Free to run, the alligator did not move. It lay there as torpidly as ever, its skin as parched and gray as if covered with ashes.

"Are you going to untie his jaws, Jim?" Dunn asked.

Bowie turned his smile on the regidor. "If I didn't know you were my friend, John, I'd swear you were in a hurry to see me swallowed up by this gator."

The crowd backed up another few paces as Bowie slipped behind the alligator and sliced through the ropes holding its jaws together. He tossed the ropes aside, but the alligator still did not stir, just lay there in the clearing with a stillness and indifference that was hypnotic to the by-standers, and more frightening in its way than the sudden lurching movement they expected. There was no sign of respiration, no heartbeat or pulse pressing against its thick hide.

Bowie began to circle cautiously around the monster. He was a big man, but his movements were swift and precise. Edmund watched him, feeling by comparison as sluggish as the alligator. Like many of the questionable characters Edmund had known, Bowie possessed a beguiling physical presence, a lightness of form that matched his effortless manners. And he had demonstrated an amused fondness for Edmund ever since their awkward first meeting, at the Ve-ramendi house years ago as Bowie was just beginning to insert himself into Béxar society.

"James Bowie!" a flabbergasted Edmund had exclaimed on that occasion. "I'm well aware of your reputation, sir."

"I've got all sorts of reputations, Mr. McGowan," Bowie had said cheerfully. "I hope you're referring to one of the better ones."

"Well, of course I had in mind your discovery of *Clivia nobilis* growing on the Quagga Flats."

"The Quagga Flats?"

"To say nothing of *Sinningia speciosa*. Or of the jacaranda tree."

Bowie let his smile linger, but his pale gray eyes grew disturbingly guarded for a moment, as Edmund began to realize his mistake. This was not James Bowie, the famous botanist and plant collector for Sir Joseph Banks, whose discoveries in Brazil and in Southern Africa had given him a triumphant notoriety. This was the other James Bowie, the renowned knife-fighter, slave smuggler, and land swindler whose fame was even greater.

"I've been accused of a great many things, sir," Bowie had roared, delighted, when Edmund apologized and explained his confusion, "but you have the honor of being the first to accuse me of being a seedsman!"

Bowie had gone around Béxar repeating the story for months, and never failed to remind Edmund of it whenever they met. In the years that followed, Bowie was on the move even more than Edmund, searching for Spanish silver in the Comanche country, hustling land grants and stirring up trouble in Coahuila. He still had his lethal charm, but he seemed to Edmund more than a little frayed. Bowie had loved the young wife he had gained in his opportunistic marriage, and her death had rattled him, though not enough for him to forget about the inheritance he thought he was due from her. He was at an age—forty or so—when the clouds begin to gather. His drinking binges left him vulnerable to illness, and the frenetic scrambling that was necessary for him to stay ahead of his legal and financial problems gave him a subtle but perpetual air of anxiety.

But all his troubles seemed forgotten now that he was face to face with this gargantuan reptile, with a curious audience gathered around the perimeter of what they imagined to be the alligator's striking range. After a good deal of taunting, Bowie finally induced the alligator to open its mouth and hiss. He then contemptuously rapped it on its snout with a stick.

"Now he's starting to wake up, by God," Bowie said. "Everybody stand back."

The crowd obligingly shuffled back a few paces, more to keep in spirit with the entertainment than from any real fear of the beast, whose lethargy was still profound. Bowie got it to hiss once or twice more, and then, swift as a panther, jumped onto its back and grabbed its jaws, holding them closed as he drew the creature's head back to his chest.

"Want to take a turn, John?" Bowie grunted at the regidor, but Dunn just laughed.

"Now that you're in that fix," he said, "how do you plan to get out?"

"Why, it's the easiest thing in the world," Bowie explained, the veins in his neck bulging with exertion as he grappled with the alligator's massive head. "I simply roll him over and put him to sleep."

In one movement, he twisted the gator onto its back and slid out from underneath. The animal lay in an even greater state of repose, the skin of its belly so shockingly pale that the sight of it made Edmund want to avert his eyes, as if from some grotesque and unfathomable display of human nakedness.

Bowie stared at the inert alligator theatrically for a long moment, then slowly and carefully stood up.

"What'd you do to him?" someone in the crowd called out.

Bowie put his finger to his lips, and then spoke in a whisper.

"I put him into the arms of Morpheus."

He grinned. There was bemused applause. Bowie accepted Dunn's handshake and his cigar. The alligator lay there on its back ignored as Bowie smoked the cigar halfway down and chatted with the citizens of Refugio about the famous Sandbar fight in which he had survived being run through the rib cage with a sword-cane. Several people produced knives and asked if they were authentic bowies, but Bowie sadly informed them that they were cheap British imitations. The genuine article, he said, was made by a secret tempering process perfected by the ancient Damascans. Further, he advised them to avoid the newly popular salons in New Orleans where young men were instructed in the code duello and the art of knife-fighting. These salons were not authorized to use his name in their promotions, and his attorneys were looking into the matter.

"Besides, there ain't no 'art' to a knife-fight," he said. "You stick your man and you cut his heartstrings if you can, and that's about as fancy as it gets."

As Bowie held forth, Edmund let Professor off his leash and walked over to the alligator. It still lay there like something eternal, its underside almost pink in the failing light. Professor sniffed around it cautiously, barked once or twice, but the reptile still did not stir.

"You ain't worried he'll wake up and eat that dog?" Terrell asked Edmund.

"He won't wake up. When an alligator's upside down it squeezes off the air to his brain."

The boy looked down at the alligator, pondering this.

"You can touch him," Edmund said, as he bent down and stroked the gator's belly. He looked underneath at the creature's open eyes, the dark vertical slits of the pupils staring out at him, perhaps aware, perhaps not. Terrell bent down beside Edmund and gingerly ran his hand along the alligator's pale underside. The boy seemed to be composing a question in his mind, but before he could ask it John Dunn walked up with his rifle, loaded and primed.

"If you gentlemen would stand at a safe distance," Dunn said, "I will slay the beast."

Edmund pulled Professor away, and walked with Terrell to the shade of the dogtrot. Dunn fired a ball into the vicinity of the alligator's brain. What haunted Edmund was the way the creature barely acknowledged its own death: a spasm no stronger than a hiccough, an aimless waving of its feet, an imperceptibly deeper stillness settling into its body.

"TEXASIANS!" thundered Mr. Despalier as Terrell served the coffee. "That is the term, sir! That is the term par excellence!"

The evening was clear and warm, and Mary had dinner served in the dogtrot to take advantage of a breeze filtering up from the river. Extra chairs had been set out to accommodate the dozen men who had lingered after Bowie's contest with the alligator. She herself sat in a rocking chair nearby, half-listening to the blustery political talk, her spirit restless in a way she could not quite identify. Terrell moved among the men silently, as stealthy and respectful as a waiter in a fancy restaurant in New Orleans. A quiet boy, wary of tragedy. She wondered when it was she had lost the ability to see into her child's mind. Up until a certain point, it seemed to her, she had owned his thoughts with a mother's regal, all-knowing power. But his mind had grown intricate and distant as it absorbed and pondered the tragedies that befell them—Susie's death, and then Andrew's, and then this recent affair with the Karankawas, which had shaken him badly. When she tried to penetrate his consciousness now, she imagined her poor child frantically engaged in anticipating disasters and formulating charms to avert them.

"Tex-ass-ians," Bowie was almost wheezing with laughter. "We can't call ourselves Tex-ass-ians, Despalier."

"It's the natural term."

"Texicans," Dunn suggested, after a moment of rigorous thought. "There's your word, if you must have one."

Someone else proposed "Texanians," but scant attention was paid to him, since at that moment Bowie took his coffee cup and, with that intoxicating casualness of his, walked away from the table and sat on the edge of the dogtrot, looking out toward the river. His dinner companions watched him expectantly.

"Texians," he muttered finally to himself, slurring and softening the *x* in his impeccable Spanish, so that the word came out sounding more like "Hessians." "The word suits us well enough, and we should stick with it."

"Texans," someone else suggested, but Bowie ignored him.

"Mrs. Mott," he said, turning to Mary with an amused smile, "your dinner was a testament to the civilizing hand of Woman. It was, ma'am, celestial."

"Never had a meal to touch it," Despalier said, "and I've eaten lamprey and peas at the Bishops Hotel."

"And real coffee!" Dunn said. "Not parched corn, by God!"

They regaled her with a spatter of applause. Mary had served them no spiritous liquors—they would have to retire to the saloons for that—but they seemed drunk all the same, brimming over with the simple satisfactions of being men and well fed.

"What do you think, Mr. McGowan?" Despalier asked after a moment. "Texican, Texasian, Texanian, Texian, or—what was that last one?—Texan! Your vote will settle the matter, sir. What should we call ourselves when we break away from Mexico?"

"Don't waste your time with Edmund," Bowie spoke up. "It don't matter to him if it's Mexico or Texas, so long as there's flowers growing on it."

Edmund smiled good-naturedly but said nothing. Mary watched him, annoyed at the way he teetered backward on one of the good side chairs that she and Andrew, bright with hope and schemes, had brought with them from their home in Kentucky. Mr. McGowan was a sort of man she was unaccustomed to, a man apparently without schemes, quiet and still. And arrogant, she thought, in the way he chose to hold himself apart from the discourse at the dinner table, staring inscrutably at a saucer of bee bait set out on a tree stump while the others thundered on about taxes and customshouses and Santa Anna's treachery in crushing any whisper of opposition to his centralist government.

"Would there happen to be another dove on the clock-jack, Mrs. Mott?" John Dunn said. "Watching Jim with that alligator has given me a wonderful appetite."

Mary nodded to Teresa, Fresada's grown daughter, a dutiful and silent young woman who helped with the cooking. Teresa walked to the kitchen with a profound limp, the result of a snakebite when she was a girl that had killed the nerves in her calf.

"Breaking with Mexico is a bad idea in the first instance," Dunn said. "A bad idea, sir," he repeated to Edmund, as if his silence meant he was eager to be persuaded one way or the other. "It is a fine way to show our gratitude."

"Gratitude," Bowie scoffed. "What are you grateful to Mexico for, John?"

"They gave us land."

"They gave you land, and now they want to tax you off it. They want to make it worthless by denying you your right to own slaves. They want to make *you* a slave instead, sir. How can a free man tolerate what Santa Anna has done? Shutting down state governments, overthrowing the Constitution of 1824. It is tyranny pure and simple, and contrary to every American principle."

"But this is Mexico," Edmund said nonchalantly, crushing a few grains of Mexican sugar into his coffee.

"So saith the sphinx," Bowie grinned. "But you have the truth of the matter, Edmund. The fact that this is Mexico is precisely the problem. Texas wants to be part of the States. God knows it and Hickory knows it and you know it too. Even the Little Gentleman himself knows it!"

The "Little Gentleman" was the infinitely patient Stephen

F. Austin, the great empresario who had led the first American settlers into Texas and done his best to see that they conformed to the contractual demands of their Mexican hosts. Bowie hated him, as he must, since Bowie was famously rash and Austin was a man of Byzantine subtlety.

Edmund had always liked Austin. He and Terán had met him during the Boundary Commission survey, when they stopped at his colonial capital of San Felipe, which at that time was just a half-faced camp of lean-tos and hastily thrown-up log huts with clapboard roofs. The streets, however, had been laid out with a measuring tape, and Austin had bordered them prettily with *Melia azedarach,* which he kept referring to mistakenly as Louisiana lilac. He was a wiry, intense man who brimmed with energy.

"You find me in a bachelor's household," he had told Edmund, ushering him into his grim little cabin. "Nothing but confusion, dirt, and torment." And books. Somehow in this remotest stretch of Mexico Austin had managed to squirrel away a library. Edmund remembered the books stacked against the walls and resting on tarps on the dirt floor—works by Herodotus and Shakespeare and Aristotle and Theophrastus (not just the *Historia,* Edmund was amazed to find, but *De Causis Plantarium* as well) and all forty-seven mildewed volumes of Rees's *Encyclopedia.* The next day, Austin had taken Edmund and Terán exploring along the Brazos when the water was low and had shown them large bones in the riverbed that he swore had belonged to a mastodon.

Austin had been arrested a year and a half ago, when he had gone down to the City of Mexico to try, in his genial way, to win separate statehood for Texas and to overturn a repressive set of laws blocking further American immigration. Frustrated by the government's obstinance, he had committed one of the few intemperate acts of his life, sending a letter decreeing that Texas should organize an independent state government no matter what Mexico thought of the matter. The letter had soon come to the attention of the Mexican authorities, who had interpreted it as a call to revolution, and Austin had been thrown into one gloomy prison after another.

"Speaking of the Little Gentleman," Bowie continued, "I have some news. He's on bail."

"Out of prison?" Edmund asked, surprised. The news cheered him. Stephen Austin was a clearheaded, far-thinking man, and if there was any hope of averting a war it lay in his influence.

"Not exactly," Bowie said. "Santa Anna's still got him in Mexico City. But he's free to flit about the streets."

Edmund ignored Bowie's choice of words. Bowie was never shy about suggesting that Austin, with his inscrutable mild temper, was at heart a sodomite.

"Austin will return," Dunn said, "and put an end to this independence nonsense."

"By the time Austin gets back," Bowie said, "independence will already be a fact, or we'll all be dead or in prison ourselves. Santa Anna's been planning to invade Texas since he came to power, and he's going to do it this year."

"Let him come!" Despalier announced. "He'll find a free people determined to die in the cause of liberty."

"Tex-ass-ians, by God!" Bowie said. "Isn't that right, son?"

He was speaking to Terrell, who was walking up to the table carrying dessert, an ashcake Teresa had baked that morning.

"Yes, sir," Terrell said.

Bowie stood and walked over to Terrell and put his hand on his shoulder.

"We don't have to worry about Texas, not with War Dogs like Terrell here and old alligator wrestlers such as myself."

Mary watched as Bowie kneaded Terrell's shoulder with

his big hand. She could sense the boy's pleasure in being noticed, in being included in Bowie's gruff goodwill. But it irritated her, and it frightened her too. By the mere act of setting his hand on Terrell's shoulder, Bowie had a claim on her son. She knew how spellbinding such a claim could be to isolated or unsettled or unformed people. Maybe that was why she had trouble meeting Jim Bowie's eyes this evening, because she herself had fallen under his claim one night eight months ago, and still could hardly believe her daring bad judgment.

Her ribs were hurting now, and another headache had begun to gather inside her skull. Terrell and Teresa began to clear the dishes; Fresada went to the springhouse for washing water. The men argued on, about the price of cotton (five dollars the arroba, a price Andrew had predicted two years ago), about the militia the government was supposed to provide to prevent Indian attacks like the one that had befallen her, about separate statehood versus independence. Bowie said Mexico was now the enemy of Texas; Dunn said Mexico could no more be Texas's enemy than a man's body could be the enemy of the heart within it.

All of the conversation seemed curiously distant to Mary tonight, though her livelihood and the well-being of her son depended directly upon the fate of Texas. She sat in her rocking chair, the pain tightening inside her head, and after a while her attention focused again upon Mr. Mc-Gowan, who remained coolly apart from the discussion, looking out over the yard. Following his eyes, she saw he was no longer contemplating the saucer of bee bait. He was looking at something beyond. It was the alligator carcass. Dunn and the other men had stripped it of its leathery hide, and now it hung from the stout limb of a live oak. Without its skin it was grotesque and troubling. Perhaps he knew she was watching him, because he turned in her direction, and their eyes met for an awkward moment. And it seemed to

Mary that in this glance he was setting forth a proposition. There is the world of war and Mexico and Texasians, the proposition stated, and then there is the world of this alligator swinging from a tree limb, pale as a salamander in the weak moonlight.

CHAPTER FOUR

✹

MARY LAY AWAKE in her bed in the dwelling house, listening to Terrell's shallow snores from the loft above, and to the distant, anxious music of wolves, their voices rising and tumbling in a melody too complex and raw for her to grasp. One moment it was a beautiful lament, the next a fiendish chaos.

But when Andrew was alive they had slept countless nights in each other's arms with the wolves howling on the prairies, and then it had been almost a lullaby. It was pain that kept her awake tonight, not wolves. She tried not to draw air through her shattered nose, but she felt closed up and vulnerable, like a child underwater with only a reed to breathe through. So she let in the air, and the pain coursed in with it. Her burns were healing without too much discomfort, but her cracked ribs still tortured her, especially at night, when there was nothing to do but lie rigidly in her bed guarding against any unanticipated movement.

She had disciplined herself not to think too much about the incident with the Karankawas. El Pinto was dead and the colonial militia had tried to track down his followers, but these Irish farmers were hardly frontiersmen, and the Mexican presidial troops that were supposed to put an end to Indian depredations were thinly scattered and poorly equipped. Mary believed the rogue band of Kronks had escaped across the bay and were working their way up or down the long, narrow sea islands that stretched from Galveston to the mouth of the Bravo. They had the whole Texas coast to ravage, if they chose to be so bold again, and she did not rationally fear that they would return to the scene of their misfortune.

Nevertheless, she was still in the grip of a dull terror, and sometimes she was glad for the sharp physical pain that overrode it. She saw the attack over and over again, so that her sickening fear, her trembling hands as she had tried to load the musket, her shameful whimpering weakness, kept passing through her mind like a feverish dream. It was as if her imagination had been polluted and could never purge itself.

She took a deep breath and managed, in slow, agonizing stages, to rise out of bed. She pulled an old scarlet blanket around her shoulders and reached up to the cupboard for the cigar that Bowie, in his familiar, insinuating way, had presented to her after dinner. She stirred the coals in the hearth with an oak twig until it glowed, then lit the cigar with it and walked out into the night.

It was well after midnight and well before dawn, a cradle moon high in the clear, dark sky, the stars spanning the vault in great luminous swaths. She walked to the river to her favorite cypress and sat down on a commodious root and smoked her cigar, remembering the look in Bowie's eyes as he had handed it to her, a look that said, "I know the kind of woman you are."

But her own look in return had been opaque, and Bowie—so coarse in some ways, so subtle in others—had not pressed her in the slightest degree. She did not regret in principle the moment she and Bowie had shared on a moonless humid night by this same river, with fireflies providing a fitful, tantalizing light that danced about their unclothed bodies. Mary was not on terms with the view that the act of human congress was a distasteful thing that must be obscured with grim propriety. She had been raised in a household in which even the naked limbs of the piano (her mother would never have been able to bring herself to use the vulgar term "legs") had to be covered with frilled pantalettes. She had always found this sort of caution peculiar and shameful on its own, and when she had finally met Andrew on their wedding night she had taken a forthright pleasure in exposing her body to him, and in touching every part of his, believing in her heart that this was a happiness that God Himself had willed her to know.

The hardest thing about Andrew's death, his continuing eternal absence, was the feeling that a significant part of her own physical self was gone as well. After he had died— of the vómito while travelling to Monclova, where he intended to petition the distant land commissioner for a final ruling on his empresario contract—Mary had been stupid with grief, experiencing events in a dull, leaden way that made her feel that the responsive half of herself had been stripped away and buried with Andrew in some nameless campo santo deep in the deserts of Mexico.

Bowie had helped restore some of that spirit. For a scoundrel, he was not an insensitive man, and during that night of the fireflies he had let her weep in his arms without feeling the need to embarrass her by inquiring why. But that one night was quite enough. Mary was a practical woman, and Bowie's limitations as a man were painfully clear. He was a drunkard, a victim of self-infatuation, and more of a villain than not.

Andrew, of course, had been something of a promoter himself, and perhaps she was drawn to the type by the demands of her own nature. The son of a rootless and inattentive father, he had roamed as a child through the Mississippi forests with his Indian friends and his blowgun, as free as any leatherstocking. When she first met him, he was twenty-two, touring Kentucky and Tennessee with a company of Choctaw ballplayers, a hopeful entertainment scheme that quickly foundered in Lexington when the Indian athletes grew weary of travelling and peremptorily demanded their pay of five pounds of bacon apiece.

Even as his enterprise fell to pieces around him, Andrew

had behaved with infectious good cheer. He projected a sense of absolute license, a sense that his life was his to do with as he pleased, and that although he might fail repeatedly at petty schemes he would never fail at the one great thing that would finally count. He had a way of drawing people to him, his young face already creased with laugh lines around his eyes, his manner steady, kind, and amused.

Mary's father, who owned a prosperous cotton-bagging manufactory in those days before his health gave out, had arranged for the bacon to pay off the Indians, and as head of the school committee he promoted Andrew to fill the vacancy left when a previous schoolmaster was blinded in a hunting accident.

Andrew was a vigorous teacher, inspiring his students during the day, schooling himself in the classics in his rooming house at night. They had married on nothing, on the promise of his brilliance. After a year he grew impatient with the tiresome, mechanical process of drilling information into children's brains. He left the school and read for the law with an old gouty judge for six months, then gave that up too, deciding to become a steam doctor instead. He invested all their savings in a volume of Thomson's *Guide to Health,* which in those days sold for the astonishing price of twenty dollars the copy. Together they scoured the woods for his medicines—lobelia, cayenne, skunk cabbage, bayberry. He actually cured a patient or two, sunken gray-faced men and women who were suffering less from their diseases than from the bleeding and poisoning that were the hallmarks of the old allopathic medicine he meant to supplant.

But Andrew had been impatient with doctoring, too, fearing it would be a settled life that would lead only to routine happiness, and not the grand, obscure destiny he so infectiously craved. His formal education was sparse, but throughout his rootless life he had read deeply and zealously. When two philosophy professors at Transylvania

College met early one morning on the College Lot and
killed each other in a duel over a quadroon chanteuse, Andrew was available to fill one of the emergency vacancies,
and his temporary appointment developed over time into a
secure position.

The wife of the president of the college was Stephen
Austin's cousin, and it was at a dinner in the president's
house that they had first met Austin and learned firsthand
about the possibilities of settling in Texas. Austin had invited them to join his colony, but Andrew's ambitions were
grander. He became a Texas empresario on his own, daz-
zling investors with his sudden, almost messianic energy.
His idea was to recruit his allotment of families from
among the dispossessed Irish immigrants flooding into
New York, enticing them with the prospect of free land in a
Catholic realm.

They followed him eagerly, gratefully, but it had all
come to nothing so quickly: the dreadful sea passage from
New York, the cholera that had infested their packet ship in
New Orleans and travelled with them to the Texas coast,
where it took little Susie away as she screamed and swatted
at the sand crabs that crawled over her body; their horrible
hunger afterward and the weevilly corn they had brought
from New Orleans whose grains had to be charred in the
embers of campfires and then husked in lye before it was
even fit to cook; the arguments, amounting once or twice
almost to open warfare, between rival empresarios—each
with his own boatloads of pasty, underfed Irishmen and his
own outraged claim to the land on which Andrew and Mary
and their colonists had landed. And then finally Andrew's
mission to Monclova, which resulted in nothing but his
death and the political triumph of his enemies.

Along with Andrew, she had allowed herself to be baptized a Catholic under the terms of the colonization laws,
but that dark and intricate faith fundamentally repelled her.

She did not practice, she did not profess, she did not believe in any God except the one she knew: a sensible, companionable presence who directed her onward while keeping a consoling hand on her shoulder. So she was a Protestant stranded in a papist wilderness, a tavern keeper struggling for a living in a colony whose title had once been in her husband's name.

But Texas agreed with her in mysterious ways. It was lush, open, boundless—a place that would kill you and all you loved but would somehow never defeat your hopes. The sky overhead tonight was almost fierce in its beauty, more brilliant than any sky she had known in Kentucky or even on the open Gulf as they had sailed their cholera ship to the Texas coast. The river below her was calm, and so clear that if the moon had been full she would have seen the bottom through eight or ten feet of water. She snuffed out her cigar against the cypress root, set her head against the trunk, and listened to the soft flapping of a night heron's wings as it sailed down the river. A stray breeze moved solemnly through the anaqua and huisache leaves, and through ageless tufts of Spanish moss. A big gar broke the surface of the water just below the spot where she was sitting, but the abrupt noise was soothing rather than startling.

But something else made her freeze: a shuffling sound coming from the other side of the tree, upwind from her. That familiar hollowness visited her body again, and she saw her hands begin to tremble in her lap. She had not brought her rifle; that had been a bad mistake. She looked up the sloping river terrace to the inn. She was a hundred yards away. Whatever was on the other side of the tree—a marauding Indian creeping through the grass, a dangerous wild hog—had probably not yet seen her, and if she took off now and ran screaming to the house she thought she could probably make it. If it was Indians, they would meet with formidable resistance if she could raise the men in time. Bowie was as famous for fighting Comanches as he was for settling debts of honor with his knife. Fresada was dependable and cool. And Mr. McGowan struck her as a fundamentally effective man, just as Mr. Despalier struck her as a fundamentally useless one.

But Mary did not move. She wanted to determine first what she would be running from. She took a deep breath, feeling the air squeezing against her cracked ribs, and peered with infinite caution around the trunk of the tree. A human form was making its way toward her through a thick curtain of ragweed, patting the ground with its hands, muttering to itself.

"Mr. McGowan," she said.

He looked up, surprised but not startled, his face half-hidden by swaying ragweed stalks.

"Oh," he said. "Good evening. I wasn't aware anyone was nearby."

"I can understand your wanting to carry out your odd little ritual in private," Mary answered, her voice still tremulous with fright.

Edmund stood and brushed his dirty hands against the thighs of his pantaloons, and detached himself from the tiny thorns of a wait-a-minute vine.

"I was looking for a species of night-blooming cactus," he announced. "It's an inconspicuous plant at best, and its flowers are infinitely small."

"You're more likely to find poison ivy, crawling around like that in the dark."

"Fortunately, I seem to be immune to poison ivy."

"Terrell's had it bad once or twice," she said. "And my husband was in torment once for an entire week. Even the vinegar rubs didn't work."

"Males seem to suffer more from the plant than females," Edmund observed. "Particularly when—"

He broke off suddenly, and shifted his attention to the river.

"You are well situated here, Mrs. Mott. A very favorable location indeed."

"Particularly when what?"

"Well," he said nervously, "when the toxin has affected the lower regions of the body."

"The feet?"

"No, not that low. The private areas."

"The testicles."

"Precisely."

She began to subject him to a long, appraising silence. He noticed that the bandage masking her face glowed faintly against the darkness.

"There's something peculiar about you," she said at last.

He felt called upon to defend himself. "I don't often crawl around on my hands and knees in the middle of the night."

"No. Something else. You don't wear a hat."

Edmund explained once again how the coyote had stolen his hat. Mary laughed at the thought. He looked at her burned neck, covered with some kind of salve that glistened in the starlight.

"I could sell you a hat," Mary said. "A plain round hat or a fancy beegum. I think they would be a fit, and they've never been worn. My husband ordered them from New Orleans, and they arrived a month after I received word of his death."

"I don't care for a beegum," Edmund said. "But a round hat would suit me. Have you been a widow long, Mrs. Mott?"

"Two years."

He nodded and sat down on a nearby cypress root without invitation. He looked down again into the river, regarding it with a penetrating scrutiny. Another gar broke the surface. Mary waited for Edmund to speak, but he seemed to be in no hurry to end the silence. He was still weary and ravaged from his illness, and this produced in her an unanticipated feeling of kinship. In recent days, they had each come very close to oblivion, and it seemed to Mary that they met tonight nearly as ghosts.

"What are you looking at?" she said. Her voice sounded inappropriately casual to herself, even intimate, as if she were talking to an old acquaintance.

"Nothing in particular," he answered. "Just the water. This is a fine place to sit late at night."

"I often do so, especially since the incident with the Indians."

He looked up at her, a steady look, though his eyes were hidden in night shadow.

"Will you recover completely?"

"I will, though I'll be ugly."

"Well, I would hardly . . . ," Edmund fumbled.

Mary brushed away his attempt at gallantry. "It's my mind I wonder about. Whether I'll always feel so unsettled. You have certainly killed men, Mr. McGowan?"

"I haven't. Botany rarely requires it."

"It's a horrid thing, to have killed another human being. And the most horrid part is . . . a feeling of satisfaction."

This admission, blurted out to a stranger, astonished Mary into another prolonged silence that Mr. McGowan did nothing to relieve. She was about to stand and walk back to the inn, deeply embarrassed, when Edmund threw a rock into the river. They listened to its pleasing hollow splash, and this somehow joined them again.

"It's thought that turtles are left-handed," Edmund offered.

"There are people who think about that?"

"Oh, a natural philosopher would ponder away forever on a question like that. I shouldn't say all turtles, just the soft-shelled variety. A man named Lincecum told me he had caught thirteen of them one winter in a beaver trap. Twelve of them were snared by the left forefoot."

"But the thirteenth was right-handed?"

"That can't be concluded, since he was caught by the neck."

She laughed, a painful wheeze. He laughed as well, with the guardedness that had been his lifelong aspect among women. Mrs. Mott's sudden lighthearted tone, its implications of a developing friendship, disturbed him to the same sharp degree that it enticed him. He had had few such friendships. His solitude, when it came to women, was particularly deep; it was nearly absolute. From an early age he had set out to conquer himself, to master his own desires with the same force of mind and constancy of will with which he had mastered his science. It had seemed to him, long ago, a necessary thing to do, as necessary as a saint turning from the clamorous demands of the flesh in order to discern the voice of God. And in Edmund's mind his own great pursuit—of perceiving and chronicling the variety of creation—required that same state of worthiness, of holy intent.

"Shall we settle down to business, Mr. McGowan?" Mrs. Mott asked chidingly. "As long as we have all this idle time on our hands, I should like to come to terms on your new hat."

"I haven't seen it yet."

"Yes, but I've been taking note of the shape of your head while we've been philosophizing about turtles. I do think it will answer very well. I'll sell it to you for seven dollars and fifty cents."

"I've never paid such an extravagant price for a hat, which I regard only as a utilitarian necessity."

"It's of dove gray felt, with a smart silk band and a little card in the crown on which you may write your name."

"Perhaps you should sell it to Bowie," Edmund said. "He's more accustomed to such finery."

"No, I think I'll sell it to you."

"Well, the client you've settled on does not have seven-fifty to spare."

"It's a fair price," she protested. "You know what Mexican tariffs are these days."

"Indeed. We're about to fight a war over them. But five dollars is all I can pay, Mrs. Mott, and I'll feel like a dandy doing so."

They agreed on five seventy-five, and went on to discuss the fee Mrs. Mott would charge for boarding Cabezon and Snorter while Edmund was gone to the City of Mexico.

"I'd like to leave my dog with you as well. Professor's never forgiven me for the last sea voyage I took him on."

"Terrell will be pleased to look after him," she said. "How long do you plan to be gone?"

"Perhaps two months."

"A great deal may happen in that length of time, I'm afraid. If Jim Bowie's right, Santa Anna will have invaded by then."

"I wouldn't call it an invasion. He can hardly invade his own country."

"Plenty of people will see it so. And hotheads like Mr. Travis will suddenly be turned into respectable patriots. And everything we've built up will be gone to satisfy their greed for conquest."

Edmund knew of Mr. Travis by reputation, a young lawyer from Alabama who had almost succeeded in sparking a revolution several years earlier when he had gotten himself arrested by the senior military officer in Anahuac. Travis was one of the most aggrieved men in Texas, always tensely in wait for any hint of injustice or tyranny.

The young lawyer was not entirely wrong, of course. Edmund thought that Mexico had, on the whole, badly mismanaged her Texas problem with arrogant and despotic officials, idiotic laws, and overall incompetence. But these inept solutions had arisen to combat the undeniable fact that Texas had always been a dangerously unstable place.

"What time do you suppose it is?" Mary asked him.

"Three-thirty or four," he said. His watch had been eaten by an ostrich two years ago in New Orleans. The ostrich had been on display as a zoological attraction and had snatched the watch out of Edmund's hands as he was winding it. Edmund was embarking that afternoon for Texas, and the keeper promised to send it to him when the bird voided, but of course he never did. He heard later that the ostrich had drowned at sea, swept overboard during a storm in the Gulf.

"I should go up to bed," Mary said without conviction.

Edmund did not feel it his place to register an opinion on this matter. He waited to see if she would rise and walk back to the inn; meanwhile he made a point of thinking about that great clumsy bird churning furiously in the dark ocean.

She observed him in his concentration. She had thought him unremarkable-looking at first, but now she was not so sure. He had a well-sculpted nose, his ears were not overlarge and were pleasingly situated close to the side of his head, his lank brown hair was roughly but conscientiously barbered, probably by his own hand. None of this added up to handsomeness, but there was a striking composure in his features whose source she could not quite locate.

"Where is your dog?" Mary asked him, having silently revoked her decision to stand up and walk back to the house.

"Curled up at Bowie's feet. Jim has a way with dogs."

"Do you feel abandoned?" she teased.

"I prefer your company, ma'am, to that of my dog."

"Your flattery is overwhelming."

He smiled at her. The night heron flew back up the river, uttering an intoxicating high-pitched *whawk! whawk!*

"I never met your husband myself," Edmund said. "But often heard his name spoken. He was well liked."

"He was easeful around people," she answered, with a confirming nod of her head. "He was trustworthy and intelligent and had many friends. He would have been a great man of Texas had he lived."

"I am sure you miss him a great deal."

She was not much moved by this purely rhetorical comment, but something in his voice jostled her emotions, and she began to cry, quietly at first and then in great heaving convulsions. The more she tried to contain the outburst, the stronger it grew.

Edmund moved closer but did not touch her. She could feel his soft eyes watching her, and though this eruption of sentiment startled her, she did not feel ashamed to have this particular man witness it.

Her own weeping gasps were so loud she was not sure whether she heard his voice, or only imagined it. In any event it was a calm, suspiring sound that came to her, rather like that of the river below—"Shhh. Shhh."

"I'm very sorry," she said at last, after long, long minutes. "How rude of me."

"I should never have introduced so disturbing a topic."

"No, it was not your questions that set me off. My emotions have been in a churn ever since the Indian attack. No doubt I would have exploded sooner or later anyway, but I do apologize for doing so in front of you."

She stood up. She moved a finger under each side of her bandage to swab the tears away.

"If you are not too shaken," she told him, "I will leave you to your search for the night-blooming cactus."

"Good night, Mrs. Mott," he said. She nodded good night in reply, and then smiled at him from beneath the bandage before turning to climb back up the river terrace toward the inn.

CHAPTER FIVE

✷

TERRELL HAD CARRIED a madstone in his pocket for years. Fresada had given it to him soon after he came to work for his father. Terrell had seen plenty of madstones and bezoars back in Kentucky, and knew that this one—the size of a walnut and as polished and milky as a cue ball—was probably a gallstone from the stomach of a deer. But Fresada insisted it was formed when a beloved stallion in a Comanche chief's remuda had been bitten by a snake and shed a single crystallized tear before it died.

Terrell could not stop himself from believing in charms and signs. He had seen the comet that passed overhead in the cholera year, gliding silkily across the heavens like some poisonous star. Somehow, he thought, the star had killed his sister. He remembered how his father had taken Susie's body and paddled across the lagoon to bury her in the desolate sands of St. Joseph's Island. The colonists had argued that she and the rest of the cholera victims should be buried at sea to reduce the risk of contagion, but Terrell's mother had turned as ferocious as a wolf when she heard this. No child of hers would be buried in the dark, lonely ocean. She won the concession that Susie could be taken to the island, where in that windswept wildness she would at least rest with a marker above her head.

The weather that day had been warm and still, the sky and the surface of the lagoon blended together in blazing whiteness. His mother stood with him as they watched his father paddle the canoe away from shore. She could not bear to watch Susie be buried, and she clung to Terrell so tightly that he later had bruises where her fingertips had dug into his arms. The canoe travelled with infinite slowness across the pale satiny water. Not a breath of wind stirred, not a wave rose. Only the all-consuming whiteness of this strange land weighing down on them all like a press. Around his neck, hidden beneath his shirt where his mother could not see it, Terrell wore a copper amulet as a defense against the disease that had taken his sister away.

His mother had taken all the usual practical steps to protect them against cholera—filtering their drinking water through burnt bread, fumigating their tent with gunpowder smoke—but he knew she would have disapproved of the amulet. She did not trust the unseen. Her world was visible, tactile, clear. Death did not belong to it, did not rise up from it. Death was an invader from some other realm.

His mother's world, as far as he could see, had no secret corners. But what solace Terrell found came from the invisible: the Irish praying their rosaries, proclaiming their Joyful and Sorrowful Mysteries, singing in their lugubrious Latin; the unredeemed Kronks with their ecstatic mitotes, listening to the gods whisper in their ears; his own little madstone, so perfect in its shape and color, so complete and powerful, somehow offering to share its power with him.

Before Jim Bowie had left last week with Mr. Despalier, he had pulled all the teeth from the dead alligator's mouth and distributed them to the children of Refugio, riding like a prince through the mud streets and placing a tooth into each child's outstretched hand. He had saved one of the big fangs for Terrell, tossing it to him casually as he mounted his horse.

"Drill a hole through that tooth," Bowie instructed him, "and it'll make a pretty necklace for your sweetheart."

But the tooth was more than an ornament. It seemed to Terrell to be a charm as well, with all the inscrutable, indifferent power of that dead alligator packed into it.

He had left the house before daylight that morning on a

hunting excursion with Fresada and Mr. McGowan, who had been staying at the inn for the last week waiting for the packet ship that would take him to Mexico. Terrell was not sure whether he had come along on the hunt out of boredom or barter, since the extra week's lodging had been an unanticipated expense. Though Mr. McGowan was not an especially talkative man, he did ask a fair number of questions, mostly about vegetation and insects and the tidal fluctuations in the bays, but also about the makeup of the local ayuntamiento and the availability of smuggled goods from the States.

Terrell did not mind answering the questions, those he knew the answers to, but he found Mr. McGowan to be rather ponderous company. He was used to Fresada's silent, self-sufficient presence, and if anyone else were to join them he would have preferred an entertaining talker like Mr. Bowie.

So at midmorning, feeling solitary, he branched off from the party and headed a few miles north to see what he could do on his own. He was riding Veronica, the fine horse his father had bought from the Tejano rancher Carlos De La Garza just before the fatal trip to Mexico. She was what the Tejanos called llegüa tordilla picada, a speckled gray mare with intelligent, wide-set eyes and long, straight legs whose hooves seemed barely to graze the earth when she ran, light as a spirit, across the luxuriant prairies. Terrell's father had also bought a magnificent saddle from De La Garza, with the leather skirts known as quadralpas that flared out protectively over the horse's rump like the illustrations Terrell had seen in books about ancient knights. In the old days, De La Garza had said, the law decreed that such a beautiful saddle could be ridden only by Spanish nobility. But here in Texas, where everyone—Tejano or norteamericano or Irishman—could think of himself as a bold frontiersman, such laws about protocol and nobility did not take root.

Terrell had shot a little deer around noon with the Ken-

tucky rifle, and a turkey an hour later, and now he was riding back to Refugio with both animals balanced awkwardly
behind him on the saddle. Mr. McGowan's dog had preferred to follow Terrell when he split off, and he trotted industriously a few paces in front of the horse. Professor had
taken no part in the hunting, merely stood quietly down-
wind as Terrell had crept up to a small congregation of deer
at the edge of an oak motte. Terrell had used Veronica for a
blind, concealing his slow steps behind hers. The deer he
had chosen never moved or displayed any interest in the
horse, and Terrell had managed to place the ball just where
he wanted it, an inch from the root of the left ear. It had
been a gratifying shot, and though he could hardly have expected the dog to admire it, he was disappointed that Professor displayed so little interest in the whole event.

Terrell stopped at a shallow creek to give Veronica a rest.
He removed the deer and the turkey and then the heavy saddle, and then poured cool water over the mare's sweaty
back. Professor settled himself into a little pool formed from
a coiling tree root at the water's edge and watched Terrell
with some slight degree of expectation, now and then cutting his eyes to the deer.

"Don't think you're going to get any of that backstrap,"
Terrell told him.

He took out the alligator tooth and studied it. Some old
Irishman had told him that the luckiest thing a man could
own was the back tooth of a horse. But you couldn't just
pry it out of a horse's skull. You had to come across it lying
on the ground all by itself. The back tooth of a horse
seemed like a common enough object to Terrell, but though
he had seen a multitude of bleached mustang skulls on the
prairies he had never found a single dislodged tooth.

Some things were precious, and some were not. An ordinary stone, a feather, the random objects in a Comanche's
medicine pouch—these could guide your life. They could
bring you power and watch over you like God Himself. Ei-

ther they had this power from the beginning, Terrell thought, or you invested it in them somehow, by the simple way you looked at them or held them.

He fingered the alligator tooth, scratching the flesh of his thumb against its sharp, simple point. The tooth did not gleam like his mad-stone, and he could barely feel its weight. It was as lustreless and brittle as an old hollowed-out bone. He did not like it, and he felt that the longer he possessed it the greater the claim it would make on him, and so he impulsively tossed it into the creek. The gesture caught Professor's attention, and the dog turned his eyes to the spot where the tooth had hit and watched it slide slowly beneath the surface. The water here was shallow and sluggish, with a mucky bottom. Very likely, Terrell thought, the alligator had known in life this very creek where only its tooth now resided.

He sat back and pondered whether he should have thrown it away or not. Professor watched him, as if silently joining in the argument, and then the dog suddenly leapt to his feet and barked at a presence on the other side of the creek.

It was the Foley girl, mounted on a ragged old mule that had one ear missing. Her homespun dress was frayed in half a dozen places, and the butternut dye had faded to the color of old parchment. She wore neither bonnet nor hat. Her black eyes stared at him like an animal's.

"What did you throw in the creek?" she asked.

"An alligator tooth." Terrell flirted with the idea of lying, but he could see no reason to.

"An alligator tooth, was it?"

Terrell nodded. Edna Foley continued to stare at him as if he were holding something back. And perhaps he was, though he didn't know what.

"And is it true, Terrell, that your mother killed a Kronk Indian?"

"It's true."

"I heard it spoken of, though no one will talk to me about it. No one talks to me about anything. Uncle Con and Uncle Dennis tied me to my bed with a hair rope. They wouldn't talk to me or look at me while they were doing so, so ashamed were they. Will you talk to me, Terrell?"

"All right."

She slipped off the mule, hitched it lightly to a tree branch, and sprang over the narrow creek to stand beside him. Terrell had rarely spoken to her, though he had known her from the beginning of his Texas life. Her parents and brother had both died on the cholera voyage, but she had been strange even before that, a sullen, distracted girl who kept to herself, absorbed in some awful private need that no one could identify.

She stood very close to him now on the creekbank, looking into his eyes with a steadiness that made him uncomfortable. Her face was small and round, overwhelmed by a disorderly mass of lush black hair. She was slender, and small as a child. The top of her head hardly reached his chin.

"Who chewed the ear off your mule?" he said, and was relieved when she took her eyes from him and trained them on the animal.

"It was a jaguar that did it, we're told. When he was quite young, deep in Mexico. He's old now."

She bent down to pet Professor. The dog rolled over on his back to present his belly.

"This is the dog of the man who's staying at your mother's inn. The man without the hat."

"You know a lot about what's going on."

"I watch things. Nobody tells me anything but I have my eyes to see. I saw you leave to go hunting this morning, and now I see you returning with a deer and a fine turkey for your mother's table."

"You want some crackers?" Terrell said.

He got the crackers out of his haversack, and they sat

there eating them in silence, with Professor looking on expectantly. Terrell handed the dog one and he sniffed it contemptuously, took it lightly on his teeth, and then dropped it on the dirt, where he studied it with an absorbed look.

"I watched them bury Mr. O'Docharty," she said. "He killed himself out of despair because I wouldn't marry him."

"I heard that," Terrell said.

"He was a cruel man. Cruel and with a wicked temper. And not a tooth in all his head."

"Why did you decide to marry him, then?"

"My uncles decided it for me. They told me he was ill-tempered only because he was lonely, and that he had a set of teeth carved from the tusk of a hippopotamus. But that is not the same as having your own teeth, and besides he would wear them only on Sunday because they hurt his gums, he said."

Terrell grunted quietly in response. She waded into the creek with her shoes on, the water soaking the hem of her dress. At this unexpected intrusion, a multitude of tiny fish burst outward from where she was standing, making the surface of the water seem like the twitching skin of something alive.

"I did not want him for my bridegroom," she said quietly. "I'm sorry he's dead. I hope he made a good act of contrition before he died, and is happy in heaven. What are these little fish called?"

"I don't know."

"Perhaps they're so small they have no name."

"Maybe."

"I've seen Our Lady twice. She's come to me twice."

"What lady?"

"The Blessed Mother."

She was looking at him again, her black eyes shining and vulnerable. "Do you believe me?" she asked.

"What did she look like?"

"First say you believe me."

"I got no reason not to," Terrell said.

"I saw her the first time at the fade of day. I thought the sun was going down, but it seemed to stop in the sky, and there she was at the top of a little hill, looking down at me. Her feet were bare, and they did not touch the earth at all. She said, 'Come here, child.' And I came to her, and she said, 'Are you lost?' and I said, 'Yes, Mother, I am in a strange land far from Ireland, and all that love me are dead.' And she put out her arms for me."

Standing in the middle of the creek, she turned her expectant eyes toward Terrell again, leaving it up to him to break the moody silence she had decreed.

"Did you touch her?" he asked.

"I don't think so, Terrell, but I felt her in some way. Her cloak is blue, as you know, and she wrapped it around me, and it was as if the sky itself had embraced me, such an embrace it was. 'Don't you worry about Mr. O'Docharty,' she told me. 'Don't you worry about anything, child. For you are home with me, and it will always be so.'

"Would you like to see her, Terrell?" Edna said suddenly. "We could go to the hill. It's not far away. Perhaps she will come to us again."

"I ain't much of a Catholic," he said. "We only got baptized because of the colonization laws."

"You don't believe in Our Lady?"

"I don't know."

"She probably won't appear to you if you don't have faith."

"I guess not."

She said nothing else for a long time, and then she sat down in the creek and lay on her back and spread her arms wide. The water was only a foot or so deep, but it enveloped everything but her pale face. Watching her hover there with her arms outspread, the water seeping over the bodice of her dress, Terrell was seized with disquiet.

"You better get out of that water," he said after a while.

"Why?"

"I don't know. Stay in there if you want to."

The afternoon sun fell through the swaying branches overhead and lit her floating form in lazy currents of light.

"You can leave if you want to," she said. "I'm just going to stay here."

"I'll stay for a minute," he answered. "I've got to get this game home, though."

She said nothing to that, just kept lying in the water looking up at the sky. In a moment they heard a distant chorus of skyborne voices, some sort of trumpeting or bleating that had an order to it Terrell could perceive but not decipher. The girl looked over at him with an odd kind of smile, as if something was about to occur that she had been expecting. The voices came nearer until he recognized them as swans, and by that time the birds themselves were overhead, many thousands of them flying no higher than thirty feet, their brilliant white forms coasting magically through the air. They were so close to the ground he felt he could stand up and grab one, but instead he lay on his back and watched them pass. Veronica stamped her feet and the girl's mule pulled at her rope and Professor barked for a minute or two, but after a while even he fell silent and seemed to gaze up into the sky in mute wonder. For ten minutes or more they flew overhead, their wings beating the air with such commotion and cyclonic force that Terrell thought he might suffocate in the vacuum they created in their passing. Then all at once the last wave passed and the sky was clear again, so suddenly empty of all life that it seemed unnatural and eerie beyond expression.

Neither he nor the girl spoke after that, not for a long time. And when finally Edna stood up in the creek, her hair and dress streaming water, she looked at him as if they had been together in the presence not just of a flight of swans but of some holy visitation.

"I want you to see my naked body," she said.

Nothing in Terrell's life had prepared him for this statement. Her words were so strange and so unbearably provocative that his mind refused to accept them as real and he thought he was in the middle of a startling daydream.

"Did you hear what I said?" Edna asked, her voice shaky. Terrell felt light-headed. There was a hum in his ears.

"Yes."

"Will you look at me?"

"All right."

His instinct was to look away while she disrobed, but she told him, "No, watch," and so he fixed his eyes on her as she unfastened the flat metal buttons of her bodice and then pulled the sopping dress over her shoulders and let it fall into the creek and stood there in her threadbare shimmy and pantalettes. She pulled down the pantalettes first and then in one swift intoxicating motion removed the shimmy and so stood there before him with her body bared unnaturally to the light and the atmosphere and the faint gusts of wind coursing up the creek from the open prairie. Her clothing lay at her feet in the shallow creek, discarded and forgotten as if she never meant to pick it up and wear it again.

"Don't take your eyes away," she said. "Please."

And so, as instructed, he stared at her. The female body was much as he had imagined, though he had never guessed that ever in his life he would see it so starkly revealed.

She walked slowly toward him, and he stood up helplessly to meet her, still feeling strangely light as all the blood in his body seemed to leave his head and flow insistently to his groin. She came very close, close enough for him to feel her slightly sour breath against his face. Her body was still wet from the creek, and there were goose bumps along her arms.

"She told me to," Edna said.

"Who?"

"Our Lady. She told me it would not be a sin with you because you were kind and would look after me."

Suddenly anxious, he looked away toward the clothes in the creek.

"You better get dressed," he made himself say. "You need to get your clothes dry before it gets dark or you'll catch a chill."

"Hold me in your arms."

"I better not."

He was ashamed of his insistent male organ, stiff and pounding against his canvas trousers. If she drew any closer to him she would feel it, and his helpless lust would be exposed to her.

But instead she took a step back, and it was she who appeared ashamed, standing there naked and unwanted in the full glare of the limitless world. She began to cry. Terrell knew she was crazy, and knew that what was about to occur was a calamity. He reached out to her, touching that shocking expanse of flesh, still covered with sliding droplets of water. She pressed herself against his chest and against his swollen groin.

"Oh, please," she whispered.

Together, they stripped off his clothes. Not since childhood had he stood naked in the presence of another person, and there was a kind of glory in it. Still he felt vulnerable and exposed, and he clung to her as much from a need to shelter himself in the flesh of another person as from outright desire.

The act itself seemed to Terrell an event of appalling urgency. He knew vaguely what was expected on his part but felt he should take more pleasure or devotion in it. As it was, it seemed to be happening to someone else, and the climactic moment took him by surprise and left him stranded in bewilderment and almost instant regret. He lay on top of her by the water's edge, the tears still fresh on her face. The sour breath that had obscurely enticed him only moments earlier now repelled him, and her dark eyes looking into his own filled him with anxiety.

"It was too fast," she said. "It was over too soon."

"I guess it don't take that long," Terrell replied, standing up and then turning his back to her as he pulled on his clothes.

"Don't get dressed yet?" she said. "Be naked with me."

"I've got to go home." He fastened his pantaloons and then, barefoot, waded into the creek to get her clothes. He spread them out over tree limbs and bushes while she continued to lie there on the ground, watching him.

"Did it feel good, Terrell?"

"It felt fine," he said nervously. "These'll be dry in half an hour."

"Uncle Dennis and Uncle Con will tie me to my bed again tonight, after all my roaming."

"I'm sorry to hear that," he said.

"But I'll have you to think about."

He put on Veronica's saddle cloth and then the heavy quadralpas saddle. Professor had been lying in his tree root basin, but now he stood up in anticipation of leaving and yawned. Terrell avoided the dog's eyes, fearing there would be some sort of judgment in them.

"And you'll have me to think about," Edna said.

"You gonna be all right?" Terrell said with his back to her as he tightened the cinch. She didn't say anything, but walked up to him from behind and put her arms around his waist and her chin on his shoulder.

"Stay with me till my clothes are dry, and we'll ride back together."

"I've got to get on home. I'll leave you the rest of the crackers."

"Can I live at your house?"

"I think you'd better live with your uncles."

"I'll come visit you. Tomorrow."

"I'll be out hunting again tomorrow."

"Where?"

"I don't know."

"I'll visit your mother till you come home."

He turned to face her. She still clung to him, and she looked into his eyes with a hunger that made Terrell ashamed and desperately confused. She was shivering.

"What's the matter?" he said. "Are you cold?"

"I'm afraid. I'm afraid to be all alone."

He tried hard to think of something to say to reassure her, but nothing would come to his agitated mind.

"Your mother will take care of me, if she knows we're sweethearts," Edna persisted.

"My mother's still hurt from that Indian fight," he told her firmly. "She can't take care of anybody right now."

"Then maybe I could nurse her instead."

"She's too proud for that. Maybe you could put your clothes on now and let them dry on your skin. There's plenty of daylight left."

"Don't you like looking at me this way?"

"I just ain't used to the sight of it."

He pulled away from her, swung up into the saddle, and looked down at her. Still unclothed, she grabbed his leg and held it in place between her breasts. Once more, he felt the suffocating warmth of her flesh enclosing him like a trap.

"You know the way back?" he asked.

"Yes."

"Are you all right?"

"No."

Tears were flying out of her eyes. He got down off the horse, picked up her dress from the bush where he had set it out to dry, and draped its wet fabric around her shoulders. He held her for a good five minutes without saying a word while her body quaked with her sobs.

"Will you at least say a Hail Mary with me?" she said.

"What's a hell mary?" he asked. Terrell's Catholic education had taken all of two minutes, and had been conducted by a drunken priest—the only priest in all of the colonies—that his father had found lying on the floor in a grog shop in San Felipe. The priest had agreed to travel to Refugio to baptize the family in exchange for an old bumbledick horse and several crocks of jam.

Edna got on her knees and pulled Terrell down beside her. The dress hung loosely from her shoulders and she did not hold it closed in front, so that her body was once again exposed to his troubled sight. She said the first part of the prayer, and then had him repeat the second part. It was a very short prayer but it had its effect on her, and she looked at him with eyes that were freakish and calm.

"You should go now," she said. "She's going to come to me again."

She kissed him fiercely, the dress fell away, and she knelt down again, unclothed and locked in some secret reverie.

"Good-bye now," Terrell said to her as he mounted the horse again, but she kept silent, her eyes fixed on the ground and her hands clasped in ferocious prayer.

TWO MILES OUT of Refugio he encountered Fresada and Mr. McGowan returning home. They were on foot, leading their horses. Each of the horses had a deer carcass draped over its back. Mr. McGowan wore his new hat, the hat that Terrell remembered seeing his mother cry over when it arrived after his father's death. It seemed to Terrell rather coldhearted of his mother to sell it, but his father had never worn it in life and anyway his mother was not the sort to let the house fill up with useless relics.

"I see that you're a lethal hunter as well," Mr. McGowan said when Terrell rode up to them with his own load of meat. "And you have a turkey."

"Yes, sir," Terrell said. He still felt numb and disoriented, and it seemed that Mr. McGowan's voice was coming to him from a far place.

"I tried to lasso a turkey," Mr. McGowan said. "Without success."

"Lasso a turkey?" Terrell said.

"It's not impossible. I've seen vaqueros do it a dozen times. As you know, a turkey will fly but once. After that it flees on foot. A man with a horse swift enough to follow the bird's initial flight can put himself within range. All it requires from there is a certain artistry with the rope itself, which Fresada can testify I don't possess."

Fresada smiled discreetly, and even in his agitated state of mind Terrell could not keep from picturing this unusual man earnestly racing a turkey across the prairie.

Terrell dismounted to walk with the two men. The country had ripened in the last few weeks, and the late-afternoon sun threw a sumptuous light on swirling bands of wildflowers. Mr. McGowan did not comment on any of the plants, but Terrell noticed his eyes searching vigilantly for any interesting specimen that might be visible in the sea of mesquite grass or on the fringes of the oak mottes.

"The mare's sidebone is nearly healed," Mr. McGowan said to Terrell, glancing back at one of Cabezon's front hooves. "She hardly favors the foot now at all."

"We'll put a dressing on tonight to be sure," Terrell told him. "She may have aggravated it a bit chasing that turkey. When are you leaving on the packet?"

"The day after tomorrow, if it doesn't run aground on the bar."

"You still want me to tend to the dog while you're gone?"

"Unless you've taken a dislike to him, which is perfectly understandable, given his arrogant ways. If not, he'll be grateful for your hospitality. Professor gets violently ill at sea. I can't say I look forward to it myself. Have you ever been seasick, Terrell?"

"No, sir. Most of the people on our passage was, but it never troubled me."

"I'd rather have the ague again. Or even the bloody flux."

Terrell nodded agreeably, his mind in a secret torment. At worst, a baby might already be forming in the girl's body; at best, his own life was now bound up with Edna's in a way that made him feel foolish and despairing. He could still see her looking up to him in the saddle, squeezing his leg between her breasts. He was already a prisoner of her commanding need.

He had no notion of what to do, and there was no one to consult. His mother, should he dare to mention his problem to her, would only be embarrassed and perplexed by his weakness. And Fresada, he was sure, would have no sympathy for him either. He was a solemn man by nature, so solemn that when he was Terrell's age the mission friars had given him the honor of carrying the tabernacle key. The friars had left years ago, abandoning the mission and leaving Fresada and the rest of his conquered people to fend for themselves, a fortunate few like Fresada finding honorable work among the colonists, the rest falling into drunken servility or desperate attempts to revive their wildness. Shortly before the mission was abandoned, Fresada had told Terrell once, a group of Kronks, feeling betrayed, had broken into the church and shattered the tabernacle with their war clubs. But Fresada kept the key, and he wore it around his neck to this day. Walking along beside him now, Terrell felt the Indian's calm self-possession almost like a reproach.

He wished Mr. Bowie had not left Refugio. He supposed Jim Bowie was not a man to be easily shocked, or to be quick about passing judgment on others over matters of earthly temptation.

Perhaps he could speak to Mr. McGowan, who appeared to Terrell to be a kindhearted man. But Mr. McGowan was also oddly disconnected. You never knew where his thoughts were.

They came to the road that ran beside the river, the dog trotting ahead, the moods of the horses brightening as the inn came into sight in the distance. His mother, he could see, was busy in her nopalade, a small cactus orchard where she had been trying for months to cultivate the cochineal insects that, when pulverized, made a fine crimson dye.

"I see you've had more success with your beasts than I've had with my insects," she said to them as they approached. She was smiling at them somewhat apprehensively, and it took him a moment to realize why. She had removed the bandage covering her face. The bridge of her nose, which had once been high and straight, was now a flattened knot, and there were ugly yellowish bruises seeping away on either side of it.

"I'm happy to see your face, Mrs. Mott, after all this time," Mr. McGowan said.

"Do I look monstrous?"

"Not in the slightest degree."

"Do you think so, Terrell?"

"No," Terrell said, though he did think so, a little. It had been a disconcerting day, and now here was his mother's face, the first face he had ever looked at, smashed and contorted.

"Your mother's poor nose," she said, seeing the look on his face, and then she suddenly brightened, almost as if her new appearance pleased her.

"Mr. McGowan," she said, "let me show you the pitiful results of my husbandry."

Terrell took Cabezon's reins from Mr. McGowan as the botanist stepped up to inspect his mother's cactus orchard. She searched through the cactus pads and pale yellow flowers for one of the insects, and then brushed it with a hair pencil into a cup of water and held it up for Mr. Mc-Gowan's inspection.

"A lean specimen," she said.

"I don't know that anyone has ever succeeded with a proper nopalade in Texas," he said.

"Why not? Prickly pear grows abundantly. enough."

"It does, but the cochineal does not seem to grow on the prickly pear without coaxing. It may be the heat, or the sea breeze. Then, of course, your plants are young. They won't be proper hosts for the cochineal until their fourth year."

Terrell listened as they talked, though he felt so strange and detached with his own worries that their voices seemed distant and strange to him, like the voices from a faraway shore resonating across the flat surface of a lake. Mr. McGowan was recommending the use of a tent to shield the plants from the sun; he advised that any leaves with a healthy crop of bugs be kept out of the elements in the winter in their own special house.

"I have to build them a special house?" Terrell's mother protested.

"Unless you want to lodge them with your guests."

His mother had not laughed since the Karankawa attack, but the removal of the bandage seemed to have lightened her heart, ruined though her face was. And Terrell saw that Mr. McGowan kept glancing at that face, discreetly but continually. In the last few weeks, during Mr. McGowan's stay at the inn, Terrell had noticed the mocking, half-ironical tones in which his mother and the botanist had begun to speak to one another. He had barely given these habits of speech a thought, but now he realized that they existed for a reason, that they were in fact a kind of private language of attitude and inflection—a language that served to both mask and express the same sort of desire that he himself had felt for Edna Foley earlier in this terrifying day.

"I THINK something is troubling him," Mary said to Edmund, as she watched Terrell lead the horses to the stable.

"Is there? What?"

"I don't know. Did he say anything to you?"

"No."

"He's too silent. And his skin—it looks flushed."

Edmund had noticed nothing; he hardly knew the boy. But he did not doubt Mrs. Mott's maternal acuity. He glanced at her face as she stared moodily at the departing form of her son, and then he glanced again, at the moment when her eyes swung back to his. He had not anticipated her direct gaze, and it startled him like a collision.

"There's something he doesn't want me to know," she said.

"It's natural for a boy that age to have his secrets."

"Yes, I'm sure that's true. Have you had children?"

"No."

"Or been married?"

"I have not."

"And what were your own secrets at Terrell's age, Mr. McGowan?"

"Ah," he said, with an evasive lilt to his voice, "they are my secrets still."

She smiled and decided to return her attention to her snails. Edmund McGowan remained standing several yards away from her in the cactus orchard. A breeze coasted above the lustrous grass of the prairie; a lizard, gray as pewter, scurried past the point of Mary's shoe.

"I do not think I require experience with children of my own," Mr. McGowan said, "to know that you have been a fine mother to that boy."

She turned to him, caught by a surge of gratitude. He was holding the brim of his hat—Andrew's hat—against the breeze, and deliberately looking elsewhere.

"Thank you," she said.

She pulled off her gloves and with her bare fingers touched the bridge of her nose. It was less sensitive with each passing day, and to her puzzlement she found herself missing the pain a little, the way she sometimes missed the fright of a violent storm after it had swept harmlessly past. The swelling had subsided considerably as well, and would continue to do so, but she knew that beneath the swelling there now lay a shattered bedrock. She doubted that she would ever willingly peer into a looking glass again, and it made her uncomfortable just now to feel Edmund Mc-Gowan's eyes upon her.

"I'm afraid you are more convincing about my virtues as a mother," she said, "than you were about the appearance of my nose."

"You keep insisting that I ought to be shocked," he admitted. "But you must remember I never knew you without a broken nose. So to me your appearance only improves with each day."

He remained where he was, some yards away, one thumb hooked in the pocket of his waistcoat. He was a man, Mary thought, who seemed to know how to talk to a woman but not how to stand next to one. In the short time he had been at the inn she had come to like him, she had come to like him a great deal, though she could not have expressed precisely why. There was a tentativeness about him, physically speaking, at least when he was around her. He seemed to always be standing just a step or two farther away from her than she considered mannerly. The men she had known in her life had been bold in their proximity, they had claimed it without a thought—Andrew standing, grinning, only inches away from her at their introduction; Bowie with his intrusive self-confidence.

It was only in her presence that Edmund McGowan seemed to lack such boldness. As long as he was not standing next to her, he seemed to regard the earth as his own, to be at ease upon it, and to know about it in ways that other men had never considered. They had taken a dozen walks together in as many days, sometimes following the course of the river, sometimes embarking upon the open prairie for a mile or two, with Professor burrowing ahead of them through the deep mesquite grass. She had found herself talking to him with an openness that sometimes embarrassed her when she thought about it afterward—telling him things she had never told anyone but Andrew: how when she was a girl her three-year-old sister had disappeared and Mary had been the one to find her body floating facedown in a spring; an unforgettable dream she had had as a young woman of raising her arms and magically lifting herself a few inches above the ground and hovering there for as long as she cared to remain, the dew of the pasture grass cold against the soles of her bare feet and blue fog swirling down out of the hills to coil around her like a blanket. She told him of the nightmarish voyage to Texas, the packet filled with dying men and women, the ocean at night so dark and limitless, but sometimes twitching and pulsing with light whose source no one could name. One night early in the voyage an old Irishman died, a bachelor colonist with no family, who was the first to perish of cholera, and the captain had insisted on burying him at sea at once lest the contagion in his body run rampant through the ship. Mary had stood at the railing as the prayers for the dead were said over his wrapped body. The water below sparkled with this fantastic interior light; the ocean swells for as far as she could see stirred with greenish luminosity. When the man's body was dropped overboard, it was like the pounding of a blacksmith's hammer on red-hot metal: the ocean exploded in sparks. Then the twinkling sparks cohered around the sinking body, around the dark core of this human shape, so that the passengers of the ship could see it drifting downward fathom after fathom, the burning outline of a man falling to the bottom of the sea.

"It is called phosphorescence," Edmund had told her as they walked, supplying her with a rather pedantic exegesis of the light-producing properties of certain fish and lowly forms of marine life. He seemed to enjoy educating her in such scientific matters, and she sensed he took some refuge in it, preferring to expound upon these objective topics rather than upon intimate chapters from his own life. But this reticence did not dampen her own conversation. In a country of blustery men Edmund McGowan's attentive stillness had its effect on her. He was somebody to talk to.

And the more he kept his awkward distance, the more she felt his nearness of spirit. She had never expected to feel such a thing again after Andrew's death, especially in the company of such a perplexing and elusive man.

"I will be sorry to see you sailing away," she said now, as they walked out of the cactus orchard toward the inn. He did not answer at first, but bent down to examine some speck of vegetation hiding in the grass.

He stood up, after silently deeming the plant to be of no consequence, and after they had walked on for a few more paces he said, "Then I suppose I must make an effort to come sailing back."

EDMUND ACCOMPANIED Terrell that night to the stable to check on Cabezon. He watched in silence as the boy soaked the hoof and then bound a dressing to it. As he worked, Terrell could see the man reflected by lantern light in the globe of the mare's eye.

"Your mother and I agree on a fee of a dollar a week," Edmund said. "That's for the mare and the mule both."

"I guess that's a fair price," Terrell said.

"And then there's the dog."

"The dog's no trouble. You got a sand crack starting in that mule's hoof. You want to see?"

Terrell led Edmund to Snorter's stall and lifted the mule's right leg. He pointed to a hairline crack in the wall of the hoof.

"It ain't that big yet," Terrell said. "I can probably stop it with a hot iron. Might have to stitch it together with a nail till it heals."

"You're pretty skillful with animals," Edmund said.

"I guess," Terrell answered. He looked at the swallows sweeping in through the open stable door with fuzzy moths in their beaks.

"I believe that animals have souls," Edmund said.

Terrell looked up, surprised. He had never heard anybody make such an unlikely pronouncement.

"I never thought about it," he said.

"I travel too much. When you ride on horseback for weeks at a time all by yourself you tend to spend your days in a kind of mesmeric sleep, thinking about the oddest things. Whether it is possible to fly to the moon."

"Fly to the moon?"

"In an aeronautical car, suspended by a balloon. Both the car and the balloon would have to be sheathed with copper to protect against meteorites, but I've talked to people who say the thing could be done."

"How would you come back?"

"I think you'd have to stay."

Edmund smiled, though Terrell did not know if he had meant his moon balloon as a joke. Terrell got up and closed the stable doors. His father had designed the stable, and the crib as well, in a manner to confound marauding Indians, with stout doors that fastened from the inside. When the doors were closed, it was necessary for Terrell and Edmund to climb up a ladder through a hole in the roof.

"There's a fine breeze," Edmund said when they had reached the top of the stable. He stood there with his feet braced against the sharp pitch of the roof in no apparent hurry to climb down. He took a seat against the purlin logs and contemplated the slurry of stars overhead.

"You go on in if you want," he told Terrell. "I believe I'll take advantage of the elevation for a moment."

"I don't care," Terrell answered him, and sat down as well. Below the stable, Professor was looking up at them, faintly curious. There was a light burning in the dwelling house, and he could see his mother sitting in her chair, holding up a sheet of music to her eyes.

"Does your mother play?" Edmund asked.

"She had a pianoforte back in Kentucky, but we couldn't bring it to Texas. She still likes to read music, though. She says she can hear the sound of it in her head."

"And are you musical-minded as well?"

"I don't know. I like it when I hear it, I guess."

Edmund nodded and said nothing. Terrell wished he would speak up again, ask him another question. He had never felt so isolated in his life. His mind was thick with anxiety, and the lust that had ruled him earlier in the day seemed now like a poison seeping through his body.

"Are you married to anybody?" he said. He kept his eyes straight ahead, but he could still sense the mild surprise, and perhaps a kind of tension, in Edmund's face.

"No."

"You ever been?"

"No. I lead a wandering sort of life, and I doubt that it would be congenial with marriage."

Terrell looked down at Professor; the dog was patiently staring up at them as if eavesdropping.

"I need to talk to somebody." The announcement hovered there between them, and Terrell wished he could withdraw it.

"Would you care to talk to me?" Edmund asked.

"I made a mistake with this girl today, and now I don't know what to do."

"What mistake?"

He didn't even know what word to use. He had heard Bowie and others say the word "fuck" in this regard, but it was too jarringly coarse, and his mind could locate no palatable alternatives.

"I laid down with her, over by this creek while I was out hunting."

Terrell pushed the words out and then waited for a reply, his heart pounding in the silence, his soul filled with shame.

"Laid down," Edmund repeated at last. "To what degree did you and she . . ."

"Well, I guess we went the whole hog." A tall hackberry grew beside the stable, and Terrell could hear its branches scraping in the wind against the gable logs.

"Well," Edmund ventured, "such a thing might be ill-advised, but it's not unprecedented."

"There's something wrong with her. She's not right in the head. She has these visions of the mother of Jesus. I don't know what to do."

"Well, you must distance yourself from her, in a kindly way, and let that be the end of the thing."

"She doesn't seem to me like a person you can distance yourself from. And what if there's a baby?"

"The likelihood of that is not great, and there's certainly no profit in worrying about such a thing unless it comes to pass."

Terrell could sense the sympathy in Edmund's voice, but his attempt at reassurance rang hollow and tentative. He remembered Bowie's big hand on his shoulder, he remembered the confidence of his own father's stride, his patient voice as he pointed out the constellations or showed him how to make a Choctaw blowgun. After his father died all the ballast seemed to have gone out of Terrell's character, and now he felt himself foundering in his own weakness and ignorance.

"I'm ashamed of what I did," he confessed to Edmund.

"You were taken by surprise, by a very powerful appetite."

"How do you keep that from happening?"

"Vigilance," Edmund said. "Strength of character and vigilance. It's an unfair struggle, since the human urge to procreate is so strong and the benefits of not doing so at any particular moment are so obscure."

Terrell tried to digest this statement, but its meaning kept eluding him. Scared though he was just now, it didn't feel true to him that the procreative act was something to be avoided, something to triumph over. But he could detect the vigilance in Mr. McGowan's own demeanor. The subject of sex had made him alert and wary, when what Terrell had needed was an easy manner, a friendly joke, a reassurance that what had happened today would have happened to any normal person, and would not necessarily mark his life forever.

Edmund turned his face to the boy in the darkness. Terrell could see the kindness in his eyes, but also a look of uncertainty, an obscure unfinished struggle that made Terrell regret that he had confided in him.

"I feel certain that things will turn out fine," Edmund said.

"But what if they don't?"

"Well, then it's up to you to resolve the situation in an honorable way."

Terrell knew what this meant: marrying a deranged girl, fathering her children, feeling the life squeezed out of him day by day.

"You won't tell my mother about this, will you?" he said.

"Of course not. I presumed from the first that this was a confidential matter between the two of us."

In this, at least, he took some reassurance. Mr. McGowan could be trusted, But Terrell had risked something in speaking to him, and now could not help feeling deflated and exposed. He recognized this as his fault more than Mr. McGowan's. He should have known better than to confide in a man who would never have allowed such an unseemly event to occur in his own life.

"I guess I'll go on into sleep," Terrell said.

"Would you like to talk some more?"

"No, I'm pretty tired."

"No doubt that's one reason your mood is so grim. You'll feel more hopeful in the morning. But I wish I could be more successful in easing your mind for the present."

"That's all right," the boy said. "Thank you for talking to me."

He stood up and climbed down the ladder on the side of the stable, leaving Edmund still on the roof. Professor sniffed Terrell's legs with scant interest, and then followed the boy into the dwelling house.

EDMUND DID NOT MOVE. Watching Terrell walk back to the house in the darkness, he felt paralyzed with failure. What could he have said that he did not say? What could he have known, had he lived a more conventional life, that he might have been able to impart? Terrell had come to him for help, and, although Edmund had done the best he could, it was clear that his words had not only not helped, but had somehow left the boy more troubled than before.

It had been a mistake to offer any advice at all. Terrell had clearly sensed that in the matter at hand Edmund was like a physician who had never been sick, a preacher who had never once strayed into sin. How could such people, who kept themselves apart from the failings and frenzies of ordinary life, ever be taken seriously as counselors?

And yet Edmund had determined from an early age to experience more than most men, and the book of his life was filled with mortal peril and rapturous discovery. Only one page had he left blank.

He hail been raised to believe in the governing majesty of the mind. Orphaned as a young boy in Philadelphia, he had been taken in by a scientific colleague of his father's, an avid widower named Thomas Necessary. Mr. Necessary had no children—his wife having died before she could give him any—and so he and Edmund lived alone in an echoing house whose parlor was covered with vast wall-paper scenes from Greek myth: Odysseus setting sail from Ithaca on one wall, returning ravaged and old and luminous on the other. There were also grim portraits of Necessary's parents by Hesselius, and of a Lenni-Lenape chief under whose tolerant, godlike gaze Edmund passed the long years of his childhood.

Thomas Necessary could not have been sixty, but seemed to Edmund as eternal as that Indian chief. His hair was full and shiningly silver, with streaks of black that contrasted as sharply as mineral veins in rock. He had been a powerful man in his youth, and he was hardy still, great-chested, thick-necked, his face florid with excitement as he looked up from his book or laboratory bench to regale Edmund with some new discovery. He sailed from the crest of one enthusiasm to the next: beetles, field mice, raptors, carnivorous plants, cacti, Roman emperors, geology, trains; he made building plans for icehouses and threshing barns and diving suits and a mechanical "wake-up" bed that tossed a sleeper rudely onto the floor when the clock to which it was attached struck a predetermined hour.

Edmund thought Mr. Necessary would die of joy the day they stood together in a lot behind a Philadelphia tavern, gazing up at the camelopard on display there, the creature's deeply feminine face looking down at them from atop its towering neck, a neck so impossibly long that Mr. Necessary declared it must have something akin to pump stations within it to deliver the blood to the creature's head.

When Edmund was older he accompanied his foster father to meetings of the Philosophical Society, where Mr. Necessary was greeted with warm fellowship by the other members, and where Edmund heard lectures whose themes varied in grandeur from the function of the opossum's pouch to the age of the Earth.

They spent long, tranquil hours together in the herbarium, where Edmund learned the arts of drying and sketching and classifying, where exotic seeds arrived on a regular basis from the far stretches of the world, sent home to Mr. Necessary from one or another of his wandering friends. Most of the seeds were small, shipped across the oceans in screws of waxed paper or animal bladders, but sometimes the seeds were large and singular and wrapped with such fastidious care that the opening of the box—itself smeared with a protective coating of sublimate of mercury— brought with it an unbearable suspense. Not all of the seeds germinated—many were destroyed by vermin, many had decayed in the shifting climates through which they had travelled—but from those that survived there sometimes emerged riotous, improbable forms that brought as much mystery to Edmund's heart as the sight of that camelopard.

"Why is a peach stone like a regiment?" Mr. Necessary would ask as they worked together in the herbarium nurturing these seeds or organizing their dried specimens. "Why is a man opening oysters like Captain Cook firing upon the savages?" He must have known two thousand conundrums by heart. Edmund never heard a single one repeated, nor did he ever hear one whose answer was, to his literal mind, quite successful. But he loved the sound of Mr. Necessary's voice speaking his riddles, as he loved the sound of the violin he played each night, or the singing of the birds in his garden; and the touch of his patron's hand on his shoulder as they worked together in the herbarium helped draw his mind away from its terrors of loneliness and grief.

But it was in the herbarium that this ease between them one day disappeared. Edmund was twelve. He had been scouting for plants all morning along the Schuylkill and had raced home breathless with news of some unlikely specimen growing in the floodplain. Mr. Necessary was not in the house, and so Edmund ran into the herbarium without a thought. There he found Thomas Necessary wholly unclothed on the plank floor with a woman whose own nakedness was so commanding that Edmund could only stand there numbly gazing upon it. Mr. Necessary made desperate sounds as he coupled with the woman; Edmund could see sweat glistening in the white hairs of his powerful chest. He could see the straining in his face, a furtive bestial desire that seemed to wipe away all of his mentor's wit and kindness and patience and replace them with an expression as blank and unreflective as death.

Groaning, Mr. Necessary raised his eyes and saw Edmund standing there. Edmund saw the man's pride, his wonderful confident bearing, dissolve in an instant's time.

That night Edmund was called into the library.

"What you saw today," Mr. Necessary began. "What you saw today was . . ." He tried several more times to continue, but his lip trembled like a child's and he began to weep, confessing his shame, lamenting his weakness, begging forgiveness from a bewildered boy.

"I am not strong, not strong," he cried, "and now you have seen me in my wretchedness, and can respect me no more."

Edmund protested that he would respect him always, and Mr. Necessary nodded his head in gratitude as he wiped the tears from his face with a handkerchief. And Edmund did continue to respect him, and even to love him, as they worked in the herbarium together, or rambled through the countryside on botanizing expeditions, or attended the lectures of the Philosophical Society. But something easeful was lost, and something formal had taken its place.

Edmund wondered now, as he sat on the roof of the Motts' stable, if his own life might have been different if Mr. Necessary had looked up from the floor of the herbarium that day with a different expression in his eyes, an expression not of shame but of amused complicity. If he had been able, with an untroubled glance, to invite Edmund into the realm of human desire. But what Edmund had seen in Mr. Necessary's eyes, and in his unsettled composure later, was a warning never to enter, never to expose himself to such devastating weakness.

And so Edmund—a grave youth who would grow into an uncommonly serious man—took this warning to heart, and heeded it far beyond the point in life where another man would have freed himself from it. Edmund remained hostage to his own stony will. On his many botanizing expeditions, in the rough towns of the frontier or in the Indian villages beyond, while his companions were in the brothels or bedded down in a brush lodge with a wife or daughter that a chief had bestowed upon them for the night, Edmund had remained steadfastly apart and alone. Often enough he watched those companions as they were married, surrendering to the comforts of domesticity after a terrible season or two in the wilderness. But Edmund did not surrender; there was too much fire in him, his need for greatness was too clear and terrible. And as the years passed, the struggle to command himself, to withhold himself, became something that he prized, something to set beside hunger and thirst and cold in the gallery of privations he had endured.

But he was aware, increasingly aware, that this battle he had waged in his mind for so long was no longer necessary. It never had been. Edmund had allowed an episode of childish revulsion to grow into what he imagined was an heroic conviction. To an important degree, he had set his life by it, but now his life felt inadequate and incomplete. And rarely more so than tonight, when he could find no words to comfort a tormented boy, when Mrs. Mott's face—still visible in the lighted window of the house as she frowned in concentration at her sheet music—seemed as distant to him as a star.

CHAPTER SIX

✳

THE ROAD to El Copano led across a flat coastal plain graced by an occasional rise of land no higher than an ocean wave. It was a military road, fairly well maintained, since the route from the port of El Copano to the garrisons at La Bahía and Béxar was a vital supply link, and would be even more vital if Santa Anna decided to send an army by sea to suppress his troublesome colonists.

Mary and Edmund drove through fields of lantana and expanses of shimmering wildflowers—cloth-of-gold and dandelion and lovely blue dayflowers that grew along the edges of the brilliant yellow blossoms like the border on a quilt. The air was thick with the fragrance of these flowers, and on the edges of the salt marshes flocks of shorebirds came cascading down from the sky—pink spoonbills and willets and pelicans whose preposterous bodies were as white as bed linen.

Mary and Edmund rode in the oxcart, with Daniel hauling them patiently across the landscape. Fresada rode horseback a quarter-mile ahead. He had never been much of a horseman, and Mary watched him jounce in the saddle as Veronica, in high spirits, danced along the road.

Mary was going to Copano to take Mr. McGowan to his packet boat, and to buy whatever useful objects or provisions the boat might have brought from New Orleans. They were in no particular hurry, since the boat would not embark until the next morning, and Mary and Fresada had the whole afternoon to make their way back to Refugio after dropping off Mr. McGowan at the decrepit old customs-house.

"It's strange to see saliferous plants so far inland," Edmund said to her, after a tedious silence. "We must still be four or five miles from the coast."

"About six. That stand of oaks in the distance is the mid-point."

"There are a great number of plants belonging to the family *Chenopodiaceae,* which I would not have expected to see for another few miles yet."

"And why is that?" she asked, tapping Daniel on the rump with a thin piece of cane.

"They are mostly maritime plants, Mrs. Mott. They require sodium carbonate and sodium chloride to stay alive. There must be a good deal of salt in these soils, since I don't smell it in the air."

"I would prefer if you called me Mary, and I called you Edmund."

"That would be my preference as well," he said.

But they did not speak again for quite some time. She considered it his turn to say something further, to put her at her ease, and she interpreted his silence as thoughtlessness. When she glanced at him, she saw him self-consciously sweeping the plains with his eyes, the brim of his new hat turned down to shade his face against the morning brightness. She let the silence grow, wondering how long it would take him to break it.

"What will you do if war comes," he asked finally, "and the Mexican army marches up this road?"

"There are few enough War Dogs in this colony," she said. "We should be safe here if we keep our heads and don't get pulled into this independence nonsense."

"I'm not sure it's nonsense."

She was genuinely surprised. "Surely you don't think it's a good thing to take up arms against Mexico?"

"No, I think it's the worst sort of vainglory. I only meant

that the idea of independence has great currency, and should not be dismissed. It is, after all, the fundamental American trait. If Mexico had granted Texas separate statehood, this desire for independence might have been satisfied for a while. But now nothing less than a total break will do."

"So you think we are destined for a full-blast war?"

"I think we are destined for a tragic, catchpenny war, in which Santa Anna will be the victor. That's why I worry about you living in such a conspicuous place."

"I will continue to be an inconspicuous innkeeper."

"It's difficult to simply sit there and cut the patching while war is raging around you!"

"Have you been in a war, then, Edmund?"

"Not a war as such. I have been in the way of some bitter quarrels, and seen a man or two plant his lead in another. But I stay away from real wars as much as possible."

She said nothing in response, and in the silence he glanced covertly at her face beneath its bonnet, the misshapen nose that drew him rather than repelled him, the brown hair at her temple lying sodden in the humid coastal air, the clear sweep of her jawline.

He was not in the best of spirits this morning. The conversation with Terrell on the roof of the stable last night still troubled him. He despised feeling useless. And he despised his own envy—envy for a young man who, no matter how complicated his present situation, had already experienced the supreme act of human intimacy. As Edmund sat in the cart beside Mrs. Mott, close enough to her to feel not just the fabric of her dress against him but the very warmth of her body, he was aware of a gathering sorrow.

He had grown comfortable at her inn in the last few weeks as he recovered from the ague, and now he was overcome with a superstitious dread of leaving. In fact, such sensations were not strange to him. Like many perpetual ravellers, he was driven on across the world as much by homesickness as by curiosity. The early death of his parents had marked him, and he had suffered all his life by a feeling of having been cast out at some crucial moment before the image of what a home was supposed to be had quite congealed in his mind.

"Are you of a morose turn of mind today?" Mary guessed. "Or are you merely preoccupied with botanical matters?"

"I was thinking about this splendid countryside, and how sorry I am to leave it for the monotonous sea."

"The sea is beautiful," she said. "Or at least I think so."

"Beautiful when observed from the shore, certainly. But from the deck of a schooner during a squall it's a different matter."

"I'm sure you'll have splendid weather all the way to Vera Cruz, Edmund. Perhaps you'll even see a whale, or a leaping devilfish."

"Perhaps so," he said, as if to himself.

It annoyed her that he had not yet used her Christian name, though she had pointedly spoken his at least twice.

"I hope I've not been forward in claiming you for a friend," she said rather coldly. "After such a slight acquaintance."

"Not at all, Mrs. Mott."

"Not at all, Mrs. Mott," she mimicked him.

He turned at her chiding tone, and she saw his face redden.

In another mile they could smell the salt in the atmosphere, and could hear the sound of crashing waves from far away on the barrier islands. The road made its way through glittering marshes, the mute, repetitive songs of unseen bitterns rising from the cordgrass.

"I had a conversation with Terrell last night," Edmund told her.

"About what?"

"About nothing in particular. About horses and mules. He's a young man of the best sort."

"He is overly sensitive. He takes everything too much to heart."

"There are plenty enough boys who are coarse and heartless."

"His grammar is wretched. It's a matter of principle with him, I'm afraid."

She hesitated a moment, reluctant to voice her greater worry.

"If war comes, I fear he won't be able to keep a level head. He may be swept up in it."

"If we're fortunate," Edmund said, "there will be plenty of calm voices for him to listen to. The Irish will stay neutral, I think, and very few Tejanos will see much advantage in fighting against their own government."

"Yes, but which government will they be loyal to? Civil war has already begun in Monclova."

"All of that may be to your advantage. The more obscure the cause, the easier it will be to stay out of the fight. Excuse me, will you please stop the cart for a moment?"

She did as he asked, but before she could coax Daniel to a full stop Edmund had already leapt to the ground and dashed away to inspect a clump of yellow flowers growing at the base of a sandy hillock.

"Have you found something of interest?" she asked when she walked over to join him. He already had a notebook out and was jotting down scientific remarks in a patient hand.

"An aster I've not seen before," he replied. "Do you recognize it?"

Mary inspected one of the soft golden flowers swaying on its tall, rank stalk. The flower was somewhat sticky to her touch and not particularly aromatic, but it was touchingly symmetrical—its pale rays spreading out from a deep golden disk.

"No," she said. "It's beautiful, but I've never encountered it."

"Nor has science," Edmund said, smiling at her. "Until this moment."

Mary watched him cut away several samples of the plant and wrap them in oilskin—he would dry them properly later, he explained, once he was aboard his ship. He made a few more notations about the vicinity in which the discovery had been made, asking her help in gauging the exact distance between this anonymous spot and Copano.

Then they continued on, and within the hour they could see the blue expanse of Aransas Bay and then Copano itself, a dilapidated collection of white shell buildings and jacales standing on a bluff above the water. The ruins of an old Spanish fort were visible on a spit of land several hundred yards farther along the curve of the bay, and there were a few rotting wharves below the bluff, with the packet anchored just beyond.

Fresada was waiting for them at the customshouse, a one-story building of shell concrete whose exterior was crumbling like a stale cake. There was no one inside, and no furniture except for a rough wooden table on top of which sat a few unguarded sacks of mail from the packet. The crew was busy filling water casks from a large cistern, and the few seasick passengers were lying on cots beneath a canvas awning spread against the customshouse. Edmund and Mary walked to the edge of the bluff and looked down at the wharf.

"That's the captain," she said, indicating a man standing on the dock who was instructing a woman and her young son in the art of fishing. "Captain Wittliff. His schooner's called the *Pangaea*. Often he will spend the night at the inn, along with his passengers, but he seems to be in a hurry today."

"Am I in good hands with Captain Wittliff?" Edmund asked.

"He's skilled enough when sober. As often as not there's

no one here to hoist the signal flags, so he must judge for himself when the tide is high enough to cross the bar."

"There's no pilot?"

"He drowned last summer. Some say he was taken by a shark, right from his boat, since his body was never found. But I doubt it. The bay is shallow, and it would be an uncomfortable fit for a shark large enough to eat a man.

"Where is the customs officer?"

"In La Bahía. He rarely has the energy to make the trip. There is a Mexican garrison at Lipantitlán, but the soldiers come here only to meet the supply ship. As a result this part of the coast is open to contraband."

Indeed it was. When Captain Wittliff came up from the dock, Mary was able to buy quantities of goods that would have been forbidden or subject to exorbitant tariffs at the more closely watched ports, like Galveston or Velasco. The captain was eager to sell her all the contraband he had on board, since his next stop was up the coast at Velasco, where his manifests would be subject to the most scrupulous inspection. Fresada and Edmund loaded eight casks of fine flour into her cart, and several gallons of pickles, as well as a tortoiseshell music box that played ten tunes and a luxurious Brussels carpet. After they were through, Fresada wandered off to sit in the shade of a mesquite and smoke a cigar, looking out at the glittering bay.

"Don't set your heart on any more such foofaraw," the captain warned her. "I won't risk it. The Mexican cruisers are as thick as gulf-weed these days. If they had caught me with this cargo they'd have confiscated my vessel and thrown me and my crew into some hellhole of a jail. Maybe even the passengers too." He gestured at the young woman and her son still fishing off the wharf. "Maybe even Mrs. Travis and her boy down there."

Captain Wittliff was anxious to get under way in case the customs collector in La Bahía managed to rouse him-

self, and he told Edmund the winds looked favorable for
departure tomorrow.

"I will leave you, then," Mary said to Edmund, after the
captain had gone to see to the taking on of water. They
stood by his baggage in an angle of shade cast by the customshouse. Mary felt the need to avoid his eyes, and she
looked out toward the bay. A long crescent of oyster reef
stretched out into the shallow water, and a raft of pelicans
near the middle of the bay looked like the foam from crashing waves.

"I should return for my animals in a matter of a few
months," he said.

"I look forward to having you as a guest again."

Impulsively, she gave him a kiss, grazing her lips against
the dense hair of his side-whiskers. It was a chaste gesture,
but more of a gesture, she realized with sudden embarrassment, than he was prepared for. His response was to stand
there as immobile as a tree. The fact was, she felt an unsettling tenderness for him, and leaving him here in this sun-
blasted ruin of a port seemed like more of a good-bye,
more of an ending, than she had anticipated.

Uncertain what else to do, she turned and began walking
toward the oxcart. Edmund followed her, and offered his
hand to help her up, and then afterward stood there stupidly
with nothing to say.

"Are you ready, Fresada?" she called to the Indian, who
was already walking toward them, leading Veronica.

Fresada shook hands with Edmund in good-bye and
mounted his horse. The Indian glanced at Mary and she
nodded for him to go ahead.

He spurred the mare forward and Mary took up her
length of cane, and she and Edmund sat there for a moment
listening to the shouts of the sailors on the wharf. They
watched a tern attack Fresada as he rode past its simple
nest. The bird came soaring down out of the sky, pulling

away from its assault when its sharp beak was only a few inches from Fresada's hat. Fresada swiped at the tern with his hand and laughed, riding on.

"I should like to thank you . . ." Edmund fumbled, "for your . . . agreeableness."

She might have laughed at his awkwardness if she had not been so disappointed by it. She would have appreciated a parting sentiment that was a bit more thoughtfully composed. She would have preferred him to be a man who, when he was kissed by a friend, did not act as if he had been sprayed by a polecat.

"Good-bye, Edmund," she said. "May you have a safe voyage."

She spoke to Daniel and tapped him gently with the cane, and the cart lurched forward as Edmund stepped aside. She did not glance back until she had gone several hundred yards up the road, and by then he had disappeared into the customshouse to get away from the midday sun.

She rode all the way home in sagging spirits, the landscape that had been so lovely earlier in the day now mute and ordinary, her own temper turning in on her. She stopped at the edge of the salt marsh once just to stand there and look out at the stippled surface, the tiny wind-driven waves whispering through the grass. She waved at Fresada when he came trotting back toward her in concern, and told him to ride on, that she would catch up.

Some great anxiety was weighing on her heart, along with a disappointment she would not allow herself to name. She felt more alone and isolated than she had since the early months after Andrew's death, and the dangerous state of the country figured in her imagination as a stalled hurricane, a dark cloud gathering momentum for its first capricious surge.

In this grim mood she climbed back into her cart, passing once again the fields of wildflowers, their blossoms either folded up now or washed out in the full glare of the

sun. She returned to the inn by midday. Terrell, she knew,
would be hunting today, and she expected to find no one
there but Teresa. But for some reason the Foley girl was
standing in her yard, arms at her side, smiling at Mary as
she approached, as if to welcome her home.

CHAPTER SEVEN

✦

"THE FIRST TIME I ever turned back in my life!" William Barret Travis fumed. In disbelief, he stared out the window of his room at Peyton's Tavern, watching the inexhaustible rain sweep down on the streets of San Felipe de Austin. No one was out on those streets today, which were already a knee-deep bog.

Joe set down his tray on the pine table, handed Mr. Williamson his coffee, then presented the other cup to his sopping master, who stood there shivering in his blanket, his brown hair plastered to his face.

"Excellent. Thank you, Joe," Travis said, rousing himself for a moment out of his self-pity. He was habitually courteous, even to slaves, and this was one trait of his that Joe had not yet found tiresome.

"First time in my life I ever turned back, Willie!" he repeated to Williamson, who stood teetering on his peg leg on the other side of the room, holding his porcelain cup above its saucer like a New Orleans dandy, dressed though he was in coarse homespun. Williamson winked at Joe in complicit good humor, as if Travis were an exasperating friend that they shared, rather than the legal owner of Joe's body and soul.

"Put it out of your mind, Buck," Williamson said. "The rain will let up soon enough."

He clomped over to the table on his wooden stump, the crippled lower half of his right leg drawn up at the knee and secured to his thigh with a rawhide band. Three-legged Willie, they called him. He had been that way since childhood. Joe thought his parents should have done him the favor of having some doctor saw off the useless half of his leg right after he was born, so he wouldn't have had to carry it around like that for the rest of his life.

Williamson, however, didn't seem to mind in the slightest.

"What are these, Joe?" he asked, looking down at a plate on which three strange circular objects resided.

"They's meat biscuits, sir," Joe answered.

"What the hell are meat biscuits? Never heard of such a thing!"

"Borden brought them over last night," Travis explained. "They're his latest invention. He takes beef, removes all the water from it somehow, and mixes it with flour. The result, he claims, is a perpetual meat that cannot spoil. He wants to start a manufactory. If Santa Anna invades, our entire army can live off his biscuits indefinitely."

"How do they taste?" Williamson asked, sniffing one.

"Like shit, of course," Travis said.

Gail Borden, the publisher of the *Telegraph and Texas Register,* had stayed in Travis's rooms until very late the night before, chattering on about his meat biscuits and some plan he had to reduce the volume of milk by condensing it, and his designs for what he called a terraqueous machine, a wagon that could propel itself across the land and the water both.

Mr. Travis could have used the terraqueous machine this morning, Joe thought. His master had started off for the other side of Mill Creek to spend the day with his sweetheart there, but the skies had opened up and the creek had flooded so wide in a matter of a few hours that it was impossible to cross, and he had come back looking like a drowned cat, as furious and full of curses as Joe had ever seen him.

"God *damn* it!" he said now, after slurping the last of his coffee and handing the cup to Joe for more. When Travis was in a lustful frame of mind—which was most of the time—he needed relief more than anybody Joe had ever seen.

"Go see her tomorrow," Williamson said. "She'll still be in a receiving mood."

"I can't! I have to go to Brazoria tomorrow. My wife is coming from Alabama."

He sat down in a chair, pulling his blanket tighter, sulking with theatrical intensity.

"And my son!" he said. "What am I supposed to do with a six-year-old boy?"

"Poor old Buck," Williamson said, winking at Joe again. It was easy to make fun of Travis, who could grow as pouty as a child when things did not go his way. He had more energy than any soul Joe had ever known, but it sometimes seemed there was no lightness in him at all. He stayed up hours and hours every night, long after he had dismissed Joe for bedtime, working on his law cases and writing angry letters and proclamations about Mexican customs laws and tonnage duties and other things that Joe had no understanding of and paid no attention to. Sometimes, though, he would hear Travis and Williamson talk about slavery; and he would lend an ear to that. Slavery was forbidden in Mexico, and Texas was a part of Mexico, and Joe lived half in hope and half in anxiety that someday a boatload of Mexican soldiers was going to come up the Brazos and tell him he was a free man. He'd been told by other slaves that all a negro had to do was run away from the colony and out of Texas and the Mexicans would release him from bondage and let him join the army. The idea appealed to Joe, but he was farsighted enough to imagine all the dangers and disappointments that might come out of it. He didn't speak Spanish, he had a suspicion that a nigger was a nigger anywhere, whether he was called a slave or not, and he was not clear in his mind exactly how being a soldier in the Mexican army would be all that different from being a slave.

And Travis was a tolerable master, more than tolerable. Joe had never experienced the base cruelty he'd heard about from other slaves—the nine-tailed cat, the terrible torture machines, the barrels whose insides were studded with sharp nails, and into which misbehaving negroes were placed and rolled downhill. Joe's mother and brother had been sold away when he was six, and that had been hard, he remembered, but there was mind pain and there was body pain, and if you started feeling sorry for yourself about mind pain you wouldn't have room in your life for another thought.

He had been raised a house servant in Mississippi on a struggling plantation ruled by an unhappy family. His first master, Mr. Halpatter Tines, had been a good-hearted but worthless man, a drunkard who had lost the respect of his wife and children. One morning, after Joe had cleaned the vomit off Mr. Tines's pillow and was setting out his clothes, his master had turned to him and said, "Let's you and me go to Texas, Joe," and that's what they did, without so much as a note to Mrs. Tines.

They had travelled overland along the trace, Mr. Tines on a blooded mare, Joe on a quick-witted mule. They stayed a week in Nacogdoches and then continued down the road to Austin's Colony, where Mr. Tines thought he could get a grant of land and be shielded from his American creditors. But the Land Office was closed because of all the troubles with the Mexican government, and no new colonists were being admitted, and so before a month had passed, Mr. Tines had lost the horse and the mule in a monte game and sold off Joe to a man in Harrisburg to buy passage for himself back to Mississippi. Joe was with the new man for only a month or so before he was turned over to Travis in payment for a legal fee.

"There are worse things than having a son," Williamson was saying. He had taken a bite out of one of the meat biscuits after all and was chewing it appraisingly. "If we can ever get this place out of Mexico's hands you can make him a splendid fortune."

"Yes, and if we don't, his father's just as likely to be shot as a pirate. I'm going to board him with David Ayers at Montville. At least he'll be safe there."

"And out of your hair."

Travis said nothing, simply looked out the window at the soft curtains of rain. He was not the sort to mind frank talk, not if it was true, and Joe knew that Travis was looking forward to the arrival of his wife and son with a great deal of annoyance. He had gone to a lot of trouble to build himself a nice bachelor's life here in San Felipe, where he advertised himself as a widower and had a reputation as the fieriest lawyer in a town where, as far as Joe could tell, the inhabitants had no real business other than the suing of each other.

"These ain't so bad," Williamson said. "Try one, Joe."

Joe lifted one of the meat biscuits to his mouth and took a bite. It tasted hideous: powdery and rancid.

"Joe and I like them just fine," Williamson declaimed, while Joe was still gagging on his. "I never want to eat any other kind of food in my life."

"You speak for yourself," Joe said, smiling at Travis to enlist him in the banter. But Travis would not let himself be distracted from his brooding.

"How long will your wife be here?" Williamson asked him, taking a seat on a wooden chair. Because of his tied-up leg, he had to sit awkwardly on one hip.

"Only long enough to drop off the boy and collect her divorce."

"Don't think you can get me to feel sorry for you, Buck. You've already chingabad every possible woman in the colony, you've got a fair young maid waiting for you across the creek, and a wife into the bargain. Your wife ugly?"

"Not particularly."

"Well, there's my point. You're a favored man, Travis. A
ew days of enforced celibacy will do you good."

"What'll you be wearing today, Mr. Travis?" Joe asked.

"What have I got that's not soaking wet?"

"Your linen coat. I got your white pantaloons mended.
The red waistcoat."

"I don't care."

"Well, if you don't care I don't care," Joe said, opening
he wardrobe. He took out the clothes, and laid them on the
bed. It was an unusual day when Travis was not concerned
with what he wore. Joe knew his master, who came from the
backwoods of Alabama, was more of a frontiersman than
most of the men who paraded around San Felipe in their
greasy buckskins and ring-tailed hats. But somewhere
along the line he had developed a fine taste in clothes.

"Joe," Williamson pondered, "you think your Mr. Travis
would like to share any of his honeydew tobacco with his
good friend Mr. Williamson?"

"I'm sure he would, Mr. Williamson," Joe said. He took
he twist out of a drawer and handed it to Williamson, who
bit off a mighty chunk and sat there gnawing on it for some
moments, studying his sullen friend.

"By God, sir, you are a miserable companion today,"
Williamson said.

"Why don't you leave, then? Why don't you both leave?"

"Because it's raining. And if Joe and I left you unat-
ended you might die of horniness."

Travis shot Williamson a look, a little light coming into
his blue eyes at last. He was such an intense young man that
any ray of brightness warmed people out of all proportion,
and made them like him more than they expected to.

"Zacatecas is going to rise," he announced, perhaps
changing to this grim subject so that he would not have to
be pulled too quickly out of his mood.

"Should we rise with it, do you think?" Williamson
asked, his own mood shifting.

"The time isn't right. Austin's situation is uncertain, the people in the colonies are divided, it's just as well to wait. Better to wait. Even if we join with the Mexican federalists and help them defeat Santa Anna, what are we left with? Even if we achieve separate statehood, what are we? A remote Mexican state? Who wants to be that? The days of fighting against Mexico for the right to be a *part* of Mexico are over. We should fight to be free."

"Where's the cuspidor?" Williamson said.

Joe went out into the rain and fetched it. He had been polishing it that morning until the sky opened up. He set it within spitting range of Williamson, who thoughtfully worked up a gob of honeydew and, with masterful inattention, let it fly into the shining cuspidor.

"Fighting to be free of Mexico. You're a little bit ahead of everybody else there. As usual."

"It's utterly impossible for two peoples so diametrically opposed in everything to be amalgamated, Willie. Independence is the only answer. Everybody knows it and is too afraid to speak it. But after Santa Anna puts down Zacatecas he will send his army here, and there won't be any honorable course except to fight. And there's no honor and no profit in fighting for the Mexican union!"

"He's reviving, Joe," Williamson said, and even Travis parted company with a laugh.

But the next day, as they rode along the road to Brazoria, Travis's frame of mind was bleak all over again. He had stayed up most of the night, working on his autobiography. Joe, in his one-leg bed on the other side of the room, had not been able to sleep for the scratching of Travis's pen and the powerful gloom of his thinking, which pervaded the atmosphere like swamp gas.

Joe didn't know exactly what Travis wrote in his ledger book every night, but whatever it was he suspected it was not entirely the truth. He was a closed-up man about his past, as so many in Texas were. Joe had heard stories that Travis's wife back in Alabama had fallen in with another man, and that Travis had killed the man and fled to Texas to escape a trial.

Joe didn't believe the stories—he figured that Travis had probably just gotten tired of being married and left—but he could see how it had taken root. Travis had a fondness for rash actions, for big gestures. Joe hadn't been in Texas when the famous Anahuac incident had taken place, but he'd heard about it often enough: Travis and Patrick Jack taken prisoner by the imperious customs collector, staked out on the ground with a dozen Mexican soldiers pointing their rifles at them, under orders to fire if Travis's friends persisted in attacking the customshouse; and Travis lifting his head off the ground and yelling, "Go on and attack, boys! Let them kill me!"

The trip to Brazoria was a long one, and as there were no habitations in the vacant stretch of land between the Old Fort and Columbia, they had to spend the night on the open prairie. Joe disliked camping, feared the open night with its quavering wolf cries and the uneasy sense it churned up in him that the world was limitless. People lived in houses or they would grow insane contemplating the immensity of the heavens and the prairies, the endless intricate darkness of the forests. Anything could happen, any frightening thought could become real.

Travis would not have a tent. He lounged in the open blackness, his head against his saddle, tracing the constellations with the glowing tip of his cigar.

"A year from now the case will be resolved, one way or the other," he said. "Texas will be a free land or it will be broken and enslaved by tyrants. And my own course will have come clear as well."

He turned his head to Joe, as if startled by an unexpected thought.

"I may very well be dead, Joe."

Joe nodded sympathetically, so tired he was barely able to think straight, but too fearful to fall asleep.

"Dead," Travis repeated, with a wondering tone.

Joe got up and walked over to the other side of the fire to piss. The sound of wolves rolled across the prairie, and he thought he heard the rustling of snakes in the mesquite grass.

"I'll be twenty-six," Travis called to him.

"That ain't old," Joe said. He himself was twenty-two or twenty-three, as close as he could calculate.

"It's old if you're dead."

Joe buttoned his pants. "You're just as easy to die from a snakebite as you is from a Mexican soldier. Or some wild Indian might come up and take your scalp off your head."

"Look at you. Living your life in fear of what might happen to you."

"You was the one talking about being dead."

"I wasn't talking about death," Travis said, with a contemplative draw on his cigar, still looking up at the speckled heavens. "I was talking about destiny."

They rode on the next morning, through the big cedar forests and then on into the canebrake. The cane grew so high above their heads it shut out all the light, the stalks twitching and creaking in the darkness. Joe was not a fearful or superstitious soul, but he was a cautious one, and as they rode through the cane he kept a careful eye on the road, knowing if they strayed from it they would be lost forever in this smothering forest.

But they emerged into the light on the other side, and by early afternoon they were in Brazoria, an orderly little town of log houses with mudcat chimneys. There were now one or two brick buildings as well, but they had been constructed of handmade brick, variably colored and misshapen, that made these structures look somehow primitive and ravaged by time.

They found the boy in the parlor of Mrs. Long's public

house, playing billiards with one of the passengers off the
schooner, a man whose face was still pale with the seasick-
ness. The boy looked up at them when they came in, his
eyes bright and curious, a far more pleasant and less complicated being, Joe saw at once, than his father.

"Are you Charles Edward?" Travis asked him.

"I used to be, but now I'm Charlie."

"I'm your father, Charlie. I'm William Travis."

Travis walked across the puncheon floor and held out his
hand. The boy shook it, then looked up at Joe.

"This is Joe," Travis said, "my body servant. How was
your crossing, son?"

"Mr. McGowan got sick, but I didn't," Charlie said, nodding toward his billiards partner.

"It's kind of you to entertain him," Travis said, and offered his hand. "I'm Buck Travis."

"Edmund McGowan. Your son is merciless at billiards."

"We cut open a shark," the boy said, and went on at a
breathless rate to relate how Captain Wittliff had given him
the shark's still-beating heart to hold in his hand. He told
his father about the flying fish they had seen, and the dying
dorado that had changed colors as it lay gasping on the
deck, and the barracuda one of the crew had hauled up on
his line, a fish whose favorite food, Captain Wittliff said,
was the nuts of male bathers.

Edmund took a seat on the horsehair sofa, still holding
his billiard cue as if for support. During the four days of
their sail to Velasco, the boy had never shut up, even when
Edmund had been leaning over the side casting up his account. But he was a likable child, eager and open, whereas
his notorious father exuded a certain grimness.

Yet Edmund liked this young man too. A high-minded
prig, he saw at once, but there were plenty of prigs who
were not high-minded. And though Travis had a reputation
as a hothead, Edmund's impression was that he was deliberate and calculating.

"I wonder if you have seen my wife?" Travis asked him.

"She's gone on a walking tour of the town with Mrs. Stephenson, the hostess here. I suppose they're down by the Brazos, but likely to return any moment."

"I'll wait for her, then," Travis said. He sat down in a chair, his eyes darting nervously about the room, unsure whether to look at his son or not. Mrs. Long's inn was a venerable building by Texas standards, capaciously built of cottonwood logs, expertly hewn to a glassy smoothness. The parlor was mostly vacant at this hour of day: a couple of would-be planters in frayed linen coats going over their business plans in the corner, spitting their tobacco juice onto the floor without regard to the cuspidors; a spindly man in a beegum—another lawyer, probably, waiting to meet with a client—reading the latest outrages in the *Telegraph;* a fastidious slave who came in every few minutes to inspect the room, trying to determine if she might be needed for anything. All of the crew off the schooner except for Captain Wittliff, who was secretary-treasurer of the New Orleans Temperance Society, had gone to the grog shops.

"Why don't you take my cue, Mr. Travis," Edmund said, "and see if you can beat your son at billiards? I'm having no luck at all."

"Well, he stands no chance against me," Travis said, with a mischievous glimmer in his eyes that Joe had rarely seen. He took up the cue and proceeded, with calculated frustration, to snub every shot, causing the little boy to giggle in triumph.

He carried on a polite conversation with Edmund as he went about the ritual of losing, a conversation touching on Edmund's errand to the City of Mexico, the dispute between Saltillo and Monclova over the location of the state government, the rumors that England was planning to join cause with the Mexican centralists to quell the disturbances in Texas, and finally the endless duplicity and tyrannical instincts shown by Santa Anna.

"I saw General Lafayette when I was a boy," Travis said, carefully lining up his shot. "He came to our little Alabama town to give a speech. There was a man who knew a thing or two about resisting tyranny."

Artfully, Travis sent the shot athwart, and put on a helpless expression for his delighted son.

"I'm going to beat you," the boy said, standing on his crate and taking careful, endless aim. "I beat Mr. McGowan, and I'm going to beat you, too."

"Or perhaps 'tyranny' is too complimentary a word," Travis said to Edmund as they waited for the boy to shoot. "A tyranny at least has a fixed purpose. Whereas Mexico has a plundering, robbing, autocratical, aristocratical, jumbled-up government which is in fact no government at all—one day a republic, one day a fanatical oligarchy, the next a military despotism, then a mixture of the evil qualities of all. But as an employee of that government, perhaps you have a different opinion."

"I'm a disenchanted employee, Mr. Travis. But it would be unfair to fault Mexico on its incompetence where I am concerned, since all governments are by nature incompetent when it comes to petty matters."

"If the fate of Texas were a petty matter, I would share your patience."

There was no missing the annoyance in his voice. Edmund turned his eyes to Travis's slave, who had helped himself to a seat on a fine mahogany chair and was watching the billiard game with weary detachment. He had a deep black complexion, a well-proportioned body, and the excellent posture of a lifelong house servant. Also a keen, insouciant look in his eyes, or so Edmund suspected as they flickered briefly in his direction.

"We'll want the horses fed, Joe," Travis said.

"What kind of horses?" Charlie said.

"Actually only one horse, Charlie. I have a black Spanish mare named Señorita, and Joe here is riding an excellent mule who has never had a name at all."

"Can I name him?"

"Sure you can. If Joe doesn't mind. He's the one who rides him. You go over with Joe to the stables and see if you can think of a good name on the way."

"My wife is making me a bargain," Travis said to Edmund when Joe and the boy were gone. He continued playing billiards by himself, without inviting Edmund to participate. "She will give me a divorce on the condition that Charles Edward comes to live with me for a period of time while she sets herself up in the millinery business."

Edmund nodded as if this were news to him, though in fact Mrs. Travis was even chattier than her son and had spent most of the voyage relating to the other passengers the exact circumstances of her husband's many indiscretions, and her deep bitterness at his continued existence. She was a firm-minded woman, but Edmund could see she was no match for this young empire builder.

"What sort of future a woman like that would have in the millinery business, I can't guess."

"She seems clever enough," Edmund said.

"Clever, and devious, and demanding, and can't sew a button on a shirt. Her looks have not gone, I hope?"

"Certainly not," Edmund said. "She is quite comely."

"She was a beauty when I taught her in school. A very distracting condition for a schoolmaster."

He tapped the cue ball with the point of his stick, sending it whispering across the felt. A sure touch, Edmund thought, the touch of a gamesman with long, idle years of practice in saloons. Travis's face was full, almost round, immaculately shaven. But the hands that held the cue were square and coarse, not pampered at all. A complex, compelling, dangerous young man.

"Will you take something to drink?" Edmund asked him, taking a sip from his coffee cup. The coffee had grown cold during his billiard game with the boy, and he walked over to the urn to refill it.

"No, thank you," Travis said. He put down his stick and went to the window to look down the street, waiting nervously for his wife to appear.

"Will you see Austin in Mexico, do you think?" he asked distractedly.

"Possibly so," Edmund said, taking his seat again.

"As patient and accommodating all these years as a man can be, and his reward is to be thrown into the calabozo. I hear it's ruined his health. You might tell him—" But he broke off and sat in the chair across from Edmund, appraising him with pale blue eyes.

"Momentous events are about to happen, sir," Travis said. "I encourage you to take a part."

Edmund sat back in the sofa and took a breath, trying to quell a wave of nausea. The thought of going back on that boat filled him with a kind of despair, and he was in no mood to be bombarded with zealous political opinions.

"It seems to me the events, will be more calamitous than momentous, and that a good many people will die for no particularly good reason."

"Freedom from a tyrant's oppression? You don't consider that worth dying for?"

"I have been inconvenienced, Mr. Travis, but not yet oppressed."

"You will, sir! I can guarantee it!"

Edmund smiled patiently, and looked over Travis's shoulder to see Roseana Travis entering the inn with Captain Wittliff and Mrs. Stephenson.

"Your wife," he whispered.

Travis leapt like a shot deer, standing up and turning around in the same motion to face his wife, who stood there wearing a riding cap that sprouted a plume of ostrich feathers. Her handsomeness was marred, or perhaps redeemed, by a slight underbite, and her lower lip trembled slightly as she looked at her husband with unforgiving eyes.

"Roseana," Travis said. "How sweet to see you again."

"I'm glad to see you have met Mr. McGowan, William," she said, in an attempt to keep the conversation cool. "He has been so kind to Charlie these last few days. Where is Charlie?"

"He's at the stables with my man."

"What sort of man? Do you have a nigger now to look after you, William? You must be prosperous indeed."

"Is it not true, Mrs. Stephenson," Edmund said, addressing himself to the stout proprietress of the inn, "that you have a room available for Mr. and Mrs. Travis to discuss their arrangements apart from our prying ears?"

"I do indeed," she said, and when Travis and Roseana followed her up the stairs the atmosphere in the room was as light as the air after a squall.

But when Joe returned with Charlie to the inn a few minutes later, the voices of Travis and his wife could be clearly heard raging from the upstairs room, an endless aggrieved carping about money and women and lawyers and broken promises of support.

"Let's go noodlin'," Joe said to the boy, and took him down to the Brazos and showed him how to probe under the banks with his bare hands for catfish. They found none, but the thrilling uncertainty of whether his hands would touch a catfish or a water moccasin kept the boy's mind off the battle between his parents, whose voices Joe could still hear faintly on the wind.

In the end it was settled more quickly than Joe had expected: divorce documents signed, money paid over to Mrs. Travis, and Señorita and the mule (which Charlie had named Buzzard) saddled and ready for travel by midafternoon.

Joe stood apart with his master as Mrs. Travis knelt

down beside Charlie in the boardinghouse, whispering urgent messages in his ear, the boy nodding just as urgently as if it was his task to reassure both of them. It brought a memory to Joe's mind of the time his mother had said good-bye to him, wailing that she was so glad he was so grown now and could take care of himself and that Jesus in heaven was looking down on him all the time so there was nothing in this life ever to fear.

Then Mrs. Travis had rushed upstairs and poor Charlie was shaking hands good-bye with Captain Wittliff and Mr. McGowan, and then his father lifted him up onto the back of his saddle and they rode out of Brazoria.

"This is a fine country, Charlie," Joe heard Travis say as they passed a struggling plantation where a hoe gang was harrowing the earth in a cornfield. The slaves were singing "Hi ho ug, hi ho ug," a chant Joe remembered from his earliest days on earth. He had been born with it in his ears, he speculated, the same way he had been born to the sound of his mother's heartbeat.

"A fine country to be a boy in," Travis was saying. "When you're a bit older, you'll have your own horse, and you'll have the prairies for your play yard."

A few hundred yards farther on he reined in Señorita and paused dramatically, sweeping his arm across the landscape. "This is a gift for you, son. Texas. I am going to take it from Mexico and present it to you with a ribbon tied around it."

Charlie looked at his father peculiarly, and for the first time the enormity and strangeness of his new circumstances seemed to overcome him, and he appeared as if he might cry.

"He don't understand that kind of talk," Joe said.

"Where are we going to sleep?" Charlie asked, his voice starting to quiver a little.

"On the open ground," Travis said. "Upon the bosom of your new country."

"Don't pay no attention to the way your daddy's speakin'," Joe told the boy.

"Are there rattlers where we're going to sleep?"

"They's rattlers all over this country," Joe said. "But if you make a circle around yourself with a hair rope they can't come in to bite you."

"Why not?"

"They's superstitious."

The boy was glum for another mile or so, but it did not seem to be in his nature to be quiet for long, and soon he was talking again—about a fifty-pound honeycomb he and his uncle had found in the woods last year, about the wicked schoolmaster who had beaten his friend Topper Nutt bloody with the hawse, about a little girl back home who'd taken gangrene in her arm and had it sawed off by a doctor who put her into a mesmeric sleep so she didn't feel a thing. And then there was Captain Wittliff's son, who had been in a battle with Comanches and had his cap pinned to his scalp by an arrow.

The boy stopped talking only when they were swallowed up by the unnatural darkness of the canebrake, and in the silence the cane vault creaked above them, and unknown birds called to each other in desolate voices.

CHAPTER EIGHT

✦

AT FULL STRENGTH, Blas Angel Montoya's cazador company was supposed to have a hundred and twenty men, but in his six years in the Mexican army Blas had yet to see any company operating at full strength. The army was swollen with officers, and because so many of the nation's resources were needed to maintain their privileged lives, scant attention was paid to the common soldados who served under them.

Of the eight companies in the Toluca battalion, all were seriously undermanned, but Primer Sargento Montoya's cazadores had the thinnest ranks by far. Over the winter the company had dwindled to thirty-six men.

Here in San Luis Potosí, where the Army of the North was busily re-forming in anticipation of a military rescue of Texas should the norteamericano pirates try to steal it from Mexico, Blas had managed to add thirty more men, but good recruits were hard to find. Convicts, bewildered villagers seized by press gangs, Indians who had never spoken a word of Spanish in their lives—these might do for a fusilier company, where marksmanship counted far less than the ability to march in disciplined ranks, fire on command with a British musket, and remain standing during the recoil. Cazadores, on the other hand, were sharpshooters and skirmishers. Their weapons were British as well—old Baker rifles, most of them—but at least they were made for picking out targets and shooting them down, rather than just contributing anonymously to an advancing wall of fire.

There were six new recruits today, men who had distinguished themselves sufficiently in the line companies as marksmen, heroes, or irritants to warrant reassignment to the elite cazadores. Blas had left Epigenio Reyna, his humorless sargento, in charge of that morning's skirmish drill and led the new men to a hillside cluster of boulders from which they had a fine view of the city and the altiplano beyond. The sharp desert air still bore traces of the evening's chill, and the sun had not yet faded the luminous blue of the sky. Blas, who had grown up in the sodden heat of Tampico, still regarded the stringent atmospherical clarity of the desert as an unnatural blessing.

Arriving at the boulders, Blas took out a tobacco pouch and passed it around, saying nothing for a while as he and the men looked down at the vast encampment, the line companies drilling in their white cotton fatigues, the cavalry units wheeling across the open ground in the distance, their lance points visible above the rising dust. And all of this faraway movement accompanied by scraps of sound that travelled with strange precision through the dry air: orders, curses, bugle calls, a rumble of hooves hardly more audible than his own heartbeat.

He felt confident about the new men. Half of them, he saw at a glance, were native northerners who had been bred through many generations to Indian fighting and the bitter ways of the frontier. He didn't know where the others were from—their time papers hadn't yet been brought up—but they too seemed solid and self-possessed. One of the northerners had a swollen cheek, and from time to time he spat a gob of blood onto the ground. And another, judging by his mildly disagreeable smell and the way he perspired in the fresh morning air, was probably coming down with the spotted itch.

It was Blas's custom to take new recruits aside like this, to sit and smoke with them and give them an easy half-hour or so in which they could take his measure and he could take theirs. He tapped his wooden staff against the sole of his brogan, letting his gaze linger as if casually on the dusty pageant below. He felt the recruits' eyes on him, but did not speak to them until it felt time to do so.

"You are no longer line soldiers," he said finally. "You are cazadores. We are a preferred company, and we treat one another with the respect due to men of skill and courage."

He held up the wooden staff. "I do not like to strike men with this, and it is rare that I must do so. A cazador does not need to be beaten like a sheep. He knows his duty and he follows his orders without hesitation. In return he receives twenty-one pesos, four reales, and eight granos a month. Allowances for bed-and-light and for laundry and tobacco are increased as well. He receives superior powder for his rifle."

Blas picked up a Baker rifle and held it up in front of the men.

"This is the weapon we are privileged to use," he told them, as the first man reluctantly passed the rifle to the next. "It is far superior to the muskets you are used to. Its range is two hundred yards, twice the range of the Brown Bess, and it can be shot with accuracy. And our powder is of finer quality. We don't use the overloaded cartridges they use in the line, so the recoil is easy."

He attached a bayonet to the rifle's muzzle, a long, slashing blade with a brass handle and guard bow.

"This is the sword bayonet," he told them. "And it too is more deadly than the pig-stickers you have used before."

Blas handed the rifle to one of the Tlaxcalans. With the sword bayonet attached, it towered over the man's head. He tested its weight in his arms, admiring it as if it were an object of priceless beauty, flipping up the sight, tracing the shape of the swan neck and the filigree of the brass patch box with his fingertips.

Blas studied the men as they passed the rifle around. It was the first time in their lives, he knew, that most of them had held an object of such worth and quality.

"Your fellow soldiers in the company are experienced men," he told them. "Men who were at San Agustín del Palmar, at Casas Blancas and San Lorenzo, and at the last battle of Puebla."

"And at Tolomé," the man with the swollen cheek said.

"Yes, and at Tolomé."

It was at Tolomé that Blas had lost the top half of his right ear, sliced off by a cavalryman's sabre, though the fighting had been so intense and confused that Blas had not even noticed the wound at the time. Later, on the long march back to Jalapa in defeat, he had been in unspeakable pain. For a long time, they had thought General Santa Anna had been taken prisoner and executed, and that the civil war in which he had led them had come to nothing. But then he was discovered to be alive, and it was not so long after their defeat at Tolomé that they came marching in triumph into the City of Mexico. There were men in Blas's battalion now who had fought against him and Santa Anna in those battles, and though the nation was still divided between federalistas and centralistas, the army for now was reasonably united. Last week, six battalions of infantry, along with three regiments of cavalry and the Zapador battalion, had defeated the state militia in the federalist stronghold of Zacatecas, and it was believed to be only a matter of time before an even larger force, including the Toluca battalion, marched north to Texas.

"What is your name?" Blas asked the man with the swollen cheek.

"Alquisira."

"And what happened to your face, Private Alquisira?"

He spat out another gob of blood before answering. "Three men robbed me two nights ago in town after a cockfight. One of them hit me with his barracks cap."

"His barracks cap?"

"He had filled the cap with musket balls, Sargento. Four of the teeth were broken off."

"Open your mouth," Blas said.

Alquisira opened as wide as he could, not complaining of the pain. Blas saw that the gums on the right side of the mouth were a tortured mass of swollen tissue, oozing coagulated blood as thick as candle wax, with the foundations of the shattered teeth showing through in places. The teeth on the left side, however, were strong and whole. That was a consideration. Though cazadores generally loaded their weapons with loose powder, in the intensity of battle they sometimes had to rely on the pre-loaded cartridges, and a soldado who did not have enough teeth to tear open the paper of the cartridge was useless and vulnerable. Blas might have sent another man back for this reason alone, but he liked Alquisira's steady, uncomplaining mien.

"With permission, Sargento," said one of the others, a short-legged, broad-chested man with pitted skin whose name was Hurtado. "What is the range of a norteamericano rifle?"

"The nortes are not an army," Blas said. "They are adventurers, and so there is no standard weapon. Many of them, I've been told, own Kentucky rifles, which can hit a man at two hundred and fifty yards if well aimed, but many others have only shotguns. And still others only Indian tomahawks and scalping knives."

"Do the nortes scalp their enemies?" one of the other recruits asked.

"I don't know," Blas said.

"They do," another said. "And cut off their scrotums to use as coin purses."

The men began to argue among themselves, some saying that the nortes were wild and undisciplined and greedy, and therefore could be easily defeated, others that their savagery was a crucial advantage because there were no rules of conduct or morality to restrain them. Blas sat down again and listened to the high-pitched bickering of men who were growing eager for war, and apprehensive that war might pass them by. He felt affection for them already, for the way they looked to him to answer questions, to calm them and shape them, to protect them in the hellish days that he knew in his soul were coming.

"True, the nortes are as vicious as wolves," Alquisira was saying. "But a wolf is a very intelligent animal."

"If they were intelligent," said the youngest recruit, "they would know that God is against them."

"There is an intelligent animal," another broke in, pointing up in the sky at a vulture coasting in the rising heat. "It is said that a vulture can be taught to answer to its name like a dog."

"Maybe they have better rifles, but there is more to fighting than weapons," Alquisira said, paying this odd comment no mind. "Skill matters more than firepower. Isn't that true, Sargento?"

Blas ground out his cigarrillo on a flat, bleached rock.

"Alle Kunst ist unsonst," he recited, "wenn ein Engel in das Zundloch prunst."

They presented him with worried looks, as if instead of repeating a borrowed scrap of a foreign language he was harboring some devilish spirit that chose to speak through his mouth. In fact, he had learned the phrase from a captain of artillery—a Prussian looking for opportunity in Santa Anna's rebel army—who had died of gangrene after he had misjudged the velocity of a rolling cannonball and jokingly tried to stop it with his foot.

" 'All skill is for nought,' " Blas translated, " 'when an angel pisses down your touchhole.' "

The new men pondered this blankly, all except Alquisira, who smiled with his ruined mouth.

"Now go down the hill," Blas told them, retrieving the rifle from the last man, "and report to Sargento Reyna."

THAT EVENING Blas went into town to report to Captain Loera, who had formed a mess in a house near the plaza with a few other officers and a retinue of female cooks, soldaderas, children, and various hangers-on. About once a week Loera would show up in camp to make an inspection, but the rest of the time he seemed to pass his days as idly as a dog panting in the sun. His contentment made him good-natured, however, and an afternoon's steady drinking tended to make him almost boisterously agreeable. When he greeted Blas this evening in the courtyard, he was drinking wine and attempting to tune a violin.

"One moment, if you please, Sargento," he said, as he remained seated in his chair alternately plucking a string with his finger and turning the knob that controlled it. He paid thoughtful attention to the tone, and took a sip of wine.

"What do you think?" he asked Blas. "Is it in tune?"

"I don't know, sir."

"Like me, you have no ear." He suddenly looked stricken with embarrassment. "Of course, I mean no reference to your glorious wound."

Blas gave a slight, gracious nod. The captain handed the violin to a little girl, who carried it away into the house.

"How many new men did we receive?"

"Six."

"All acceptable?"

"Yes, sir."

"No more desertions?"

"No, sir."

"Excellent. Train these new men well, Montoya. I want you to concentrate on target practice and skirmish drill. Four-man teams. If we march on Texas, we will be fighting in prairie country and in forests, I am told. The nortes will fight Indian style, from behind trees and rocks, so rifle teams may well determine the outcome. It is unlikely that

there will be concentrated battles, or massed attacks against
fortifications. The nortes have no forts except for a few old
missions that are unsuitable for defense."

Blas nodded indulgently. Loera was presenting all this
to him as if it were new information, when in fact talk of
the Texians and their likely strategies had consumed the
camp for weeks. The captain would have been a ridiculous
figure—with his plump little belly and his hair combed
dramatically forward at the temples into two swirling eagle's
wings—if Blas had not seen him in battle, cool and savage
and exquisitely alert.

"Seat yourself, please, Sargento," the captain said finally, after seeming to drift away for a moment into a private reverie.

Blas took a seat on a severe wooden chair and waited
while the captain studied his wine.

"From Parras," he said. "Do you know it? There is a remarkable winery there, built only a hundred years or so after the conquest when this land was all wild Indians and
waste desert.

"Maria," he called to the little girl who had taken the violin. "Bring the sargento a bottle of pulque."

In a moment the girl showed up with the bottle and
handed it without ceremony to Blas. He thanked her and
held it in his two hands. The captain did not offer him a
glass, and if he had, Blas would have been shocked beyond
speech. Officers did not drink with enlisted men, nor did
they routinely hold them in their presence for such a long,
awkward duration as this was turning out to be. Blas
glanced up uncomfortably at the sky above the courtyard,
the sumptuous fading light in which an eerily large moon
was as sharp and commanding as a silver spangle. There
was music drifting now from the plaza, and the smell of
meat being cooked on braziers.

"I do not recall ever seeing you with a woman, Sargento," Loera said at last.

Blas could think of nothing to say in reply to this strange comment, and so he merely tilted his head.

"You have no wife?" the captain persisted.

"No, sir."

"Nor a woman?"

"No, sir."

"If we are given the honor of marching to Texas, who will carry your boots?"

"I will carry my own boots, sir."

Loera smiled and gently shook his head. "It is a very long way to Texas, Sargento. You will grow tired of those boots. And let me say this candidly. Our country is bankrupt. To prosecute this war, His Excellency Santa Anna will have to borrow money at outrageous prices from unscrupulous men who have no sense of patriotism, and from the Church, which has even less. As a consequence, rations will be short on the march to Texas. A man who wants to eat will need someone to forage for him, someone who can travel with the camp followers and bargain for food. Without a soldadera to help you, it will be a very unpleasant journey.

"You ask why I say these things. It is because my good friend Pomposo Garza, a captain in the Querétaro battalion, was killed last week at Zacatecas. We were imprisoned in Perote together after Tolomé. We played chess endlessly, for months at a time, using chessmen we made from the cartridge paper the guards threw away. He kept my spirits up during an anxious time, and now I would like to do a good deed in his name."

Loera drained his wineglass, picked up the bottle from the ground, and filled the glass again. A lizard moved in cautious stages around the circumference of an old fountain in the center of the courtyard, negotiating its way across fields of broken tile.

"There is a woman. She's Mayan. A girl really, only fifteen or so. Who knows where Pomposo got her? He had friends who were officers in the Jiménez battalion; most of the men in that unit are conscripts from Yucatán. Maybe they passed her along to one of the officers, who lost her to Pomposo in a game of whist. He had a passion for whist and all things English. In the end, he fell in love with her and would not let her go with him to Zacatecas. He had a premonition about his death. Or rather, she had the premonition. As I understand it, she's some sort of a witch."

Loera inserted a cigar into a pair of golden tongs and lit it with a lucifer match. A cloud of smoke erupted and momentarily concealed his head.

"And so," the captain said as his face swam into view again, "I have her in my keeping, and I offer her to you. She is not a creature of luxury, and a primer sargento's pay will support her well enough."

Blas sat there in motionless silence, clutching the pulque bottle.

"Sir," he began, "I have many responsibilities . . ."

"The girl can help you with your responsibilities. She will be no trouble at all; she'll be a blessing. I'd keep her myself, but we already have quite a menagerie here. I could turn her out, but I hesitate to do that. As I said, she's a witch. Who knows what harm could befall one if she were not treated with kindness?"

"I have no place to keep her."

"She'll live in your jacal. She'll sleep on the ground if you want, but she's not bad-looking at all, and I think you'll want her in your cot soon enough."

"Where is she now?"

"Out with the women somewhere. Shopping or washing. I'll have her brought to you tonight. Be at the cathedral an hour or so after dark."

The moment to say no seemed to have slipped away without his recognizing it. Perhaps because he did not want to say no. Blas had often thought of having a soldadera, a woman, even a wife, but there was something shy or wary in his nature. He was twenty-three. His relations with women had always been comfortably confined to whores, though unlike the other men in his unit he had never gloried in the need for this sort of release and in his heart had always been obscurely shamed by it. He had lived as a soldier since he was seventeen—most of his adult life—time enough for him to have developed a dependence on the rhythms and petty certitudes of army life. His ordered days, his grave, methodical privacy, the unvarying drills, and the simple, unchanging language of bugle calls and ritualized commands—these were the charms that somehow convinced him he would survive the unstructured hell of actual war.

"Her name is Isabella," said Loera. "She doesn't speak Spanish at all, just some Indian language. But she's alert enough, and she understands what's expected of her."

"An hour after dark, in front of the cathedral," the captain repeated. "I'll have Maria bring her to you."

Blas stood and took his leave, clutching his bottle of pulque. He walked aimlessly through the city. The plazas were crowded with promenading youths, with women wrapped in their chinas poblanas against the chill; the jardines teemed with soldados from the great encampment outside of town. The clear evening air inspired him with a sense of destiny and expectation.

He encountered two sargentos he knew from the Morelos battalion, and they sat down together in a little fonda by the Alameda and ate dinner and shared the bottle of pulque and talked about the victory in Zacatecas. The units that had taken part in the battle had not yet returned, except for one cavalry regiment that had come in only hours before and brought stories of the wholesale looting that Santa Anna had allowed after the city had fallen.

"Zacatecans needed to be taught a lesson," one of the men from the Morelos battalion said. "They've always considered themselves superior to the rest of the country."

"Maybe so," his friend said, "but it took courage to rise for Hidalgo."

"It's one thing to fight against the Spanish. It's another to fight against Mexico itself."

Blas listened to the arguments without commenting much. He did not approve of the sacking of Zacatecas, if that was indeed what had occurred, because he knew war well enough and the awful license that it could grant. What appealed to him about the army was the restraint that it imposed, the way it was supposed to hold the demons of human nature in check, rather than release them in all their savagery. War was not glorious to him, as it was to the officers, yet he craved the order that could sometimes be perceived in the chaos of battle the way he had craved the beautiful hallucinations that had come to him out of the hunger and pain during that long march from Tolomé in defeat.

"I saw Hidalgo's head when I was a boy," one of the sargentos said. "On the walls of the Alhóndiga in Guanajuato. It was there for eleven years."

"What did it look like?" his friend wanted to know.

"Dried out, like a mummy."

They talked on about the best way to preserve the head of a bandit or revolutionary. There was a general in Tamaulipas who was said to fry them in oil like pork rinds, another who displayed them in a jar full of alcohol. This led to a discussion of the fourteen bandits the other sargento had once seen hanging from trees on the road from the City of Mexico to Puebla, and from there they talked about the crucifixion of Christ, and how much His death might have been hastened if the Roman centurions had broken His legs, and whether He would have actually walked on those legs after the Resurrection or simply glided inches above the surface of the earth.

Blas left the two sargentos arguing the matter and walked through the streets of San Luis Potosí. Though his own feet were firmly on the ground, he felt strangely light-headed and expectant as he approached the cathedral. There was the usual crowd of aggressive léperos at the entrance, reciting their afflictions and extending their hands for centavos. Blas dropped a coin or two into their palms and went inside, into the immemorial stillness of the church.

He knelt at a rail near the entrance and looked at the distant gilded altar, its golden encrustations twinkling in the candlelight, the carved images of Christ and His Mother and tortured saints looking down from their niches in hollow agony. He was not to meet the Mayan girl for another hour yet, but he was content to pass the time here, kneeling on a hard wooden plank in this great church where the very mind of God seemed to loom overhead like a fog.

Blas set his forehead upon his clenched hands and closed his eyes to pray, but instead of prayers there came yearnings and unguarded memories. He found that deep in his soul he was anxious for war. He imagined leading his cazadores through an open field, taking shelter behind rocks and trees as they skirmished far ahead of the lines, confounding the norteamericano riflemen with unexpected stealth and marksmanship. He imagined a great bayonet charge like the one at Tolomé, his eyes and nostrils burning from gunpowder, his isolated terror giving way as they ran across the cobbly ground to a general elation, an unsustainable pitch of glory.

During his boyhood in Tampico he had often seen crews of norteamericano sailors roaming through the streets on shore leave—men who even when sober were painfully coarse and boisterous, and whose massive, hairy, heavy-boned bodies seemed to him an expression of natural belligerence. As an enemy, what would they be like? Disorganized, surely, but full of fierceness and bravado. A race of near giants who believed that not just Texas but the entire continent was theirs to seize.

Blas had never fought against anyone but fellow Mexicans, during the almost unbroken episodes of civil war through which Santa Anna had risen to power. He had been too young to fight with Hidalgo or Morelos against the gachupíns, but he knew firsthand the galvanizing hatred of foreigners. When he was seventeen the Spaniards had invaded Tampico, his home, sending down an infernal rain of canister and shell. He had been at the reservoir when the bombardment began, meeting with a group of other boys who were planning to march off that night to join with the army that Santa Anna was raising to repel the invaders. When Blas ran down to his house, climbing frantically over the rubble that now blocked the streets, he saw that it had been destroyed. His parents and four sisters had been crouched beneath a table and that was where the eighteen-pound exploding shell had found them. He ran up to where his house had been and then let his uncle drag him away before he could see his dead family. All that he saw—and this he remembered as if from a dream—was a severed head lying in the street, its face turned away from him, its black hair covered in masonry dust. Whether it was his mother's head he had seen, or his father's, or one of his four sisters', he did not know. Nor had he, in the long solitary years since, ever wanted to know.

He walked out of the cathedral and stood by himself in front of its ornate facade, waiting to receive the Mayan witch who would be his woman. Finally he saw the little girl Maria leading her across the plaza by the hand. She was not much taller than Maria, and with her small, wiry body, her broad face with its luminous eyes, she reminded him startlingly of a deer. She walked across the plaza on wide, splayed feet, carrying her few belongings in an old army knapsack of half-rotted leather. Slung across her shoulder was a shooting pouch made from the skin of a jaguar.

She did not look at him, and Maria said nothing by way of introduction, just let go of her hand and stood there waiting, Blas thought, to be dismissed.

"Is it true she speaks no Spanish?" Blas asked Maria, who merely nodded.

"How do you speak to her?" he persisted.

"Like you speak to an animal," she said. "If you call her by her name, she'll come to you. If you point to something you want her to carry, she'll carry it."

"And her name is Isabella?"

The girl nodded again, her indifference beginning to annoy him. Blas gave her half a centavo anyway, and she turned and disappeared, leaving the witch standing there alone, with no hint of pleasure or apprehension on her face.

"Isabella," he said. "Come with me."

She followed him through the streets, and he was aware of her insubstantial body behind him as if it were a spirit. On the way out of town a group of pleasantly drunk soldados from the Galeana battalion who had commandeered a cart stopped to ask him if he had heard any details about the glorious victory in Zacatecas. He said he had not, but they insisted on giving him and the girl a place in the cart, and so they rode the last mile into camp listening to the singing soldados try to reconstruct a corrido they had heard in town that night about a crystal bird that came to life at the touch of a human breath.

"Who is she?" Epigenio Reyna wanted to know as Blas led the girl through the camp toward the cluster of jacales that served as noncommissioned officers' quarters for the battalion.

"Someone to carry my boots," he said.

He lit a candle in the small jacal and set it on a table he had made himself from the discarded wood of a packing crate. He had also built a rude cot, and now it occurred to him that it would be a good thing to have Isabella around to watch over his two pieces of furniture, since firewood was a precious commodity in the encampment.

The girl looked around at the little hut without betraying a single thought, then turned to him, gesturing with her head toward a bare space of ground on the other side of the jacal from his cot.

He nodded. He had an extra blanket, much frayed at the edges and worn thin through years of use, and he took it off his cot and spread it down on the spot she had selected. Isabella took off her knapsack and jaguar pouch and set them on the ground as well. Out of the knapsack she took another faded huipil like the one she was wearing and a comb, and set them beside the blanket. Then she brought out a cloth bound together with a string, and set it down as well. That was all she had.

Sitting on the blanket, she looked up at him. There was a strange, satisfying perfection in the lines and angles of her small face. She might have been beautiful to him if she were not so unnervingly alien, a creature from very far away in both distance and thought.

"Let me see," he said, gesturing to the bound cloth.

Without hesitation, but without hurry, she picked up the cloth, untied the string, and opened up the little bundle to reveal perhaps a dozen small stones of various shapes and colors. Blas looked at the stones for a long moment, as she seemed to want him to, though he had no idea what their purpose was. He assumed they had something to do with her powers as a witch, and he was relieved when finally she bound them up again into the cloth and tied the string.

Then she handed him the jaguar pouch. The pouch was empty, and though it was pleasingly and strongly made, its appearance produced in him a faint tremor of nausea. He did not like the sickly yellow background of the jaguar's hide, nor the formless black blotches that decorated it. Yellow and black were the cholera colors. In 1832 he had been with Santa Anna's rebel army during the siege of Chapultepec, and he remembered the yellow and black banners that hung everywhere in the city, announcing the presence of the dead, the grotesque contagion that travelled in some unknown manner, like an evil spirit, from one human soul to the next.

He handed the pouch back to the Mayan girl, but she shook her head and indicated to his surprise that it now belonged to him. It was a fine pouch, but he was not sure that he wanted it; on the other hand, to refuse such a gift would bring unknown consequences. So he merely nodded his thanks, careful not to look directly into her eyes. He had a powerful desire to do so but was uncertain what she was capable of, whether she planned to draw his gaze and then fix him with the evil eye.

He did not know what else to do or say, and so he blew out the candle, took off his brogans, and lay down on his cot, too modest or vulnerable to remove his fatigues in her presence. Moonlight leaked through the stick walls of the jacal, giving her dirty cotton huipil a ghostly radiance as she stood up from her pallet and moved lightly out the door without speaking. Blas heard the sound of her pissing against the rocks a few yards away, and then she came back inside and lay down on her blanket, untroubled and self-possessed and ready for sleep.

CHAPTER NINE

✹

TELESFORO VILLASENOR, the third son of a Puebla wool merchant, was blessed with a grandiose temperament. He believed in his own destiny with an infectious fervor that bound other men to him, and he knew instinctively the value of the striking gesture that could vault a soldier out of the anonymity that, for Telesforo, was a graver and more conclusive fate than death.

His role in the battle for Zacatecas had been a success, due both to his own initiative and to his good luck in receiving a remarkable wound. Telesforo Villasenor was a lieutenant in the engineer battalion known as the Zapadores, a unit that was well respected in the army not just for its mapmaking and bridge-building skills but for its peerless fighting spirit. Usually the Zapadores were held in reserve during a battle, since Santa Anna was reluctant to put his most highly trained and motivated troops in jeopardy unless he needed them in a crisis.

At Zacatecas, however, the plan had been different. In fact, the real fighting had not taken place in Zacatecas at all, but in a village called Guadalupe that guarded the entrance to a long ravine that served as the main avenue to the capital city. A series of barren hills ran along either side of the ravine, and the enemy line extended from the base of the foremost hill across the town to the edge of a steep, impassable arroyo.

It was a strong position. For an attack to succeed, one or both of the enemy's securely anchored flanks would have to be turned, and for that to happen defenders had to be drawn from the flanks to the center of the line. When the order of battle was made known, Telesforo and the other officers of the engineer battalion had been gratified to see that the Zapadores would have the honor of attacking the center. They would not be held in reserve this time; rather, they would be used as the most convincing diversion possible while Santa Anna himself, on one side, and the cavalry, on the other, assaulted the flanks,

The night before the battle Telesforo decided to sneak through the enemy lines, climb one of the hills, and see for himself how the commanders of the Zacatecan militia had laid out their defenses. After making sure that his men had eaten their supper, that their bayonets were sharpened and their cartridge boxes full, he slipped out alone, carrying only his sword and a pouch filled with paper, ink, and watercolors.

He made his way north for a mile, around the base of the foremost hill. The moon was perilously bright, and he moved step by step with exquisite alertness. Several times he heard the close-by voices of enemy sentries, and once he had to lie flat on the ground as a troop of cavalry passed within a few yards, the horsemen grimly silent but their gear clanking and creaking like some sort of ghostly machine.

The enemy had built campfires at regular intervals around the bases of the hills, but he soon saw that most of the fires were unmanned and were there only to provide the illusion of more men. From a distance, watching behind a screen of thorny ocotillo stalks, Telesforo studied one of the fires for a long time. When he was satisfied that no one was near, he crawled across the cool desert floor past the fire, not daring to stand up for another twenty yards in case the flames might suddenly reveal his silhouette.

He climbed the hill known as Matapulgas, staying as low to the ground as possible as he approached its summit of craggy, splintered rock. It was not until he reached the

summit that he heard voices below him on the eastern flank
of the hill, two scared teenaged privados tending a fire.
Telesforo could hear the dry wood popping, and once or
twice explosions of sparks vaulted into the air, reaching the
promontory on which he lay as still as a lizard. Below him,
the boys argued about what they should do if their position
was overrun. One said they should surrender as soon as
possible. The other said if they surrendered they would be
shot anyway. They should fight back, street by street, house
by house, giving up their lives dearly and gloriously. Neither of the boys, Telesforo observed, seemed to have any
confidence at all that Santa Anna's army could be repulsed.

Very carefully, he opened his pouch and took out his paper and ink and watercolors. The moon was bright enough
to give contour and shading to the village and the landscape
below him. Inside the town, soldiers were running back and
forth, bringing furniture from the houses to reinforce the
breastworks. He could hear officers calling out orders, he
could smell the odors from a hundred cooking fires, he could
see groups of panic-stricken civilians fleeing Guadalupe,
headed down the road toward Zacatecas.

As the two anxious soldiers talked on below him, Telesforo drew a map of the enemy's position—the silent, serene
hills, the fortifications, the major houses, the deep arroyo.
He worked quickly. He was a natural and facile artist, a gift
that God had granted to him, Telesforo had always believed, in compensation for his unfortunate order of birth.
A third-born son, if he had any pride, had to make his own
way in the world. Telesforo had joined the army without
fully realizing the value of his gift. Originally assigned to a
line company made up of convicts, he had amused his fellow officers by painting their portraits on ivory disks cut
from pilfered billiard balls. It was only a matter of months
before a captain in the Zapadores had heard about Telesforo's talent, requested his own portrait, and then arranged

'or the artist to be reassigned to the engineer battalion as a
napmaker.

But there were other mapmakers in the battalion, less
:alented than Telesforo, whose unashamed flattery of supe-
:ior officers consistently awarded them the most favored
assignments. Telesforo had seen the map of the Zacatecan
militia's defenses at Guadalupe that Santa Anna had used
to devise his battle plans. It was a poor piece of work, in his
opinion, giving no real information on the crucial contours
of the land—the intricate chain of hills, for instance, with
their strategic peaks and skirts, were depicted as just a series of wrinkled uplifts on a flat plane. The houses of the
town were mere boxes, with no perspective and therefore no
indication of probable fields of fire. Worse, the map had
been aesthetically displeasing: no pleasure taken in line or
shading, no subtlety or fidelity, no interest in the landscape
beyond its starkest strategic features.

Working only by the light of the moon, with the voices
of the enemy in his ear, Telesforo could not produce the
map he wanted. But inadequate though it inevitably was, he
thought anyone would clearly see it was the product of skill
and daring. He had no notion of showing it to anyone, at
least for the present. He had risked his life for his own satisfaction.

He had made his way down from Matapulgas and back
to his own lines without incident, and was even able to calm
himself sufficiently for a few hours of sleep before the
army was awakened at four o'clock. The battle began three
hours later. The Zapadores waited in formation for some
time as the artillery cut the enemy line into tatters and the
cavalry began the process of turning the right flank. Watching from a distance, Telesforo felt no anxiety at his first
major action but an almost eerie sense of well-being. Everything was happening as Santa Anna had ordained, as a classic maneuver against the rear, like Alexander at Chaeronea,

that for all its distant chaos and piercing screams was as plain as the illustrations in the tactical manuals Telesforo had studied.

Telesforo watched as the battle ripened, and he guessed at almost the exact moment they would be ordered to charge. Then when the order came he raised his sword into the air and led his men across the desert, a direct bayonet charge into the demoralized heart of the enemy line without even a pause for a volley. He could see muzzle flashes from the torn-up breastworks a hundred yards ahead, he could hear men near him grunt as they were struck and skidded to the ground. Meanwhile the velocity of the living men continued to increase, until Telesforo felt the way he had felt as a child, running in open fields with exhilarating swiftness, believing that at any moment he could suddenly take flight. He pointed his sword at the breastworks as they closed in on it. It was thinly defended now, the furniture barricades blown up into splinters by Santa Anna's artillery, and body parts littering the ground in front. Telesforo saw—or did he imagine he saw?—a head lying upright in front of them as they charged, its lips still moving, uttering silent words like a distracted old man mumbling to himself.

He scrambled nimbly up the barricade, yelling for his men to follow. An enemy militiaman appeared above him, raising the butt of his rifle to strike. Telesforo thrust upward with his sword, and the point caught the man under the chin and came out his mouth. At that same moment the barricade collapsed on them both, and by the time Telesforo had dug himself out of the rubble of blown-apart furniture and cart wheels and sacks of dirt his antagonist had already been bayoneted by a dozen men.

Once over the barricade, the Zapadores swarmed into the village, but the resistance had all but evaporated. Individual cavalry men rode through the street, cutting down retreating enemy militia, and the frenzied line troops were already breaking down the doors of the houses, searching for plunder and people to kill.

A privado standing next to Telesforo in the plaza was hit in the center of the face by a ball that struck downward through the visor of his shako. Telesforo looked up, quickly factoring the trajectory, and saw a dispersing cloud of gunpowder smoke near an upper-story window. He lifted his left arm, pointing toward the window. He had just opened his mouth to warn the nearby soldiers about the sniper when another cloud of smoke erupted and he found himself on the ground, his arm suddenly alive with strange erratic pulses of energy that took him a moment to recognize as pain. The ball had entered at the back of his wrist and plowed up the entire length of his arm.

Ashamed to be lying in the dirt, he somehow sprang to his feet before his men could reach him. He felt deliriously light-headed, though his awareness was grounded by a searing weight of pain. He vomited. He asked for his sword. When it was set into his hand he led his men across the square. The door of the sniper's house was firmly barricaded, but a captain from the Battalion of Public Security had his men roll up a captured eight-pounder and fire. Telesforo was first through the shattered doorway. One of the militiamen inside lunged at him with a bayonet, the blow glancing off the leather of his map case as Telesforo sliced deep into the man's neck with his sword, unleashing a black jet of blood.

Telesforo fell to the floor as his own men shoved him from behind in their fury to get through the broken doorway and kill whoever was inside. There were a half-dozen militiamen defending the house, wild-eyed teenagers, and Telesforo heard them squeal as they were bayonetted and saw them run around the room slipping on the entrails that were falling out of their torn bodies. It all seemed to be happening at a very great distance.

He stood again as the killing went on, all the energy and

bloodlust suddenly drained from him. The tile floor of the house, from wall to wall, was already coated with blood, and his entire arm was a sopping mass of tissue that sent out pulses of pain so wild and strong he could hardly believe he was experiencing them.

Through the screams, he heard a shuffling movement in a dark corner of the house. Lifting his sword, he walked across the blood-soaked floor to find an old man and woman cowering behind a heavy wooden table that had been overturned.

"Who are you?" he said.

"Citizens of Guadalupe," the woman said. The man was weeping with fear and could not speak. "This is our house. Please do not kill us."

Telesforo swayed back and forth on his feet, trying to fix his eyes on the trembling couple.

"Don't be afraid," he said. "Here is a hand and a heart to protect you."

The chaos had subsided behind him. He called to two privados he recognized from his company and they came forward, their shakos gone and their hair and faces and uniform fronts coated with blood. They looked like demons, but there was a glassy calm in their eyes.

"These are innocent citizens," he told the soldiers. "Do not hurt them. Find out where the other civilians are and escort them there."

"You're hurt very badly, Teniente," one of them said.

"I know. Take these people to safety."

The two men walked the old people across the slaughterhouse that had been their living room and led them out through the broken door. Telesforo was about to follow when he saw an ornate wooden box that had tumbled out of one of the drawers of the overturned table. He slipped his sword into the scabbard and bent down and picked it up with his good hand. The little casket was a marvel of Oaxacan artistry, covered with carved and painted flowers and birds and animals, all of them glued into place with gum arabic. When he opened the lid he found nestled within the box fifty packets of the most expensive chocolates, each one decorated with the same themes of nature found on the outside of the casket.

His friend Robert Talon, a Frenchman stranded in Santa Anna's army, came running into the house. Telesforo noted the look of shock on Robert's face.

"They said you were wounded," the Frenchman said in his expert Spanish. "And now I see."

"The bone is not broken," Telesforo said dreamily. He tried to lift his blood-soaked sleeve to demonstrate, but he could no longer command his arm to move.

"Come," Robert said. "We will find you a doctor. Not some army butcher, but a real doctor who can perhaps save your arm."

The two of them left the house, Telesforo still dumbly clutching the box of chocolates. He tried to make his mind split itself away from the breathtaking pain of his wound, but the pain ruled his entire consciousness and would give his thoughts no peace.

All around them soldados were bayonetting the dead and breaking into houses, and running through the streets with whatever they could carry. No one was stopping them. A thick haze of gunpowder still lay heavily on the plaza, and the air was rank with the smells of sulfur and blood.

"Where are the ambulances?" he heard Robert call to someone. "Where are the stretcher bearers? Here is a wounded officer! My God, is there no one to attend him?"

Telesforo felt his consciousness surging and receding like ocean waves at the shore. All around him men were running about frantically, looting and butchering. He could hear the screams of women.

Then through his fading awareness he saw Santa Anna himself, conferring with a group of his officers on the other side of the plaza. He stood dismounted next to a black stallion with an artful blaze on its face. The president of Mexico was tall and lean. Beneath his towering cocked hat, with its crest of plumes in the colors of the Mexican flag, his hair was raven black. His eyes were alert and commanding, his face open. Telesforo knew Santa Anna to be in his early forties, but he seemed a decade younger as he spoke to his staff, issuing orders with fluid urgency.

"Hold this," Telesforo said to Robert, handing him the casket of chocolates. With his good hand he reached into his case and took out the folded map he had drawn the night before.

"Open the lid of the casket and put this inside," he told Robert, handing him the map.

"What are you doing?" Robert said. "You're very badly hurt, Telesforo."

"Put the map inside with the chocolates."

Robert did as he asked.

"Now give me back the casket."

Holding the casket, Telesforo began to walk across the plaza. His movements were slow and unreal, and it seemed like it would take him forever. He kept his eyes focused on Santa Anna, who stood with one thumb hooked theatrically in his blue silk sash, nodding gravely as he listened to some exhortation from one of his staff.

"Where are you going?" Telesforo heard Robert saying behind him, but he did not have the strength to explain or even to wave the question away. He kept stumbling ahead, as El Presidente pointed in the direction of Zacatecas, issued a final directive, and then turned to a groom for his reins.

It was then that Santa Anna happened to catch sight of Telesforo as he staggered forward holding the flowery casket of chocolates in his good hand, his mangled arm limp at his side and the entire left half of his uniform soaked in blood.

"Your Excellency," Telesforo said.

Santa Anna gave his reins back to the groom and walked toward Telesforo, looking at him with dark, appraising eyes.

"You are badly hurt, Teniente," he said.

Telesforo swayed on his feet. He locked his eyes onto the face of the president of Mexico and somehow managed to keep upright.

"Would you do me the honor," he said, holding up the casket, "of accepting this gift from an anonymous and unworthy soldier? They are chocolates from Oaxaca."

Santa Anna took the chocolates and studied for a moment the carved flowers and birds that decorated the box. When he raised his eyes to Telesforo, they were moist with tears.

"What is your name, Teniente?"

"Telesforo Villasenor, Your Excellency."

"You have been grievously wounded, and yet your first thought was of my happiness. Your gift has touched me deeply, my friend, and I accept it with a full heart."

He handed the chocolates to his aide and embraced Telesforo, taking care not to touch the wounded arm. Telesforo smelled the pomade on the president's hair. When Santa Anna pulled away, the front of his blue coat was covered with Telesforo's blood, a fact that did not seem to concern him in the slightest.

"Take him to my personal surgeon," Santa Anna said to the aide, and then mounted his black horse and spurred it toward Zacatecas.

THE DOCTOR was young, less than thirty, but marvelously skillful and swift as he pulled clothing fibers out of the the long, furrowed wound in Telesforo's arm, and then sewed the whole limb back together with a series of ligatures that reached from his wrist to his shoulder. Even as he writhed on his cot in agony during this interminable procedure, Telesforo had noticed and been reassured by the doctor's steady concentration. Now, the fourth day after his surgery, though he still burned with fever and his arm was still inflamed, he knew himself to be emerging from his inferno of pain, and there was a sense of gladness and well-being in his heart that was almost sacred in its intensity.

He lay in a makeshift hospital somewhere in the center of Zacatecas. He had no memory of being brought here, though he remembered the operation on his arm more vividly than any other experience of his life. He worried intermittently that his conversation with Santa Anna, and the president's embrace, had been only a fever dream, but Robert and the other friends who had come to visit him and marvel at his miraculous wound had spoken of the event, confirming its reality in his own grateful mind.

"It was a subject for a painting," Robert said. "You could not know how horrible you looked—your face as pale as a fungus, your arm mangled and completely soaked in blood—and yet there you stood, offering His Excellency a box of chocolates. What a magnificent gesture! How did you think to make it?"

"It's well known that the president has a fondness for chocolates."

"A subject for a painting," Robert repeated. "David should do it: 'Villasenor Presents Santa Anna with Chocolates at the Conquest of Zacatecas.'"

Robert stayed longer than Telesforo wanted him to, chattering on about a scheme he had to create and market something he called the "Antiquity Globe," which would be made of transparent glass and would display, beneath the representation of every modern country, a palimpsest of vanished civilizations. Robert had come to Mexico to explore the ruins of Palenque, deep in Chiapas, but his little expedition had been routed by bandits only two days out of the City of Mexico, and he was left penniless and forced to join the army to survive. He still burned with the longing to explore the ancient cities of the Maya, and he had grown tiresome on the subject of those temples mouldering away in their jungle solitude.

"If only Santa Anna would march south," he said, "and conquer the Mayan regions, instead of north to Texas, where there is nothing of interest to see at all."

Robert talked on until dark, and then finally bid Telesforo good-bye. The Zapadores were marching on to San Luis Potosí in the morning, he said. He would see Telesforo in a few weeks, when he and the other wounded were strong enough to make the journey.

Telesforo wondered how many of the others with him in this hospital would survive their wounds. Next to him lay a mortally wounded captain, whose constant tormented mumbling had finally silenced, and whose face was now filled with simple stupefaction and despair. There were four other men in close proximity, one with a bandaged face where his cheek had been sliced away by a sword, two with amputated legs, one with a bayonet wound to the lower bowels that filled the room with the stink of pus and excrement.

Late at night the man with the bayonet wound let out a hideous screech, a heartbroken wail of agony accompanied by an eruption of noxious body gases. Telesforo thought he had died, but though his life was near its end his dying was far from over. He wailed on through the night. The doctors were gone—who knew where?—and twice Telesforo struggled to his feet and walked to the soldier's cot to hold his hand and try to speak to him, but the man had no awareness beyond his pain and could not be reached or comforted.

He died in the early hours of the morning, and the silence that finally fell on the hospital was as pure and luminous as the air after a rainstorm. Telesforo lay on his cot, unable to sleep. He kept recalling his meeting with Santa Anna, remembering it in endless feverish variations, examining it from every angle like a glowing, faceted crystal. In his fantasies he saw the president suddenly appearing in the doorway, striding in to inquire after the welfare of his heroic Zapador officer.

He knew, however, that Santa Anna would not come. He had already gone on to the City of Mexico, and from there he would retire to his estate at Manga de Clavo to ponder his next move against the nortes.

The next night the captain died, but the other patients steadily improved, and in another week they were all put into an ambulance and carted across the desert on the long journey to San Luis Potosí. Telesforo gained strength on the trip, and when they arrived in the main plaza of San Luis he was able to step down out of the ambulance and walk on his own to the little house several streets away where he and Robert were billeted. It was there that his orders were delivered the following morning.

"Excellent Sir," they read. "Upon receipt of these orders, and subsequent to your recovery of the wounds received during the battle to liberate Zacatecas, you are to be conveyed to my present headquarters, where you will join my staff as a mapmaker."

The letter concluded with the phrase "God and Liberty," beneath which was the signature of Antonio López de Santa Anna.

CHAPTER TEN

✦

SEVERAL WEEKS had passed since Mary had driven Edmund to Copano, and she had not been to the bayshore since. Before the Karankawa attack, she had enjoyed visiting her favorite oyster-gathering places along the coast, but now the sight of all that open water haunted her. Driving the oxcart today above the shell bluffs, she could not train her eyes away from the bay's surface, that great blue blankness from which so many threats could arise.

And yet the beauty of the place defiantly lifted her heart. The water had a slumbering calm, and there was a briny edge to the air that tickled the shattered bones of her nose. Herons stalked the shoreline, and in the deeper water farther out Mary saw a porpoise fin arching above the surface; and she remembered how when she had lain on the ground expecting to die it was this same sight—of this same singularly unknowable being—that had momentarily erased the terror from her soul.

"What is he barking about?" Edna said, as Professor began a furious, indignant yapping a hundred yards ahead. The dog was at the water's edge, hidden from sight below one of the bluffs.

"Wait here," Fresada said, and kicked his horse forward, leaving Mary and Edna behind with the cart. Not wanting to frighten the girl, Mary resisted the impulse to grab her rifle, but she took careful note of where it lay behind her in the cart, and mentally rehearsed the action of picking it up in one swift movement and firing a ball at an attacker. In a moment, though, Fresada turned and waved them ahead, and they joined him at the edge of the bluff, looking down at a long serpentine oyster reef that the meager tides in the bay had exposed.

Professor was barking at a massive, wriggling fish stranded on the surface of the reef. Mary judged it to be almost twenty feet long, with about a third of its length given over to a peculiar flat snout that the fish swung side to side in confused fury.

"What is it?" Edna asked.

"I don't know," Mary said. "I've never seen such a fish before."

"A sawfish," Fresada told them.

Mary and Edna followed him down the bluff to the water's edge, where Professor danced around in agitation, still howling at the great fish. The exposed scrap of reef lay twenty yards out into the bay. The fish thrashed so wildly that it had lacerated its underside on the sharp oyster shell, and its blood covered the reef Mary saw that the odd snout was indeed a kind of saw, studded all around with teeth that pointed straight out from the edges, and in its dying delirium the fish seemed to be lashing out with this weapon at the air itself.

After a moment, Professor could bear it no longer, and he began to wade into the shallow water with the intent of swimming toward the reef. Fresada reached out and grabbed him by the scruff of his neck and threw him back to shore.

"That fish will cut that dog in two," he said.

Professor did not venture into the water again, but he kept up his howling.

"Hush!" Mary told him, and the dog grudgingly obeyed, uttering now an agitated whimper.

"Is it a whale, then?" Edna asked.

"No," Mary said.

"What if it comes after us?"

"It's dying," Mary said impatiently. Any reasonable person could see that the fish was in no condition to attack them, even if such an attack was within its nature. The girl had the wild, unquenchable fears of a young child. And yet the sight of this wondrous and hideous fish dying in such torment before them left Mary a bit unsettled as well.

"Is it edible?" she asked Fresada.

"You can eat it," he said. "And there's good oil."

Mary thought for a moment about wading out into the water, standing a safe distance away from the reef, and shooting the fish. But she had no idea how many balls she might waste trying to penetrate the creature's atlas. She had heard of fish with multiple brains, like the multiple stomachs of a cow, and there was no telling where this monster's consciousness resided.

"We'll wait for it to die," she announced, and they sat there for some time in silence watching the beast slash and heave on the oyster reef. Her father had told her once that fish could not feel pain, but she had always doubted this. They felt something as they were torn out of the water on a hook, or hauled up gasping in a net. If they felt nothing, it had always seemed to her, their dying would not concern them nearly so much.

"How long will it take, Mrs. Mott?" Edna asked her.

"I don't know, child."

"I don't like watching it."

"Well, then, turn your head."

But Edna kept her eyes on the dying fish. She would turn her head only if Mary did so. She did everything that Mary did, not in the way of a copycat but in the way of a child who sought security in matching her movements and expressions to those of a wiser and more powerful being. To Edna, Mary realized, the slightest gesture of independence carried the threat of isolation. Mary had never seen a girl who hungered more for love, for simple human contact. This constant need annoyed Mary, but it spoke to her heart as well.

When she had turned up at the inn several weeks ago

there had been such a trusting, imploring look in her eyes that Mary could not have turned her away in any case, even if she had not announced that she was carrying Terrell's child.

"Can I live with you now?" she had said. "Will you take care of me?"

Flabbergasted, Mary had questioned the girl closely about the date of her last courses, about soreness in her breasts, and other signs of pregnancy, but Edna's answers had been so opaque that it was clear that her being with child was more of a wish than a reality.

At first Mary had been disinclined to believe her claims that Terrell had had relations with her as well, but the stricken look on his face when he entered the dwelling house that afternoon and saw Edna there emptied Mary of hope in this regard.

She had ordered Edna to stay and drink her tea and told her son to come with her. They walked down to the river without speaking. Terrell, his face tight, bent down to gather stones, and then stood up to toss them idly, one by one, into the water.

"Is she telling the truth?" Mary said. "Were the two of you together in that way?"

He tried to speak, but his embarrassment was so crushing he simply nodded his head while the tears began to spill out of his eyes.

"Oh, Lord," she sighed. "Why would you do such a thing, Terrell? She's disturbed. She has no wits at all. Why would you take advantage of such a simple girl?"

"I didn't mean to," he said.

"She said she's with child."

The look of terror that came into her son's face broke her heart. Impulsively, she reached out to hold and protect him, but he broke away, too ashamed of himself and too angry with her to allow it.

"I didn't mean to," he repeated.

"It's all right. I don't believe she's really going to have a baby. I think she's making that up."

He would not look at her. In the long silence that followed, he furiously rubbed the tears from his eyes.

"I've never spoken to you about these matters," she said gently. "About the love between men and women. It's my fault for not giving you more guidance. I always expected you would learn about such things from your father."

She could see in his face how unbearable this was to him, to have his mother lecturing him on the most private of human affairs.

"Please," he mumbled, as she opened her mouth to continue. "Please don't talk about this anymore."

"I wish we might never have had to talk about it at all, Terrell," she said.

She meant to say more but held her tongue. She held her thoughts as well, not wanting to picture her son and Edna Foley in their misbegotten intimacy. She was angry with him but also heartsick on his behalf, because she knew that the glory of sexual love had now necessarily been poisoned for him right from the start.

"I'll let her stay the night," Mary announced, "and then take her back to her uncles in the morning. She'll sleep in your bed, and you'll sleep in the public house."

"All right," he said, and threw another stone into the river.

Terrell took his supper by himself that night, and the next morning he woke up well before daylight and rode out onto the prairies to hunt.

Mary let Edna help Teresa cook breakfast for the inn's only guests—a pair of brothers from Tennessee, both of whose wives had been killed in the same fire and who had wandered to Texas in search of some way to start their lives anew. They wore buckskins and frayed hunting shirts and ate their breakfast in polite, gloomy silence. After the meal was over and the dishes cleaned she drew Edna aside and explained firmly to her that she was taking her home. The girl made no reply other than a devastated nod of her head, and seemed to sit there resignedly as Mary saddled her mule for her. She saddled Cabezon as well—Mr. McGowan's mare was always glad of an opportunity to leave the stable—and brought the two mounts to the dogtrot where Edna sat in numb despair.

"Come on now, child," she said.

Edna obediently mounted the mule and followed Mary as she rode along the path by the riverbank. Edna's uncles, Mary knew, lived about five miles up the river on good bottomland, where they raised corn and range hogs and pursued their religion in such a harsh and mortifying manner that they were sealed off even from their fellow Catholics.

For most of the way, Edna rode in solemn, bewitched silence. But when they drew near to her uncles' land she reined up her mule and began to sob.

"What is it?" Mary said, turning Cabezon around to face the girl.

She was crying as piteously as a three-year-old child.

"I don't want to go back there," she wailed. "Please don't make me, Mrs. Mott."

"Hush, now. It's your home."

"What about my baby?"

"There is no baby, Edna."

"Yes, there is! Don't cast me out, Mrs. Mott! I have no one. No one to look after me."

"Nonsense. Your uncles will look after you."

"No, they won't! They think I'm possessed by the devil!"

"Surely they think no such thing."

"But they do! I swear they do!"

The girl was crying so hard she had given herself the hiccoughs, and now she sat there in the saddle, as forlorn and despairing a creature as Mary had ever seen.

"Please don't make me go," she repeated, between spasms of hiccoughing.

In the end Mary had not had the will to force Edna to return home. The girl was fragile and disturbed, but that was all the more reason not to send her back to her cruel life with her uncles. Whether they believed the devil was in their niece or not, they were well known around Refugio as bitter and unfeeling men. As she turned her horse around and led Edna back to the inn, Mary tried to convince herself that this was a sound decision, but she knew that little good could come of it. The girl would doubtless be more of a nuisance than a help, and her presence would be deeply troubling to Terrell. But Terrell would have to bear his troubles. It was because of him that this situation had come about in the first place, and Mary reasoned that an act of charity toward this witless girl was an excellent way of teaching him responsibility for his deeds. But beyond all that was the fact that it was just not in her to look at that suffering child and refuse her what she needed most and what Mary knew she had within herself to give—a steady, consoling adult presence. She realized now, riding back to the inn, how deeply she had wanted to mother Susie into womanhood, and how her death as a child had left something in Mary forever unfullfilled and unexpressed.

"I don't know how long she'll be here," Mary had explained to Terrell that evening. "All that's certain is that she's in need, that she's looked to us, and that we have a Christian obligation toward her."

Terrell said nothing in response, merely nodded his head in resigned affirmation. Mary could not help but feel that she was somehow betraying him. Deep in his heart, she imagined, he had counted on his mother to restore matters to normal; instead she had invited into their home this girl, who could do nothing but remind him of his own corrupted nature.

Mary's initial anger with Terrell had abated. She knew, through the example of her own character, how helpless men and women could be when tested with sexual desire. She forgave this impulse in her son, as she forgave it in herself, but she knew that Terrell could not help viewing his mistake as a grave, burdensome, debasing sin.

She had no worries about the sin being repeated; Terrell's shame was too great for that. In the weeks that Edna had been staying with them, he had hunted or gone about his chores in moody isolation, hardly talking to anyone, even Fresada, and avoiding his mother's eyes as if he feared them, as if her gaze saw right through his body to his sordid soul. It broke her heart to see him drifting away, but when she tried to speak to him or touch him she felt only the rigidity of his body and the ceaseless anxiety of his mind.

WHEN AT LAST, after half an hour or so, the big fish finally stopped moving, Fresada waded out to the reef and kicked the creature hard in its side behind its stubby, wing-like fin. He was poised to jump away in case the fish came to life again, but it did not stir.

Mary and Edna waded out onto the reef and stood there inspecting the sawfish as Professor boldly sniffed its hide. It was indeed as large as a whale, Mary thought. She wished she had paper and ink with her to sketch it, or that there was some feasible way to haul it back to Refugio in one piece to put it on display, since she was sure few people in the town had ever seen anything like it, or could even guess that such a monstrous beast inhabited these familiar waters. She looked at Professor, running from one end of the fish to the other, barking at it now as if trying to rouse it from its death slumber. The dog made her think of Edmund McGowan, and the obscure resentment she still held toward him. He would be deep into Mexico by now, if his packet had not sunk in the Gulf or been boarded by pirates, if he had not caught yellow fever in Vera Cruz or been killed by bandits on the road to the City of Mexico. At this very moment, no doubt, he was declaiming about some obscure flower or shrub to an uncomprehending audience of mule drivers or to some bored hacendado. She looked forward, upon his return, to telling him that while he had been admiring the natural marvels of Mexico he had missed seeing a twenty-foot sawfish stranded on a reef, an event that he could certainly not expect to see repeated in his lifetime.

"We'll butcher it here," Mary told Fresada, "and haul the meat back in the cart."

They had only two knives, and so Mary assigned Edna the task of hauling the meat to the cart as she and Fresada cut it away from the body. The fish's hide was rough to the touch, and its flesh was very firm. It could be smoked like mackerel, she thought, or poached. They worked for several hours, until the cart sagged under the weight of the meat.

"What will we do with it all, Mrs. Mott?" Edna asked, exhausted but uncomplaining, happy to be included in the work. "There's so much."

"There are always hungry families in Refugio," Mary said. "But we must hurry. It will spoil if it's not cooked or preserved soon. Where will we find the oil, Fresada?"

"In the liver," Fresada answered as he sawed off one of the stubby fins on the other side of the fish's body.

Mary bent down and sliced open the belly of the fish with her bowie knife, letting its guts fall out of their own weight. The liver tumbled obscenely onto the oyster shell, a massive flaccid shape as large as a human child.

"It must weigh seventy pounds or more," she said. "We'll have to tie it up to Daniel and have him drag it onto—"

Her words were cut off by Edna's sudden scream. Mary leapt to her feet, grasping the knife, and Edna stepped behind her and clutched her around the waist.

"What is it?" Mary said to her. "What is it, child?"

"Down there!" Edna screamed.

Mary looked down and jumped back. A half-dozen miniature sawfish were wriggling at her feet, and more were slipping out of the body cavity of their mother. The baby fish were perfectly formed, fully alive, all of them flailing about in bewilderment.

Edna's panicky sobs annoyed Mary, but there was something nightmarish, something sinister, about all these orphaned monsters twitching on the oyster shell.

"They won't hurt you," Mary said. "Go on back to the cart now. Go on."

"You come with me, Mrs. Mott. I don't want to be alone."

"For heaven's sake, Edna, they can't hurt you."

"I don't like them! I hate them!"

"Don't look at them, then. Go on and leave."

"It's the work of Satan, Mrs. Mott!"

She peeled away Edna's clinging arms and gave her a gentle shove off the reef. The girl waded to the shore, wailing in fright and confusion all the way.

"I've never seen a more excitable creature," Mary said to Fresada as the two of them watched her climb up on the shore and stand by poor Daniel the ox as if he were capable of comforting her. "Everything scares her."

"She sees the devil in it," Fresada said. He stared down at the infant sawfish that were still emerging from their mother's stripped body as if in some ghastly parody of human birth.

"And do you as well?" she asked him.

Fresada did not answer. He just looked down at the struggling forms. Something about them reminded Mary of a deep, ancient fear that she herself had once harbored. When she had been near her term with Susie, she had had a dream that she gave birth to a malevolent, unrecognizable thing that was not human at all. But the fear she recalled now seemed to come from farther back, from the vapors of her own earliest childhood, a time when the world was new

her and unreliable and a sense of menace could emerge
om any quarter.

She bent down, picked up one of the small fish by the
il, and tossed it into the water. Then she began to do the
ame for the rest, taking care to keep clear of their tooth-
udded snouts. Fresada joined her in the task, and in a few
oments they had released all of the gasping babies into
e sea.

"Why are you doing that, Mrs. Mott?" Edna called out
om the shore, but Mary ignored her. She had no reason to
scue them, other than a bias against letting suffering crea-
res die for no reason. And even if they were the devil's
hangeling children, it was clear they were in distress.

Between them, she and Fresada managed to carry the
sh's monstrous liver to the cart without enlisting Daniel's
elp. Then she directed Fresada to wade out to the reef one
ore time and chop off the lethal-looking bill, so that they
ould take it home as a curiosity. Before they set out for
efugio, Mary knelt down at the water's edge to wash the
sh's blood and bile off her arms. She could hardly see the
arcass now, so thick was the cloud of gulls that had de-
cended to strip it clean.

On the way back to Refugio they met two vaqueros from
e La Garza's ranch, and Mary gave them a good ten
ounds of fish, warning them to cook it as soon as they
ould get it back to their camp, since she worried that it
ould spoil in the hot sun. In town, John Dunn accepted a
onation of sawfish meat on behalf of the ayuntamiento
nd promised that it would be distributed forthwith to the
eedy residents of Refugio.

"You are an admirably lethal woman, Mrs. Mott," Dunn
aid as he inspected the sawfish bill. "First you kill a ma-
auding Kronk, and now this fanciful creature."

"I didn't kill it, John. It stranded itself on a reef and died
ll on its own."

"A fish could do some harm with this," he said, hefting

the bill like a weapon. "And a man could as well, by God.
reminds me of an Aztec sword."

"The meat will be quick to spoil," Mary reminded him

"I was just reading in the *Telegraph* about a firm i
Boston that has set itself up to supply ice to the governmer
of Malta at a little more than two cents a pound. And to th
pasha of Egypt as well. Imagine that. If ice can be sent t
the land of the Pyramids surely it could be sent to Texas a
well! We could eat fresh fish till Saint Brigid's Day."

"If we cared to pay the tariff."

"Well, you have a point there, Mrs. Mott. One shoul
think hard before paying permanent money for such a tem
porary commodity as ice. And have you heard the news?"

"No. What news?"

"Santa Anna has raised the veil of Mokanna."

"He has what?"

"Attacked his own countrymen at Zacatecas. Not merel
conquered the city but plundered it as well. The man Austi
thought would uphold the Constitution of 1824, the ma
we all believed to be the federalist savior, turns out to be
centralist tyrant after all!"

THAT NIGHT the fall of Zacatecas figured only briefly i
the dinner conversation at the inn, though Mary's mind wa
plagued by the scenarios for disaster it portended. The tw
brothers from Tennessee were neither political-minded no
particularly intelligent, and were either unwilling or unabl
to credit the fact that Texas belonged to Mexico and not t
the United States.

"This is American soil," said Rice, the younger, sallowe
brother, "and no pepper-belly president ought to think h
can take it away from us."

"If that don't take the dilapidated linen!" his olde
brother, Montroville, said with an exasperated sneer. "Yo

st got here two weeks ago, and now you're ready to fight
anty Anny."

"This is peach and cane land if I ever saw it, Montro."

"It's pepper-belly land, is what it is."

Montro helped himself to another sawfish steak.

"I hope the fish is not too dry for you, Mr. Gleason. It's a
ype I've never cooked before."

"No, ma'am," he said. "Me and Rice is used to much
oorer fare."

"We've eaten nineteen kinds of animals on this trip,"
Rice said. "To wit: buffalo, mustang, domestic horse, wild
ow, deer, antelope, panther, bear, wildcat, mountain cat,
olecat, leopard cat, beaver . . ."

And on he went, droning out his hunting exploits as if he
vere reading a page from a Crockett Almanac. He and his
rother soon fell into a lively argument about whether the
erm "animal" included fish, turtles, and poultry, or whether
applied only to creatures with hair.

Terrell sat quietly during dinner, avoiding Mary's eyes,
miling thinly when the sawfish bill was passed around the
able to be admired. In the past, she had expected Terrell to
elp Teresa with the serving and the clearing, but now that
dna was here that task had passed to her, and Mary had
oped that Terrell would take advantage of this fact to try
ut the role of host. But his mood was so anxious these
lays, and the company tonight so poor, that it was a
roundless expectation.

She noticed that he was especially careful not to glance
t Edna as she took his plate away, or even to raise his eyes
intil she was safely in the house. His attitude toward her
vas one of thorough avoidance, and Edna in turn seemed
ontent that it be so. She had latched on to Mary instead,
nd the safe harbor of another human being's kindness
eemed to be all that she now craved in the world.

"Good night, Mrs. Mott," she said when it was dark and

she was on her way to the jacal she shared with Teresa. She
held a candle, cupping it with her hand against the breeze
and the glow from the flame made her small, vague features
seem pretty.

"Good night, Edna," Mary answered from the dogtrot
where she sat sewing a patch onto one of the Gleason
brothers' hickory shirts.

"Is Terrell awake, then?" she said.

"He is in the house. I'll tell him good night for you."

She watched the girl walk in her bare feet toward the jacal along a path Mary and Terrell had—one idle afternoon—
bordered with fossiliferous rocks from the riverbed. She was
not an unappealing girl, in a physical sense, and though
this did not excuse Terrell's misconduct with her it made it
seem, in some indefinable way, less crude.

After she had finished her mending she stood up to go
into the house. As he did every night, Professor looked at
her with sober expectation as she opened the door. He
seemed to believe it was his right to be invited into the
house to sleep, and night after night he did not waver from
this hopeless conviction.

Inside, Terrell was lying on his bed in the loft. Though
the floor of the loft hid him from her sight, she knew from
the candlelight that he was reading.

"What book do you have up there?" she asked in a neutral voice.

"Ivanhoe."

"Do you still like it as much?"

"Not as much."

"The Tennessee gentlemen are leaving tomorrow after
breakfast," she told him. "They're going to San Felipe and
then up the Brazos to the buffalo country."

"All right," Terrell said.

"Today is your father's birthday."

"It is?"

"Yes," she said, taking a seat in her horsehide chair. "He would have been thirty-nine years old."

A screech owl called from outside, its hollow, anxious voice seeming to fill the house.

"Would you like to move away?" she asked her son, saying the words as soon as the thought flew into her head. "Back to Kentucky?"

He did not answer for a long time, though in the silence she was somehow aware of his deliberating mind.

"I don't know," came his voice at last from the candlelit nook above her.

"Will you look at me when you speak?"

"I don't know," he repeated, his face now appearing over the edge, his fine hair tousled where he had been resting his head against the wall during his reading.

"It's hard to know if what happened in Zacatecas will calm all the war talk or inflame it," she pondered out loud. "The wisest course might be to go back to the States and take what we can along with us, before we're driven away with nothing."

"They can't take this place away from us."

"They can, Terrell. And they can take our lives as well."

"If they try there'll be hell to pay and no pitch."

She kept herself from smiling at this heady talk from her gentle, peaceable son. And yet maybe the talk was genuine. Maybe he was not so gentle and peaceable, not at the core. She had imagined him, after all, to be as innocent and chaste as a boy in a storybook until the incident with Edna Foley had revealed that he was otherwise; not evil, certainly, not corrupted, but brimming with ungovernable desire. And as for fighting, she knew very well the solitary pleasure he took in hunting, the quiet that seemed to come over his soul after taking the life of another creature. In his heart, she thought, perhaps he was a warrior, waiting for the war that was coming like a hunter waiting in a blind for a deer.

"Won't you come down and talk to me?" she said to the loft. "Let's sit and talk face to face, and not hoot at each other like a couple of owls."

"I just want to go to sleep," he said.

"Terrell, why do you insist on acting as if I'm punishing you over Edna, and then on punishing me in return? I wish it could all be forgotten. I wish I could send her back to her uncles, but I can't find it in my heart to do that."

"I know," he said. "I just want to go to sleep."

He blew out the candle and said, "Good night," and she said it in return, and then sat there in the darkness with a silence between them, knowing full well that his mind was as restless and incapable of sleep as hers.

Nevertheless, she got up and changed into her nightclothes and lay down on her bed. Closing her eyes, she encountered with unnatural vividness the great fish on the reef, its writhing babies pouring out of its dead belly. And it was the thought of those primitive infants, swimming boldly out into the bay, that finally soothed her into sleep.

CHAPTER ELEVEN

✷

THE SMELL OF FLOWERS, saturating the morning air with sudden intensity, woke Edmund like a thunderclap. He had settled himself in a nameless mesón not far from the Plaza Mayor, and for almost two days had tried to banish in sleep the memory of his unremarkably hideous journey to the City of Mexico: the tempestuous passage to Vera Cruz in a high-tempered sea, the passengers crammed into the hold like figs in a drum, an old man yammering without end to Edmund about having been a pirate in the service of Lafitte, and about his present aspirations to become a scorpion hunter in Durango, where these venomous creatures were such a threat that the Mexican government paid a generous bounty for each one killed; and then the equally seasick land voyage, days and days in a mule-drawn diligencia that swayed like an ocean vessel as its wheels crested each and every stone on that endless road.

Though Edmund's exchequer was not yet perilously low, he was certainly not in funds, and it would have been foolhardy to lodge himself for an indefinite time in the Gran Sociedad, the city's only half-decent hotel. His room in the mesón had no amenities: no meals, no washing facilities, no laundry or cleaning services, no furniture, not even a bed. He had had to arrange for all such things himself upon his arrival, after dragging his weary and jostled body from the diligencia station on Calle Dolores.

But his lodgings did have the advantage of proximity, being just a block or so away from the Plaza Mayor and the palace and government offices where he would make his

petitions. And the bracing climate of the City of Mexico—
the sharp, perfumed air, the brilliant light that made the
snowy summits of distant volcanoes appear sumptuously
close at hand—erased his awareness of his squalid surroundings.

It was only an hour or so after dawn, but already the
street below his window was crowded with wandering
vendedores and cambistas advertising their wares—coal
and lard and salt beef and shirt buttons and cotton balls—
in piercing fragments of song. Edmund washed his face in
a basin of water that the proprietors of the inn had grudgingly provided for him, cleaned his teeth, dressed in his
best clothes, and walked down to the market, nudging pigs
out of the way at every step.

Ravenous from his long sleep, he walked through the
labyrinthine stalls of the market, breakfasting on his way.
He ate several gorditas that an old woman passed into his
hands straight from a stone oven, and nibbled at unknown
fruit that he selected from glittering mounds garlanded
with poppies. He drank a morning cup of chocolate as he
watched a column of smoke from one of the faraway volcanoes drift lazily across the blue sky. The richness of his
sensory surroundings—the smells of flowers and tortillas,
the squealing of pigs and the rote pleadings of the léperos
("Señor! Señor! For the sake of the most pure blood of
Christ! For the love of the most Holy Virgin!") and above
all the piercing purity of the air—all this threatened to
overcome him. By comparison, Texas suddenly seemed like
a meager, empty, and far-distant place.

His spirits were buoyed by the teeming industry all
about him, and by the sterling atmosphere, and at another
time in his life he would have found himself dazed with
happiness just to be walking through these exotic streets.
But his mind was weighted with anxiety about the success
of his errand, and still obscurely troubled with thoughts of
Mary Mott, and their unsatisfactory parting in that ragged

port some weeks ago. He had blundered with her, and he could not put the thought to rest. The few days at sea when he had not been sick had still been clouded for him with a chronic feeling of regret. He remembered the touch of her lips against his cheek, that benign gesture of farewell that in his imagination, in this instance, had seemed almost unbearably provocative. Was it meant to be so? That was the question that had visited him incessantly during the Gulf crossing and the overland journey in the diligencia. He knew without doubt that in some way—through some failing in himself, some craven inability to meet her on her own forthright ground—he had earned her anger. And this anger gnawed at him in a way that was new to his experience, and for which he could imagine no relief.

At Jouvel's barbershop in the Calle Plateros the talk was of the suppression of Zacatecas and of Santa Anna's triumphant return to the city. Edmund's barber, a grave, alert man of fifty or so who snipped each hair with painful deliberation, expressed his sadness that things had come to such a turn. Would Mexicans never stop fighting one another?

"It makes one weary," he said, his soft voice barely audible over the buzzing political talk in the crowded barbershop, and over the high-pitched grunts of a man several chairs away who was having a tooth drawn. "All of these risings and declarations of a new order. The Plan of Iguala. The Plan of Casa Mata. The Plan of Montano. The Plan of Puebla, Jalapa, Orizaba, Oaxaca. And yet Mexico is eternally the same."

As if in agreement the dental patient grunted again, and as the barber twisted the turnkey Edmund could hear the faint grinding and squeaking sound of the tooth being pried out of his jaw.

"But you are an American," the barber said, "and so are impatient with things that do not change as they should."

"It's true I have remained an American, since I have

never aspired to own land in Texas. But the colonists there are Mexican citizens, as the law requires, and many are sincere in being so."

"Ah, but these days one can only be a Mexican in one's soul. It is very difficult to be a citizen when one's government is so inconstant."

Having been barbered and shaved, and having declined the offer of a tooth examination and a phrenological assessment, Edmund set off walking for the National Palace, determined to win an audience with whichever minister there now had the authority to renew his commission. As he mentally shaped the speech he would make before the clerks—"I am here on a matter of some consequence concerning the natural resources of Texas, and it is vital that I speak without delay to an appropriate officer of the government"—he lost his way in the maze of crowded streets, whose names, in the maddening Mexican fashion, changed with every block.

Eventually, however, he made his way back toward the plaza and found himself passing through one of the portales near the Casa Municipal, entering a bazaar of cafes and flower stalls and shops already teeming with customers at this early hour. The sheer profusion of goods—jewelry, liquor, European fashions, chocolates, toys—seemed unreal to him after so long a time in Texas, where few such objects were readily available. A bookseller's stalls spilled out onto the street, the bright leather spines of the volumes gleaming in the sun, and there were many more stalls leading back into the darkness of the arcade, an unbelievable bounty of knowledge that called forth in Edmund such a sudden, sharp appetite that he felt troubled and even ashamed.

He was examining a Spanish translation of Erasmus Darwin's *The Temple of Nature* when he happened to look up and notice a startlingly familiar gentleman burrowing through the books at the next stall.

"Stephen?" he said.

Stephen Austin lifted his sharp face in Edmund's direction, peering at him uncertainly for just a moment until his hazel eyes grew warm with recognition.

"Edmund McGowan!" he said, pumping Edmund's hand. "What a joy to see you, sir! Only the other day I was remembering our great expedition in search of the mastodon."

"You're looking extraordinarily well," Edmund told him, though in fact he looked much diminished, paler and weaker, his curly hair thinning a bit so that his naturally high forehead now loomed unimpeded above his eyes. "All your friends rejoiced to hear that you're free."

"Free of the dungeons, but still confined to the city until they can figure out what to do with me. My attorney promises I'm to be released under a general amnesty, but the amnesty keeps being postponed and so in the meantime I'm condemned to a life of unaccustomed idleness. You've come from Texas?"

"Yes."

"What is the state of the country?"

"Apprehensive."

"Even before the news from Zacatecas?"

"There is a good deal of talk about independence."

"A dangerous notion. It's Houston and Wharton and that crowd, all the newcomers with their dreams of avarice and grandeur. I grant you, Zacatecas is a profoundly disturbing development, but as far as I know I'm still on friendly enough terms with Santa Anna. A little patience, a little temperance, a little real diplomacy instead of bombast, and we might still see this thing clear."

They strolled aimlessly through the Parian. Austin was hungry for news of Texas, the child he had nurtured with such monastic devotion for so long and whose fate now depended on so many things—the ruthlessness and capriciousness of Santa Anna, the intrigues of American land speculators and politicians, and above all the general expectation in the atmosphere that it was time for something definitive to happen.

"It is a building storm, there can be no doubt," Austin said as they entered the Plaza Mayor, the great cathedral looming before them across the sunstruck vacant expanse. They heard a bell ringing to their right, and turned to see a procession coming their way—a mule-drawn coach driven by a priest and followed by a dozen chanting friars.

"I must kneel," Austin said, "being a loyal Catholic. They are taking the Host to someone's deathbed."

Austin got down on one knee, an act that seemed to require undue exertion and emphasized how little strength he had. Edmund knelt as well, preferring not to be conspicuous, but he bowed his head only slightly and did not make the sign of the cross as Austin did.

"We Catholics believe," Austin said with a wry little smile as they stood and resumed their walk, "that the Host is in fact the body and blood of Christ. Our faith is such that we do not question how so much ghoulish matter could be compacted into such a flat disk.

"You hear the irony in my voice, and the bitterness as well, I suspect. I am afraid I don't possess the stone heart that is the first requirement of a public man. My loyalty to Mexico has brought me nothing but heartbreak and ruin. They treated me abominably, Edmund. Not Santa Anna, who is strangely cordial for a tyrant, but the federalists, the *liberals*! They were the ones who threw me in the calabozo. It seems the only thing that unites Mexicans these days is their suspicion of Americans, and I don't blame them, with all the speculators and revolutionists trying to steal their lands away through one scheme or another. The problem is they can't seem to tell the difference anymore between the pirates and the legitimate settlers that are in Texas at the invitation of the Mexican government. I am an officer of that government, I have hazarded my life for it time and again,

I have cooled the tempers of my people whenever a crisis threatened. For God's sake, I have even chased American filibusters out of Mexico with my own militia!"

"You were much abused in prison, I take it?" Edmund asked.

"I was in solitary confinement for the first few months. That was the cruelest part. No lawyer. No hint of the charges against me and hence no way to prepare my case. No books! Can you imagine that? I finally managed to embolden my guard to accept a bribe, and he got me a biography of Philip the Second. If there is any detail you wish to know about the life of Philip the Second, no matter how trivial, you will find me a fount of knowledge."

They stopped to inspect the Aztec calendar stone that had been mounted on the side of the cathedral as a pitiful reminder of the other-worldly empire that Cortés and three hundred years of Spanish dominion had tried to erase from the earth. The plaza where they now stood, Edmund reflected, had once been the site of towering pyramids and temples to unthinkable gods, a place of feathered warriors and gruesome priests whose function was to rip the palpitating hearts out of screaming human bodies. And this ancient Mexico, with all its fatalistic wonder, still seemed alive to him in almost imperceptible quantums of mood and thought, as eternal a presence as the volcanoes on the horizon.

"But in my rudeness I have spoken only of myself," Austin said as they turned away from the calendar stone and began walking along the Paseo de las Cadenas toward the government buildings. "What has brought you to the city, Edmund? Are you collecting in the neighborhood?"

"No. Like you, my life's work is Texas. And like you, I have come to petition the government. My commission has expired, and I need desperately for it to be renewed. Otherwise my years of work on the Texas flora will have been wasted."

"Who are you planning to see?"

"I don't know. The names have all changed. The last man I knew in authority was Terán."

"God rest his tortured soul," said Austin. "But surely you were not thinking just to walk into the palace and present yourself?"

"I had no better plan."

"It will never do. They will keep you waiting for the rest of your life. And many of the clerks you would encounter are high-minded, fastidious people who cannot be bribed. No, you need to see Almonte."

"Almonte?"

"He's a colonel in the army, highly placed. He came through Texas last year. I'm surprised you didn't meet him then."

"For much of '34 I was down near Ciudad Guerrero, studying the chemical properties of the creosote bush."

"He's a brilliant man, and has quite a lineage. He's a bastard son of Morelos, the insurrectionist priest. The old man had him sent away to the States for his education. Then when Mexico won its freedom and became a republic, he was sent on a diplomatic mission to England. As polished and engaging as a man can be. He was in Texas supposedly to gather statistical information—climate, crop potential, navigable rivers, and so on—but everybody knew he was really there as a spy. If Santa Anna invades, it's Almonte's information he'll be using."

"Is he not your enemy, then?"

"Hard to say. The mood I'm in these days, with all the thieves and jackals around, an honorable, even-tempered man like Almonte has to be considered a friend. There are a thousand possible alliances and enmities, all of them in constant churn. That's what your Houstons of the world don't care to consider. My task is not to rip Texas away from Mexico, as they want to do, but to make it into a garden. And gardens, as you botanists know better than I, require meticulous care."

They arrived at the doors of the National Palace. Even from outside, Edmund could see it was a place of buzzing protocol, a formidable hive of soldiers and plenipotentiaries in splendid uniforms and European fashions, all of them bustling about in a manner that seemed strangely out of phase here in the invisible sanctum of Aztec thought.

"No, you don't want to go in there!" Austin said. "Come over to my house for dinner tomorrow night, and I'll send my card around to Almonte and see if we can entice him to join us. Nothing gets accomplished here without cards, Edmund. My necessary first errand, on getting out of the dungeon, was to have some done up at the printer's, so that I could be perceived as officially at large. I dare say Almonte will come if he's in town. When he was in Texas he developed a fondness for good southern cornbread, which is hard to come by here in the land of the salamander taco."

GOOD SOUTHERN CORNBREAD was served, its preparation meticulously supervised by Austin himself in the little house he had rented near the Alameda. Since there were several Americans present, not just Edmund and Austin but the American consul general, a Mr. Wilcocks, the meal quickly degenerated into a slightly rowdy informality, of which Juan Almonte seemed to heartily approve. The colonel pushed back his chair from the table and stretched out his legs in front of him, and for a moment Edmund thought he might be planning to let out one of the roaring belches with which clients in the lower-class fondas announced their appreciation of a meal.

"But you must!" he was saying to Austin. "You must buy a box and take all three of them! My dear Austin, just because you are a prisoner in this city is no reason for you not to have fun when the opportunity presents itself."

"Los boletos cuestan demasiado," said a beautiful young woman on Austin's right, who slipped in and out of English with a caprice that they all found fetching. Her name was Luisa Alvarado. She and her less lovely sister and their widowed mother—the three of them puffing furiously on cigarritos—were, in some enigmatic arrangement, the "wards" of Mr. Wilcocks, who from time to time during the course of the meal exchanged discreet, knowing smiles with Señora Alvarado, an elegant sharp-eyed woman in a black mantilla fastened by diamond aigrettes. There seemed nothing terribly enigmatic about Austin's relationship with Luisa, however, judging by the familiar, almost absent way in which she now and then touched his forearm, as if testing to make sure this fine-boned, high-minded, ethereal man had not evaporated away into the air. So much, thought Edmund, for Bowie's crotchety assessment that Austin had no native desire for women.

"How can you speak of expense," Almonte chastised Luisa, "when you have an opportunity to look history in the face? A man rising from the earth in a balloon! Esteban—my dear Stephen—you must take these ladies to the ascension!"

Almonte was a little drunk on Austin's wine. They all were, except for Edmund, who feared few calamities more than the sudden loss of his composure. He sipped his wine judiciously as he listened to the talk about the French aeronaut and his marvelous balloon, which had eclipsed even the conquest of Zacatecas as the talk of the city. Could a balloon, indeed, Edmund wondered, rise as far as the moon? There would have to be some sort of steering and propulsion mechanism, surely, for use in the black, windless regions beyond the atmosphere, but once that was in place, and the contraption safe in its copper sheathing from meteorites, it seemed to him the moon could be chased down easily enough through dead reckoning.

But he took these idle musings as a sign that he had better put down his wineglass altogether.

"An apple pie!" Almonte exclaimed, when one of Austin's servants brought dessert to the table.

"A rendition of it, anyway," Austin said, noting the deflated crust. "My cousin's recipe, though who knows how it has been mangled in translation."

"I find it impossible to hire a decent cook in this country," Wilcocks proclaimed. "We had a French boy at the consulate, couldn't write his own name, but he had a way with pastries, and the first thing we knew somebody had slapped a 'Don' on his name and set him up in a restaurant."

"Marvelous," Almonte said as he scooped up his pie. "And yet nothing can ever surpass the peach pie your colonists served me in San Felipe, Stephen."

"Here's to peach and cane land, then," Austin said, raising his glass for a toast. "To Texas."

"The most valuable possession of the republic," Almonte offered. "May it prosper in peace under the Mexican flag."

"Under the Mexican flag," Austin repeated, without a trace of hesitation, and drank his wine.

Almonte had the dark skin and sharp eyes that Edmund imagined were traits from his incendiary father, but there was a gentleness in his face as well. Like Austin, Edmund thought: men of purpose who were also men of feeling.

"And now, I hope," Almonte said, looking to Edmund, "you will tell us something about the present temper of the place. Much has happened in Texas, I'm sure, since my last slice of peach pie."

"Its temper would be vastly improved by the swift return of its most creditable citizen," Edmund said, with a tilt of his head toward Austin. "You will find varying degrees of opinion toward Mexico among the colonists—from complete loyalty to wild talk of outright revolution. There are idealistic hotheads who are, in my view, too ready to fight, legitimate though some of their grievances may be; and then there are mere scoundrels who want to make themselves rich by seizing the land or buying it away piece by piece."

"As to the grievances," Almonte said, "what more can the president do? He has all but revoked the provisions of the 1830 law that the colonists found so odious. Immigration has been reopened, it is now legal to speak English, a blind eye has been turned to the practice of the Protestant religion, the laws of indentured servitude have been postponed so that your great cotton empire can be built upon the suffering of black slaves. Yes, there are still tariffs. But doesn't a nation have a right to impose tariffs on foreign goods? Doesn't even the wondrous United States protect its economy in such a manner? And as for the issue of separate statehood—the issue which resulted in our friend being thrown unforgivably into jail—it can comfortably be decided at a later time."

"I think not," Austin said. "For that is the core issue. Whether we will be ruled by a centralist government that is hopelessly distant and callously indifferent to our needs, or whether we will have some degree of authority to regulate ourselves as we see fit."

"And after Zacatecas," Edmund added, "the colonists are more likely than ever to believe that Santa Anna is nothing more than a centralist tyrant."

"I am very disturbed by the reports I hear about that incident," Austin said. "The plunder and rapine and wanton slaughter."

"Those reports are fictitious, Stephen, and where they are not fictitious they are exaggerated. And in any case, as you know only too well from your battles against the Karankawas, insurrections require a firm response."

Edmund thought he saw Austin's pale face take on a choleric flush, but the Little Gentleman kept a diplomatic silence. Almonte was Austin's friend, but he was also Santa Anna's man, and the topic of insurrection was an awkward one in this company.

Wilcocks leapt into the breach and proposed a song from the less beautiful sister, whose name was Sarita.

"Certainly nothing could be more desirable," Austin said in his perfect Spanish, "but I am embarrassed to say there is no instrument in the house."

Even so, Sarita required very little coaxing, singing "Aforado" with such piercing clarity that all agreed afterward that any accompaniment would only have sullied the purity of her voice.

"I regret extremely that His Excellency requires my presence at an early hour tomorrow," Almonte said after the sixth or seventh song, this one a stirring anthem to the Mexican Republic, though the music was a relic of the recently discarded monarchical Spain. Otherwise I should stay and beg Señorita Alvarado to sing us to the dawn.

"Perhaps you would be kind enough to share my carriage," he said, turning to Edmund, "and we can talk over a few matters of business on the way to your hotel."

ALMONTE'S CARRIAGE was a sprightly little English curricle pulled by a matched pair of the stately white horses that the Mexicans called frisones. Though the little coach boasted a velvety suspension, its slightly surging motion still whispered to Edmund of the gruesomely uncomfortable diligencia ride he had recently endured. Left on his own, he would have much preferred to walk, wandering through streets lit by the feeble, wavering light of turpentine lamps, with chihuahua dogs—those that had survived the cooking pot—yapping in outrage at his foreign presence.

But he would not have thought of refusing Almonte's invitation, and the opportunity it presented to artfully press his case. The young colonel was full of wine, and even in the strange, tinctured light from the lamps Edmund could see his face was flushed.

"I thought she would never stop singing," Almonte said, continuing in his impeccable English. "Was I rude?"

"Not at all."

"I was terrified she was going to start singing the 'Jota Aragonesa,' with its infinite annoying verses. We would never have gotten away. But her voice is sweet, and her beautiful sister has helped to leach some of the bitterness out of our friend Stephen's recent experiences. It was a disastrous thing, his imprisonment. Disastrous and unfair, since Mexico can have no truer friend in Texas. But we've had enough political talk. What about your vegetables?"

Edmund told him about his *Flora,* his massive ongoing compendium of the plants of Texas, and the crucial importance it would certainly assume through the generations in fixing the location of species of commercial or medicinal value, and in the discovery of unknown plants whose beneficent effects could not yet be predicted. Almonte nodded his sleepy, friendly face as Edmund made his points. He was receptive, Edmund saw. Almonte was no natural philosopher, as Terán had been, but he had an alert mind, and his recent inventory of Texas had helped educate him to the material value of the plant kingdom.

When Edmund finished his petition Almonte merely smiled his approval, gave a brisk nod, and then retreated for a moment to the vault of his own thoughts. When he emerged, it was Santa Anna, not plants, that he wanted to talk about.

"He is not a tyrant," Almonte asserted, as if in response to a challenge, "though he is without a doubt too forward and powerful a personality to suit the American taste. I am very fond of Americans, Edmund, but they have a habit of carrying their Constitution in their pockets, expecting it to be honored by every other country, expecting every other leader to mimic their own. But your President Jackson could not govern Mexico for an hour. This country is owned by the Church and by the military, and a president must appease them both while at the same time creating a credible hope that their reign is coming to an end. This requires more than strength or political skill. It requires a certain amount of caprice, and that is a quality that the president has in abundance. Remember that this is the man who, as a young officer of twenty-eight, embarked upon the courtship of the emperor's sixty-year-old sister. His vanity, his transparent flattery, are exhilarating. He has spirit. He inspires hope. He drove the Spanish royalists out of Tampico, and if necessary he will drive the norte pirates out of Texas."

"Send Austin back," Edmund repeated, "and perhaps it will not be necessary."

"We will. The amnesty will be signed soon. But here is your destination."

Edmund stepped down from the curricle into a pile of pig shit in front of his mesón and shook hands with Almonte through the window.

"I leave for the United States at the end of the week on government business," the colonel said, "but I would welcome an opportunity to speak with you further. Will you visit me at my office in the palace tomorrow afternoon?"

"Certainly."

"We'll talk about the particulars of your commission, and if I start in on politics again you are obliged to kick me in my trousers."

EDMUND SPENT the next morning in a restless ramble through the city, unable to concentrate his thoughts on any-

thing except what might come from his appointment with
Almonte that afternoon. If his commission was renewed, as
Almonte had given him every reason to expect, it seemed
reasonable that he would be given an immediate advance,
with which he could purchase the many quires of drying
paper he would need in the years ahead, as well as a quantity of Wardian boxes constructed to his specifications, and
several new suits of durable clothes. After supplying himself, he would start out for Texas without delay, retrieve his
horse and mule and dog from Mrs. Mott, return to Béxar and
recruit an escort of Indian or Tejano assistants, and strike
off to the east, beyond the Brazos into that unending forest,
rich with undescribed orchids, known as the Big Thicket.

The thought of entering this gloomy wilderness filled
him with vigor, though his imagination was still clouded
with pestering thoughts. He worried about the safety of his
collections back in Béxar, particularly if the situation in
Texas worsened and the town was invested by one faction
or the other. He was not certain he looked forward to another interview with Mrs. Mott, whose censure he had
somehow earned.

But in the main his mood was bright. To pass away the
hours before his appointment he stopped in at the museum
and had a look at the artifacts of the conquest—the armor
suits of Cortés and Alvarado, the obsidian swords and indecipherable hieroglyphs of the Aztecs, and the great sac-
rificial stone upon which many thousands of hearts,
boasted the attendant, had been ripped from their bodies.

He walked along the paseo by the canal, keeping pace
with the Indians as they poled their canoes laden with flowers from the floating gardens of Xochimilco and Chalco.
The air was thick with their smell, and with the smell of the
soil that had nurtured them. It made him feel like an infant,
coming to awareness in a world of overpowering sensations. Indeed, his earliest memory, when he considered it,

was of the scent of flowers, of the strange ripe tinge in the air when as a very young child in Philadelphia he had been taken on an outing to Bartram's Garden. And it was Bartram's Garden, as well, that was the site of his final memory of his mother. He could not have been older than four on that occasion, a day of perfect happiness as his adult mind remembered it. It was late in the century, the fashions had not yet turned, and though Edmund could not call to mind his father's face, he remembered vividly his wig and knee breeches. His mother, too, was a vague physical presence, indistinguishable in some way from the loamy smell of the garden, and the sharper and more insistent aroma of flowers, which seemed to course through the air like music. The three of them travelled along the garden paths down to the broad, shining river, his father hoisting him over a patch of mud, his mother laughing, all of them bound together in a mood of unanticipated well-being and contentment. Perhaps the whole day had been this way, bright and careless, perhaps just this one moment, but Edmund remembered the swelling happiness in his mother's voice as she bent down to him by the river.

"I will tell you a secret," she said. And when she whispered it he could feel her breath tickling the hollows of his ear. "You are splendid."

When she died that next week—in childbirth, delivering a baby girl who lived for only a day—he repeated the secret to himself as if in saying it he could reproduce the whispering breath of his mother. Soon after, when his father caught his hand in one of the apple crushers in his cider mill and died of the infection, Edmund's unformed mind had told him to hold the secret tighter, and to be wary of those moments of unguarded happiness.

He had not yet acclimated himself to the rhythms of Mexican dining, and though it was too early for a proper *almuerzo* his American stomach was hungry for a meal. He

stopped at a fonda not far from the canal that featured a gar-
ish, peeling mural depicting the apparition of the Virgin of
Guadalupe to Juan Diego. The figure of the Virgin was
awkwardly drawn, but with his mind so recently occupied
with thoughts of his own mother Edmund found this exotic
icon unexpectedly moving. He was too proud a man, too
strict with his own thoughts, to believe in a conventional
God or a formal hereafter, but he did not quite believe either that the souls of the dead simply disappeared; rather,
he thought, they evaporated like dew and rained down upon
the world as companionable and protective spirits, like this
mute Virgin in her blue cloak, or perhaps the owl with its
blanched face that had so frightened the Comanches.

FROM THE INSIDE, the President's Palace was not nearly
so imposing as it appeared from the plaza. Massive but
threadbare, it was as charmless as a factory, with pinched
light barely leaking in through a multitude of undersized
windows.

The urbane lieutenant who escorted Edmund to Almonte's
office led him down one noisy, chaotic corridor after another,
passing the ministries of war, finance, justice, and the public
treasury, every office and hallway in the palace teeming with
industrious uniformed attachés and civilian clerks, with peti-
tioners of every sort, the air foul with smoke from their ciga-
rillos and the light still oppressively weak.

"There you are!" Almonte said, setting down his pen as
Edmund was shown into his office. The colonel rose from
behind a beautiful mahogany desk whose legs were carved
in the shape of Mexican eagles. "Please sit down if you
like, but you will have to bounce up right away. The president wants to meet you."

"The president?"

"Yes, I happened to mention you and your plants to him
this morning when we were discussing the Texas matter,

and he took an unexpected personal interest and wanted to see you. I sent around to your hotel to ask you to come earlier, but you were out. In any case, if we go now we will still find him in his office, I believe. He's off to his hacienda tomorrow, so today is our only chance for an interview."

The president's reception room was as opulent as the rest of the palace was meager. A hundred feet long, Edmund guessed, with high ceilings and generous windows looking out onto the plaza and the cathedral, and all the furnishings in gold and crimson. Edmund was studying a massive portrait of Napoleon, on horseback amid swirling clouds, and was on the verge of commenting to Almonte about Santa Anna's famous ambition to become the "Napoleon of the West" when the president himself sauntered unannounced into the room.

"Señor McGowan, it is very kind of you to call on me at such short notice," he said, shaking Edmund's hand with a studied norteamericano firmness, and looking into his eyes with a soft, penetrating gaze. "Please seat yourself. Will you take a glass of orangeade with me?"

"With pleasure."

"Colonel? An orangeade?"

"If you please," Almonte said.

"I am so delighted that you fell into the keeping of Colonel Almonte," Santa Anna said, seating himself on a velvet sofa. "He is the ablest man in Mexico."

"He has been very kind to me in my brief stay here," Edmund said.

"Kindness has little to do with it. Almonte knows an extraordinary man when he meets one, and it seems you have caught his eye. And just in time too, because I am off to Manga de Clavo in the morning. That is my little hideaway near Jalapa."

"I believe I may have passed near your lands, sir, on my way from Vera Cruz." He did not mention that the diligencia driver had said that all the land for as far as the eye could stretch on both sides of the road belonged to the president, along with every cow and chile patch.

And what did you think of the country?" Santa Anna wanted to know.

"I have seldom seen a more beautiful place," Edmund said, not lying, though he had admired the scenery through a veil of nausea. "It was a brilliant day, and with one sweep of the eyes I could see the whitecaps on the Gulf and the snow glistening on Mount Orizaba."

"You are making me homesick, señor," Santa Anna said. "Oh, how I long to get away! I love our capital but I am a simple soldier at heart, and if I stay here I will be expected to go to the opera night after night."

The president leaned back on the sofa with his long legs crossed, seeming perfectly at repose except for one slipper-clad foot that bobbed up and down like a metronome. In manners and appearance, Edmund decided, Santa Anna was the most compelling human being he had ever seen. The president was elegantly lean. His face was sallow from tropical disease, and his handsome features had a strange tinge of melancholy. He looked as sad as a poet, yet his worldly confidence appeared absolute. Edmund did not think he was a simple soldier by any means.

They chatted on for a few moments as they sipped their orangeade. Discovering that Edmund made his home in San Antonio de Béxar, Santa Anna brightened and said he knew Béxar well, having been there with Arredondo as a young lieutenant during the troubles of 1813. Did the young women of the town, he wanted to know, still continue their charming custom of bathing unclothed in the beautiful river?

Yes, Edmund wanted to answer, and the old women still remembered Arredondo's brutality in suppressing the rebellion. He wondered if Santa Anna, with his kind and noble countenance, was one of the officers who had sanctioned the beating and raping of the women who were imprisoned to grind corn for Arredondo's army. One of the city's main streets was named for the horrible sadness of that time: Dolorosa.

"That was a cruel episode in our history," Santa Anna said, as if reading his thoughts. "But your countrymen do not seem to have learned from it. They have been invading Mexico ever since through one avenue or another, and so we have come to look upon them as the Romans looked upon the Goths. I am sure I do not offend you by speaking so frankly. The United States is a miraculous country, an example for the world, and yet like every other country it has its grasping and unprincipled elements."

"All the more reason for the Texas colonies to flourish," Edmund said. "If the people there feel secure as Mexican citizens, they will form a natural buffer against the Americans."

"The lawful citizens of Texas have nothing to fear from me," the president said. "Nothing. I am already weary from campaigning. I want to go home to my fighting cocks and my fruit trees."

He smiled gently, looking at Edmund as if this new acquaintance were his most trusted friend in the world.

"But politics has no place in our discussion. Colonel Almonte has told me of your magnificent project to write a compendium of the Texas plants. How long will such a work take you?"

Edmund set down his empty glass onto a napkin decorated with the seal of Mexico, and as he pondered Santa Anna's question the future seemed, to rise up before him, expansive and oppressive at the same moment.

"I have already made an excellent beginning," he said. "At home in Béxar I have notes and specimens representing almost ten years of collecting. I have no doubt the rest of the work can be accomplished in my lifetime."

"You take a long view, señor, for your unit of measurement to be a lifetime."

"Texas is a big place."

Santa Anna smiled again, and then stood up, lithe as a cat. Edmund thought the interview was suddenly over, and he and Almonte began to stand as well, but the president waved them back into their chairs.

"Please remain seated, gentlemen," he said, as he walked across the room and retrieved an ornate flowered box from a desk drawer. When he sat down again he took the lid off the box and held it out to Edmund.

"Will you take a chocolate, señor?"

"Thank you," Edmund said, extracting a piece out of its nest of white paper. The chocolate was crowned with an intricate marzipan dove.

"Colonel?" Santa Anna turned to Almonte, offering the box.

"Exquisite," Almonte said.

"They are from Oaxaca," Santa Anna explained. "A teniente of the Zapadores, seriously wounded at Zacatecas, presented them to me after the battle. An extraordinary gesture, don't you think?"

"And an audacious one."

"I like men with ambition," the president said, tossing a whole chocolate into his mouth. When he had finished chewing and swallowing it, he leaned forward to Edmund, his soft eyes suddenly harder and more appraising.

"If the Mexican government is to support your botanical enterprise, what can it expect in return?"

"A fundament of knowledge," Edmund replied.

Santa Anna peered into the chocolate box again, deliberated a moment over his choice, and then ingested another piece of candy.

"Mexico is a very poor country, Señor McGowan," he said after a moment's thoughtful silence. "We are always in need of revenue, and never more so than at the moment, when the government is being financed by unscrupulous moneylenders who, if the tide is not stemmed, will soon hold a mortgage on the entire country. The import duties that the Texas colonists are so upset about make up one source of income, but we are also desperately in search of products to export."

"Certainly Texas has very many useful plants—the candelilla, to name only one, which renders a marketable wax. And there are many more waiting to be discovered."

"Good. Knowledge for its own sake is to be commended, but at this point in her history Mexico can hardly afford to indulge in trivial flower gathering."

"You are speaking of the science of botany, sir, which is not a trivial thing."

"Of course. I meant only—"

"I am greatly offended by that remark, as you would be if I were to slight your own achievements with such an inconsiderate choice of words. Trivial, indeed, sir!"

In the flabbergasted silence that followed, Almonte appeared to stop breathing, his eyes examining an expanse of blank wall behind the president's desk. For his part, Edmund was careful to meet Santa Anna's furious gaze. The president's kind, wounded eyes were now as hard as ebony. For half a minute he slashed them back and forth between Edmund and Almonte, and then finally lowered them as the blood ebbed in his sallow face.

"If I have inadvertently insulted you, señor, I am inconsolable."

"If that is an apology, I am very happy to accept it."

Santa Anna seemed to smile, or at least the steely look in his eyes diminished. Edmund glanced at Almonte, to see if it was time for them to take their leave, but Almonte still sat there with his legs crossed and his spine erect.

"Señor McGowan," Santa Anna said at last, after another theatrical silence, "I would like to talk to you about chewing gum."

"Chewing gum?"

"You are certainly aware of the human compulsion to gnaw upon things without swallowing them. I have yet to have the honor of visiting your United States, but Colonel Almonte tells me the practice of tobacco chewing is almost universal there."

"That is unfortunately so," Edmund said, still puzzled. "The floors of the saloons, of the theaters, of every public place are generally awash in the juice of that particular plant." He was aware once again of how bestial a creature an American must seem to a Mexican.

"And yet tobacco is only one of many substances used for this purpose," Santa Anna said.

"Certainly," Edmund replied. "The Eskimos chew whale blubber, the ancient Greeks chewed the wild mint *Mentha sativa,* though Aristotle disapproved of its supposed aphrodisiac effects. The sap of *Boswellia carteri*—the frankincense of the Bible—is famously aromatic. Then of course there are the betel nut, the resinous branches of the *Gouauia domingenis* tree, the mastic shrub of the Mediterranean, and common dirt, which is the delight of geophagists all over the world."

"And do you know the chicle tree, señor?"

"*Achras zapota?* I have never seen it in Texas, but it is considered common in the tropics of Mexico, and I have heard that its resin can be chewed like spruce gum."

"Indeed it can," the president said. "In fact, it is the finest substance for chewing ever known. If this gum were flavored somehow, so that it was not just a tasteless wad in one's mouth but a confection like candy, and if it could be produced in quantities sufficient for export, I believe that the chicle tree could one day be an important resource for Mexico. And that is why I want you to go to Yucatán."

"To Yucatán? My work is in Texas."

"I understand that very well. But I would like you to go

to Yucatán first, to gather information on the chicle tree—its abundance in the wild, the best time to harvest the sap, the feasibility of creating chicle plantations, and so on. After this time, a period of only a few months, I am sure, your commission to Texas will be restored."

Before Edmund could take this in, Santa Anna rose briskly from his sofa and offered Edmund his hand.

"Is that agreeable to you?"

"It is," Edmund said without any enthusiasm.

"Excellent! I will see to it that you receive all the proper paperwork and vouchers immediately."

"And now, gentlemen," he said, walking Edmund and Almonte to the door with a hand on each of their shoulders, "I must dress for tonight's interminable opera. What is it called again, Juan?"

"*Belisarius,* Your Excellency. I'm told there are horses in it."

"Well, if there are horses perhaps I can stay awake."

At the door Santa Anna offered Edmund his hand once more, and gripped his guest's upper arm at the same moment, looking at him with the warmth of a brother.

"Your devotion and your candor are remarkable qualities. May I speak of one more thing, since we have been so honest and at ease in one another's company?"

"Of course," Edmund said, dreading what it might be.

"You know Texas well, and many of its inhabitants. By the time you return from Yucatán I expect the situation there to be fully resolved, but if it is not I hope I can feel free to call upon you for advice."

"I will not be a spy, Your Excellency."

"Of course not! Do you see, Colonel, I have insulted him again. You are not a spy, Señor McGowan, but you are an employee of the Mexican government. If war should occur between Mexico and the norte pirates in Texas, I know that you will consider that fact in deciding where your loyalties lie. But surely there will be no war, and the next time we meet it will be as friends discussing the chewing gum tree."

"IT MAY SEEM to you like purgatory indeed," Almonte stressed to Edmund as they walked back to his office through the congested corridors of the palace, "but it is really only a very small favor the president is asking."

"It is a very long journey to Yucatán," Edmund responded, still so agitated he could barely speak. "And a maddening disruption of my work. Chewing gum!"

Almonte laughed and set a hand on Edmund's shoulder as they walked.

"At least he will think carefully before ever dismissing another botanist as a—what was it?—'flower gatherer.' You were very bold in the defense of your profession, Edmund. I thought we might both be stood up against the wall and shot."

But Edmund was far too dispirited and angry to find this amusing. Almonte had spoken of Santa Anna's capriciousness, and now here it was, sentencing him to six months in the fetid jungles of Yucatán.

"I must return to my work, alas," Almonte said at the door to his office. "But we will talk again before I leave for New York. Please do not be so disheartened. The important thing is that your work can continue, with only this minor interruption."

"Yes, of course. It's just that I'm agitated at the moment. I am very grateful to you."

"I will have someone escort you out," Almonte said as they shook hands. "This building is a hopeless maze."

"I can find my way," Edmund assured him.

But in fact he lost his way almost immediately, blundering into the offices of the mint and then into the Chamber of Deputies, empty except for a pair of ancient senators arguing heatedly beneath the sword of Iturbide. A set of stairs then led him to a dingy corridor and a massive wooden door he hoped would open out onto the street. But when he passed through the door he found himself in a dreary court-yard overgrown with dusty plants. A sign nailed to a manita tree read "Jardín Botánica."

Edmund surveyed this pathetic place in disbelief. The botanic garden of the Palace of Mexico was cramped, air-less, light-starved, and populated with meager, untended specimens—a guanacaste tree, with its black reticulated bean pods, a few unremarkable epiphytes and orchids, a se-lection of blighted cacti. Edmund said "Buenas tardes" to an ancient, spidery attendant, but the man simply looked at him mournfully and returned to his task of raking the dirt clean of fallen leaves.

Edmund was overcome with the uncomfortable convic-tion that this garden had been placed in his path simply to mock his profession, or to foreshadow the gloomy outcome of his life's work. In general, he was not a man given to useless or oppressive thoughts, but here in this decrepit place he felt sharply, for one of the only times in his life, the certitude of his own demise. He was only forty-four, but forty-four was far from a young age, and it struck him all at once that the years of his remaining existence were ap-pallingly few. There was a time when the prospect of an ex-pedition deep into tropical Mexico would have thrown him into a, delirium of anticipation, but now the idea just made him tired and apprehensive.

"Is there another door?" he asked the attendant.

Edmund followed the old, man's pointing finger and found—behind a screen of parched willows—an open gate leading out onto the plaza. The square was crowded at this hour of the afternoon. Men trudged by carrying earthen jars of water on their backs, or tiered cages crowded with chickens; bare-breasted women patted out tortillas; escri-banos sat in the shade of their makeshift awnings writing love letters for illiterate clients.

All of this clamoring activity, the cries of the vendedores piercing the air with the purity of birdsong, helped to revive him, and his unaccustomed mood—of despair, of brutal emptiness—began to evaporate like an old nightmare.

"DEAR MRS. MOTT," he wrote a week later while sitting in the comedor of the Gran Sociedad drinking a cup of chocolate. "As you will recall from our discussions, I had anticipated an early return to Texas upon the completion of my business in the City of Mexico, but circumstances now demand my presence for some months in the region of Yucatán, where I am engaged by the Mexican government to study the chicle tree, whose resin is famous for its masticatory appeal. I expect now to return in December, and beg you to extend your care of my animals until that time. The enclosed draft, when presented to the ayuntamiento of Refugio, will provide you sufficient funds for their upkeep both past and future.

"I have had the good fortune of encountering Stephen Austin here and renewing our friendship. He is out of prison, as you have heard, and only a few days ago we rejoiced in the news that his liberty is now fully restored and he is free to travel to Texas as soon as he desires. I believe he will be leaving within the next few weeks. Santa Anna has invited him to his estates near Vera Cruz for a final interview before he leaves the country, to explore a peaceable solution to the problems of Texas.

"I hope that the political conditions there have not deteriorated since my departure, and that this letter finds you and your son in a comfortable situation. I think often of your hospitality and of your generous and amiable spirit, and accuse myself of deficiency in these same categories. I regret that my ignorance of common manners resulted in your unmistakable annoyance during our last interview in Copano, and I hope you will not think ill of me altogether.

"Last night Mr. Wilcocks, a friend of Austin's, led us on a moonlight boating party down the canals to the floating gardens of Lake Chalco, with a band playing all the while and a picnic dinner under the stars. It was extraordinarily agreeable, but it did little to erase my longing for Texas, and I will confess to you that I regard this expedition to Yucatán with an unaccustomed anxiety. My life's work is in Texas, and I think my life as well.

"The arrangements for this expedition—the gathering of supplies, the hiring of arrieros, a thousand other tedious details—must force a close to this letter. Please remember me to your son. And if the sound of my name does not continue to cause you annoyance, you might whisper it in my dog's ear from time to time, so that when I do manage to return he will not have forgotten me entirely. I look forward to seeing you, Mary—if you have not withdrawn the privilege of my calling you by that appellation—and to conversing with you once more in the breezeway of your inn. In the meanwhile I send you a token of our brief trip to Copano, when we discovered a flower together growing on the coastal plain. The enclosed specimen is dried, of course, but I believe I have managed to preserve its essential color and form. As you will see by the attached label, it is now known to science as *Chrysopsis marymottiae*— named for you, its co-discoverer. Look for me in December.

"Edmund McGowan"

PART TWO

CHAPTER TWELVE

✭

"**H**E THANKS YOU once again for your kindness and generosity," the young captain translated as General Martin Perfecto de Cos stood at the head of Mary's table twirling an empty wineglass. "He understands that the last few weeks have been difficult ones for the good citizens of Refugio, and he rejoices in your patience and in the patriotism you have displayed to the Republic of Mexico. For your many sacrifices, please allow him to make this small recompense."

The general turned and nodded to a pair of Indian soldiers in dusty uniforms who stood at attention at the edge of the yard. The soldiers reached down, picked up a heavy crate, and lugged it to Cos's feet. From the straw-lined crate Cos withdrew one of a dozen bottles and handed it to the captain to open.

"It is champagne," the captain—whose name was Luis Montemayor—said to Mary as he withdrew the cork and filled her glass. "I am sure it is of the best variety."

When all the glasses had been filled, Mary's and John Dunn's and those of the rest of the members of the ayuntamiento of Refugio, Cos offered a toast to his brother-in-law, President Santa Anna, and then proposed they drink to the spirit of amity that would forever bind the loyal citizens of Mexico to one another, a spirit that could not but vanquish the forces of divisiveness and greed.

Mary sipped her champagne and thought what a strange sort of war this was turning out to be. The Mexican army had finally arrived in Texas last month, five hundred sol-

diers jammed into a single fetid troop ship that had sailed
into Copano Bay one bright September afternoon. The
army had quickly invested Refugio without a single vocal
complaint from the Irish residents. All the town's carts, including Mary's, had been commandeered to haul baggage
from the port, and those citizens with commodious homes
were soon sharing them with Mexican officers. Twelve
men, Captain Montemayor among them, had been billeted
in her inn for several weeks, nonpaying guests that the government of Mexico expected her to feed and shelter in exchange for a "writ of subsistence" redeemable at some
unspecified point in the republic's future. The common soldiers had set up camp along the banks of the river, chopping down trees for firewood and for crude windbreaks,
digging sinks, blasting away at squirrels with their heavy
muskets and littering the ground with expended wadding.
To Mary the soldiers seemed like bewildered and deeply
homesick young men. With their dark skin and stoic Indian
features, their small, nervous, tensile bodies, they clearly
belonged to a conquered race as much as to a conquering
army.

Cos had assured the citizens of Refugio, in an address he
gave in front of the old mission church shortly after his arrival, that his army had come only to ensure the peace and
to protect the colonists against the radicals whose only interest was in hurling Texas into a war from which only they
would gain. No one believed him. Everybody knew that
Cos's men formed the advance guard of a massive invasion
force. But it was safer to share in the fiction, to provide
whatever services and goods were required for the moment
and to wait warily to see which course events were to take.
Patience had been the best strategy, and now it was paying
off. Cos and his army would leave tomorrow for Goliad,
and from there most of them would probably march on to
invest Béxar, so that the serious fighting, if it came, would
take place far away from Refugio.

The Irish offered several toasts in return, including John Dunn's artfully ambiguous "Here's to absent friends, and here's twice to absent enemies," and then Cos had a threadbare regimental band, with its strangely discordant bassoons and hautboys, play a musical salute to their hosts. The songs were a selection of leftover anthems from the French Revolution, apparently the only sheet music the Mexican army had available. They played "Let Us Watch O'er the Safety of the Empire" and "I Love Onions Fried in Oil," and concluded with a soldier—as pure a Mexican Indian as Mary had ever seen—singing "The Song of Roland" with strangely solemn conviction. After the formal festivities had concluded, Cos drifted among the populace, expressing his apologies individually to everyone, regretting extremely the grave inconvenience he and his army represented.

"To you he says he is especially grateful," Captain Montemayor translated as Cos spoke to Mary in Spanish. She understood the language to some degree, but could not keep up with Cos's rapid, silken speech patterns, or with what she took to be an overly rich vocabulary. He was a slight man of no more than medium height, his skin as smooth as a baby's. His black hair was thin in places but nevertheless dramatically coiffed, Bonaparte style, and his head rested like an egg in an egg cup on the high gilded collars of his dress uniform. He smiled at her with his brilliant teeth.

"He says the rest of the champagne is for you," the captain said. "No one has given more or been more discomfited."

"Please convey my gratitude, if you will, Captain, and tell him once more how much I appreciate the delicacy he has shown in an awkward situation."

In fact, Mary did like the general. He had occupied Refugio with more tact and consideration than she would have thought possible. And yet it was becoming clear to her that he was the enemy after all. The simple fact of the army's arrival, its commandeering of goods and services, its unannounced and uninvited presence, felt like a violation. For weeks she had been required to billet troops in her inn, when she depended for her livelihood on paying guests. Neither could the army seem to feed itself. Its levies from the citizens of Refugio in terms of meat and corn and milk were enormous, and its blundering hunting parties had driven the game farther and farther out onto the prairies, so that Terrell and Fresada—in their own hunting expeditions to feed the officers at the inn—were now gone for days at a time.

The tremendous inconveniences, and the loss of revenue, frightened her deeply. Had it not been for the overly generous draft that Edmund McGowan had sent from the City of Mexico, she would have no currency at all. But something troubled her more. It was a growing and not entirely defensible feeling that this was her soil and not theirs. These soldiers with all their weapons and demands, acting on the orders of a government so distant and uninterested in her particular welfare that it might as well have been on the moon, stirred up an anger in her she had not expected to feel. And somehow General Cos's solicitousness, his kind words, and his crate of champagne, only made that anger more acute.

The Irish colonists felt it too, but perhaps because of their long experience in their native land of living under the heel of an occupying power, they had been remarkably even-tempered. Mary knew, however, that Dunn and the rest of the ayuntamiento were playing it both ways, that they were secretly in contact with the rebels in the more openly volatile parts of Texas, informing them of Cos's every move.

"He is very sorry to once again have to ask you—along with all the other kind people of Refugio—for the loan of your cart and ox," the captain said, "but he is unfortunately obliged to do so if he is to get the army's baggage to Goliad."

"He is welcome to the cart. I am sure he will return it promptly in good repair."

Cos smiled at her as this was translated, and kissed her hand in gratitude. One more night and they would be gone. In the meantime there was another feast to clean up after, another breakfast to serve in the morning to the departing officers.

It was only early October and the days were still moderately long, but the farewell party did not end until long after dark, and there was such a pile of dishes that Edna and Teresa would have been up until dawn washing them without Mary and Terrell's help. Captain Montemayor and some of the other officers billeted at the inn insisted on helping to clear the tables and succeeded in breaking two of her china plates.

"I am speechless with grief," the captain said as he handed her the broken plates.

"They can be mended," she assured him, keeping her deep agitation to herself.

"Yes, but they will be scarred, and they will always remind you of our clumsiness."

"Sometimes they can be boiled in milk, and the seams will hardly show."

But this feeble attempt at reassurance did little to soften the desolation in Captain Montemayor's face, and a few moments later he reappeared with a bottle of oil mangoes, unopened, the cork still cemented in place. Would she do him the great honor of accepting this trivial gift?

"You have a long march ahead of you, Captain. I think you will need these mangoes more than I."

"Please," he said.

She took the bottle and smiled her thanks. He bowed slightly, saying he must now see to the readiness of the troops for the morning's departure, and expressed once again his gratitude, his apologies, his—but he could find no English word to finish his sentence. She liked Captain Montemayor, but he was a rather tedious young man who had been recently rejected by a girl in Matamoros he had hoped to marry and was now infatuated with his own broken heart. During the course of the last few weeks he seemed to have grown dependent on Mary's consoling words about the situation, and now as he disappeared into the darkness it crossed her mind—a fleeting thought like the swoop of a bird—that he might be a little bit in love with her. But she quickly pushed that foolish notion out of her thoughts.

"I don't think they'll get to Béxar without a fight," Terrell said when the captain was out of earshot. He was scraping the grease off the plates into the soap-making barrel.

"Perhaps not, Terrell," she whispered. "But there seems to be no army to oppose them."

"They're raising an army up at San Felipe."

"They're only talking about it."

"Well, they better talk fast, or else Austin and Travis and all of them are going to get hunted down and shot."

"Keep your voice down, dear, or we'll be hunted down ourselves."

"I don't see why we can't say what we want in our own yard," he said.

Edna came out of the house to collect another stack of plates to put away; and Terrell and his mother stopped their discussion by silent agreement. As a matter of course, they did not discuss anything of consequence around the girl. She was not inquisitive about the political situation, but she was alert to any shift in the air, and deeply frightened of any unexpected change. In some ways, this worked to Mary's advantage, because Edna's uneasiness made her a devoted worker. As conditions in the colony grew more and more uncertain and even dangerous, Edna sought security in the familiar rhythms of her housekeeping chores. Over the summer, Mary had taught her to spin at a little sitting wheel that had once belonged to her own mother back in Kentucky, and the anxious girl had soothed herself by producing a quantity of cotton yarn. When the Mexicans had gone, Mary told herself, she would teach Edna about dyes and mordants, and perhaps she would even get around to repairing the loom that Andrew had made so that she could put her to use in weaving.

"They are going, then, Mrs. Mott?" Edna asked her this evening, with a little tremor in her voice, as she took another load of dishes into the house.

"They say they are leaving in the morning. I expect it will take a long time for them to get on their way, but by the end of the day they should be gone."

"And they won't be coming back?"

"We don't know, Edna. But everything will be fine. There is no danger."

"There is no danger." Mary wondered how many times she had said those words to Edna during the course of this very dangerous summer. For a time, even after the centralist suppression of Zacatecas, it had seemed as if Texas had grown calm, but it was only the weird, anticipatory stillness of a coming storm. The events of the last five months had followed one another in a sequence that Mary now regarded as inevitable, an orderly march toward chaos. A schooner from New Orleans, loaded with contraband goods, had been seized by a Mexican warship in Galveston Bay. In retaliation, William Travis had stirred up a mob and ousted the Mexican garrison at Anahuac. And when after his long imprisonment Stephen Austin finally sailed home into Texas waters, his vessel was fired upon by a Mexican gunboat. The incident brought an end to Austin's famous patience. He would have no more to do with the tyrannical centralist government or with the duplicitous Santa Anna. When the citizens of Brazoria held a banquet to welcome home the lost father of Texas, he had stood up and called for a general consultation of the colonies, which everyone—particularly Santa Anna—understood as a call for war.

War. And yet no one, so far as Mary knew, had been killed. It was a war so far of icy propriety, polite toasts, smoothed-over crises. A war of manners. Ever since Cos and his men had arrived she had been taut with worry, waiting for the hostilities to finally begin, for Terrell to be dragged into it on one side or another. But the calm had mysteriously held, and now tomorrow they were leaving.

It was almost midnight when they finished washing the dishes. Edna and Teresa walked off to their jacal. Mary went to her bed, as weary as she could ever remember being, and as she went to sleep her body felt like a stone falling through the dark waters of a lake.

BUT TERRELL could not sleep. On the eve of its departure, the army scattered up and down the length of the river was restless, and Terrell lay there listening to occasional shouts and scraps of song and angry voices in Spanish calling for quiet. Terrell had avoided the Mexican soldiers ever since they had come. There was something about them that made him uneasy. They did not seem to belong here. With their small bodies and their wary, apprehensive faces they seemed to come not from Mexico but from somewhere far beyond the rim of the earth. The Mexicans he knew best— the Tejanos who had lived in Texas for many generations— seemed to belong to the landscape. The vaqueros who worked for Carlos De La Garza had a sense of grandeur and confidence that Terrell had always envied. They rode across the prairies in their cueras and serapes, with rosaries looped around the crowns of their hats, as if they had been called forth by the earth itself. By contrast the Mexican soldiers looked out of place and ill at ease in their grand, awkward uniforms, their tall shako hats crowned with pompons, contrasting meanly with their threadbare sandals. The officers seemed more assured, more adventurous, but they were steeped in privilege and treated his mother with a kind of fussy chivalry that Terrell found annoying.

Lying in his bed, Terrell heard the limbs of the oaks and anaquas creaking as a gust of wind swept down the river. It would not be long before the season's first norther. More Mexican voices tumbled along in the wind, and from the stable he heard one of the horses wheeze with approval as the breeze swept through the window that Terrell had left open.

From Professor's sleeping place on the breezeway he heard a low growl, and then the sound of a female voice shushing the dog before he could bark. Terrell sat up in bed, listening, but heard nothing more except the continual scraps of sound from the encampment. When the army had first arrived, Professor had been in a state, barking furiously as the soldiers, in their confounding multitudes, ceaselessly came and went. But Professor was a perceptive dog and he had soon made his peace with the army's presence. Why was he growling now?

Terrell got out of bed, pulled on his trousers and slipped his brogans onto his bare feet. He climbed down out of the loft and walked softly to the front door, picking up the Kentucky rifle on the way.

"Terrell?" his mother inquired from her bed.

"I'm just going to check on the horses," he said. "There's a wind come up."

"Be careful," she said reflexively, and then sank instantly back into sleep. Terrell lifted the frizzen of the rifle and tested the powder with his thumb, and then checked the seating of the flint. When he pushed open the door, Professor trotted over and looked up at him with an air of expectation. Terrell listened carefully and glanced in the direction of the smokehouse. The soldiers were pretty well disciplined, but that was no guarantee one or two of them wouldn't try to steal some backstrap or a ham for the march.

But the noises he heard came from the direction of the river: several male voices whispering to one another in urgent fragments of Spanish, and mixed in with them a womanish groaning that Terrell interpreted as distress. He pulled the hammer back to full cock and crept across the yard, down the broad river terrace toward the timber. The moon was bright enough until the tree branches began to filter it out, striating the darkness with bands of light that were as subtle as the tiger stripes ornamenting the maple stock of the rifle.

He moved closer to the sound of the voices, thinking they were farther ahead than they were. He came upon them before he was prepared: two Mexican soldiers, their white fatigues ghostly pale in the filtered moonlight, one of them in the act of buttoning his pants; Edna Foley lying unclothed on her back beneath a cypress tree on the quilt Terrell's mother had given her, lying there with a strange dull compliance while a third soldier lay on top of her, thrusting and quivering. There was something about the mechanical indifference of the scene—the animal twitching of the soldier's loins, the blank contentment on Edna's face as she stared up at the cypress branches, that maddened Terrell with disgust.

Professor bared his teeth and growled, causing the four faces to turn and look in their direction. The soldier on top of Edna stood. He was wearing only his fatigue jacket; his dark, spindly legs were visible beneath it, and his stiff pecker, obscenely glistening.

Terrell's first instinct was to strike the soldier in the chest with the butt of the rifle, but a Kentucky was too fine and fragile a weapon to use as a club. So he checked himself from advancing but levelled the octagonal barrel at the half-dressed soldier. He could think of nothing to say.

"Señor . . . ," the man said, "por favor, señor . . ."

"Did they make you do this?" Terrell said to Edna, who still lay on her blanket with her head against the cypress.

"No."

"How many?"

"Just the two, Terrell. Don't hurt us, please."

One of the men, the one who hadn't yet had his turn, tried to run, but Terrell stepped forward and kicked him hard in the knee as he ran past, knocking him down so that he fell against a cypress root. The soldier was fifteen years older than Terrell but not much bigger than half his size, and he went down with surprising velocity. Terrell swung the rifle around and placed the barrel an inch or so from the would-be fugitive's eye. Professor erupted into a barking fit.

"What are you going to do, Terrell?" Edna asked over the dog's piercing barks.

Terrell didn't answer her. He kept the rifle levelled at the one soldier's head and checked on the other two with quick darts of his eyes. They appeared paralyzed, simply stood there barely breathing. They had no weapons that Terrell could see.

"Get your pants on," he said to the soldier who was standing there in only the top half of his fatigues. "Pantalones."

The man eagerly complied.

"You get your clothes on too, Edna," Terrell said.

"Don't shoot them, Terrell." Her voice was choked with a child's terror.

"You be quiet and get your clothes on."

The man he was holding the gun on could not make himself meet Terrell's eyes. He bowed his head as if in submission, and Terrell could hear him quietly weeping. It amazed him that the man actually thought he was going to fire a bullet into his brain. And then Terrell wondered if that was indeed what he was about to do. He could not bear the revulsion and shame that had come over him when he had seen Edna on the ground. He could not bear the thought that his own lust had once been so openly displayed, and that to an intruder it would have looked no less raw, no less callous.

The soldier who had just put on his pants was the most composed of all of them.

"Señor—" he said again.

"You shut up!"

"Señor, si usted—" and as he took a step toward them Terrell backed up and swung the rifle in his direction. The gesture did not slow the man down but only caused him to quicken his advance, and in the critical moment Terrell could not convince himself to pull the trigger. The soldier grabbed the barrel of the Kentucky and tried to twist it out of Terrell's grasp. Terrell held on with both hands. With what must have been a foot, the soldier gave him a shuddering blow to the underside of his jaw, but Terrell never let go of the rifle. Finally his assailant simply abandoned his own grip and ran off, unbalancing Terrell enough to send him sprawling back against the cypress knees. He landed on top of the rifle, knocking the powder out of the frizzen and preventing an accidental discharge, but also breaking the precious maple stock in half at the slender neck.

He looked at the broken rifle in desolation, and then spat out a piece of one of his back teeth. He lifted his eyes to Edna, who was struggling to get into her clothes. Professor was still barking, and Terrell could hear inquiring voices, including his mother's, from the direction of the inn.

"Hurry up," he told Edna.

"Don't scold me, Terrell," she sobbed. "Please don't scold me. It wasn't a sin. It wasn't!"

She had not finished buttoning her dress, and her shoes were still off. Terrell's mother was calling his name.

"You stay here for a few minutes and then get on back to your jacal," he said. "Don't tell anybody what you did."

He didn't look at her again, but he was aware that she

was quivering with fear and confusion. He picked up the two pieces of the broken rifle and headed back up toward the inn. His mother was advancing from the edge of the yard, and Captain Montemayor was walking out of the public house holding a dragoon pistol.

"Terrell, is that you?" his mother called. "Are you hurt? What's all the commotion about?"

"I'm all right," he said. "I thought there was somebody in the smokehouse, and then I heard voices down by the river, and I went to look. But there wasn't anybody there."

"Is anything missing from the smokehouse?" the captain asked.

"No, nobody took anything. I just made a mistake."

He held up the broken stock of the rifle.

"I broke the rifle. I wasn't watching where I was going, and I tripped and fell on it."

In the moonlight he saw the baffled look on his mother's face.

"I'm sorry," he said.

"It can be mended. But are *you* all right?"

"I broke off a tooth, I think."

"Come into the house and let me see. Captain, thank you for your vigilance. Good night."

The captain gave a slight nod, said good night in turn, and walked back into the public house. Mary led Terrell inside and examined his tooth as best she could by candlelight. His swollen jaw felt numb and prickly. But a nerve had been exposed beneath the broken tooth, and the slightest circulation of air within his mouth caused a wild trill of pain.

"You've lost a big piece of your tooth, and there's a sharp point that will need to be filed," his mother said. "I'll seal it with beeswax for now, so that it won't hurt you so much."

He gripped the sides of the chair as she worked, his eyes flashing inevitably to the ruined Kentucky rifle lying on the floor near the fireplace. His father's prized rifle. The stock could be replaced, but here in the colonies it would have to be made of oak, not maple, and Terrell doubted that the subtle tiger stripes on the old stock could be duplicated in oak.

When his mother had finished sealing the tooth, Terrell ran his tongue over its broken surface. It felt strangely magnified, and his mind could not help perceiving it as a vast range of jagged mountain peaks.

"Is it better?" she asked.

"Yes."

"I'm afraid the filing will not be pleasant. But we can leave that for a day or so. What happened out there, Terrell?"

"Nothing except what I said."

She looked at him sternly, the planes of her face sharp and vivid in the candlelight. He wanted to tell her everything that had occurred, but he felt protective of Edna, and also of himself. His revulsion at his own lasciviousness still ran so deep that he thought he would rather die than ever touch upon such a conversation again.

"I've never known you to stumble over your feet with a rifle in your hands," Mary said.

"Well, I guess I did," Terrell said, and then announced through his clenched and swollen jaw that he was going to bed.

THE ARMY marched out of Refugio the next day as promised, on its way to invest Goliad and then to strike out west for Béxar. Goliad commanded the coast road, Béxar the old Camino Real leading up from the interior of Mexico. Those were the two essential avenues into Texas, and in a matter of days Cos would have possession of both and could begin the task of uprooting the rebellion before it had a chance to flower.

It seemed to Terrell that it was all over, and that the rebellion in the end had been little more than a rumor. Refugio's streets were still scarred and rutted from the passage of the army, and there was still a bad odor from the sinks the soldiers had dug up and down the river, but the disaster they had all anticipated had never occurred, and the conflict once again seemed distant and of no direct concern to the peaceful colonists of Refugio. Even the carts and wagons commandeered for the march to Goliad had been courteously returned, driven by arrieros and escorted by a contingent of heavily armed vaqueros from the Tejano ranches.

Terrell wanted to feel relief but felt only frustration instead. The long fearful anticipation of an event that had never come to pass made the world seem unbearably static. If the war had come, he would have fought in it, though he was still half a child. Every day he grew more distant from his mother, burdened with a man's secrets and silences. He did not speak to Edna and continued to evade her eyes even when they were cast imploringly in his direction. He wished the loathing he felt could be for her and not for himself, for the universal male baseness he carried within him like a disease. Over and over he recalled how that Mexican soldier—with his contemptuous confidence—had grabbed his rifle and kicked him in the jaw and sent him sprawling to the ground. The soldier's power had seemed to reside in his shamelessness, in the way he had stood there without embarrassment while his organ dangled in front of him as if on display.

Something stirred in Terrell when he learned, only a few days after Cos's departure, that real conflict had finally erupted in DeWitt's Colony, where a group of colonists in Gonzales had fired upon a detachment of presidial troops who had been sent from Béxar to confiscate a cannon.

"The war is in the open at last, Mrs. Mott," John Dunn said two nights later, when he and the other members of the Refugio Committee for Safety and Correspondence convened at the inn to discuss strategy. There were twelve of them present, including Mr. Westover, the captain of the municipal militia, and a Mr. Linn, who had ridden down that day in haste from Victoria and whose overtaxed horse was now recuperating in the stable. "The war is in the open, and now it is time for a man to declare where his loyalties lie. Will you pass me the macaroni once again, Captain Westover?"

"And where do your loyalties lie, John?" Mary asked.

"My father fought for a free Ireland at Oulart and Enniscorthy. He taught me to fear the tyrant. I grant you that the Texas colonies are filled with grasping, scheming, and ungrateful men, but I see only one tyrant, and his name is Santa Anna. Under Santa Anna, Mexico will merely be another England, a more backward England at that, and here in our new country we will once again be at the mercy of the landlord and the goddam tithe proctor."

Terrell hovered at the edges of the conversation after the plates were cleared. The men conferred by candlelight, Westover sketching with a stub of pencil and speaking so softly that Terrell could barely hear him. But he understood the main part of it. One of the sketches was of the Goliad road, and of the rendezvous point where they were to meet a party of men from Matagorda. The other sketch was a plan of La Bahía, the presidio at Goliad, which they were going to attack.

"God protect them," his mother said that night after they had gone, and that was all she said about the whole matter, though her voice was taut with worry. And God did protect them, because in less than a month Westover and Dunn and most of the rest of the Refugio contingent were back. Goliad had been taken without the loss of a man, Westover reported to the town in a speech in front of the mission. Not only that, but Austin's army had arrived at Béxar and was preparing to lay siege to the city and run Cos and his men back to Mexico. And tomorrow Westover was leading a force down to the Nueces to attack the Mexican garrison at

Lipantitlán, and any man with a horse and a rifle was welcome to join him here at six o'clock in the morning.

Terrell packed that night while his mother supervised Edna in the kitchen. He did not know what to bring. He did not know if they would feed him or if he would be responsible for his own meals. He decided he would take some bacon and a sack of cornmeal. He stuffed his extra hunting shirt into his father's old haversack, filled his wooden canteen, gathered his powder horn and shooting pouch, and got down the Kentucky with the new oak stock that the elderly blacksmith, Mr. Berney, had finished just a few days before.

"I'm going with Mr. Westover tomorrow," he told his mother after dinner.

He saw the frozen look on her face in the firelight where she was sewing a shirt for Fresada. She was silent for a long time, though she kept working the needle through the gingham fabric without a pause.

"God forgive me for not leaving this place when I should have," she said at last.

"I feel like I ought to go," he said, and he was annoyed at his words, as if he were trying to justify it to himself.

"You're sixteen years old, Terrell."

"I know it."

She stopped her sewing and stared into the fire. He saw the tears starting to spill down her cheeks, and she seemed to have no intention of wiping them off.

"You've changed so much in these last few months," she said. "You're so full of secrets it sometimes feels strange to me that you could be my child."

"This ain't a secret. I'm telling you about it."

"You know nothing about fighting, and the men you'll be riding with know little enough themselves."

"They took Goliad. I guess they can take Lipantitlán."

"Terrell, even if they do, and even if Austin drives Cos out of Béxar and there's not another Mexican soldier left in

Texas, how long do you think that victory will last? Santa Anna will be here with a far larger army as soon as the grass rises in the spring, maybe even before, and everyone who took up arms against him will be set up against a wall and shot!"

"So what am I supposed to do, go and fight for the Mexicans?"

"There's no point in fighting for anyone! If everybody would stay calm, the situation would resolve itself."

"The war's already started, Mother. It's time to choose sides, and sixteen is old enough for that."

His mother did not answer, and the two of them sat there in silence for a full ten minutes.

"I'm going for a walk," she said at last. She stepped out the door and was gone for an hour, and when she came back he was still sitting there by the fire, taking an obsessive mental inventory of all the things he had packed in his outfit, and starting to fret about what might not be in there but should.

"I've asked Fresada to go with you," his mother said.

"What!"

"I've asked him to, and he's going."

"I don't need Fresada to—"

"Hush!" she commanded.

She crouched down before his chair and laid her hand against his cheek.

"Do this one thing for me," she said, "and you can ride off tomorrow with my blessing, and with your mind at peace about how I feel."

In truth the news that Fresada was coming worked on his anxious mind like a balm, and when he went to his bed that night he was even able to sleep a few hours. He coasted from one fitful, provocative dream to the next, always aware of his mother sitting by the fire below the loft, locked into a stony wakefulness.

Long before sunrise she had baked two skillets full of

cornbread, and what Terrell and Fresada didn't eat for breakfast they took with them, wrapped up in tea towels and still warm against Terrell's hip where he carried it in the haversack.

He did not look back at his mother's grieving face as they rode to the mission. It was still half an hour before the six o'clock rendezvous time, but there were already fifteen or twenty men gathered there, and Captain Westover was leading them in the rosary.

CHAPTER THIRTEEN

✴

"WHY, 'TIS no fort at all," Billy Tool said as he and Terrell and the rest of the weary expedition walked through the earthen breastworks of Lipantitlán with their rifles and shotguns on full cock. "'Tis a fucking anthill!"

Billy was a loutish boy of eighteen who had attached himself to Terrell on the long ride down to San Patricio and now shadowed him wherever he went. He was ill provisioned for war, with only an old Spanish scopet to shoot and a mule to ride and a lance made of a cane pole with a sharpened file lashed to the end. He clearly resented Terrell's Kentucky rifle and the rest of his outfit and seemed determined to make him feel unworthy of it. "We'll see how you handle that pretty rifle and that pretty mare when the balls are flying about you," he had said to him during that day's tense ride along the lower San Patricio road, as they expected to be attacked at any moment by Mexican dragoons. Terrell didn't understand the source of Billy Tool's resentment except that maybe it was a way he had of stifling his own fear. The more insistently he had hectored Terrell, the closer he had ridden to him on the narrow road, so that their knees kept touching.

They had taken Lipantitlán without firing a shot, since most of the troops quartered there were out on the Atascocita road looking for the very force that had now eluded them and invested their garrison. There were fewer than thirty Mexican soldiers in the place tonight, and they stood with their hands in the air and their backs to a big bonfire as the colonists entered the fort. A few dozen muskets were piled at their feet, and there was a four-pounder cannon without any powder or shot anywhere near it.

"Son todas las armas?" Westover asked a frightened corporal who seemed to be at least marginally in charge.

"Si, todas," he said.

Terrell looked at the ragged men and their pitiful arsenal, feeling a nervous sort of relief. There had not been a battle, but the Mexican force could return at any time and turn the tables on the rebels, laying siege to them in the fort. Terrell had wanted out of this place almost as soon as he entered it. It was merely a crumbling dirt redoubt shored up on the inside with timber, and a few ragged tents and lean-tos scattered about for shelter. It stank of moist earth and human waste.

Under the terms of the surrender agreement, Westover let the Mexicans go, with the promise that they would not take up arms again against the rebels. They were out of the fort by midnight, their worn leather knapsacks slung over their shoulders, on their way to Matamoros to deliver the news of their disgrace.

For days, Terrell had kept a piece of his mother's cornbread in reserve, thinking that an emergency would arrive and it would be all he would have to eat. But as it turned out, Westover's little army was well enough provisioned, and the distribution of food was fair and efficient. Tonight there was not only salt pork but bread and even cakes appropriated from an old Irish woman across the river in San Patricio.

They were eating the bread when the woman rode up on a broken-down mule and started cursing.

"And what kind of army is this?" she said in a loud, imperious tone to no one in particular. "Why, I see nothing but filthy spalpeens sitting about in the dirt eating my bread!"

Terrell was sitting up against the earth wall of the fort between Fresada and Billy Tool. Blank with exhaustion, like everyone else, he just stared at the woman. A part of his mind acknowledged her grievance at the outright theft of her comestibles, but a larger part of his mind was just too weary to care. The air was turning sharp, and he was getting a sore throat, and though he was not far from home in terms of miles he felt a constant dull pang of homesickness that was strangely debilitating.

"And why did you come here in the first place?" she demanded to know. "What gives you the right to come here to meddle in San Patricio's affairs?"

"We're after saving the country from tyranny," Westover finally answered her, without much interest or conviction.

"Ach, what tyranny? What tyranny is that, I ask you?"

San Patricio, Terrell had seen plainly enough, was far from united in its support of the rebels. Riding through town, they had received sullen looks and grudging courtesies from the citizens, who seemed to feel that these insurgents from Goliad and Refugio were doing nothing but bringing trouble into their midst. Indeed, there was a rumor that the San Patricio alcalde himself was out riding with the Mexican dragoons, ready to fight his fellow Irishmen and put down the rebellion.

"I want to be paid for my bread," the woman said after a long silence in which no one answered her question about tyranny.

"You've been given a receipt," Westover told her.

"A receipt, is it? What good is a piece of paper from such rabble as you? I want money for the bread you stole from me."

She harangued the men for ten minutes or more until John Dunn finally gave her a coin and told her to shut up and be on her way. When she was gone Westover addressed the men, telling those who had picket and guard duty that the lives of the entire expedition depended on their vigilance tonight, as the Mexican cavalry could not be far away.

The rest should get as much sleep as possible, because tomorrow they were going to dismantle the fort.

Fresada drifted into sleep right away, and after a few moments Billy Tool was unconscious as well, but Terrell lay there for a long time keeping a nervous eye on the guards who patrolled the dirt walls, making sure they did not shirk their duties and leave them open to surprise attack. As the night wore on, sleep began to seem further and further out of reach, as his imagination, flaring up in his exhaustion, pictured the returning Mexican troops pouring soundlessly over the walls, killing them all silently with knives and bayonets and lances. He had to piss, but he was afraid to get up and walk to the latrine for fear that one of the sentries would mistake him for a Mexican and shoot him, and so he lay there under the torture of his brimming bladder, succumbing again and again to dark waking dreams of being overrun by the enemy. He could face a nighttime battle, he thought, if his bladder were not so full. But he knew he had no skills to bring to such a fight. He knew how to shoot a rifle, but in a dense, furious battle such as the one he expected he knew he would be lucky to get even one shot off, and then it would be a matter of knives and tomahawks and choking hands, and no one had told him anything about that. He had thought there would be training and drilling and discussion, but nothing of that sort had yet occurred in this thrown-together army.

Despite all his anxiety and discomfort, he fell asleep for an hour or so before dawn, waking to the calls of mourning doves and the smells of frying meat. He ran outside of the fort to piss, carrying his rifle with one hand and unbuttoning his trousers with the other, and finally stood there emptying his bladder beneath a huisache tree as he shivered in the cold air. Behind him he could hear rustling and grumbling as the men came awake.

Captain Westover came and stood next to him, unbuttoning his own trousers and making water in a great hissing arc.

"Good morning, boy," he announced.

"Good morning, Captain," Terrell replied.

"'Tis a fine rifle you have there," Westover said.

"It was my father's."

"Can you shoot true with it?"

"I believe I can."

"If we have an encounter with the enemy today, as I think we will, those of us with rifles such as that can't be shy about using them. Those old Paget carbines and Brown Besses that the Mexicans have won't do much harm past a hundred yards or so. It's up to us long rifles to keep them at a distance. Can you do that, boy?"

"Yes, sir."

"If you can do that, we don't have a problem in all the world."

They spent the morning trying to reduce Fort Lipantit-lán. While some of the men burned the jacales in front of the fort, Terrell and Fresada and Billy Tool joined with those attempting to tear down the timber that shored up the earth walls. Others attacked the hard-packed walls themselves with shovels, but after several hours not much damage had been done. The stout embankments of dirt still towered over their heads. Terrell guessed it would take a week to destroy the place, and then only another week for the Mexicans to build it back up.

A few of the men had crowbars, but most of them had only their bare hands to rip the timber out of the hard earth. Terrell's nails were already torn and bleeding, and a gusting cold wind sent stabs of pain along the exposed nerves in his fingertips. His sore throat was worse, and there were sharp, gassy pains in his abdomen that he supposed came from worry.

"If I'd wanted to haul wood, I would have stayed home," Billy said as he and Terrell dragged a tangle of lashed-together timbers out of the fort and threw it on a bonfire. They lingered there for a moment, catching their breath and warming themselves by the leaping flames. Billy's face was streaked with dirt, and his nails were raw like Terrell's. "What kind of fucking army is this, that we have to work like fucking tenant farmers?"

"I don't know," Terrell said absently, pulling himself away from the fire and walking back to the fort. He wanted away from Billy's hectoring voice more than he wanted the warmth of the fire and the brief respite from the work.

"They might have brought along some proper tools," Billy said, "seeing as how they had such a piece of work in mind."

"Maybe you should just leave," Terrell said.

"Just leave, is it?"

"You didn't sign no papers, did you? They can't make you stay."

"They can shoot me for a deserter if I leave."

"Well, if you won't leave, stop complaining," Terrell said.

A scout rode up on a lathered, wheezing horse and slipped out of the saddle in front of Westover. He scratched the back of his neck with his quirt as he made his report, and Terrell could see the concentrated look on the commander's face.

"You men stop eavesdropping and get back to work," Westover told the volunteers, and then he took the scout aside out of hearing distance, where they were joined by John Dunn and a few other men who seemed to have a claim to being the expedition's leaders.

"What do you think's going on?" Billy said. "Are the Mexicans nearby?"

"I guess they'll tell us when they want to," Terrell replied. The words in his mouth sounded calm, but his skin felt clammy and the knot in his abdomen grew tighter. He turned his eyes to Fresada, who was working calmly a few yards away, and desperately wished he could at least mimic the Indian's apparent lack of turmoil.

In five more minutes the scout got back on his horse and galloped off in the direction he'd come from. Westover walked over to rejoin the men. He did not have to ask for their attention, since they were already gathering in around him, setting down their tools and unstacking their firearms.

"Gentlemen," Westover said. "The enemy have been sighted on the road to the Nueces crossing. If you will follow me, it will be my pleasure to lead you to them."

WESTOVER DIVIDED his force in two, sending half the men across the river with the caballada, leaving the other half behind to guard against a Mexican flanking attack. Terrell, Fresada, and Billy Tool were with those who crossed the river in canoes, and when they reached the far bank they were instructed to scatter themselves amidst the timber and to use the steep riverbank for protection.

"Here," Fresada said, pointing out a hackberry tree with a good stout trunk. "This is a good place."

"Where are you going?" Terrell asked.

"Over here," he said, indicating another tree a few yards away.

Uninvited, Billy Tool took up a position next to Terrell, using the same tree for cover. Terrell was annoyed, but he said nothing. He set his powder horn on the ground beside him and checked the contents of his hunting bag: vent pick, brush, patching, balls. He made sure his loading block was filled and that his flint was free of grime and damp. Ordering his killing tools in this way helped to calm him, but he could feel a hollow dread rising in him anyway. He did not like having his back to the river. He could swim, but if the Mexicans overran their position the rebels would be easy to shoot as they struggled in the water.

"Shite, it's going to rain!" Billy Tool said as he looked at the gloomy sky overhead.

"Not for a while yet," Terrell answered.

"And how are we supposed to fight in the rain with wet powder?"

"Their powder'll be wet too. I guess we'll have to stab each other." He remembered his butcher knife in its scabbard, but he did not want to think about having to use it.

"Oh, Christ Almighty," Billy said under his breath. "Do you think they'll charge us on their horses?"

"Not into these trees, if they've got any sense," a man a few yards away said as he lit his pipe. "They'll come after us on foot. We ought to have the range on them, those of us with rifles. But if they get in close all hell will break loose when they start using those short swords of theirs. They probably have bayonets for their muskets, too."

Westover walked up and down the line, joking with some men, slapping others on the back. His voice was calm and ordinary, and his mood and the mood of the men was one of good cheer and self-conscious high spirits. Terrell felt a sudden sharp fellowship for the men lying with him in these trees. It was a feeling that extended even to Billy Tool.

"Our scouts say the Mexicans are four or five miles down the road," Westover said chattily to Terrell and the other men who had stationed themselves in the center of the line. "Time to take a shite if your bowels are feeling loose."

A few of the men laughed, but Terrell was not grateful for the comment, since it reminded him anew of the digestive turmoil going on inside him.

"Are they going to want to talk first?" Terrell asked him.

"I don't know, son. Maybe so. But my guess is they're going to dismount and come straight for us. You just keep shooting them down with that Kentucky of yours, and we'll be fine."

He walked on, strolling down the line of men.

"You got anything to eat?" Billy asked Terrell.

"I got a stale piece of cornbread."

"Give it to me."

"You can have part of it. I ain't givin' it all to you."

He broke off a piece of the cornbread and handed it to Billy, feeling suddenly generous toward this tiresome and unwanted companion.

"I'll be right back," he said to Billy.

"Where are you going?"

"Just to talk to Fresada."

Terrell walked across the twenty-yard gap of open ground to where Fresada lay behind his tree, silently fingering his rosary beads.

"You want a piece of this cornbread?" Terrell asked.

"No," Fresada said.

"I was thinking," Terrell said. "Maybe you should take the Kentucky, and I should take your shotgun."

Fresada was silent a long time while considering it. "No, you go ahead and use the rifle."

"You shot that Kronk with it."

"I know."

"I'm afraid I'll miss," Terrell whispered. "I'm afraid my hands will shake."

"They won't shake that bad. Look at mine. They're shaking a little bit too."

"I don't like having our backs to the river."

"I don't either, but that's where we are."

"What were you talking about?" Billy demanded when Terrell came back to his position.

"Nothing," Terrell said.

Someone down the line said, "There they are!" and Terrell and Billy looked up to see the Mexican dragoons arriving in a pale, dispersing cloud of dust three hundred yards away. The Mexicans reined up and dismounted in a waist-high expanse of brush, a few feathery huisache trees towering over their heads and blowing in the cold wind. Terrell was startled by how close they appeared, how particular each man and each horse seemed even from this distance.

Terrell watched as some of the dragoons gathered the horses and led them away and the others deployed behind the screen of brush. Most of them wore red coatees with green trim, and leather helmets. The helmets were crowned with goat-hair crests. The dragoons seemed to be in no hurry. One of the officers stood on a little promontory looking through a glass at the rebel lines, now and then turning to a man in a frock coat and straw hat—the alcalde of San Patricio, Terrell guessed. They seemed to be calmly chatting with one another. The mayor was eating something, though at this distance Terrell could not see what it was.

"There's seventy of them," Billy said. "That's how many I counted."

Terrell said nothing, though they were all thinking the same thing. Half of the rebel force was on the other side of the river defending the horses. There were fewer than forty men here to meet the charge when it came.

But it seemed as if it might never come. The two men on the grassy hillock—the Mexican officer and the Irishman—appeared to be taking all the time in the world to chat about the situation.

"I think they're starting to lose their nerve," one of the men called out. "I believe they're going to absquatulate on us here before too long."

There was some nervous, spotty laughter in response, and then Westover's voice—still calm and casual—answered.

"No, gentlemen, I believe we will not be disappointed. They will certainly want to try us before dark."

Some of the men had found pecans on the ground and were tossing them down the line. Billy caught one in the air and cracked it in his teeth.

"You want some?" he asked Terrell.

"No."

"I don't either. Why are they taking so long? Now I've got to piss."

"Well, just go ahead and do it, and stop telling me every thought in your head," Terrell said.

Billy stood up and walked a few paces down the sloping bank toward the river and opened his trousers. Terrell heard the first splash of his piss on the ground and then almost immediately John Dunn called out in an excited voice, "They're coming!"

There was no gunfire, not yet. Just a silent advance of the uniformed figures on the other side of the meadow. They moved cautiously, a few yards forward at a time, searching out whatever cover they could find. Billy came running back and threw himself down on the other side of the tree trunk, panting with excitement. He rolled over on his back to button up his trousers. When he had done so he made a quick sign of the cross and rolled over again, aiming his scopet at the advancing forms.

No one spoke, and no one fired, until one of the men on the far right flank tried a shot with his Kentucky, and one of the distant figures seemed to fold up like a leaf and disappear into the deep grass.

The Mexicans, in response, opened up with a spattering fusillade, and their advancing line was immediately obscured by an eruption of white smoke from their inferior gunpowder. Terrell heard the balls from those carbines and muskets falling harmlessly into the grass forty yards ahead of the rebel position, but the Mexicans rushed out of the heavy smoke and charged forward.

"Shoot!" Billy Tool shouted at him. His own musket was useless at this distance, and he looked at Terrell's rifle with wide, frightened eyes.

"Shut up," Terrell told him as he lifted the Kentucky and sighted it on the midsection of an officer who was standing at the summit of a little rise, holding a sword. He pulled the trigger, and the hangfire seemed to last for an eternity as the powder sizzled in the moist air, but then he felt the familiar kick as the ball rocketed out of the barrel and the rank smell of gunpowder rose into his nostrils. His aim was rushed. The ball hit the officer not in the trunk but on the inside of his thigh. Terrell saw the man look down at a pulsating fountain of blood, stumble for a pace or two, and then fall. He was lost to sight in the tall prairie grass, but the blood still geysered above the dry wintry stalks.

Terrell reloaded. His hands did not shake as he had feared, and he felt a strange, calm exhilaration. A Mexican musket ball hit him in the cheek but bounced off without even breaking the skin. Other balls whistled in the air above them and dropped like hailstones a few yards beyond their position. But Terrell knew that as the Mexican line crept closer those balls would become deadly, and it was up to the men with long rifles to keep their attack from closing. He fired again at one of the leading dragoons and missed, and as he was reloading, Billy Tool's musket belched in his ear.

"Don't shoot yet!" Terrell yelled at him, "They're still out of range!"

"I put in a double charge!" he yelled back.

"You're still just wasting powder!"

As Terrell rolled onto his back and rammed his next charge down the barrel he glanced over at Fresada, who lay patiently behind his tree, watching the progress of the battle, waiting for the enemy to come within his range.

"On the left!" he heard Westover scream, and rolled over in time to see a desperate charge of Mexican dragoons and Irish loyalists trying to attack and roll up the defenders' left flank. Terrell levelled his rifle and pulled the trigger, joining in a general broadside that brought seven or eight of the attackers down and sent the rest running back to whatever cover they could find. He was fairly certain it was his ball that caught one of the Irishmen in the hipbone, and he watched him crawling brokenly and calling out in pain under the low yellow cloud of gunsmoke.

Directly in front of them now there came another charge, led by a brave officer who ran several yards in front of his men, fully exposed, until a fusillade from the rebel line cut him down. The rest of the dragoons fell prone upon the grass and fired a ragged volley, their muskets now finally in range. Terrell pressed his face to the base of the tree as the bullets seethed in the air above him. He heard Billy Tool screech but could not see him for a moment because of the thick, coagulating smoke all around them. The rancid expended gunpowder poisoned the air and made his already sore throat unbearably dry. The touchhole of his rifle was fouled, and he groped around in the obscurity for his vent pick and brush as the Mexican balls continued to pepper the leaves all around him and Billy kept screaming in his ear.

He managed to clean the pan and touchhole and to reload, but by the time he was ready to shoot again the Mexicans were already beginning to fall back in careful stages, unable to tolerate the accurate fire that the rebels kept pouring at them from their protected position in the trees. Terrell put his rifle on half-cock, saving the shot in case another charge came from another quarter, and then turned at last to Billy, who was staring in horror at his right hand, which had only its thumb and little finger left and from which blood ran in gently pulsing sheets.

"They shot off my fucking fingers, Terrell!" he said. "Oh Christ my fucking fingers!"

Terrell took a handkerchief out of his coat pocket and reached for Billy's mangled hand.

"Don't touch it!" he screamed. "Don't touch it, for Christ's sake!"

"Well, do you want to bleed to death?" Terrell said.

"Just give me the fucking handkerchief," Billy spat out

at him. A chorus of cheers and huzzahs erupted up and down the line as the Mexicans continued their retreat. Billy wrapped the handkerchief around the bloody stumps of his fingers and squeezed the mutilated hand beneath his armpit, then rolled around on the ground, groaning in agony.

"They shot his fingers off," Terrell said to Fresada when he came running up to their position.

"Let me look," Fresada said to Billy, prying Billy's wounded hand out from under his arm. The handkerchief was already saturated with blood.

"Find the doctor," Fresada told Terrell.

Terrell picked up his rifle and began to run down the line. He had only gone a few yards when he noticed something dropping from the folds of his hunting shirt. He looked down on the ground and saw that the object was one of Billy's fingers, drained of blood now and eerily pale, with dirt packed beneath its ragged nail. He could think of no right thing to do with the severed finger, and so he just left it there and continued running as cold rain finally burst through the heavy clouds overhead, washing the priming powder out of his rifle pan and streaming down the back of his shirt. When he located the doctor, a tall, astringent man in a visored cap, his teeth were chattering so much from the cold or the delayed excitement of the battle that he could hardly make himself understood.

BILLY TOOL was the only rebel casualty of the fight, and so the doctor was eager to attend him. While the other men went out onto the field in the rain to inspect the bodies of the Mexican dead, Terrell helped set up a tarp to create a dry space for the doctor to sew up what was left of Billy's hand. Terrell and Fresada held down his shoulders during the operation, and Billy bore the pain with a stouter resolve than Terrell would have anticipated.

"We beat them back, though, didn't we?" Billy said in a breathless, hysterical voice.

"That's right, son, we did," the doctor replied. He was seated on the ground, using his knees like a vise to hold Billy's trembling arm still as he passed the needle through the gouged and tattered flesh of his hand.

Terrell looked away, to the meadow where the other rebels were walking in the rain among the dead. The Mexican dragoons had retreated out of sight, somewhere beyond this thick curtain of rain. Terrell thought the officer he shot in the thigh probably died, all his blood expelled in that obscene spouting. The Irishman he hit in the hipbone perhaps would live, if he had gotten off the field before another ball caught him. Terrell found himself wondering what he should feel, because no coherent reactions presented themselves to him. The awareness that he had likely ended a human life kept crowding in on his mind, but it was so enormous a thought it could find no purchase, and so he let it drift away. And though he certainly felt sympathy for poor Billy Tool, panting in agony and then finally openly screaming as the surgery went on endlessly, Terrell felt more keenly a sense of relief at his own miraculous wholeness and lethal competence.

They crossed back over the narrow river in canoes, the rain falling so heavily now that Terrell could barely see the opposite bank. He shivered in the frigid downpour, and his throat was so raw and swollen he could barely swallow. By the time they marched into San Patricio his head was swimming with fever. They were led into a house where the furniture had all been shoved back against the walls and a fire was roaring in the hearth. A woman and a girl took their cups away and brought them back filled with soup, but Terrell's throat was so tight and swollen he could get very little of the soup down, though he was desperately hungry and cold and the hot liquid was like an unreachable balm.

Fresada made him pull off his wet clothes and wrapped

him in a quilt that the woman gave him. Terrell lay awake all night in the crowded room at the foot of the fire. The men talked and laughed for hours, all of them giddy and amazed to be alive and chattering away like children about the battle. In the end they all drifted off to sleep, and so did Fresada. But the choking pain in his throat and the wracking chills in his body made sleep impossible for Terrell. The elation he had felt in surviving the battle had now faded, and he lay there in as deep a physical misery as he had ever known. He was preoccupied by a sharp fear that he might die after all, not from a musket ball but from putrid throat.

On the other side of the room Billy Tool kept moaning like some sort of beast.

"Oh, please," he kept saying. "For the love of God, oh, please."

"There's nobody awake," Terrell finally told him through his closed-up throat. He thought he could smell his own fetid breath as he said the words.

"Oh Christ Terrell it hurts so bad."

"I know it does."

"I've only got the two fingers left. And 'tis my right hand!"

"I guess you'll have to be left-handed from now on."

"Where are my fingers? Are they just laying out there on the river bank?"

"Probably," Terrell said. "Don't ask me to talk anymore, Billy. It hurts for me to talk."

"But just listen, then. Don't go to sleep and leave me alone."

"All right," Terrell said. "I'll listen." And so he lay there shivering in his quilt on the floor. The fire burned down, but he didn't have the strength to stand up and get more wood. Billy's voice, droning on across the room, became like some hectoring presence within his own head, assaulting him with its fears and opinions throughout every minute of this endless night.

CHAPTER FOURTEEN

✶

"I RECKON I'm well enough to do some work now."

Gaunt, pale as a grub in the bright wintry daylight, Terrell appeared in the doorway and spoke to Mary as she and Edna and Teresa did the washing in the yard. Mary looked up at him with a strange twist in her heart. His terrifying illness was behind him, but her son still looked like an ashen-faced old man, and when he walked to them across the yard his every footfall had a probing, testing quality to it, as if he was not quite sure yet where the ground was.

"You need another few days before you start thinking about work," Mary told him. "And a few more meals into the bargain."

Terrell opened his mouth as if he were planning to contradict her, but said nothing and simply sat down on the edge of the porch. The full sunlight of this brilliant December day fell upon his colorless face.

"Is there any news?" he asked her.

"If there is, I haven't heard it. As far as we know, they still have the town surrounded."

A contentious volunteer army had been besieging Béxar for weeks. Their goal was to oust General Cos and his men and drive them back across the Bravo, but apparently no one could decide whether to force them out by assault or by starvation, and the army itself had been undermined by bickering, ineptitude, and outright mutiny. The last Mary had heard, from several Refugio men who had quit the siege in disgust, was that Sam Houston and his various operatives were succeeding in all sorts of underhanded ways to strip General Austin of his authority and steal the army away from him.

Most of the men who had accompanied Terrell on the Lipantitlán adventure had gone on to join up with the army that invested Béxar. Terrell would have gone himself, Mary felt sure, if he had not already been half-dead from quinsy. He had come home to her in a cart, wrapped like a mummy in the quilts that Fresada had commandeered in San Patricio, his throat so shockingly raw and swollen that he could barely draw a breath.

Twice during those first few days after his arrival she thought her son was on the verge of suffocation, and she had steeled herself for the unbearable recourse of opening his windpipe with a knife. But to her great relief his anxious, shallow breathing held its pitch. It was a long time before he was out of peril, many nights of pepper-and-vinegar swabs and volatile liniments of her own desperate concoction, but in the end she had saved him, and now he stood before her like some ravaged spirit, no longer a boy or even a youth but a young man who in the last month alone had not only killed other men but had visited the precincts of his own death.

"You need a jacket," she told him now. He was wearing only his shirt.

"It's not cold."

"It's cold enough to give you a chill. Edna, fetch Terrell's jacket."

Edna put down her scrub board and raced into the house, returning with his jacket and holding it out for him to slip his arms through as if he were a lord. The girl's eager need to please had not diminished, and in fact Edna had been a comfort to Mary during the trial of Terrell's illness. Simple though she was, she was a natural nurse, and on several occasions when Mary knew she was reaching her limits of exhaustion she had trusted Edna to stay up with Terrell during the night, confident that she would shift the poultices before they blistered him or awaken her if there was a drop in his fluttering pulse or a change in his breathing.

"I ought to do some work," Terrell said, but his weakened body did not seem eager to rise to the occasion. He sat there on the steps watching the women heft the bed linens out of the boiling water, the smell of soap sharp and bracing in his nostrils. Several times during his illness he had felt the closeness of death, but it had been no more frightening or strange to him than the touch of his mother's ministering hands. Dying, he discovered, was a familiar sensation after all, a gray, sumptuous presence like a storm cloud, with something thrumming inside it, something that beat with the urgent rhythm of a bird's heart.

Professor walked up to him and collapsed against his feet. Terrell rubbed the dog's chest for a moment. When he took his hand away, Professor growled in outrage.

"Don't give in to him," Mary warned her son with a smile. "He's demanding enough as it is."

But Terrell resumed scratching the dog's silky chest. Professor's eyes closed against the sunlight, and his tail beat with steady contentment against the warped oaken boards of the porch. Terrell fell into a reverie of his own: the Mexicans advancing across that field above the Nueces, Billy Tool screaming beside him, and Terrell loading and shooting his rifle with dreamlike precision, untouched by all the terror and chaos of the battle. The killing efficiency he had discovered in himself that day was the most satisfying sensation he had ever known, and the more he remembered it the stronger his cravings were to experience it again. He knew he could not last here in Refugio many more days, when great events were about to unfold in Béxar.

The rhythmic thumping of Professor's tail suddenly stopped, and the dog lifted his head and sniffed the air with consummate interest. For a long moment he sat there, tensely alert, emitting an agitated growl, and then all at once he leapt off the edge of the porch and ran barking along the road that led toward town.

"What's troubling him now?" Mary said.

"Perhaps 'tis that man coming," Edna answered.

It was Edmund McGowan, walking toward the inn and leading a decrepit mule. He was still wearing the hat Mary had sold him months ago, though it had been much abused. He had lost weight, she saw at once, and his face—which once had a malarial pallor—was now deeply tanned by the tropical sun.

Professor raced toward him and made a flying leap against his chest, which frightened the mule to such a degree that Edmund almost lost control of it as he tried, laughing, to respond to his dog's extravagant greetings.

Professor was still dancing at Edmund's feet when Mary walked up, wiping her soapy hands on her apron. She meant not to smile in greeting him, but could not stop herself. The specific nature of her dissatisfaction with him seemed remote now that he stood before her. He was not a noticeably handsome man but he was generally well made, and his burnished skin, she thought, improved his looks to a considerable degree.

"Good morning, Mrs. Mott," he said.

"Good morning, Mr. McGowan. You have arrived just when you predicted you would."

"You received my letter, then?"

"I did. And your generous draft. Along with the flower you named for me."

"I hope it was not presumptuous in me."

"It was. It's the height of presumption to confer immortality onto someone without consulting her first. But I forgive you. And thank you.

"Your animals are all well," she went on, "and as you can see, Professor has not forgotten you. How did you come?

No Mexican ships have dared call at the port since the war started."

"I had to disembark at Matamoros and make my way overland on this disagreeable mule. All the while dreaming of your cornbread."

"It's still warm from breakfast. Though we've long since run out of coffee, I'm afraid."

"I happen to have a small sack of coffee in my outfit, Mrs. Mott, and would be pleased if you would join me in a cup or two while we eat your cornbread."

"THERE ARE TEMPLES everywhere," Edmund said to Mary as they ambled along the river after lunch. "Though you have to train your eye to see them, since most of them are so covered in vegetable matter they seem little more than mounds rising out of the jungle floor. I saw traces of great roads as well, and stone tablets twenty feet high with strange carvings of feathered men."

"Could I trouble you to walk faster?" she said, as he bent down to examine some plant that interested her not at all. "It's been months since I've had coffee, and now I find that I'm so unaccustomed to its effects that the blood is racing in my veins."

She had drunk four cups. The coffee had tasted so supremely good that she had had no more willpower than an opium eater, and as a result she felt that she was about to leap out of her skin.

"I liked the place, all in all," he resumed as they walked faster and her heart finally began to find its rhythm. "Very much, in fact. Particularly the coastal regions, where the water in the lagoons is so clear and bright it hurts your eyes to look at it. And of course one could spend a lifetime studying the epiphytes alone!"

"And what about your gum tree?"

"The sapodilla is common enough, but is generally inaccessible, slow to mature, and hard to cultivate. You can't grow it like cotton in a plantation, and no sooner have you harvested the resin from the wild trees than it begins to decompose in your bucket. Nevertheless, I've made what suggestions I could: grafting, and so on."

She half-listened as he rambled on. The sapodilla fruit, which was the basis for a drink as refreshing as lemonade; the great sinkholes, filled with water and shining like jewels in the floor of the jungle; the flamingoes that paraded through the sky overhead, and the leaf-cutting ants that swarmed below; the glorious orchids; the coral reefs; a two-headed sea turtle kept by an Indian in a fish weir.

She became aware, at some point during this walk, that his conversation had a nervous quality she had never noticed before. She felt as if this rush of words was an attempt to hold some other topic of discussion at bay. It annoyed her, as did so much about this man, but she could not deny that curious currents of thought and feeling ran between Edmund McGowan and herself. With another man she might have recognized these currents as forthright romantic impulses, but with Edmund she did not quite know what they were, and she thought perhaps that it was this uncertainty as much as her overindulgence in coffee that made her pulse beat so ungovernably fast.

For just the briefest moment, she had a strange feeling that all was well. A hawk glided above them, casting its shadow through the cypress limbs. The water of the river glistened like ice in the full glare of the sun. She walked along beside Edmund, their steps now in rhythm, their bodies somehow closer, more allied, than if they had actually been touching. She knew to a certainty that she had nursed Terrell through his grave illness only to face the prospect of watching him ride off to another battle, but for this instant that chronic fear was no longer preying on her mind. She saw the hawk whose shadow had passed across them a few paces back. It flew low over the treetops on the other side of

the river, never beating its wings, merely shifting weight
with its shoulders as it glided along on its current of air.

They talked about the war. In the City of Mexico and on
the road from Matamoros he had heard only unreliable
rumors—that the rebels had executed the Mexican soldiers
they had captured at Goliad, that Béxar had already fallen,
that the Comanches had joined with the centralists to drive
the norteamericanos out of Texas forever. All these rumors
were false, Mary told him, but the tone of her voice indicated
that they were not far from the realm of possibility and that
similar events were certain to come true sooner or later.

"When did you last hear anything about the siege at
Béxar?" Edmund asked.

"Four days ago. There was an assault planned, but it was
cancelled, and now everything is in chaos. Jim Bowie is
there, but he is hardly a stabilizing force, and I think has
been a thorn in Austin's side. Meanwhile General Cos has
fortified some old mission near the river."

"The Alamo."

"Do you know it?"

"I know it very well. It would make an indifferent
stronghold."

He drew to a stop at a slight promontory that looked
down upon the river. Its banks were steeper here than downstream, and the vines linking the trees were as stout as ornamental iron. A doe was drinking at the water's edge on
the far bank. When it caught Edmund's and Mary's scent it
crashed up the slope in a burst of panic, its white tail flashing through the tangled vegetation.

"I'll leave tomorrow," he announced, when the tapping
of the deer's feet in the underbrush had died away.

"Tomorrow? Why?"

"I want to see to the safety of my notes and specimens.
They're sitting in a house in Béxar. I hired a man to look after them before I left, but I can't expect him to risk his life
for my sake if an assault is made."

"You won't be able to get into the town."

"Maybe not, but at least I'll be in the vicinity."

Mary said, with a crossness in her voice, "We had hoped for the pleasure of your company for a few more days. This has not been a happy place since the war began."

He said nothing, though she could tell by the look in his eyes that he had registered her chastening tone and, as usual, had no idea how to respond to it. He reached into the pocket of his waistcoat and removed a small paper-wrapped bundle.

"Would you like to try it?" he asked.

"Try what?"

"The chewing gum."

He unwrapped the paper and held out to her a whitish substance about the size of an egg.

"It's been flavored with mint," he said.

With the tip of her fingers, she pinched away a bit of the gum and put it in her mouth and began to gnaw on it.

"Do you like it?"

"No. And I don't see what purpose it serves, other than to keep one's mouth busy."

She chewed the gum a little while longer in silence as they walked back toward the inn, and then finally removed it and pointedly tossed it into the river.

"How does Terrell look to you?" she asked.

"I thought perhaps he had been ill. He has lost weight, and his skin is very pale."

"He went with the rebels to Lipantitlán and was in a battle. When he came back his throat was septic and he almost died. And any day now he will be riding off to Béxar to join Austin's army, and it will be useless for me to try to stop him. He's a man now, I guess, and entitled to his adventures just like any other man."

Edmund was silent for a moment, quite aware of the undercurrent of anger in her voice.

"Even if he does go," he ventured at last, "he will probably arrive too late for any real fighting, particularly if Austin—"

"I'm not interested at the moment in hearing any more of your predictions about this war. As I recall, you said the Irish would remain neutral, but it was Irishmen who swept Terrell up into the raid on Lipantitlán and almost got him killed. I have no confidence in your talents as a seer, Edmund. In fact, I think you like to prognosticate simply to hear yourself talk!"

"Very well," he said. "The future will unfold without any further commentary from me."

It took a few more moments of testy silence before Mary was ready to speak to him again.

"I am sorry," she said. "I was so glad to see you—to see a friend—walking up the road. As I told you, it has not been a happy time. Your declaration about leaving tomorrow caught me unprepared. Of course it is none of my business when you leave, and I am embarrassed to have been so sullen about it."

"You were sullen because I was thoughtless, and so the apology rests with me."

They finished their walk in slightly better temper. Edmund was somewhat unclear why an apology on his part had been necessary, but Mary Mott's anger had not really put him off; it had in fact stirred him, and now as he walked beside her back to the inn he struggled to keep down the troubling thoughts generated by her nearness, by the intimate tone of her anger, that kept threatening to rise in his mind.

Edmund walked into town later that afternoon to buy a pair of woolen socks and a patch knife to replace the one he had lost in an accidental tumble into one of those jungle sinkholes. There was only one knife available for sale in Sullivan's store, a useless antler-handled showpiece that was almost as long as a Mexican espada, but there were two pair of socks and he bought them both. The clear December sky had turned steely, and a norther was coming on. It was rare to have a fierce winter in Texas, particularly this far south, but Edmund and the hatchet-faced storekeeper were allied in their suspicions that raw weather would soon be settling in.

There was no news of events in Béxar, though the storekeeper was of the opinion that by now the siege must inevitably have collapsed, given the quarrelsome nature of the rebel army. Walking back to the inn, Edmund thought of Stephen Austin trying to hold these contentious volunteers together in one place and hone them into a single instrument. Austin was a persuasive man, but his health was uncertain and after so long away from Texas he had perhaps become more a symbol than a leader. And he was fundamentally guileless, unlike Sam Houston, his most formidable rival, whom Edmund had never met but who was regarded as a supremely devious man during his periodic fits of sobriety. As much as he wished for Austin's personal success, Edmund thought the best thing in the long run might be for the rebel army to fall apart and melt away from Béxar before any more blood was shed and Santa Anna sent a much larger force into Texas to destroy every trace of resistance to centralist authority. There was still a chance, he thought, for an all-out military suppression to be averted; still a chance for Béxar—and his precious botanical documents—to escape the flames of war.

HE WAS the only guest at the inn that night; the only guest at all, he understood, in quite some time. Mary was extremely civil to him at dinner, seemingly eager to discuss with him his work, where and how he would move his papers and specimens from Béxar, where he would begin his expedition and whether it would be better to use Tejano or Caddoan guides when he ventured into the fastness of the Big Thicket. But in her conversation there was no trace of that sharp attentiveness, that vague and awkward sense of expectation, that had underlain all of their meetings so far.

Tonight he was merely a guest at her inn, someone who would continue on his journey in the morning and most likely never return.

Terrell was mostly silent during dinner. He had cleaned out the horse stalls that afternoon, defying his mother's orders to remain still during his recuperation, and this evening both his appetite and his strength were tentative. He left the table early, and retired to his bed. Edmund felt a certain coldness from him as well, and remembered with some distress how singularly unhelpful he had been months before, when Terrell had taken the risk of confiding in him about his misalliance with a disturbed girl.

Edmund was not sure, but he thought that the Irish girl who had helped Mary prepare the dinner and had made up his bed in the public house was the same person that Terrell had described. There was something disconcerting about Edna. She had the puzzled, pleading look of an animal whimpering at the door. Her eyes were too luminous, her smile too lingering: a young woman who seemed that she might seize on any act of kindness with a crushing embrace.

Edmund knew immediately, when a series of piercing, hysterical screams woke him a few hours before dawn, that it was Edna's voice he heard. He picked up his shotgun and ran barefoot across the cold ground, following the screams to a jacal on the other side of the dwelling house. Lantern light spilled through the gaps in the stick walls, and when he looked inside Edmund saw that Mary was there already, and that she and Teresa were holding the girl's hands to keep her from striking her own face as she writhed in fear and pain on the ground.

"What is it?" he asked.

But Mary was too involved in struggling with Edna to answer. Edmund put down his shotgun and went inside to help. The ground and the girl's nightdress were thickly stained with blood, and her eyes were wild. She was calling out, in piteous shrieks, to the Blessed Mother.

CHAPTER FIFTEEN

✦

"**T**ENIENTE VILLASENOR! What can you tell me about this mission General Cos has supposedly turned into a fort?"

His Excellency spoke to Telesforo without raising his eyes from the sheaf of orders on which he was scrawling his signature: orders for the leasing of carts and oxen, for the hasty reassigning of men and horses and artillery and gun carriages and field forges—orders for the war that was at last coming in earnest.

"Mission Valero, Your Excellency," Telesforo said, as he stepped forward into the crowded room with his map case. "Though everyone calls it the Alamo. We've had a presidial company stationed there for years, but it is hardly a—"

Santa Anna, lost in sudden concentration over one of the orders on his desk, held up a hand and Telesforo accordingly fell silent, casting his eyes discreetly about the room. The Governor's Palace of San Luis Potosí had been commandeered by Santa Anna immediately upon his arrival yesterday in the city, and already the immaculate offices were a shambles, the carpets caked with mud from the boots of countless couriers, the haircloth of the furniture destroyed by spilled coffee and chocolate and neglected cigars, charming landscapes and silhouettes of the governor's family carelessly removed and stacked in the corner to make room on the walls for maps to be hung.

The room was filled with important men. Colonel Almonte, recently returned to Mexico from New York, sat in a chair by a window with his legs crossed, looking out over the clean streets and stolid stone buildings of the city, tapping a rolled-up newspaper on his knee. General Filisola, Santa Anna's second-in-command, stood over a map of the route to Leona Vicario with General Arago. And there were a half-dozen adjutants and senior aides as well, all of them toting up figures or poring over documents. Telesforo was by far the most junior officer present.

"Yes, I know the Alamo," Santa Anna said at last, lifting his eyes to Telesforo and handing the revised order to Ramón Caro, his civilian secretary. "But I have not been to Béxar in over twenty years, and I must confess that as a young officer I was more interested in cockfights than picturesque old missions."

"General Cos has fortified it, Your Excellency."

"That I would assume. But how well?"

Telesforo had just that morning ridden into San Luis from Leona Vicario, where he had spent two days interviewing a remarkably perceptive dragoon captain who had been sent out by Cos as a courier the week before. The captain had described the repairs made to the Alamo and the dimensions of the makeshift fort with such exactitude that Telesforo was able to draw maps that he was convinced were almost as reliable as if they had been done from the field. One map showed the Alamo compound itself as seen from above, another a sketchy plan of Béxar, showing the mission sitting in relative isolation among the cornfields and jacales just across the San Antonio River from the town.

"With permission, Presidente," he said now, removing the maps from the case and setting them out on Santa Anna's desk as Almonte and Filisola and the other officers began to crowd around.

"Please remember, Teniente, that I am not at the moment your president. I have left that title in the safekeeping of Señor Barragán while I prosecute the war."

Telesforo acknowledged this correction with proper gravity, though he saw Almonte and Filisola exchange an amused look. It suited Santa Anna's schemes to fade in and out of office periodically so that he might remain as elusive as a firefly, but nobody who had ever met him could believe that he would voluntarily relinquish even the smallest portion of power over his fellow creatures.

"Here is the river," Telesforo said, tracing with his finger a thick blue line. "The Alamo is located about two hundred varas east of the river's bed. The surface of the site is higher than that of the city and can dominate it easily. General Cos has apparently cut down much of the timber along the riverbank to further that end. The only higher elevation is an old Spanish powder house and watchtower here to the southeast."

"The friars always situated their missions with a surprisingly strategic eye," General Filisola said. He was Italian-born, and the faintest Italian inflections teased their way through his perfect Spanish.

"The friars had Spanish soldiers to help them," Santa Anna corrected him, with a good-natured lilt in his own voice. "Left on their own, they would have built their missions in floodplains, or on the tops of sand dunes. How high are these walls, Teniente?"

"No more than four and a half varas, Your Excellency. The north wall is in very bad shape. General Cos has reinforced it, and he has filled in this gap between the church and the south wall with a defensive parapet and platforms for artillery."

Santa Anna nodded and leaned his head closer to the map, peering at it with a conjuring intensity, smoothing the paper with his fingers as if attempting to touch the contours of the Alamo itself. Telesforo spoke when he thought it appropriate, pointing out the roofless shell of the church, the various lunettes and esplanades and tambours that Cos had built in an attempt to convert this hopelessly broken rectangle into a workable fortification.

His Excellency grunted from time to time as Telesforo spoke, and then continued to regard the map with solitary scrutiny for a full five minutes, completely unmindful of all the other people in the room who were hostage to his wandering concentration. Finally he lifted his head and sat back in his chair, idly stroking a surging curl of hair at his temple.

"General?" he said to Filisola.

"I would not want to defend it, Your Excellency."

"I agree. But if the rebels manage to defeat General Cos in the streets of Béxar, he may very well have to retreat to the Alamo and make a stand there. And I don't think such a fortress can hold out for long, even against Austin's norte rabble. As for a well-disciplined army, it could storm the place in half an hour."

He turned to Telesforo.

"How is your arm? Are you fit for a campaign, Teniente?"

"Any chance to serve would be an honor, Your Excellency," Telesforo said, reflexively straightening his back, his left arm hanging weightily at his side. The ball had killed various important nerves, and though Telesforo could clumsily move the arm he could not raise it above his chest. He was in more or less constant pain, a dull, bristling pain varied by searing currents that moved up and down his arm at unpredictable moments. These wild flashes of agony had filled him with dread in the first few weeks of his recuperation, but now he found himself strangely craving them, perhaps as proof that his arm was still alive.

"Then you will leave tomorrow with General Filisola's forces," Santa Anna said, looking not at Telesforo but to Señor Caro, who—recognizing the tone of an order—was already furiously scribbling Santa Anna's words into a copybook. "And at the first opportunity you will ride ahead to join the vanguard led by General Ramírez y Sesma, which is already on the march toward Béxar. I will follow with the rest of the army in a few weeks' time, and when I arrive in Béxar I will expect you to have already completed even more excellent maps and diagrams of the situation there."

Santa Anna flashed his eyes at Filisola. "I trust your troops are ready to set out tomorrow?"

"We are doing everything we can to make them so, Your Excellency. But I must say again that the route you have proposed is a long and dangerous one, and there is very little money to provision them properly for such a—"

"DO YOU THINK I'M A FOOL?" Santa Anna erupted, pounding his fist on the governor's desk with enough force to send an inkpot over its edge and onto the carpet. Telesforo flinched instinctively, but he was not so alarmed as he might have been a few months earlier. Since joining the president's staff he had seen a dozen such outbursts, and though they were fierce while they lasted they were quick to evaporate, almost always ending in a crafty apology by Santa Anna to the poor rattled subordinate who had provoked his rage.

"Do you think I have no conception of what an army needs for a proper campaign?" the president roared. Caro was on his way to the spilled inkpot, but Santa Anna waved him away and walked around to the front of the desk to clean up the mess himself. "Do you think I have been idle on the matter of finances?"

"No sir, I merely—"

"Have I not just signed a note, General—on my own security—so that our soldiers can receive their overdue pay before they march off into the despoblado? Have I not been working myself into a fever trying to raise the four hundred thousand pesos it will cost to prosecute this campaign? Do not lecture me about provisions, sir, when I hazard my reputation every day negotiating with thieving moneylenders in order to buy food for my troops! Ramón, find someone to clean this ink stain off the governor's carpet before it sets."

Telesforo slipped out of Caro's way as the secretary set out on this impossible errand with a panic-stricken look on his face. Filisola, on the other hand, did not appear in the least intimidated by Santa Anna's outburst, though his face was mottled with anger.

"I have given you my opinion of this matter repeatedly, Your Excellency. An overland march to Texas is a far more expensive and dangerous undertaking than sending the troops by sea. We would not have to cross four hundred leagues of wilderness, we would not have an exposed and isolated line of operations, subject to attack by wild Indians at every point, to the peril of mountain and desert both, to—"

"Yes, by all means, General, a pleasant sea voyage, and when the troops arrive in Béxar they will find Cos and all his men slaughtered and the nortes in secure possession of every village in all of Texas!"

"There are no hospitals established on the line of march," Filisola pressed, his anger rising but his voice studiously calm. "Furthermore, we have few surgeons, and no money to hire them, and no medicines. The welfare of the troops—"

"The welfare of the troops depends upon a short, swift, decisive campaign, and a quick return home before the unbearable Texas summer catches up with us. Do not forget that this is an emergency, General. A day's delay—an hour's!—could be fatal. And I am sure your men will gladly accept any risk, once you have explained to them that our national honor is at stake."

While Filisola searched his angry brain for a reply that could not be considered insubordinate, Santa Anna returned to his seat behind the governor's desk and brushed a fleck of lint off the knee of his trousers. All the fury had suddenly evaporated from his face, and in its place was the mild, reasonable look that Telesforo knew so well: the lethal calm of a reposing alligator.

"I am sorry to have lost my temper, General," he said to Filisola, whose own jaw muscles were still lividly pulsing. "A better man would not have lashed out at you like that.

Your concern for the safety of your troops shows you to be a leader of the finest moral acuity."

Santa Anna stared vacantly at the top of the desk, as if suddenly struck by an unbearable sadness. And then he sprang to his feet and offered his hand to Filisola, who had no choice but to take it and face the president's soft black eyes.

"I will see you in Béxar, my friend," Santa Anna said, and then added, when the still-fuming Filisola was almost to the door, "God and Liberty."

"I AGREE with the president," Robert Talon said that night in the minuscule room he shared with Telesforo. The Zapadores were billeted in a drafty old deconsecrated convent whose plaster peeled off the walls like dead skin. Telesforo had long since finished packing—his spare shirts, fatigue jacket, socks, shoe brushes, combs, scissors, and boot grease precisely stowed in his cylindrical saddlebag, his raincoat and map case lying neatly on top, his rarely worn shako secured in its protective hatbox, and his sweat-stained sombrero hanging from a peg by the door. He was walking around the room trying to break in a pair of riding breeches with an antelope-skin seat that he had just received from the tailor's and that were as stiff as sailcloth and likely to chafe him on the long ride tomorrow with Filisola's army.

"The great object is to reconquer Texas in the shortest time possible," Robert said, as Telesforo stole a glance at himself in the mirror. He had ordered the breeches made to regulation, but there was a rakish irregularity to the whole outfit that pleased him. Neither cavalryman nor dragoon, but simply a mapmaker on horseback, he felt free to choose which components of uniform pleased him best, though never forgoing the sash that identified him as a member of Santa Anna's staff.

"Yes," Telesforo answered him, "but I'm afraid Filisola is right as well. The army is not properly provisioned, and it is not disciplined enough for such a long march. For every seasoned unit like the Zapadores there are three more made up of convicts and recruits who have never shot a musket except in pantomime.

"And then there's nonsense such as this," he said, holding up an old Spanish drill manual, unchanged since the wars of Napoleon, except for the new title page bearing the Mexican eagle.

"At least when you join Ramírez y Sesma, you'll be in the vanguard. By the time the rest of us catch up you'll have already secured Béxar and the war will be over. Have you seen Tornel's decree in *El Mosquito*?"

"What decree?"

Robert picked up a folded newspaper from his cot and handed it to Telesforo.

"It's on the second page."

The decree was a statement from Minister of War Tornel—to whom Santa Anna was now technically subordinate since he had temporarily resigned the presidency—that began with the usual trumpet blast of rhetoric decrying the foreign usurpers of Texas and reminding the soldiers who were about to march north into the wilderness that the nation would adorn their tombs with flowers if they should fall in this most righteous of wars.

"The usual verbiage," Telesforo said.

"Read Article Two."

"There is established a military order to be called the Legion of Honor," Telesforo read aloud with renewed interest. The Legion of Honor, the decree intoned, would be the highest award a Mexican soldier could merit, and only those who had served in the Texas campaign or in similar wars of foreign aggression with the greatest bravery and distinction could hope to receive it.

Tornel's proclamation went on to describe in great detail

the Legion's insignia: the golden medal emblazoned with crowns of laurel and the republic's coat of arms, and the proud name of the campaign for which it was given. What would that name be? Telesforo wondered. The War for Texas? The War of Northern Liberation?

"I predict that when this war is over and Texas is restored to the nation," Robert said, taking out a whetstone to sharpen his sword, "a man who can wear that insignia will find his way enormously eased."

"His way where?"

"Wherever he should like to go. You are a political creature, I think, once all is said and done. I can see you with your Legion of Honor rising to a level where you are eminently qualified to be poisoned or shot by your rivals for high office."

Telesforo smiled along with him. His yearning to raise himself above other men, to live apart from them at a higher pitch of feeling and experience, was not something he had ever disguised from his friend, or been too solemn about to laugh at himself upon occasion. This boiling need to be noticed, he assumed, was a trait of all exceptional men. No doubt even Samuel Houston, the nortes' vain and hopeless commander in chief, reviled in all the papers as a drunkard who had abandoned his wife, would be a kindred spirit in this one regard. More than once, Telesforo had imagined himself gravely accepting General Houston's sword on some blood-soaked swath of Texas prairie.

Telesforo sat on his cot, reading the decree again, picturing with an almost lustful vividness the physical thing that this Legion of Honor would be. He wanted the medal for what it would represent, for what it would buy him in terms of prestige and advancement, but he also wanted it simply for what it was: an object that he could hold in his hand, that his grandchildren could hold in theirs. He realized, with a sudden sharp thrill, that he had never wanted anything so much in his life.

"And you'll be in the vanguard," Robert was saying, "where at least you'll have a reasonable chance of distinguishing yourself. By the time the rest of us make it to Texas, the fighting will probably be over."

"It may not be as brief a campaign as you anticipate, especially if the United States decides to help its fellow countrymen in Texas."

"Now *that* would be a war," Robert said wistfully. "It could last years and years. A grand conflagration like that would set us both up nicely."

"If we live through it," Telesforo said.

"We must trust in God." Robert lifted his wineglass as if in salute. "And in your case God has given you such an outstanding wound that I very much doubt he would care to bother you further."

Telesforo smiled, though his friend was starting to sound tiresome to him, and a little drunk.

"In such a war we could march all the way to New York and liberate the oyster saloons!" Robert said. "Are you hungry, by the way? Let's get something to eat."

"You go. I want to stay here and go to sleep."

"It's your last night in San Luis. You should have a good meal."

"I'm not hungry, Robert."

Robert sighed, pulled on his shoes, then stood and paused at the door.

"Very well. But be sure to wake me in the morning so we may say our au revoirs before you march off to win your Legion of Honor."

"We will both wear that medal when this war is over."

"Perhaps. But you for sure, Telesforo. I see it written on your brow."

Robert left. For an hour Telesforo sat on the edge of his cot, not moving, not thinking, just sitting in the cool air and the moonlight that drifted in through the open convent window. He sat there in an anticipatory stillness, knowing with certainty that the great events of his life were about to commence. When he closed his eyes he saw the sketches he had presented to Santa Anna that afternoon: shored-up walls, the broken-down facade of a church, a failed mission sitting alone in a cornfield. A mute, mysterious ruin, waiting for him in a far land. He felt keenly that in sketching this place he had somehow stumbled across an emblem of his own destiny. Would this mission be the scene of his death? The thought failed to trouble him. He was prepared to die, as eager in some ways for the glory of oblivion as for the continuing grandeur of life. He was at peace with his fate. His only anxiety was to see the place where it would be decided. With a sharper desire than almost any he could recall, he wanted to see the Alamo.

CHAPTER SIXTEEN

✦

"**H**OW IT IS POSSIBLE to be so simple, so completely—inattentive?" Mary said as she and Edmund sat in the dark at the edge of the dogtrot, looking down at the high bank of trees screening the river. "To have a baby growing inside you, and not know of it!"

Edmund had no authoritative answer, and since he had no wish to venture an idle one, he remained silent, holding Professor's squirming head between his knees while he snipped the hair above the dog's brows with a pair of Mary's shears. Edmund had noticed Professor bumping into things since his return—a laundry bucket, a mound of firewood that Teresa had gathered and dumped in the yard—and realized that it was long past time to trim the curtain of hair that tended to grow over the dog's eyes.

"You need some light," Mary said in a moment. "You might poke his eye in the dark like that."

But Edmund was already finished. He stepped off the porch and threw the dog hair out into the yard, where a chill night breeze bore it away. Professor meanwhile had run under the house in outrage.

"He doesn't care for my barbering skills," Edmund said, hoping to lighten her mood. But it had been a grim day, and Mary managed no more than a polite smile in response. She pulled her shawl tighter around her shoulders.

"Do you happen to have a cigar?" she asked.

"No. I don't have the vice."

"Well, I do," she said with some defiance.

Edmund stepped back onto the porch and took his chair, waiting for her to speak again.

"I suppose it's a blessing," she said at last. "If she was going to lose the baby, it was far better for it to happen so early. And though you may think me cruel for saying so, it was far better for the baby to be lost than to be born at all."

"I don't think you cruel, Mary," Edmund replied.

She turned her face toward him, and her voice was suddenly gentle.

"You were going to leave today for Béxar."

"I doubt that delaying the trip a day or two will make that much of a difference," he told her, though his anxiety about what might be befalling his collections in Béxar was increasing by every hour.

"I hope you will feel free to leave as early in the morning as you wish," she said. "There is nothing more you can do here, in any case."

She reached across and lightly touched his arm.

"For what you have done, though, I am very grateful."

In truth, he had done little during this tortured day except to stand silently by. He had taken it upon himself to gather up a recognizable form from the bloody discharge staining the dirt floor, wrap it in a tea towel and bury it at the edge of a meadow a mile or so away from the inn. When he came back that morning Edna was still hysterical. It was only after she had quieted and fallen asleep, late in the afternoon, that the icy silence between Mary and Terrell had finally erupted into an open quarrel. The boy had refused to defend himself as his mother lashed out at him, accusing him of breaching every form of responsible conduct—lying with the poor girl again when he had pledged he would not, giving no thought to her future and paying no heed to his own reputation and sense of honor.

Terrell—with a look of shame and fury on his face—had ridden off on his speckled mare just before sundown.

Afterward, Edmund had given Mary a wide berth. There had been no supper that night, and he had walked into town on his own and eaten a wretched meal of dried catfish and cornmeal waffles at one of the grog shops. When he returned, he had found Mary sitting on the porch, gazing off into the darkness.

"I'm sorry to have given you no supper," she said now.

"I am well provided for, but you must be hungry yourself."

"I ate some crackers a few hours ago. I will of course deduct the price of a meal from your account. I want you to have honest value for your money. Have you seen this?"

She handed him a folded piece of paper.

"What is it?"

"A courier rode through early this morning, while you were off on your . . . errand. It's a circular from Sam Houston. Wait here a moment, and I'll bring you a candle."

Edmund read the florid proclamation, his eyes straining to make out the words in the weak, fluttering candlelight. He had never met Sam Houston, but he saw him plain enough in his rhetoric: an excitable, theatrical man, believing himself to have arrived at the high tide of his own destiny. The oppressors must be driven from our soil. The usurper shall see the fallacy of his hopes of conquest. The sanctity of our firesides must be preserved from pollution.

"What do you think?" Mary asked.

"It makes me weary."

"It makes me afraid."

"That too," Edmund said. His hopes that this minor insurgency on the Mexican frontier might simply sputter out were becoming increasingly dim. Houston was a trumpet blower, and he was Jackson's man, and he would be sure to raise the stakes as high as they could be raised. After his marriage scandal in Tennessee, and his long drunken debauch afterward among the Cherokees, his political career in the States was surely over. But Houston, Edmund suspected, was determined to find another country to rule. And it was implicit in this aggrieved proclamation that he thought Texas already belonged to him and not the "usurper" who was its president.

Edmund handed the proclamation back to Mary who folded it and tapped it distractedly against the arm of her chair.

"I'm going to look in on her," she said, then rose and took the candle and walked purposefully across the yard to Edna's jacal. She was gone for only a few moments, and then Edmund saw her returning, her hand in front of the candle flame to guard it against the wind, her careworn face illuminated in its shifting light.

"She's sleeping just as soundly as she was hours ago," she said. "She hasn't even changed her position."

"Do you expect Terrell back tonight?" Edmund asked her.

"I don't know what to expect of Terrell anymore." She turned to him, her face still glowing in the candle flame. She looked as vulnerable and in need of solace as a frightened child, and the urge to reach out to her and draw her head against his chest was so forceful that Edmund felt that in resisting it he was defying an imperative of nature.

"I'm so confused," she told him. "I'm so unhappy."

"I know. It has been a very difficult day for you."

"Please touch me," she whispered. "Just for a moment. Just touch my cheek with your hand."

He did as she asked. Her skin was cool, and setting his hand upon it felt to him like a startling act of intimacy, even of trespass. He could feel the minute, invisible hairs along her jawline. His thumb brushed against the impossibly tender flesh of her lower lip, and when it did she compressed her mouth lightly into what may have been a kiss. And then she smiled, took hold of his wrist, and gently pulled his hand away.

"You are leaving tomorrow, then?" she asked.

"Yes."

"Then I will be sure to send you off with a proper breakfast. Good night, Edmund."

She blew out the candle—careful to save the precious tallow—and walked into the dwelling house.

Edmund was too agitated to go to bed himself. He picked up his chair from the dogtrot and carried it across the yard to the edge of the river terrace, where he could hear the sound of the water running in its channel and the tree branches creaking overhead as the wind fanned through the leaves. He buttoned his jacket and tried to concentrate his thinking on matters of immediate and vital concern: rescuing his collections, relocating them if necessary, organizing his expedition in time for the spring. But these thoughts seemed to evaporate from his mind as soon as he proposed them, and in their place insistently appeared all the things he meant not to think about: the strange unborn creature, small as a mouse, with its looming, featureless head and paddle-shaped limbs, that he had buried this morning in the tea towel; or the feel of Mary Mott's skin under his hand, and the pressure of her lips upon his thumb.

He was mentally attempting to sort through his specimens from the prairies west of the Brazos—*Euphorbia corollata, Cassia chamaecrista, Eryngium aquaticum,* and so on—when he heard footsteps on dry leaves and turned in his chair to see a girl's dark form wandering between the house and the river in a cotton shift. She was barefoot and her hair was untied and matted from her writhing on the dirt floor of the jacal. It was Edna Foley.

"Hello," he called to her. "You mustn't be out. There is a chill, and you're still weak."

The girl turned her eyes to the sound of his voice.

"Who are you?" she said.

"My name is Edmund McGowan. Are you walking in your sleep?"

"I heard the Blessed Mother calling me. Was she calling you too? Is that why you're here?"

"No."

"Will you take me to see her? Do you have a wagon I could ride in?"

He stood up and touched the girl's elbow.

"Come with me," he said. "I'll take you to your house and you can go back to bed."

"No, she wants to see me."

"You are walking in your sleep."

"No, no, no," she whimpered, but did not pull away from his touch. "'Tis awake I am. I see you. I see everything. How can I be asleep? Where is Terrell, then?"

"He is away. He hasn't come home."

"Does he know about it?"

"About what?"

"The baby."

"I believe he does. Come with me now."

He led her back along the path lined with fossil stones. She did not resist him. Her face and manner were numb, compliant, dazed. Teresa heard them coming as they approached the jacal and stood at the door, waiting.

"See that she goes back to bed," Edmund said to her in Spanish. Before he turned to leave, he felt Edna's forehead for fever. It was cool. As he was walking away, the confused girl called out to him.

"I saw it," she said. "Everyone thought I didn't see it, but I did."

"What did you see?" he asked.

"I saw what came out of my body. What the devil had put in there to grow."

Edmund was too startled to respond.

"You took it away, didn't you?" she said.

"Yes."

"Are you an angel, then?"

"No, child. Go to sleep now."

The girl allowed Teresa to lead her back into the jacal. Edmund replaced his chair on the porch, then went into the public house and stretched out under his blankets and tried to will himself into sleep. But he merely lay there listening to the calls of night birds and watching the faint silvery light that leaked in through the shooting holes. Every time his restless mind began to sink into the pool of sleep it suddenly bounced away again like a skipping stone. But to his surprise, just before daylight, he found himself being aroused from a slumber he had not known he had achieved. Professor was whimpering outside his door, and when Edmund opened it he found his normally composed and indifferent dog in a state of high agitation, whining and lifting his nose to the wind and looking at Edmund for some sign of assent.

Edmund pulled on his shoes, took up his shotgun, and nodded to the dog. Professor ran barking past the stable, following the sloping ground upriver. Edmund thought about saddling Cabezon, but something told him the trouble, whatever it was, was nearby. Trotting past the stable, he realized the horses and mules were aware of it as well. He heard them huffing nervously in their stalls.

He could see the sun rising, fierce and naked, through the tangled oak limbs to the east. Ground fog clung to the grasses beneath his feet, and the calls of mourning doves reverberated through the cold air. Edmund felt heavy as he ran uphill, his breath wild and unregulated, his soul sluggish with fear. The rising sun sent a harsh wave of light across the predawn grayness of the landscape, and Edmund tilted his head so that the brim of his hat would shield his eyes.

He ran for perhaps a half-mile, following an old deer trail through brittle grass and dense brush. Professor stayed ahead of him by a hundred yards, and as he was just about to disappear from sight over the crest of a low hill Edmund called him back, and the dog reluctantly retreated a few paces in his direction, but then defiantly took off again before Edmund could catch up to him.

As soon as Professor vanished over the hill he began howling and barking in an uncontainable manner. Edmund stopped, took a moment to scan the hilltop and cock his shotgun, and then advanced again with a mounting feeling of unease, trying to clear his ears of Professor's maddened yelping and concentrate instead on what his eyes might find revealed beyond the summit of the hill.

He saw what looked to him a lake of blood, unnaturally sharp and vivid in the heightened morning light. It fanned out from the body of the girl for perhaps twenty yards before pooling in the gnarled and exposed root system of a solitary live oak. Wolves had crowded in around the roots to lap the blood or lick it off the grass. Edmund had never shot a creature in anger in his life, but he levelled his shotgun at one of the wolves that was tugging at the body. He pulled the trigger with a terrible hatred, and the animal cartwheeled back into the grass, yelping and snapping at the air as it died.

The other wolves fled fluidly away. Professor started to chase after them, but Edmund yelled, "Stay still!" in the harshest tone he had ever used with the dog. Professor held up immediately and sat down on his haunches, squirming in confusion and excitement, looking back at Edmund as if some explanation were forthcoming.

"Stay!" Edmund said again to the dog. He reloaded the shotgun in case the wolves came back or the vultures that were coasting vigilantly overhead decided to descend. Then he walked over to where Edna Foley lay on her back with her eyes staring flatly up into the sky.

She had stabbed herself to death. One hand still fiercely gripped the handle of the butcher knife embedded beneath her ribs, and there was a quantity of less lethal gashes all along the front of her blood-saturated dress. The smell of blood was so nightmarishly pungent that for a moment Edmund felt himself unable to breathe. He set down his shotgun and walked a few yards away and got down on his hands and knees to vomit. Looking up from the ground, he found himself staring into the eyes of a bold wolf that was skulking back toward the body. But as soon as he moved his hand toward the shotgun the wolf disappeared.

He stood again and stared down at the girl. He had no doubt that she had done it to herself, chaotically stabbing and slashing, hitting bone, missing the vital spots, screaming in pain and wild fear but all the while listening to some voice tell her to do it again and again until she managed to destroy one of the great vessels that fed her heart. He could see it all with grotesque clarity in his mind, could see the evidence with his eyes, but he still could scarcely understand that such an act was possible.

He looked down at her face, at her open eyes and open mouth, the lips drawn back against the teeth as if she had died in the act of taking an arduous breath. He did not know what to do. He noticed his hands were shaking, and not just slightly. Ashamed, he bit into the heel of his right hand to shock it back into composure, and then sat down and tried to think.

Somehow he would have to take her back. It was not all that far to carry her but he hated the thought of shocking Mary Mott by staggering up to the inn with the girl's bloody corpse in his arms. He would prefer to walk down to the stable for his mule, but that would mean leaving Edna's body here with the wolves, and that he could not do.

He was bending down to pick her up when he heard Mary calling his name and then saw her and Fresada appear at the top of the hill. She opened her mouth to scream when she saw the body, but no sound came. The blood drained away from her face, leaving a blank white mask.

"It would serve no purpose for you to come any closer," Edmund told her.

But she walked forward anyway, and stared down at the girl. She took hold of Edmund's elbow with both her hands and squeezed hard.

"Dear Lord," she said. "Oh, dear Lord."

"This is how I found her," he said.

Mary stared at the body for a moment more, then let go of his arm and walked a few steps away. In a moment she looked over at the dead wolf.

"Did you kill this wolf?" she asked Edmund.

"Yes."

"We heard your gun. I knew something bad had happened. I thought that perhaps—"

She stopped speaking and anxiously scanned the empty prairie.

"Where is Terrell?" she asked Edmund. "Have you seen him? Did he ever come back last night?"

"I don't think so."

"He wasn't with her when this happened! He couldn't have been!"

"No, Mary, of course not. She was alone. She did it to herself."

"I'll get a horse," Fresada said in a moment. "And a blanket to wrap her in."

He turned and walked heavily down the hill. Edmund could see the inn in the distance, and thin smoke from the chimney that was hardly more substantial than the vaporous early-morning fog that drifted in off the river.

"Are you cold?" he asked Mary as they stood there in grim silence, waiting for Fresada to return.

"She was walking about last night," Edmund said, when Mary did not answer. "Sleepwalking, as I thought. She seemed to believe that the baby had been the devil's child. I took her back to her jacal. I should have been more vigilant, but I could not have imagined that—"

"Of course not," Mary said. "No one could have imagined such a thing. She used to tell me that she spoke to the Virgin. I think this is where their meetings took place. It must have been the Virgin who told her to do this to herself.

"Do you think she is with God now, Edmund?" Mary asked. Her teeth chattered as she spoke.

IT WAS close to noon when Terrell returned. He had spent most of the previous day aimlessly riding along the bayshore. He told himself he was hunting, but except for a squirrel he shot for his supper he killed nothing all day, and spent the night wrapped in a blanket beneath a tree and staring into a driftwood fire he'd assembled with elaborate care, having no other task to occupy him. The squirrel had not been enough to eat, but hunger and privation suited his mood. What should he do now? he had wondered. His mother thought that Edna's unborn child had been his, and though he knew it had been conceived on that night of the Mexican soldiers he had no urge to convince her of the truth. Let her think what she wanted. He had no interest anymore in cultivating his mother's opinion of him. So much had happened to him in the last few months that he felt as if he had leapt across a divide, and that returning to his previous cast of mind would not be just a step into the past but a step into oblivion.

He was light-headed with hunger and lack of sleep when he rode home. There was no one in sight, though it was laundry day and he had prepared himself to encounter his mother at work in the yard. Professor trotted over to greet him as he arrived, which meant that Mr. McGowan had not yet left for Béxar. Terrell started to lead Veronica to the stable, but the unusual stillness, the absence of his mother or Fresada or Teresa, made him suddenly apprehensive. He wrapped the mare's reins around the rail in front of the public house and walked to the dwelling house, more convinced with each step that something was wrong.

Probably his mother was just sitting in the house waiting for him, waiting to rebuke him once again for his craven nature and his base appetites. But the day and a night he had just passed in solitary deliberation made him feel stronger than otherwise. He had made up his mind that no matter what his mother said to him he would not answer beyond a civil word or two. He would climb into his bed and go to sleep, and leave everything until tomorrow to be sorted out. And then tomorrow or the day after he would ride to join the army at Béxar, where he should have been long ago.

But when he opened the door of the house he saw the unclothed body of Edna Foley lying on a board, and a sudden weakness came to his legs, and he staggered to the floor.

"Oh, Terrell!" Mary cried. She put down the cloth with which she had been washing the body and rushed to help him stand, but he was already on his feet again, and he pushed her hand away. He gaped in disbelief at the girl's naked corpse as Teresa pulled a blanket over it, leaving the dead and bewildered face exposed.

"What—" he said.

"She killed herself, Terrell," his mother said. "We found her this morning."

She tried to grasp her son, but he was already backing away from her out the door.

"Terrell, darling. Wait."

But he didn't respond. The strength was back in his legs, and he could feel the blood moving through his limbs in an uncontainable surge as he made his way to the rail where Veronica was tied.

"Terrell! Stop!" his mother cried. She was clinging to him as he walked.

"Let me go!" he shouted, without meeting her eyes. "Let me go, Mother! Now!"

He shoved her away from him, untied Veronica's reins, and mounted the weary horse.

"Where are you going?" she pleaded with him. "At least tell me that, Terrell."

"To Béxar," he said, and kicked the mare forward without looking again at his mother's weeping face. On the way into Refugio he passed Fresada and Mr. McGowan, returning from the carpenter's with a coffin loaded into the cart, but he did not look at them either, merely took in their surprised gaze as he thundered past them, heading toward Béxar and the seat of the war.

CHAPTER SEVENTEEN

✦

E TOOK the Horse road toward Goliad and did not stop until he came to the banks of San Nicolás Creek, eight or ten miles away. He held on to Veronica's reins while she drank, though the horse was too tired and hungry to wander far. Terrell drank as well, repeatedly dipping his tin cup into the creek. The water was cold and flowed in sheets across the flat stone bed of the crossing. A black snake glided along the surface on the opposite bank, barely penetrating the veil of water beneath it.

He removed the heavy quadralpas saddle from Veronica's back and let the poor exhausted mare rest for a while, though Terrell himself felt that if he had to stay idle for longer than ten minutes the panicky energy in his body would poison him. He looped a rope around Veronica's neck and tied it to a tree branch, then walked up and down the bank, fingering his madstone, forcing his thoughts forward in order to stay sane. He would need food and rest. It was not reasonable to suppose he could ride all the way to Béxar in this condition. Goliad was twenty miles farther on. He had no money, but he thought he could sell the saddle if he had to or give it in trade for a night's lodging and provisions for his journey. Béxar was west of Goliad, ninety or so miles away on the far frontier. He had never been there, but he knew it was an old Spanish mission town, far older than most of the towns in Texas that had been settled in the last few years by American and Irish colonists. He supposed the road there was decent, and well enough marked so that he would not lose his way. The siege could

not last forever. Sooner or later the rebels would try to take
the town, and the thought of that happening without him
filled Terrell's frenzied mind with alarm.

After half an hour, he threw the saddle back on the horse
and rode on. He passed cattle from one of the Tejano ranchos grazing on the mesquite grass, but he saw no vaqueros, nor anyone else on the road until he was within a few
miles of Goliad and he could see the fortified mission
standing by itself on a hilltop above the roofs of the town.

Two men came riding up to him out of the trees. One of
them carried a rifle and had a pistol in his sash. The other
had a shotgun and a short Spanish sword.

"What's your business, pard?" the one with the rifle
asked. He had a coarse American accent, and Terrell supposed he was one of the volunteers from the States that had
been streaming into Texas ever since word got out that the
Texas colonists had risen up against Cos.

"I'm going to Béxar," Terrell said.

"You got orders to go to Béxar?"

"I don't need orders to go anywhere. I ain't in the army."

"If you ain't in the army we can press that mare of
yours," the man with the shotgun said. "Saddle too. We can
have your whole outfit if we want it, and if you try to stop
us by God we'll beat you all hollow."

But he said this in such an oddly conversational tone that
Terrell didn't perceive it as a threat. The man shifted his
shotgun to the crook of his arm and began to bite a callus
off his thumb.

"You know where Jim Bowie is?" Terrell said.

"We don't know where the fuck anybody is, pard," the
man with the rifle answered. "And if we did we wouldn't
tell you, because nobody knows who the fuck you are. You
come on with us into town. If Colonel Dimmit decides not to
shoot you for a Mexican spy, maybe you'll get some dinner."

Terrell never saw Colonel Dimmit, though he waited
outside his headquarters at the old Spanish presidio for

more than an hour while two soldiers stood guard over him as if he were a prisoner. The guards were amiable enough, but Terrell was in such a sullen and distant mood that they soon stopped trying to make conversation with him. He sat cross-legged on the ground, shivering in the cold air, and watched a company of volunteers drilling on the parade ground of the old presidio while an officer stood apart thumbing through a little book of infantry tactics.

Terrell was so hungry he thought he might faint, but his pride kept him from asking the guards for food. After another hour of waiting for Colonel Dimmit to appear, his vision began to dance, and he thought he saw faces emerging from the rough stone wall of the chapel. When a monstrous old snapping turtle began lumbering across the parade ground he thought he was imagining that too. The turtle had an aggrieved expression like an old man and dragged a tail that seemed to Terrell to have the girth and length of his own forearm. The drilling volunteers, who were trying to form themselves into a square, began to laugh as the creature labored past them, and they called out to it as if to a familiar.

"What is that?" Terrell asked one of the guards, his curiosity finally rousing him from his angry silence.

"Well sir, that's Mr. George Robicheaux," the guard said as he gnawed off a bite from a twist of tobacco with his side teeth. All his front teeth were gone.

"No, I mean that turtle."

"That's who I'm talking about, son. That turtle's name is Mr. George Robicheaux. We had a company of volunteers here for a while from New Orleans. The New Orleans Greys. They had their own fancy uniforms, their own flag, hell, they even had damn canteens just alike. And they had that there snapper as a mascot. They carried him all this way in a tub of water, but when they got sent on to Béxar a few weeks ago they decided they'd had enough of hauling Mr. Robicheaux across Texas and left him here with us."

"He could eat a whole chicken in one gulp if you'd let him," the other guard said.

A man in a chewed-up planter's hat and a sword ambled over and walked into the headquarters. It was the first person Terrell had seen enter or leave the place since he had been sitting there.

"Is that Colonel Dimmit?" Terrell asked.

"Don't you worry about who's Colonel Dimmit and who's not," the guard with the missing teeth said.

Just then the man in the planter's hat came out of the door holding a rolled-up map.

"If you fellas are waiting for Dimmit, you're in a bad way," he said.

"He ain't in there?"

"He ain't been in there all day. He's over in town holding a court of inquiry about who owns all that smuggled tobacco they found at the customshouse. And when he's through with the court of inquiry I'd bet my bonnet he'll go on and have his supper."

"That's it for me," Terrell said. He stood up, but was so light-headed that for a moment everything turned black and he had to fight to stay conscious and standing. Then he started to walk across the parade ground.

"Where are you going?" the guard said.

"To find my horse."

"You won't have much luck finding your horse with a ball in your head."

"I'd just as soon you shoot me as waste my time like you've been doing," Terrell said, without looking back. He heard a rifle being cocked but he kept walking, and no shot came. Instead, the two guards came running up, and each one grabbed one of his arms. Terrell tried to shake them off, but they were both big men and they had him tight, and in the process of struggling all he managed to do was accidentally bump heads with one of them.

"Let go of that boy!" he heard a familiar voice call out, and when the guards complied he turned and saw John Dunn walking hurriedly toward them across the parade ground.

"He tried to escape," the man with the missing teeth said.

"If he was trying to escape from you, Ratliff, he was demonstrating uncommon good taste in the company he chooses to keep. Now you men go on about your business. I'll vouch for Terrell Mott not being an enemy agent."

Mr. Dunn, noting Terrell's famished appearance, led him out of the presidio and down into the town. They passed a detachment of volunteers digging a ditch from the presidio to the nearby river, and then a series of boarded-up stone houses belonging to the wealthier Mexican families who, Mr. Dunn explained in his jabbering way, had mostly retired to their ranchos to wait out the results of the war rather than hazard their fortunes in a fight against their powerful invading kinsmen. Beyond the stone houses, in the poorer districts of the town, were jacales whose veneers of whitewashed plaster reflected the afternoon sun with a blinding intensity that made Terrell, in his light-headed condition, feel as if he were walking through a corridor of mirrors.

He followed Dunn across a plank spanning an eroded street and into a little fonda where they were the only patrons except for a young Tejano man with long, flowing hair, dressed in a fancy linen shirt, who sat there doing nothing, as if waiting for somebody to come in and admire him. Dunn greeted him heartily in Spanish, and the young man nodded indulgently in return.

"He's a tobacco smuggler," Dunn said after a ten-year-old boy had led them to a table and brought a platter of tortillas. "That was an excellent business for a while, but I'm afraid it's going the way of the mastodon, which is perhaps why our friend there is looking so portentous. No matter who wins this war, Texas will no longer be ignored. One nation or another will vigorously police it, and our fine smuggler's paradise will be no more."

The tortillas were soft and thick and still so warm from the comal that when Terrell bit into one steam rose into his mouth. He ate six or eight tortillas in rapid succession as Dunn ordered cabrito and a bottle of pulque.

"I don't have any money, Mr. Dunn," Terrell said, in a sudden embarrassed revelation.

"I have money in plenty," his host answered. "And there can be no higher use for it than to entertain the son of the indomitable Mrs. Mott. Especially when he is so gratifyingly hungry!"

Terrell braced himself for a barrage of questions that mercifully never came. Although Dunn asked about the welfare of Terrell's mother, he did not inquire too deeply as to what had brought her son to Goliad in such an agitated and ill-prepared state. He took Terrell's wish to join the army at Béxar at its face value, or at least pretended to. Perhaps this was out of kindness, or perhaps Mr. Dunn had simply grown used to not asking such questions, since it was widely known that most of the volunteers rushing into Texas were fleeing circumstances that they vigorously did not care to discuss.

"You should find no obstacles on the road to Béxar," Dunn said. "None, that is, except for Texian patrols—we're calling ourselves Texians now, by the way. Bowie is certain to be there, or at least in the vicinity, but down here we get very little reliable news. Austin is said to be on his way to the States to raise money. Houston, our noble commander in chief, is said to be drunk. He is always said to be drunk, of course, but they are saying it now with hushed conviction. Ah, here is our cabrito!"

Terrell ate ravenously, lifting the food to his mouth with trembling hands, while Dunn went off on a discourse about what fine eating the Mexicans were capable of—this infant goat as a case in point, grilled to perfection—and what a shame it was that all those volunteers from Kentucky and Tennessee sullenly looked down on the local cuisine. They would rather subsist for months on weevilly bread and salt pork than even consider sampling the food of their pepper-belly enemies.

Dunn stopped talking long enough to say good-bye to the tobacco smuggler, who had finally risen from his moody reverie and was walking out of the fonda with his oversize spurs clinking.

"Now, lad," Dunn resumed in a more serious tone as he gnawed on a cabrito rib, "tell me why you are going to Béxar."

"To get in the fight."

"Well, we all want to get into the fight, don't we? We've had the devil of a time keeping our boys here in Goliad when there is such a fine mob assembled in Béxar ready to attack the place at any moment if they could only agree among themselves who is in charge and how the thing should be done. But allow me to offer you a golden word of advice, Terrell. Stay here with us in Goliad. Join my company. Interesting things are afoot in this part of the realm. There is talk—serious talk by serious men—about an expedition to Matamoros. Now that would be a bold stroke, by God, to take the war out of the colonies and into the very heart of Mexico itself! You do not want to be mired down in Béxar when such an opportunity arises."

"I guess I'd rather just go on to Béxar," he replied.

Dunn looked him over with an examining eye.

"Are you all right, son?" he said at last. "Has something happened to you?"

"I ain't had much sleep is all."

Dunn let the matter drop. "You are most welcome to lodge with my company tonight in our barracks," he said, "and if you're still so keen to go in the morning you will go at least with a few pesos in your wallet. No, no, 'tis merely a loan, till the Army of the People takes you into its bosom."

Dunn lifted his glass and smiled broadly. "And then it's good luck to ye, Terrell, and may the saints preserve your lovely hide."

HE WAS two days on the road to Béxar. Once he encountered what he supposed to be a courier heading in the opposite direction toward Goliad, but the rider wouldn't speak to him or even bother to stop. He just held up a hand in an impatient greeting as he thundered down the road. Terrell thought the courier might be bringing Dimmit news of some important development in the siege. Maybe the battle was under way at last, maybe the town was already taken and the war won. But then he reasoned that couriers were probably sent up and down this road all the time, and that the presence of one galloping rider did not necessarily mean an urgent development in the fighting.

He saw no one else. No Mexican soldiers, to be sure, since all the men who had entered Texas with Cos were now bottled up in Béxar. Though he passed through several ranchos he saw no cattle, and he assumed the vaqueros had rounded them up to protect them against the ravening Texian army. Terrell had heard that the Tejanos in this part of the country were on the federalist side, ready to fight against Santa Anna and his centralist forces, but he didn't know if that was true or not. In any case the road was eerily vacant, and the blue river beside it shone brilliantly in the December sunlight. The weather was mild enough, though not warm, and he was grateful whenever the road veered away a little from the tree-lined river and out into the open sunshine.

He was so impatient to reach Béxar that he would have ridden through the night if there had been a moon. But the road was indistinct in places, and he was worried that he might lose his way in the darkness. He camped on a rocky plateau above the river. He did not make a fire, in case Indians might be nearby, and as he lay on his back all night with the cold wind on his face and the unfathomable stars overhead he felt so alone and despairing that it seemed to him he was the only soul left on the earth and that he would never again hear the sound of another human voice.

But he managed to sleep a few hours, during which he endured a series of dreams in which Edna Foley was frantically present. He was on the road again before the sun was high enough to dry the dew on the grass, or to warm his shivering body. He was not sure how far he was from Béxar, though Mr. Dunn had told him there was an old Spanish barracks at the Carvajal crossing on the Cibolo, and that when he came to it he would be about halfway. Dunn had assured him that the few Mexican presidials who had been stationed there had abandoned it, called to the defense of Béxar. It was inhabited now only by several families from the vicinity of Las Animas Creek, who had moved into the vacant buildings thinking they would provide better protection against the Comanches, who might begin raiding again under cover of the war.

Terrell came to the place late in the afternoon. It was an old fallen down wooden stockade whose barracks buildings had been taken over by Mexican families. At first nobody noticed him when he rode up. All the people in this minuscule village were clustered excitedly in the far corner of the compound, where a group of heavily armed Texian rebels were dragging a middle-aged man out of one of the jacales. The man's hands were tied behind his back, and he kept falling to his knees as the rebels hauled him across the dirt, with a group of crying children following behind and throwing rocks at the abductors.

Terrell searched the rebels for a familiar face and saw none until his eyes fell on Bowie, who was arguing heat-

edly in Spanish with a sobbing woman that Terrell took to
be the man's wife.

Terrell didn't know what to do, so he just sat there on his
horse until somebody noticed him in all the commotion.
The first person to do so was the only Tejano among the
rebels, a round-faced man in cut-off pantaloons with a
shredded cigar in his mouth.

In his surprise the man put a hand on the pistol in his belt.

"Don't pull that gun on me, mister," Terrell said. He had
his own thumb on the hammer of the Kentucky, and meant
to use it if he had to.

"Goddammit, Plácido," Bowie suddenly said, looking up
from the scuffle, "if you shoot that boy things are going to
get even uglier around here."

Bowie walked up to shake Terrell's hand. A five-year-old
girl threw a dirt clod at him, but he ignored it.

"How are you, Terrell?" he said heartily. "What are you
doing out here all by yourself?"

"Looking for the war."

"Well, by God, son, you've found it. You come on with
us. As soon as we get this gentleman on a horse we'll be on
our way."

Several of Bowie's men wrestled the captive Mexican
onto a horse and tied him to the saddle while the others
stood there pointing their guns at the angry villagers, who
continued to spit and hurl rocks, though so far none of
them had produced a serious weapon.

"I believe you're gettin' to be unpopular in this place,
Jim," one of the men said to Bowie as he mounted his
horse. Bowie only grinned like he was enjoying the abuse,
turned to Terrell and told him to follow along, and then they
all rode out of the old fort at a gallop as the angry screams
of the man's wife and children and neighbors faded away.

They rode for about five miles, backtracking along the
road and then branching off on a well-worn cattle trail that
Terrell guessed led to the heart of one of the mission ran-

chos. They finally stopped on the far side of a stony uplift and staked their horses near a grove of live oaks. Two of the men started to build a fire; some of the others dragged the prisoner off his horse and laid him down at the base of one of the trees, trussed up with rope. His eyes were darting from one man to another in panic, but Terrell tried not to look at him.

"I'd like you men to meet a friend of mine," Bowie announced, and he introduced Terrell to each one of the men under his command. They shook his hand in an open fashion, as Bowie praised his mother and told them of her ferocity during the Karankawa attack. Bowie's convivial mood and the welcoming friendliness of his men contrasted so sharply with the terror of the man tied up beneath the tree that Terrell did not know how to respond except with a blank, uncertain smile.

"Now as for out quest here," Bowie said, "he's got some information that we want. We're looking for some dragoons that Cos sent out of Béxar on a scout, and we were told that this man knows where we can find them. Trouble is, how do we convince him to tell us?"

"We could cut his balls off," said one of the Texians.

"No, I'm not one to interfere with a man's sacred parts," Bowie said. "Let's give him a few hours to think about it. Maybe he'll just decide to tell us out of courtesy. Have you got yourself a cup, Terrell?"

"Yes, sir."

"Good. Then you can join us for coffee. I always tell my men you can soldier without a gun easier than you can soldier without a cup."

The coffee was watery and bitter, but it was real coffee nonetheless, which Bowie said he had liberated from an officer of a Mexican column he and his men had recently attacked on Alazan Creek. Terrell listened as the men reminisced and joked with each other about that fight. They had been convinced that the mules in the column were loaded down with silver, but after a hot skirmish that lasted the better part of the day they discovered that the packs the mules carried contained only grass.

"There were some long faces amongst us when we opened those packs," a man named Roth said.

"Why grass?" Terrell asked.

"Because we've had Cos shut up in that town for so long he's running out of feed for his horses," Bowie explained. "So he had to send out his dragoons to get some. Grass is worth more than silver to him right now."

"It ain't to me," one of the other men said.

The men then fell into a heated discussion about the siege, complaining about how poorly it had been managed, first by General Austin and then, after his departure, by General Burleson.

"I'll tell you one thing right now," Roth said. "If they'd had a fair election after Austin left we'd have Jim Bowie in charge, and the town would be ours by now, and Cos would be on his way home to Santa Anna with his fucking tail between his legs."

Terrell listened as the men thundered away on this grievance. They seemed to believe that the election had been stolen from Bowie, though exactly why this was so was unclear—something to do with the deviousness and cowardice of Austin, the paralyzing lack of nerve in the army in general, and the fact that, Terrell gathered, Bowie had been dead drunk during the election process.

While they talked Terrell kept stealing glances at the prisoner, who was lying on his back with his hands tied behind him, looking up at the sky as if waiting for something to appear out of the clouds and rescue him. The man kept grunting and shifting his weight. His breathing seemed heavy.

"I think his hands are hurting him," Terrell said to Bowie. "They're digging into his back."

Bowie looked at the man, thought for a minute, then drained his coffee cup and stood.

"You got that rope, Plácido?" he said to Benavides. "Let's see if we can get our friend's attention."

Terrell watched with a gnawing sense of dread as Benavides produced a rope and began crafting a noose at one end.

"I don't like this," Terrell was glad to hear one of the other men say. "I don't approve of it."

"I ain't asking you to," Bowie replied. "just stand out of the way if it offends your principles."

Terrell watched the man consider. For a moment, there seemed to be a possibility he might try to stop Bowie, but then he thought better of it and walked off into the trees.

"Don't worry, Terrell," Bowie said, perhaps catching the anxious look on the boy's face. "We ain't going to hang him. Just stretch his neck an inch or two."

Benavides placed the noose around the whimpering man's neck and threw the other end of the rope over a stout limb of the live oak under which the prisoner lay. Three of the men grabbed it as it cleared the limb and pulled it till it was almost taut, and Bowie almost cordially helped the man to his feet.

"Dígame, amigo," Terrell heard him say to the man. "Dónde están los soldados? Dónde están los caballos?"

Terrell understood that much, but the man spoke too fast, and with too much convulsive sobbing, for Terrell to follow any of the Spanish words that came flooding out of his mouth in reply.

"What's he saying?" a man named Sparks asked Bowie.

"Oh, about what you'd expect. He *thinks* he may have seen a few dragoons way off in the distance two or three days ago, but his eyesight's so bad these days he can't be sure. That's a load of shit for sure. I'll bet you my grandmere's fine china that those dragoons rode into his village, and he led them to some pasture somewhere close by, and that's where they are right now.

"All right, gentlemen," Bowie said to the men holding the other end of the rope, "let's put him up on his tiptoes."

The men pulled on the rope, the Mexican felt the noose tightening around his neck and opened his mouth to plead, but before any words could come out he was already in the air, the ends of his sandals kicking the dirt and the swollen whites of his eyes starting to bulge out of his head. Terrell was close enough to hear the strange mechanical-sounding wheeze that was the result of the man's breath being choked off in his throat.

"How long do you reckon he can stay up there like that without dying on us?" Roth wanted to know.

"Oh, let's give him to the count of ten or so," Bowie answered.

Terrell took a step or two back, and looked at the ground in disgust and confusion. He thought about running forward and grabbing the rope from the hands of the men who held it, and easing the suffering man to the ground on his own authority. But he knew he lacked the resolve and the moral confidence to do any such thing. All the confidence belonged to Bowie, who was torturing this man with such a characteristic ease of manner that any objection would seem simply peculiar.

It seemed to Terrell more like a full minute before Bowie finally told the men to slacken the rope and the prisoner collapsed onto the earth, gulping for air like a dying fish while the blood slowly drained from his engorged head. Bowie leaned down and spoke to him in a quiet, intimate, reasoned voice, as the man choked and sobbed and shook his head, still pleading ignorance.

"We'll give him a few minutes to collect himself," Bowie genially announced, "then I guess we'll hoist him again."

He walked over to a nearby limestone rock and took a seat with his back toward the gasping prisoner, looking out over the winter prairie. The sun was low on the horizon now, just touching the tops of the trees on a high swell of ground in the distance. Bowie pulled off one of his riding boots, shook it out, and snaked his hand down inside, looking for rocks. He made a point of taking his time, then he pulled the boot back on, stood up, and spoke to the men standing by the rope.

"All right, boys, let's try again."

Terrell caught the disbelieving look in the man's eyes as he was lifted up again. This time it seemed to last even longer, and when he was lowered back to the earth he was allowed to remain there for only a few moments until Bowie ordered him strung up again.

Afterward he lay on his back wheezing and sobbing, with all the skin on his neck trussed up grotesquely under his chin, and his face as swollen as a frog's.

"Why don't you talk to him this time, Plácido?" Bowie said, and they all waited as Benavides leaned down and spoke to the man in Spanish, his manner harsher and more insistent than Bowie's had been. Sprawled on the ground, the noose still around his neck and his hands still tied behind his back, the man nodded pitiably as tears and snot dropped from his face onto the dirt.

Terrell noticed that several of the other men looked away, though whether out of disgust or disquiet or simple indifference he could not say. Finally, after a long silence, the prisoner began to speak.

Bowie immediately walked over and crouched beside him, and as the man told what he knew he looked up at Bowie with an expression of sad relief on his face, as if he had forgotten that Bowie was his torturer and now believed he was a trusted confidante. And Bowie was shrewd enough to play that part. When he had taken the man's confession he removed the noose from his neck and gave him a reassuring pat on the back that, to Terrell's astonishment, turned into a hearty embrace of reconciliation.

"Gracias, mi amigo," Bowie told him. "Mil gracias."

"The dragoons are over on Leon Creek," Bowie announced to the men with a grin on his face. "We'll go after them first thing in the morning."

"What are we going to do with him?" Roth asked, nodding toward the prisoner.

"I think it'd be prudent to keep him with us for the night. We'll let him go when we ride out. He shouldn't have any trouble finding his way back."

"I think it'd be prudent to shoot the sonofabitch," Sparks said. He was tall and redheaded and half-bald and wore a fancy calico hunting shirt.

"No, Sparks, I think I'll give him some dinner and let him go. Wouldn't want him to think ill of us."

They ate a meager meal that night of salt beef and crackers, Bowie insisting that the Mexican have a share. Afterward, when they had talked some more about the siege and about the treachery of their fellow rebels, they all turned economically to bed. Sparks sat away from the others, enduring their ridicule while he exhausted himself by blowing into a nozzle, slowly inflating a portable bed made of Indian rubber.

"Are you in a mood to capture some Mexican horses tomorrow?" Bowie asked as Terrell was spreading his blankets.

"I guess so," Terrell answered. In the past Bowie's powerful hand on his shoulder had felt like a friendly benediction, but now he detected a subtle coercion in the gesture that made him not just uncomfortable but afraid.

"Good," Bowie said, with a thin-lipped grin. "When we join up with the rest of the army we'll find you some enlistment papers. In the meantime, you can consider yourself a member of my company. Plácido here will wake you up for guard duty."

And a few hours before dawn he felt Benavides's hands shaking him, waking him from a consoling dream that evaporated like a rainbow the moment he opened his eyes.

The night had grown colder, and the fire had been allowed to burn down to a few gleaming coals.

"What am I supposed to do?" he asked Benavides.

"Watch the prisoner. And stay awake and listen," he replied. "Sit on that rock over there. It's a good place."

Terrell wrapped himself tightly in his blankets and put on his shoes and walked over to the rock. The ground cold had seeped into his body, and he could not stop shivering. He watched Benavides crawl under his blanket, and it was not long until his snoring joined that of the other men. The Mexican prisoner still lay with his hands tied behind his back. He had no covering, nothing to protect him from the cold wind except his thin cotton shirt. And he was awake. Terrell could see the whites of his eyes shining in the moonlight as he stared straight up at the night sky.

After a while Terrell pulled one of the blankets off his shoulders and walked over to the Mexican and laid it on top of him.

"Gracias," the man said.

"De nada."

And then the prisoner continued to talk, mistakenly believing that Terrell knew more than a phrase or two of Spanish. When he saw Terrell's blank look, he was silent again, and Terrell went back to sit on his rock and wait for the dawn to warm him.

CHAPTER EIGHTEEN

✳

MARY SENT WORD to Edna's uncles, informing them of their niece's death and of her own intention to see to the details and expenses of the girl's burial. The uncles did not object. They rode into town on the morning of the service, and stood there holding their hats as Edna's unsanctified body was lowered into the ground in front of the old mission. After the varying torments of the last few days, Mary's primary emotion as she watched the coffin disappear into the earth was a seething anger. She felt contempt for these weak and selfish men who had been Edna's closest earthly relations, and an unsettling hostility toward the members of the ayuntamiento, who had presumed to engage her in debate on abstruse points of Catholic theology before they would allow Edna to be buried in the campo santo. In the end, she had worn them down, had—she hoped—shamed them. What kind of God was this, she demanded to know, who would create such a tormented girl in the first place, and then deny her even the comfort of a grave when she could no more triumph over her own confused nature than she could fly like a bird?

And so her burial had taken place in holy ground, with the mourning left to Mary, and the two uncles standing there with the placid indifference of official witnesses. Afterward they had climbed onto their cart and ridden off without a word of thanks to her, nor with any request for further information; the bare explanation of Edna's death that Mary had included in her letter seemed quite enough for them.

"I am going with you to Béxar," she startled Edmund by announcing as they rode back to the inn in her cart.

He was lost for a moment in brooding silence.

"I understand your anxiety," he said at last. "But travelling just now to Béxar—travelling into the eye of the storm, so to speak—is a poor solution to your problem."

"And what do you suppose my problem is, Edmund?"

"Well," he answered, "you are fretful about Terrell's welfare."

"That is not a problem. That is an emotion. My problem is that my son has gone off to this insane war believing that his mother has judged and condemned him for causing that girl's death. He thinks I have withdrawn my love from him."

"Surely he thinks no such thing."

"I saw the look in his eyes, Edmund, when he walked in on us when we were washing her body. I saw in his eyes that he thought I had somehow cast him out of my heart."

"If I may say so without offending you, you are being dramatic."

"I am being supremely practical. If Terrell is killed in the war, if he dies thinking he has lost his mother's love, then I will live the rest of my life in a state of mental torture."

Tears came to her eyes, but her heart was solid with resolve. She had made herself a goal, and the thought of reaching that goal was the only thing that gave her any relief from the quavering dread that had enveloped her for the past few days.

"I had planned to leave within a few hours," Edmund said finally.

"The sooner the better," she said. "He's already been gone for three days."

And so by two o'clock that afternoon they left, Mary riding a buckskin gelding that Andrew had bought not long after they had come to Texas and named Gar for his long, bony head. She left behind her bonnet and replaced it with a man's wide-brimmed planter's hat that she tied under her chin with a scarf. She wore her riding skirt and Andrew's thick wool jacket with a quilted collar that she could turn up against the cold. She tied a sash tightly around her waist to use as a pistol belt. The butt of the pistol pinched the skin over her hipbone, but she was willing to put up with the discomfort for the feeling of security it gave her. Edmund tied her Spanish musket, cartridge box, and clothes satchel to his pack mule, along with a tent square of waxed canvas that she and Andrew had last used when they camped on the beach after their desperate passage from New Orleans.

They rode side by side on the road to Goliad, with the mule trailing behind and Professor ranging ahead with such a wild joyfulness that it was as if he were discovering the world anew. She found it strange to be riding next to a man across open country; it felt illicit in a way she could not quite identify. Cabezon and Gar were, in the mute, mysterious protocols of horses, agreeable to one another, and they kept pace in a way that would have made for easy conversation between their riders, had easy conversation been on either of their minds. In fact, both were sunk in silent anxiety—Mary for her son, Edmund for his collections—and after a few miles of strained observations about the landscape they tended not to say a great deal.

Once or twice Mary hummed a little snatch of a song, until she remembered the weight tugging at her heart and let the cancelled notes drift off into the air.

Some miles before they reached Goliad, Edmund reined Cabezon to a halt and turned to Mary. The wind had been blowing incessantly, and his lips were chapped, and there was windburn on the planes of his face.

"Shall we get off our horses for a moment and have a consultation?" he said.

Seeing that they were dismounted, Professor came trotting back to them as if they had called him in for his opinion. Mary walked in circles in the grass, trying to work the saddle cramps out of her muscles, and feeling the press of her bladder.

"What is it that you want to consult about?" she said.

"There is a trace up ahead, a cattle trail really, that we can use as a cutoff to avoid Goliad."

"Why should we avoid Goliad?"

"Because the town is garrisoned, and for all we know martial law has been declared. They might try to press our horses, or our weapons."

"But Terrell might be in Goliad."

"Possibly so, though I think it more likely that he's already in Béxar."

Mary remembered the heedless look on her son's face when he had ridden away from the inn. It seemed to her that he was searching for the war as if for a vortex to drown himself in, and the war just now was in Béxar. And in searching for him, she was of the same heedless spirit. The idea of being detained in Goliad for even a day was an oppressive thought to her.

"I agree," she said to Edmund. "Let's take the cutoff. But first I must excuse myself and disappear from your sight behind that rise."

Edmund nodded gratefully, for he had the same pressing complaint. When she was out of sight he unbuttoned his pantaloons and pissed on the dry mesquite grass. He prayed that in the awkward days to come she would continue to take the lead in such topics, because the thought of him confiding such a base necessity to her—no matter how roundaboutly he phrased it—was a matter of graver concern to him than having his horse stolen by the rebel army.

The cutoff led through a confusing welter of cattle and game trails, but the country was open enough that Edmund had no worries about getting lost as long as they could strike the Béxar road before dark. They rode through a stretch of hog-wallow prairie, where scattered declivities in the grass took on a peculiar allure as the shadows lengthened, reminding Edmund of a fanciful illustration he had once seen of a cratered valley on the moon's surface. Beyond the hog wallows the prairie resumed its featureless splendor, the grasses so high that the spent seedheads brushed against the bellies of their horses. As the light continued to fade the canopies of the isolated oak mottes grew so dark against the pale grass that they looked inverted, as if they were not stands of tall trees but deep pits that led from the tawny prairie to the blackest depths of the earth.

They struck the road an hour before the light gave out, and rode on a few more miles toward Béxar. There was a well-known camping place in a bend of the river—a hardwood meadow as glady as a park, with a fine spring seeping out of a rocky grotto—where Edmund had often passed the night on botanizing expeditions. But when he and Mary passed through the place as the sun was setting he saw too many signs of recent habitation—banks of ashes with squirrel bones nearby, cartridge paper, droppings both equine and human—to feel comfortable about setting up camp. So they continued for another two or three miles until they wandered off the road into a lush bottomland much to Edmund's liking, with splendid walnut trees catching the day's last light in their yellowing leaves.

They unpacked and hobbled the animals, and after much experimentation succeeded in erecting Mary's square of canvas so that it resembled something like a tent. For dinner they fried bacon in a skillet and then made fritters in the grease with the cornmeal Mary had packed. And though Edmund felt unaccountably nervous about the fire, he kept it going, both as a source of warmth and as a device that somehow made the silence between them seem more contemplative than strained.

"We are here in the wilderness together," she said at last in a sharp tone. "We might as well speak. Are you still angry at me for inviting myself along?"

"I was never angry. Only concerned about your well-being."

She stared into the flames, as if looking there for instruction in framing her thoughts. Edmund noticed that in the firelight her face was as unlined as a girl's.

"Have I been an impediment so far?"

"Of course not."

"But I make you nervous."

"Not in the least."

"All women make you nervous, I think. Why that should be, I haven't reckoned out yet."

"There are certainly more compelling subjects for your speculations."

"Yes," she said, smiling for the first time that day, "there certainly are. But they are all too grim. Why have you never married?"

"It never occurred to me to do so."

"Are you hostile to companionship?"

"I have tried to be indifferent to it."

"Why?"

"Because my work so often requires . . . so much of me. And I have found that once people begin to dwell on any form of privation—hunger, or thirst, or loneliness—they can no longer concentrate with any effectiveness on the task before them."

"I keep receiving the impression from you that we human beings are an especially tedious race."

He smiled, though not quite openly enough to suit her.

"What will you do after you see your son?" he asked.

"I hadn't thought that far ahead," she responded. "I suppose I will simply turn around and go home to Refugio and pray that the war doesn't take him."

"You will have come a long way to say a few simple words."

"Do you think my business is in any way less urgent than

yours, Edmund? Don't you routinely go a long way just to observe a weed growing up from the ground?"

This time he laughed, and the anger that had suddenly flared up in her subsided. She took out a handcloth to wipe the skillet free of the bacon grease the fritters had not absorbed. Then she put the skillet into a bag with the utensils she had assembled for their cooking kit, and hung it from the limb of a tree to discourage thieving wildlife.

When she had finished she stood there surveying their little campsite, as if trying to determine what else needed to be done. But when no further chores recommended themselves she simply glanced at Edmund and said, "Good night."

"Good night," he said in response.

Mary walked over to her tent. He did not think it seemly to stay in the vicinity while she arranged her bedding, so he stood up and went to check on the two horses and the mule, which were all well hobbled and peacefully foraging in a field of wild rye. He gathered up his blankets and surveyed the site for a place to set them.

"I wish that I had two tents," she said as he was standing there. "That way you would have some shelter as well."

He assured her that he was a veteran of the open air, bid her good night again, and began walking with his blankets to a grove of trees some fifty yards across the meadow where the horses were picketed.

"Edmund," he heard her calling when he was almost to the trees. "Why are you going so far? I can hardly see you."

"Well, I just supposed, as a matter of propriety . . ."

"Propriety, I think, can be somewhat relaxed in our circumstance. I'm not accustomed to sleeping out-of-doors, and I would like to be able to see you in case some emergency arises."

So he set his blankets down on the other side of the fire ring. Professor settled as usual at his feet, but after a few minutes he stood up and trotted over to the tent to join Mary.

"You may have your dog back if you'd like," she called out to him after a while. There was a lightness in her voice for the first time that day.

"You are more than welcome to his company," Edmund replied. Mary laughed briefly and then was silent until, a quarter of an hour later, he could hear her exquisitely faint snoring.

They were off the next morning not long after daybreak, travelling at a resolute pace along the better sections of the road, with the river always visible beside them. Late in the morning a cold rain assaulted them, but they broke out their mackinacs and rode through it, determined not to surrender any more time than necessary. Edmund wanted to reach the old Spanish barracks on the Cibolo before dark, where they would be that much closer to Béxar and where they would have decent shelter if the weather remained disagreeable.

But the place was farther than he remembered, and it was several hours after sunset before he finally spotted the outlying fields in the moonlight and then the clusters of jacales and barracks buildings up ahead beyond the curve of the road. He could smell food cooking and could see the glowing coals in the ovens outside the houses, but otherwise the place seemed ominously vacant and quiet.

They rode into the old parade ground, Edmund calling out a hearty "Buenas noches." There were shuffling sounds in several of the houses and apartments but no answering greeting. Edmund turned and looked at Mary. The ears on her horse were beginning to lie flat in apprehension.

"Is something wrong?" she whispered to him.

"I don't know," he said, but at that moment an old man appeared at one of the doors, holding a Spanish musket. In the darkness Edmund could see that the man's hands were trembling and that the musket was on full cock.

"Cálmate," Edmund said. "Somos amigos."

Professor growled at the man but did not attack. A few

men and women appeared at the entrances to the other
dwellings, some with machetes and hoes in their hands, but
this musket was apparently the only firearm in the village.

Mary sat quietly on her horse, careful not to make any
moves that might excite the man with the gun. She could
just make out the shape of the beehive ovens that were lined
up in a row on the ground. Edmund and the man talked for
a while in Spanish, and though she tried to isolate every
word and phrase so she could hold them for translation in
her mind the conversation went by far too quickly for her to
understand it. She heard the words "Bowie" and "jefe," and
then at some point in the conversation, in reply to something Edmund said, the man peered sharply into the darkness, grinned, put the musket on half-cock and walked over
to Edmund with his arms outstretched.

"We are safe enough now," Edmund said to her as he dismounted and accepted the man's welcoming abrazo.

Several women and boys came forward to see to their
horses, and then Mary and Edmund were led into one of
the larger rooms in the old barracks building and given a
dinner of tortillas and thin caldo while the entire village
crowded around them, gossiping good-naturedly with Edmund in Spanish. Mary once again tried to be alert to the
meaning of the conversation, but after the day's exhausting
ride her mind was simply not keen enough for the task. One
of the older women kept pushing a young child forward,
trying to coax her to speak to Edmund, but the girl was shy
and could offer no more than a forced smile, though her
eyes met Edmund's in a steady and relaxed way.

"These people seem to like you well enough," Mary said.

"I spent a few days with them last spring," he replied.

"And who is the little girl?"

"Her name is Lupita. She had been captured by the Comanches, and I was able to be of some service in obtaining
her release."

"El señor es un hombre de Dios," one of the women whispered to Mary.

"God sent you? Is that what she's saying?"

"She is substantially overstating the case."

Mary meant to question him further on this subject, but her attention was diverted when a gaunt-looking man walked painfully into the room out of the darkness. The others cleared a space for him, and he sat down on the dirt floor in front of the two guests and smiled without speaking. There was a poultice of some sort around his neck, and when he spoke in greeting the sound of his voice was barely detectable.

One of the women began to speak rapidly to Edmund, her voice gaining in pitch and anger as she recounted some event Mary could not understand. From time to time the man interrupted her and corrected some detail in the story, his voice exquisitely faint and raspy, and then he lowered his eyes again and let the woman's impassioned narrative wash over him as if he played no part in it.

"This man's name is Flores. He has been much abused by both sides," Edmund said when the woman had finished and the man had nodded solemnly in confirmation. "Some Mexican dragoons rode into the village last week, confiscated a pig and some chickens and made a nuisance of themselves for the better part of a day, and then had Señor Flores here guide them to a pasture up toward Sulphur Springs so they could cut grass for Cos's horses. He had to walk home for two days with nothing to eat, and when he got here the rebels were waiting for him. They demanded to know where the dragoons were, and when Señor Flores wouldn't tell them—he had been promised there would be reprisals on the village by the Mexicans if he did—they took him away and kept hanging him from a tree limb until he told."

"That is torture," Mary said.

"He does not disagree with your characterization. His

windpipe is damaged. He is worried that he may never draw a proper breath again, and he has not slept since the incident, since he fears that if he loses consciousness he will surely suffocate. He says the man who did this to him was Bowie."

"Bowie?"

"He is well known in this vicinity, as everywhere."

"Jim Bowie would not do anything so cruel."

Edmund's impatient look startled her. "I think he would, Mary."

She sat silently for a moment, accepting the truth of this. She had never seen directly beneath Jim Bowie's veneer, even when she had lain in his arms, but if she were true to her own memory she had to admit that there had been something frightening about him, some fury slumbering within that made his gestures of kindness all the more provocative.

"And Terrell?" she suddenly realized. "Was Terrell with him?"

She listened frantically while Edmund described her son and his outfit—the only word she could grasp was "joven," a word that sounded so vulnerable as to melt her heart in her breast—and then sat there in tormented suspense as the villagers speculated on the subject, several of them nodding their heads and Señor Flores with his painful voice seeming to conclude with an authoritative anecdote.

"Several of them say they saw a young man on a speckled horse ride up as Señor Flores was being abducted. He did not seem to be part of Bowie's group, but he went with them when they left. Señor Flores believes it was this same young man who gave him a blanket later that night. He remembers it as an act of distinct kindness."

"Where would Bowie and his men be now?"

"Off in search of the dragoons and their horses, most likely. Our best strategy is still to ride on to Béxar. Bowie's sure to show up there sooner or later."

Edmund halved a tortilla and sopped up the last of his caldo. The bowls they ate from, Mary saw, had been good china once, though they had been broken and glued back together so many times their surfaces were as intricate as cobwebs. From what little of the design she could still make out, they were of French origin. Probably some ancestor of these people had traded for them a hundred or more years ago, when the French were still rivals with Spain for the possession of Texas.

Terrell was with Bowie. The knowledge did not soothe her anxiety in the least. Bowie was the sort to go out of his way to look for a fight, and he would drag Terrell along in his train. And if he did not get her son killed, he would very likely corrupt him. There was a warrior in Terrell. Was there a torturer as well?

"Will you tell Señor Flores, Edmund, how horrified I am by what happened to him? And how deeply I wish for his complete recovery?"

The man smiled at her when this was translated, and said something in reply that neither Mary nor Edmund could hear. She was weighing the decision of whether to ask him to repeat it, given the trauma to his windpipe, when she heard a faint drumming sound in the distance—so faint she was not certain she heard it at all. It was a sound as deep as thunder but without the sustained cause-and-effect cadence of thunder, without the music. Rather it was disturbingly erratic: low, billowing rumbles that came to no resolution and seemed to have nothing to do with one another.

She saw from Edmund's face that he heard it too.

"They are attacking Béxar," she guessed.

"I believe you are right." He turned to the villagers and conversed with them for a moment.

"They say they've heard it off and on all day. They don't know where the battle stands. They are equally apprehensive whether the rebels take the city or the centralists drive them out."

Everyone in the hut grew quiet for a moment, listening to the distant sporadic rumbling.

"Only big guns could be heard so far," said Edmund. "I know of at least one sixteen-pounder at Béxar. Cos seems to be making fair use of it."

They heard the firing for another quarter of an hour—the abstracted sounds of death reaching them from the edge of the world—and then the night grew silent again. Mary was shown to a mattress of Spanish moss in one of the jacales. Four or five women and girls shared the room with her, including the girl that Edmund had somehow liberated from the Comanches. Though Mary was exhausted from the day's long ride her fretful mind woke her at intervals throughout the night, and each time she came awake she saw this same girl sitting up in her own bed, open-eyed and vigilant, like someone who feared sleep more than death.

BY THE EARLY AFTERNOON of the next day they had ridden to within twenty miles of Béxar, but no more reports of ordnance reached them. Indeed, the closer they came to the city, the more ominous the silence became.

"The battle is very likely over," Edmund said. They had veered a few yards off the road to water their horses at a shallow bank of the river. "Now it is a question of who holds the city. I think the rebels may have carried the day. If they had been routed there would be a quantity of refugees already on this road."

Unless the fighting had been such a disaster they had all been killed or taken prisoner, Mary thought before she could stop herself.

He sawed off a piece of dried beef with his knife and handed it to Mary. She worked it around in her mouth, but she had no appetite. If the rebels had indeed taken Béxar, and Terrell was with them when it happened, he might still have fallen in the fighting, his body torn to pieces by one of those sixteen-pound balls they had heard rumbling through the night. And if the battle had gone the other way, to the centralists, he was very likely dead or—if he had been captured—soon to be, since it was a well-established fact that Santa Anna had decreed that any colonists who joined in the federalist uprising were to be considered pirates and executed.

She walked upstream a few yards, away from the cloudy residue stirred up by the horses' hooves, and dipped her hands into the cool river and rubbed them over her face. The water's bracing feel against her skin carried with it something like a warning. In her grim and superstitious mood she felt as if any pleasure, however slight, might be subtracted later from the possibility of a happy resolution. But to acknowledge such a premonition, she decided, meant that she was already giving up, and so she dipped her handkerchief into the river and squeezed water down the back of her neck so that it trickled liberally down her dress.

She heard Professor suddenly erupt in a barking fit and then just as suddenly stop. "Buenos días," Edmund said in a strangely neutral voice that sent a shiver through her. Why would he be talking to her in Spanish?

When she looked over to him she saw that he was holding Professor tightly by the neck and watching eight or nine uniformed men carefully advancing down the bank, several of them with carbines on full cock. Mary looked down the lethal bore of one of those short barrels. It was pointed at her abdomen. She knew to a certainty that if the frightened man, as short as a jockey, who held the weapon felt compelled to pull the trigger it would blow her completely in half.

"No somos rebeldes," she heard Edmund say. The men stopped advancing five or six yards away from them and stood as quiveringly still as tuning forks. A few of them wore helmets with long goat-hair crests that blew sideways in the wind. Some of them were holding lances.

"El cuchillo, por favor," one of the soldiers said to Edmund. He wore the same red coat and ragged overalls as the others, but there was an epaulet on his shoulder of the sort that Mary had seen on the sergeants who had encamped at her inn with Cos's army. Of all of them, though, he appeared to her the most nervous. He had a broad, austere face that might have once been fat. He looked sallow and apprehensive.

Edmund handed the man the knife with which he had been slicing the dried beef, and then offered the meat itself, but the sergeant waved it away impatiently, as if offended at Edmund's silent proposition that this be a civilized encounter. He then spoke to his comrades, and several of the men walked up to the horses and the mule and took their reins.

When all weapons and horses had been thus summarily appropriated, the sergeant said, "Siéntese," and Mary and Edmund sat on the ground, Edmund still holding Professor in a firm grip. The troopers remained standing. The sergeant walked around for a moment in a tight little circle, thinking, and then he sat down as well and spoke a few admonitory words to Edmund with his head inclined toward the growling dog. Mary understood that if Edmund could not get Professor to calm down the dragoons would be obliged to shoot him. After another exchange in Spanish the sergeant tentatively put out his hand and the dog just as tentatively sniffed it, and a wary truce was established.

The sergeant smiled. "Es un perro muy inteligente."

"No tiene enemigos en esta guerra," Edmund replied. "Como nosotros."

Mary cobbled together the meaning of this: the dog had no enemies in this war, and neither did they.

The sergeant did not seem to disagree, but the conversation soon turned so tense that the other troopers began clos-

ing in, as if anticipating that they might be called upon to
kill the prisoners. Edmund reached into his haversack for
his wallet and removed from it a piece of paper that he
thrust with some authority into the sergeant's face.

"That's my commission from the Mexican government,"
he told Mary as the sergeant studied the paper with a degree of perplexity that made it apparent he could not read.
In a moment, he stood up, indicated with gestures that Edmund and Mary were to stay where they were, and walked
up the riverbank to the road.

"What's going on?" Mary asked.

"These men were out on patrol a few days ago," Edmund
responded, "when they were attacked by rebels and their
horses were run off—probably by Bowie and his men. When
they tried to get back into the city early this morning they
found that it had fallen and Cos and his men were now prisoners. So naturally they are filled with the greatest anxiety."

"Where has he gone with your paper?"

"I don't know."

The sergeant returned and ordered them to stand up and
follow him. He led them up the riverbank to the road, and
then about twenty feet farther on where a wounded officer
was hidden behind a broad live oak trunk. The officer, attended by two more troopers, lay on a crude litter made of
blankets and cavalry lances. His leg, Mary saw at once, was
badly broken below the knee. Though it was immobilized
with a splint, it had not yet been set, and a sharp tip of bone
emerged from the skin. He had been shot as well, apparently, since his shirt and jacket were completely soaked in
blood, and there was a crude poultice over his side.

The officer gave them each a look that was wavery with
pain as he studied Edmund's commission. While he and
Edmund conversed in Spanish, the officer let his eyes drift
vaguely to the paper from time to time, but finally handed it
back to the sergeant. At that point Edmund's voice grew
aggrieved and insistent, and he picked up a stick and

started to draw a map in the dirt, but the officer dismissed
this effort with a wave of his hand.

"You must tell me what is happening," Mary said.

"They are cut off from the rest of their army and concerned they will encounter a rebel patrol at any moment.
And, as you can see, the lieutenant here is seriously injured.
He has heard that there is a rancho in the vicinity whose
owner is friendly to the centralists. I tried to show him how
to reach it—it's Espinosa's place, about forty miles east of
here—but he insists we accompany him and his men in
person."

"Tell him I won't go," Mary said firmly. "I'm sorry for
his situation, but I have urgent business of my own."

"We have no choice in the matter. The truth is they cannot find the place by themselves, and he knows it."

"Didn't he read your document?"

"He says I will be free to resume my commission after
he and his men are out of danger."

Mary turned abruptly to the lieutenant. "Lo siento," she
said, "pero no voy con usted."

The wounded man wearily shook his head, and directed
his reply to Edmund.

"He says he will kill you if you don't come. Take him seriously, Mary. These men are desperate."

The other troopers brought the horses up from the river,
and after briefly consulting again with the sergeant, Edmund pointed them back down the road in the direction
from which he and Mary had already ridden the greater
part of the day. The lieutenant ground his teeth in pain as
four of his men lifted his litter.

"There is a little-known contraband road that runs to Espinosa's rancho," he told her as they set out on foot, with the
troopers' carbines trained on them and the sergeant and two
other men scouting ahead on the captive mounts. "I doubt it
will be patrolled, but we will make poor time hauling the
lieutenant on his litter."

"His leg needs to be properly set and the ball removed from his wound, or he will die before we get there." She said this indifferently. In abducting them, the lieutenant had proven himself to be an enemy, and she found to her surprise that she truly did not care whether he lived or not.

"Do you suppose they will let us go when we reach the rancho?" she asked.

"I don't know," he said. "If I were in the lieutenant's place I might not, since he would have no guarantee we would not give him away."

"Then we must escape."

"Yes," Edmund replied. "Of course we must."

CHAPTER NINETEEN

✴

WHEN BLAS heard that one of his cazadores had been shot by Indians, he had to backtrack against the marching columns of soldiers for half an hour before he found him. Private Alquisira was lying on the side of the road with his back propped up against the wheel of a baggage cart, staring down with a trace of morbid amusement at the arrow protruding from his leg. He was singing to calm himself. "The little Indians," he chanted under his breath, "the little Indians are coming through the canebrake . . ."

"What happened?" Blas asked Hurtado, who was standing over Alquisira, holding the wounded man's rifle.

"There were four of us guarding the flank of the mule train," Hurtado said. "But then Salas collapsed—he has the tele, I think—and Pretalia took him off to the ambulance wagon. The Indians must have been watching, because as soon as Salas and Pretalia were gone they attacked. They got four mules. Alquisira shot one of the Indians. His body is lying over there."

Hurtado gestured to a place about fifty yards distant, where a group of soldiers and mule drivers were standing around kicking at the body of a dead Comanche lying on his back with his mouth open as wide as if he were yawning. Just at that moment a mounted patrol of presidial troops that had joined the march in Monclova galloped by in pursuit of the Indians, stirring up a choking cloud of dust that hung suspended for a long time in the windless atmosphere of the desert.

Blas bent down to inspect Alquisira's wound. The arrow had entered the meaty part of the calf just below the knee. There was little enough blood, but the shaft was so firmly lodged that Blas was certain the point was buried deep in the bone.

"Don't take me to the ambulance, Sargento," Alquisira said.

"No, of course not," Blas replied. The ambulance wagons were safe enough for men who, because of dysentery or tele—a dangerous fever brought on by drinking stagnant water—could no longer walk. But someone with a real wound to be treated should avoid them at all costs. For a time, during the long march from Leona Vicario to Monclova, the fifteen hundred men of the First Brigade had had the services of a drunken German doctor who for unexplained reasons had been living as an outcast in some nameless pueblo on the edge of a water hole. The doctor, tired of the unendurable thirst and nonexistent hospital facilities, had promptly deserted, but his brief presence had emboldened his assistants to think of themselves as practitioners, and they had already sawed off the limbs of three men that Blas had heard about, all of whom had subsequently died in the greatest agony.

"Go back to the chusma," he said to Hurtado, "and find Isabella."

Hurtado set down Alquisira's rifle and headed for the towering cloud of dust several hundred yards down the road that marked where the chusma—a ragged congregation of soldaderas, peddlers, children, and domestic animals—was currently located. As Blas and Alquisira waited by the side of the road, several fusilier companies of the First Brigade marched past in their ragged columns of four, staring at the wounded man in alarm. The soldiers were ghostly—from their white shako covers to the pale, powdery dust covering their sandaled feet. They were only a few miles out of Monclova, but already all the life seemed

to have been leached out of their bodies, and Béxar was
still unimaginably distant, across a waste desert of mud-
holes and fouled springs and not one town of any size
where provisions and shelter could be obtained. As bad as
it was, as bad as it had been, each of them knew it was going to get far worse. The arrieros and private purveyors
were deserting every day in disgust, taking their wagons
and mule teams with them, and the one blessed rain the
army had experienced had destroyed a month's worth of
provisions, since some unconscionable contractor, trying to
squeeze every peso he could from the government, had
stored the food in cheap cotton sacks rather than in water-
tight barrels. Alquisira was by no means the only soldier
not on his feet. The road was littered with dozens of men
who had collapsed today from thirst and fatigue, unable
any longer to support the weight of their heavy muskets.
But the sight of Alquisira with an arrow sticking out of his
leg was a new horror to the men who were marching by.

Blas's canteen was long empty, as was that of every
other soldado in the First Brigade, so he could offer
Alquisira no comfort other than a few idle words, though
speaking was painful when his tongue was so parched and
raw and his throat so swollen. The wounded man simply
nodded in reply. Blas crouched down next to him on the
balls of his feet, but found that he could not keep his balance. Thirst did that to you as well. So he stood up again
and put out a hand against the wagon for support. It was interesting to him that he found it easier to march than to
stand still. He closed his eyes for just a moment to shut out
the sun, and in the gauzy darkness he started to lose consciousness. The sounds of the men's feet hitting soft earth
and the shriek of ungreased cart wheels became intolerably
loud, and he found himself staring at a creature with the
skin of a jaguar that walked upright like a man across the
desert floor.

When he opened his eyes again the vision was gone and

Isabella was there in its place, walking toward him with a steady stride, her small face as thin as a bird's after weeks of privation.

With a tilt of his head, Blas directed her attention to Alquisira's wound. After these months together they had still not learned one another's speech but had discovered a common language of silence and gesture. The Mayan girl looked at the arrow as if it were a commonplace sight, slipped off her knapsack, and knelt down next to Alquisira. She touched the shaft of the arrow to feel how deeply it was buried, and Alquisira flinched more in anticipation of the trials to come, Blas thought, than in actual pain.

Isabella withdrew a knife from the knapsack and wiped the dust off the blade with the hem of her shift. Alquisira shifted his eyes uneasily to Blas.

"Why can't you just pull it out?"

"The arrow point is in the bone."

Isabella reached out her hand to touch Alquisira's face. She was far too shy to look at him at the same time, and so it was a strange gesture, as if she were distractedly comforting an animal. But there was a power in it too. Alquisira trusted, as they all had learned to, in the Indian witch's healing touch. Every night she doctored their blisters with nopal sap and did her best to soothe their fevers with teas brewed from desert plants she had learned about from the curanderas who travelled with her in the chusma. So far Blas's company had been fortunate. There had been no broken bones, and no real wounds except for bites from the scavenging dogs that trotted along at the edges of the column.

With the knife, Isabella cut away Alquisira's pants leg and gently folded the cloth out of the way. Then, because the wound was in an awkward place, she pushed Alquisira a little until he was lying on his side and the wounded leg was flat on the ground. Hurtado held down his foot and Blas secured his knee. Alquisira chewed on the strap of his knapsack as Isabella cut down through the meat of his calf,

exposing what was to Blas a fibrous, oozing, undifferentiated mass of flesh, but which to her probing eyes seemed to
be made up of identifiable components. When she reached
the gleaming white bone, she took a length of wire and
passed a loop down the length of the arrow until she had
snared its point so that it would not remain buried in the
bone when the shaft was extracted. With the snare in place
she rocked the arrow gently back and forth to loosen it in
the bone, and then—with a look at Blas and Hurtado that
admonished them to tighten their grip—she suddenly
tugged hard in a swift, straight motion. Alquisira gave a
surprised yelp and then lay there, his whitened face covered
by a sheen of perspiration.

Afterward she sewed up the wound, and then used the
same needle and thread to repair his bloodstained trousers
where she had cut them. Then Blas bribed a field blacksmith to give Alquisira a ride, and they squeezed the
wounded man into a wagon between a portable forge and
an oven for baking communion wafers. When Blas left him,
he was staring up at the white sky overhead and singing
once again the song about the little Indians stealing through
the canebrake.

Isabella went back to the chusma, and Blas and Hurtado
continued the march. They did not catch up with the company until after dark, and by that time they were both hallu-
cinating wildly—sensing Indians behind every creosote bush,
seeing a grasping hand in every clump of lechuguilla—and
made so dizzy by thirst that they were hardly able to keep
their footing. The army had made its bivouac at a bolson
fed by seeping springs and bordered by green marsh grass,
but by the time Blas and Hurtado got there the shallow
spring waters and the grass had been trampled into a paste
by hundreds of horses, mules, oxen, goats, and dogs, and
the animals' droppings covered the surface of what little
water remained in liquid form. Even so, Blas drank gratefully. His throat was so swollen that he could barely swal-

low, and it took a long time for this infuriatingly slow trickle of water to relieve his thirst.

The men, under the direction of Sargento Reyna, had made their camp in surprisingly good order considering the day's various ordeals. Now they clustered around Blas and Hurtado as they came back from the water hole, wanting to know about Alquisira, and about the welfare of Salas and all the other men who had collapsed with tele and were no longer marching in the column with them. So far, none of the cazadores in Blas's company had died, though each day's route led past the fresh graves of men in the vanguard who had succumbed to this same stretch of desert. Blas noticed how his men had grown increasingly protective of one another, even as their tempers had grown short. The first death among them, he knew, would be a serious blow to their morale, and to his. Even now he fretted about Alquisira like a mother, troubled that he had no idea where the blacksmith's wagon might be bivouacked, and no energy to check on the wounded man even if he had known where to find him.

Blas sat down near the fire in a stupor, his thirst still haunting him even though his stomach was bloated with the fetid water from the spring. He forced himself to eat something, but his tongue was still so dry that when he chewed his stale tortillas he felt a lacerating pain across its surface. Isabella came to him, as she did every night, to minister to the soles of his feet, both of which had been plagued since the beginning of the march with suppurating blisters. He watched her face as she worked. The camp was strangely silent, except for the incessant barking of dogs and the music of distant coyotes. Most of the men were already asleep, and those who were still awake merely stared off into the black desert, either out of vigilant fear of an Indian attack or out of simple mental blankness.

In the firelight the girl's eyes were luminous as she bound his foot with strips of cloth. Skin was peeling off

along the planes of her cheeks and her lips were cracked
and bleeding, but otherwise she seemed to have absorbed
the sun's punishment with nothing worse than a deepening
tone to her already dark complexion. The touch of her
hands on his bare feet was light, as gentle as a breeze. He
remembered when she had climbed into his cot one night
in San Luis Potosí, less than a week after he had brought
her back to camp: the look of frank intent in her eyes, the
sharp angles of her slight body, the careful ministrations she
brought to the act of love, as if it too were a form of healing.

When she had finished wrapping his feet and was putting away her things, Blas gestured with his eyes to the
small cloth bundle that held her collection of stones.

"Show me," he said.

Without hesitation, but without enthusiasm, she opened
the cloth and spread it out on the dirt with the stones lying
on top. It seemed to Blas that there were considerably more
stones now than there had been when she first showed them
to him, though where she had acquired them he didn't
know. He supposed they were divining stones of some sort
and had to have unusual qualities of shape and color, but
perhaps she had just picked random rocks off the ground
and in the mere act of her selecting them they were invested
with the power she required.

Isabella divided the stones into tour small piles and then,
with great absorption, began redistributing the members of
each pile in accordance with some design that only she
could see. It was a soothing thing to watch. Blas had long
been fascinated by how almost everything she did, every
gesture she made, seemed so harmonious and deliberate.
And yet he was not quite sure that he truly trusted her. The
creature he had seen today in his delirium of thirst—the
jaguar walking upright across the desert floor—could have
been a meaningless figment of his tortured mind or it could
have been Isabella in a more dangerous and provocative
form. Such things could happen, he reasoned, just as surely

as Christ could rise from his tomb or the Virgin could appear out of the empty blue sky.

Isabella moved the stones around for quite some time, muttering prayers in her language, and then at last she stopped, as if their placement finally satisfied her, or she could think of nowhere else to move them. She sat there looking at them, absorbing the information they gave to her.

"What do they say?" Blas asked.

In response, Isabella only glanced briefly in his direction. If she was concerned or alarmed about what she saw in the arrangement of the stones she did not show it. She simply swept them up with her hands and tied them once again in the cloth bundle. And then, as she did every night, she arranged Blas's bedding and placed his personal objects—his falling-apart shoes, the jaguar shooting pouch she had given him—at the foot of his blanket. And without a word passing between them she walked off in the night toward the women's camp in the chusma, carrying the secrets of the future with her.

THE FIRST BRIGADE suffered no more Indian attacks as it continued the march north the next day toward the Rio Grande, though thirst and sickness were constant. Blas had long since trained himself not to dwell on the enormity of the journey before them, and he worked hard to instill this essential present-mindedness in his men. He made sure that they marched in column, although other companies around them had long since degenerated into straggling groups of demoralized individuals. At the beginning of the march the men in Blas's rifle company had talked incessantly of their destination and the progress they were making toward it, but now their minds were occupied with nothing but the next few footfalls, and Blas supposed that this was a healthy thing.

Beyond the presidio at the Rio Grande there were still

another hundred frightful leagues of desert before they
reached the town of Béxar, which the norte rebels had
seized from General Cos, and whose fall must now be
avenged by Santa Anna. Blas had seen Santa Anna when he
had reviewed the troops in San Luis, and then later during
the early days of the march when the commander in chief
and his staff and cavalry escort had flown past the column
on swift horses, racing ahead of the First Brigade to join
General Ramírez y Sesma's vanguard, which even then was
rumored to have crossed the Rio Grande. Blas had waved
his shako along with his men and shouted "Viva El Presidente" as His Excellency rode by, but the enthusiasm they
displayed that day seemed now like some quaint excitement
of childhood.

In fact, the only legacy of their previous enthusiasm was
the brutal pace they maintained—eight, ten, sometimes
twelve leagues a day, with few provisions to support them
and breakdowns, desertions, and suffering at every step.
Last night even more of the civilian arrieros and carters
had disappeared, and the road today was jammed with the
balky animals they had left behind. Blas led his column
past a team of orphaned mules harnessed to a cannon lim-
ber that an artillery crew was trying to force back onto the
road. The poor creatures—beset by thirst and fatigue and
tongue sickness—bleated miserably and merely shuffled
angrily in place as the ignorant soldados prodded them
with the tips of bayonets.

An hour later, when a halt was called, the men collapsed
into the dust on the side of the road to drink the last water
from their canteens and gnaw on tortillas. Blas used the
stopping time to visit the ambulance wagons, which he located by the clouds of vultures circling above them. The
half-dozen men in his company who had contracted tele lay
groaning in the wagons along with all the other sick men,
their uniforms caked with dried vomit and their fatigue
pants soiled from diarrhea. The stench was violent, so pow-

erful that the coasting vultures overhead seemed to be feeding on the smell alone. The men raised their heads a little
and smiled when they saw Blas's face, and one or two even
managed to sit upright and ask for news of the company.
Salas, the most recently afflicted, also appeared to be the
most gravely ill, but even he was alert enough to listen with
interest as Blas told them about the Comanche attack and
Alquisira's arrow wound.

Alquisira himself was nowhere to be found. Blas
searched for the blacksmith wagon as he made his way
back to the company, but he knew the chances of finding it
in any particular place were meager. The First Brigade was
strung out for miles along this rough desert road, an endless
column of stumbling, thirst-crazed men and beasts and
broken-down conveyances. The wagon could be anywhere
within that train, or lying abandoned somewhere by the
side of the road, its oxen dead or its wooden wheels split by
the dry air. Or the arrieros who had been driving the wagon
might simply have grown tired of their wounded passenger
and turned him out. Alquisira's unknown fate and whereabouts tortured Blas's conscience. He should have gone
looking for him last night, instead of succumbing so readily and completely to his own fatigue. And now with every
passing moment he began to feel certain that Alquisira was
already dead—that his death was in fact what Isabella had
seen last night in her stones and with her fatalistic acceptance had found unremarkable and not worth speaking
about.

As Blas stumbled back to his company he passed fields
of prostrate, gasping men, The soldados who had enough
energy to take full advantage of the halt had made sun shelters out of their thin blankets, propping them up on the
ends of their muskets. Others were crowded beneath the
beds of the wagons, but most of the men simply lay there
exposed to the white sun, too tired and sick to seek escape.
Lost oxen, bellowing in thirst, threaded their way through

the column, and savage dogfights erupted everywhere with such frequency that the men didn't bother to even turn their heads to watch.

When he reached the Toluca battalion, Blas saw that Captain Loera had come to pay his company a rare visit.

"Ah, there you are," the captain called out to him. He was standing among the men, holding the reins to a dazed-looking mule. "Sargento Reyna said you were off visiting our sick comrades. That is commendable. And how are they? Improving, I hope."

"So far none have died, sir."

"Excellent." He suddenly turned to the men, as if just noticing they had been grudgingly standing there at attention since his arrival. "Please, please, my friends, sit down. You need your rest."

He then proceeded to attempt to raise their spirits, praising them for their uncomplaining endurance, informing them of a fine hacienda only two leagues distant where the army would bivouac for the night along the banks of a clear stream bordered by cottonwoods, and how with each step they were moving closer to a glorious victory over the rebels in San Antonio de Béxar.

The men were not much moved, though they grunted and nodded their heads when it seemed politeness called for some reaction. Captain Loera for his part uttered his remarks as if he were reading them from a book. Though he had the wondrous advantage of a mule to ride and a tent to sleep in, he too had suffered on the march. It showed in his sagging face, and in the once-plump body that had been made thin by the ravages of diarrhea.

When he had finished speaking to the men, Loera climbed back on his mule and looked down at Blas.

"A word with you, Primer Sargento," he said.

Loera kicked at the mule's flanks and turned its head around and managed to make the weary beast move. Blas followed the captain as he led him away from the road and some fifty or sixty varas into the raw desert, where the men could no longer hear them. Still sitting on the mule, Loera took off his shako and patted the top of his head where his thinning hair lay in sweaty strands. When he replaced the hat and looked down at Blas, deep gray bags appeared under his eyes.

"It is true what I told the men about tonight's bivouac," he said. "There will be good water and perhaps a quantity of edible beef. But I fear that will be our last bit of good fortune on this march. The supplies we were expecting at the Rio Grande are evidently not there, and since the hardtack we are carrying with us is almost depleted, the men must be prepared to forage all the way to Béxar."

"There is nothing to forage on, Capitán," Blas said. He was looking down at the ground, trying to hold back his despair, as small lizards darted across the desert floor with such swiftness that his mind and eye could barely register their passage. He wondered if there was any way such creatures could be caught in a trap, and if there was enough meat on their slight frames to justify the effort. Besides the lizards, he saw nothing that could provide any possible sustenance, just endless fields of wiry creosote plants, and the shadows of coasting vultures.

"Further ahead there are mesquite forests," Loera said, gazing out at the monotonous and fearsome landscape, rumpled hills rising on either side of the parched desert valley, the men of the column splayed out at rest as far as the eye could reach along the road, looking less like an army on the march than one that had been massacred and left on the field. "Mesquite beans are said to be nutritious to some degree. And I fear there will be plenty of dead mules and oxen for us to feast upon before this journey is over."

Loera flashed his eyes back down to Blas. "And your witch," he said. "How is she? Still alive, I hope."

"Still alive, sir. She is a good nurse, and the men trust her."

"I am delighted to hear it. Didn't I tell you you would find her useful, Montoya?"

He reached down to pat Blas paternally on the shoulder.

"Do what you can for the men," he said. "Keep them alive and ready to fight. Remember, there is still a war waiting for us on the other side of this purgatory."

With his heels, the captain launched several ferocious blows on the flanks of the mule, until the creature consented to bear him away to the comforts of his tent and the society of his fellow officers.

WHILE THEY WERE CAMPED along the stream that night Blas and Isabella again went in search of the blacksmith wagon, and after many inquiries they finally found it lying up for repairs outside the walls of the hacienda. The men Blas had paid to look after Alquisira had been true to their word, and he found the wounded man lying comfortably on a blanket beside the wagon, heartily gnawing on a piece of seared beef and drinking water from the canteen his hosts had filled for him from the spring.

"How are you, Alquisira?" Blas asked with more casualness in his voice than he felt. The grim premonition that had afflicted him for much of the day—of Alquisira dying and neglected, or already residing in a shallow trailside grave—had suddenly vanished like an oppressive fever, and he felt not just relief but a strange conviction that all was well and might continue to be so.

"The wound is painful, Sargento," Alquisira said, "but walking is painful too. So I suppose I am doing as well as anyone."

As he spoke, he looked down rather anxiously at Isabella, who was unwinding the dressing on his leg. She removed the nopal poultice and held a candle up to the wound to inspect it, and after a moment looked up at both Blas and Alquisira with a pleased expression.

"There's no infection," Blas said.

"It's the dry air," Alquisira answered. "Things don't rot here."

Isabella put another poultice on the wound and began to bind it again with strips of cloth.

"Without her, though," Alquisira said to Blas, "I might have died. I think she is good luck."

"Yes," Blas agreed.

"She'll see to it that we all make it to Texas and back in one piece."

Isabella smiled in the light of the candle. Blas did not know if she understood the substance of their conversation or not, but there was a contentment in her eyes. Blas felt the way he imagined a husband and father must feel at the end of the day, when the household is quiet and secure and all the many children are sleeping in their beds. Despite all the privations they had suffered so far, despite those that he knew still loomed ahead, Blas felt charmed. Looking down at Isabella, her lips cracked and swollen but her eyes shining with an unearthly sympathy, he felt happier than he had expected ever to feel in his life.

THEY PASSED more graves along the side of the road as they marched north, graves marked with crude white crosses, sometimes with the dead man's rosary looped on the arms, or his shako plate hanging from a string. There were many dead animals as well—oxen, horses, mules, and sometimes dogs—and there was a continual litter of wrecked carts and abandoned equipment, and mounds of spoiled hardtack. Observing all this wreckage, Blas wondered if there would be anything left of the army when they reached Texas.

As they drew closer to the Rio Grande, the pure desert gave way to a tangled brush country, thick with thorny mesquite trees. Blas pulled some of the pods from these trees and tried chewing the beans as Loera had suggested, but they only made him retch.

At the end of one day they came to a camping place named El Sans and made their beds as usual under a clear sky. It was February now. The night was chill, as all the nights had been during the march from Monclova. But the cold deepened as the night wore on, and deepened even further as the sun rose through the skeletal mesquite limbs. The clouds Blas saw that morning were unlike any he had seen before. They covered the sky like some billowy vault, gray and sumptuous, bearing some beautiful turmoil within.

As they marched that morning Blas could not stop looking at the clouds. They had the richness of something encountered in a dream, though he could sense the threat in them as well, the lowering heaviness with which a nightmare begins. The temperature kept dropping. The men broke out their tunics, and then covered themselves in their blankets. Their feet grew numb in their sandals, and Blas called a halt so that they could change into their brogans. Isabella ran up to him carrying one of his shoes in each of her hands. She herself had no shoes, and her thin body quivered beneath her cotton shift. Blas draped his own blanket around her shoulders. She protested, shaking her head. Her cracked lips were now blue and her teeth were chattering. He made her take the blanket and sent her back to the chusma, where perhaps she could find some degree of warmth by climbing into a wagon or at least walking behind an ox in the lee of the wind.

The wind grew ferocious. It caught the soldados' shako covers and made them billow like sails, and those who had not thought to fasten their chin straps saw their headgear bounding across the tops of the creosote plants. It cut through Blas's woolen tunic, through the cracked leather of his shoes, as rending and violent as a sabre stroke. The sky grew tighter and darker, and in the late afternoon snow came. He had never seen snow before. Very few men in the company had. Had they not been quaking with cold and terrified of the brutal night to come, they might have regarded the silent snowflakes as a heavenly blessing.

But in only moments, it seemed, the soft snowfall intensified into a churning white void. It was the most unlikely thing Blas had ever thought to encounter. He knew blizzards existed, but in his mind they took place far to the north, on the empty plains where Coronado had searched for his golden cities, or in the wild mountain country of Alta California. In this desert south of the Rio Grande a blizzard was as unexpected and fantastic a thing to behold as an elephant.

The men's feet were already buried in snow. The road no longer existed. Blas could see no more than a few varas in front of him, and once or twice the violent, swirling snow cut off his vision entirely, leaving only a gauzy, suffocating whiteness.

The men were calling out in terror and loneliness. Blas stumbled into an ox that had lost its bearings and crossed the line of march. He fell and sliced open his knee on a rock.

"Cazadores!" he called out as he stood up. "Take hold of the crossbelt of the man in front of you! Walk slowly and carefully!"

But the howling wind took his words as soon as they came out of his mouth and bore them away. He kept stumbling over bodies of men who had fallen. He slapped the terror out of them and got them back on their feet. Men hung on to his own crossbelt as if on to the skirt of their mothers. Several times he fell, bringing five or six men down with him, then rallying them back onto their numb, bruised feet to march into the whiteness that led nowhere, neither forward nor back, only deeper within its borderless self.

Finally it became apparent that the army could travel no farther. The road was lost beneath the snow, and in the tumultuous whiteness all human instincts about which way to go were buried as well. The word came down for the men to bivouac for the night wherever they were standing. When Blas announced this order to his cazadores they crowded around him as if he might have some kind of answer to their misery. The men looked as frightened and bewildered as if they had suddenly found themselves standing on the moon instead of the familiar earth. They cringed in the cold wind, clutching their pathetically thin blankets over their shoulders. Their mustaches and eyebrows were sheathed in ice. Each one of their faces bore a look of perfect, abject pain.

Somewhere with the army there were carts carrying firewood, but no one knew where they were. Blas sent two platoons out to gather wood, though the mesquite trees surrounding the road were only intermittently visible in the blowing snow, and though he knew the limbs would be green and hard to burn. He ordered the bugler to sound assembly every five minutes, so that the men in the firewood details could find their way back. Then he took twenty men and groped through the storm until he located four of the company's supply carts. He ordered the arrieros to empty the carts and cache whatever could not be used immediately for shelter, and then turned the carts over on their sides to form a windbreak. Soon, with wood stolen from crates or from the least essential parts of the carts themselves, they had fires going, and in time they were hot enough to catch the green wood that the firewood gatherers, numb and nearly lifeless, brought back from the mesquite forests.

Then there was nothing to do but endure it. The men

clung to each other in the lee of the overturned wagons. Few of them could move anymore, or even speak. The strength kept shivering out of them. Blas tried once or twice to get them singing, hoping to rouse their spirits, but none of them took it up, and he was not sure if his voice was even audible beyond the confines of his own skull.

The fires burned down at an alarming rate, and the flames seemed to consume the green wood without producing any perceptible heat at all. Blas organized another wood-gathering expedition, selecting the strongest men, the ones he thought had the best chance of surviving it. The sun had long since set, the cold was immeasurably sharper, but the night itself was strangely invisible. It was as if the day's horrible whiteness had simply grown deeper and more impenetrable.

The men moaned as he led them out into the biting wind. All at once the negligible warmth of the fires seemed like a luxurious refuge. Blas felt the cold as a savage assault. He could not feel his grip on the hatchet he carried and worried that it had already slipped out of his hand. Behind, holding on to his crossbelt, matching each step to his, was Hurtado. The other teams had been swallowed up. They came to the trees. The bean pods rattled in the wind. The snowdrifts were almost up to their knees, and Blas knew that the chances of finding dead wood on the ground were poor. They had to cut the living limbs, which were thin and wiry and drooping with snow. Thorns bit into their hands. Blas and his men had neither the strength nor the tools to chop through the trunks of the trees to procure the big heartwood logs that would allow them to survive the night almost in comfort. All he and Hurtado could do was to try to cut off the smaller branches, which danced in the wind like whips. Blas held the limbs steady, lacerating his hands on the thorns, while Hurtado held the hatchet in both hands and, weak and blinded by the snow, chopped at the place where the limb joined the tree. As often as not, his blows missed, sometimes striking air, sometimes merely scarring the trunk.

After an eternity of effort they had amassed only a spindly stack of wood, enough fuel for perhaps ten minutes of this long night. But it was all they could carry, and Hurtado was quaking uncontrollably.

"Let's go back," Blas said. Hurtado nodded his head and started to walk off in an indiscriminate direction, his mind as numb as his body. Blas grabbed him and held him in place until they heard the bugle call, and then they set off in that direction. Others from the wood-gathering detail came out of the storm and joined them on the way back, each man cradling a load of wood in his bleeding and swollen hands. Finally they could see the fires glowing softly in the haze, the most welcome sight Blas had ever witnessed. He dropped his wood directly on one of the fires and made the bugler keep sounding assembly until he had satisfied himself that all of the wood gatherers had made it back. And then he collapsed near the flames. The fire awakened his bloody, frozen hands to shrieking pain. The sudden warmth, the towering flames as the new wood was consumed, was almost worse than the cold. The way that the pain in his hands kept building in intensity reminded him of some hellish bugle call, a shrill, eternal note, never changing in pitch, never breaking off into music.

"Sargento," Reyna said, after perhaps an hour had passed. He was pointing with his head toward a figure on the other side of the fire, standing there just beyond the hunched and miserable forms of the cazadores that were crowded against the flames. A slight, trembling figure, wearing only a cotton shift and sandals, and with a single blanket for protection against the cold.

"Let her in!" Blas shouted. "Let her in!"

The men shuffled beneath their blankets, clearing a path for Isabella. Blas stood and grabbed her and folded her like

a child into his lap as he sat down again. He squeezed her
so hard to keep her warm he was afraid he might break her
bones. She said nothing, just shivered in his arms. She had
been mad to leave the chusma, he thought, mad to go out
into this wild, smothering night. It had been a miracle that
she had found him, a miracle that she was not already
dead—this girl from the distant Yucatán who had grown up
knowing only the sodden heat of the forests and never
imagining such a thing as lethal cold.

Blas did not scold her for walking out into the storm; he
just tried to keep her alive by holding her. After a long time
he began to perceive some degree of warmth kindling in
her body. And then he could feel that warmth spreading
back to him, as if they were sharing this hideous night in
one flesh. Incredibly, he slept; from time to time the frozen
wind simply sheared away his awareness. And then he
woke up again into the unabating storm, still clutching Isabella to his chest while men huddled against them on
every side. Some of the men groaned in pain and despair;
others waited for the morning in grim silence. In his wakeful moments Blas worried anew about the sick men in the
ambulance wagons, about Alquisira lying next to his field
forge. But there was nothing he could do. And having Isabella with him gave him hope. It was true; she was life itself. She had stepped out into the storm to come to him, to
bring him confidence and strength. Because of her he would
survive, and because of him his men would survive—not
just this night, but the long war that was coming.

He sailed off into sleep again until a desperate strangled
sound brought him back.

"What is it?" he shouted reflexively, before he even understood that he was awake or remembered their hideous
situation.

"It's that mule," Hurtado said.

A veil of blowing snow parted and Blas could see the
form of a mule standing outside the fire and the tight circle

of men hunched around it. The mule continued to emit a tortured bray that was keen enough to pierce through the wind but still strangely muffled. The animal disappeared from sight in a fresh gust of wind and then was revealed again more clearly, a bright sheen of ice covering its nose.

"Somebody shut that mule up!" one of the cazadores cried. "Somebody shoot it."

"My hands are too numb to pull a trigger," someone else replied, after a long silence in which the mule continued to torture them with its cries.

"It can't breathe," Blas said. Hurtado was sitting next to him and he slid Isabella into his arms, then stood up on his stiff, cramped legs and grabbed a hatchet. He staggered through the snow-covered mounds that represented his men and approached the mule. The creature was still braying in panic, but it seemed to know enough not to run away as Blas reached out and grabbed its ear in one hand and with the other struck it on its frozen nose with the blunt end of the hatchet. The ice covering its nostrils broke like window glass, and the mule began to snort and gasp and, intoxicated now with the miracle of breath, began to prance back and forth in the weak glow of the firelight.

Blas went back to his place and took the girl once more into his arms. Throughout the endless night the mule kept coming back, with the ice once again covering its nose, and the cazadores took turns standing up with the hatchet and restoring its breath. Since Blas had saved it, no one wanted to see it die.

CHAPTER TWENTY

✦

JOE LIKED San Antonio de Béxar better than any place he had ever been. It gave him a feeling of peace to walk through its streets, even though those streets were ravaged by war. There had been heavy fighting within the city when the Texians had taken it from Cos—several weeks before Joe arrived with Travis—and whole buildings were now no more than heaps of adobe rubble and splintered furniture. Many of the buildings had odd gaping holes in their sides, put there by the rebels as they had advanced with crowbars from house to house, demolishing walls as they went. And there were still a few cannonballs lying around, though most of them had been gathered up and taken into the Alamo, where they would be used again against Santa Anna, who everyone seemed to think would be arriving with his army in only a matter of months to take back the town.

But a calmness lay at the heart of Béxar that all the destruction could not reach. Joe felt it again this morning as he walked down Potrero Street toward the river. This was a Mexican town, perhaps that was it: the low, faceless buildings of adobe or stone, never more than one story high, that seemed as cool and dark inside as springhouses; the lack of any bustle or urgency in the streets, just people going about their errands as if the day were spread out before them like a gift; and the way those people looked at him as he passed, with nothing more than a matter-of-fact curiosity. They did not seem to care one way or another that he was a negro. He felt that he could walk up and boldly begin a conversation with any of them whenever he chose, if he could only speak the Spanish like Mr. Travis.

Joe found it hard to believe that he was still in the province of Texas, so different was Béxar from San Felipe. It was not just the language, not just the attitude toward his black skin. Here was a place where everything was on the inside—people seemed to carry their thoughts within themselves in the way they built their houses with secret courtyards that could not be seen from the streets. In San Felipe everything was visible, everything was fulminating talk and action, and the tall wooden houses with their white paint seemed to be clamoring for notice.

He crossed the wooden bridge that spanned the river. The river was narrower than the Brazos, maybe thirty yards across, but the water was so icily clear that looking into it was like looking into a chasm. Fish hovered in the transparent water. The banks were lined by the stumps of cypress trees—Cos had cut them all down to provide a better field of fire between Béxar and the Alamo—but where the river looped back into town the leafy branches formed a kind of tunnel above it. The day was cold. Clouds as solid as pewter hung over the rocky hills to the west, hills laced with crevices and shadows that Joe had a strange new urge to explore. He thought of what it would be like to take a horse or a mule up into those hills, with a sack of cornmeal and some bacon, with no intention of ever returning to these Texians and their war.

The Alamo stood a hundred yards from the river, with the hills in the distance beyond it. The cornfields all around it had been trampled in the fighting, and the dirt was bare and hard under the winter sun. Joe did not know what a fort was supposed to look like but thought it ought to give an impression of strength and not of weakness. Even from close up, the Alamo looked like something you could almost step over. The mission's walls were low, only a few feet higher than his head in most places, and they formed a long, spread-out rectangle that, it seemed to Joe, would be hard to defend with as few men as they had. The men in general were worn out. The ones with energy had long since marched off to try to capture Matamoros, and they had taken most of the garrison's supplies with them. Joe wasn't sure how many men were left—a hundred and fifty or so, and a lot of them were sick, or recovering from wounds they'd received in taking the town from the Mexicans. But the news that Santa Anna's army had reached the Rio Grande seemed to have put some life into them, and there was more activity at the fort than he had seen since he had arrived here with Travis ten days ago.

Joe crossed a plank bridge over a water ditch and walked up to the south gate, where a dozen men were reinforcing a stone redoubt in front of the gatehouse. Major Jameson, the engineer who was in charge of turning the Alamo into a real fort, had a shovel in his hands like the rest of them.

"Mornin', Joe," he said. He was a cheerful, broad-chested man whose side-whiskers were so bushy they seemed to pinch his face. "Feel like piling up some dirt with us?"

"Colonel Travis give me this note for the congressman."

"I think you'll find the honorable Mr. Crockett working yonder on the abatis."

"That nigger don't know what you're talking about," one of the other men said, noticing Joe's blank look. "He ain't never heard of no abatis."

"An abatis is a barricade of felled trees, Joe," Jameson said reasonably, nodding in the direction of the chapel. "Such as Montcalm used at Ticonderoga."

"He ain't never heard of Ticonderoga either," the other man said.

Joe put his anger at this man quietly aside, as was his custom, and passed through the gate and into the Alamo courtyard, saying that word over and over again in his mind: "Ticonderoga," a creaking sort of word, like the call of a raven. There was the smell of bacon grease from the small house that served as the kitchen, though breakfast was over and the Mexican women inside were already patting out tortillas for the garrison's dinner. Another redoubt stood just inside the gate. Captain Carey was trying without much success to train a gun crew, calling out "Attention!" and "To action!" as the cannoneers fumbled about with their lint stocks and sponges.

Joe found Crockett standing in front of the church, sighting with his rifle through a chink in the palisade that had been built to bridge the gap between the outside edge of the church and the south wall. A few days ago there had been nothing but bare ground here, nothing to stop the Mexicans from running in as they pleased, but now the palisade looked to Joe even stronger than the rest of the fort. It was made of upright timbers and packed earth, and out in front of it stretched the abatis, a deep tangle of thorny mesquite that would put a stop to a charge by the Mexican cavalry.

"You're piling it up too high, Bill," Crockett was yelling to a man standing on the far side of the timber. "Spread it out more so a man can hit something besides tree limbs."

Joe wasn't sure whether to address Crockett as Mister or Congressman or Honorable. Some of the men had taken to calling him Colonel, though he kept insisting he hadn't ever been a colonel of anything and didn't intend to be. Finally Joe just handed him the note and said, "Here's a paper, sir, from Colonel Travis."

"Had your breakfast yet, Joe?" Crockett said as he unfolded the note.

"Yes, sir."

"I'm finding those tortillas of theirs more and more tolerable." Crockett kept talking as he read, as if even a moment of silence made him nervous. "Think I'm turning into a pepper-belly?"

"I don't know, sir."

Crockett handed the note back to Joe. It was written on a blank page torn from an old gazetteer. Paper was short in Béxar. "I'd be delighted to confer with Colonel Travis," Crockett said. "Let me just get my coat."

Crockett disappeared into one of the nearby buildings and came out wearing a black hat and a coat of dark brown wool, the most splendid garment Joe had ever seen. The coat reached all the way to the congressman's ankles and flowed behind him when he walked. Joe had not been warm for a minute since the last norther had hit, and the sight of this voluptuous greatcoat left him weak with longing. He marvelled not just at the coat itself, but at Crockett's easy ownership of such a magnificent thing. He wore it with no more regard than if it were an old patched-up hunting shirt.

"I bet Travis is as wrathy as a painter," Crockett said as he and Joe crossed the bridge into the town, "after that business with Bowie yesterday."

"He ain't happy that I can see," Joe said.

Crockett laughed and gave Joe's shoulder a companionable squeeze with his big hand. Joe divided white men into two categories: those who paid him not much notice at all and those who seemed to want to use him as an audience when they were in a humorous frame of mind. The men in this second category did not seem to want Joe to laugh at their jokes, just to be there when they were said, as if his sober presence somehow made them funnier. Some of these easy-humored men were hateful at bottom, but Crockett was not that way at all. He had a soft heart, it seemed, and he took an interest where another man might not. Joe liked him, and all the other men at the post did too, though some of them still couldn't believe he was standing there in front of them in flesh and blood, the most famous man in America except for President Jackson.

Even the people of Béxar, Tejanos who spoke not a word of English and had no notion of the distant politics of the

States, glanced with interest as Crockett walked by, and he in turn gave them all an easy smile and waved as if he were in a parade all his own.

"Buenos días," he said to a pair of old ladies walking arm in arm. "You learned any of the Spanish yet, Joe?"

"I know them words you're using, for good morning and good night. And I can say cómo estás, and muy bien if somebody asks the same of me."

"My ears for a heel tap if it ain't the comeliest language I ever heard. Of course, when old Santy Anny starts speaking it to us I might hold a different opinion entirely. Travis ever been in a war?"

"He was in the militia back in Alabama, and he's been in a scrape or two since."

"A scrape or two," Crockett repeated, and then seemed to chew this over as if Joe's thoughts really mattered to him. The congressman had a sharp nose and dark hair that he parted in the middle and wore down to his shoulders. There was no gray in his hair, though Joe had once heard him say he was almost fifty years old. He was tall and well made but getting a little fleshy around the middle. As they walked, Crockett's coat threw a shadow on the street that looked like a pair of black wings. Joe looked away when he saw this. Crockett was one of the few men in this army who gave him any confidence at all, who seemed untroubled by fear and cloudy prospects. But that shadow on the street made it look like death had already enveloped him.

FOR HIS HEADQUARTERS, Travis had taken a house on the Plaza de las Islas, just a door or two down from San Fernando Church. There was a healthy fire burning in the hearth when Joe and Crockett walked in, and Travis and Captain Baugh, his adjutant, were standing over a table studying a map and shelling pecans.

"Thank you for coming, Colonel," Travis said as he pumped the hand of his distinguished guest. Travis, Joe had noticed, was always a bit agitated in Crockett's presence, as if he couldn't quite believe the man was standing in front of him.

"You're the colonel, sir," Crockett replied as he pulled off his heavy greatcoat and handed it to Joe. "I'm just a miserable private. The more you order me around, the happier it makes me."

Crockett sat down on a high-backed chair and teetered on it with his back against the wall, as if he planned to do nothing else the whole day but sit there and talk.

"That's a handsome coat," Travis said as Joe hung it on a peg near the door.

"It's New England wool, Colonel, and so snug-finished I reckon it'll stop a cannonball. Joe, reach inside one of those pockets and see if you can't call forth a spirit."

Joe removed a whiskey flask from one of the coat's many inside pockets and handed it to Crockett. The congressman held the flask out to Travis, who gave a polite shake of his head. Travis was particular about his vices, pretty much limiting himself to fornication.

Baugh turned the flask down as well, saying he'd had a fiery Mexican breakfast that morning and his digestion was on the corrosive side. But Baugh had a light manner generally, and Joe thought he looked like a man who might take a drink now and then. He'd marched to Texas with the New Orleans Greys, and he wore his unit's handsome uniform, though the jacket was ripped and frayed and he'd lost so much weight the faded trousers sagged in the seat like an old man's.

They talked for a bit about the progress of the fortifications at the Alamo. Crockett said he'd been in a fort or two during the Creek War and it looked to him like Jameson knew what he was doing.

"But I tell you what, Colonel," he told Travis, "I don't like forts generally. I tend to be an open-air man. And if we're planning on defending that place and not getting killed in the proceedings I'd say we need about four times the men we got. And it might be nice to have a dollar or two from this so-called Texas government so these boys wouldn't have to parade around in rags and could maybe even have a bite to eat every now and then."

"I sent a letter to Governor Smith yesterday and another goes out this afternoon."

"Last I heard, Governor Smith was getting himself impeached."

"Yes, but he has deposed the council that impeached him."

Crockett laughed and cracked two pecans against each other in one of his big hands. "You're making me nostalgic for politics, Colonel."

He took his time picking the meat out of the pecans, and then stood up and threw the shells into the fire.

"If you want my advice," Crockett said, "I'd say let's get the hell out of here. I'm with Houston—let's blow the Alamo up. We ain't got the men to defend it, and we ain't got a government worth a shit to back us up."

"Nevertheless, it's the only government we have. And it doesn't agree with Houston, and neither do I. Béxar is the key to Texas, Mr. Crockett."

There was a defiant note in Travis's voice that Joe was glad to hear. It showed Travis was getting his confidence back. The last few months he'd been a trial to be around. For someone who'd wanted war to break out as bad as Travis did, he had a troublesome time getting used to it. First he fretted that he wouldn't get a good commission, then that his law practice would fail while he was in the army, then that he couldn't get enough men to join his cavalry troop. He hadn't wanted to come to Béxar in the first place, thinking that all the fighting from now on would take place somewhere else. But the thrown-together Texas government had ordered him to go, and he hadn't been here a week when the commander of the garrison, Colonel Neill, had to leave to look after his sick wife. When he left, Neill put Travis in charge, and at first that had made Travis as nervous as a goose. With good reason, Joe thought, since Travis was only half as old as Crockett and hadn't even been in a real war yet.

The only time Joe had seen Travis in a good temper at all in the last few months was when they went to visit his boy in Montville. Travis and Charlie would sit out on a tree bench at the edge of the yard reading a book together, and that seemed to settle the colonel's mind a bit. But when they went to Montville for the last time, and then rode on to Béxar, Travis had been even more agitated than usual. On the way he apologized to Joe for his bad temper. He said it was because he thought he might get killed fighting the Mexicans and would never see his boy again.

"This post is the frontier picket guard," Travis was saying now to Crockett, "and men died to secure it. If we give it up now we open the door for Santa Anna to march right through to the colonies."

Crockett shifted his eyes to Baugh. "What do you think, Captain Baugh?"

"I think Béxar must be held at all costs, sir."

"Well, gentlemen," Crockett said, casting an amused glance in Joe's direction, "let's just hold the damn place."

"The question is," Travis said, "what do we do about Bowie?"

"I figured you were working your way around to that. Is he out of control again today?"

"No, he's safely drunk at the moment, passed out at the Veramendi house, but when he wakes up you can be sure he'll start sowing havoc all over again. And I won't tolerate it, sir."

Travis launched into a recitation of Bowie's recent offenses. Travis had been irritated about being ordered to

Béxar in the first place, and secretly fretful about being placed in command, but the minute Jim Bowie had tried to steal that command away from him he made sure to hold on to his new authority as if it were the dearest thing in his life. There was bad blood between the two men, one of them an aspiring pillar of propriety and the other a natural thief. Yesterday Bowie had gotten himself into a drunken panic because he'd heard from one of his Tejano informants that the Mexican army had already left the Rio Grande and would show up in Béxar any day. He had taken it upon himself to declare martial law, and he and his men then proceeded to parade around like barbarians, shooting off their rifles, letting people out of jail on a whim, ordering the law-abiding citizens of Béxar off the streets and back into their houses.

"I saw what went on yesterday," Crockett said, interrupting Travis's list of Bowie's transgressions. "It was a disgraceful row, no doubt about it. But Bowie got agitated for a reason. Somebody like that—somebody who's kept a step ahead of the law his whole life—he starts to grow feelers like a doodlebug. And when Bowie's feelers tell him the Mexicans are farther along than we thought, it might do us some good to listen."

"Santa Anna will not be here for at least a month," Travis almost shouted. "He can't leave the Rio Grande until the grass rises and Bowie knows it! This has nothing to do with the location of the Mexican forces and every goddam thing in the world to do with Bowie's flagrant desire to usurp my authority over this post! And I will not stand for it! He will put himself and his volunteers under my command or we will have a reckoning on these streets before Santa Anna ever arrives."

"I give you credit, sir," Crockett said. "You are a fiery sonofabitch. But if you start talking like that to Bowie he'll pull out that knife of his and your cake will be dough."

"That's why I need someone of your gravity to talk to him for me," Travis said. "There is a common purpose here, and he needs to be able to see it."

Crockett took a final swallow from his flask and then tossed it to Joe to put back in his coat.

"All right," he said, "but I ain't about to start waving a bone in front of Jim Bowie's face unless there's a little meat on it."

"What do you suggest?"

"Joint command. You're in charge of the regulars. He's in charge of the volunteers. You sign orders together."

Travis looked uncertainly at Baugh.

"We're not likely to agree on which orders to sign."

"That ain't a problem," Crockett said. "In the event of an honest difference of opinion, both parties agree that common sense will prevail."

"Who decides what's common sense?" Baugh asked.

"I do," said Crockett. "By virtue of my long experience of the matter in the United States House of Representatives."

"I JUST DON'T like it, Joe," Crockett mused as they walked together down Soledad Street. "I've killed too many bears in their dens not to get a little nervous about holing up in a place like this."

The congressman was on his way to the Veramendi house to talk to Bowie. Joe had a bundle of Travis's clothes under one arm that he was taking to a Mexican laundress who lived in a hovel at the far western edge of town, and who was sure to want money for her services, not the receipt from the Provisional Government of Texas that Travis had told Joe to try to pay her with first.

"I ain't never seen a bear," Joe responded, not knowing what else to say.

"Well, you got to go out in search of 'em," Crockett said, as if he were mildly annoyed with this comment. "They usually ain't of a mind to come to you. Tell me this: can you shoot a musket?"

"I can shoot a musket and a rifle both, but I don't know if I can hit anything."

"Well, you understand Colonel Travis may call upon you to do so? Hell, you may find yourself firing a cannon, short of men as we are. When those Mexicans start coming at us like the locusts of Egypt you can forget about your launderin'."

"Yes, sir."

"And what will you think about that?"

"I don't know what you mean."

"I mean what will you think about shooting down men who say they're coming up here to free you from slavery? Think you can still pull the trigger?"

"I guess so," Joe said. That very thought had occurred to him several times already, but there was no point in speculating about jumping over to the other side, because he knew he wasn't going to do it.

"Well, then you're a patriot," Crockett said as they walked up to the Veramendi house, "and Travis is a lucky man to have you."

Joe had heard people call the Veramendi house a palace, but to his eyes it was just a bigger version of the other houses in Béxar: a long building perched on the edge of the street, as plain as a box except for its towering wooden doors and narrow windows. There were a couple of Bowie's men guarding those doors, looking as if they expected an attack at any minute not only from the Mexicans but from Travis's men. But they were friendly to Crockett—everybody was friendly to Crockett. They greeted him with big grins and pushed open a smaller, man-size entrance that was cut into the massive doors. When Crockett had gone inside, Joe continued walking down Soledad Street in the biting winter wind. He felt something stirring in his blood, some great change looming, but as much as he could he set his mind to normal earthly thoughts, for fear that this tumultuous feeling might be nothing more than death whispering in his ear.

BEHIND THE VERAMENDI PALACE, Terrell was digging up a chest of household silver that had been buried in the garden at the edge of the stone coach house. He and Sparks had been working for an hour, and they had only now unearthed the broad, flat rock that covered the treasure like the lid of a sarcophagus.

"By God, she's in there snug," Sparks said as he expectorated a great wad of tobacco into the ruined garden. He took a moment to remove his hat and mop the sweat off his bald forehead with the sleeve of his shirt. "You want my opinion, Bowie ain't gonna find a better hidin' place than that."

While Sparks stood there and stared contemplatively at the hole, Terrell stepped down onto the rock and began shovelling the dirt away from its margins. He had been listening to Sparks's opinions for the entire hour they'd been digging—opinions about whores, military strategy, ice skating, phrenology, fox grape jelly, Baptists, and iron plows—and he was not in the least interested in hearing Sparks debate about whether or not the silver should be moved. The point was, Bowie wanted it moved. The silver had belonged to Governor Veramendi, who had perished with all his family—including his daughter, Bowie's wife—in Monclova during the cholera year. Now the great house and everything in it belonged to Bowie. He had ordered the silver buried in the garden when he had heard Cos was on his way to Béxar, and it had remained there undiscovered throughout the siege and battle for the city. But now Bowie had begun to fret about, it, worried not only that the advancing Mexican army might hear about it and dig it up, but that Travis might beat them to it, confiscate the silver for the government of Texas, and give him a worthless receipt in return. Terrell's orders were to unearth the chest, transport it under armed guard to the Seguín ranch, and bury it again.

It took another half-hour for Terrell and Sparks to shovel away enough dirt to free the rock and then to pry it up with a crowbar. The silver chest lay beneath it, wrapped in mouldy canvas.

"You better get Mrs. Alsbury," Terrell told Sparks after they managed to wrestle the chest out of the hole. "She wanted to have a look at it."

"She wanted to make sure we didn't steal any of it, is what you mean," Sparks said. He wiped some more sweat off his forehead, put on his jacket, and walked into the house, Terrell helped himself to a seat on an iron bench that looked down the sloping ground toward the river below. He had been working hard enough to break into a considerable sweat himself, but now that he was still he was aware of the cold, bitter wind. Since all the trees on both banks had been cut down during the siege, he had a clear view across the river to the Alamo from the back of the Veramendi house. A work crew was shoring up the crumbling north wall of the mission with timber and dirt, and Terrell could hear their voices and the echoing blows of their hammers in the wintry air. He had spent some time working on the Alamo defenses when he had first arrived in Béxar and had gotten friendly with a few of the regulars—some of whom were close to his age—but lately the members of Bowie's volunteer forces had kept mostly to themselves and stayed mostly drunk.

Something was wrong with Bowie. His color was off, his

temper was high, he could not seem to stay sober. And his lack of self-control had spread to his men. Yesterday had been a disgrace, Bowie storming about like a madman, maliciously drunk, sowing confusion and panic everywhere as he ordered his men to blockade the roads. Terrell himself had had to turn back a dozen families who were trying to flee Béxar before the fighting erupted again. He had gone to bed last night remembering their tear-streaked faces and imploring Spanish voices, and the shame he felt kept him from sleep. At least he had been sober enough to feel shame. Some of the volunteers, encouraged by Bowie's wild dissolution, had staggered back and forth in front of the plaza, demanding the release of prisoners from the jail, and afterward a few of them had even sold their rifles for more aguardiente.

Sitting on the bench, looking across to the Alamo, where so much industry and order was in evidence, Terrell was tempted to lay down his shovel and report for duty as a regular soldier under Travis. Since joining up with Bowie, his status in the army had been informal. He was officially an "unattached volunteer," and unattached was the way he felt. Most of Bowie's volunteers had started out together as members of a company. Sparks, for instance, belonged to the United States Invincibles, which had been formed in Mississippi and had marched and drilled and bivouacked together before setting off to liberate Texas. Terrell had no company. He had simply stumbled upon the army all on his own, and after spending two months scouting with Bowie's volunteers he still felt isolated. Partly this was because his instincts told him to hold himself apart. The ceaseless drinking of these men bothered him; it made them, he thought, vulnerable, and obscured whatever principles may have led them to this war in the first place.

Terrell spent a lot of time thinking about his own conduct. The great issues of the war mattered less to him than private issues of character that he believed the war would determine. The weak and dissolute side of his character had already displayed itself vividly enough to him, and he had by now seen some of the sordidness of war. But the conviction lingered that there was something fine within him as well, something that had not yet emerged, and that could emerge—could shine clear—only in the heat of some great extremity, some great battle. It did not much matter to him if he survived such a battle, as long he could have even a glimpse of his true self. More than once he had pictured the face of his mother upon learning of his honorable and selfless death.

He heard the door squeaking on its heavy Spanish hinges and turned to see Mrs. Alsbury and her sister, Gertrudis, walking with Sparks across the yard in his direction. The fallen leaves were so thick on the ground that the women's feet were obscured and they seemed to float on the hems of their dresses. Both women were young. Gertrudis was slender and pretty but cross-looking. Mrs. Alsbury was stouter and had a kind voice, but she always seemed to Terrell to be weighed down with aggravation. She held her baby boy against one hip, but he kept writhing and twisting to be let out of her arms, and when she would not allow it he banged his head against her chin.

"Ábrelo, por favor," Mrs. Alsbury said to Terrell as she stood there wrestling with the baby.

"Excuse me?" he said.

She gestured with her free hand for him to unwrap the canvas from the chest. If she knew any English, Terrell had not yet heard it. She had an American husband, a doctor named Horace Alsbury, but Terrell supposed he hadn't had time to teach her the language, since he had only recently married her and now he was out on a scouting mission. Mrs. Alsbury's given name was Juana. She and Gertrudis were members of Béxar's powerful Navarro family and had been raised together with their cousin Ursula, who had been Bowie's wife. Bowie considered himself their guardian and treated them as if they were his own sisters.

Terrell lifted one end of the chest off the ground as Sparks struggled to slip the half-rotten cotton sacking off. The chest was made of some kind of gleaming, heavy wood—mahogany, Terrell thought. The word "Veramendi" was elaborately carved into the lid, which was secured by a large heart-shaped lock.

Juana Alsbury nodded to her younger sister, who knelt down and opened the lock with a key she had brought from the house. Then Terrell and Sparks stood there in polite silence as the two women sorted through all the plates and candlesticks and place settings of silver until they had accounted for and discussed every piece. Mrs. Alsbury set her baby down beside her. He was not walking yet, but he leaned on the wall of the chest for support and fished inside with his clumsy hands. He held up a spoon and waved it at Terrell, and Terrell, feeling as if he should respond, simply nodded his head.

When she was certain that all the silver was still there, Mrs. Alsbury closed the lid, picked up her son, looked up at Terrell, and whispered "Gracias." There were tears in her eyes, and in her sister's too. He supposed he would feel emotional too if the house he had grown up in had been taken over by rebel soldiers who didn't even speak the same language, and if the dishes off which he had eaten all his meals as a child had to be buried and moved from place to place.

Terrell and Sparks each took hold of one of the handles on either end of the chest and hauled it up the sloping yard to the house. It was so heavy they had to pause and renew their grip every few yards. Mrs. Alsbury and Gertrudis waited patiently for them but did not think to lend a hand. Finally they managed to manhandle the chest through the back door and into the sala, where they set it down as gently as they could on the gleaming tile floor.

"What have you boys got yourselves there?" Roth said. He and two of the Invincibles were sitting on the floor in front of the hearth, yawning and eating cold tortillas and warming their bare feet.

"What do you care what it is?" Sparks told him, after he'd gotten his breath back. "I didn't see you helpin' me and Terrell dig it up."

"Where's Colonel Bowie?" Terrell asked Roth.

"He's back there talking to Crockett," Roth said, gesturing toward the other end of the house. "We just took them a pot of coffee."

Terrell thought he should let Bowie know that the chest was out of the ground, but he knew better than to interrupt him during a conference with Crockett. He and Sparks sat down with Roth near the fire and tried to get warm. The big room was bare except for a long table, some barrels of crackers and piles of tack and blankets. Most of the furniture and decorations had already been carted off to Seguín's ranch, and the grand house was gradually being turned into a warehouse for Bowie and his men. Daylight shone through a hole near the ceiling where a cannonball had struck during the siege, and rubble and masonry dust that had never been cleaned up were still lying within the room.

Mrs. Alsbury and Gertrudis disappeared, but a little while later Gertrudis came back with cups of coffee for Sparks and Terrell.

"What about the rest of us?" Roth said to her.

"Qué?" she replied.

"The rest of us. Nosotros, dammit."

"She ain't a maid, Roth," Terrell said. "She's just doin' us a favor 'cause we did her one."

Terrell nodded his thanks to Gertrudis. She smiled politely and left the room.

"Look at her grinnin' at you," Roth said. "You're a little

young for her, but she's thunderstruck under the tailbone all the same."

"Shut up," Terrell said quietly.

"I'm just givin' you my opinion is all. You've got a golden opportunity, boy."

"A golden opportunity for Bowie to cut his pecker off with that knife," Sparks said.

Some of Seguín's men were supposed to show up with a cart this morning and lead them to the ranch, but nobody was here yet and Terrell didn't know what else to do, so he just sat in front of the fire with the others waiting for Bowie to show up. After an hour or so he and Crockett finally emerged. Terrell and the others stood up. They were used to being casual with Bowie, but Crockett was another matter. You couldn't help paying court to him, even though he kept insisting he was just a man from Tennessee who was out of a job.

"Now these boys've got the right idea," Crockett said, shaking hands with each of them in an easy, habitual manner as he walked through the room. "I don't believe there's a better use for a man's energies than staring at a fire and drinking a horn or two.

"How are you, son? I'm David Crockett," the congressman said when he took Terrell's hand. Terrell had seen him before but never up close like this, and he thought that no one in his life had ever looked at him with such lively interest.

"Terrell Mott, your . . . honor," he stammered in reply.

"Your honor! If I look like a judge, I wish I may be shot right now."

"I didn't mean . . ."

"You call me David like everybody else, Terrell. We start bowin' and curtsyin' to each other we might be too busy to notice when the Mexicans slip into town.

"Now you boys look after your colonel here," he said,

gripping Bowie by the arm, "there ain't but one of him, you know."

Bowie looked gray and hungover. And with the alarmingly vital Crockett standing next to him and holding on to his arm he seemed oddly subservient. After he had escorted the congressman to the door, he came back with his pale eyes narrow and glowering. Whatever Crockett had said to him in private had left him in a foul frame of mind.

"You men go on over to the Alamo and report to Major Jameson," he said.

"The hell you say," Roth declared. "I ain't about to go dig trenches for that fuckin' Travis. If he wants me to—"

Before Roth could get another word out Bowie grabbed hold of both his ears and hurled him across the room. Roth's head hit the wall with a disturbingly loud thud. He teetered on his feet for a second and then, feeling his balance start to give, sat down on the floor and took a moment to figure out what had happened to him.

"That's a goddam stone wall you threw me at, Jim," he said.

"Get up off the fucking floor and report to Major Jameson like I said," Bowie replied. "And don't you say another insubordinate word about Colonel Travis."

Roth started to get up, but thought better of it.

"You all right, Jacob?" Bowie asked him. The deadness had gone out of his eyes, and remorse was seeping in. Gertrudis and her sister were standing in the doorway, looking alarmed. Bowie avoided their eyes.

"I'm all right, Jim. I'm just dizzy."

"Take your time," Bowie said in a contrite voice.

"No, I got 'er now," Roth said. He waved off Bowie's hand and drew himself to his feet.

"I'm sorry to be rough with you, Jacob," Bowie told him, "but we've got to have some discipline around here or we won't stand a chance when the Mexicans show up. Now you men go on across the river and tell Major Jameson I said to put you to work on the defenses. And if I see anybody drunk from now on—including me—he'll spend the rest of this fucking war in the calabozo."

Terrell started to file out of the house with the rest of the bewildered men, but Bowie called him back and told him to stay a minute. Terrell stood there expectantly in the empty room, but Bowie didn't say anything at first. He just opened the lid of the chest and stared at the silver for a long time as if it weren't even there.

"Ursula and I ate many a fine meal off these plates," Bowie said at last, turning his eyes to Terrell. He had a dispirited and shamefaced look this morning. Probably this was the result of Crockett's lecture, but Terrell also thought the man looked actually sick. Bowie's skin had always been fair, but now it looked as white as caliche dust, and the physical effort of throwing Roth across the room had taken a toll as well.

"Gertrudis," he called out toward one of the other rooms, "trae una silla, por favor."

"There ain't a stick of furniture left in this house," Bowie said to Terrell as Gertrudis rushed in with a chair and set it next to Bowie. "This was a grand place once, but you wouldn't know it now, would you?"

"I guess not," Terrell replied.

"No, you wouldn't. And you'd never guess the happy times we had here. They were fine people, the Veramendis, and by god I'll cut the heart out of the man who says a word against them."

He looked once again at the silver plate and candlesticks and closed the lid.

"I want this buried a good four feet beneath the cookhouse on Seguín's ranch. You go along with 'em to make sure they do it right. And I want the names of every man who sees where it goes. That way if it ain't there when I come for it I'll know who to go after."

Terrell nodded soberly. Bowie slumped against the high

back of the chair and looked vacantly at the wall. He reached down and tossed another oak log into the hearth, though the fire was already giving off too much heat.

Gertrudis asked him in Spanish if he wanted something to eat. He told her no, he wasn't hungry. Gertrudis went and got her sister, who held a hand to Bowie's forehead.

"Tienes fiebre," she said. "Tienes que irte a la cama."

"I'm not going back to bed," he told her in English. "Hell, I just got up."

Bowie suddenly stood and rushed out the back door into the cold air. Terrell heard him vomiting on the grass. In a minute he came back and sat down on the chair again, with Gertrudis and Mrs. Alsbury hovering anxiously around him and pressing wet rags to his face.

"You all right?" Terrell said.

Bowie nodded his head, but he didn't answer. He just sat there for a long time, taking deep breaths. After a while he politely waved the women away, and they retreated into the next room.

"They're like sisters to me," he said absently. "That silver's all I've got left, and I mean to provide for Juana and Gertrudis with it. That's why we have to keep it out of Santa Anna's hands."

"I'll hide it for you as good as I can," Terrell answered, but Bowie didn't seem to hear. He seemed to be looking past Terrell, studying the bare walls of the grand sala.

"I've set a poor example for you," he said at last. "Your mother wouldn't be happy with me about that."

"It ain't my mother's business," Terrell replied.

"I have a weakness for spirits. If you care to hear the truth, I'm almost as bad a drunk as Sam Houston. And it was idiotic of me to try to steal this command away from Travis. We don't stand together, we're dead men. You hear me?"

"I do."

"But that don't change the fact that that goddam teeto-taling lawyer don't know shit about fighting a war. Santa Anna ain't gonna wait on the Rio Grande for the grass to rise, like Travis thinks he will. I'll guarantee you he's on the march now. And when he gets here things are going to get serious fast. He doesn't intend to take any prisoners. He's made that plain. As far as Santa Anna's concerned we're land pirates. And you know what the penalty for piracy is?"

"I guess it's death," Terrell said.

"I guess you're right."

Sweat was beginning to trickle from beneath Bowie's widow's peak of chestnut hair. He took another few deep breaths and fought back the need to puke.

"When you get to Seguín's ranch," he told Terrell, "I want you to keep riding south."

"Where?"

"Anywhere. Back to Refugio. Go home and help your mother out with her inn."

"Why?"

"'Cause I got the feeling things ain't gonna turn out too well around here."

"They'll turn out worse if everybody leaves."

"I'm not talking about everybody, Terrell. I'm talking about you. I don't want to have to explain to your mother how you got stood up against a wall and shot."

Terrell was casting about in his mind for a phrase or two of ringing defiance when Bowie abruptly stood up from his chair and raced out into the yard again. Terrell followed and found him on his hands and knees.

"Fucking dry heaves are about to turn me inside out," Bowie said. He turned his head and looked up at Terrell. The skin of his high forehead was prickly and beaded with sweat. "Were you listening to me? About leaving here?"

"I was listening," Terrell said. "But I ain't going to do that."

"Then don't blame me when you've got a Mexican bay-onet stuck in your gut."

"We better get you out of the cold," Terrell said. He and Gertrudis and Mrs. Alsbury got him back on his feet, but when they let go of his arms he almost collapsed onto the ground again before they could catch him.

"Never had a hangover to beat it," he said. He meant it to sound light but his voice was shaky, and his smile was thin. "I believe I might go back to my bed after all."

CHAPTER TWENTY-ONE

✦

"**W**HAT IS the true purpose of this rebellion?" Don Osbaldo Espinosa droned on rhetorically as he filled his wineglass yet again. He then seized a nearby taper and held the flame to the end of his cigar, working his thin cheeks like a bellows until the air around him was thorcoughly beclouded. Edmund knew Don Osbaldo well enough by now to understand that the filling of his wineglass and the lighting of his cigar were calculated pauses meant to arouse suspense in his guests' minds as to what his next glittering pronouncement might be. But the pronouncements were never brilliant, the guests were in reality prisoners, and with each interminable evening their imprisonment was growing more and more tiresome.

"At first the rebels proclaimed that they merely wanted to restore the Constitution of 1824," Espinosa said, settling back gravely in his chair. "That was transparent nonsense, of course. The real object is to break away from Mexico and perhaps to take two or three Mexican states with them. Then they will join the United States, or create their own slaveholding republic. Because that is what these sons of Jefferson, these supposed believers in the rights of man, truly desire: an empire for slavery."

Don Osbaldo went on, as he did almost every night, reminding his dinner guests that slavery had not been necessary to either himself or his forebears, who for many generations had devoted their toil and blood—*their* blood, not that of some innocent and uncomprehending negro—to the safety and prosperity of this land.

Edmund cast a glance across the table at Mary. She was listening to Espinosa's harangue with an alert interest that had nothing to do with what he was saying and everything to do with a desire to improve her Spanish. During the month they had spent as hostages at Espinosa's rancho, Mary's grasp of the language had grown far more assured, her accent and vocabulary both impressive, though she had as yet no real command of the verbs and spoke in an eternal present tense.

Espinosa was a widower. He was in his late fifties, Edmund guessed, his body still powerful and taut from ceaseless ranch work but his face starting to collapse like an old man's. His young wife, like Mary's daughter, had been carried away by the cholera, leaving behind two mute and glowering children, a boy and a girl, who were required to sit at dinner every night with their spines in rigid conformance with the hard, straight backs of their Spanish chairs. Besides Edmund and Mary, the other perpetual guest was the dragoon officer who had abducted them, Lieutenant Arechiga. Arechiga was still frightfully thin and frail, but it was a testament to Mary's remarkable healing skills that he was alive at all. He had almost died several times during the four days it took for the dragoon patrol and their prisoners to reach the Espinosa ranch. Upon opening the officer's tunic that first afternoon, Mary had discovered a wad of congealed blood large enough to fill a milk bucket, and after she had casually tossed it aside, to the horror of the troopers, she probed with her fingers in the wound until she found the rifle ball that had incarcerated itself just below the ribs. She also set and splinted the compound fracture below Arechiga's knee as Edmund and Sergeant Paredes and several troopers held the screaming man still. Though everyone, even Mary, expected him to die, his fever was broken and his wounds were discharging laudable pus by the time they reached Espinosa's fortresslike hacienda on its high bluff above the Atascosa River.

"Please take another glass of wine, Mrs. Mott," Espinosa said to Mary. It was a nightly rhetorical ritual, this urging of his benevolence upon his captives. "Please humor me in my poor attempts to make you feel at home."

He sat there grinning, with the wine bottle raised in her direction. Edmund knew that Mary could not quite follow her host's decorative Spanish, but she caught the gist of it, and with a practiced dismissive gesture she merely laid the palm of her hand across her wineglass.

"Once again I am devastated," he said good-naturedly. He filled the lieutenant's glass, and then his own. He had long since given up trying to press his wine upon Edmund.

"And who are these men who think they have the right to tear Texas away from us?" Espinosa thundered on. "They are ingrates at best, colonists who do not have the grace to appreciate the gifts of land and citizenship freely given to them by the Mexican government. At worst they are mere fugitives and opportunists. But foreigners all, Señor Mc-Gowan, foreigners all."

"You forget that there are Tejanos among the rebels as well, Don Osbaldo," Edmund said. "The Seguíns, for instance, and—"

"Political schemers!" Espinosa shouted, so loud that the children winced and the parrot in its cage behind the hacendado's chair ruffled its neck in alarm. "Political schemers and traitors! I will thank you not to violate my hospitality by mentioning the Seguíns in my own sala!"

Edmund caught Mary's eye. Her look was sharp and chastening: Didn't he know better than to let this volatile and self-important man draw him into an argument?

"Please excuse my rudeness," Espinosa said tightly after a moment, his ivory bridge clacking angrily in his mouth. "Of course your opinions are always welcome. You are a man of great intelligence, and I am merely a backwoodsman and Indian fighter whose only accomplishment has been to hew a poor living from the wilderness. But I hope I do not offend you, Señor McGowan, when I note that your commentary is almost always theoretical. Unlike Lieutenant Arechiga and myself, you have not troubled yourself to declare an allegiance or to take a part in the war."

"If I am so neutral and inconsequential," Edmund said evenly, ignoring this ornate insult as he had ignored dozens over the past weeks, "then why am I still your prisoner?"

"It is very simple, and you are no doubt wise enough to understand this without my pointing it out. I do not trust you. The Texians know that I am quietly loyal to Santa Anna, but they do not know that my vaqueros are spying on his behalf. If you betray me, the rebels will come here in force, and there will be a battle I would much prefer to avoid. Children, you are excused. You may attend to your studies."

The two solemn children stood without a word and passed out of the room without a parting glance at any of the adults. When they had first come to Espinosa's rancho Mary had made an effort to notice the children and speak warmly to them, but they had lived in this arid and haughty environment for far too long for her kindness to have any effect, or even to be noticed.

Edmund thought it the unhappiest home he had ever known, ruled by a needling windbag who mistook his own coarse self-interest as liberal enlightenment. The vaqueros and the servants in fact lived in fear of him, of his exquisite temper and his sarcastic whimsy. He paid them well, Edmund supposed, or they would surely all have deserted him long ago. The sala in which they were sitting tonight was dark, with only a few meager tapers burning, but it was darker still in the daytime, since the main house had been built as a fort, with stone walls three feet thick and only a few narrow windows, so that almost the only light that seeped into the house came from the shooting holes spaced every three feet at shoulder height. The roof of the house was crenellated for defense, and all the outbuildings were connected by a wall ten feet high, so that the whole hacienda was one tight and self-protecting structure, as formal, impenetrable, and cold as the medieval castles Edmund had seen illustrated in books.

Only the parrot seemed to possess any liveliness or genuine humor. It was a compact green creature with alert, knowing eyes. The parrot's name was Medardo. It seemed to register and understand everything it saw, and to lock this knowledge away in the alien vault of its brain where no human being could ever trespass.

"Ah! Qué bonitos son los enanos," the parrot crooned in its strange timbreless voice as the children left the room. Ah, how lovely are the dwarves. It was the first line of a song that had been fashionable during Edmund's first visit to the City of Mexico, years ago.

"Someday perhaps he will learn the whole song," Don Osbaldo laughed. "Shall we let him out of his cage?"

He stood and opened the iron door of the birdcage. Medardo hopped on his shoulder and then, as soon as Espinosa had seated himself again, leapt onto the table and began walking up and down as if he were on parade.

"He wants to be admired," Espinosa said. "He is very vain."

"What did he say?" Mary nervously whispered to Edmund as the parrot waddled between them. "I couldn't understand half of it."

"That he thinks we will betray him if he lets us go."

"Please," commanded Don Osbaldo in Spanish from the head of the table. "Texas is still Mexico, my friends. Therefore I will ask you to speak the language of the country."

Espinosa turned his thin face toward Mary and told her, in Spanish simple enough for a child to understand, that she and Edmund would continue to remain here as his guests until Lieutenant Arechiga was well enough to travel.

"What do you mean?" Edmund said, feeling a new throb of foreboding. "Travel where?"

With a mischievous tilt of his head, Espinosa directed Edmund's and Mary's attention to Arechiga, who was sitting in his usual nimbus of silence, studying the bright green parrot on the table.

"I want you to accompany me and my men to the Rio Grande Presidio."

"Rio Grande!" Edmund shouted. "Why?"

"Because the army is said to be there. And I do not know the way."

"Don Osbaldo's vaqueros can show you the way."

"I'm afraid my men are busy at the moment, Señor Mc-Gowan," Espinosa replied. "Between their patriotic duties and the routine demands of operating the ranch, they have no time to serve as scouts. And besides, you and Señora Mott are nortes, and as such are of some strategic value should Lieutenant Arechiga have the misfortune to encounter a rebel patrol."

"Rio Grande is over two hundred miles away," Edmund protested to Arechiga. "Your men have no horses, and Don Osbaldo can spare you none. It will take weeks to get there, and the chances are the army will have already moved on by the time you arrive."

"Then we will continue on to Monclova, and you will go with us."

Espinosa laughed, and as he did so held out his open hand to the parrot. Medardo hopped onto his fingers, and Espinosa passed him along to Enrique, the decrepit old mozo who waited on Don Osbaldo with singular vigilance throughout the course of every interminable meal.

As Enrique placed the bird back into the cage, Edmund felt Mary's eyes on him and turned to look at her. She had understood. In the weeks of their captivity together they had developed a strange unspeaking accord. Espinosa had been careful to keep them apart from one another, locked away most of the day in their individual rooms at opposite ends of the compound, letting them walk about in the yard for an hour or so in the afternoon, always under the guard of his own vaqueros or Arechiga's troopers. They were allowed to speak, but curiously, they did not tend to say much, just walked together in the shadow of the stone walls with Professor trailing alongside, their shoulders sometimes brushing, their very minds—it seemed to Edmund—silently converging. It occurred to him more than once during these afternoon walks that this was what marriage must be like—this sense of a corresponding consciousness, of another person magically absorbing and understanding your moods.

Now, as he met Mary's alarmed eyes across the table, her thoughts could not have been more clear or urgent. They must escape, and soon, before Arechiga's health improved enough for him to drag them deep into Mexico.

But how? In his grim little room that night, lying on a thin mattress and looking out his lone shooting hole at a tiny star-filled circle of sky, Edmund rehearsed the possibilities once again. He had a small powder flask. During their first night after being taken captive by the dragoons a blundering feral hog had torn through their camp, sending everyone into a scurrying panic. In the midst of the confusion one of the men dropped the flask, and Edmund had promptly picked it up and concealed it in the waistband of his trousers. Miraculously, it had never been discovered, and it was now buried in the dirt beneath his mattress. His own shotgun, along with Mary's Spanish musket and pistol, were locked up in the armory room, but on their afternoon walks he had often had occasion to pass by the open door of the small one-room house belonging to Espinosa's ranch foreman. The foreman's wife was always there, shelling corn into a bowl or patching up her husband's shirts, and behind her was a bare shelf. Just visible to him as he walked by, flush with the edge of the shelf, was the curved stock of a horse pistol. Day after the day the pistol lay in the same position. Nobody ever moved it. Possibly it was broken and useless, but it was just as possible that it was not, that it was kept on the shelf for protection against a nighttime intruder. Edmund could not see the barrel from his vantage point, but he thought it likely it would accommodate the four deeply pitted musket balls that he had found discarded in a trash barrel outside the armory.

He could conceivably steal the pistol. With his powder and defective shot it would probably serve as at least some sort of weapon, but then what? There were hams hanging in the smokehouse, but the odds of stealing both a pistol and a ham were long indeed. And what about horses? Cabezon and Gar were now part of the rancho's caballada, kept in a walled corral fifty yards away from the main hacienda, and usually securely guarded by the vaqueros, who bragged of never losing a horse to an Indian raid.

But if he had a weapon, if he had food, if he had horses for him and Mary to ride, Edmund knew precisely what he would do. There was an old contraband road shown to him years before by a friendly whiskey smuggler he had hired as a guide on one of his expeditions. Edmund remembered the road as hardly more than a track, overgrown and washed out for much of its length, and it was probably in worse shape now, but that was to his advantage. None of Espinosa's men, he felt sure, would suspect him of knowing about it. Perhaps they did not even know about it themselves. He was fairly sure that a shallow tributary of the Atascosa crossed the road no more than ten miles west of the hacienda. If he could make his way to the road without being detected, if he could recognize its faint presence, then he was reasonably sure he could get away. The road stretched north for sixty miles, where it struck Sandies Creek and then intersected the Gonzales road at an isolated but well-provisioned cabin owned by a man named Castleman, where travellers between Gonzales and Béxar often spent the night.

"I will not allow those men to drag me to Monclova,"

Mary whispered to him the next afternoon as they walked back and forth below the stone wall. The structures of the hacienda were built into the wall. There was a small chapel, the smokehouse, and the tiny dark rooms—like the ones in which Mary and Edmund were imprisoned—where the vaqueros and their families lived. The foreman's house was one of these, and once again its door was open. The foreman's wife sat at a table with her daughter picking the pebbles out of a great pile of beans. Behind them on the wall shelf the pistol still lay with its curved stock facing outward.

"It's too dangerous to try to escape," Edmund reasoned.

"There's a seeping damp in one corner of my room. The mortar is rotted. I've already dislodged several stones and in one or two more nights of work I can make a hole through the outside wall. Then there is the question, of course, of how to get you out. But if we could escape the compound during the night without attracting attention, if we could get our horses, we could be far away by the time anyone noticed."

"I've been having a similar daydream," he said. "But I think it's better to wait." He did not tell her about the pistol, or the powder flask, or the almost unknown road through the wilderness.

"Better to wait for what?" Mary said.

"I don't know precisely. If Santa Anna is really on the march toward Béxar, Houston is likely to rally the whole army there to defend it. An army like that will need provisioning. Espinosa has plenty of beef, and since he's openly loyal to Santa Anna the Texians may very well come here to raid the place."

"That's just hopeful speculation, Edmund. And even if such a thing did happen we'd probably already be on our way to Monclova."

She was right. Lieutenant Arechiga was improving daily and in two or three weeks would probably feel well enough and impatient enough to be on his way. And neither Edmund nor Mary trusted him. He was an excitable, ill-tempered man, holding a commission that, like so many in the over-officered Mexican army, had little to do with his abilities and everything to do with his family's means. Sergeant Paredes was a competent enough soldier but hadn't the least spark of initiative or perspective. The prospect of a long, hazardous, and unpredictable journey under the shaky leadership of these two men inspired Edmund with a sharp sense of doom. And he was aware—again, with that mysterious closeness of thought—that Mary had the same uneasy conviction. They would not survive. They would be the first to starve when food gave out, the first to drown when a river crossing needed to be investigated. They might be shot by accident by a rebel patrol, or even killed on purpose by Arechiga if Edmund aroused his panic by guessing wrong about the location of a trail or the distance between springs; and even if by good fortune they made it to journey's end they still might be arrested on some cause or another and left to rot in a Mexican jail.

No, he did not want to go. And yet the hazards of escape were, if anything, even greater.

The clouds of the day before had scudded away, and the sky was a glaring blue. Through the open gate of the hacienda winter leaves flared along the river, and smoke from distant branding fires drifted upward on the windless horizon. It had been cold earlier in the day, but now the sun's warmth was seeping through, and Medardo the parrot had been given his freedom, as was the custom on fine days, to perch and sing in the branches of a struggling peach tree. The bird's wings had been clipped to prevent him from soaring away; but he spent much of the day shifting from one foot to another on the bare branches as if continually gauging his weight and trying to summon the courage for an attempt at flight.

"Abra la puerta encantada! Abra la puerta encantada!" the parrot called in an anxious voice as Edmund and Mary walked by. A barefoot little girl in a tattered shift—the daughter of one of the goatherds—was standing on tiptoe at the bottom of the tree, repeatedly tossing a raisin to the bird, but Medardo showed only casual interest in catching it.

"How are your shoes?" Edmund asked Mary as they watched the girl pick the raisin off the ground and toss it up again to the parrot.

"Serviceable enough, though the laces are rotted."

"And your mackinac is within easy reach?"

"Why? Do you have a plan?"

"No. But there's no reason not to be ready, in case an opportunity happens to present itself."

"I'm ready," she said.

DON OSBALDO WAS troubled with an intolerance to cedar pollen, and he presided that night at the dinner table with visibly red and teary eyes and an even more caustic demeanor than usual.

"I believe I have come to understand you very well during our weeks together, Señor McGowan," Espinosa said as he cut into a thin beefsteak, his knife scraping and screeching on his silver platter. He took his time chewing the meat and then washed it down with wine from a goblet made of blue Puebla glass, creating his usual resonant pause. "But Señora Mott, I am afraid," he said, when he finally resumed his monologue, "is still something of a mystery to me."

"In what way?" Edmund asked. Mary had an anxious look of incomprehension—Don Osbaldo's Spanish had as usual been too swift for her.

"You are a man, as you say. of principled neutrality, serving the higher cause of science. This I accept as more or less true, though I think it is less a matter of neutrality with you than indifference to the struggles of your fellow men. However, with Señora Mott, I detect a more vital interest—a personal interest."

"Indeed you do. The war directly threatens her livelihood."

"That is not quite what I mean."

Mary had by now caught enough of the conversation to be worried about its drift. From the beginning she and Edmund had maintained to their captors that she had been on her way to Béxar because she had heard that, in the panic after the rebels took the town, a stock of furniture and bed linens she had recently purchased had been confiscated by the ayuntamiento. They had invented this fiction because the truth struck them as dangerous. As the mother of a rebel soldier, she would be perceived as a different kind of hostage, and if Terrell's name were discovered, and passed along by Don Osbaldo's centralist spies it might make him a specific target if Santa Anna's army gained—as it was of course likely to do—the upper hand.

"I mean that she has a stake in the cause," Espinosa went on, talking once again about Mary as if she were not at the table but sequestered in another room. "What that stake is, I don't know, of course. Perhaps she has a husband. Perhaps he is an officer in the United States Army, stationed at the Louisiana border, and he has sent her into Texas so that she can advise him of the proper moment for the Americans to invade the sovereign Republic of Mexico in support of the rebel cause."

Edmund made a point of looking amused. "That is a fanciful thought."

"Or perhaps," Espinosa went on dryly, "her husband is an agent for one of the unscrupulous American land companies and—"

"Is he saying I am a spy?" Mary demanded of Edmund.

"Yes, perhaps you are a spy, Señora Mott," Espinosa replied in slow, deliberate Spanish. His voice was genial.

His swollen, reddened eyes gave the false impression that this sort of speculation was painful to him. "I do not mean to say that is such a bad thing. I am a spy myself. But if you have acquired information that might cause the deaths of Mexican soldiers it is my duty to keep that information from circulating."

"By shooting me?" Mary said in English, not having the Spanish for such a conditional thought. Her eyes flashed to Edmund. "Ask him if he is planning to shoot me!"

When Edmund translated, Don Osbaldo laughed. With the corner of his napkin he wiped away the mucous discharge that had almost glued his eyes shut.

"Of course not," he said. "Do you think I am a barbarian? Surely during the time we've been in each other's company you've managed to form a better opinion of me than that."

And then he excused himself to dissolve into a fit of sneezing.

EACH MORNING at dawn Edmund had grown accustomed to seeing Don Osbaldo Espinosa ride out to work with his vaqueros, sitting erect on a splendid Spanish saddle, his feet encased in ornamental wooden stirrups carved in the face of a lion. But the next morning Don Osbaldo did not appear. The vaqueros left without him. Sitting in his room, Edmund overheard the mozo telling one of the women that Don Osbaldo was stuttering so greatly from the pollen sickness that he could not leave his house.

He had still not emerged when it came time for Edmund and Mary's afternoon walk around the compound. Lieutenant Arechiga, however, continued in his improving health.

"Good afternoon," Arechiga said, riding up to them on horseback. On Cabezon, Edmund noticed, with a bitter anger that he knew he must suppress. The mare shifted and settled her mild bluish eye on her owner. A look of chastisement, Edmund thought.

"I hope you do not mind that I have borrowed your horse," Arechiga said. "It is a fine day and I think a ride will do me good."

"Not at all," Edmund forced himself to say in a pleasant tone. "Though you should ride gently. It is still possible you could tear open your wounds."

Arechiga smiled, dug his cruel Spanish spurs into Cabezon's flanks, and rode out the open gate. Professor ran after them for a few yards, barking, until Edmund called the dog back.

"I hope he does tear open his wounds," Edmund said to Mary as they resumed their walk. One of the dragoon privates trailed along several paces behind them. His name was Solis, Edmund had discovered, one of many sons of a wayward Franciscan friar from Querétaro. Solis was their usual guard and he had grown bored with the habitually uneventful duty of escorting them around the grounds. Although Edmund was sure the private could not understand a word of English, he and Mary were always careful to keep their voices as low as they could without attracting his suspicion.

Mary did not reply. Her thoughts, Edmund knew, were still on the dinner conversation of the night before, on the way Don Osbaldo had seemed to be hinting at some new level of peril.

As they walked, the shadow of a coasting hawk rippled across the nubby ground in front of them. Edmund looked up to see the bird flying low in the clear winter sky, so low that he could see its piercing eyes as it scanned the earth. Medardo the parrot was singing in his peach tree, ruffling his plumage in the sun. This would be the last fine day for a while, Edmund reckoned. There were close-knit clouds visible above the western horizon that would soon cover this blue sky like a blanket.

"If what he says is true," Mary said at last, "if he suspects me of operating as a—"

But she broke off, feeling, as Edmund did, a sudden strange tension in the air. Both of them turned instinctively to the peach tree they had just walked past, in time to see a dark form drop out of the sky and collide with the parrot in a muffled eruption of green feathers. Medardo shrieked. The hawk that had seized him spread its wings and began to beat them frantically, trying to lift its stocky prey into the air.

Edmund and Mary and Private Solis stood there watching in amazement as the parrot, with the hawk's talons holding its body in a piercing grip, was slowly borne aloft, flapping its own useless wings and screaming in terror.

From every corner of the compound women and children came running, along with the soldiers of Arechiga's dragoon patrol, all of whom had become fond of Medardo. Above their heads the two birds battled in the air, the parrot struggling fiercely to free itself, the hawk simultaneously fighting to keep its grasp and to gain altitude.

Children were throwing rocks and sticks at the hawk now, and several of the dragoons took aim with their carbines and tried to shoot the bird down, but the balls went wide and finally the hawk got enough purchase on the writhing parrot to begin to slowly bear it away over the walls of the compound.

Edmund and Mary ran outside the gates along with everyone else. The children sobbed and the dragoons continued to discharge their weapons into the air as they raced along the ground trying to keep pace with the hawk. With Medardo fighting to escape, twisting his body and pounding his wings, the hawk could not seem to reach higher than twenty or thirty feet above the ground.

Then all at once Medardo broke free, to the cheers of the people below, and began a broken descent to the ground on urgent wingstrokes. But before he could reach the treetops the hawk plummeted and struck again, and the horrified observers could once again hear the cushioned violence of the blow, and more green feathers drifted down to the earth.

"Help him! Help him!" the children cried to the dragoons as everyone kept running along below. Edmund watched Solis load his carbine and fire at the hawk, and thought he saw the ball take away a few feathers from the forward edge of one of its wings. But that was the closest anyone came to bringing the hawk down, and it continued its strangely slow process, dragging Medardo over the tops of the live oaks.

"Ah! Qué bonitos son los enanos!" Edmund heard the parrot's eerie emotionless singing as it beat its wings against the treetops, fighting for its life.

No one was willing to give up. The parrot had gotten away once, perhaps it could do so again. Everyone kept up the pursuit, firing carbines and throwing rocks, all their eyes fixed on the battle in the sky.

Edmund suddenly stopped and grabbed Mary by the arm.

She turned to him, and seeing his eyes she gave a sharp, frightened nod of understanding.

"Go to the smokehouse," he whispered. "Grab something for us to eat. Then meet me in the chapel."

They stood where they were for just a moment more to make sure the confusion held. It did. Solis and the other dragoons were still running through the brush with everyone else, their eyes trained on the eerie struggle in the air above them.

"Now!" Edmund said, just as the pursuers passed over a swell of land that hid them from sight.

The compound was several hundred yards away. Mary ran for it with her skirts clenched tightly in her fist. Edmund could hear her wild, unregulated breathing. Her face was drawn taut in fear and exertion. Professor ran a few yards ahead of them, composed and silent, as if the urgency and danger of their situation were perfectly apparent to him.

They ran through the gate. The compound was empty, and gunfire still sounded from the distance, where the battle to save the parrot continued. Edmund glanced at Mary, and she ran in the direction of the smokehouse, stumbling briefly on her skirts but hardly breaking stride.

Out of breath, Edmund entered the foreman's house through the door that had been left open. There was no one inside, and he grabbed the horse pistol off the shelf as he had rehearsed doing a hundred times. It was a heavy wide-bored German model with a sawed-off barrel—a powerful weapon but, he discovered with a sense of aggravation, an unloaded one.

He slipped the pistol in his waistband and ran along the wall of the compound to the room where he was kept confined. With the heel of his shoe he quickly dug up the powder flask and the four pitted balls and loaded the pistol, trying to keep his hands steady and his movements sure. When it was done he glanced out the door, saw no one, and ran to the chapel.

It was a small, dark room with an altar at one end covered with an embroidered cloth, and above it a crucifix depicting Christ in openmouthed agony. Wooden statues of the saints stared at him from the walls, and the metal milagros attached to them glittered in the meager sunlight from the open door. He had not been there half a minute when Mary ran inside to join him. She was wearing her jacket and held something wrapped in her mackinac.

"I have a ham," she said. "Is that enough?"

"'We will make do with it," he said. "Did you see anyone by the corral?"

"No."

Edmund listened and reckoned. He could still hear gunfire and shouting in the distance. There might just be time to saddle horses and ride away.

"Run to the tack room," he said.

But as she turned to go, Don Osbaldo suddenly filled the

frame of the door and struck her down with a hard blow
from his leather quirt. As she fell out of the way he raised a
cocked pistol in his other hand and levelled it at Edmund,
hesitating just long enough as he searched for his target in
the dark interior of the church for Edmund to pull his own
pistol and shoot him instead. Edmund had no opportunity
to aim, and had the ball not been so severely pitted he
would have hit nothing but the wooden doorjamb, but as it
happened the shot went off course and struck Don Osbaldo
squarely in the chest of his quilted dressing gown. He leapt
backward through the door like an acrobat and lay there as
blood from his ruptured heart poured out of his mouth and
ears. Don Osbaldo looked upward at the gunsmoke and cotton fibers swirling above his head. His eyes were still
swollen with pollen sickness. He emitted an amazed groan,
looked at Edmund with an intense interest, and then
seemed to die.

Professor erupted in barks and nervous whines, but Edmund was too stunned to notice. Mary kicked the dog
squarely in the ribs to silence him.

"Help me get him inside!" she said to Edmund. Her
voice sounded distant to him, and as they dragged the body
of Don Osbaldo Espinosa out of view into the chapel he
felt his own body moving in a numb, methodical way that
seemed independent of his reasoning mind.

They closed the door to the chapel. Mary started running
for the corral, but Edmund held up his hand and whispered
"Wait!" He listened for more gunfire in the distance. There
was none. But he thought he could hear the sound of returning voices.

"There's no time for the horses," he told Mary. "We have
to go now."

They ran out the gate and to the rear of the compound,
then scrambled down the steep bluff above the Atascosa
and plunged into the river. The water was shallow except

for one narrow channel in which it rose over their heads. He had not thought to ask Mary if she could swim, but it seemed that she could, after a fashion, by the way she kicked herself unhesitatingly through the deep water. Professor churned along behind them, his face peeking above the waterline, his expression as calm and unsurprised as if this escape had been his idea all along. They were almost across the river before Edmund realized he could have taken Don Osbaldo's pistol and, in his fright, had not thought to do so.

On the far bank a tributary intersected the creek forty or fifty yards downstream. They swam and stumbled to the tributary's mouth and then continued along its rocky bed. The water of the creek grew shallower as they proceeded, until it was no more than knee-deep.

"Why don't we get out of the water?" Mary asked, gasping for breath.

"It'll be far easier for Espinosa's men to track us on land," he told her. He wasn't particularly worried about the dragoons. Their tracking skills seemed to him minimal. But Espinosa's vaqueros would be back at the end of the day, and could not help but notice the footprints and gouges he and Mary had made in their hurried descent of the riverbank. But with good fortune Don Osbaldo's body would not even be found until late in the afternoon, and when the vaqueros rode out to hunt for his murderers they would naturally assume that the fugitives had followed the downstream course of the river to the place where it crossed the main road.

THEY WALKED UP the shallow tributary for several hours, until Edmund judged it safe to step out of the water and leave footprints. From then on they walked along the bank, hoping to strike the contraband road before making their camp, but as the day wore on Edmund decided to stop, worried that the faint wilderness path they were seeking might not be apparent in the feeble evening light.

They found a cypress with a hollow, bell-shaped trunk, and after they had pulled out the spiderwebs they climbed inside and piled up Spanish moss for their beds and ate ravenously of the ham. They did not think of making a fire. The norther had come in and the weather was cold, but the bitter wind did not touch them in the cypress trunk.

Mary had never known such weariness. They had walked miles through the water, and the muscles in her legs quivered spasmodically, remembering the exertion. There were blisters beginning on the soles of her wet feet, and her hunger was vast. Edmund hardly spoke, except to inquire about her comfort and to volunteer to make more room for her in the hollow tree. She responded with an appreciative grunt; speaking suddenly seemed as much an effort to her as trudging another hundred yards through the creek. Edmund was silent too, but not from fatigue. In the tightness of their confinement she could almost feel the tortured pondering of his mind.

"I am sorry you had to kill that man," she said at last. "I know that you have never done such a thing before."

"No," he said simply. "Not until now."

She waited for him to say something else, but if he did she was asleep before the words came.

By midmorning the next day Edmund had found the contraband road, though if he had not been looking for it with such precise attention it would have never come to his notice. The road was the width of a single oxcart, weeded over and washed out, and they had not travelled on it for a hundred yards until it disappeared altogether in a tangle of agarita. But they breasted through the tensile shrubs— Edmund regretting that it was early yet for the tart berries, which he had known to make an excellent jelly—and found the trace again.

They walked for a day and a night and another day, the
road growing more and more apparent to their discriminat-
ing eyes. They met no other travellers and began to grow
confident that they were not being pursued, though Edmund still found it advisable not to build a fire. The temperature held at an endurable level, despite the cutting wind
and the constantly deepening clouds above them. The ham
was gone by the end of the second day. The soles of Mary's
shoes had begun to split and the blisters that had formed
the day of their escape up the creek had become a serious
concern. But there was nothing she could do except to bind
them and continue walking awkwardly on her heels or the
sides of her feet. The unambiguous pain of the blisters
served to take her mind off the more complex sensations of
hunger and exposure. But she did not think of resting.
There was no point to it. She felt all would be well if she
could only continue going forward. The only fear she felt
was that they might take a wrong turning or lose the road
altogether and find themselves backtracking, surrendering
ground so painfully won.

He talked more than she would have liked, pointing out
where Mexican plum would be leafing out in a month, or
where purple horsemint would be blooming, or commenting how the root of a particular flower, if he could find it,
would make an excellent poultice for her blistered feet. The
effort to listen to him, to respond with even a grunt, made
her angry, and finally she told him so, and he walked on in
a chastened silence that made her angrier still.

Late in the afternoon of their third day on the contraband road the temperature dropped suddenly and sharply—
below the freezing mark, Mary was sure. The wind grew
savage, and before dusk she had lost feeling in her hands
and feet.

They made camp in the lee of two live oaks whose
trunks had grown together and formed an extended windbreak. But the temperature kept dropping and they both

knew that tonight a fire would be worth any risk. Edmund had been collecting tinder all along the route. Though his fire kit was back at Don Osbaldo's along with his other possessions, all that was necessary was to plug up the touchhole of the horse pistol and set tinder in the frizzen instead of powder. When he pulled the trigger he got a fine spark, and then he carefully transferred the glowing tinder to a cradle of dry twigs.

He left Mary tending the fire and then, while it was still light, ventured out with Professor to search for something edible. He loaded the pistol just in case, though the chances of finding any game in this cold were slim and of hitting anything with one of the three defective balls slimmer still.

He gathered some hawthorn fruits that he found on a creek bottom. They would be mealy, but there was real nourishment in them. Empty pecan husks still clung to the branches of the trees overhead, or were scattered about the ground, but the nuts had all been gathered up long ago by wildlife. Had it been any other time of the year there would have been a bounty of food available in this vicinity—dewberries in the spring, wild grapes, Jerusalem artichokes, and plentiful nuts in the fall. But he did not dwell on what was not available. He had been hungry before, and he knew that his body—and Mary's too—had reserves of strength that would see them through the three or four days of walking it would take to reach Castleman's place on the Sandies. And as usual the early stages of hunger had created in him a burning alertness. Searching along the ground for food, he found several surprises—a *Ficus indica,* smaller and without the downward-projecting thorns he had seen in others of its species farther west; a large *Opuntia* that he realized he had mistakenly identified last year as *Oresticus turcica; Lythrum,* though not *foliosum* as he might have expected, growing on stones in the water.

It was almost dark when a squirrel bounded across the grass ten yards in front of him, and he fired at it with the pistol without a conscious thought. The wayward ball shot off one foot of the squirrel as it leapt onto a tree. The animal fell to the ground and ran brokenly away, too fast for Edmund to catch but not for Professor, who had the writhing creature in his teeth in an instant, and who glowered in disbelief when Edmund spoke to him sharply and made him surrender it.

They cooked the squirrel on sticks over the fire, reserving the meat for themselves and letting Professor have the lights and the bones. They kept the fire up as well as they could, but the cold kept growing fiercer. Mary faced the fire with her arms folded across her trunk, her frozen hands nestled in her armpits. Sitting next to her, Edmund did the same, with Professor burrowed under his mackinac.

"We can't get warm like this," she said at last, over the sound of the wind.

Without asking what he thought about the proposal, she pulled herself tight against him, burying her head beneath his chin, wedging her hip into his lap, gripping him tight with her arms. After a surprised moment he returned the emergency embrace, and they clung together in silence. After half an hour Mary felt better. Not comfortable, certainly, but she could sense the blood in her veins again and for the first time that night was aware of some other sensation besides pain and unappeasable hunger.

"We need more firewood," Edmund said after a time, and stood up and wandered outside the circle of light and warmth, leaving her there alone before the fire. She worried that when he came back he would not take up his previous station, but he did so without a word, shielding her from the freezing wind. Her body continued to grow warmer, both from the fire and from the proximate heat of his. His arms held her, as clumsy and unyielding as tree limbs at first, but gradually with a more deliberate purpose. He drew them tighter around her body, pulling her closer and closer until her cheek rested against the buttons of his waistcoat. He pulled the flap of his jacket over her face and touched her hair with his hand. She felt the scratch of his chin against her cheek and neck. She felt his lips graze the crown of her head. And she settled deeper into the hollow of his body and raised her chin so that his lips would touch her own.

Against the curve of her hip she could feel a part of him stirring. It did not surprise her, and it gratified her to know that his whole body was coming to life for her. But Edmund suddenly turned as still as a statue. He broke off their tentative kiss and shifted his weight in an attempt to hide this helpless human reaction from her. But as he tried to move from beneath her, she clutched him tighter to hold him in place.

"It's all right," she whispered.

"I am sorry," he replied.

"It's all right."

She slid a hand inside his waistcoat and felt the contour of his chest through his shirt. She kissed him on the neck, to calm him. But his tension only grew.

"Am I undesirable to you?" she asked.

"No."

"Perhaps because I so much wanted you to take an interest, I assumed too much. I was lonely and my face was ruined, and I thought no man would ever again want to—"

"You were not mistaken, Mary. Please do not think that. What you wanted me to feel is what I felt. It's what I feel now."

But he kept shifting his body, trying to conceal from her the physical evidence of his words, as if it shamed him. She accommodated him by moving her hip. She relaxed her own arms so that they were no longer embracing, merely huddling together for warmth. She sat there for a long time, aware of the cold again, thinking about this man who seemed so afraid of the demands of his own body.

"Have you never been with a woman?" she finally asked. She did not expect him to respond, and he did not, though the answer was clearly expressed in his silence. She wondered how a person could live through so many years without the consoling touch of another. It had been so hard for her since the death of Andrew, but a willing lifetime of such isolation?

She said not another word. Here was the opportunity, plain enough, if he wanted to come down from his ether and join the world of men. She would have him. There was a strange power in him, she had known that from the first—and a fineness of feeling she had not seen in any other sort of man. But this strange forbearance—it was an affliction. An affliction of pride.

She didn't even know that she was crying until she heard his soft voice speaking into her ear.

"Only a few more days," he was saying. "Only two or three days more and we will be out of this wilderness."

So he had changed the subject. But she was too tired to be disappointed. She was too cold and weak and hungry. She no longer noticed his arousal, or indeed her own wakefulness. She was asleep, and in the morning she awoke in his arms, cramped and bone-cold, and the fire had burned down to a white mound of ash.

TWO DAYS LATER they came to a little wooden bridge spanning a creek. There was a hill of red sandstone on the other side, and on its summit a commodious cabin with corrals and outbuildings.

"Castleman's," Edmund said.

She was startled to be standing here. It seemed hardly possible that they could be at the end of their journey. She had grown so accustomed to stumbling along a faint trail on her blistered feet that she had begun to feel there could be no other condition of life.

"Hallo!" Edmund called out as they stood at the far side of the bridge. "Hallo the house!"

Immediately four savage black dogs came bounding down the hill after them. Professor ran out to meet them and launched himself into a snarling tangle with the leader, just as Castleman himself appeared to call them off and wave the tattered travellers forward.

"I HOPE YOU ain't intolerant of the society of females, sir," Castleman told Edmund at supper the next day. "Because by God that's about all we got around here." Castleman was a rangy backwoodsman of middle years, starved for talk, whose spacious cabin served as a kind of inn for travellers on the road that ran from Gonzales to Béxar. Edmund and Mary were the only guests at the moment, but even so the table was crowded, since Castleman had not just a wife and four daughters but a sage-looking mother-in-law who rarely spoke but took in everything with piercing eyes.

It had been this woman, Mary recalled now as if the last twenty-four hours had been a dream, who had supervised the household's reception of these two frightening strangers, setting out bowls of steaming hominy for them, finding them clothes, shepherding them upstairs to the bedrooms, where she saw to it that they were left undisturbed for fourteen hours.

When Mary had finally awakened, she found the mother-in-law wrapping a poultice on the sole of her left foot, where the blisters were the most severe. It had been a trial making her way downstairs to supper. Castleman's stairs were as sharply pitched as a ladder, and Mary's feet now hurt so badly that every time she let their blistered surfaces touch the ground it sent brilliant darts of pain through the core of her body. Fortunately Castleman had an old crutch—he had made it, he said, after a disagreement with a rattlesnake—and using it she was able to hobble from the stairs to the dining table.

"I must confess to you," Edmund said now as Mrs. Castleman filled his plate with sweet potatoes and roasted turkey, "that neither Mrs. Mott nor I am in funds at the moment."

"I didn't expect so," Castleman said. "Not as raggedy as the two of you looked coming out of the woods. But I'd be a poor enough Christian not to offer you food and shelter for gratis. Susan and the girls'll mend your clothes as best they can, and if you want to keep the clothes I loaned you I can put it to an account."

"Thank you," Edmund said. "And as soon as Mrs. Mott and I can be on the road to Béxar, the sooner we can repay you. Would you have a spare horse or two to add to our account?"

"Now there I will disappoint you, sir. If you'd come here six months ago you could have had your pick from my caballada. But I had to sell all but four of my horses to this outfit that calls itself the Texian cavalry—sell 'em or have 'em pressed outright. So I must leave you afoot."

"How long will it take us to walk to Béxar, Mr. Castleman?" Mary asked.

"Three long days, I'd guess, ma'am, if your feet were healed up. But they won't be of much use to you for another week, is my medical opinion. And I'd caution you both not to go out on that road alone. There's people looking for you."

"Who's looking for us?" Edmund said.

"You girls take the dishes away," Mrs. Castleman said to the four daughters. There was a silence as they gathered up the tableware and went outside to feed the scraps to the dogs and clean the dishes. Castleman waited until they were gone to resume the conversation, and when he spoke it was hardly above a whisper.

"Some of the vaqueros from Espinosa's ranch rode by here three or four days ago. They were lookin' for you. They said you murdered Espinosa, shot him dead in his own chapel while he was prayin' to God."

"That's not what happened at all!" Mary cried, before Edmund could respond. And she went on to provide the Castlemans with a detailed account of their imprisonment and lethal escape. Mrs. Castleman listened with horror, and her mother sat there as stern as a judge, staring down at the thick plank of the dinner table. Castleman himself merely nodded his head in a neutral manner from time to time, and when the story was finished he gave a kind of shrug and called for more coffee.

"I'm glad to hear the true version, Mrs. Mott," he said. "But that ain't what's being passed around. If I were you I wouldn't go to Béxar. That's where the Mexican army's headed, and if Santy Anna gets hold of you, and finds out you killed one of his biggest friends in Texas—shot the man down in church—he'll by God plant some lead in your heart."

Castleman took a sip of his coffee.

"My advice to you two is to stay here with us till your feet heal up and then head away from Béxar. Go to Gonzales, find yourself some horses, and ride across the Sabine into the States where they ain't never heard of no Mexicans."

The children returned with their piles of clean dishes, affecting a casual manner as if they had not been standing outside the door eavesdropping, and Castleman dropped his whispering tone and heartily changed the subject.

"Who would care for music? We ain't got no pianoforte, Mrs. Mott, but Mother Satterfield here will torture the catgut for us if we ask her polite. "

It required no asking, polite or otherwise. Castleman's mother-in-law stood without a sound or a change of expression, retrieved her fiddle case, and set the instrument under her formidable chin.

"I will play 'The Children of the Wood,' " she announced,

as if all that long evening and its troubled talk had been just a prelude to her performance. She played with admirable rigor but without much art, and the hard-won music that resulted cast Mary's troubled mind adrift. She found herself unable to concentrate on her worries about Terrell, or about Castleman's ominous warnings regarding their own welfare. All she could think about was Don Osbaldo's parrot, and of the song about the loveliness of the dwarves that it had been frantically singing as the hawk wrestled it away into the sky.

PART THREE

CHAPTER TWENTY-TWO

✦

A T SEVEN O'CLOCK on the morning of February 23, Telesforo Villasenor stood on the summit of a modest rise of land known as the Alazan Hills and looked down for the first time at San Antonio de Béxar. He had not slept all night, but he was at a strange pitch of alertness, and sleep was far from his mind. Here it was at last. It amazed him to be standing here, since during the last month he had grown so accustomed to the likelihood of death by thirst or cold or simple exhaustion that he had all but forsaken the possibility of actually reaching his destination. But now he had, and the bulk of the army—shattered though it was by the terrible ordeals of the march—was not far behind him. Santa Anna and the rest of his staff had caught up with the vanguard, and were camped on the Medina River twenty-five miles to the west. The First Brigade under General Gaona was several weeks behind them, probably just now embarking on the punishing stretch of waste ground between the Rio Grande and the Medina, and Andrade's Cavalry Brigade was somewhere out there as well. Telesforo calculated that when they all caught up, Santa Anna would have somewhere in the neighborhood of four thousand men here at Béxar, not including the force under General Urrea that was sweeping toward the rebel positions along the coast.

Last night, Telesforo had been ordered by Santa Anna to ride ahead to Béxar with General Ramírez y Sesma and a reconnaissance detachment of a hundred lancers and presidials. They had left just after midnight, their clothes still wet from the afternoon rain of the day before, and had ridden through the darkness on muddy roads, expecting at any moment to be ambushed by a rebel patrol. But no such resistance occurred, and they had arrived at Alazan Creek just as the sun was sweeping over the eastern prairie. When Telesforo climbed the hill on foot to look down at Béxar, he was blinded for a moment by the new daylight glaring off the surface of the river that looped its way through the center of town.

It was much as he had pictured it: the bands of greenery along the river and the irrigation ditches, the whitewashed adobe houses lining the streets, the stone church with a plaza on either side, the jacales standing alone in fields and garden plots at the fringes of the town, smoke rising into the sharp air from a hundred cooking fires, dogs barking, cattle and goats grazing in the pastures.

In the center of town the river formed a large, meandering loop to the east, and on its far bank sat the mission known as the Alamo. Telesforo recognized it immediately and was glad to see that the proportions supplied to him by the dragoon captain from Cos's army were fundamentally correct. There were differences, of course. The main rectangular courtyard was larger than he had expected—not a problem, if the Texians had as few men to defend it as a captured rebel spy had told them—and the gap between the church and the south gate, as well as the tambour guarding the gate itself, had been considerably strengthened. And, through General Sesma's glass, he counted eighteen pieces of artillery, including the eighteen-pounder that Cos had left behind and that the rebels now seemed to have mounted on the southwest wall. Nevertheless, the place looked more vulnerable than it had on his map, and of surprisingly indifferent strategic value. Now that he had seen it with his own eyes, the Alamo seemed to Telesforo a place hardly worth taking.

And it seemed unlikely to him, at that moment, that they

would need to. No one seemed to be stirring in the Alamo itself, and across the river the streets of Béxar were somnolent as well, except for a few Tejano families who seemed to have gotten word of Santa Anna's proximity and were anxiously loading up carts and trying to steal away from town.

"What do you see, Villasenor?" the general said as he joined Telesforo. The rest of the men waited, dismounted, behind them, out of sight below the crest of the hill.

"I think the nortes are still asleep, General," he said. He handed Sesma the glass. The general took off his cocked hat and set it on a rock. Its protective oilskin covering was muddy and much abraded. Sesma stood there for a long time peering through the glass at the town. He was a spare, solitary man of forty, pale and thin from the flux, as so many of them were, and weary from the night's long ride. The mud churned up on that ride by the horses' hooves had spattered his face and left his white uniform trousers caked almost solid with grime.

"We've caught them by surprise," Telesforo ventured. The general merely grunted ambiguously, still studying the town.

"You're of the opinion we should attack them at once? With a hundred men?" Sesma said finally, handing the telescope back.

"They don't have many more than that, General," Telesforo said. "And as soon as they become aware of our presence they'll retreat into the Alamo, and we'll be faced with a siege."

Sesma thought about it for a moment, but then shook his head.

"No, it's too rash, Teniente. The rebels might very well be aware of our presence already, and we would be riding into an ambush. We need more information."

"By the time we get it, sir, the—"

"Thank you, Villasenor. I have made up my mind. We'll

wait for His Excellency to come up with the army and
make a proper assault."

He turned and walked down the hill. Telesforo stayed
where he was, boiling with impatience and frustration at
Sesma's misguided caution. There was no ambush. The
rebels were asleep. The town could be taken in half an hour.

Telesforo found a comfortable rock to sit on and got out
his map case and began to sketch the Alamo and its ordnance. And as he sketched, his anger started to seep away
and the conviction overtook him once again that there
could be no wrong turning of events. This was where he
was meant to be. Something he could not yet know was
meant to happen here. The map of his own destiny had already been drawn by an unknown hand, and he had no duty
other than to be patient and courageous and see what would
be revealed.

"WAKE UP, goddammit!" Bowie was yelling. Terrell
opened his eyes to see him stomping around the sala of the
Veramendi house, kicking at the soles of the feet of his
sleeping men. "Wake up, you lazy bastards! Something's
happening!"

"What's happening, Jim?" Roth asked in a groggy, disin-
terested voice.

"Oh, not much to speak of, Jacob. Except for the fact
that the Mexican army is already on the Medina."

The men scrambled to their feet and started to pull on
their boots and run outside to piss, their hangovers forgotten
before they could even register. There had been an interminable fandango last night in honor of George Washington's birthday. Bowie had relaxed his sobriety regulations
for the occasion, and the whole garrison had started out
drunk early in the evening and stayed that way until some
indeterminate hour near dawn. Terrell dimly remembered
Crockett making an inebriated speech, but could not recall

the subject. He himself had drunk just enough aguardiente to pass the evening in stupefied watchfulness, fearing that at any moment the carousing garrison would be taken by surprise and overrun. Travis, he was glad to see, remained judiciously sober during the evening. Though the commandant danced as eagerly with the Bexareñas as any of his men, there was an unquenchable vigilance in his eyes that filled Terrell with a measure of comfort. In his opinion Travis was too young for the position he held, and his military experience was thin at best, but at least he was alert.

Bowie had not attended the party. He was still sick, and getting worse. It seemed to Terrell that Bowie had lost a troubling amount of weight in the last week or so. He ate little and spent half the day in the outhouse and had fallen into a mood of constant surliness and sarcasm.

"Who told you they was at the Medina?" one of the men was asking Bowie.

"Half the goddam town told me. Unlike the rest of you, I happened to wake up this morning and look out the door. And what I saw is people running away from this place as fast as they can."

Bowie sank exhaustedly into one of the few chairs remaining in the room and turned his eyes to Terrell.

"You pull on your shoes, son, and go find Travis. You give him my compliments and ask what the hell is going on and what the hell he plans to do about it."

Terrell ran all the way to Travis's headquarters on the plaza. The streets were congested now with fleeing Bexareños, some with carts hitched up to milch cows, others simply with their possessions in their arms, heading blindly for the countryside, where they would not be bombarded by Santa Anna's artillery. Running along, Terrell wove in and out of the commotion with a fluid, purposeful energy that thrilled him. He felt no panic, though he knew he should. The Béxar garrison was absurdly small, demoralized, divided, hungover. But the prospect of action, of something happening at last after a month or more of ill-tempered stasis, filled him with an expectation of release that his logical mind could not counter.

Travis, he was told, could be found in the bell tower of San Fernando Church. The church had been heavily damaged in the fight for Béxar, and there was so much rubble blocking the entrance to the winding stairs that the only way to reach the summit of the bell tower was to scramble up a scaffolding that had been erected on the outside.

When Terrell had climbed the scaffolding and squeezed through the arches at the top, he found Travis standing there with Baugh and Crockett, all of them studying the hills to the west. Crockett turned and gave him a warm grin in welcome, but Travis kept peering through his telescope with a tight look on his face.

"Colonel Bowie's compliments, sir," Terrell said to Travis, "and he asks if you know what's going on."

"Where the hell is Bowie?" Travis replied sharply. "How come he isn't here himself?"

"He's pretty sick, Colonel."

"Is he worse, Terrell?" Crockett asked gently. Terrell was astonished that the congressman knew his name.

"Yes, sir, I think he is."

"Well, I'm sorry to hear it. I told him he should go see Dr. Pollard. I don't suppose he ever did, though."

"I don't think so, sir."

"Well, I can't blame him. I've never been too fond of doctors myself. Once had a doctor bleed practically every drop of blood out of me till I was white as a toadstool."

Crockett's voice was as casual and unworried as ever. Nobody said anything for a moment more, while Travis continued to study the gentle hills in the distance through his telescope. He seemed composed enough, but when he finally turned to Terrell and spoke there was a faint tremor in his voice.

"You tell Colonel Bowie that the Mexican army has not

yet been sighted, but we have several reliable reports they reached the Medina last night and are probably already on the march. I'm sending scouts out immediately on the Laredo road to look for them, and I'll order a full-scale reconnaissance as well. In the meantime, tell Bowie I want his volunteers and the rest of the garrison in the Alamo as soon as possible."

"THE LAREDO ROAD!" Bowie thundered when Terrell reported back to him. "What the hell is he talking about? If the Mexicans are coming from the Medina they'll take the Leon Creek road. Did Travis say anything about sending scouts out toward Leon Creek?"

"No, he didn't," Terrell said.

Bowie shook his head wearily. For a moment he looked like he was going to stand up and storm around the room, but then he just slouched back in his chair and was silent for a long time, breathing deeply and carefully as if trying to keep himself from puking. Gertrudis Navarro appeared with a wet tea towel and swabbed Bowie's forehead, and the few men who were in the room drifted away, disturbed or embarrassed to see Bowie in such a helpless state.

"What else did Travis say?" Bowie asked finally.

"He said you should get everybody into the Alamo right away."

"God help us," Bowie said. "We've got less than a hundred and fifty men."

"Can you make it over there?"

"Not walking, that's for damn sure. They'll have to haul me in a cart like an old viuda. Here's what I want you to do, Terrell. Get on your horse and ride out the Leon Creek road. You see anything that looks like it might be the Mexican army, you do a quick count and turn around and ride like hell and report to me about it."

"Where will I find you?"

"Well, by God, son, I guess I'll be in the fucking Alamo like everybody else."

TERRELL FOUND himself alone as he followed the Leon Creek road. The fleeing populace of Béxar was headed in the opposite direction, toward the ranchos to the south and east. After the rain of the day before, the road was boggy, and pools of rainwater glistened in the sun. The weather was more agreeable than not, though the wind had a bite to it and his ears were cold under his hat. He buttoned the collar of his woolen coat. He held his father's Kentucky rifle in his lap.

He passed fields where the farm implements stood hastily abandoned and corrals where the stock had been left without any provision. Goats peered out at him from their pens as if expecting him to provide an answer for the abrupt departure of their human owners and the sudden tense quiet that had descended over the city.

Once he had passed the outlying jacales and cornfields and was out onto the prairie he felt as vulnerable as a mouse. He wished that Bowie had thought to send someone with him. He kept his eyes in a constant sweep not just of the country ahead but all around him, knowing that at any moment a Mexican cavalry patrol might appear from any quarter and stab him to death with their lances. Veronica was a fast horse and well rested. If lancers started to chase him he thought he could outrun them back to Béxar, but not if they cut off his retreat. And the farther he advanced the more likely that situation began to seem.

He had gone about a mile when he came to the base of the Alazan Hills, a long swell of broken rock that rose abruptly but not too imposingly above the landscape. There was juniper growing in the crevices of the hills, and there were ferns and mats of bright green moss that marked where springs seeped out of the rock. Terrell reined Veronica to a stop at the base of the hills and listened. He heard no bugle calls, no shouting, no sounds that he would associate with thousands of marching men.

The road veered off to his right, meandering gently between limestone boulders toward a series of fissured terraces that marked the summit of the hills. But there was a game trail leading off in the other direction, narrower and steeper, that Terrell decided to follow instead. He slipped out of the saddle and held his rifle in the crook of his arm as he led Veronica by the reins up the trail. The mare's hoofbeats on the bedrock sounded like reverberating drums to him, and as he ascended he began to realize that with each step his situation was growing more dangerous and exposed. He kept his eyes on the broken ridgeline above, rehearsing what he would do if he saw the silvery flash of a dragoon's helmet appear there. He would scramble back down the trail until he and Veronica were on open ground, and then he would leap on her back and spur her mercilessly in her flanks and not look back or take a breath until he had crossed the river and passed through the gates of the Alamo.

Near the crest of the hill he tied Veronica's reins to a stout branch and crept on without her, hiding himself as much as possible in the rocky crevices. He stopped once or twice to look back toward Béxar. He saw no enemy patrols between him and the town, but there was a stream of refugees visible on the Gonzales road, and Potrero Street was a churning line of dust as the Texians drove cattle along it and into the Alamo.

He reached the top of the hill and followed its broad, sloping crest toward the far side, concealing himself as best he could behind the weathered boulders scattered across its summit. When he was finally able to see what was below him on the other side of the Alazan Hills his body responded with a startled flinch, and suddenly his mouth felt as dry as cloth. He remembered his instructions to count the enemy, and he started with the cavalry. They were dismounted. Their horses were spread out along the banks of the creek, drinking. They were maybe a half-mile away. Terrell counted the horses instead of the men. He counted them in groups of three, anxiously losing count twice before he was able to come up with an approximate number: three hundred and fifty. The infantry was just coming along the road behind them. They were dressed for battle in their blue coats and marched four abreast in reasonably good order. Terrell counted the ranks of four men, but they extended over the horizon, and as more and more came into view the precision of the ranks deteriorated. Desperate to get away, he made an informed estimate: sixteen hundred men, including cavalry. He thought he saw eight artillery carriages, but they were hard to make out in the milling mass of blue-coated infantry.

He looked back, trying to judge whether it was better to race back over the edge of the hill on two feet or to crawl slowly along on the ground. In the end he ran. He did not have the courage to be patient and careful. And just as he reached the concealing, jumbled boulders at the apex of the hill he felt a presence nearby and looked up to see a Mexican officer sitting on top of one of the rocks with his legs crossed. The man had a refined, handsome face, and he was looking off toward Béxar and drawing or writing something on a sketching pad.

The Mexican saw him at the same instant. Terrell lifted his rifle with trembling arms and would have shot the man off the rock without hesitation if he hadn't been afraid the report of the rifle would alert the enemy army to his presence—and if the officer's expression hadn't been so strangely mild and fearless. He sat there holding his pen in his hand, looking down at Terrell with no more alarm than if they had encountered each other while out on a picnic.

"Quiere rendirse, señor?" the man said.

"What?" Terrell responded, hardly able to form the words in his dry mouth.

The officer didn't understand him either, and didn't reply. Incredibly, he pulled his eyes away from the boy pointing a rifle at him and returned his attention to his sketch.

Terrell couldn't think of anything to do but leave. He ran down through the tumbled rocks to where Veronica was tied, and then led the mare down the game trail to the base of the hill, expecting at any time that the Mexican officer would shoot at him from above and put a ball in his spine. But no such thing happened, and a moment later Terrell was on Veronica's back and galloping down the muddy road to Béxar. He kept glancing back to see if any dragoons were behind, but they were not. When he realized there was no immediate danger of being shot and captured, his concern shifted to slowing his breath and quieting himself, so that he could give a calm accounting to Travis and Bowie of what he had just seen.

A CRUMBLING old Spanish watchtower stood on a hill to the east of Béxar, guarding the Gonzales road. Edmund and Mary and the men they were riding with reached the structure at about one in the afternoon, and from the summit of the shallow hill on which it stood they had their first glimpse of the city. The whole population seemed to be on the move. Dust from their horses and carts drifted in the wind above the trees.

"Why is everyone leaving?" Mary asked Edmund.

"I think it must be because the Mexican army is close by," he answered in a flat voice. His eyes were trained on an isolated cluster of houses at the southern part of the town, on the near bank of the looping river. It was there, in the neighborhood of La Villita, that his own little house stood, and within it the voluminous collection of documents and

specimens that seemed to Edmund at that moment as crucial to his being as the blood running through his veins. But
he could not make out either his house or its condition from
this distance, and the neighborhood itself was obscured
along with the rest of the town by curtains of dust.

"By the look of things, we're going to make a stand in
the Alamo," David Cummings said to them, as his horse
danced defiantly beneath him, eager to gallop into town
and join the commotion. Cummings was one of the eleven
men with whom Edmund and Mary had travelled from
Castleman's. He and his companions had arrived in Béxar
last month and then gotten leave to ride east and scout for
land they could claim as their headright once the wax was
over and Texas was won from Mexico. They had been on
the Guadalupe when they got word from one of Travis's
couriers that the Mexican army had reached the Rio
Grande and might already be on the move. The group had
quickly turned back to Béxar, stopping at Castleman's just
long enough to rest their horses and eat a hasty meal. They
cheerfully agreed to take Edmund and Mary along with
them to Béxar, as they had five extra horses that they had
stolen from a Comanche hunting party.

They had ridden through the night at a hard pace. The
blisters on Mary's feet had healed during the week she and
Edmund spent at Castleman's place, and after the first few
days of idleness their fatigue had disappeared as well.

"I do not like to see the two of you going into the lion's
den," Castleman had told them as they prepared to ride off to
Béxar with Cummings and his friends, but neither Edmund
nor Mary would seriously consider another course. Edmund
marvelled at his own obdurate fearlessness. The lion's den
was where he wanted to go, and as they rode that night to
Béxar he saw the same bewitched eagerness in the faces of
their companions. His plan was to hire a cart, hurriedly
load it with his collections, and withdraw a safe distance—
perhaps to New Orleans—to await the resolution of the

war. But even with this practical errand at the front of his thoughts he felt an unreasonable impatience to arrive in Béxar, to be present at the place where so many years' worth of resentment and ragged conflict seemed to be reaching a culmination. The men who accompanied him along the dark road spoke little; they did not complain or joke. They simply rode forward with a brooding anticipation. They all seemed to be heeding a summons, all of them except for Mary, whose errand, Edmund knew, held nothing of grandeur. She only wanted to see her son again, and to speak to him with a mother's voice.

"If you'll come with us, ma'am," Cummings said now, turning to Mary "We'll ride down into the Alamo and ask after your son. He might be there already, or he might be engaged in bringing in stores."

He gave her a direct look. "I think you should get out of this place as soon as you can, Mrs. Mott."

Mary replied with a thin, appreciative smile. She and Edmund had both come to like David Cummings on the short trip from Castleman's. His companions were polite enough but were coarse adventurers at heart; they had come to Texas as much for a fight as for free land, and subscribed to the common fiction that Mexico was trying to steal Texas from the States, and would not listen when Edmund tried to tell them that the situation could be considered in the reverse. Cummings, by contrast, was quiet and deliberate and took keen notice of everything.

Mary turned to Edmund. Her hair had long since fallen loose. She still wore her man's planter's hat and woolen jacket, and the same riding skirt she had been wearing when they left Refugio, though it had required considerable patching by Mrs. Castleman.

"What about you?" she asked.

"I'll need at least two hours to find a cart to hire and load up my notes."

"You may not have that long, Mr. McGowan," Cummings said. "Not if the enemy is as close as they seem to be."

Edmund nodded in agreement, but he did not see how he had any choice in the matter. Turning around now, when he stood almost at the door of his house, with all his precious documents inside, made no sense at all.

"I'll look for you in the Alamo," he said to Mary, then he spurred his horse forward, forsaking the congested Gonzales road for the open cornfields.

Mary and the others continued on to the Alamo. Mary's horse—one of the ones taken from the Comanches—trotted along in a nervous attitude, frightened by all the traffic on the road and by the water ditches they had to cross that were spanned only by narrow boards.

They approached the old mission from behind, and it looked to Mary to be no more than a random cluster of houses and broken-down buildings, connected in some places by walls and in others by earthworks. It did not appear half as strong as Don Osbaldo's fortified hacienda, and she remembered Edmund's observation of months ago that it would make an indifferent fort. If Santa Anna had artillery—as he certainly must—he would immediately blast it into even less prominent pieces of rubble. Although she knew nothing of military matters, Mary could see no point in trying to defend such a place. Why were they all rushing into this death trap when they should be escaping as fast as possible into the open country?

"The goddam Mexicans are just over the hills!" a man shouted out to the new arrivals from the rear of the roofless, broken-down church. Others on the walls yelled to welcome them. Mary galloped along with the men of Cummings's party, even sharing a little in their heedless exaltation as they raced over the uneven ground, dramatically passing the refugees that were streaming the other way down the road. There was an expanse of standing water behind the mission, and one of the men's horses slipped and fell at its boggy edges. But the man was unhurt. He climbed back into the saddle laughing at himself, and as he quirted the horse to keep up with his companions the mud that covered him flew off his body in long, wet tendrils.

Mary was almost out of breath when they finally stopped and dismounted in front of the gate, which was itself guarded by a half-moon artillery battery whose narrow entrance they had to carefully walk the horses through. Inside, men were furiously engaged in mounting artillery pieces and unloading barrels of provisions, but she was alarmed at how few men there were. Fewer than fifty or sixty were visible, and the compound was vast.

An officer yelled down from the roof of the gatehouse for Cummings and his men to put their horses in the corral and set to work.

"I'll see to your horse, Mrs. Mott," Cummings said to Mary, taking the reins from her hand. "You go and find your son."

"Where is he likely to be?"

"With his company, I expect. You say he's one of Bowie's men?"

"I think so."

"Then Bowie would be the man to speak to."

She walked down the center of the compound, hoping to see Terrell among the men preparing the defenses. What was she going to say to him, if she suddenly encountered him? Though she had been driving herself to this moment for weeks and weeks with the unquestioning resolve of a migrating bird, she realized now she had prepared no words, and no plan beyond the simple declaration of her presence. She had always assumed the moment would resolve itself naturally enough, but now she was beginning to lose that conviction, and indeed the hope of a substantial conversation seemed increasingly frail. An attack might come at any moment, and would surely occur very soon unless the garrison had the sense to surrender. And if they surrendered, their perils would only be beginning. She herself—an accomplice in the murder of Don Osbaldo Espinosa, the loyalist hacendado—would very likely be shot.

Nervous young men were rushing out of the powder magazine carrying cannonballs and canister shot to the artillery batteries. When Mary asked one of them where Bowie was, he said he didn't know but thought he might be in the hospital, as he was said to be sick.

Holding the cannonball in his cupped hands and shuffling like an ape, the young man pointed with his chin across the yard to the most substantial building in the complex, an old stone convent of two stories just north of the collapsed church. Mary found the hospital on the second floor. It was a long, dark room lined with perhaps two dozen men lying on pallets. There was a stench as thick as a curtain, the product of fetid wounds and unemptied chamber pots. One man at the end of the row was on his knees vomiting onto a pile of straw. Others, bandaged but ambulatory, were helping two able-bodied men nail a stiff cowhide over the open windows.

"Excuse me," Mary said to the nearest of these two men, "is Mr. Bowie here?"

"No, ma'am, I've sent him to private quarters." The man backed away from the cowhide curtain and walked over to her and gave a curt nod of welcome. He was older than most of the men in Cummings's group but still young; not much over thirty, Mary suspected, with a lean face and impatient eyes.

"I'm Dr. Pollard," he said. "What is going on outside? Has the enemy been sighted in the town yet?"

"I don't think so," she said. "But it appears the men of the garrison are putting up defenses."

"Well, you see our defenses," he said, pointing to the stiff hides that robbed the cheerless room of all light. "I doubt they will stop a cannonball, but they might keep out a stray musket ball or two."

The man who had just vomited into the straw turned over on his back and groaned. Mary could no longer see him.

"Are all these men sick?" Mary asked Pollard.

"Some are, some have wounds sustained when we ran the Mexican army out of Béxar. We treat them as best we can, but we have few medicines, and few tools other than what Dr. Reynolds and I happened to have in our kits." He gestured toward the other able-bodied man, who had already disappeared down the dark corridor to ease the groaning patient back onto his pallet. "We'd come here to fight, you see, not to practice our ancient craft. We thought there would be regimental doctors, but of course in this make-believe army there are no regimental anythings."

"Is Mr. Bowie sick or wounded, Dr. Pollard?"

"He is seriously ill, I am afraid, Mrs.—"

"Mott. Mrs. Andrew Mott."

"Very pleased to know you, Mrs. Mott, though you could not have arrived at this outpost at a more dangerous time." He lowered his voice to a whisper so that the wretched men behind him could not hear. "If I may say so, you should leave immediately before the enemy traps us inside this place and begins a bombardment. Some of these walls are stout enough, but they will be no match for siege weapons."

"Thank you. What is Mr. Bowie's illness?"

"I don't know," Pollard said, whispering ominously. "I fear typhoid fever, though in Bowie's case there is as yet no telltale rash. But I have four other patients here with the same set of afflictions—not including the man I lost a week ago."

Mary thanked Dr. Pollard and hurried downstairs again and crossed the courtyard to the room in the gatehouse he had pointed out. She knocked on a thick door that sagged on a leather hinge.

"Pase," a female voice said.

Mary pushed open the door and walked inside. The room was small, and she could not see Bowie at first because of the two young Mexican women who were standing over him. When they noticed her and stood aside, Mary almost gasped. She did not recognize Jim Bowie. He had lost an alarming amount of weight, his ruddy skin was ghostly, and his hair was limp and drenched in sweat.

"Jim?" she said.

"Who's that?" he answered in a parched voice. "Goddammit, whoever you are, move away from the door. Don't make me stare into the sun to look at you."

"It's Mary Mott," she said, stepping aside and closing the door behind her.

"Mary Mott?" Bowie replied in an astonished voice. "What the hell are you doing in Béxar? Don't you know the Mexican army's on the edge of town?"

"I'm looking for Terrell, Jim. Do you know where he is?"

"All the way here from—where is it, Mary? I can't think."

"Refugio."

"Refugio." He pronounced it in the proper Spanish way, not in the garbled approximation of the Irish colonists. "Our Lady of Refuge. I'm burning up with fever, Mary."

She walked forward and touched his face. She could feel the furnace heat rising through his skin. The two women looked at her as if for explanation. One of them, Mary noticed for the first time, held a sleeping baby.

"You've got medical wits, as I recall," Bowie said to Mary. "What do you think's got ahold of me?"

"I don't know, Jim. Have you kept any food down?"

"No, I'm a puking fool, Mary. And it ain't no better at the other end, if you'll pardon my indelicacy. Pollard thinks it's typhoid, but he won't look me in the eye and say it."

Mary replied with a pondering nod. She felt Bowie's pulse. It was slow as a clock. She lifted his sodden shirt and put her hand on his abdomen. It felt tight and distended, and he jerked back in pain when she touched it.

"Tender?" she asked.

"Considerable."

She lifted the shirt higher. The rash that Pollard had been waiting to see was now visible, a spattering of round pink spots that extended up to the chest. Mary had never seen typhoid, but she remembered reading about it in Andrew's medical book. She lifted her eyes and found Bowie staring fixedly at her face. The fearless knife-fighter looked terribly frail and scared.

"What do you think?" he asked.

"I think it could be typhoid," she said. "But it might be something else. In any case there's nothing to do but treat the fever."

"Pollard's been doing that, but he ain't got much in the way of medicine. A handful of blue pills and some Dover's powder. I guess I'll just ride her out and see what comes of it."

Mary turned to the woman holding the baby.

"I think you should . . ."

"She don't speak English, Mary. Neither of them do. They're my late wife's cousins, and they won't leave my side, though I keep telling them they ought to get out of this place as fast as they can."

"She should certainly take the baby from the room. He might become infected with your illness."

Bowie explained this to the two women, and they looked even more frightened than before, but did not move toward the door.

"Take them with you, Mary. Take them with you and get out of Béxar."

"I can't. I have to see Terrell first. Where is he, Jim?"

"I haven't seen him since he rode in from the Alazan Hills. He's the one who saw the Mexican army camped out there as brazen as you please. If I hadn't sent Terrell out, Travis would still be waiting for Santa Anna to march up the Laredo road."

"Where is he now?"

"If he ain't in the fort he's probably in the town, going

through the houses looking for provisions. There's corn in plenty in some of those houses."

"Where would I look?"

"I don't know exactly. When you find him, though, you tell him he's got orders from me to escort you and these ladies all the way to Gonzales. Sparks!"

A tall man in a calico shirt came into the room. The front of his hat brim drooped down nearly to his chin, obscuring most of his face.

"Sparks, this is Terrell's mother, Mrs. Mott," Bowie said to the man. "You take her into Béxar and help her find her son."

"We're about a whisker away from them Mexicans ridin' into town, Jim."

"You telling me you're afraid to help this woman?"

"I ain't saying that," Sparks said in a hurt voice. "That's an ugly thing to say about a man, Jim. Godalmighty."

"I'm sorry, Sparks. I'm a little off my head."

Sparks gave Bowie a gruff nod and turned to Mary. "I'm ready to go whenever you are, ma'am."

Mary thanked him as he slipped outside. She looked at Bowie again before leaving.

"What are you going to do, Jim? What are you going to do when the Mexicans get here?"

"Well, Mary," he said, "there ain't much choice that I can see. We make the best terms we can and surrender the garrison."

SPARKS HAD a long stride, and in his agitation he walked so fast that Mary could barely keep up with him as they made their way into Béxar. There was only one narrow bridge across the river, and it was so crowded with people fleeing the town that they had to squeeze their way against the flow and take care that they were not pushed off. Men from the garrison were hurrying through the streets with bundles of rifles or sacks of corn, and other men were on horseback driving three or four longhorn cattle at a time toward the river fords. Many of the houses had been damaged in the fighting of the month before, and some had been blown apart entirely.

"He might be down by the plaza," Sparks said as they made their way down Potrero Street. "That's where Travis has his headquarters. On the other hand, he might be anywhere at all."

Sparks's voice was dry and thin. Mary could almost hear his heart pounding in his bony chest. She knew herself to be afraid as well, but her sharp resolve to find Terrell made the fear seem oddly distant.

"Seen Terrell Mott?" Sparks yelled at a passing rider who was harrying a steer.

"No," the man replied. "And you better not spend any more time lookin' for him, neither. The Mexicans ain't but four or five miles away."

The man spurred his horse and hawed to the steer, which lurched and balked and then ran through a gap in a fence and through someone's yard to the riverbank.

"Well, you can stay there, you sonofabitch!" the rider called out to the steer. "I ain't gettin' killed on your account." Mary and Sparks watched as he turned his horse and rode up Potrero Street toward the bridge.

They were almost to the plaza when they encountered a young man on horseback. He was wearing a red waistcoat and held a portable writing desk under one arm, and was accompanied by a negro loaded down with bulging valises.

"Where are you going?" the man said in a harsh voice. "Haven't you heard my orders? Everyone is to retreat to the Alamo at once."

"We're tryin' to find this lady's son, Colonel Travis," Sparks said.

Travis turned to Mary and touched the brim of his hat.

"Is he a soldier, ma'am?"

"Yes, he is. His name is Terrell Mott."

"Yes. One of Bowie's men. But there's no sense looking for him here. He'll turn up in the Alamo, along with everybody else."

Travis looked down sternly at Sparks. "Take her across the river at once. The Mexicans will be upon us at any moment."

"He's in command?" Mary said to Sparks as Travis and his slave rode off.

"Him and Bowie, more or less. But Jim ain't in too good a shape, as you know yourself."

The hopeless feeling Mary was trying to hold back suddenly flooded through her. She knew Travis by reputation as an unreflective firebrand. What she had not known was how young he was. Standing there in the middle of the street, she suddenly realized how completely her life and Terrell's now depended upon the judgment of this hot-tempered boy.

"We'd better get out of here, Mrs. Mott," Sparks said. He didn't wait for a response. He just took her arm and led her back the way they'd come. The street was almost vacant now, though a half-mile up ahead there was still a good bit of congestion at the bridge.

"Oh, merciful Lord," she heard Sparks proclaim in a shaky voice. He was standing still all of a sudden, looking back toward the plaza and the church.

"What is it?" she said.

"Look there. Toward those hills yonder."

At first sight it looked like a slow-moving, silver trickle of water. It took her a moment to comprehend that what she was seeing was the lance points and polished brass plates on the helmets of the Mexican cavalry gleaming in the sun.

A woman was screeching from a half-opened door, speaking to Sparks in heavily accented English—"You will all be killed!"

Sparks took off running, and Mary followed. With his

long legs he naturally outdistanced her, and every few seconds he looked back peevishly to see how far behind she was and forced himself to slacken his pace so that she could catch up.

Ahead of them, the bridge was still jammed. The people there were jostling each other and looking back toward the west, where the cavalry was coming on at a frighteningly steady pace and the infantry was just pouring over the hills behind them.

"There's a ford over by La Villita. We'll have to wade across, but I'd a damn sight rather get my feet wet than get a lance in my back."

She followed him as he ran down a side street. A dog ran out from one of the yards, silently and purposeful, and bit Sparks in the meat of his calf. He yelped and leapt in the air but kept running. The dog came after Mary too but only managed to catch its teeth in her skirt, and after that did not pursue them any farther.

Twenty or thirty yards up ahead the street pitched down toward the ford, and they waded across the cold, knee-deep water and scrambled up the other side, where there was an outlying neighborhood of adobe houses. She followed Sparks down one of the streets and they passed a heavily damaged house with its roof and most of its walls missing and Edmund sitting in the center of it in a splintered chair, looking down at the floor, with Professor curled at his feet.

"Edmund!" she called. She entered the house, walking on the fallen door as if it were a drawbridge. He looked up at her in acknowledgment, but his eyes were numb.

"We've got to get into the Alamo now!" Sparks was calling from twenty yards up the road. "I can see 'em from here. They're already in the plaza!"

She turned and looked back to the town. They were on a slight rise of ground, and through the trees she could see the Mexican cavalry entering the town at the gallop and could hear their shrill bugle calls and the cries of their officers.

"Go on!" she told Sparks.

"I ain't supposed to go back without you, ma'am,"

"Go on. Tell Colonel Bowie I wouldn't go with you."

Sparks debated for a second or two, and then tipped his hat and broke out into a run.

Edmund continued to sit there as if entranced.

"Was this your house?" she said.

"Yes. It appears to have been destroyed in the fighting."

"And your papers? Your specimens?"

"I have found a few scraps of things. I don't know what happened to the bulk of it. It is gone, that's all; what was not destroyed outright was scattered by the wind."

"Edmund, I am sorry."

"My life was in this house, Mary. All of my work for twenty years and more. I am nothing without it."

He looked up at her as if noticing her for the first time.

"Did you find your son?"

"Not yet."

"You will. I'm sure of it."

He looked down at the floor again. She knew there was nothing she could say that would rouse him from his despair. All she could do was to try to save their lives.

"Edmund," she said, "we must go into the Alamo at once. The Mexicans are in the town. They will take us prisoner and they will have you shot for the death of Espinosa."

He answered with a hollow nod, as if the saving of his life was an unpleasant duty he was required to perform. He stood and untied the reins of his horse from an iron hitching ring that had been upended and was lying in a pile of rubble in front of the house. She mounted first and they sat double on the saddle, with Mary squeezed between his lap and the high wooden pommel. From this new height, she had a clearer view of Béxar. Lancers were riding through the streets, and artillery limbers were being unloaded in the plaza. From the bell tower of the cathedral, a long red banner was waving.

"What does that mean?" she asked Edmund.

"It means no quarter will be given," he answered as he gave the horse a sharp kick and rode hard toward the Alamo.

CHAPTER TWENTY-THREE

⁕

NO ONE stopped them from entering the mission, though there were over a dozen men stationed within the artillery battery in front of the south gate, and it seemed to Mary it might have been a prudent thing to challenge anyone who rode in.

"Here comes a dog too," one of the men said as Professor trotted in behind them. "That makes it one dog and two cats."

"Well, the Mexicans don't stand a chance, then," one of the others said, and there was some thin, nervous laughter.

Edmund was leading his borrowed horse through the gate when he was almost knocked off his feet by a booming eruption. The horse jerked violently upward, striking the flat of its head against the archway of the gatehouse, and then pulled the reins from Edmund's grip and raced in panic across the open courtyard.

"Get down!" he called to Mary, and the two of them crouched in the relative safety of the archway. The men in the tambour outside had hurled themselves against the embankment, expecting an enemy barrage, but there were no further explosions, and it was soon obvious that the noise had come from the Alamo's own artillery

"Gentlemen!" they heard someone calling from the southwest corner of the compound. Edmund crept out from under the gate and saw William Travis standing at the summit of an artillery ramp while a dense cloud of powder smoke ravelled away from him like a spirit.

"That sound you just heard," Travis was saying, "was the

report of our eighteen-pounder. It was in answer to that red flag you see in the distance, at the summit of the cathedral. It was my way of telling the Mexicans that we do not intend to surrender, we do not intend to run, and that by God they may go straight to hell!"

Travis stood there as if waiting for a roaring chorus of approval, but most of the defenders seemed unnerved by the sudden cannon blast, and others—those stationed on the earthen ramp at the back of the church, for instance—were too far away to hear their commander and were turning to each other with puzzled expressions.

Edmund looked at Travis as he stood by the cannon, one hand on his sword hilt and the other theatrically waving his hat. He would have looked almost comical, Edmund thought, had it not been for his intensity, which betrayed nothing of fear or self-doubt. Edmund remembered the uncomplicated certainty that Travis had displayed during their one meeting in San Felipe last year, and his spirits fell at the thought of this rigorous young man presiding over their fates in a situation that could be redeemed, it seemed to him, only by the most exquisite diplomacy.

A strange silence hung over the Alamo after Travis's cannon blast. Most of the men were clustered near the batteries, or stationed thinly atop the walls, lying at full length with their rifles trained on the town and watching the Mexican troops as they continued to march into the plaza and set up artillery emplacements. Mary looked from one man to the next, hoping to spot Terrell, but could not find him. Surely he was in the Alamo, though. He might very well be inside one of the buildings, or stationed at the fortifications inside the church or along the palisade, locations that were both out of her line of sight.

"That is a stout building," Edmund said, pointing to the convent whose second-floor hospital room Mary had visited earlier. "Go there and I'll meet you as soon as I can."

"Where are you going?"

"To get that horse." He pointed to the far end of the courtyard, where his renegade horse was prancing in nervous circles by the shallow and decrepit-looking north wall.

"I want to see Bowie again first," Mary said. "His room is just down the way, and Terrell might have reported to him while I was gone."

Edmund nodded vacantly. Despair over the loss of his life's work had seeped into his veins, and some part of him marvelled at the fact that he still cared to live. In any case, the present circumstance did nothing to encourage that expectation. It seemed to him that only two outcomes were possible: the Mexicans would attack and everyone would be killed, or Travis would come to his senses and surrender the garrison, and perhaps some would be spared—though not he. He would be stood up against the wall and shot for murdering the centralist patriot Don Osbaldo Espinosa as he knelt in prayer in his chapel.

He felt Mary's hand on his face, the briefest touch, and then she was gone without a further word, disappearing through a door in the wall of the gatehouse. Edmund picked himself up and started to walk across the courtyard to retrieve the horse.

"Is that your horse?" said a man—an officer, Edmund supposed—who was standing at a battery of three small cannon that were raised on a shallow ramp of earth just inside the main entrance. The officer had a slow match in his hand, ready to fire at the enemy if they managed to break through the main gate.

"Yes, it is," Edmund replied as he walked by.

"Take it to the corral immediately. We can't have horses stampeding in the courtyard. Whose company are you with? Don't you have a rifle?"

Edmund did not bother to answer. He walked to the other end of the courtyard in the solitude of his own hopelessness. The horse was frightened but did not run from him, merely stood there with its reins trailing on the ground, waiting on his approach, waiting for the solace of a human touch. Edmund resolved at that moment to mount the horse and ride out through the gate and down the Gonzales road. He did not want escape so much as he wanted privacy and silence in which to contemplate his own enormous heartbreak. This war would go on perfectly without his participation. However, as he reached down for the reins he felt a leaden conviction that he would never see Mary again, that his riding out of the Alamo without stopping to say goodbye or to explain himself would be understood by her as a rebuke that could never be repaired.

The horse must have heard the deep cramp of the distant howitzer an instant before he did. As he was about to take hold of the reins the animal jerked them out of the dirt, and Edmund looked up into its eyes and saw them white with fear and then heard the grenade arcing toward the walls of the Alamo with its lit fuse sputtering in the air.

The ball grazed the sloping thatch roof of one of the buildings on the west wall and rolled down onto the ground ten yards from where Edmund and the horse were standing. The Mexican gunners had guessed wrong about the duration of the grenade's journey and had cut its fuse too long, and so instead of exploding in the air as it was meant to, it lay there spinning frantically on the ground in tight circles.

There was a pile of mouldy canvas and splintered crates lying on the eastern side of the courtyard and Edmund turned on his heel and ran toward it for the scant protection it offered. He heard someone shouting "Bomb!" and "Get down!" and saw men all around him scrambling futilely to find a less exposed position.

The grenade exploded before he reached the canvas. If there was a noise he didn't hear it, though he was aware of an intense white flash and the sound of jagged metal as it made a rapid, spattering rain against the stone walls behind him. Professor, running along just ahead of him, yelped and turned a cartwheel. Edmund was struck in the back by something powerful and blunt that seemed to lift him off the ground a few inches and send him coasting upright toward the pile of gray tarps. He landed hard on the other side of them, plowing into the bare winter dirt, and lay there for a moment with his ears buzzing wildly as he slowly considered the proposition that he might not be dead.

"I can walk," he told the two men who came running out from the shelter of the barracks to grab him by the shoulders and drag him off. They paid him no heed and kept dragging him anyway. Their faces were tight with fear, the sky was filled with the noise of another grenade. This one exploded properly, in the air, only seconds after they entered the barracks. The three of them threw themselves onto the stone floor. The room was long and dark, with only two shuttered windows. Dozens of men were crouching against the walls, holding their rifles, and in the light that leaked through the cracks in the shutters and through the crudely dug loopholes Edmund could make out the carved figure of a saint in the corner, staring down at him from an entablature over the hearth, its bloodless wooden face regarding him with supernatural scrutiny.

"Whose company you with?" one of the men who had rescued him said, trying to sound casual as the bombardment continued. To Edmund's reverberating ears he sounded as distant as someone calling out to him across a river.

"I'm not in a company," Edmund said.

"I thought I saw you come in with Cummings and them," the man said. "That's Cummings's horse lyin' out there anyway."

The man was holding the door ajar for him and when Edmund peeked through it he saw the horse lying splayed and broken in a field of blood. Its great chest was still slowly moving, and its eyes were open and staring into the sky as if it had decided to roll over on its back and contemplate the clouds as they drifted by. One of its legs was broken as sharply as the leg of a kitchen table, and another was missing entirely. Edmund spotted it lying twenty yards away, atop the canvas heap he had been running toward for protection.

"That gave you a pretty good lick, I guess," the man said.

"What do you mean?" Edmund said.

"That horse leg," the man replied, after another shell had exploded overhead. "It hit you in the back like a club. Or maybe you were too busy to notice."

"Where's my dog?" Edmund said, suddenly aware of Professor's absence.

"I've got him right here," someone called out. When Edmund turned in the direction of the voice he saw a middle-aged man in expensive clothes holding Professor in his lap. The dog was staring at Edmund as if he didn't recognize him, his scalp laid bare by shrapnel and hanging in a bloody flap over his left eye. "I suspect his thoughts are a bit addled, but he should turn out all right," the man said. "He'll need some sewin' up, though."

"Someone get Congressman Crockett a needle and thread," one of the men said.

TERRELL WAS in the horse pen next to the chapel removing Veronica's bridle when the bombardment began. He had worked the mare hard today, riding her out to the Alazan Hills and back and then joining in a mad horseback dash to the close-lying rancho of a friendly Tejano to bring in a dozen cattle. They had just managed to squeeze the little herd into the corral when Travis's eighteen-pounder erupted, throwing the cattle and horses both into a panic.

Veronica was trained to gunfire but not to bellowing explosions, and when the cannon fired she danced about the corral with her ears laid flat against her head, and it took

Terrell a few moments to calm her and lead her away from the terror-stricken cattle to the horse pen on the other side of the adobe wall.

"Why did he shoot off the cannon? Are the Mexicans attacking already?" he asked a man named Crossman, a Pennsylvanian with the New Orleans Greys who had been on the cattle expedition and had ridden into the fort a few minutes earlier than Terrell.

"Hush a minute," Crossman said. Terrell listened. He could hear Travis making a speech, his voice travelling weakly from way over on the other side of the fort.

"I can't hear him," Terrell said.

"Neither can I," Grossman replied, "but I'll be damned if I'm going to stay out here in this horse yard any longer than I have to."

He was hastily uncinching his saddle. His forage cap lay flat on top of his head like a parcel, and his stiff, unwashed hair hung down to his shoulders.

Terrell lifted the heavy saddle off Veronica's back and carried it to the old monk's cell that now served as a makeshift tack room. Saddles and horse blankets lay on the floor on top of each other, and the bridles were all tangled up in a corner of the room. Some of the men had carved or burned their initials into the saddles so they could find them again, and Terrell wished he had thought to do so, because from now on, he suspected, there would be nothing but commotion and men grabbing whatever outfit came first to hand.

He was removing Veronica's bridle when he heard the first grenade hiss across the sky and explode on the other side of the barracks. The fifteen or twenty horses in the pen, Veronica among them, fell into a churning panic, and Terrell and Crossman had to fight their way around their shifting bodies to reach the safety of the tack room.

The second shell exploded at the corner of the church, only a few yards away from them, and Terrell could feel the hot metal slicing through the air and horseflesh all around him. Bats were streaming out of the church and flying witlessly over the heads of the frightened horses.

They reached the tack room at the same moment, as a third shell detonated above the churchyard and another exploded too high in the air to do much damage but sent shards of hot metal raining down on the roof above them. Terrell looked out the door. The horses were miraculously all standing, though some were bloodied, and the gunners in the ramp at the far end were starting to sit up and check themselves for damage.

"You hit, boy?" Crossman asked him.

"I don't think so," Terrell said.

"I believe I got a piece of something in my arm here," Crossman said, digging a dull wedge of metal out of his forearm, admiring it for a moment and tossing it aside.

"You got hair all over your shirt," Terrell said.

"Well, ain't that the most curious damn thing you ever saw?" Crossman said, inspecting a strange half-moon of shed hair that covered his shoulders. He lifted his hat. "Did it all come out? I still got any left up there?"

"You got plenty," Terrell said, and then realized to his overpowering shame that his own body had turned on him in its panic. He clenched his jaw and looked away, filled with revulsion at his own helplessness.

"I shit my trousers once too," Crossman said with calculated casualness. "When we took Béxar I was standing next to Ben Milam when they blew his head off, and I couldn't have held on to it if you'd offered me a box full of gold."

He smiled kindly, brushed the hair off his shoulders and held out his hand.

"Give them to me, son. I'll take them over to the trough and fix them up for you and nobody'll know the difference."

"I appreciate that," Terrell said, pulling off his trousers. He was more grateful to Crossman than to anybody he'd ever met in his life.

AFTER CROSSMAN brought his trousers back the two of
them waited a while longer, and then when it seemed like
no more shells were coming they went out into the churchyard.

"Crossman, take your rifle and get up there on the wall at
once," a captain named Blazeby said in an English accent
as he jogged past them toward the north battery.

"And you," he said to Terrell. "What is your affiliation?"

"Sir?"

"Which company?"

"Bowie's company, sir."

"Have you been assigned to a post?"

"Not yet, sir."

"Well, then, report to Bowie or Baker and get one as
quickly as ever you can."

IN BOWIE'S ROOM the two Mexican women were patting away the fine dust that had fallen from the ceiling and
covered the colonel's blanket. Their hands were shaking as
they did so, and the baby had not stopped screaming since
the first of the explosions.

Mary stood in the corner, trembling, waiting for the next
bombardment or for an outright attack. She could hear officers outside calling to their men, and footsteps on the roof
above as sharpshooters returned to their positions on top of
the gatehouse, but all the activity seemed ragged and unco-
ordinated to her. She had the feeling that there was no core
to this garrison, no guiding force. Travis himself, from that
one glimpse she had had of him, struck her as a man trying
to command a whirlwind.

"Goddammit, why did Travis shoot off that cannon?"
Bowie was raging from his sickbed. "Did he think the Mexicans needed a little more provocation?"

Bowie was considerably livelier than he had been when the bombardment started. When Mary entered his room he was lying in bed groaning and staring at the ceiling and when he looked at her it took a while for his mind to clear.

"Did you find your brother, Mary?"

"It's my son I'm looking for, Jim. Terrell."

"Oh, hell, yes," he had said, and then the first grenade had gone off and men started pouring through the door and crouching against the walls.

One of the men who had come running into Bowie's quarters for shelter was a captain named Juan Seguín, who entered into a long, vociferous discussion with Bowie as the shells exploded and the screaming bits of metal flew against the walls and embedded themselves in the wooden door.

Now that the bombardment was over Bowie was dictating a letter in Spanish to Seguín, who sat in a hard-backed chair with one leg draped elegantly across the other, writing down the words in a fluid hand, now and then suggesting a change of phrase. Bowie spoke slowly enough that Mary thought she could make out the essence of the letter. It seemed to be an apology for Travis's cannon shot and an offer to parley. When Seguín had taken the letter down he held it out for Bowie to sign. The sick man's hand shook so badly that Mary walked over to his bed and steadied it for him, and even so his signature was as scrawled and ragged as if setting it down had taken the last of his mortal strength away.

Bowie told Seguín in Spanish to show the letter to Travis and have it delivered to the Mexican lines.

"Of course that idiot Travis will probably just tear it up," Bowie said to Mary when Seguín had gone. He looked at her with his feverish, straining eyes.

"I never thought to be in such a hobble with you, Mary," he said. "As I recall, our adventures were on the pleasurable side."

"You'll come through this all right, Jim."

"I wouldn't mind dying so much if I could do it colorful."

She was searching for words to counter his fatalism when there was a knock on the door and Bowie called out "Come in," and Terrell was standing there in a grimy hunting shirt and jacket and the faint tracery of a beard on his face. He held his father's rifle. He was looking at Bowie and did not see Mary in the corner of the room.

"Captain Blazeby said I should ask you about where to put myself. I can shoot this rifle pretty well and it seems to me we need sharpshooters over by the—"

"Good God, son," Bowie said. "It's a rude man who won't say hello to his own mother."

CHAPTER TWENTY-FOUR

✴

THEY STOOD talking in a corner of the fort, at the base of an earthen ramp leading up to the southwest battery. Men labored up and down the ramp, hauling cannonballs and powder, preparing for an attack. Major Jameson had walked out of the Alamo with a white flag, carrying Bowie's letter, and the men on the walls waited tensely for him to return, arguing with each other whether it would be better if he returned with an honorable surrender or if there was no choice but to hold the fort and pray for reinforcements.

Their speculations drifted down to Mary and her son, but they paid them little attention, both knowing that this might be the last conversation they would ever have. Terrell had lost weight and now had the gauntness and hardness of a man. His features had sharpened and to her tender eyes seemed cruel. He had begun shaving last year. She had seen Fresada instructing him in the yard, and her heart had lurched at the sight, thinking how it should have been Andrew passing on such masculine lore to his son. Terrell had obviously not shaved in months, but even so his chin was mostly clear, with only his side-whiskers forming an unruly smudge down to the jawline. His eyelashes were still youthfully lush. When he blinked she could not help thinking of him as an infant, asleep in her lap by the hearth, earnestly dreaming behind his sealed eyelids while she trailed her fingertip across the frondlike softness of those lashes.

Alert to his embarrassment, she had not run to embrace

him when he first discovered her in Bowie's room. And she did not do so now, though her longing to hold him—to pick him up in her arms and carry him away, to carry him back through the years so that he was a trusting, confiding boy again—was as sharp and savage as any emotion she had ever felt.

"I've come a long way to speak to you, Terrell," she began carefully.

"You shouldn't have."

"But I did. What happened with that girl—"

He looked away, desperate to be with the other men.

"What happened with that girl was not your fault. No one could have imagined she would do such a thing."

He nodded indifferently, but there were tears building in his eyes. He turned his head and pretended to train his attention on the opposite end of the fort, where the wall was broken and shored up with timber and dirt.

"You considered it my fault," he said at last.

"I know I did, and I am sorry, Terrell."

She put a hand on his forearm. How strange that a mother's touch had come to this—so tentative and skittish. She truly felt that if she moved closer or increased the grip of her hand he would run like a rabbit.

"Major Jameson's coming back!" one of the men called down from the battery. There was a long silence during which everyone waited for Jameson to walk up from the river. In a few minutes he walked through the gate, holding a white flag made from a torn bedsheet.

"What did they say, Green?" the men called down to him from the walls. But Jameson wouldn't even answer, or look up at them. He walked past Mary and Terrell and down the courtyard to one of the houses on the west wall—Travis's quarters, Mary guessed—and disappeared inside.

"Looks like they ain't going to let us surrender," Terrell said. "You have to get out of here."

"It's too late."

"No, it's not. They won't harm a woman for leaving. They let Major Jameson out with a white flag, and they'll let you. But you have to do it now."

"I need to speak to Mr. McGowan first," she said. She had not yet told him about the death of Don Osbaldo, or her role in it.

"Mr. McGowan is here?"

"We came together."

She tried to look into his eyes, but he still would not let them fall on her.

"Please, Terrell . . ." she whispered.

"What?"

"I only want . . ." But she did not know what she wanted, and so she just stood there dumbly, as this crucial moment drifted away from them and someone began to play a bleating, insistent call on a bugle.

"That's assembly, I think," Terrell told her. "Nobody uses bugle calls much. They usually just say it."

They watched as Travis strode out of his headquarters, mashing his hat on his head. Jameson and another officer were with him, and his slave followed a step or two behind, silent and apprehensive.

"Everybody gather in the church! All except the pickets!" the officer with Travis and Jameson was calling. "Hurry! Right now!"

The men in the battery above them walked down the ramp and trotted toward the empty, roofless church. It was almost dark now. There was a wind blowing and the air was fresh, but Mary could still smell the gunpowder from the exploded shells, and a rank, mildewy odor clung to the old stone walls of the mission.

"I have to go," Terrell said. "I can't stand here and talk anymore."

"I know," she said.

But Terrell stayed where he was.

"What is it you want me to say?" he asked. "I'll say it."

Mary shook her head. All she wanted was to seize him in her arms, but she knew if she did such a thing she might not be able to let go, and he would have to pull away from her as if she were a crazy woman who had run up to embrace a stranger on the street.

"I can't fight and worry about you at the same time," he said, when she did not respond to his question. "I can't do that, and it ain't fair of you to expect me to."

"We'll talk later," she said at last.

"We can't talk later. You've got to get out of here, Mother. They may attack tonight, and I can't protect you."

"Stop worrying about me, Terrell," she said, with an unexpected firmness in her voice. "I've done what I came here to do, which was to say I was sorry about the way I spoke to you, the way I thought of you. It was my weakness and not yours I worried about. You are my son and I love you without regret, no matter what has happened in the past or what will happen here. Now go with the others to the meeting, and try not to worry about me. And when it comes time to fight I want you to fight without distraction."

He hesitated. She kissed him on the cheek and whispered "Go," and that seemed to release him. He met her eyes glancingly as he picked up his rifle and walked toward the church, indistinguishable from the other scared and grimy young men who were congregating there.

She watched him pass through the open doorway of the church. In the deepening shadows of this winter evening that arched opening looked like a human mouth in a frozen expression of anguish.

Mary felt her body quaking. She could not control it, and she could not stop the hiccoughing sobs that threatened to rend her in two. With her back against the wall, she sank down onto the dirt and gathered the hem of her dress against her face. She had come all this way and had still not reached him, had pushed herself farther away from him than before. In a normal time she could have abided this aching distance, but it was not a normal time and in the next hours or days one or both of them might be dead, and the painful, embarrassed estrangement of mother and son would linger on—resounding, unconcluded, eternal.

She pressed the dirty dress hard against her eyes, trying to stanch the tears, and when she released it she saw Professor sitting in the dirt beside her, quietly contemplating her misery. The dog's face and snout were thick with caked blood, and somebody had done a gruesome but effective job in reattaching his scalp to his head. She reached out with her hand in a consoling gesture, but Professor yelped and danced away as if he were afraid she meant to put more stitching in his skin.

Then Edmund appeared, standing next to Professor, looking down at her. Without thinking about it, she reached up her hand. He took it and pulled her to her feet and drew her head against his chest as her sobs began again. She wrapped her arms so tightly around his waist she thought she might squeeze off his breath, but he just stood there and allowed it, and after a moment she was able to gain back her self-possession.

"Did you find him?" he asked.

She nodded, but said nothing, and he did not press her for details. She looked down at the wounded dog.

"What happened to Professor?"

"A piece of metal from one of the grenades. David Crockett sewed him back together."

"Crockett? From Tennessee? What is he doing in Texas?"

"He came here for land, I suppose, like everyone else."

When she became aware that she was still clinging to him, she relaxed her arms and stepped back a few paces and leaned against the wall. Except for the pickets stationed outside the fort watching for an attack, everyone had already gathered in the church. Standing behind the corner of the gatehouse in the growing dark, they were certainly unobserved, but even so Mary felt conspicuous.

"It was a mistake to come into this fort," Edmund said. "You have to get out. The Mexicans have possession of the town, but they don't yet control the roads. Travis sent a messenger out earlier, and it is probable he got through to Gonzales. If you leave tonight, staying off the main road, there is a good chance that you can make it as well. If you are captured, you can say that it was I who murdered Espinosa and forced you to flee."

"And what about you?"

"I have no choice but to take my chances in the fort."

"Where you will be either killed in an assault or taken prisoner and executed."

"If Travis's messenger got through, reinforcements are probably already on the way. In any case, your staying will not help my situation, or Terrell's either."

"I will not leave here, Edmund."

"Why not?"

"I don't know."

She said it again in a whispering voice—"I don't know"—with such emphasis that it sounded like a declaration. In truth she had never felt more helpless or confused. But she knew that she wanted to stay in the Alamo, because all that was left to her was within these walls. The thought of making her treacherous way back to Refugio, leaving her son here to be slaughtered by Mexican bombs or bayonets, was intolerable to her, more intolerable than the thought of remaining here and watching while it happened.

Edmund's own mood was much the same: grim and static. His work, the high purpose of his life, the thing that differentiated him from other men, had evaporated, and in a way it was perplexing to him that he still desired to live at all. All his life he had driven himself forward, through every sort of adversity both material and emotional, toward the simple, single goal of greatness. And now that the possibility of reaching that goal had disappeared, he felt stranded and idle, with neither the conviction to stay nor the will to escape.

He looked toward the church, where the men of the Alamo had gathered, and felt keenly his and Mary's isolation in this dark corner of the fort.

"We should go and hear what Travis is telling them," he said.

She nodded, wiping the sheen of tears from her cheeks, and then walked with him to the church as though they were two people strolling down a city street, late for a performance of the theatre.

The door to the church was an open archway, its doors long since gone. When Edmund and Mary passed through, they saw Travis standing on the long ramp of packed earth that ran the length of the building and ended in an artillery platform. The men stood below him, their backs to the walls, ready to scramble through the doors leading to the baptistry and sacristy should another bombardment begin. Those rooms had stout stone roofs. The chapel itself was open to the cold night air, all its churchly trappings long since hauled away or used for firewood, so that it looked as empty and haunted as the Roman ruins Edmund had seen pictured in books. Travis, standing on his ramp, might have been Antony on the Rostra, mourning the death of Caesar.

But Edmund was heartened to see that Travis had not taken this opportunity to be theatrical. Rather, he was speaking to the men in a contained, conversational tone of voice, and they responded with an accepting silence. Several of them shifted their eyes to the doorway as Edmund and Mary entered without paying them a great deal of interest, since there were already plenty of refugees and castaways inside the fort. Edmund noticed five or six Tejano women and their children, and one young Anglo woman whose baby's piercing cries of discontent and fear threatened to drown out Travis's words.

"—eighty bushels of corn," he was saying, "perhaps more. Almost thirty beeves. We have more than enough provisions, enough powder and shot, to hold out here until help comes."

Travis paused, looking down at the men from his makeshift stage. His eyes met Edmund's briefly, a disconcerted look as he struggled to place him, and then swept on. Edmund saw Terrell for the first time, standing near the rear of the church with some of Bowie's men, looking no younger really than the rest of them with his hat brim dipping below his eyes and his jacket buttoned up to the collar. He had seen his mother enter but studiously avoided looking in her direction.

"And help *will* come," Travis said. "I say this to you with perfect assurance. As soon as the enemy was in sight I sent a courier to Colonel Fannin at Goliad. He has over three hundred men under his command and will surely hasten to our aid. And in only a few hours another courier will be arriving in Gonzales, and an express will be sent from there to General Houston in San Felipe. Reinforcements will be here in a very few days. Our countrymen will not forsake us. Our charge is to hold Fort Alamo until they can arrive. This, gentlemen, is the decisive ground. This is where the fight for Texas will take place."

"Where's Bowie?" one of the men standing with Terrell called out.

"Colonel Bowie is ill," Travis said. "I trust he will be on his feet again in a few short days, but in the meantime I continue to consult with him about the command, and you may consider every order as originating from our common understanding.

"Congressman," Travis said, turning to Crockett, "is there anything you would like to say to the men?"

"Well, if I'd know'd I was to make a speech I'd of brought a leetle of the creature to embolden me," Crockett said, climbing the ramp. He said the present situation reminded him of another scrape he'd been in—a literal scrape in which all the skin had been peeled off his body when friends pulled him out of the pilothouse of a sinking flatboat, and how he'd had to wrap himself in an alligator hide while he swam down the Mississippi looking for his skin, and finally found it, face and all, hanging from a tree branch. By the time he'd finished telling the story, the men of the garrison had collapsed into wheezing laughter, and the Tejanos who didn't speak English were looking on in confusion and a degree of alarm.

"Mr. McGowan, I believe?" an officer said to Edmund when the men were dismissed and returning to their posts.

"Yes?"

"My name is Baugh, Colonel Travis's adjutant. The colonel would like to see you and Mrs. Mott immediately in his quarters."

"PLEASE SIT HERE, Mrs. Mott," Travis said when Baugh ushered them into the dingy headquarters room. The colonel set his writing desk aside and dragged a sturdy-looking chair from beneath a window that had been mortared shut against enemy shells. "It is the one chair in the room I can vouch for. There was no time to bring any furniture over from my headquarters in town, and I am afraid we have a wobbly selection."

Travis cordially shook Edmund's hand and gestured to the second-best chair, while Baugh took a seat on a dusty cot and Travis's slave remained standing. In the dim taper light the room was as gloomy as a dungeon. It did not appear to have been used as a dwelling place for years, and whatever ornamentation might once have lightened it was long gone. Several sheets of precious foolscap had been nailed to the wall, and spread across them was a bird's-eye map of the fort and the important buildings in the town.

"We have met before, sir," Travis said, "in San Felipe."

"I remember."

They heard a piercing bugle call from the Mexican lines on the other side of the river. Travis excused himself, picked up his shotgun and went outside with Baugh. He was gone for only a few moments, and then walked briskly back into the room and set his shotgun against the wall.

"It was nothing," he explained. "Probably just their version of a call to mess. We are at a disadvantage, since no one in our army knows Mexican bugle calls."

"Do you fear an attack tonight?" Mary asked him.

"I don't think so, Mrs. Mott. They have had a long march and from what we can put together the bulk of their force has yet to arrive. That little bombardment we experienced today was more like an opening salute. I doubt we will see an attack in force for several days, at least. They will surely want to test our defenses on a smaller scale beforehand. Do you agree, Mr. McGowan?"

"I am not a military man."

"Yes, of course. You are a civilian. A civilian, if I remember our conversation in San Felipe correctly, with a personal commission from Santa Anna."

Edmund tilted his head in agreement, realizing now why he had been called in for this interview.

"And now I find you in my garrison," Travis said, "and am curious as to whether I should consider you friend or foe."

"I am here by accident, Colonel Travis," Edmund replied, and then offered a brief account of their abduction by the dragoons and the shooting of Don Osbaldo Espinosa. Travis listened without interrupting, though Edmund could detect his lawyer's mind assessing each element of the story as soon as it was presented.

"You have come to a poor place for sanctuary," Travis said when Edmund had finished. The colonel leaned back in his chair, pondering the matter while he stared at the map on the wall.

"I can offer you two choices," he said at last. "You may leave, or you may fight. Do you have a gun?"

"No. It was lost."

"Captain Baugh will take you to the armory. We have a quantity of firearms that were captured from the Mexicans. Then you will report to Captain Baker as a volunteer private. Is that acceptable?"

"Yes," Edmund said vacantly.

He did not look at Mary, but he could feel her eyes on him. He knew himself to be in a state of moral as well as physical exhaustion. The fact that he was suddenly an anonymous volunteer in a hopeless little war, now that the grand enterprise of his own life no longer existed, seemed only the natural culmination of this ruinous day.

Travis shifted his attention to Mary.

"As for your own situation, Mrs. Mott, all I ask is that if you want to stay in the Alamo you attend to your own safety. The other women and children are quartered in the chapel rooms, where the walls are thickest."

"I can be of some use in the hospital, I think," she responded.

"Good. I'm sure Dr. Pollard will be grateful for your help, as am I."

Travis walked outside with them into the strangely still night, and they stood there at the edge of the old grown-over ditch that had once channelled water into the mission. There were men on the walls, their forms outlined against the winter stars, but so few of them that the Alamo looked unpopulated. Edmund could hear the horses snorting in the corral behind the barracks just across the courtyard. He looked at the north wall, which was hardly a wall at all, just a crumbling adobe facade shored up with dirt and timber. Tarpaulins had been strung up at its base, and below them some of the men were clustered around cooking fires. Oth-

ers were taking their turns digging a defensive trench that
ran from one side of the courtyard to the other. The artillery
crews were huddled in blankets at the bases of their cannon
and gunnades. Someone was playing a fiddle on the other
side of the broken wall that separated the main courtyard
from the churchyard where generations of mission Indians
rested silently in their forgotten Christian graves.

The suspended peacefulness of the scene filled Edmund
with foreboding. He wondered what Travis's plans were for
defending this awkward fortification against an attack, or
indeed if any plans were possible. Edmund was no soldier,
but it seemed obvious to him that a forceful assault would
necessarily succeed, and that once the walls were breached
there would be nowhere for the defenders to rally where
they could not be blasted out by artillery. Reinforcements
would forestall this conclusion, but if he were General
Houston he would certainly question the wisdom of placing the bulk of his army behind these fragile walls.

He was rescued from these unwelcome reflections by the
sound of Travis's voice, which was suddenly low and confidential. As he spoke, he took Edmund's arm and led him a
few paces away from where Mary was standing with Captain Baugh.

"Officially you are a rifleman, Mr. McGowan, but since
you know Santa Anna himself and speak the language and
are a man of some substance and reputation, I might require other services from you on occasion."

"What services do you mean?"

"I don't know yet. Perhaps I will need a sort of plenipo-
tentiary, though I fear we have left diplomacy far behind."

Edmund said he would of course do anything within his
power to help resolve the crisis. Travis nodded his thanks
and chewed on his lip. He looked more certain of himself
in the dark, his round, youthful face lengthened by shadow,
his jaw more sharply delineated.

"I believe the story you told me earlier," Travis continued, his voice now a whisper. "But I will be honest with you and admit I cannot be absolutely certain of your intentions. Therefore if you are seen leaving the fort without my permission I will order you shot immediately as a spy for Santa Anna. Is this clear to you, Mr. McGowan?"

"Of course it is clear to me," Edmund said, not caring particularly to keep the disdain out of his voice. There was steel in Travis, but also a youthful pomposity that made Edmund nervous, and he suspected it had the same effect on the rest of the garrison as well. The men accepted Travis's leadership, they had listened to his speech in the church without dissension, but it was plain they had all felt more secure when it was Crockett's turn to address them.

When Travis returned to his headquarters Baugh turned to Mary and offered to situate her for the night in the church.

"Thank you," she said, "but I'm sure I can find a place to sleep without taking you from your duties.

"Good night, Edmund," she said with striking brevity, but there was a frightened, imploring look in her eyes as she spoke the words. And then she walked alone across the courtyard in her patched-up riding skirt and jacket. She was bareheaded, and tufts of her unbound hair danced in the wind. She still tended to walk somewhat on the outsides of her feet to avoid the massive blisters that had plagued her ever since they escaped Espinosa's rancho, and now this awkward gait was so plaintive to him he could hardly bear to see it. At the close of this day in which he had lost so much, he realized that, by not reaching out to possess her, he had lost her as well.

BAUGH TOOK HIM into the armory room, where a hundred or more Brown Bess muskets captured from General Cos's army lay in a heap on the floor.

"There were a few Baker rifles here as well," Baugh said, "but they were claimed pretty fast."

Edmund sorted through the muskets until he found one
that was reasonably well maintained and looked as if it
would shoot true. He collected a cartridge box as well,
though Baugh warned him that the Mexican powder was so
inferior he would need a horn in addition so that he could
double-charge his shots.

"We're fixed well for ammunition," Baugh said, "but low
on flints. Make sure you keep the cock tight and check it after every five or six shots. Have you ever been taught the
use of the bayonet?"

"No."

"Better not to deal with it at all, then. It will only throw
off your aim. But you might want to have one near at hand,
in case the fighting grows close."

Baugh then took him into the barracks and introduced him to Captain Baker, the Mississippian—a good ten
years younger than Edmund—who was now in command
of Bowie's men.

"Do not quail at my appearance," Baker said, shaking
Edmund's hand. There was a lump on his forehead the size
of a peach, and in the dim light from the few tapers in the
room it appeared even larger and more grotesque.

"A piece of flying rock struck me during the cannonade
this afternoon," he explained. "It is not painful, but it both-
ers me that I cannot wear my hat. I have not been without a
hat since I was in hippins."

Baker introduced him to the men sprawled on blankets
on the dirt floor. Clemuel Sparks, Jacob Roth, two Tejano
scouts named Esparza and Fuentes, four or five others
whose names Edmund did not register. They were friendly
and shook his hand, but he was aware that they were unsettled by his arrival, by this intrusion upon their seamless
comradeship. He looked around in the darkness for Terrell,
but did not see him.

"We'll do our sleeping in here," Baker told him, gesturing around the dark room, whose floor had been dug up to

make trench works, with a mound of dirt in front covered with cowhides. "Though I suspect none of us is in much of a mood to sleep. There's no strictual time for meals. We'll take them when we can. Colonel Travis has assigned us the north end of the west wall. If you scrunch down low enough on top of those buildings there's fair cover. Keep your pan clean and your frizzen down, and leave the blankets up there for the next man. If you see the Mexicans coming, scream like the hound of hell, and we'll be out to join you."

"Ain't you the one who came into the fort with Terrell's mother?" Sparks said, with his eye on Professor, who had invited himself into the room and was now lying on his back against the wall with his paws up in the air as if he were dead. "And ain't this the dog that Crockett sewed up?"

Edmund told Sparks he was right in both instances.

"Where is Terrell?" Edmund said, turning to Baker.

"Out on the wall. He will be relieved at dawn."

"I'll join him," Edmund said, hefting his heavy musket, careful not to ask permission. Baker looked at him with a degree of surprise but did not stop him as he left the room and walked out into the darkness.

He found Terrell on the roof of the officers' quarters across the compound. The boy was wrapped in a blanket, sitting behind a barricade of empty powder barrels filled with sand, his rifle cradled in his lap and his eyes on the town across the river.

"Good evening," Edmund said, sitting down next to him. There were other men spaced along the roof, but none closer than ten or fifteen yards.

"You better crouch low there, Mr. McGowan," Terrell said, after he'd gotten over his surprise. "I expect they've got sharpshooters out there somewhere."

Edmund stretched himself down at full length. The wall rose above the roofline for several feet, and some previous marksman had chipped a V-shaped shooting crevice out of

it. Setting the barrel of his musket into this declivity and
hiding the rest of his body behind the wall, Edmund felt
reasonably protected, but he knew he could not lie for long
like this without cramping.

"My mother told me you were here," Terrell said.

Edmund nodded and said nothing. The nearness of
Béxar fascinated him: He could hear the voices of Mexican
soldiers across the river as they built earthworks behind the
Veramendi house. There were lights burning in some of the
houses, and campfires scattered throughout the town, and
silhouetted shapes walking back and forth in front of them
as if in some feverish shadow play. It was cold and Edmund's teeth were already chattering, though he wore his
jacket and a blanket of coarse wool around his shoulders.
The sky was startlingly clear above them, with only shreds
of fast-moving cloud, and when an owl teetered silently in
front of his position his body jerked in alarm, and he tightened his grip on his musket and then just as quickly subsided into an embarrassed stillness. He watched the owl
coast downward in the darkness toward the river, and remembered what Bull Pizzle had told him a year ago when
he was still half-delirious with malaria, and the Comanche's
words seemed to have a spectral, divining authority: "You
have owl medicine, Tabby-boo."

At the time he had assumed that this owl medicine, if he
indeed possessed it, would somehow shield him as he made
his way down his life's true path. But tonight it seemed that
the owl, instead of shepherding his steps, had led him
astray, and delivered him to this terrifying and ignoble
place where he would be destroyed and utterly forgotten.

Edmund withdrew the sword bayonet that Baugh had
given him from the waist of his trousers and set it down
within easy reach. Here in the dark, with the enemy voices
audible to his ears, the use of this hideous weapon did not
seem abstract at all. If the Mexican attack came swiftly

enough, he and the other defenders would have barely enough time to get off a shot or two, and then it would all degenerate into savage grappling with whatever killing implements lay near to hand.

"I can see men on the bridge," Terrell said to him.

Edmund shifted his eyes to the south, where there were indeed a half-dozen shadowy shapes walking about on the far end of the bridge.

"They are probably engineers," Edmund said. "Inspecting the bridge to make sure it will support artillery."

"We should have blown that bridge up," Terrell said. "If they can get their cannon across it they'll put up a battery over there in the Alameda. Then they'll start surrounding us. I think we ought to break out of here while we still can and fight in the open."

"I think so too," Edmund said, though he was sure the Mexican cavalry was waiting for them in the hills. The Texian army was no more prepared to fight a battle on open ground than it was to endure a siege.

A long time passed before Terrell spoke again, a half-hour or more, as the two of them swept their eyes across the trampled cornfields in front of them, looking for a moving shape or a glint of metal in the starlight that might be the advancing form of an enemy skirmisher.

"What happened to her, Mr. McGowan?" Terrell finally said, whispering so that none of the other men could hear. "How did she kill herself?"

"With a knife," Edmund replied.

"Stabbed herself? With her own hand?"

"Yes."

"I never heard of anybody doing that."

"She was insane, Terrell. The day before, she had lost her baby and seemed to think it had been the devil's child. She spoke to me about it. I should have seen through to what she was capable of, but I did not."

Terrell was silent again for a long time. It was long past
midnight now, and Edmund's teeth still clattered in the
cold.

"That baby wasn't mine," the boy said at last, with an aggrieved, defiant tone. "I never touched her again after that
first time. It was some of Cos's soldiers who did that to her.
She let them. I got into a scrape when I tried to run them off."

"Did you tell your mother that?"

"No."

"Why not, Terrell?"

"Because it didn't matter to me what she thought. I was
tired of her thinking about me at all."

Edmund could think of no way to pursue the topic without sounding like a lecturing boor. He looked over at Terrell, at the boy's sharp, vigilant face. There was less fear in
that face than in many that Edmund had seen today, and
certainly less than in his own. But Edmund thought that
Mary had been right to come all this way to see him, had
been correct in her supposition that she had made Terrell
unsure of her love. She had come to Béxar to spread some
sort of balm on her son's troubled soul, though the urgency
of the moment had defeated her, and they would all be fortunate indeed if they survived with their mortal bodies.

Toward the dawn the owl came back from the river, flying low and silently over the fields, searching for mice.
Then it flew over the courtyard of the Alamo and back out
again, where some nervous, half-awake picket stationed in
the lunette outside the walls took a shot at it, alarming the
whole garrison. But as far as Edmund could see, the owl
was not hit, and it streamed away to the south toward the
treetops of the Alameda.

CHAPTER TWENTY-FIVE

✦

THEY CANTERED across the bridge in the glare of the noon sun, the president buoyantly in the lead on his black charger, followed by his generals and staff, with a cavalry escort behind. Telesforo rode beside Colonel Almonte, who had followed Santa Anna's example in abandoning his unwieldy bicorne for the occasion and replacing it with a wide-brimmed straw hat. Santa Anna had also left behind his blue general's sash; a prudent decision, Telesforo thought, since they were passing within rifle shot of the Alamo. Though the norte rebels were more than two hundred yards away, it was not unthinkable that one of these backwoodsmen could, through a combination of luck and skill, hit such a desirable target.

The defenders were preoccupied, however. A new Mexican battery had been completed this morning just north of Potrero Street, and now was steadily bombarding the fort. As the reconnaissance party crossed the bridge and headed up the road toward the Alameda, one of the six-pounders in the battery emitted a percussive roar that caused Telesforo's grulla mare to break stride in fear. When he looked to his left, Telesforo caught sight of the round sailing over the river, moving almost sluggishly, it seemed—as if through water rather than air. The solid shot made an oblique strike on the top of the west wall, sending up a spray of brown dust and flying rock, then continued over the courtyard and corrals before dropping like a hailstone into the marshy lake on the other side. The eighteen-pounder on the southwest corner of the Fortin del Alamo boomed out in response, though Telesforo was moving too quickly in the opposite direction to determine if it did any damage to the Mexican works.

The procession continued on through the Alameda, a long colonnade of cottonwood trees growing on either side of the road, and then the road emerged onto open country, and Santa Anna spurred his horse into a gallop. Telesforo bounded along with the rest of the staff, delighted to be a part of this reconnaissance, though as his body coasted rhythmically in the saddle ragged bolts of pain shot through his damaged arm with far more than the usual intensity. He had slept little last night, despite the fact that for the first time in weeks he had lain on a real bed in the house of a norte storekeeper who had abandoned all his goods in a blind panic to leave Béxar. It was the pain in his arm that had kept him awake, or so he told himself. But it had been an eventful day and perhaps his wakefulness was just the result of his agitated mind refusing to let go of its grip. Every time he had closed his eyes he had found himself on that rocky escarpment looking down at the town, which stretched out below with such precision and order it was as if what he was seeing was somehow his own creation. Once more, he was staring into the eyes of that boy soldier who had happened upon him while he was sketching, and once more—his heart pounding with fear in his chest, his horse pistol unprimed—he brazenly asked the flabbergasted boy in a courteous voice if he wished to surrender.

Telesforo had kept the incident to himself. He was friendly with most of the other members of Santa Anna's staff, and had shared many hardships with them during the long march to Texas, but none had the particular slant of humor that he found so valuable in his good friend Robert Talon. Unfortunately, Talon was not here to listen to his stories. He and the rest of his Zapador company, along with the other companies of the First Brigade under General Gaona, had not yet arrived. They had suffered even more than the vanguard, Telesforo had been told, enduring Indian raids and desperate thirst made even worse by the fact that the troops ahead of them had carelessly fouled the water holes. Ranging far ahead of the main army with Santa Anna and his staff, Telesforo had missed the full force of the terrible norther that had descended upon the First Brigade, but the stories made it quickly up the line. Telesforo heard of men and animals freezing to death, of a soldier's toes turning black and numb with frostbite and then snapping off as he pulled on his shoe.

Telesforo hoped Talon had survived, and he hoped the First Brigade would reach Béxar before Santa Anna ordered an attack, so that his friend would not miss his opportunity to win the Legion of Honor.

The party galloped past the turning for the Goliad road and continued up the flank of a modest hill on whose summit stood a watchtower and powder house and long-vacated barracks for Spanish soldiers. There was a luncheon already waiting on field tables, and several spyglasses sitting on tripods.

As they dismounted, horse holders raced up from the cavalry escort to relieve them of their mounts, and soldiers handed them cups of wine. The president drained his in one or two appreciative swallows, declined the offer of more, and walked over to one of the spyglasses without saying a word and peered down at the Alamo for quite some time.

"What a nuisance to have to assault this place," he said at last without looking up from the eyepiece. Colonel Almonte, standing next to Telesforo on the lip of the hill, arched an eyebrow and shot a glance at General Ramírez y Sesma, who stood alone with his arms folded and his face angrily set. Santa Anna had harangued him yesterday afternoon, in full hearing of his staff, for not investing Béxar immediately with his cavalry instead of waiting for the infantry to come up. His delay, as Telesforo had predicted, had resulted in the rebels running to ground in the Alamo, precipitating what might be a lengthy siege and a costly assault.

"How far out are you sending your patrols, General?" Santa Anna said now, looking up from the spyglass and speaking to his humiliated general in a disconcertingly pleasant voice.

"Five leagues in every direction, Your Excellency."

"Increase it to seven. Teniente Villasenor!"

"Yes, Your Excellency," Telesforo said, hurrying over to the president's side.

"Let me see your map."

Telesforo unfolded the map on a camp stool and positioned it to the proper orientation. Santa Anna knelt down on one knee to study it, lifting his eyes continually from the paper to the fortress itself sitting in the valley below. The bombardment from the battery had ceased for the moment, and the hazy clouds of dust and gunpowder that obscured the Alamo were starting to blow peacefully away. Telesforo could see men running about in the courtyard during the lull.

"This is remarkably detailed," Santa Anna said after a moment more of comparing the map to the actual thing it represented.

"Thank you, Your Excellency."

"Tell me about those houses." The president was pointing to a haphazard grouping of ten or twelve jacales clustered outside the southwest corner of the Alamo.

"It is a little neighborhood the Bexareños call Pueblo del Valero. The houses are not substantial. They are mere huts, and most of them have been abandoned since the fighting in December."

"Still, we can't allow the rebels to occupy them. They are too close to the road. What about water?"

"There are two wells within the compound, one still under construction. At present they have plentiful water from the acequia, but since they are digging a well they obviously expect us to cut off their supply."

"And we will not disappoint them, Teniente," Santa Anna said cheerfully as he turned to his staff. "Gentlemen, shall we have our luncheon?"

The day was mild and they ate in the open air, looking down upon the besieged fort. Santa Anna, having discharged so much anger at Ramírez y Sesma the day before, bantered genially with his officers throughout the meal, as completely at ease as if they were all dining in a fine hotel rather than on a hilltop in the remotest stretch of Mexico. When he had finished his custard he set down his tableware with a ringing finality and called for coffee.

"We must cut the roads," he said, when he had his cup in hand and had shuffled his field chair away from the table to face the plain below. "Tomorrow, Colonel Ampudia, you will construct entrenchments in the Alameda. That will give us control of the roads from Gonzales and Goliad, which is the likeliest avenue for reinforcements. What road is that, Villasenor? The one leading off to the northeast?"

"The road to Nacogdoches, Your Excellency," Telesforo replied, surprised and flattered to be asked a question that Cos or Ramírez y Sesma or any of the other generals present could have answered as well.

"We'll put the next battery there, and build some sort of dam in that acequia to deny them water. Now who is this man I keep hearing about, this Crocker?"

"Crockett," Colonel Almonte said. "A clownish American politician. Quite successful with his backwoods affectations but no match for Jackson, who engineered his defeat."

"Have you met him?"

"No, but I saw his portrait exhibited in Washington, and when I was last in New Orleans there was even a play up about him."

"And why did he come to Texas?" Santa Anna wanted to know.

"The same reason they all did," Almonte replied. "To run away from failure—or disgrace. Still, I gather that Crockett is not quite a spent force. He would make a very interesting prisoner for us."

"No," Santa Anna answered firmly. "He will be killed along with the rest."

Almonte looked away, and no one else chose to break the uncomfortable silence that followed. They were quite aware of His Excellency's position on the matter of quarter; he had been very specific on numerous occasions. Women and children would be spared, of course, and negro slaves as well, who by definition could not take part in this rebellion by the dictates of their own will, but every man who had taken up a weapon against the Republic of Mexico would be killed in battle or executed thereafter, even the sick or wounded in their beds. There would be no exceptions, nor would Santa Anna listen to any special pleadings or discussions of this point. The red flag he had ordered to fly from the bell tower of San Fernando Church, the flag of no quarter, should be regarded as what it was: not a decoration but a statement of clear intent.

Telesforo had never heard any of Santa Anna's senior officers challenge the president on this issue, though they felt secure to argue points of strategy or supply. He suspected that this was because the standing order of extermination somehow shamed them, and that they believed that the less it was discussed the more it could be put quietly aside when honor dictated a more generous course. Telesforo himself had a soldier's tolerance for killing, but no appetite for it. He believed in war, he accepted its grotesque particulars. War was the one stage upon which a man could proclaim his courage, his nobility, his final unequivocal worth. And what troubled him about Santa Anna's pitiless decree was that it made him feel that something had been taken from him: the chance for the magnanimous gesture, the opportunity to extend the hand of soldierly fellowship to a vanquished foe.

The president rose from his chair, walked over to the edge of the escarpment and stood there staring down at the Alamo with Telesforo's map spread wide in his arms. The other officers naturally clustered around him, some smoking cigars, some still with wineglasses in their hands. Santa Anna himself, Telesforo noticed, had left all such beguilements at the table and was looking at his objective with the single-minded intensity of a bird of prey.

"I do not want a long siege. I want to get this over with as soon as possible, before they are reinforced."

"It will be a week at least before the First Brigade arrives," Cos said.

"I am aware of that, Martín. But in the meantime we will not be idle. The fort's vulnerable point is obviously the north wall, but tomorrow we will make a probe to the south with the Matamoros and Jiménez battalions to gain control of those jacales and test the nortes' skill at enfilade. If these land pirates are as undisciplined in a fight as I suspect, we may even be able to force our way through that palisade by the church and carry the fort."

A good, cautious plan, Telesforo thought, with the possibility of a bold finish. But it only served to make him nervous. His own battalion was a hundred leagues away and it would be an impertinence, when Santa Anna's mind was so beset with innumerable details, to beg leave to join in the assault.

The generals gathered around the map and began to discuss with Santa Anna the details of tomorrow's action and the personnel and equipment that would be needed, as well as the logistics of supplying the troops that would occupy the batteries on this side of the river. Telesforo stood humbly apart, as did Colonel Almonte, who was restless with such details and was more a diplomat at heart than a soldier, even though it was said he was the bastard son of Morelos and that his father had taken him by the hand when he was a young child and had led him onto the battlefields after each engagement to show him the dead bodies of his royalist enemies.

Almonte strolled over to the spyglass, still resting on its tripod, and looked through the eyepiece. In a moment, he looked up and called softly to Telesforo, so as not to disturb the deliberation of the generals.

"Can you explain something to me, Teniente?" he said. "What do you suppose is the meaning of this flag?"

Almonte stood aside and invited Telesforo to look through the spyglass. It was an excellent instrument, and he was startled at first by the intimacy it afforded. During the lull in the artillery battle, the men of the Alamo had come out of their shelters and were swarming about their errands: digging the well, hastily clearing away debris from the last barrage, positioning their own artillery for a response. The lens of the telescope made them seem almost comical, racing here and there in their silent urgency, but also uncomfortably human and particular. An officer stood at one end of the courtyard, vigorously addressing unseen defenders within the stone building of the convent; a man took advantage of the lull to rush into the outhouses at the edge of the cow pens; a gunner at the artillery position at the rear of the church ran down the ramp to speak to a woman holding a baby. Telesforo even saw a dog trotting along in the courtyard, following close on the heels of one of the defenders.

The flag Almonte referred to was a Mexican tricolor hanging over the chapel, with the Mexican eagle removed from its white field and two stars sewn there instead.

"Do you see it?" Almonte asked.

"Yes, sir."

"What do you suppose the two stars are meant to represent?"

"The union of Coahuila and Texas, I suspect, Colonel."

"Perhaps. If so, that flag is sadly out of date. You can be sure that very few men in that garrison want Texas to remain a part of any sort of Mexican federation. That was yesterday's cause. Those men down there are fighting for an independent Texas republic that they can deliver to the United States of the North. Or they are fighting just for the opportunity to be in a war. In either event," Almonte concluded, with an amiable smile, "they should make themselves a new flag."

The colonel continued to chat, and Telesforo listened with pleasant deference, though with one ear attuned to the tactical minutiae being discussed over his map. Colonel Almonte reflected on his previous experiences in Texas while conducting a survey for the government; of the suspicion he had harbored for the United States of the North, but also of his helpless admiration for that nation's abundant and indiscriminate energy. He spoke of his particular friendship with Stephen Austin, a reasonable and honorable man who perhaps would not have made his disastrous declaration against Santa Anna had not his poor health confused his mind. Though Almonte expected an early resolution to this war, it was possible they would be in Texas for several months yet, by which time the peaches would be ripe on the trees, and he urged Telesforo to search out a norte dish called peach pie, which would more than compensate him for all the weary miles he had travelled from San Luis Potosí.

"He is watching you," Almonte then said unexpectedly. His head was inclined toward Santa Anna. "He has spoken to me about you, about your act of gallantry in Zacatecas."

"His Excellency is kind to remember me," Telesforo said.

"And how is your arm?"

"It troubles me very little, Colonel. I have some inconsequential pain, and am not yet able to lift a rifle or musket with it. But my right arm is strong, and effective with both sword and pistol."

"You are eager to fight, Villasenor."

"I am, sir."

Almonte smiled and clapped him on the shoulder, and as he did so the bombardment began again from the Mexican battery. They heard the deep, rhythmic roar of four pieces discharging almost at once, the sounds echoing and rumbling across the valley, the gray smoke rising above the trees of Béxar.

Two of the exploding rounds burst over the south courtyard as the defenders scrambled once again to safety. The solid shot from one of the guns plowed harmlessly into the dirt beyond the north wall, but one struck squarely in the southwest corner, and when the smoke cleared Almonte peered through the spyglass and turned to the officers with a grin on his face.

"We've dismounted the eighteen-pounder," he said.

THOUGH THE young man's face was swollen to almost twice its size, and the features were lumpishly distorted, Mary recognized him as one of the men of David Cummings's party with whom she and Edmund had ridden to Béxar. He had been shy on the route and they had not spoken, but Mary remembered that his last name was Perry.

He was the first casualty of the bombardment. For most of the day, the people in the Alamo had huddled indoors, but this afternoon they had grown increasingly bolder in the intervals between barrages, rushing outside on errands urgent or trivial. Mary herself, hearing the mistaken information that the well had been completed, had run out of the hospital with a bucket—the patients being desperately thirsty—only to find that water had not yet been struck. Two of the New Orleans Greys, however, eager and self-consciously gallant, had taken her bucket and several others and then risked their lives by slipping through a window in the west wall and crawling out to the acequia.

The Greys made it back into the compound without being killed by Mexican sharpshooters, and it was well into the afternoon before the hospital received its first casualty. Private Perry—a member of the gun team manning the eighteen-pounder on the southwest corner—had been struck in the jaw by a piece of splintered rock when a cannonball burst through the upper part of the wall and took away part of the gun's left wheel and carriage.

Perry babbled excitedly as his comrades carried him to a bed, though his words were incoherent. He tried to smile at Mary in a display of bravado as she put a pillow behind his head, but he had not much left to smile with, only a few teeth remaining on the left side of his face and his upper jaw badly splintered.

"Kahnna be fissed?" he asked one of the men who had brought him into the hospital. With each word he tried to form, Mary could hear the gurgling, backed-up blood in his throat.

"What are you saying, Dick?" the man replied.

"Don't encourage him to talk," Dr. Pollard said.

"Kahnna be fissed?" the wounded man repeated.

"He wants to know if the cannon can be fixed," one of the other men said. "Is that right, Dick? You're worried about the eighteen-pounder."

Private Perry nodded, and his friends all gave him warm smiles of admiration, dazzled by his selfless courage. But soon enough they were gone back to their posts, and the young man was thinking of nothing but his own pain as Pollard probed with his fingers among the wreckage of his jaw, removing teeth and bone spiculae and tiny fragments of rock.

Mary simultaneously tried to hold down his head and soothe him with kind words while Pollard went about his work with pitiless absorption. Dr. Reynolds stood at Pol-

lard's side, listening to the older man as he lectured about
the importance of probing carefully for fragments, since
broken teeth and bones often buried themselves in the soft
tissues of the mouth, giving rise to fistulae that could cause
the patient grievous problems in his recovery.

"You were indispensable, Mrs. Mott," Pollard said when
the ordeal was at last finished, and the injured man was lying in quiet agony on his cot with his face obscured beneath
a bandage and a splint fashioned out of scavenged wood.
"Indispensable and unperturbable. You are a most welcome
nurse."

In fact, Mary felt weak. She had always considered herself practical and unsentimental when it came to medical
matters, but Private Perry's condition affected her greatly.
Pollard seemed confident that his face would heal—he
would be more confident, he said, if he had not used up the
last of his muriated tincture of iron two weeks ago—but
only after months of grinding pain, and the end result, it
was plain, would be considerable disfigurement. And Perry's
wound, she was sure, was only a harbinger of horrible
wounds to come. What would happen when these men were
hit not by flying rock but cannonballs and canister and
grapeshot? What if Terrell were brought to her with his arm
torn off, or his vitals ripped from his body?

"The chamber pots must be carried out," she said to Pollard, partly to distract herself from these thoughts, though
the necessity of emptying the room of these foul recepta-
cles was urgent enough. In this confined space where the
cowhide stretched across the windows cut off any possibility for ventilation, the stench had grown to be intolerable.

"I'll take them, Mrs. Mott," Reynolds volunteered, looking up from a patient whose wound he was palpating.

"You can't take them all yourself," she responded, and
was reaching down to pick one up when another shell
screamed through the air. Mary dropped to the floor and
pressed herself against the wall with her hands covering

her head. Pollard and Reynolds did the same, and the patients who were able to do so rolled over onto their backs. The bomb exploded in the churchyard, just behind them, sending shards of metal and debris raining against the cowhide curtain.

"What? What?" a man named Main cried out, rising halfway out of his cot. He had been shot in the fighting at Béxar, and the ball, which Pollard had been unable to recover, had become encysted and inflamed. He was now in a state of delirium, and all day long had been reminiscing with feverish excitement about a trip he had apparently taken as a boy to view an underground cataract.

"What happened to the light, Uncle Caiphas?" he screamed now. "I can't find the way out!"

Mary crawled across the floor to take his hand as another shell exploded to the north.

"I can't see my hand in front of my face, Uncle!" Main was crying. "We have to get out of here! We have to get out of here before it falls in and we're trapped!"

Mary wanted to say something to the deranged man, but she could think of nothing, and her mouth was so dry and cottony with fear she did not know if she could even form the words. Her hand, clasping his, shook rather violently. When at last the bombardment was over and he was calm enough for her to let go, she found that her hands were still trembling. She knotted the fabric of her skirt in her fists, trying to force them to be still.

Mary and Señora Losoya were the only noncombatants lending their help in the hospital. There were a half-dozen other women sheltered in the chapel, but most of them had small children and would not leave them even for a moment. Like Mary, Señora Losoya had a son among the defenders. Her English was better than Mary's Spanish, though not by much, and for much of the morning they had worked silently together, giving what comfort they could with what few supplies and medicines were available.

Señora Losoya pulled back the hide curtain to look down at the area in front of the chapel where the bomb had gone off.

"No one is on the earth," she said to Mary and the doctors in her imperfect English. Mary took this to mean that no one was lying on the ground dead, but the strange forlorn words seemed to sum up exactly her own sense of terror and isolation. She knew that Terrell and Edmund both were charged with defending the west wall, and from time to time when the bombardment was in abatement she had looked out through the hide barriers covering the window to see if she could see them across the compound, but neither ever appeared.

Now she stood and waited for the wounded from this last barrage to be brought to her, her heart surging wildly in her breast with the anticipation that the next mutilated man, or the next, might be her son. Or it might be Edmund. And as she waited she began bargaining in her mind. She would trade Edmund's life for her son's, of course. If either of them must die, it should be the complicated and aloof man who pretended to be a stranger to every simple human want. And yet the thought of Edmund's death caused much the same turmoil in her blood.

But no more wounded came to them. Unbelievable as it seemed to her, the Mexican shells had fallen harmlessly. And there followed a long interval in which they were able to carry the chamber pots out to the sinks and to feed their patients from a bucket of tasteless stew that some of the defenders carried up to them.

"You ladies must leave now and spend the night in the church," Dr. Pollard said when night had fallen and they had at last had their own dinner.

"You may need us," Mary replied, thinking that she would just sleep on the floor against the stone wall.

"I will send for you if we do. But if there is an attack

tonight you will be far safer with the other women and children in the church."

"Surely they will not attack the hospital," Mary said.

"Surely they will," Dr. Reynolds returned, in a slightly mocking style of voice that she decided she disliked, "if they mean to kill us all."

It took all her will not to go searching among the rooms or along the ramparts for Terrell. Instead, she parted with Señora Losoya and raced across the exposed courtyard to Bowie's room. Pollard had visited the stricken man earlier in the afternoon and had returned with a grim look and the confirmation of what Mary had already ascertained, that the illness was typhoid and that the expectation for recovery was slim. Tonight, she found Gertrudis, the younger of the two Navarro sisters, sitting by herself against the wall next to Bowie's cot. The older one had apparently taken Mary's advice and removed her young child.

Mary asked Gertrudis in her blundering Spanish how Bowie was faring, but the girl just inclined her head toward the cot, as if his condition required no comment from her. She had a rosary in her hands but did not seem to be praying on it, just twining it through her fingers. The cannonade had badly unsettled her, and like everyone in the fort she had not slept in the past day and a half.

"Ha comido?" she asked, indicating Bowie and taking a wild guess at the proper verb form. It must have been close enough, because Gertrudis readily answered that Señor Bowie had refused food all day long.

Mary walked over to him and felt his hot, flushed face.

He opened his eyes and looked at her.

"Hello, Jim," she said.

"What do you mean, the signatures are suspicious?" he said. "By God, sir, if you are accusing me of forging those grants then tell me so outright!"

In his agitation he almost sprang at her from his bed, but

she held him gently down by his shoulders and began to swab his face with a rag, and in a moment he was on the verge of lucid thought.

"They're throwing bombs at us," he said. "I heard them."

"Yes, but not now. It's quiet now."

The door opened, and Travis and Crockett walked in. Seeing Mary, Travis greeted her with a merely civil nod of the head, but Crockett introduced himself with a broad smile, inquiring about her health, her origins, her present circumstances, complimenting her on what a fine son she had—he'd met Terrell only briefly, but looked forward to a closer acquaintance—and finding her own courage and fortitude to be of the most admirable and inspiring sort.

She smiled in return, for the first time in a week. She recognized Crockett's pleasantries for the habitual politicking they were, but it was a tonic to meet a man who put a value in reaching out to people.

"Colonel Bowie," Travis said when Crockett had finished with his effusions. Bowie stared up at him, squinting, as if Travis were standing a far distance away.

"Yes?" he said.

"Congressman Crockett is here too," Travis said.

"Those grants have the seal of the King of Spain on them. They are real as real, and you will be dead as dead, by God, if you think you can—"

"Jim!" Crockett said.

"What!" Bowie answered in the same sharp tone, and then seemed to recognize his visitors for the first time.

"Don't surrender," he said in a slurry, defiant voice to Travis. "Let the sonsofbitches try to come on and take us."

"I believe we can get a courier through, Colonel," Travis answered. "The Mexicans haven't completely surrounded us yet, and we believe the Gonzales road is open beyond the powder house. I've written a letter for general circulation. If there is anything you would like to add, a letter of your own you would like to send, please tell me. Due to your illness

I've had to take over command of the garrison, but I am sensible to the fact that you and I agreed to share the position and—"

"Read the letter," Bowie muttered.

Travis produced a sheet of paper, unfolded it, and lifted the candlestick from Bowie's bedside to illuminate the letter as he read.

"To the people of Texas and all Americans in the world," went the audacious salutation. The letter was succinct, defiant, bombastic, somehow brilliant. "*I shall never surrender or retreat,*" Travis pronounced, and Mary shuddered at the arrogance of that "I," this young man ready to doom them all in order that "all Americans in the world" would not forget his heroism.

"Victory or death," he declared at the end, and then folded the paper again and leaned down to Bowie.

"Is there anything you wish to add, Colonel?" he repeated.

"What?" Bowie said.

"Is there anything—"

"Give me the goddam paper," Bowie bellowed, reaching out as if to grab the letter from Travis's hand, "and I'll prove it ain't no forgery."

But Travis held the letter back, away from Bowie's grasping hands. He looked at Mary and then at Gertrudis, and then shifted his eyes to Crockett. The two men communicated with a silent look that was plain enough for Mary to read: there was no longer any necessity to consult with Bowie about the leadership of the Alamo.

"It is a ringing letter," Crockett said to Mary afterward, after Travis had gone off to consult with his couriers. On hearing she was on her way to the church, the congressman had insisted on accompanying her. "Travis knows how to tickle a phrase."

"It is a proclamation of suicide," Mary countered.

"I do not think so, Mrs. Mott. The language is excitable,

but perhaps it needs to be to cause excitement in others. A man could not read that letter and fail to come to our aid."

She was not nearly so convinced, but decided to keep her thoughts to herself. Crockett removed his hat as they walked and threaded his fingers through his gritty hair. They kept close to the walls and to the sides of the houses. There were lights burning in some of the rooms, but most of them were dark. She could hear the sentries on the walls speaking softly to each other. Four or five men were standing around a brazier behind the palisade, waiting for coffee to boil in a pot, and they spoke out to Crockett as he passed and asked him what he thought might happen next. "Boys," he said, "if I could read the future I would've prognosticated myself into a feather bed in a New Orleans hotel." They laughed at the remark—too eagerly, Mary thought. At the entrance to the church Crockett gently took her elbow to steer her around a pile of rubble.

Moonlit streaks of cloud were visible above the roofless church. Crockett looked up at the men huddled against the cannon at the top of the artillery ramp and called out a hearty "Good evening," but as he escorted Mary to the baptistry he dropped his voice to nearly a whisper.

"Bowie is in an awful hard way," he said.

"Yes," Mary agreed.

"I hate for him to miss the fight. I hear he can be savagerous with that knife."

Mary nodded. She lingered at the door to the sacristy. They had been in a hurry crossing the courtyard, lest the unpredictable cannonade start again and catch them in open ground, but now that they stood at the entrance to the safest room in the fort she felt considerably more at ease.

"Why are you here, Mr. Crockett?" she asked without preamble.

"Why, because I am a wayward, wandering soul, Mrs. Mott," he laughed, and then spoke more seriously. "I lost an election, you see, and it hurt my sensibilities to have such a quantity of people say they could no longer stand the thought of me. And the only cure that's ever worked for me when I'm feeling hollow like that is to move on to a new country."

She could not see Crockett's eyes in the darkness and shadows of the church, but she supposed them to be bright with self-delusion—a shattered fifty-year-old man still hostage to his boyhood dreams of flight and renewal. It had been that same unquenchable confidence that had caused Andrew to lead her to Texas, where all had come to ruin.

"And why are you here, Mrs. Mott?"

She found herself confiding in him, telling him more or less the whole story of her own delusions—that she had come to the Alamo to heal the obscure but unendurable rift between herself and Terrell, and if possible to save his life.

"Does your son know the country?" Crockett said after she had finished, in a still softer tone of voice, so that she could barely hear him.

"What do you mean?"

"Does he know the roads, and can he find his way from one place to another without them?"

"He is sensible that way. And has spent some months scouting with Bowie in the vicinity of Béxar."

"Good. Then I will try to get him out of the Alamo."

"How?" she asked.

"Travis wants me to have some men ready. As soon as we have some word that reinforcements are on the way we will leave the fort to meet them and guide them back in. I won't say it ain't dangerous, Mrs. Mott, but once we're at the Cibolo crossing I can send your son ahead with dispatches, and with luck on his side he won't be here if the Mexicans overtake the fort."

"Thank you!" she said. The words exploded out of her mouth, and tears burst from her eyes at the same moment.

"I can't say it'll happen exactly that way. But if the opportunity sprouts up, I'll save your son if I can."

"Why are you doing this for me?" Mary asked.

Crockett grinned. "I've been in the politicking business too long, I guess. Every time I see an unhappy face it makes me nervous about my own prospects. You should try to get some sleep, Mrs. Mott, before they set in to blowing us up again."

And she did sleep, for perhaps an hour, in the cool darkness of the sacristy. There were only a few beds in these rooms, and they had been claimed by other women and their children, but Mary scarcely minded. She lay down on a mound of straw and fell at once into a perfect sleep, despite the high-pitched fretting of Mrs. Dickinson's baby girl across the room.

It was Mrs. Dickinson herself who roused Mary shortly afterward. She was a woman of not much more than twenty, the wife of one of the artillery officers, and Mary had spent much of the previous night trying to soothe her mounting panic and loneliness.

"Mrs. Mott, wake up," she was calling now. "Do you hear that? What is it?"

Mary opened her eyes into a darkness that seemed at first absolute, until she was able to see the contours of the vaulted roof overhead, illuminated by the barest wash of moonlight seeping in through the high window above her head. Susannah Dickinson's face was above her, her lips trembling, her baby squeezed to her breast. Behind her were the dark forms of the Tejano women—Mrs. Esparza, Mrs. Gonzales, Mrs. Losoya—all of them shrouded like statues in their shawls, and all of them seeming to look to Mary for some sort of explanation.

"What are you speaking of, Susannah?" she said at last when she remembered where she was.

"That music," Mrs. Dickinson said.

Mary did not have to strain to hear it. It was loud and strident, the music of a sizable band playing an incongruously jaunty and brassy air. No sooner had the song ended than it started all over again, this time with more insistence, and with its shrillest instruments following their own wayward tangents.

"Does it mean they are going to attack?" Susannah said.

Mary shook her head as this absurd, belligerent concert echoed off the stone walls of the sacristy.

"No," she said. "I think they just want to keep us from sleep."

And then above the music they heard the distant crump of one of the guns in the battery across the river, and the shelling started again. Susannah Dickinson began to sob, and Mary put out her arms and drew the terrified girl and her baby into them. White light from the exploding grenades throbbed through the windows, and through the entire cannonade the band continued to play with malevolent fervor.

CHAPTER TWENTY-SIX

✵

THE MEXICANS ATTACKED at ten o'clock the next morning, small groups of skirmishers advancing steadily under cover, firing as they went, taking shelter in the abandoned houses that extended along the plaza south of the Alamo. From his position next to Travis at the southwest battery, Joe could see the faces of the enemy. He could see their smooth skin and lank black hair and sparse sidewhiskers.

Most of the men defending the Alamo had rushed from their positions to the south end of the compound to meet the attack. The shooting holes that had been cut into the walls were all taken, and so men crowded together behind the ramparts on the roofs, so close that they burned one another with the barrels of their guns when they pulled them in to reload.

"Goddam it, nigger, quit crowding me," a man next to Joe said as he shoved against his shoulder, inching him closer to a gap in the defenses where he could hear the Mexican rifle balls ripping through the air.

It had started out to be a lazy, tentative fight, with the Mexicans hopping from cover to cover, and the rebels—those like Joe who were not armed with long-range hunting rifles—mostly holding their fire.

"They are testing our defenses, gentlemen!" Travis had called out in a clear voice to the garrison as the Mexican soldiers filtered onto the field. "Keep a steady hand and show them what we have to offer!"

But the fight was hotter now, and Travis was crouched

behind the ramparts with the rest of the defenders as rifle and musket balls steadily raked the top of the wall. The colonel was yelling something to Captain Carey, but Joe could not make out the words. He lay on his back with his musket charged and cocked, telling himself that at the next moment he was going to twist around and fire. The Mexicans were just under the walls, having found shelter in the abandoned houses, and the incessant snapping of their muskets and the occasional thunderous discharge from one of the Alamo's artillery positions pushed all other sounds into a feverish distance.

Carey gave Travis a sharp nod and then took off at a crouching run to carry out whatever order it was he had been given. He scrambled down the dirt ramp as rifle balls scythed through the air above him.

The metal storm had barely passed when Captain Dickinson, commanding the twelve-pounder that had been hauled up to replace the damaged eighteen-pounder, rose up and shouted "Fire!" One of his crew lurched forward to apply the slow match, and the piece erupted with such astonishing noise that Joe thought he would never hear again. But soon the popping sound of the musket and rifle fire returned, though the dense, sulfurous cannon smoke would not clear. Joe found it odd that the atmosphere could be so still and windless when all he could see around him was tumultuous movement. He opened his mouth to take a breath, and the poisonous fumes he inhaled coated his already parched throat.

"Keep up a steady fire!" Travis shouted as he moved from man to man on the rampart, slapping each on the shoulder to wake them once again to action. Crouching next to Joe, Travis pulled back the hammers of his shotgun and stood up to discharge a volley.

"Take a shot, Joe!" Travis yelled as he began to reload. "We've got to drive them back from those houses."

Joe took a breath and did as he was told. His hands were

shaking so much as he exposed his head over the rampart
that he felt he was not so much aiming the heavy English
musket as wrestling with it. At first he saw only the same
suffocating cloud of smoke, but then a wounded Mexican
rifleman staggered into sight just below him. The man had
been hit by the canister from Dickinson's recent volley and
the whole bottom half of his face was gone, just gone, so
that all that was left to his features were a pair of staring
eyes on a bloody stalk. He looked up at Joe with those eyes,
and Joe, as startled as if he'd seen a man rise from the
grave, slunk back down behind the parapet without firing.

"Don't let up!" Travis called to the men, and Joe forced
himself back into firing position. The staring man was
gone, but a detachment of Mexican soldiers was now sallying from the nearest house to attack the tambour at the
south gate. Joe fired along with everyone else. One or two of
the invaders dropped in midstride, another stumbled as if
he had tripped over a stone and then tried to right himself
but couldn't because one of his feet was gone.

There was a general hurrahing as the Mexicans fell back
to the safety of the houses, dragging the dead men but
leaving the detached foot on the field. Dickinson's twelve-
pounder fired again, and the riflemen on the walls and in
the lunettes and palisade kept up a rapid, heartening fire
that drove the Mexicans out of the jacales nearest the fort
and back to the more substantial adobe houses beyond them.

Joe reloaded and fired again. His thirst was so great, the
smoke and its acrid vapors so dense, that what frightened
him most about being killed was the thought that he would
die without ever again having a drink of water or drawing a
clear breath.

Nevertheless, he found himself sharing in the jubilant
spirits of the men around him. The Mexican attack was wavering. Not one of the men defending the Alamo, so far as
Joe knew, had yet been hit, and they were pouring down a
volume of fire now that the retreating enemy could not

counter or withstand. Joe heard more canister passing over his head, and a solid cannonball struck the wall below them, sending up a dark geyser of dust and chipped rock, but he kept loading and shooting until his flint came loose and fell out from between the jaws of his hammer.

He blinked hard to expel the grimy paste of gunpowder and sweat that was burning his eyes, and then groped around among the rubble for the lost flint.

"Quit wigglin' around!" the man next to him commanded as he took another shot with his rifle, the spark from the pan flashing against Joe's cheek.

"I'm lookin' for my flint," Joe tried to explain, still struggling to avoid being pushed into the breach. The Mexicans may have fallen back, but they were not retreating, and if anything their fire had grown more intense.

Joe opened the flap of his captured Mexican cartridge box and rooted around in it for an extra flint. He found one wedged among the paper cartridges and fitted it into the jaws of the hammer, but his hands were shaking so badly that when he tried to twist the tightening screw the new flint fell out as well and tumbled down off the rampart and bounced off the hat brim of the man at the shooting hole below him and landed in the dirt.

He was about to scurry down the ramp after it when he felt Travis's hand gripping his shoulder.

"Joe!" he shouted. "My shotgun is fouled. Take it back to my room and bring my rifle."

Joe took the gun from Travis and ran with it and the musket along the west wall of the Alamo toward the headquarters room. The Mexican batteries were still spraying canister at the walls, and the defenders on the roofs above him were bent down with their hands pressed upon their hats like men caught in a furious rainstorm. As he ran he caught sight of Crockett scuttling from man to man, slapping each on the back, shouting words of encouragement that Joe could not hear. He was more exposed than any of the men, but he seemed so calm and unhurried that Joe yearned to be up there with him, dangerous as his position was, rather than down in the sheltered courtyard where he was alone with his fear.

A bony yellow cat, one of two cats that Joe had seen in residence at the Alamo, sprinted across the ground in front of him as he reached the door to Travis's quarters. With a firearm in either hand he pulled the door open with his foot and hurried inside. When he saw the Mexican soldier with a crowbar in his hand who had broken through the bricked-up window he yelled like a child calling out in a nightmare. He had two useless weapons in his hands and though in an instant he had dropped the shotgun and was levelling the Brown Bess at the Mexican, it felt to Joe that he was in the grip of a frantic decision that took an eternity for him to resolve.

No word of Spanish came to him, nor even of English. He simply stood there with his musket pointed at the man who had just tumbled out of the window and bared his teeth and said "Haah! Haah!" as if he were a teamster trying to give orders to an ox. The man on the floor tightened his grip on the crowbar. His own rifle was on the floor along with his shako where he had dropped it coming through the window. Another soldier was crawling through behind him, and this one had a rifle in his hand. Joe shifted the barrel of his musket from one to the other, praying that they were as frightened as he was and did not notice the missing flint in the hammerlock.

The soldier with the rifle, the one still halfway in the window, kept his eyes on Joe and boldly pulled himself through and stood upright. He pointed the rifle at Joe and said something in Spanish in a calm, insistent voice. He used none of the few Spanish words that Joe knew, but from the way he kept saying "naygro" Joe reckoned that the word might be Spanish for negro and that it referred to him.

"No!" he shouted to the first man when he started to reach out for his own rifle on the floor. "No!"

The gunpowder sweat was pouring into his eyes again, stinging them violently, and his throat was so raw and dry he felt that single word—"No!"—scraping up and down it like sharp glass.

Not one of the three of them knew what to do to break this impasse, and they stood there for what seemed like a long time listening to the rattle of gunfire and the yells of the Texians on the roof above them and the violent, mysterious bugle calls hectoring the Mexican soldiers forward into peril.

The man with the rifle shifted his weight from one foot to the next, then started to lift the weapon. Joe held his musket tight to his shoulder and squeezed his eye and sighted along the bayonet lug at the end of the barrel. Even though he knew the weapon would not fire, he needed to impress this fearless invader that at any moment he could blow away his head. The man's face had pox marks and a jagged white scar along the chin line where perhaps a dog had bitten him as a child. A scant satiny mustache grew on his upper lip.

The soldier lifted his free hand a little more, until it was hanging in the air. Joe blinked more sweat out of his eyes. Then the soldier moved his fingers, gesturing, beckoning Joe forward. The soldier on the ground nodded. He spoke some more words in Spanish.

"Ven con nosotros," they were saying. "Ven con nosotros, negro."

He understood now what they were saying: to come with them, to go out through the window with them and leave the Alamo behind.

The thought was enormous. Inside this room he was a slave. If he went out with these men through the window, he would be free. It was true, then, what was said about Mexico. Though it was, as Travis had insisted a hundred times in Joe's hearing, a country ruled by tyranny, there was no special tyranny set aside only for black men.

He did not plan to nod his head or to lower his musket. He did so without factoring out the reasons or arguing the case in his head. His body knew before his mind could catch up with it that he could choose to die as a slave in the Alamo or live out his life as a free man.

He allowed the man on the floor to retrieve his rifle and his shako. The other soldier gave Joe a curt smile of welcome and led the way out the window. He was halfway through when he was cut down by flanking fire from the rooftops and shooting holes along the west wall. Joe heard him say, very softly, "Ahhh," as first one ball, and then another, struck him in the spine, and a third passed through his head and blew off his ear.

His dead body was almost out the window, and now it teetered on the sill and then slid like a bundle of wet laundry to the earth below. The other Mexican soldier had been on the point of following his comrade, and now he turned to Joe with a wild look and a flood of excitable Spanish coming out of his mouth. Joe did not understand a word of what he was saying, but the sound of it and the gestures he was making were plain enough. He wanted Joe to find them another way out. But there was no other way out, and now he could hear shouting and footsteps on the rooftop as the men up there began to realize there might be more infiltrators in the rooms below them.

"Amigo!" the man was saying. "Ayúdame!"

Joe threw down his useless musket and grabbed Travis's rifle from a wooden shelf above the cot. He cocked the rifle and pointed it at the soldier and told him in English to drop his own weapon and put his hands against the wall. The man understood and was surprisingly compliant, but the look he gave to Joe was harsh, and Joe was glad when the other men burst into the room and he could take his eyes away from his prisoner.

AT THE PALISADE between the gatehouse and the church, Edmund watched as the Mexicans dragged away their dead and wounded from the field. The men in the Alamo were under orders not to fire during this procedure, and Edmund assumed there were probably a few for whom this order was necessary. The Texians' blood was up. They had completely routed the attacking Mexican riflemen, and in the last stages of the skirmish some of the defenders had sallied out with lamp oil and lucifer matches and set fire to the closest jacales so that they could not be used again for cover. The smoke from those burning houses was black and thick, but its smell was clean compared to the corrosive odor of gunsmoke.

"Would you care to come back, lads?" a private named Bourne, an Englishman, was shouting out to the retreating Mexican soldiers. "Would you care to come back and join us for a lemonade and a nice mixed biscuit?"

Men were starting to peel away from the firing line and run over to the water trough that had been hammered together next to the just-completed well. But Baker and some of the other officers headed them off and ordered them back.

"Stay at your posts," Baker called out. "Stay at your posts in case they attack again."

"We're a thirsty bunch of lizards, Captain," Sparks told him.

"You'll have your water. It will be brought to you in an orderly fashion. But for now you must stay at your posts."

Edmund turned his back to the field and slumped down against the palisade, reflexively swallowing to work up some moisture in his mouth, but he could not produce even a drop of spit. The thick, rancid taste of gunpowder coated his tongue.

The men with him behind the palisade were laughing and congratulating each other and shaking hands, and though he meant to hold himself apart from this exhilaration he could not. When hands were offered he shook them, and one of the hands belonged to Terrell. The two of them had been at their posts on the west wall when the attack began, and had run down with most of the other defenders to take up firing positions at the south end. They had been at the palisade side by side for much of the fight, except when Terrell and several other men had been pulled off by Baker to reinforce the tambour outside the gate. Edmund had been aware of the boy's steady presence next to him, methodically loading and firing his Kentucky rifle. He was fairly certain that at least one of Terrell's shots had found a mark, but in this moment of riotous celebration when the men all around them were boasting and arguing about who did or did not shoot which enemy soldier, Terrell kept a careful silence.

For his part, Edmund had shot as true as he could, defending his life with a fervor he thought he had lost. If he had killed anyone through the fog of powder smoke with his heavy, unfamiliar musket, he did not know it or care to.

"There is your mother," he said to Terrell. With some of the other women and older children, she was filling buckets at the well and bringing water to the men on the line. Her eyes were on them both, and as soon as her bucket was full she brought it to their part of the palisade. Sensitive to Terrell's feelings, she did not give the bucket to him first but to another man farther down the line, and it was passed from hand to hand as the defenders drank straight from the rim. By the time it reached Edmund and Terrell it tasted, like everything else, of gunpowder. Nevertheless, Edmund took a deep drink.

"Have you received many wounded into the hospital?"

Edmund asked her after he had passed the bucket on to the next man.

"Not a one," she said, moving her eyes back and forth from him to Terrell. "It seems impossible, but no one was hurt."

"Perhaps our good fortune will continue," Edmund said, though he was convinced it would not. It was plain to anyone who wanted to contemplate the matter that the Mexicans had sent only three hundred or four hundred men against them today, when they had perhaps two thousand already in the town and scattered among the artillery works, and still more on their way. The attack today had been only a test, a way to gauge how securely the Alamo was defended, and what points were most or least vulnerable. Because the attack had been limited to the south end, the rebels had been able to meet it with concentrated force and disciplined fire, but how could they, with their few numbers, defend the Alamo against a general assault on all points involving ten times the men they had faced today?

Mary stood in front of Edmund and Terrell for a moment more as the bucket travelled down the line of thirsty men.

"Are you well?" Edmund heard her ask her son in a confidential voice. He nodded, looking off to the battery to avoid meeting the fierce, pleading look in her eyes. But when she allowed herself to reach out and squeeze his hand, he did not withdraw it. In a moment more they were calling to her that the bucket was empty, and she moved briskly away to refill it.

They remained on the line for another half-hour while Travis and his officers studied the enemy's movements. When it was determined that another attack was not forthcoming the bulk of the men were dismissed and allowed to go to their dank barracks for whatever brief period of sleep they might be able to obtain before the next cannonade. For Edmund this period was briefer than most. He fell asleep the moment he lay down on his pallet, his face warmed by the overheated musket barrel beside him, but within the hour he was awakened by Captain Baker and informed that he was to report to Travis's headquarters. Professor was asleep on his chest. The dog had taken up lodgings in some secret recess of the barracks buildings, and would not follow Edmund outside even when there was a suspension of the cannonade, much less an attack such as the one they had just witnessed. Edmund slid out from under Professor and left the dog lying on the pallet, staring up at him with a sleepy, chastening look. He was no doubt in pain from Crockett's needlework, the scars on his face were still livid, and it was clear he held Edmund responsible for his every misfortune.

Edmund walked across the courtyard in the evening light. He looked up and saw Terrell back at his station on the west wall, staring out toward the town as he distractedly hefted some sort of object—a stone?—in his left hand.

Travis answered Edmund's knock himself and bade him a hearty good evening. The colonel was in a buoyant frame of mind after the day's modest victory, and if he still harbored cautions about Edmund's motives he kept them to himself.

"You've met Colonel Crockett, I believe," Travis said, sweeping his arm across the crowded room. "And of course you're well acquainted with Major Baugh and Captain Baker. But have you had the chance to make the acquaintance of Captains Dickinson, Seguín, and Carey?"

Edmund shook hands all around, and was greeted with weary smiles. Joe was in the room as well, standing with his back to the officers as he replaced the bricks in the window that had apparently been knocked out in the afternoon's action.

"And this gentleman," Travis said, indicating a Mexican soldado sitting unbound in one of Travis's lopsided chairs, "was captured by Joe during the battle after he had broken through my window with a crowbar. I wanted you in the room while we interrogated him. My Spanish is serviceable but not fluent, and there may be nuances in his conversation that should not be missed.

"Juan's command of English," Travis continued, with a look toward Seguín, "is similarly limited. And Bowie, who can speak both languages without a thought, is ill. So perhaps you will do us the service of interviewing this man and interpreting for us."

The soldado, a corporal, was no more than twenty-two or twenty-three. He was frightened, of course, but had a steady bearing that did him credit, and he answered Edmund's questions as readily as if they were engaged in a casual conversation rather than a formal military interrogation. His name was Reyes, he was from a village along the coast not far from Matamoros where the people had prospered by collecting the eggs that turtles laid in the sand when they crawled out of the sea every year in vast numbers. But four years ago the turtles chose another beach, far to the south, on which to lay their eggs, and they had not been back since.

Reyes had joined the army, as had a number of young men in the village who had never considered that their livelihood as turtle egg collectors was a gift that God might one day revoke. He was now a cazador in the Permanent Battalion of Jiménez. He did not know precisely how many men were now in San Antonio de Béxar—he judged the number to be between fifteen hundred and two thousand. Besides the Jiménez battalion, there was the Permanent Battalion of Matamoros, the Reserve Battalion of San Luis, an artillery unit, and two regiments of cavalry from Dolores and Vera Cruz, as well as two detachments of presidial cavalry.

He knew little about artillery but supposed that the army had on hand some eight or ten pieces and were expecting more when the First Brigade under General Gaona arrived. Yes, it was his understanding that Gaona had siege weapons, but he did not know how many or what strength. It was said that the First Brigade would arrive in a week's time, and that their arrival would double the size of the army already in Béxar, and that the reinforcements would include a company of engineers as well as seasoned battalions such as those of Querétaro and Toluca.

The questioning went on for an hour or more. The prisoner was given water when he requested it, and when food was brought in for the officers—a platter of tortillas and seared beefsteaks from a steer that had been slaughtered that morning—Travis ordered that Reyes share in the meal as well.

"Make sure he understands that we do not want for food, or for any other necessary," Travis told Edmund as the prisoner gnawed at a strip of bloody beef.

Once or twice Seguín interrupted Edmund in his interrogation and spoke to the prisoner directly to press a point. What was the condition of the men? The horses? How were the citizens of Béxar being treated by the military? Did the decree of no quarter apply as well to the Tejano rancheros who had risen up in revolt?

After the prisoner had eaten he went on to tell of the terrible hardships the army had experienced on its march north. He himself had been bitten by a rattlesnake that had crawled into his knapsack and with no doctor or bruja to treat him had no choice other than to ignore the injury as best he could, though his arm swelled to twice its size, requiring him to slit the sleeve of his coat to accommodate it. Yes, he was recovered now, thank you. It had a been a small snake without much venom. It was his opinion that the men of the First Brigade who were coming to reinforce them would need at least two days to recover from the punishing journey before any attack in force could be mounted.

Baugh, who was musical-minded, produced a piece of paper on which he had written down the notes of the bugle calls the garrison had heard from the Mexican forces.

"Ask him if he can read music," Baugh said.

"I doubt that he can read much of anything, Captain," Edmund replied, and when he asked the former turtle egg collector if he could look at these notes and reproduce the sounds they represented, Reyes looked at him in as complete a state of confusion as if he had been asked to converse with a horse.

"Why don't you whistle the tunes for him, Captain?" Crockett suggested.

Baugh took a drink of water to wet his throat, which was still dry from the afternoon's fight, and rendered the bugle calls in a manner that soon had all of them, even the prisoner, grinning and shaking their heads in amusement. But Baugh's rendition was faithful enough, and Reyes was able to identify for them five or six calls, including Disperse, Fire, Cease Fire, and Assemble.

"But it is not so simple, señor," Corporal Reyes pleaded in Spanish to Edmund. "For instance, the call he just made is Skirmishers, I think. But it means nothing by itself. There must be another call with it if we are to know whether to come together or move apart, or whether we are to go right or left. I am trying to give them the information they want, but you must tell them how difficult it is."

Edmund relayed this information to Travis, though the commander had already understood the better part of it. In his own harshly accented Spanish, Travis told the man directly that he had nothing to fear as long as he continued to cooperate and answer their questions as best he could.

And so the session went on, as the temperature in the room began to drop and a bitter north wind swept down upon the fort, threading its way through the old mission's open doorways and half-shuttered windows. No, Corporal Reyes said, he did not know in which direction the cavalry patrols scouted—he assumed along the main roads to the norte settlements. He had not seen Santa Anna, and did not even know if he had yet arrived or was still with the First

Brigade. The only officer of note he had seen was Colonel Almonte, because there was a sergeant in his regiment who had fought with Morelos and pointed him out. The purpose of today's attack? He was not an officer and did not think in tactical terms but simply did what he was ordered to do, which was to attack in skirmish formation and then continue to attack until he heard the order to fall back.

"Are they going to kill me?" he asked Edmund in a calm voice, then shifted his eyes to Seguín with the question lingering in the air.

Edmund took a chance and assured the man that they planned no such thing, knowing that Travis probably understood both question and answer and would be irritated at Edmund's assumption that he had any right to speak to the matter. But there was no anger in his voice when he declared the session over and ordered the man taken under guard to the calabozo.

Edmund stood to go as well, but to his surprise Travis gestured for him to stay.

"What is your opinion, Mr. McGowan?" he asked. "Can we consider this man's information to be reliable?"

"He did not seem to me as if he were holding anything back, or deliberately misleading us."

"He was an affable enough fellow," Crockett said. "Anybody here ever eat a sea turtle egg, by the by?"

Travis gave him a puzzled look. Some of the other officers blankly shook their heads.

"You can cook 'em all day, I hear, but they won't ever scramble. On the other hand, they're said to be a powerful weapon in the wars of Venus."

"What?" Travis said.

"They can harden your pecker, Colonel, if you eat 'em raw and in quantity."

Travis smiled distractedly. He was far too weary for levity, whereas Crockett was far too weary to go without it.

"It is my belief that Santa Anna will attack in force one

or two days after the First Brigade arrives," Travis continued. "He will want to rest his men and to position his siege
artillery. That gives us perhaps eight or nine days. If we are
not reinforced by that time our position is lost. Captain
Seguín has volunteered to try to get through the enemy
lines before daylight tomorrow with a dispatch for General
Houston, and until we are completely invested I will continue to send out couriers."

"Slipping out of this fort is a dangerous occupation,"
Crockett said, glancing at Seguín.

"He knows the risks. Verdad, Capitán? Sabes que será
peligroso."

"Claro," Seguín said, lighting a conical Mexican cigar.

"Maybe we could help him along somehow," Crockett
speculated. "Make some kind of a commotion where he
ain't."

"You could release the prisoner," Edmund found himself
saying.

Travis turned to him with a skeptical look, and Edmund
quickly realized he had overstepped his role in this council
of war, where his presence was entirely honorary at best.
Nevertheless, he plunged forward.

"It occurs to me that releasing Corporal Reyes will serve
two vital purposes," he said with more authority in his
voice than he actually possessed. "Sending him out with a
white flag may provide a temporary distraction of the sort
that Mr. Crockett has proposed, and releasing him at all is a
gesture of magnanimity that might be remembered by the
enemy if the fort is taken."

"Such a gesture would be lost on Santa Anna," Travis
said. "He means to kill us all one way or another."

"Yes, but there are other officers on his staff of a more
liberal bearing."

"Do you know them?"

"I know Colonel Almonte. And I think if he knew that—"
He was interrupted by the report of one of the Texian

cannons and the subsequent crackle of concentrated rifle and musket fire.

"The east wall," Travis said, grabbing his hat and his rifle and leading the officers out the door. They ran across the courtyard as sleepy men streamed out of the barracks to climb onto the rooftops and parapets. Edmund followed the general rush to the horse pen next to the church, which was defended by an artillery position looking out over the marshy lake to the east. The nine-pound cannon on the ramp roared again as Edmund and the others took up positions at the wall. There was no lingering powder smoke to obscure their view tonight, since the norther was still blowing in and it carried away the smoke with even greater velocity than the racing clouds overhead.

Nevertheless, there was little to see. The night was dark and the Mexicans well concealed as they crawled forward in the mesquite grass or took shelter behind the walls of several jacales that stood fifty yards away on the other side of the shallow rainwater pond. Edmund could see only the flash of their weapons. He fired where the flash had been, then stepped back from the wall to give another man a chance as he reloaded. Beside him, other men were conducting the same unspoken maneuver, and as he joined them in moving back and forth to their shooting perches he took a strange pleasure in the coordinated fluency of the process.

The Mexicans were driven back in short order, due less to the guesswork of the marksmen than to the barrage of canister fired from the gun crews. Edmund heard excited voices out in the darkness, though he could not make out the words or, despite his recent lesson in the subject, the meanings of the bugle calls that accompanied them. There was a ghostly quiet when all the firing was finished, and the cheering of the defenders had vanished on the north wind. Edmund stayed on the wall to help provide covering fire for the half-dozen men who ran out into the darkness to wade through the knee-deep water of the marsh and set fire to the huts beyond. But the Mexicans had returned to their entrenchments, and the sallying force was not harassed.

Edmund stood with the other rebels and watched the jacales burn. He could hear the dry wood snapping, and sparks from the thatch roofs gusted away in the wind. The violent flames were reflected on the surface of the pond, so that it seemed that the dark sump was itself a sheet of fire. By and by, the men were allowed back to their barracks, though the gun crews stayed to keep watch. Edmund took up his musket and walked through the horse pen, where the terrified beasts all crowded together against the stone walls of the convent building. He thought for the first time in weeks of Cabezon, and how the last time he had seen her was when Lieutenant Arechiga had ridden her arrogantly out onto the prairie the day of their escape from Espinosa's rancho. It surprised him how much he missed the horse, and his mule too, here at this extreme turning in his life when he might have expected his mind to be occupied by thoughts that were properly consequential and grave.

He heard Travis call his name from the artillery battery, and turned to meet him as he descended the ramp.

"I have been considering your proposal about releasing the prisoner," the colonel said, pressing his hat against his head to keep it from flying away in the wind. "I think it is meritorious. We'll send the Mexican corporal out under white flag through the south gate an hour before daybreak, and Captain Seguín will use the moment to sneak under the north wall at the irrigation ditch. Will you inform the prisoner to make himself ready?"

"Of course," Edmund said.

"Thank you, Mr. McGowan," Travis said, giving Edmund a weary smile. "It seems you are becoming a Texian patriot despite your best intentions."

Travis strode out in front of the church. Edmund remained in the horse pen, in this fouled and ruined courtyard

where in decades past friars had strolled in contemplation
of their God. He sat down on the wreckage of a cart that
had been destroyed in the shelling, pulled out a pencil and
his pocket diary from his waistcoat, ripped off a page, and
began to write a secret missive to Juan Almonte.

THE LETTER WAS BRIEF: an appeal to Almonte to remember the delightful evening they had spent together in
the City of Mexico as guests in Stephen Austin's house, a
reminder that there were innocent women and children in
the Alamo in addition to armed rebels, a plea that a Mrs.
Andrew Mott in particular be extracted from the fort before
an assault was made. "You have probably heard that I was
the agent of Don Osbaldo Espinosa's death," Edmund concluded. "I will not dispute this bare fact, though were we
sitting at a friendly hearth rather than facing each other
from military ramparts I would relate the particulars of that
incident, which I trust would make you see it in a more
benevolent light. In the instance, however, it does not matter. The significant fact is that Mrs. Mott had no connection
whatever with the man's death, other than to be in the vicinity where it occurred through no desire of her own. If you
can lend the hand of chivalry to her at whatever occasion it
may be possible, I promise never to forget."

He had slipped the note into the pocket of Corporal
Reyes's tunic when no one had been watching, and whispered into his ear that he must find some way to deliver it in
person to Almonte. Reyes had eagerly agreed, astonished
as he was at his good fortune.

Now, in the predawn darkness, Edmund watched from
his firing position on the west wall as Corporal Reyes
walked with a blazing torch in one hand and a white flag in
the other out the south gate of the Alamo toward the Mexican battery that had been dug in the Alameda the night before. He called his name and unit in Spanish out into the

darkness, and Edmund could hear the soldiers calling in return and officers ordering the pickets to hold their fire.

At almost the same moment, Juan Seguín was crawling out through the irrigation ditch on the north wall. From where he was standing, Edmund could not see him, but there was a knot of men, including Travis and Crockett, standing silently and attentively below the artillery emplacement on the northwest corner. Edmund supposed that Seguín was already twenty or thirty yards out, and if he had not been discovered by now would probably make it all the way to the river, since the area to the north and west of the Alamo was as yet thinly guarded. There were friends waiting for him with horses on the other side of the river, and if they managed to circumvent the Mexican patrols they could be in Gonzales by nightfall.

After a few moments Travis and the others walked away from the wall and went back to their quarters. Edmund stayed on guard. He had relieved Terrell at four, having slept no more than an hour or two in the last day and a half. His mind in consequence was frantically keen, to the point that it had started to strain at the boundaries of reality and perceive the world that lay beyond them. He looked across the river at Béxar, at the fires burning in the Mexican artillery emplacements, the smoke rising laterally from the chimneys in the cold wind, the dogs trotting through the streets on silent errands. He heard wolves howling on the distant margins of the town, he felt the cold wind gusting across his face. And each of these sensations joined with the others in a kind of harmony, forming an elusive music comprehendible heretofore only to the mind of God—but now, perhaps, to his mind as well, if only he could be alert enough.

Then the thought evaporated like the dream it had been, and he was sitting alone on an adobe roof in the cold, his life verging toward its violent and inconsequential close. In a little while the steely darkness began to lighten, and he

turned to see the sun erupting in one swift movement above
the hills to the east. A gunner on the battery at the rear of
the church stood up and stretched and called down something to one of the men below that Edmund could not hear.
Silhouetted by the rising sun, a cat made its way along the
rooftop of the barracks with a bird in its mouth. The flag on
top of the church, stretched taut by the unceasing north
wind, was suddenly vibrant with color.

The light crept down the hills, then swam across the
shallow river valley until it reached the field where the
Alamo stood, and then moved on to the river and the village
beyond. In a cypress tree along the banks, a hawk sat ruffling its feathers, shaking off the cold that had seeped into
its bones during the night and beginning to rouse its mind
from the sleep that had held it fast. The light gave clarity to
Edmund's awareness as well, or perhaps it just made his
near-hallucinatory ruminations that much more vivid.

He surveyed the brightening landscape as if looking at
the life he had already departed: the distant hills with their
carpets of juniper and tawny mesquite grass, the riverbank
lined with elms, willows, laurels, cypresses, and, if he was
not mistaken from this distance, a species of cherry. He saw
as well the eastern variant of the persimmon that the Mexicans called níspero. There were peach orchards behind the
houses, and wiry remnants of *Vitis vinifera* from the desert
districts of Mexico that had not prospered in Texas, their
grapes producing only a mediocre wine.

He thought of the wildflowers that would cover this land
in only a few short weeks, their colors brazen beneath the
spring sky: lupine, verbena, delphinium, evening primrose.
The hawk, having shaken its wings dry of dew, rose from
its perch and flew southward along the river, and in his
mind Edmund was its companion, soaring above the bounteous flora of Texas. He passed over groves of fustic trees,
forests of mimosa, vast stretches of waste ground claimed
by mezquitales. Below him everywhere he looked were un-

described species of *Opuntia,* and strange luxuriant grasses unnoticed even by Drummond. With his hawk's vision he saw through the tree limbs and the underbrush. Here was a little *Asclepiadacea* with its winged fruits, here a broadleafed *Cooperia,* here a glorious palmetto fifteen feet high. He soared over the coastal prairies, the groves of live oaks and pecan, the fields of *Marsilea,* the dune grasses giving way to bare sand and its pavement of broken shell and finally to the quiet blue water of the bays with their rich beds of turtle grass.

And all of it lost to him. Everything he had studied, everything he had perceived, everything he had allowed to matter in his life gone in a season.

"I come to relieve you," a voice behind him said, and Edmund's body helplessly jolted at the unexpected sound. He had been so lost in this reverie that he had not even noticed that Private Herndon had climbed up behind him on the rooftop.

Herndon was a Kentuckian who had come to Texas with the Invincibles and been folded into Baker's company with the rest of his unit. He was in his thirties and was one of the few men at the Alamo who had brought along his own slave, a quiet young woman named Bettie. Edmund had heard it said that Herndon had fallen in love with her back in Kentucky and stolen her from his cousin. Probably it was true, as so many other rumors about why people had come to Texas were true. Herndon certainly spent the preponderance of time in her company, and his clothes were always smartly patched.

"Did you sleep?" Edmund asked him now, as Herndon slipped the cow's knee off the lock of his rifle and took a seat beside Edmund.

"A particle or two," Herndon said. "They didn't bomb us last night but I was wakeful all the time, thinking about when we might get help. You reckon Fannin's started out yet?"

"I don't know," Edmund said. "He'll need to provision

his men and that might take a few days. I think we should look for help from Gonzales first."

"There ain't as many men in Gonzales as there is in Goliad."

"I know," Edmund agreed.

Herndon gave a worried nod of agreement and then asked suddenly, "What do people call you? I hear Travis calling you Mr. McGowan, but by damn I won't call a man Mister anything if I'm beside him on the firing line."

"Edmund."

"Well, I'm Pat," Herndon said, and offered his hand.

They talked for a while about the previous day's fight and the chances for another one, and about whether the convention about to meet in Washington-on-the-Brazos would declare for independence. "They goddam better" was Herndon's opinion on the matter, and he explained that he saw no point in hazarding his life if at the end of all his troubles and travails he was still living under the Mexican flag and eating these same fucking tortillas and having to learn the sonsofbitches' language after all.

Edmund came down from the roof, listening to the sound of mourning doves across the river. He stopped at the well to wash his face with cold water and then, instead of heading to the barracks and going to sleep, he found himself walking through the church to the baptistry room where the women and children were quartered. The room was still dark, and its sleeping occupants were curled up against the walls.

"What do you want, señor?" he heard a middle-aged woman's voice ask in a whisper. She was sitting upright, shrouded in a blanket, her features invisible, like some punitive apparition from the Old Testament.

"Is Mrs. Mott in here with you?"

"Yes, but asleep. Do you want me to wake her?"

"Please, señora. I would be grateful."

The woman stood and shuffled carefully across the room, then bent down and shook one of the sleepers by the shoulder. Edmund saw Mary spring up with a cry, and it was a moment before the woman could calm her enough to give her the news that a visitor had come for her.

She walked out of the sacristy into the roofless church where Edmund stood, his back to the artillery ramp. Her hair was grimy and misarranged, her face pale, and her eyes correspondingly vivid.

"What is it?" she said to him. "Has something happened to Terrell?"

"No," he whispered. "But I need to talk to you."

He led her out the door of the church and into the old burial ground in front. There were a few men at the palisade, looking out toward the tangle of brush that had been erected to impede the Mexican cavalry, and there were other sentinels visible around the perimeter of the fort, but in this first hour of dawn Edmund felt as if they were alone in the world.

"I am sorry to wake you," he said.

"Don't apologize, Edmund. What is it?"

"There is something about Terrell you need to know, something he told me. It was not his child that Edna Foley was carrying when she died."

"No? Then whose, Edmund?"

"One of the Mexican soldiers who came with Cos. Terrell discovered her with a group of men one night and chose not to speak to you of it."

Mary turned away and looked at the facade of the church, at the saints in their niches holding up their hands in blessing. In silence, she reached out a hand and put it to Edmund's chest and said, "Thank you."

"It is some comfort, perhaps, in the circumstance."

"It is," she said. "What can I do, Edmund? What can I say to him?"

"I don't know."

"Will you tell him that you told me? Will you tell him that I know?"

"If you want me to."

"I have never known a better friend than you, Edmund. Not even my husband was a better friend to me. I love you. You must preserve yourself."

She removed her hand from his chest, curled it into a fist, and struck him just above the heart, not gently.

"You *must!*" she said, and when he had no ready reply she turned from him and walked back into the church.

CHAPTER TWENTY-SEVEN

IN THE WEEK that followed, Mary grew to hate the nighttime serenades of the Mexican musicians more than the continual artillery bombardment. The grenades and cannonballs kept her and everyone else in constant agitation, but there was something worse, something pointedly aggressive and malevolent, about the music, as if it were an evil spirit that followed her from place to place hectoring her about her foolishness and misfortune.

The music usually began late in the evening and continued for hours. Once some of the men in the Alamo had brought fiddles and bagpipes out into the open and tried to counter it, but no sooner had they started than the cannonade began again and drove them inside.

When the bombs were not falling the men were engaged in strengthening the fort. A number of cannonballs had already burst through the outer walls, miraculously injuring no one, and the only way to keep the walls from being penetrated further was to dig up dirt and pile it in densely packed mounds against the fragile perimeter. Most of the effort in this regard went to the north wall, which was still painfully thin in spots and could be battered down easily with artillery once the Mexicans completed their works to the north.

During the daylight hours, when Mary looked out the hospital windows and down into the courtyard she saw what looked like a dug-out colony of burrowing animals: haphazard, half-finished trenches, and fresh dirt thrown up in all directions. She thought it might be wiser, if they were

doing all this excavation anyway, just to dig an underground tunnel leading out of the fort and onto the open
prairies. Such a monumental work did not seem so far removed in effort from the indiscriminate enterprise already
in progress.

Once or twice she saw Terrell at work with a shovel at
the north wall, but in that week she spoke to him only once,
when he ran breathlessly up the stairs and appeared at the
hospital doorway late one night after an especially heavy
cannonade.

"Is my mother here? Has my mother been hurt?" she
heard him asking Pollard as she sat at the other end of the
room spooning broth into Dick Perry's shattered mouth.

Someone had told Terrell that a cannonball had passed
through the hospital walls. The information was mistaken,
though the thick stone walls had been struck twice in this
latest barrage by projectiles from the smaller enemy cannon.

When she had drawn Terrell over to the warmth of the
hearth she saw that his face was bloodless with fear—fear
for her safety. He told her with anger in his voice that she
must stay in the church from now on, where the walls were
thicker and the chances of survival greater, but she responded with firmness that she would go where she was
needed, just as he must if another assault was made on the
fort.

Of the great matters residing between them they did not
speak. Edmund had told Mary the truth about Edna's baby
when Terrell had been too proud to do so, and now, thanks
once again to Edmund, her son was aware of her knowledge. That this information had necessarily been communicated in such a roundabout way did not particularly trouble
Mary anymore. It was simply the way things were. She had
been naïve to believe that her inward and self-conscious
son would have ever confided in her about these painfully
personal matters, that he would have come to her of all

people to try to unburden himself of his shame. And here at
the Alamo, where the danger on every hand was so sharp
and tangible, she would only add to Terrell's jeopardy if she
kept the vague misunderstandings of the past alive in his
imagination.

So they had talked, in their few moments together by
the hospital hearth, of matters of the garrison. When would
Fannin's men arrive from Goliad? When would the colonies
rally to the Alamo's defense? Would there be enough water
in the wells for the men to hold out if the Mexicans cut off
the flow from the acequia? Were the enemy lines still porous
enough for messengers to get out or reinforcements to break
through?

"I think we will have help," Terrell had told her, as the
hateful, capricious music began again. Fannin would
come, as well as rangers from Gonzales and Bastrop, and
the Tejanos that Seguín would rally from the ranchos.
And General Houston was certainly on his way with whatever men he could gather, and even the politicians meeting in Washington-on-the-Brazos had probably adjourned
so that they could rush to the aid of their countrymen. The
talk of the men in the barracks was that all these disparate
groups would probably rendezvous on the Gonzales road
ford of the Cibolo and wait until they were in force before they tried to break through the Mexican lines and
enter the Alamo. Such an enterprise might take two or
three days more. It was not a simple thing to assemble and
provision so many men. But they would come. No one
doubted it.

Perhaps because the subject of their conversation had
been so neutral and so urgent, because it had placed them
on an equal plane as two frightened adults, she felt free to
put her arms around Terrell as he left the hospital, and he
had not been distant in returning the embrace.

That had been three or four days ago, and she had not

seen him since. There had been minor skirmishes during
the intervening time, but still the Alamo's good fortune
held. Not a single man had been killed or seriously wounded,
and the hospital population remained the same. Most of the
men were steadily improving, Private Perry most of all,
who had proven stoic about his pain and cheerful about his
disfigurement. When he could finally move his jaws sufficiently to mumble, he joked to Mary that as he had won no
prizes for looks when his face was intact he could not complain of his handsomeness being taken away. The case of
Lieutenant Main was more difficult. After extensive palpa-
tion, Pollard had finally found the encysted ball that was
causing such inflammation in his body, but the patient had
almost died from the operation to remove it.

"You must cut boldly in these cases," Pollard had lectured to Reynolds as he thrust his bistoury into the incision
that Mary held open with her fingers, revealing the bloody
diaphanous web of cellular tissues in which the bullet was
embedded. "You will not harm the patient if the incision is
a half-inch longer than strictly necessary, and the removal
of the object will be correspondingly less difficult." He had
spoken these words as if not hearing Main's astonished
screams, though when he was finally through he, like his attendants, was drenched in a nervous sweat.

Now the lieutenant seemed to be emerging at last from
his wilderness of pain, and his appetite was better than
Mary's own. She forced herself to eat at least once a day the
unvarying meal of tortillas and hastily cooked beef or watery soup delivered to them in the intervals between bomb-
ings. From her position in the upper room of the hospital
she could hear the longhorn cattle bawling as they were led
to slaughter in the plaza. There was a problem of disposing
of the carcasses once the meat had been stripped off them.
At first the men had thought to bury them in the churchyard, but they had shovelled down only a few feet when

they struck the bones of mission Indians that had been interred there, and so they had moved the operation to less consecrated ground in the center of the fort.

Mary did not know how many cattle were left—perhaps fifteen, and at least as many horses if it came to that extremity. Though the Mexicans had succeeded in cutting off the water to the acequia that ran just outside the walls, the wells within the fort had proven to be adequate. Powder and shot were the greater worry, particularly for the artillery pieces. Some of the men who were not engaged in the earthworks were chopping up horseshoes and mixing them with nails and random scraps of metal for use as canister, though it was said the very act of firing such ragged projectiles would pit the cannon barrels so deeply that after only a few charges they would be blown apart.

Their medical supplies were now almost nonexistent. No laudanum, no opium, no rhubarb or calomel, no adhesive plaster or catheters. They had amassed a quantity of cloth and sticks to improvise splints and dressings when the need came, but if the casualties were heavy this store of materials would soon be used up, as would the remaining quantities of everything from castor oil to castile soap.

Only reinforcements could save them, reinforcements with their own liberal supplies of munitions and medicines. But she wondered if anyone else shared her doubts about the wisdom of committing more men to the Alamo. What if Houston or the other great men of Texas had decided it would accomplish nothing to bottle their armies up within these walls when they could do more damage as free-ranging fighters? What if their plans for the Alamo were to let it fall as a sacrifice?

She was fretting over these matters during a pause in the cannonade on the fifth or sixth day of the siege when a single rifle shot broke through the afternoon's silence, and the men of the Alamo erupted into a cheer.

"What is happening?" Dick Perry said. "What's all the shouting about?"

Mary and Señora Losoya and the two doctors rushed to the windows, but no sooner had they pulled back the hides than they heard the report of the howitzers from the Mexican batteries and had to scramble for shelter. It was not until the barrage had ended and Congressman Crockett had appeared in the hospital for his nightly visit that they were able to discover what the cheers had been about.

"Why, my nephew killed a Mexican," Crockett said. "It was the comeliest shot you've ever seen, two hundred yards or more. I gave Will an old rifle of mine before we left Tennessee and damn if he hasn't made fair use of it."

Crockett went up and down the line of patients as he did every night, shaking hands, telling jokes, handing out his last stray twists of tobacco. His campaigning amused Mary, or would have in lighter circumstances. In this place and under these conditions it seemed like just another helpless compulsion, a desperate bid to reclaim a former life. Crockett had looked well fed and expensively turned out when she had first met him, but during the siege his weight had dropped and the luster had gone out of his skin. He had not shaved, and a dark beard was growing in beneath his side-whiskers, emphasizing the stark, hungry intensity of his eyes.

She tried not to think of her own appearance. Yesterday Private Perry had demanded to see his reflection in the looking glass that Dr. Pollard kept in his medical case, and after the young man's sober assessment of himself, Mary had caught a glance at her own face as she put the glass away. She saw at once that she had lost considerably more weight than she had supposed, and that her thin and sunken face did her no more credit than her broken nose. Had she looked this way on that night by the fire during their escape from the rancho when she had essentially offered herself to Edmund? It made her shudder to think of it now, the thoughtless vanity that had provided her with the illusion that a man might still find her features appealing.

"I have been to see our friend Bowie," Crockett told her as he finished his rounds of the patients. "He was more or less cognizant when I walked in the door—'Here comes the half-man, half-alligator,' he said—but then he drifted away again. He has his knife in his hand. Mrs. Alsbury and her sister told me they are under strict instructions to replace it there every time he drops it."

Crockett made free to sit down next to her on the floor. His fine hunting clothes were rank and long unwashed, but in this room with its myriad foul smells the odor barely registered.

"Bowie aims to die holding that knife, I guess," Crockett whispered to her.

Reynolds, who was afflicted with cramps, had gone out to the sinks. Señora Losoya stood by the hearth, feeding small pieces of scavenged lumber into the fire. Dr. Pollard had developed the ability to fall asleep on an instant's opportunity, and now he sat upright in a chair on the other end of the room with his mouth gaping open and emitting a belligerent snore. A few of the patients were sitting up, staring at the walls, though the majority were asleep as well, some restlessly, some with a profundity that bordered on death.

In this quiet hour, even Crockett's spirits seemed to suddenly dim. When he spoke to her again, still in a whisper, his voice had something vulnerable in it.

"I wish we could go out and fight on the prairie," he said. "I don't like being hemmed up in this fort. Back during the Creek War, I was in the attack on Tallasuhatchee. Those Indians was in the same fix that we are now, shut up in their village with us crowding them in on every side. We shot them down like dogs and burned them in their houses. You could see them firing back at us while the grease was stewing out of them. I don't care for the recollection to this day."

"I think there is a good chance we will be relieved," Mary said, less out of conviction than a selfish need to pull this fundamentally optimistic man back from the edge of doubt.

"I believe there is too," he said in return, with a quick, buoyant smile. "And if they don't want to get turned back at the gate they'd better have the sense to bring us some coffee to drink. Can I give you a letter, Mrs. Mott, in case I'm to perish?"

"Of course."

"It's to my son. I found a good place for a headright claim up on the Red, and the letter will tell him where to find it, though him being my son, he'll probably get lost in some canebrake somewhere and never find his way out."

Mary slipped the letter into a pocket of her jacket, where it joined the letter Dick Perry dictated to her yesterday from his pallet, full of high-blown language about "throwing off the yoke of oppression" and admonishments to his family, especially his dear sister, not to weep at his passing but to "rejoice" that he had been fortunate enough to give his life for Texas. Mary had taken down the boy's words exactly as he had mumbled them through his broken mouth, and she had hated their high-minded falseness. She had heard enough of these empty patriotic effusions by now to feel that the Alamo was nothing but a sinking island of rhetoric.

"I have not forgotten about your son," Crockett said, anticipating the question that she had worked hard to keep herself from voicing. "If Travis sends me out, I'll recommend him for the expedition. But I wouldn't say it's all that much safer out there, with all the lancers they've got riding around. You never know where you're going to find the short end of the horn."

———

TRAVIS WAS ASLEEP in his clothes, lying on his back beneath a blanket with the perfect repose of a dead man. There had been three explosive shells from the howitzers tonight, all of them landing within the fort but causing no serious injury except to one of the cattle, which had been blinded by flying metal. The nine-pounder across the river had also fired two cannonballs, one of them striking the breastworks at the southwest battery but failing to do any more damage to the eighteen-pounder, which had been set on a new carriage and laboriously remounted some days ago.

Joe was too shaken to sleep, fearing the barrage might begin again at any moment, and it was a mystery to him how Colonel Travis could just close his eyes and accept the chance that he might be blown in two by a cannonball before he woke. That was a terrible thought to Joe—dying in your sleep. What if death caught you in the middle of a nightmare? It seemed to him you would be locked there forever.

He wished for the music. The Mexican band had stopped playing an hour or so ago, not long after midnight, and though he did not care for the harsh tunes they played, the music at least gave his mind something to grapple to keep it from sliding into sleep. He wanted to stay awake until morning. He felt safer in the daylight, and perhaps he could have a few hours of reasonably peaceful sleep until Travis woke him and made him go to work again.

Joe was so tired in body and mind that sometimes he felt himself coasting along in a realm of thought that had nothing to do with either sleep or wakefulness, but amounted to a kind of suspension of his knowledge of his own existence. He was heading to that place now, and it was only a distant crack of thunder that pulled him back from it.

Travis did not stir. The colonel's mouth was open and he snored slightly, but his body stayed as still as a statue. Joe decided to creep out of the room and get some air as long as the shells weren't falling. He didn't see much point in sitting here watching Travis sleep.

He picked up his musket and cartridge box and walked outside. Storm clouds had overwhelmed the stars, and it was treacherous walking across the compound in the darkness. Most of the Mexican cannonballs had been taken up, but there were still jagged fragments of metal from the exploding shells, and unexpected craters and trenches. There was no rain as yet to churn all this into mud, but he could hear the angry sound of approaching thunder and smell water in the air. Lightning slashed across the sky to the north, and in these short bursts of illumination Joe could see the sentinels outlined on the walls and a steer that had somehow strayed from the pens behind the barracks standing confused in the open compound, swaying its immense horns from side to side.

Joe walked cautiously around the steer, and continued on to the north wall, where he climbed up onto one of the shooting platforms that had been erected on the dirt mound that shored up the collapsing remains of the original mission wall. To his left, on the southwest battery, the gun crew had gathered around a brazier and were loudly talking politics, decrying Andrew Jackson and bankers and something or someone called Locofocos.

He heard softer voices as well, the voices of a man and a woman along the wall to his right. Joe saw them a moment later in a flash of lightning—the man named Herndon and the slave woman he had brought to Béxar with him. He couldn't hear what they were speaking about—it wasn't talk, just murmurs, and it took his weary mind a moment more to realize what it was they were doing.

Well, let them do it, he thought. It wasn't any business of his. Joe had seen the woman on the firing line, loading Herndon's rifles while he took aim and fired, and maybe they had a closeness in everything they did, like proper husbands and wives.

The woman was comely. Joe had noticed her, though she had never bothered to cast her eyes on him, just took him in with the surroundings as if she were a white woman herself and he was just another nigger running around on this errand or that.

But her presence in the Alamo had stirred him up. He had been with women four times in his life, and each time now stood out as a blazing remembrance. It angered him to think that he was now about to die defending this crumbling fort in a cause that was confoundingly obscure and distant and that he would never know such a moment again.

The thought circled back endlessly in his mind. What if that Mexican soldier had not been shot as he was leading the way through the window? Joe imagined himself escaping the Alamo and running across the cornfield to the river. Would he have truly been welcomed? Some of the men he had seen advancing on the Alamo had skin almost as dark as his own, and running forward at a crouch under the storm of enemy fire while their officers goaded them on with raised swords they had seemed as powerless as any slaves he had ever seen.

Travis and all the other white men in the Alamo talked about freedom all the time, but Joe could not quite grasp the nature of the bondage they were fighting to release themselves from. They had had the freedom not to come to Texas in the first place, and they had had the freedom to leave it once they determined that Mexico no longer wanted them here. To Joe, this whole war was airy. But the liberation that those two Mexican soldiers had promised was not particularly tangible either. Maybe if he could leave Texas and go deep into Mexico, deep into the forests he had heard about that were full of monkeys and huge birds with glowing feathers, maybe in such an exotic realm freedom would seem like something real and not just another word that people felt they had to be excited about.

The thunder grew steadier. The lightning tore through

the cloudy fabric of the sky. Beneath the thunder, Joe heard a thin, snapping sound, and beneath the reach of the lightning he saw distant erratic flashes of light that he thought at first might be wayward spurs of electricity. It did not occur to him it was gunfire until he heard human shouting and the rumble of horses' hooves.

When he saw the men riding out of the darkness he raised his musket to fire, but for some reason he could not name he hesitated.

"Don't shoot! Don't shoot! We're Texians!" one of the riders in the lead finally called out as they galloped into sight. "Shoot the goddam Mexicans that are chasin' us."

By this time there were a dozen men on the wall, and they were starting to fire over the heads of the riders, though the Mexicans who were in pursuit of them were still not visible.

"Open the gate! Where the hell's the gate?" the leader called out as he and his men reined up beneath the wall. Even with the rattle of gunfire in his ears Joe could hear the blowing of the spent horses.

"It's on the other end of the fort!" he called back.

The force wheeled like a flock of birds and raced along the west wall to the gatehouse on the south end. The men continued to fire at the pursuing Mexicans, but they were now distant and invisible. Joe grabbed his musket and ran across the courtyard to alert Travis. He tripped on a mound of dirt and cut the heel of his hand on a piece of shrapnel, but in an instant he was on his feet again. By the time he got to Travis's door the colonel was already running through it, and it seemed the whole garrison was awake and cheering wildly as the reinforcements passed through the gate. They were on foot now, leading their horses, both beasts and men gasping for breath.

———

"WE CROSSED UP on the river below the old sugarcane mill," Captain Martin was saying as Joe entered Travis's quarters with two cups of a hot drink made from water and parched corn. "I reckoned they'd close the Gonzales road first, so we snuck way around to the north. We would've come in bold as you please if that patrol hadn't seen us."

Joe handed one cup to Martin and the other to John Smith. Martin took his with a curt nod. He was Travis's age. Smith was older, handsome and capable-looking, though like Martin he was shivering with cold and wet. Trickles of mud ran down their clothes and pooled on the dirt floor where they were sitting.

"As you can see, John," Travis said with a grin when Smith gagged on his drink, "we haven't had any deliveries of coffee since you left."

Travis had sent Martin and Smith out as couriers a week ago, soon after the Mexicans had arrived, and he was clearly delighted now to see them back, though the men they had led into the Alamo—the Gonzales Mounted Ranging Company—numbered only thirty-two. There had been thirty-four, Martin reported, but two of them had gotten separated from the main group during the fight with the Mexican patrol, and nobody knew where they were.

"We ain't all that's coming, though," Martin said. "That letter you wrote has got all of Texas stirred up."

"What about Fannin?"

"The last I heard he was setting out on the march. Tumlinson's got men too, and Seguín's out there somewhere raising an outfit. Everybody's supposed to meet up on the Cibolo."

"Where's Houston?" Travis said.

"Nobody knows where the sonofabitch is. I guess he's in Washington at the convention by now, if he hasn't gotten drunk and fallen off his horse. Here's a letter for you from Williamson."

Martin reached into his clothes, produced a piece of paper from an oilskin pouch and reached forward to hand it to Travis just as a cannonball slammed into the wall behind them. Joe had spent the better part of two days shoring up that wall with dirt so thick that the room was half the size it had been, and this crude embankment kept the ball from bursting through. But the impact blew out the tapers in front of them and filled the room with a cloud of dust so thick it drove them all coughing and gagging out into the cold air. The shells were coming down hard now, and the men all raced across the courtyard to the safety of the barracks with the twisted metal from the grenades screaming all around them.

"Christ in a kerchief!" John Smith said to Travis as they huddled against the walls of the barracks. "How do you put up with this?"

"Oh, it doesn't bother us much, John," Travis finally answered him when the explosions had stopped.

"Is everyone all right in here?" he called out to the room. A considerable number of the defenders were gathered in the barracks, but only a few of them muttered an answer. Joe heard somebody sobbing on the other side of the room.

"What's the matter? Is somebody hurt?" Travis asked.

"It's just young Bill here," Captain Carey said. "He's a little wrung out, I guess."

Joe looked across the space. There was a fire burning low in the hearth and the light was weak, but Joe could make out Carey and the shaking form of the young man he was trying to comfort, a private named Bill Smith who was no older than a boy.

"I'm all right," the young man said, though each word was separated by a kind of gasp as he fought away the sobs. "I'm sorry, Colonel."

"There is no reason to apologize. You men have been under a strain and have behaved with an uncomplaining heroism that does you all credit. Let me see that letter now, Captain Martin."

Martin produced the letter he had been handing Travis before the cannonball hit. The colonel stood and walked over to the hearth, shedding clouds of dust with every step. Joe watched with the other men as he held the letter up to the light and read it in silence.

When he was through he turned and passed his eyes over the tired men who were huddled in the room. There was a look of satisfaction on Travis's face that made Joe hopeful but also a little nervous. It was always when Travis was the most confident that they seemed to end up in the most trouble.

"Captain Baugh," he said, "will you give my compliments to the company commanders and ask them to assemble the men immediately in the courtyard?"

It was almost dawn before the word had been passed and the men were gathered. It was a strange time for a convocation, or would have been if time had not lost its meaning during the sleepless days and nights of the siege. Travis began by leading the garrison in a cheer for the brave men from Gonzales who had ridden through the enemy lines to stand beside them in this decisive and historic hour. Then he read aloud the letter he had received from Major Williamson, detailing the efforts that were under way to relieve them. At this very moment, the letter said, the colonies were responding to Travis's magnificent letter with alacrity, determination, and selfless valor. Fannin had mobilized his men as soon as he had heard of the plight of the Alamo and was now marching across the prairies to the Cibolo, where he would rendezvous with more men from Gonzales, and from Mina, and from ranchos and settlements all across Texas.

"We have succeeded, gentlemen!" Travis said as he folded up the letter. "We have fought back the enemy and endured his cannonades, and now in a very few days the Alamo is sure to be relieved."

Travis went on with his exhortations. He challenged the men to be as alert and courageous in these coming critical hours as they had been in the past. He reminded them how vital it was that the great fight should occur here at Béxar, where Santa Anna could be turned back from the very threshold of Texas so that the fair fields and settlements of the colonies would never be despoiled by his armies.

"God and Texas!" Travis shouted. "Victory or Death!"

The men cheered and repeated the call. Edmund, standing in the ranks of Baker's company in the freezing dawn, remained silent—not sullenly or contemptuously so, but from the habit of lifelong solitude. And he was half-asleep on his feet, so that he watched Travis's address as if it were a dreamlike pageant that had little to do with him.

Sparks stood next to him, waving his rifle in the air, repeating the cry of Victory or Death; Herndon next to Sparks, and then Roth and Terrell and Captain Baker, who made a point of shaking hands with each of his men as the cheer continued. Edmund returned Baker's handshake, and greeted a few of the men from Gonzales, who filtered through the ranks saying hello to old friends and introducing themselves to members of the garrison they had not yet met. All of them wanted to meet Crockett. The energy and good spirits of the Gonzales men were intoxicating. Someone brought out a fiddle and started playing. The tune was "Oft in the Stilly Night," but the words had been rewritten to celebrate the Texian victory over Cos, and those who had been part of that fight joined rowdily in.

Edmund saw Mary looking down at them from one of the windows in the hospital rooms above the barracks. Their eyes met and she smiled at him with cautious hopefulness. Most of the other women had left the security of the church and were out among the men. Mrs. Dickinson, whom Ed-

mund had never seen allow her infant daughter to leave her
arms, set the girl onto the ground and let her toddle across
the courtyard to her father. If the Mexicans chose this moment to begin another bombardment, Edmund reflected,
half the population of the Alamo would be cut down before
they could reach safety. And this thought must have occurred to everyone else as well, because in short course the
compound was once again deserted. Only those on guard
duty remained.

THE STORM that Joe had seen on the horizon in the early
hours of the morning veered off beyond the hills to the
east, the sound of its thunder growing more and more muffled within the velvety gray clouds.

Joe went into the headquarters room to get some sleep,
but found Travis in the midst of a cheerful burst of industry, sweeping the furniture clear of all the dirt that had
fallen on it when the cannonball had slammed into the wall.

"You did a fine job shoring this place up, Joe," Travis
said, "but I think more dirt is needed."

"What I need is some sleep."

"You had your chance. Don't think I didn't hear you
prowling around in the middle of the night. Why you would
want to waste an opportunity to sleep I have no idea, but
now there is work to be done. Take the other end of this
blanket."

Joe picked up the blanket and helped Travis snap it free
of dust. Then he straightened up the rest of the room as best
he could as Travis sat down to write more letters.

"I believe the tide is turning to our advantage, Joe,"
Travis said as he signed his name to the bottom of a page.
"All we have to do is hold on for another few days, and we
will have won a splendid victory here."

Joe mutely nodded his head and went on with his work

while Travis took out the copybook in which he was writing his autobiography. When he considered himself finished with his housekeeping, Joe lay down on his cot without asking for permission and went to sleep as he had so many nights before, listening to the sound of William Barret Travis's scratching pen.

CHAPTER TWENTY-EIGHT

✶

THE BELLS of San Fernando Church were ringing in welcome as Blas Angel Montoya entered San Antonio de Béxar with his cazador company. The company, along with the rest of the Toluca battalion, as well as the Zapadores and Aldama battalions, had been on a forced march for the last five days, called up on the expressed order of General Santa Anna to reinforce the men of the vanguard who were besieging the fortified mission known as the Alamo.

When the order came to advance, Blas and his men had been camped for a week on the north bank of the Rio Grande in a pleasant grove of pecan trees, lying there in stupefied relief as the life began to creep back into their exhausted bodies. Since the women in the chusma were in as bad a condition as the men after the terrible march through the desert heat and freak snowstorms, it was the women of the little town of Guerrero who brought them food and mended what was left of their clothing. The men who had suffered from the tele soon strengthened, though Salas was still weak and had trouble keeping down food any more substantial than broth. By the time the battalion was ordered on the march again, even Alquisira was able to walk, the arrow wound causing him less discomfort than the fresh blisters he soon developed on the road to Béxar.

At first it had seemed that this renewed march would be as grim and dangerous as the first part of the journey had been. The men were driven at a punishing pace through endless empty reaches of chaparral, and once again they encountered a savage snowstorm that killed a man in one of the Toluca's line companies. But at least there was food in the chaparral—jackrabbits bounding away at their every step that could be shot or clubbed—and after a few days the cold abated somewhat and the landscape grew less brutally monotonous. They camped by clear, chalky streams with magisterial cypress trees growing at the water's edge, and between the streams the terrain rolled gently under the steely winter sky.

And now at last they had arrived. As they marched in their columns past the church with its ringing bells, past the band and the cheering troops lined up along the plaza, Blas felt an almost dreamlike swell of relief and well-being. From the smiles of the faces of his men he saw that they felt it too.

Hurtado turned and said something to him that Blas could not hear above the blare of the music.

"I said we made it, Sargento!" Hurtado repeated, his wide toad face split in a grin.

Blas nodded as the column marched the last few yards to the center of the plaza. He had developed serious blisters of his own in the last few days and had walked for many leagues on the sides of his feet, but now he put his feet down flat upon the dirt, not minding the pain. They had made it. Every one of them. Blas felt sure that there were few companies in either brigade for whom such a statement could be true. There were so many graves along the way, so many men dead of tele or exposure or simple weariness. But each man of his company had survived.

The officers, Captain Loera among them, promptly disappeared into one of the nearby houses. The rest of the reinforcements were told to remain in the plaza until the baggage wagons came up and bivouac assignments were given out. No one bothered to feed them, but women from the town filtered among the new arrivals selling tamales.

Blas and his men could not see the Alamo from the

plaza, but the sound of the artillery bombarding the place was ferociously loud in their ears, and the cold air was thick with greasy yellow smoke. From men in the Jiménez and Matamoros battalions who had been in the vanguard and thus in Béxar since the siege began they learned that the rebels in the Alamo would not surrender and had determined to fight to the last man. An attack had been tried early in the siege but the rebels had repulsed it, and just two days ago they had been reinforced by thirty or forty men who had broken through the Mexican lines a few hundred varas upriver. Santa Anna had ordered trenches dug at this vulnerable point, and a new battery had just been completed to the north that could cover this approach, as well as batter the Alamo's weak north wall, but no one really knew from which direction more rebel forces might come, or how strong in number they might be. General Sesma had gone out on the Goliad road with the Dolores cavalry and a company of infantry to try to cut off any reinforcement attempt, but they had come back two days ago without encountering hostile forces. That same day a cannonball from one of the Alamo's artillery pieces had struck the president's headquarters. He was out scouting at the time and no one was hurt, but it was said that the incident had helped clarify his inclination to attack sooner rather than later.

Another two hours passed before the baggage trains arrived and the company set out on foot once more, marching to the outskirts of the town to an empty field next to the river.

When they reached the bivouac site and set down their gear Blas allowed the men to stand on the bank of the river and study the fortress of the Alamo. They were well out of rifle range but close enough so that the broken-down mission seemed sprawling and ill-defined.

"Where will the attack be made?" Alquisira asked Blas.

"They say the north wall is the weakest point, though you can't see it very well from here."

"There is no cover in that direction," Hurtado said. "No trees or rocks to hide behind."

"No," Blas answered. "We'll have to advance very quickly. Probably at night."

He tried to keep his voice casual and conversational, but he did not like what he saw across the river. Some of the artillery emplacements were clearly visible from this distance, but others were no doubt hidden within the walls. Blas suspected the norte artillery crews were not experienced, but they had a formidable number of pieces and if they managed to get off only two or three volleys there would be a terrible price to pay before the Mexican forces could cross all that open ground and overwhelm the walls. And from that point on, the battle would grow even fiercer. The nortes were tall and powerful, and violent by nature, and it was said each one of them had a brace of horse pistols in his belt, along with murderous knives and even hatchets.

It grew dark as they stood there, and Blas ordered the men to see to their camp and to their weapons, warning them that Captain Loera would appear just after reveille to make an inspection, though he knew and the men knew too that the captain was unlikely to appear before midday.

Isabella brought his dinner that night, and afterward the two of them sat on the riverbank beneath the cypress boughs and stared out at the rebel fortress. There were guard fires burning on the walls and Blas could see the silhouettes of men when they walked in front of the flames, but otherwise the Alamo was as dark as the sky behind it.

He pulled Isabella to him. They were warm enough with her blanket and his woolen tunic and the body heat they shared. He stroked her sharp cheekbones with his fingers and rubbed his chin against her black hair, and then their touching grew more purposeful, and, anticipating him as always, she spread her thin blanket on the ground and drew up the hem of her huipil. When he entered her body she moaned quietly to herself and then turned her head to look down into the deep channel of the river, as if imagining herself under the water. But when her body came to its climax she shifted her eyes to Blas and stared at him as she had never done before and furiously pressed her gaping mouth to his.

Neither of them moved for a long time afterward. When Blas felt her begin to shiver beneath him he shifted his position and allowed her to pull down her huipil and to huddle against his tunic. They could hear voices from the Alamo, distant scraps of laughter and complaint from the men on the walls.

Isabella had learned a few words of Spanish on the long march north, and now she whispered to him as she stared at the fortress.

"This enemy place?"

"Yes," Blas said.

"When?"

He supposed she meant when would the assault come, and he shrugged and said two or maybe three days. No one knew.

"Many enemy men?"

"Not many," he told her. But enough, he thought. He could not stop thinking of the screaming spray of canister that would meet his men as they ran toward those walls. He was not eager to attack the Alamo, but he knew that it was better to do the thing sooner than later, before norte reinforcements arrived and there were full crews for all the guns and more riflemen on the walls.

She shifted in his embrace, and the bag filled with divining stones that was tied to her belt pushed against him. He took it in his hand and fingered the stones through the cloth. One night when they were encamped on the Rio Grande, recuperating from the ordeals of the march, he had asked her how the stones spoke to her. He was not sure she had understood the question, and her reply was long in coming as she tried to formulate enough Spanish words to give him some sort of reply.

She had gestured to the sky, and then down to the ground, and then made a slow swiping motion with her arm through the air in front of her, as if trying to call his attention to some invisible plane.

"Stones take me there," she said, continuing to move her arm back and forth.

"Where?" he persisted.

"Place between worlds," she finally said.

It surprised him that he thought he knew what she meant. It seemed to him that at various memorable times in his life he had fallen out of the common reality and entered something like this "place between worlds." He had felt it as a boy after long hours of kneeling in church, he had felt it with the shock of his family's brutal death, he had known it on the march through the Mexican deserts, when his fretful mind had strayed and stretched into boundless realms of despair, and there was nothing left to his being but a numb, residual awareness. Sometimes this place between the worlds had seemed evil and desolate to him, sometimes in its very blankness it had been consoling. Was that where Isabella truly lived? he wondered. Did it account for her mysterious, harmonic distance? Had Blas been in this place when he saw that jaguar man walking toward him across the desert?

He untied the bag from her waist and handed it to her, wanting her to shake out the stones so that she could enter that world and tell him whether he and his men would live or die in the coming days. But she pushed the bag away and shook her head, and tightened her grip around his body.

"THERE ARE two perimeters of defense," Baker was explaining to the men of his company as they sat around him in the barracks. In the last two days they had used pickaxes and shovels to dig out a defensive trench in the stone floor, and they had barricaded this trench on either side with earth embankments covered with hides. It had made the building even more crowded and dusty, but Terrell had ceased longing for any sort of privacy or cleanliness. Most of the men in the Alamo had only one set of clothes, which they had not changed or washed for weeks, many of them had diarrhea or windy digestive eruptions rising from the unvarying diet of corn and beef, and in this fellowship of ill smells no one felt conspicuous or particularly uncomfortable. It was the lack of sleep and the constant terror from the shells, the constant worry about his mother's safety, that made Terrell feel as if the flesh of his body had melted away and left behind only a web of nerves.

The bombs were not falling at the moment. It was the night of the third of March. Two hours before, they had heard cheering and bell ringing in Béxar, along with music from the military band that was different in pitch and enthusiasm from the droning, contorted serenade that was played to torture the Texians. What this celebration meant was plain to everyone: the rest of Santa Anna's forces had arrived. Travis had immediately called a meeting of his officers, and Baker had come back grim-faced and gathered the men together.

Now Terrell sat next to Sparks, sipping beef tea out of a cracked mug with a portrait of George Washington on it that he had found in a trash heap in the corner of the barracks during the first day of the siege. Baker was using the blade of his hunting knife to draw a diagram of the Alamo in the dirt.

"We don't know from which direction they will come, probably several at once," Baker said, looking up at the men. The bump on his head had subsided considerably, but in the exaggerated contour provided by the candlelight it still looked prominent. "But Colonel Travis thinks, and Major Jameson and Mr. Crockett agree with him, that the main objective will be the north wall. Every effort is to be made to hold that position. Those of you on the west and on the east must be aware of this, and must be ready to rush to its defense unless your own position is in immediate danger of being overwhelmed.

"Now," he continued, using the blade of his knife to cut through the line representing the north wall, "if they get over the walls and into the fort, if the first perimeter is breached, there will be an immediate retreat into these rooms."

He sliced across the diagram with the knife to indicate the barracks room in which they were already sitting.

"They'll blast us out of here with our own artillery," Roth said.

"No, they won't. The gun crews will spike their pieces before they retreat. From the barracks we can command the whole plaza with rifle and musket fire and make it very dangerous for the enemy to advance."

Terrell shifted his eyes, for some reason he did not know, to Edmund McGowan, and saw in the older man's face a worried expression that matched his own thoughts. There was a calculating silence while the men came to perceive the desperation of this plan.

"How long do they think we can hold out in here?" Terrell finally asked Baker.

"A day or two. And every hour we buy is another hour for Fannin to reach us."

"I don't think Fannin's coming," Sparks said. "If he was, he'd have been here by now. It's been two days since the Gonzales men came, and we ain't heard a word about any reinforcements."

"There's nothing I can do about that, Sparks," Baker said.

"Well, it's a shitty plan," Sparks said. "Where's the plan that has us breaking out of here?"

"Colonel Travis feels that we would all be cut down by lancers before we'd gone a hundred yards."

"Well, Colonel Travis can—"

"That's a pretty picture you've drawn in the dirt there, Captain Baker," David Crockett said as he walked into the room, just in time to choke off Sparks's insubordinate remark. "You are a draftsman and a marksman both. Can I beg you to release Private Mott into my keeping?"

Baker looked at Terrell. Terrell looked at Crockett. His head felt suddenly light, and inside his skull there was a buzzing like a hive.

"Get your traps, son," Crockett said.

"Where's he going?" Roth asked.

"I ain't sure, yet, Jacob," Crockett answered. He had long since learned everyone's first names. "As my colleague in the House used to say whenever a bill was about to come up, 'The answer is hid in the bowels of futurity.'"

"I AM GROWING nervous," Travis said a few minutes later in his headquarters. Terrell was there with Crockett and his nephew Will Patton, who was tall and rangy and wore a greasy leatherstocking outfit complete with a fur cap with dangling earflaps. Captain Baugh was in the room as well, along with Colonel Bonham, who had caused a great deal of excitement earlier in the day when he had ridden down the Gonzales road and into the Alamo with a bulging bag of dispatches. Now he sat familiarly in the corner with his boots off, smoking a cigar.

"Colonel Bonham has brought us a good deal of news, some of it good and some of it bad," Travis said. "It appears we can no longer rely on General Houston. He has never approved of our making a stand at Béxar and has ordered us to fall back into the colonies, which of course we cannot do without being cut down by Mexican lancers."

"Where is he now?" Crockett asked. "Still at that convention?"

Bonham looked up from his cigar and answered Crockett in a tired, cynical voice.

"He says that's where he's most needed. If Texas is to claim independence it must have a strong constitution."

"I never trusted that sonofabitch," Crockett said. "He's pure politician. Worse than Polk himself. Seems to me a commander in chief ought to be on the field and not warming his hindquarters in some goddam committee room."

"The other news is more encouraging," Travis said with a due pause to acknowledge Crockett's uncharacteristic anger. "Colonel Bonham has brought me another letter from Williamson. Unlike Houston, he's as solid as steel. He says that Fannin has been on the march with three hundred men and four pieces of artillery for three days now, and that he himself has assembled another three hundred. The problem is, where are all these men now? We think they might already be on the Cibolo ford on the Gonzales road, but somebody needs to find them and guide them in, somebody who is familiar with the Mexican emplacements and who has the power of persuasion to make them come immediately."

"I humbly accept the office," Crockett said. "If that's what you decided to elect me for."

"Thank you. And these are the men you want to take with you?" Travis glanced at Terrell and Patton.

Crockett nodded. Travis seemed to have no particular concern about Patton, but he turned to Terrell and questioned him with a lawyer's scrutiny.

"You were in Bowie's company?"

"Yes, sir," Terrell said. It felt strange to him to be having this conversation with Travis, who had never noticed him before and was now suddenly speaking to him as if he were the most significant person on the earth.

"Do you know the country from here to the Cibolo?"

"I did a lot of scouting out that way with Bowie. There may be others that know it better."

"He's got common sense and a solid keel," Crockett explained.

"All right. The three of you will leave in an hour. Colonel Bonham managed somehow to ride in here this morning uncontested, and he might have some thoughts about the best way for you to get out of the Alamo."

Bonham's advice was plain as buttermilk. He said as far as he could tell the patrols were spotty and the best thing to do was to get on your horse and try to slip by between the powder house and the artillery works to the north, and then when you thought you might be in the clear to dig in your spurs and not look behind you.

MARY HAD SPENT an hour in the afternoon with Bowie. The delirium had passed, but he was so weak now he could barely turn his head, and when he spoke it was in a barely audible mutter that was sometimes English and sometimes Spanish.

"Does he know his visitors?" Mary had asked Juana Alsbury in her clumsy Spanish. She and her sister took turns nursing Bowie and watching out for the infant in the church.

Mrs. Alsbury nodded her head with wishful enthusiasm and spoke too rapidly for Mary to catch the greater part of what she said. The kernel of it, she gathered, was that Señor Bowie was more aware than he seemed to be, that he recognized people as they came in and out of the room, and that even though his grip was weak he still clutched his knife in his hand night and day.

"Mary," she heard him say. She leaned forward and put her ear to his mouth. His breath was foul. His eyes bulged like a salamander's.

"Where's Fannin?" she heard him say.

"We don't know, Jim. We think he's on his way."

"Stay in the church when they come. You and Juana and Gertrudis."

"We will."

"Don't worry about me. I'll carve the bastards up soon as they get in the door."

He tightened the grip on his knife for emphasis, but in the process it slipped out of his fist and onto the floor. Mary picked it up and set it back in his hand, and then left when he drifted off to sleep.

She slept for an hour or two in the church and then walked over to the hospital, where Dr. Pollard, boisterous from lack of sleep, was entertaining the patients with an account of a meeting he had attended of a New York medical society, at which a young French-Canadian man who had been badly wounded in a shooting was exhibited. A good portion of the man's outer abdomen had been shot away and replaced with a glass window through which the doctors could observe the digestive processes taking place within.

"What did it look like?" Perry wanted to know. His ruined face was still bound in dressings, but his eyes were lively and wondering.

"Well, it looked like the inside of a clock," Pollard said. "A very soft and wet clock."

Mary glided among the patients like a sleepwalker as Pollard and Reynolds reminisced about their days as medical students, where no party or frolic of any sort was ever considered a success unless a quantity of laughing gas was on hand to strip away the guests' inhibitions.

"There ain't no such thing as gas that makes you laugh," a man named McGehee said. He had been seriously wounded by a musket ball in the battle for Béxar, and this was the first time Mary had heard him join in a conversation.

"There is!" Reynolds declared, laughing himself at the thought. "And it's better than whiskey or any other spirit in the world. It directly excites the risibility of the brain."

"I bet it smells bad," Main said.

"It smells no worse than the air around you," Pollard said, prompting a spontaneous eruption of laughter from these patients confined in a room that perpetually smelled of diarrhea and vomitus.

Mary exchanged looks with Señora Losoya. This sudden, improbable levity did not suit her. She could sense the desperation in it, the mounting hysteria that was in itself a measure of how hopeless things were growing for them. But Señora Losoya broke into a helpless grin and so did she, and she was laughing when she looked up and saw Terrell walking through the door, with his hat pulled tight on his head and carrying his father's rifle and haversack.

"I'm going out with Mr. Crockett to bring in help," he told her when she had led him outside into the cold night, not wanting their conversation to be overheard by the men in the hospital. Out of nervous habit, they stood at the doorway, ready to scramble inside when the shelling started up again. But for now it was quiet, and the passing storms had scoured the sky clear, so that the stars overhead were harsh in their brilliance.

"When?" she asked him.

"As soon as we get the horses saddled."

"Terrell . . ."

But there were no words she could say that made any sense to her. Why tell him to be careful, when it was plain that their salvation, if it was to come, lay not in caution but in daring? Why tell him once again that she loved him when the enormity and timbre of that love was, as she had discovered, so clearly inexpressible?

But she said the frail words anyway, and seized him in her arms before she could convince herself not to.

The grit of his unshaven face was against her cheek, and she could feel his tears there as well.

"The Cibolo is only twenty miles away," he said, his voice trembling. "We should be back before daylight, if we can find the men we're looking for. If the Mexicans attack in the meantime, you stay with the other women and children in the church and wait till it's over."

She nodded her head and gripped the back of his neck and pressed her son's face against hers for a moment, and then she released him.

"Don't die, Terrell," she said. "Don't."

"Don't you either," he answered and turned to go to the horse pen.

THEY SADDLED their horses, but word came from Baugh for them to wait until Travis had finished another letter he wanted them to carry out.

"I hope he hurries," Crockett said. "We're so jumpy we might hop over these walls any minute."

"I think I'll go to the sinks again, Uncle David," Patton said.

"You go right ahead, Will."

"I need to talk to somebody," Terrell said to Crockett as Patton walked off.

"You go talk to whoever you want, son, as long as it doesn't take you any longer than it takes Will to move his bowels."

Terrell found Mr. McGowan at his post on the west wall. His dog for once was with him, having finally grown emboldened enough to creep out of the buildings into the open.

"I'm going out with Crockett, Mr. McGowan," he said.

"That's what I've heard, Terrell. Which way?"

"East. Along the Gonzales road to Cibolo Creek."

"Well, that's dangerous. The Mexicans will have patrols out."

"I know it."

"Have you told your mother?"

Terrell nodded. Though there was no wind tonight, there was a penetrating cold, and Mr. McGowan was shivering in his blanket. He had lost weight like they all had and had not shaved in weeks, so that his beard had almost grown in among his side-whiskers. A stranger would have seen him as no different from the other men in the Alamo, just another cornered Texian rebel, but to Terrell there was still something peculiar and remote about him. He remembered the time in Refugio when he had tried to talk to Mr. Mc-Gowan about Edna Foley. Terrell had been drawn to his kindness, to his grandeur, to what he thought was his wisdom. But now he did not think there was any wisdom in him, or he would not be here in this terrible place, unconnected and uncommitted.

But once again it was this flawed man to whom he turned.

"Will you try to save my mother?" he said.

"I will, Terrell." And as he said the words he held out his hand for the boy to shake.

THEY LEFT the Alamo on foot, leading their horses. Though the stars glared in the heavens, there was no moon and Terrell crouched low as he walked behind Crockett, drawn to the shadowy darkness of the ground. His madstone was in his pocket, and he wished his hands were free so he could touch it. The heavy leather of the quadralpas saddle on Veronica's back creaked in his ears, though the mare herself was broodingly quiet. Every few paces he would hear a distant Mexican voice—some soldier taunting another, some sergeant calling out orders to his men in the trenches.

They had gone fifty yards when they heard a voice speaking to them in a husky whisper.

"Over here."

Crockett did not risk answering but veered toward the sound of the voice. After a few yards Terrell could make out the forms of the Texian pickets who were lying in a shallow trench, watching for enemy patrols.

"How are you tonight, sir?" one of them whispered to Crockett. It was David Cummings, the Pennsylvanian who had escorted Terrell's mother and Mr. McGowan into the Alamo.

"I hope that I am as slippery as an otter, Private Cummings," he answered.

Terrell nodded to Robert Crossman, who was with Cummings in the trench, and to another man he did not know. All three of the pickets were quaking with cold, and he wondered if his own face was as bloodless and as conspicuous in its paleness as theirs.

Cummings reported to Crockett that as far as he and his fellow pickets could ascertain, the night was quiet, with no enemy movements outside of the batteries and trenches. They had looked and listened hard for any sign of cavalry, but so far nothing had presented itself.

"I suppose it's as clear a chance as you're likely to have, sir," Cummings said to Crockett. "We'll lead you out a ways to the east, past the edge of the Alameda. Then you can decide what to do from there."

They crept past the charred ruins of the jacales the defenders had burned and kept moving forward for another hundred yards, until the Alamo, when Terrell glanced back, looked like a distant island in a dark, forbidding sea. There was music coming from the church—someone was playing "Oft in the Stilly Night" again—but there was no other sign of life, not even a single forlorn fire.

"We will take our leave of you here, gentlemen," Crockett said to the pickets. They shook hands all around, and Cummings led his men back to their lonely positions outside the walls.

They kept leading their horses forward, through boggy and then stony ground and up a gradual slope where the scrubby timber gave them at least a degree of cover. When they reached the summit of the slope they passed several hundred yards to the north of the powder house, and they could see fires burning and horses silhouetted in front of them.

"Maybe the patrols have come in," Terrell whispered to Crockett as they peered at the distant horses. "Maybe the road is clear."

"Well, that's about as pretty a thought as I've heard," Crockett said.

After another fifty yards they mounted their horses and turned toward the road.

CHAPTER TWENTY-NINE

✴

THE HORSES were restive and hard to control. After almost two weeks of terror-stricken confinement in the Alamo, they wanted to run. But Crockett would allow only a steady trot. The road to Gonzales was generally in good repair, but even so, to gallop blindly along in the deep night was a heedless thing to do.

They kept to the side of the road, ready to rein off into the trees if they heard the slightest tremor of hoofbeats or rustle of tack. Thin, ragged clouds were coasting across the sky now, and the wind was up. Beneath his hat, Terrell's ears were numb with cold, and all he could do to protect them was to turn up his jacket collar against the wind. He envied Patton his absurd-looking fur cap with its earflaps, and Crockett his commodious greatcoat.

Terrell's teeth chattered and his body quaked, whether from cold or fear he could not discern. He had to fight Veronica to keep her from running, and after an hour his arms ached from pulling on the reins. No one spoke a word, though several times Crockett held up a hand and they stopped and listened and then rode on again. They heard owls and coyotes and once saw a porcupine shuffling across the road.

They had ridden for three hours or so when Crockett stopped again and motioned Terrell forward. Crockett nodded toward the dark landscape ahead. The road continued on for about twenty yards and then made a steep descent toward a thick band of trees.

"I reckon that to be the crossing up ahead," Crockett whispered. "What's your opinion?"

"I think you're right."

Crockett deliberated in silence a moment more, and then touched his heels to his horse's flanks and led them closer. They continued another fifty yards and then stopped again, hearing voices in the dark shadows of the trees ahead.

"I can't tell if they're speaking English or Spanish," Crockett said. "Can either of you?"

They listened. All Terrell could hear was a distant conversational rumble, the words as indistinct as water running over rocks. Finally, Patton spoke up and said, "English."

"You sure, Will?" Crockett said. "I'd hate to ride in there and say 'How do you do?' to a Mexican patrol."

"I ain't sure, Uncle. It just sounds like English and not Mexican to me."

They listened some more, and the more they listened the more Terrell was convinced that Will was right. The talk was loud, its rhythms slow and irregular, and was punctuated by bursts of hearty laughter.

"Sounds like it to me too," Terrell said.

"Well, we'll give it a try, then," Crockett answered. "Even though my heart's fluttering like a duck in a puddle."

They moved closer. The talk they heard from beneath the dark bank of trees became more distinct, though they could still not make out the words. Finally Crockett cocked his rifle and called out in a loud voice, "Hello!"

The talk instantly ceased. From somewhere on the side of the road in front of them a picket called out, "Who is that? Who's on the road out there?"

"David Crockett of Tennessee. And two of my friends."

There was another spell of silence, and then a different voice called out, "You and your party may advance, sir, but do so with all caution."

They followed the steep road down to the crossing, and

as they did so armed men started to filter out of the tree canopy to greet them. The men had made no fires, and their faces were still mostly indistinct in the darkness, but Terrell noticed that Juan Séguin was among them.

"Are you David Crockett for a fact?" one of the men said as he walked forward with a disconcertingly casual gait.

"I am, sir. And if you have no objection I will get down off this horse before I find myself with a case of the piles."

The man laughed and Crockett slid out of his saddle without further invitation. Terrell and Will did the same.

"Captain DeSaugue," the man in front said, reaching out his hand. "Francis DeSaugue of Pennsylvania. And this is Captain Chenoweth. Captain Seguín you already know, and Captain Tumlinson is here with his ranger company."

"I never expected to see so many captains in one place," Crockett replied. "We are well set for an ocean voyage."

Crockett took the time to introduce his nephew and Terrell, calling them his "esteemed companions in adventure."

"I hope these men are on the way to the Alamo," he said when all the handshaking was done.

"We are indeed."

"How many believers you got in this congregation?"

"We number a man or two over a hundred and fifty," DeSaugue said.

"We expected more. Are Fannin's men here?"

"Colonel Fannin sent Captain Chenoweth and me ahead with the cavalry. He was supposed to follow with the infantry, but they had to turn back."

"They turned back!"

"Their oxen wandered off when they stopped the camp, and they couldn't move the artillery. Then Fannin got worried about leaving the fort at Goliad when the Mexicans have got a whole division coming up from the south."

Terrell had never seen Crockett frustrated before, but now he stamped his foot hard on the ground and uttered an oath under his breath. The spell didn't last more than a few seconds, but it troubled Terrell to see it. He realized that Crockett was as tired and scared as he was.

"Williamson's still putting some men together up in Gonzales," DeSaugue said, hoping to raise Crockett's mood, "and maybe in a day or two Fannin will have changed his mind around."

"I don't expect we have a day or two, Captain De-Saugue."

Crockett swept his eyes across the men standing in front of him in the dark.

"Men," he said, "are you ready to ride with me to the Alamo?"

The bulk of them grinned and vigorously nodded their heads, but prudently did not break out into hurrahs for fear that their cheers would be heard by an enemy patrol.

"Then by God we'll leave in ten minutes, whether I got piles or not," Crockett said. "Just give me a chance to meet with my executive committee here."

He walked a short distance away with Will Patton and Terrell in tow. "Let's find us a place to sit that ain't covered with horseshit," he told them, and when they were seated under a tree whose trunk blocked the wind he took out an oilskin pouch and handed it to Patton.

"These are letters from Travis, Will. I want you to take them to Gonzales and see that somebody takes them on to the convention in Washington-on-the-Brazos. You know the way?"

"Yes, sir, but I'd rather go back to the Alamo with you."

"Well, you ain't. Now go on."

"Right now?"

"We're in the hurrying business here, Will. In case you haven't noticed." He stood in the manner of a powerful man declaring a meeting at an end. Will stood up with him, and Crockett shook his hand.

"I'll get back to the Alamo as soon as I can," Will said.

Crockett slapped his nephew affectionately on the shoul-

der and shooed him away. Terrell could see that the older
man was fighting back tears and looked away. Terrell shook
Will's hand himself and then sat down again in front of the
tree while Crockett unfolded a sheet of paper and took
out a pen from a writing case.

"What do you want me to do?" Terrell said.

"I want you to sit there while I write a letter."

Terrell sat there as ordered, and in a matter of moments
he was asleep with his head bobbing on his neck. He was in
the midst of a hurried, complicated dream when Crockett
shook him awake.

"Are you awake there, Private Mott?"

"Yes, sir."

Crockett smiled and pressed the letter into his hand.
"This goes to Fannin at Goliad."

"You want me to take it?"

"If you can stay awake."

"I can," Terrell said. "What do I do after I give him the
letter?"

"If it turns out Fannin can send us some men, you come
with them. If not, bring yourself back here. Williamson's
men ought to be here by then, or else up in Gonzales. Don't
try to get into the Alamo by yourself."

Ten minutes later all the men gathered on the Cibolo
were mounted and ready to ride to the aid of the Alamo, all
except Terrell, who was headed alone in the opposite direction.

"Keep a good pace," Crockett told Terrell as they parted.
"Try to get as far as you can before sunrise, and stay off the
road during the daytime. If you meet up with any Mexican
lancers out on patrol, all I can tell you is to do the best you
can to get away."

Terrell nodded. Crockett leaned forward in the saddle to
shake his hand and wish him good luck, and then he and the
rest of the men headed west along the road. Veronica
wanted to follow, and Terrell had to fight her with the reins

until she was resigned to being alone with him. Then he pulled her toward the crossing and the far bank of the creek and took off south across open country.

It was, as near he could determine, about one in the morning. Veronica was balky and irritated for the first mile or so, but she soon got her spirit back and fell into a rhythmic canter along the dark road. Terrell had not slept for days, and his weariness and fear began to weave together and he saw shadowy riders on his flanks that he could not outdistance and malevolent birds swooping down out of the night sky.

Time passed as the horse surged under him. Was he asleep? He thought it very possible. The dark riders dropped away and the frantic wingbeats of the night birds no longer troubled him. There was now only the cold wind freezing his ears and his fingers, so that he could no longer feel the reins in his hands, and the harsh sound of a voice up ahead calling out, "Alto! Alto inmediatamente!"

Before his mind could wake and catch up with the responses of his body he had already spurred Veronica in her flanks and was galloping back the way he had come with the lancers in pursuit.

He could hear their breathing and their horses' breathing behind him. He could feel the anxious shifting and creaking of saddles and the clacking sound of metal bits against the horses' teeth. No one called out to him again. They were saving their breath to run him down with their lances.

The landscape before him was black, though his fear made him see deeper into it than he might have otherwise. He was riding across open, grassy swells, paying no attention to which direction he was heading, just following the least complicated route the land offered. He coasted up a hill and then down again, and saw in the distance the margins of a forest. He steered Veronica in that direction and then lay down low in the saddle as they crashed through the branches.

The forest was only a thin belt, and sooner than he wanted they were out onto the open ground again. It was grazing land here and the grass was low, and the sound of his pursuers grew louder as the horses' hooves struck the uncushioned ground.

Perhaps they went five miles, through pasture and prairie and chaparral and then across stretches of sandy soil where the horses scrabbled for their footing on sheets of exposed rock. Once Terrell heard one of the horses behind him trip, its rider grunting and cursing as he hit the ground. The others did not break stride. They called back something to him in Spanish and rode on after Terrell.

Even though the air was cold there was a sheen of sweat on Veronica's neck, and the saddle blanket was soaked through. Terrell's legs were cramping and he was out of breath, and the lancers behind him were tireless and patient and frighteningly silent.

Veronica's breathing grew deep and hollow as Terrell kicked her mercilessly forward, but the breathing of the horses behind him was even more labored, and he could sense them falling behind. To his left was another dark mass of trees, and he debated whether it was better to drive Veronica into the forest where it would be easier to hide or to continue to try to outrun the lancers on open ground. As he was trying to make up his mind the lancers suddenly gave up the chase. He heard the heavy wheezing of the horses as they were reined up, and the clink of spurs as the riders leapt to the ground.

Terrell looked over his shoulder and saw a powder flash, and before he heard the crack of the escopeta he and Veronica were already tumbling to earth. He felt the bone in his right forearm snap, and at the same moment one of Veronica's flailing hooves crushed the hand of that arm against unyielding rock.

Terrell nevertheless sprang to his feet and with his left hand reached into the waist of his pants for the pistol he carried there, but it had fallen out and there was no time to look for it.

Veronica tried to rise but her leg bone was broken like a stick, and her foreleg dangled wildly as she struggled in pain. In the distance the Mexicans were shouting to each other in Spanish and climbing back onto their tired mounts, and Terrell knew of nothing more to do than run toward the trees, leaving his horse to her agony.

He ran heedlessly forward through the forest, once or twice stumbling on rocks but generally having the fortune to keep his feet. One of the lancers was knocked off his horse by a loop of stout grapevine, and the rest dismounted out of caution and continued after him on foot. He knew as he was running that the chase meant more to him than it did to them, and after a mile of heedless flight he no longer heard their voices behind him or the sound of their boots pounding through the underbrush.

He looked for a place where the shadows were deepest and then finally threw himself on the ground beneath several trees knit together by vines. The winter branches of the trees were so tightly enmeshed that no starlight penetrated. The pain of his arm and of his crushed hand was astonishing to him. His arm pulsed wildly—it felt like there was a frightened mouse trapped under his skin, scuttling back and forth. No matter which way he turned his shattered limb, or tried to brace it against his upraised knee, the mouse could not find its way out.

He listened for the lancers. When he heard their voices at last, they had retreated far in the distance, at the edge of the forest where he had fallen. He assumed the single gunshot he heard was a kindness they performed for his wounded horse.

CHAPTER THIRTY

✦

THE CHEAP AMERICAN CLOCK in the storekeeper's
house indicated four-thirty in the morning, but Telesforo
was so invigorated by the company of his friend Robert
Talon he had no thought for sleep. He and the Frenchman
had been sitting up all night, drinking the storekeeper's
brandy and smoking his cigars and carrying on an endless
conversation in which they took turns interrupting each
other with solemn bursts of insight on subjects ranging
from Mexican politics to the historical reliability of the
Gospels to the best way to remove a porcupine quill from
the nose of a dog.

Talon had lost considerable weight on the march, and in
the taper light his long Gallic face would have looked ca-
daverous had it not been so animated. He was draped across
a haircloth armchair, his boots on the floor and his tunic unbuttoned. He and the rest of the men in Telesforo's Zapadores unit had arrived with the reinforcements yesterday
afternoon. Telesforo had promptly found his friend and fed
him a good meal and brought him to the billet he shared
with three other officers, all of whom were now sonorously
asleep in the next room.

"Yes, it was an unforgettable journey," Robert was saying as he studied the fiery liquid in his brandy glass. "You
no doubt experienced some discomfort yourself, but travelling in the company of the president you were naturally
spared the most hellish aspects of the march. I saw men
freeze to death, Telesforo. There was a man in the Aldamas
whose nose turned as black as crepe after the snowstorm

and later just simply fell off. And the thirst! My Spanish, I hope you will agree, is excellent, but I can find no words to describe the hopeless agony of marching through that waterless desert. And yet I am grateful for every step. To suffer in such a fashion without actually losing one's life—or one's nose!—is a transforming experience."

"And how are you transformed, Robert?"

"I am stronger," Talon said, with no levity in his voice. "I am aware, as never before, of being observed by God. I am conscious of His expectations of me."

He suddenly leaned forward in his chair and looked at Telesforo with a fierce light in his eyes.

"Perhaps I will be killed in the fight for this place, this Alamo. Perhaps I will not. I am supremely unconcerned. All that matters is my conduct. Valor, magnanimity, honor—these are no longer mere words to me, Telesforo. I hear them and I hear God's voice whispering in my ear."

Telesforo smiled indulgently. He leaned forward and poured more brandy into his friend's glass.

"It may be," he said, "that God has no plans for us to assault the Alamo."

"What do you mean? What have you heard?"

"Santa Anna's senior officers are divided. Some want to attack the place right away before any more reinforcements can arrive, like the group from Gonzales that managed to sneak through the other day. But others are of the opinion that time is our ally. We should not be in a hurry. We should wait for the twelve-pounders to be brought up and simply batter down the walls from a distance until the defenders try to flee out onto the prairie."

"I am with the former group," Robert said. "A decisive, conclusive engagement, after which this Colonel Travers—"

"Travis."

"After which this Colonel Travis will turn over his sword."

"He will not be alive to do so. There are to be no prisoners."

"Oh, I've heard that talk. But when the moment comes, the president will be generous. We are not barbarian Huns."

Robert said this with such conviction that it seemed the matter was set to rest, and Telesforo was silent for a moment as he envied his friend the ennobling suffering he had experienced on his journey to Texas.

"The two of us will advance toward the barricades side by side," Robert said dreamily. "And if I fall you will send the Legion of Honor to my sister in France. And if you fall—but you will not fall. You will go on to become one of the great men of your country."

Telesforo shook his head, expressing a private worry. "I am on Santa Anna's staff. He may not allow me to participate in the attack."

"Nonsense. He knows how hungry you are. He will not deny you your chance at greatness."

They talked on for another hour, and as they grew wearier the conversation became less pompous, until Robert was talking about the Mayan girls whose mats he had shared during his private expedition to Chiapas, and about the churches and cemeteries he had visited where the bright polished bones of dead villagers were lined up like trophies, and the skulls were inscribed with petitions from the deceased, begging the living to pray for them and deliver their souls from purgatorial fire.

"When will we have breakfast?" Robert said, suddenly interrupting his own travel narrative.

"We have a woman to cook for us. She should be here in an hour or so."

"And how is this woman's cooking?"

"Neither good enough to be memorable, nor bad enough for us to be redeemed through suffering."

Robert laughed, set down his glass, put his cold cigar in his mouth and pulled himself up from the chair, announcing that it was time for him to take a piss in the yard and contemplate anew the glories of God's creation.

Telesforo walked outside with him and unbuttoned his trousers and looked up at the sky as he urinated on the ground. Dawn was near but as yet there was no light to dispel the radiance of the stars. He felt the cold but the wind had abated, and in the stillness he could hear the barking of dogs and the sounds of soldiers in the distant trenches.

"I like this Texas," Robert said. "And this place particularly. The water in the river is wonderfully limpid, and in the summer when one was hot one could simply—"

The sudden sustained crackling of rifle fire to the north caused him to fall silent. Telesforo's immediate thought was that a Mexican patrol had encountered rebel pickets outside the walls of the Alamo, but the volume of the fire indicated that this was a significant engagement.

They buttoned up their trousers on the run and went into the store to pull on their boots and grab their weapons and cartridge pouches, then joined with other officers and men running down the center of Potrero Street toward the river and the sound of the gunfire.

A captain was standing at the foot of the bridge yelling for the men to cross and form a line of fire on the other side. Running across the bridge, Telesforo factored out what was happening. A large group of enemy horsemen was charging toward them in disorder from the north, harried by fire from Mexican sharpshooters on the far side of the river. The men inside the Alamo were firing sporadically from the walls, trying to protect the horsemen, but in the darkness and confusion Telesforo doubted that any of the riflemen were finding targets.

He and Talon joined a file of fusileros who were running toward the advancing horsemen. Most of the men seemed to be from the same company because they dropped to their knees in good order when they heard an officer call out a command in the darkness. They fired in volley at the riders, creating a tangle of screaming horses that could be seen only in fitful glimpses as the powder of individual weapons ignited and flashed within the confused mass of charging men with the brevity of fireflies.

The volley caused the advancing wave of men and horses to stumble and break and veer off to the right. Telesforo saw muzzle flashes from the tambour that guarded the Alamo gate, and felt the bullets whistling through the air around him. When he heard the riflemen in the tambour calling out to the confused men on horseback—"Here! Over here!"—he understood what was happening. This was not an attack, it was an attempt at a reinforcement. The riders had been discovered to the north of the Alamo as they tried to cross the Mexican lines and now they were desperately trying to cut their way through to the gate.

"The gate!" Telesforo called to the men around him. "Follow me!" Robert joined him and together they led a charge toward the tambour, trusting in the darkness to shield them a little. They met hurried, intense rifle fire that did little damage, but when the artillery piece on the southwest corner discharged in their direction a piece of canister took off the top half of a fusilero's head. The men all dived to the ground and clung there as more canister from one of the cannon in the tambour screamed over their heads.

A hundred yards in front of them, many of the men on horseback were leaping out of the saddle and running to the safety of the tambour, where their comrades pulled them over the low ramparts into the fort. But most of the reinforcements were caught between the flanking fire from Telesforo's position and that of the skirmishers on the far side of the river. Realizing that they could not get into the Alamo, they spurred their horses into a blind run around the south wall. Telesforo ran forward with his pistol. No one was shooting from the Alamo anymore because the escaping horsemen were now in the line of fire. He cocked the pistol and shot one of the riders as he went past. The ball struck the man in the thigh and he cursed and groaned but managed to keep himself in the saddle. Telesforo threw the empty pistol on the ground and reached for his sword, but before he could withdraw it another passing horseman struck him hard with a thick quirt in his wounded arm, and the shock of the blow on those confused nerves sent him to the ground gasping in agony. The pain was so thrilling it blunted his instinct, and he had to reason his body away from the sharp hooves of the horses as they passed.

When the horsemen had disappeared into the night the fire from the Alamo commenced again. Telesforo heard Robert Talon calling his name as he and the fusileros retreated, but it was a long moment before he could gain control of the pain and answer that he was all right.

INSIDE THE ALAMO there were competing currents of hope and confusion. The exhausted defenders greeted the new arrivals with handshakes and outright embraces, but the men who had managed to cut their way into the fort were shaken by the experience and worried about the friends who had not been able to gain entry and who were now surely being pursued by Mexican cavalry.

A few of the men were wounded, though not gravely. Most were missing their horses. The reinforcements and defenders were gathered in the south end of the plaza, and as Mary pushed through the crowd looking for Terrell, she saw a man sitting on the dirt pouring blood out of his shoe.

"Have you been shot?" she asked him.

"Yes, ma'am," he said with a strange grin. "I believe I have lost a quantity of toes."

"Come with me to the hospital." As she bent down to the wounded man Edmund appeared from out of the darkness and helped her pull him up. She looked at him but did not speak.

On the way to the hospital the man—he said his name was Frazier, one of Chenoweth's Invincibles—told them what had happened. They had left the Cibolo with more than a hundred and fifty men and ridden all night, skirting around the powder house and the enemy trenches and entering Béxar from the north. Three hundred or four hundred yards out they were surprised by a Mexican patrol and made a run for the Alamo, but they were soon cut off by rifle and musket fire, and every man had to decide for himself whether to escape or try to make it into the fort. Frazier himself had determined he would run off and try his luck another day when his horse was shot and he had to sprint for the gate.

"That was when some lucky pepper-belly shot me," he said, as Mary and Edmund settled him onto a vacant cot. Dr. Pollard rushed over and unrolled his bloody sock. One toe was hanging by a piece of skin and another was missing. Pollard discovered it in the sock.

"Well, hold it up and let me see it," Frazier said.

Pollard did as he was asked.

The wounded man stared at it for a long time, sucking in his breath to cope with the pain.

"It looks smaller when it ain't on your foot, don't it?" he finally said.

"Was Terrell Mott with your group?" Mary asked him anxiously.

"I didn't know everyone by name, ma'am."

"What about David Crockett?"

"He came and got us and led us to Béxar, but I don't know if he got into the fort or not. He could be lying out there dead for all I know about the matter."

Crockett was not dead, though when Mary and Edmund finally located him at the palisade between the chapel and the gatehouse he was so exhausted and bleary he could hardly stand. He had already made his report to Travis and was standing around with Baugh and some of the other officers as he gnawed on a stringy piece of beef that someone had brought him. The sun was coming up behind the chapel, and light beamed down on the ground from the empty windows.

"Ah, there you are, Mrs. Mott," he said when he saw Mary. "Your son is well, I think. I sent him on to Goliad with a dispatch to Fannin, and from there he will most likely proceed to Gonzales."

Hearing these words, Mary almost fainted with relief. Her son was safe and the new day was coming and Edmund was standing beside her. She had to remind herself that it was impossible to be happy in this horrible place. She nodded her gratitude to Crockett, and he smiled at her and resumed recounting for Baugh and the others his adventures of the previous night. His bluff humor was frayed and he spoke in a plain voice, now and then pausing to take a bite of his rude breakfast. His best guess was that somewhere between fifty-five and sixty men had gotten into the Alamo with him, which meant that a hundred others had not. Crockett was of the opinion that most of these men were now headed back to the Cibolo, to join up with the group Williamson was raising in Gonzales. Perhaps Fannin's men would join them after all.

"I'd say there's a chance another four hundred men will try to fight their way through to us in the next few days," Crockett said.

"But for now," Baugh calculated, "we've only got two hundred and thirty effectives. And Santa Anna has three thousand at least."

Crockett smiled, a familiar smile that they had all come to learn was a preliminary to a witty remark. But this time no such remark occurred to him, and he merely shook his head and announced that he was going to sleep.

But before he could start out for the barracks they heard the voice of the howitzers in town, and he and Mary and Edmund and the rest of the men who had been standing out in the open by the palisade rushed into the church just as

two shells burst in the air. They made their way to the safety
of the sacristy. Captain Dickinson was already there, along
with some of his gunners, and he was doing his best to
comfort his screaming infant and sobbing wife. A young
woman named Ana Esparza, whose husband was one of
the Tejano defenders, hunkered in a corner with her three
small children, all of them crying hysterically. A twelve-
year-old boy, the son of a defender named Wolfe, sat alone
against the wall with his arm draped across the shoulder of
his younger brother. Neither of them made a sound, but
Mary noticed that they were both trembling in terror, and
when she sat down next to them and opened her arms both
boys clung to her without embarrassment. She in turn took
Edmund's hand in the dark room as if it were an accustomed thing for her to do so, and with each concussion their
bodies squeezed closer together.

The shells continued to fall as the morning deepened,
and each came so quickly upon the last that there were no
intervals in which a human voice could be heard. Finally
the rain of exploding shells died away, but almost immediately the new Mexican battery to the north opened up, and
instead of indiscriminate grenades they heard relentless,
concentrated artillery fire whose obvious goal was to
pound a breach in the fragile north wall.

The sound of cannonballs repeatedly striking the wall a
hundred yards away was ominous, but it did not excite the
deep terror of the grenades, and gradually the shrieking of
the Dickinson baby subsided, and the older Wolfe boy
stopped quaking and pulled away from Mary and led his
younger brother to the opposite end of the room, where
Señora Losoya was handing out horehound drops to the
children.

Crockett and Dickinson and the rest of the men who had
sought shelter in the room stood up and left. Edmund and
Mary stayed where they were for just a moment longer. She

did not let go of his hand and she could feel the pressure of his grip in response.

"They are going to attack soon," she whispered.

"Yes. They cannot allow another reinforcement. It will come at night, I think, though of course I am the furthest thing from a military strategist."

"It was I who led you here, Edmund. I am sorry."

He squeezed her hand.

"You could go over the wall tonight," she said. "Your Spanish is flawless. You could talk your way past the Mexican pickets, and then if you could get a horse you could—"

"I think I shall not, Mary," he said. "It would be a poor thing to do, not to stay here and lend a hand in the fight."

"It is not your cause."

"It might as well be now, as my own cause is dead."

He was staring down at his shoes. They were caked with dried mud, and the ends of his trousers were frayed. A shaft of sunlight from the window in the center of the room illuminated a paper wrapper for Ward's Anodyne Pearls, which Mary had seen Mrs. Dickinson using on her teething infant.

"I must go back to my position now," Edmund said. "I will try to come back and speak to you again."

"Before we are attacked, do you mean? And what will you say, Edmund? What will you say then? Is it something you cannot say to me now?"

But she herself could not imagine the precise words she wanted to hear from him, and knew it was unfair of her to be disappointed when he fell into one of his flustered, searching silences. But when he finally spoke, it surprised her.

"If it were possible for me to exchange the life I have lived for another, I think I would do so. And in that life I would want you as my companion."

He did not look at her as he said these words, and they were spoken so softly they felt to her less like a verbal declaration than a secret thought transmitted directly from his mind to hers. Another cannonball struck the distant north wall, and the thick wall of the church upon which they were leaning shuddered in response.

"You must remain in here with the other women and children during the fight," he said to her. "You must promise me not to leave. Tell the first Mexican officer that you see that it is a matter of vital importance that you speak to Colonel Almonte. He is an acquaintance of mine, and I think he will do his best to help you."

He was pulling himself to his feet when she grabbed him by the back of the neck and kissed him hard on the mouth. His lips remained rigid, he was surprised, he did not know how to respond. She thought it likely, she thought it certain, that this was the first such kiss he had ever received. And when she watched him walk out of the room into the sunlight she felt how bitter, how cruel a thing it was she had done, to confront him suddenly with what he had never known, and to taunt them both with what could never now come to pass.

THAT AFTERNOON in his headquarters on the plaza Santa Anna called his senior officers together and served them coffee and round fluted cakes and directed their attention to the maps spread out on a long refectory table. That morning, after two hours' sleep, Telesforo had hurriedly completed several new renderings of the Alamo and the terrain surrounding it, taking care to incorporate the burned-out outbuildings and any shifts in artillery placement within the fortress.

"I have taken the liberty," Telesforo said to Santa Anna as he and his generals peered at the map, "of including the parapet that is now under construction to the north. Teniente Talon, who is in charge of that particular series of entrenchments, assures me that by the end of the day they will have reached the position indicated on the map."

"Excellent. Thank you, Villasenor. Am I not fortunate, gentlemen, to have a mapmaker who can see into the future?"

He favored Telesforo with a comradely grin. "Now, Teniente, is it possible that you can also see through walls? Because I would very much like to know what sort of defenses the rebels have erected within these buildings."

"All I can offer is a guess, Your Excellency. I have of course interviewed the corporal from the Matamoros battalion who was briefly held prisoner within the mission, but he saw the interior of only one room, whose walls he said were heavily reinforced with dirt. My expectation is that the defenders plan on making their final stand here, within the barracks. That is the strongest building in the fort, and they have surely built defensive works inside it, and perhaps there is artillery concealed there as well."

Santa Anna listened to this theory in silence. Telesforo, sensing that His Excellency's mind had already veered to another concern, stepped back from the table and stood inconspicuously against the wall.

Santa Anna stared down meditatively at the map, then turned to his assembled officers. "Gentlemen, I am inclined to attack as soon as possible. Please let me know your opinions."

Generals Cos and Castrillón, along with Colonels Romero and Orisnuela, immediately took up the contrary position. It was crucial to wait, they argued, until the two twelve-pound siege cannon now with General Gaona could be brought up and positioned—say, within three days. With the twelve-pounders the weak north wall could be opened in short order. Without a substantial breach, the men would have to scale the walls and casualties would be high.

Telesforo was surprised when Colonel Almonte, the least sanguinary of the senior officers, joined with General Sesma and several others in urging for an immediate assault. It was clear from the morning's reinforcement attempt, they argued, that other rebels were in the vicinity, and if they did not secure the Alamo immediately they might find the tables turned and themselves under siege.

Telesforo listened as the officers pressed their arguments with mounting conviction, until the conversation grew so heated that Santa Anna had to raise his hand and beg for the men to lower their voices and speak in turn.

"Thank you all for your excellent opinions," he said when the last argument had been voiced. "We will meet again tomorrow at midday, at which time I will inform you of the timing of the assault and the general plan of battle."

As the officers filed out, Telesforo stepped forward to retrieve his maps. Santa Anna remained standing in the center of his room, using his thumb to dab up crumbs of cake from his plate.

"And what do you think, Villasenor?" he said as Telesforo was folding the maps into his pouch.

"About what, Your Excellency?"

"The strategic matter at hand."

"I would favor an immediate attack, sir."

"At the risk of far greater casualties?"

"We are in a hostile country, far from our line of supply. If we do not press forward at every opportunity we may find ourselves in a situation we do not control, and in such a case no one could predict the cost."

"Put out the maps again," Santa Anna said.

Telesforo did as instructed. The president peered down at the maps for a moment without saying anything. He held his coffee cup in the air, and a steward promptly arrived to fill it.

"Coffee, Teniente?" Santa Anna said absently, gesturing toward the steward.

"No, thank you, sir."

"Just as well," Santa Anna said, taking a sip and setting down the cup on the table next to the map. "It is tepid. Here is what I am thinking: one column starting here, to the northwest. One originating from our new entrenchments to the north and the third sweeping in from the northeast. A fourth column will come from the south. What should its objective be? This palisade between the church and the gatehouse?"

"In my opinion, no," Telesforo said, though his confident voice sounded like it belonged to someone else. He was dumbfounded that Antonio López de Santa Anna had chosen to solicit his opinion on a matter of such supreme consequence. "The nortes consider it their weakest point and it will be heavily defended, and this bramble out in front could become a death trap. I think the chances for breaking into the fort are better here, at the west side of the southwest corner."

"A sound enough argument," Santa Anna said. "In any case the real action will be to the north. That wall must be overrun quickly, before the pirates have a chance to spike their cannon. As an engineer, you will appreciate that the crucial weapons in this battle will not be the musket or the bayonet but the climbing ladder and the crowbar."

Santa Anna smiled and took a chair and set the heels of his boots on the table. The leather gleamed like ebony, and his trousers were hypnotically white. The manicured fingernails of his left hand drummed upon the summit of his knee.

"And now," he said, looking up at Telesforo with a sly expression, "you are going to request that you be released from my staff so that you may join your unit in time for the attack."

"If I could be of service, I would of course happily—"

Santa Anna laughed. "Do not try to hide your ambition from me, Villasenor. You have done a poor job of doing so until now, and in any case the concealment of ambition is a virtue of no interest to me. You are welcome to take part in the assault, though the Zapadores will be held in reserve and will attack only when I personally give the order."

"Of course."

"I do not want my most valued troops cut apart by norte artillery. I prefer that you survive this battle, Teniente, so that I can personally award you the Legion of Honor when the war is over."

"To have Your Excellency's trust is of far more worth to me than—"

"Please do not prattle on in this obsequious way. I pulled you from obscurity not because of your talents at flattery, and not just because of your skills as a mapmaker, but because there is a fire burning in you. Another general might have been suspicious of such a fire in such a man, but not me. I welcome your ambition, I understand it, I will cultivate it. And in return I expect a high degree of loyalty, not just on the battlefield but in the halls of the National Palace, where I have no doubt that you will someday find a berth."

"Thank you," Telesforo managed to reply, his head vacant and buzzing.

"You are welcome, my friend," Santa Anna said, and then turned to rebuke the steward for the lukewarm coffee.

CHAPTER THIRTY-ONE

✯

TERRELL DID NOT know how far he was from the Goliad road before the lancers intercepted him, and he did not know how far he had ridden across open country in the desperate chase that followed. He knew he was still north of the San Antonio River, west of Cibolo Creek, and that in all likelihood this stretch of country was heavily patrolled by Mexican troops from General Urrea's column, which was said to be advancing upon Goliad.

He had spent the night shivering with pain and cold at the base of the trees where he had come to rest, and during the course of the day he thought it prudent not to venture out of the hardwood forest onto the prairie where he would be visible to any passing horseman. It was now late afternoon, and he thought he would try to walk somewhere tonight if he could find the strength and the endurance to do so.

The letter that Crockett had given him for Fannin was in his haversack, but he thought it a bad idea to continue on to Goliad. The farther south he went the more likely he was to encounter Urrea's men, and the greater the probability he would be captured and shot. Perhaps Goliad was sixty miles away, probably more. In his tremulous state, travelling only at night to avoid detection, it might take him a week to cover that distance. Better to retrace his steps, find the Cibolo, work his way surreptitiously back to the crossing, and hope to meet up with Williamson's Gonzales group or any other reinforcements that might still be converging there.

But retracing his steps would not be a simple task. He was weak and hurt, and his mind was deeply clouded. He knew he had to go east to find the creek, but he did not know how far east he must travel, and was not sure that in his distress and confusion he could reckon out the cardinal directions from the malevolent swarm of stars in the black sky.

He needed sleep above all things, and yet sleep was unthinkable. The pain in his shattered arm and hand was too great to allow it. He had never known a pain that did not at some point subside but instead kept rising and deepening. The pain had kept him awake all night, and all during this long day in the woods. There had been times when he thought he might have been asleep, but if sleep had indeed come it had brought no relief. He tried once again before sunset, making himself as comfortable as possible in the little declivity he had found between the trees, supporting his arm upon his haversack so that the blood would not sluice downward through his broken bones. Tortured images came to him—bright, vivid, flying by too swiftly for his mind to secure them—and when they were gone there was perhaps a moment of suspended awareness until the pain woke him like a panther's shriek.

It was still daylight. Dusk had not yet fallen. He looked at his right hand and arm. Three of the fingers were swollen to twice their ordinary size, and the taut skin that covered them had bruised to a deep greenish-black. There was a large bruise as well on the back of his forearm, and a scimitar gouge below the knob of his wrist where Veronica's flailing hoof had cut him. His forearm was bent at an angle—not wildly so, but enough to confirm that it was not just his fingers that were broken but his arm as well.

The bones should be set, he knew, otherwise they would knit together in their broken configuration. He had no idea how he might set the bones in the fingers, but his arm was another matter. He had heard of men in such situations as he now found himself placing their hand or foot in the crook of a tree and pulling until the bones in the injured limb realigned themselves.

He found such a crook only a few paces from his hiding place, low enough so that he could sit on the ground while he attempted the procedure. He cradled the heel of his hand in the fork of the two limbs and then tried to pull his arm back without thinking further about it, but the slightest tug brought him such tremendous pain that he immediately removed his hand and clutched it to his chest and sat on the ground crying and trembling.

After a while he worked up the courage to try again, and if it had only been a matter of courage he thought maybe he could have accomplished it. But it seemed to him, after a second and then a third try, that the thing was impossible, that a human being could no more willingly inflict such agony upon himself than he could breathe under the water or leap above the treetops. And yet Edna Foley had done it to herself, had stabbed her own body with a knife again and again. Perhaps one had to be mad, and in some important way unaware and uncaring. Perhaps he himself would be mad soon, but for now he lay curled up on the ground, squeezing his arm to his chest in a vain attempt to quell the violent surges of pain.

Terrell lay there for another hour before he found the resolve to rise to his knees and to fashion the haversack into a sling that kept his broken arm more or less secure against his body. He had had nothing to eat for many hours now, and when he set out walking he was so hollow and weak that he had to stop three times before he reached the margins of the forest. It was almost dark by then, the temperature plummeting, the forest suddenly alive with the crepuscular meanderings of birds and animals. A family of deer moved ahead of him with stately indifference. A possum waddled across his path, rustling the leafy floor. He saw a fox as well, though it melted so swiftly out of his sight it might as well have been another of the taunting dream images that crowded into his mind whenever he attempted to sleep.

He had lost both pistol and rifle—his father's cherished rifle!—and had no weapon with which to kill game even if he possessed the strength and persistence of mind to attempt it. All he could do was walk, and with each step the blood pounded fiercely in his arm.

By unconscious dead reckoning, he emerged from the forest at almost the same place he had entered it, and there he saw Veronica's body with a crowd of buzzards perched upon it. He waved angrily at them with his good arm, and they scattered a few feet away before returning. It was a gesture on his part; he could do no more. The lancers had taken the wonderful quadralpas saddle and the bridle as well, so that all that was left was her gaseous, swollen form.

Terrell walked past her and out onto the dark prairie, crying like an infant at the loss of his horse, though less from grief than from the awesome loneliness that now consumed him. He walked all night in a direction he thought was east, though several times he found himself sitting on the ground with no memory of having stopped, and when he continued walking he found it difficult to hold a deliberate thought in his head, much less a coherent bearing. By morning he had not yet found the creek. If it had not been for the rhythmic sounds far, far to the west—the sounds of the Mexican guns battering the Alamo—he would have been utterly lost.

WITHIN THE ALAMO, the defenders were enduring the most sustained shelling since the siege began. The artillery to the north fired round after round day and night, steadily shattering the outer wall and leaving gaping holes and collapsed roofs in several of the buildings within the compound. Cattle and horses lay dead in the corrals, killed by the grenade fragments or in one case by a broadside strike by a nine-pound ball.

The Texians stayed inside, though some men were always needed on the walls to watch for enemy movements, and they protected themselves as best they could behind crudely fashioned bunkers and sandbags and scraps of wood. No one slept. Sleep was a distant fantasy. Early in the morning of March 5 a man who had come in with Crockett's reinforcement had been crossing the courtyard on his way to the sinks when a bouncing cannonball had taken off his leg at the knee. As of late afternoon, this man, so far as Joe knew, was the Alamo's only real casualty.

"Dr. Pollard expects him to recover wonderfully," Travis said late that afternoon when Crockett braved the barrage to stop by the headquarters. "His name is Petrasweiz, or something equally unpronounceable. He was one of the men you brought into the fort last night."

"I don't recall meeting him," Crockett said, "but I'll try to stop by the hospital and say a kind word to the poor bastard. Now let me ask you this, Colonel Travis. What are we going to do?"

Travis was cleaning his shotgun. He looked up at Crockett and Joe saw a flash of irritation in his eyes.

"When the attack comes we will do our best to repulse it. If our best efforts fail we will retreat to our secondary positions within the barracks and hold out as best we can until Williamson and Fannin arrive."

"I don't know about Williamson," Crockett said. "He might come through like he promised. But Fannin's already turned back once, and he's got an army in his rear and it seems to me that him coming to help us is about as likely as a lizard falling in love with a mouse. I say we get out of here tonight."

Travis worked a pick into the vent of his weapon, then wiped the tool on a rag. The room shook with the impact of another shell somewhere in the fort, but Travis and Crockett took it in stride, and Joe did too, as if they were all on a long sea voyage and the strike of a cannonball was of no more consequence than the slap of a wave against the hull.

"I do not like our position any better than you do, Mr. Crockett," Travis said at last, "but I like even less the thought of running away from it, particularly when we are tightly encircled not just by thousands of foot soldiers but by hundreds of lancers as well."

"Some of us would get through."

"Some of us, undoubtedly. But I still think the best chance for us all is to stay with the fort."

Travis's voice was firm and his look steady. Joe could see Crockett trying to decide whether to press the commander further, and he found himself oddly relieved when Crockett let the issue drop. Joe knew they were trapped, he knew that a Mexican assault could come at any moment, but the thought of abandoning the fort was too bold for him. He took some comfort in the paralysis of the moment. He did not want to force events to a swifter resolution than fate intended. And if they all ran out of the Alamo in the darkness, the Mexicans might not see that he was a negro, and would shoot him down with all the rest.

Travis and Crockett continued to talk: about Bowie's steadily deteriorating health—he could not possibly live longer than a few more days, Crockett believed, certainly not under these conditions; about the state of the trench works inside the buildings and the shattered nerves of some of the pickets; about whether to expect an attack in daylight or in darkness; and whether Travis should address the garrison and tell them plainly that the hour of crisis was near.

"The firing stopped," Joe said as Crockett and Travis were each deliberating this last question with such prolonged silence that he thought they had fallen asleep.

"It has indeed," Travis said, already on his way to the door. Joe followed him and Crockett to the ramp leading up to the southwest battery. Other defenders were by this time pouring out of their hiding places and taking their places on the wall, expecting that this sudden artillery silence foretold a Mexican attack. But no troops were on the move—only a solitary horseman crossing the Potrero Street bridge under a white flag.

Travis sent Colonel Jameson out to parley. But there was no parley. The officer simply handed Jameson a sealed letter on crisp white paper, and Jameson brought it back into the Alamo. Travis leaned back against the wooden truck of the cannon and broke the seal of the letter as every man in the vicinity watched with speechless absorption. In the distance, the rider with the white flag was galloping back toward the bridge. Beyond him, in the center of the town, the red banner was still flying from the summit of the church.

It took Travis an intolerably long time to read the letter, and when he was finally through he folded it back neatly along its original lines and turned to Joe.

"Joe," he said, "find Mr. McGowan, give him my compliments, and ask him to visit me immediately in my quarters."

EDMUND READ the letter under Travis's suspicious gaze. It was from Almonte. Angel Navarro, the former alcalde of San Antonio de Béxar and a steadfast champion of Santa Anna's cause in Texas, wished for his two daughters and his infant grandson to leave the Alamo. Would Colonel Travis please honor this devoted father's wishes and send the two women out this evening beneath a flag of truce? General Santa Anna would also be pleased at the opportunity to confer with Señora Edmund McGowan, an employee of the

Republic of Mexico who was believed to be presently in the fort.

"Why do you suppose he wants to see you?" Travis asked Edmund.

"I don't know. As I told you before, we are somewhat acquainted, and Colonel Almonte and I were on friendly terms during my stay in the City of Mexico last year."

"Maybe he's asking you over for a game of whist," Crockett said, with no particular levity in his voice.

"I will go or stay," Edmund said to Travis, "depending on your wishes in the matter."

"It is necessary for me to ask you once again, Mr. McGowan. Are you a spy?"

"No, I am not. But I have not concealed from you the complexity of my situation in regard to this war, and leave it to you to decide whether to trust me or not."

"If I send you out, will you betray our position?"

"No."

Travis lapsed into a tight-lipped deliberation with himself. The Mexican guns were still not firing, and Joe was amazed to find the stillness eerie and unwelcome.

"The truth of the matter is," Crockett said after a time, smiling companionably at Edmund, "we ain't got much of a position to betray."

Travis went over to his desk, dipped his pen in the inkwell, and began writing in his lawyer's bold hand on the back of the letter he had just received. He paused several times to contemplate what to write next, and during his unhurried composition nobody spoke a word.

"You are to deliver this letter to Santa Anna himself," he said at last, handing the letter to Edmund, "or if that proves to be not possible, to your friend Almonte. It is an offer to surrender the Alamo and all its arms and artillery on the sole condition that the garrison is spared. It is a bitter document to have written. I pray that Texas will not reproach me for it."

Edmund was touched by the stricken look on Travis's face. He would not have been surprised to see the young commander explode in tears.

"You have been splendidly defiant, Colonel," he found himself saying. "You have been heroic."

"Thank you, Mr. McGowan. And now heroism must give way to humility. Bring me an answer to my proposal if you can. Or send it by a Mexican officer. You are released from this post. It is not necessary for you to return."

THE NAVARRO SISTERS were not anxious to see their father. They were not on close terms with him, having been raised in the household of his brother-in-law, Juan Vera-mendi, and deeply formed by his liberal ideals and by the company of James Bowie, who had married their beloved cousin Ursula. Juana Navarro herself, the alcalde's older daughter, had incited her father's anger by choosing Dr. Alsbury, a prominent norte rebel, as her husband.

"Gertrudis and I have agreed," Juana Alsbury said to Edmund in Spanish when he went to collect her in front of the church, "that I alone will talk to my father. It would be wrong for both of us to abandon Señor Bowie. And I will insist on coming back into the fort."

"You should both take this opportunity to leave for good," he told her. "The two of you and your baby. There is unlikely to be a happy conclusion."

"I believe that my husband at this moment is riding to the relief of the Alamo," she countered, "and I will be here to welcome him when he arrives."

She handed her baby to Gertrudis and asked Edmund to wait a moment while she spoke to Bowie. Edmund watched through the splintered door of Bowie's room as she lit a candle by the stricken man's bedside and bent down to speak to him. Bowie's eyes were as big as a bird's in his pale, wasted face, and no part of his body was moving except for his lips, as he replied to some tearful words that Juana was whispering in his ear. After a moment Edmund looked away, disquieted and embarrassed, and saw Mary standing in front of the barracks building, watching him.

She and Dr. Pollard were supporting one of the patients from the hospital, whom they had brought out into the fresh air when the Mexican guns stopped firing. When he saw her, Edmund began to walk across the courtyard in her direction, and she left the patient in the charge of Dr. Pollard and met him halfway along the low wall that ran in front of the churchyard.

"I am leaving the fort for a while," he told her, keeping his voice low so that none of the men standing nearby could hear his words.

"Where are you going?" she asked in a voice choked with alarm.

"Into the town. Santa Anna wants to see me. I don't know why, but I believe the meeting was set up through the agency of Colonel Almonte and might be a good thing."

She did not respond at once, and he could sense her anxiously turning this prospect over in her mind. Her teeth chattered in the cold, and she drew her arms tight about her body and looked up into his eyes.

"Will you come back to me?"

"I will, Mary," he said, and turned and walked back to Bowie's room, where Juana Alsbury was standing now with Travis and Crockett and some of the other officers. Travis handed him a broomstick with a grimy square of white linen tied to it.

"I pray that you will have secured an answer in a few short hours," Travis said to him. "Be sure to tell whoever brings the reply to make sure the flag is visible as he approaches—to use a torch if necessary to illuminate himself. I would not want such an important emissary to be shot by our pickets by mistake."

"Are you taking that dog with you?" Crockett said, gesturing toward Professor, who sat now at Edmund's heels with a willful look on his face.

Edmund told Professor to stay, and the dog looked away as if wounded, but did not follow as his master and Señora Alsbury walked through the gate and out through the tambour in front and past the blackened remains of the houses that had been burned in the first few days of the siege.

It felt strange to be outside the walls after so long and intense a time within. Edmund and Señora Alsbury walked on together without speaking. He held the white flag high, feeling acutely vulnerable. The light was fading, but he could see Mexican soldiers peering at them from behind their parapets in the Alameda, and over by the river an officer was standing on the near end of the bridge in a casual pose, the wind ruffling the plumage of his hat.

The officer was Almonte. "Good evening, Edmund," he said, reaching out his hand in friendship. "And Señora Alsbury—are you quite warm enough in that rebozo? I am afraid the temperature might fall considerably tonight. Please, step into the carriage and I will convey you into the town."

They climbed up into the hack with Almonte and set off at a spirited pace down Potrero Street into the heart of Béxar. Edmund and Señora Alsbury were both in a wary frame of mind and Almonte was considerate enough not to pester them with unwelcome small talk in so grave a moment. He merely joined with them in contemplating the empty streets and the setting sun that sent flaming streaks of light across the still blue sky.

"Your father is waiting inside, señora," Almonte said to Juana Alsbury as they pulled to a stop at a house near the main plaza. He leapt out of the conveyance and put out a hand to help her down. "When you and he have finished your discussion he will know to send for me. Edmund, you and I will drive a few blocks more."

Señora Alsbury disappeared into the house without a look back at either of them, and when Almonte stepped back into the carriage he spoke to Edmund with as casual a voice as the circumstances would permit.

"I thought there were two Navarro sisters in the Alamo. And a baby as well."

"There are, but only one would come. It seems that neither sister is politically aligned with her father, nor emotionally as well."

"Yes," Almonte said sadly. "This Texas country is deeply riven, families and friends falling out everywhere one looks. I suppose that in itself makes the case that it is indisputably a part of Mexico."

"Did you get my letter?"

"Yes. But we will speak of it later. Are you hungry, Edmund?"

"There is no shortage of food in the fort."

"The question was not meant to trick you into providing information. If I wanted to know if the garrison was starving, I would have asked you directly. I only meant that I could have something prepared for you—something besides beef and tortillas."

"That is thoughtful, but no thank you."

The carriage stopped at a substantial house across the plaza from the church. The red banner on the bell tower rippled in the wind, and was made even bloodier by the brilliant sunset behind it. Almonte noticed Edmund looking at it as they stepped down onto the packed earth of the plaza.

"I am sure it seems as unimaginable to you as it does to me," Almonte said, "that less than a year after our pleasant little dinner with Stephen Austin in the City of Mexico we would find ourselves in this remote spot facing each other from the ramparts."

"No one could wish more fervently than I for a happier outcome," Edmund said.

"And now my friend Austin, the most patient and judicious man Mexico could have hoped for, is our bitterest enemy. Off raising money in the States to try to finance this preposterous war. His health is no better, I hear; in fact, considerably worse."

"Mexico destroyed his health, to her shame," Edmund heard himself saying.

The house was heavily guarded, and as Almonte led Edmund to the door four or five officers in splendid uniforms and sober expressions departed in advance of them, staring at Edmund with no more embarrassment than if he were an animal on display in a zoological park. He was suddenly conscious of his unshaven face, his ragged, borrowed clothing, and the powerful smell that must surely emanate from his long-unwashed body.

"Are we to meet Santa Anna here?" he asked Almonte.

"Yes. He is inside."

"I would prefer not to present myself in such a dishevelled state."

"I understand, Edmund, but the general has fought in many campaigns and will not be shocked."

Almonte opened the door, taking off his hat as he did so, and then beckoned Edmund to follow. Santa Anna was sitting at a desk, dictating something to a civilian secretary. The president was as long-limbed and elegant as he was when Edmund had seen him in his palace, but this time his eyes were hostile when Edmund entered the room, and he did not leap up to pump his guest's hand.

"Señor McGowan," he said simply, and then turned his eyes to the document his secretary handed him, taking time to read it carefully before bending forward to sign it with a silver pen.

"I trust you had a rewarding journey to Yucatán," he said coldly as he handed the document back to his secretary, who immediately disappeared into a back room. There was only one other man in the room, a lieutenant who stood at attention against the wall, holding a leather case in his hand.

"I sent you a report immediately after my return," Edmund replied, conscious of putting the same level distance into his voice.

"Oh? I am not aware of receiving it. But as you know, the events of the last few months have claimed most of my attention. But as long as you are here, perhaps you can tell me straight out: do your investigations lend support to the idea of a chewing gum industry?"

"I am skeptical of cultivation, Your Excellency. However, the trees exist in great numbers, and sufficient resin could probably be harvested in the wild, given a steady supply of labor and a speedy system of distribution."

"Yes," said Santa Anna in a cold, musing tone, utterly unlike the wild enthusiasm that had sent Edmund on the improbable expedition in the first place. "And did you kill my friend Don Osbaldo Espinosa?"

"I did, in the defense of myself and a woman. Neither of us had taken up arms against Mexico nor planned to do so. Espinosa unlawfully made us his prisoners, and I took his life only as he was acting to take ours."

"Unfortunately, he is not alive to verify your version of the event. And since he was loyal to me and you are plainly not, I am inclined to execute you."

"I am here under a flag of truce," Edmund responded in an angry, steady tone. He and the president-general continued to stare at one another for a strangely long time, and then Edmund broke the silence by reaching into his coat and producing the letter that Travis had given him.

"I have a letter from Colonel Travis, the commander of the forces in the Alamo."

"You may give it to Colonel Almonte."

Edmund handed the letter to Almonte, who read it in silence as Santa Anna waited with a feral stillness, his eyes still on Edmund.

"He is willing to surrender," Almonte reported, "on the sole condition that the lives of the men in the Alamo be spared. In return they will give up their—"

"How many times must I say this!" Santa Anna erupted. He turned to Edmund. "Why cannot these friends of yours understand me? There will be no conditions! This Travis may surrender if he likes, but I will not listen to his arrogant, whining pleas for his life. The red flag flying from the church is my answer. It has been there since the day I entered Béxar—could there be a plainer statement of my intent? If your commander was a true soldier, not a quivering, vacillating amateur, he would understand his position plainly and not demean himself by asking for a mercy I am in no mood to dispense."

Edmund watched as Santa Anna crumpled up the letter and tossed it into the hearth, where it rested on the edge of the coals for a moment before bursting into a quiet flame.

"Mercy need have little to do with it," Edmund ventured. "It strikes me as a matter of supreme practical sense. Why attack the Alamo when it is not necessary to do so? When the cost to your men would be so grievous?"

"My men are soldiers, Señor McGowan. They understand the risk of death, they are pleased to accept it, and I am fortunate to have their complete trust when I deem it necessary to order them into battle. Now let us stop talking about this craven surrender and turn our attention to a more vital concern."

Santa Anna shifted his eyes to the lieutenant with the map case and beckoned him forward.

"This is Teniente Villasenor," Santa Anna said as the man began to spread a map upon the table, "an officer in the engineer battalion. He has prepared some extremely detailed maps of your fortifications. The teniente is very skilled at this work, as you can see, but since he has never been inside the walls there are things he cannot know. I would like you to consult with him about the defensive works within the buildings, any tunnels or passageways connecting the structures, significant damage by our artillery that may not be visible to us—that sort of thing. In addition, I want to know more particularly about the present strength and morale of the garrison and the likelihood of more reinforcements. I do not like committing my men to action without a clear sense of the hazards that await them."

The lieutenant took a pencil out of the map case with an awkward crossover movement of his left arm—his right arm hung limp and useless at his side. There was a polite, expectant look on his face as he waited to amend the map to Edmund's specifications.

Edmund glanced at Almonte, who was deliberately looking down at the map. Santa Anna, by contrast, bore into Edmund with his raptor's eyes.

"I will not do this," Edmund said to him.

There was almost no reaction. Santa Anna's temper did not flare as Edmund anticipated; rather, his sallow face took on a mild look of disappointment and he looked away and spoke to Edmund as if from a distance.

"When we met in Mexico," he said, "when I gave you the assignment to go to Yucatán and along with it the promise to restore your commission, it was my expectation that you would be grateful and would regard me as a friend to you."

"That was my expectation as well, and I wish that events had borne it out. But I recall that I told you at the time that I would not be your spy."

Santa Anna stood for the first time since Edmund entered the room. He leaned back against the wall, like a lounging gentleman at the opera, pondering something. Then he turned to Almonte.

"Colonel," he said, "where is the building we are using as a warehouse?"

"Across the plaza, Your Excellency."

"Let us accompany Señor McGowan there. Villasenor, you will please wait here until we return."

Santa Anna took down his hat from the wall—not the imperial chapeau bras, but a battered straw—and strode out into the night, with Almonte and Edmund following in his train. Guards fell in and kept pace with them as they walked across the plaza to a doorway secured by a heavy lock. Santa Anna waited patiently, without speaking, as one of the guards produced a key and unlocked the door, and preceded them inside, carrying a lamp.

"After you, my friend," Santa Anna said to Edmund.

Edmund entered the building. It was familiar to him from his residency in Béxar, an old printing office that had been abandoned for newer quarters several years ago. Along one wall were stockpiled desks and chairs and other odds and ends of furniture, all of it draped in cobwebs. The rest of the front room was filled with cabinets, and with crates and bundles of papers of one sort or another, stacked almost to the ceiling, and ranked outward from the walls so that there was only a narrow corridor left for Edmund and the others to pass through.

"These are the archives of Béxar. Land grants, marriage certificates, court proceedings and the like. When my brother-in-law, General Cos, found himself besieged in Béxar by your pirate army, he immediately set about gathering the valuable papers of the town together into one secure room, so that the history of this place would not be scattered to the winds or casually burned by the insensitive enemy. Colonel Almonte?"

Almonte took the lamp from the guard's hand and led the group through the front room into another space, which was likewise crammed with documents.

"An officer of the local presidial cavalry," Almonte said to Edmund, "someone you know—Gutiérrez, I believe is his name—brought another collection to Cos's attention.

He was concerned that it was of considerable value and should be moved along with the Béxar archives so that they would not be destroyed in a rebel attack. These are the items to which he referred, and which are now in the safekeeping of the Mexican army."

Almonte walked to the opposite side of the room and shone his light on a mound covered by a canvas tarp. When he removed the tarp, Edmund recognized the raw material of his *Flora Texana*—stack upon stack of dried specimens, volume upon volume of drawings and notes in leather-bound notebooks of variable design. There in the benevolent glow of Almonte's lamp was the life's work that he had thought was lost. There was a hollow trembling in his body, intense enough for him to put out a steadying hand against a heavy storage cabinet. Warm tears were starting in his eyes. He felt as he had felt in dreams when he had unexpectedly come upon his resurrected mother.

"The living plants are stored in another location," Almonte told him. "Some have died, I am afraid—there are few horticulturists to be found in the Mexican army—but I believe the majority are safe."

"Thank you" was all Edmund could manage to say.

"We are all glad that such a store of intellectual riches was saved from devastation," Santa Anna said. "And may I say I am moved by the obvious happiness in your expression. I once insulted you by calling you—what was it, Juan, do you remember?"

"A 'flower gatherer,' I believe, Your Excellency."

"Yes. And you were properly vehement in correcting me. This material plainly represents a remarkable endeavor, the passion of a great and resolute mind. And I look forward to lending you a hand so that you may see your vast work through to its completion."

The bargain was evident in the consoling, congratulatory tones of Santa Anna's voice, in the hand that suddenly appeared on his shoulder. Edmund walked forward a few steps and opened one of the notebooks at random—to the *Senecionidea,* he had found and sketched one day while roving the prairies near Buffalo Bayou. He remembered the day as glorious—the prairie abounding with life, the blue sky so brilliant it seemed to waver in his sight as if it could not contain its own exuberant color. The plant was new to him, its discovery a triumph. It had yellow blossoms like a chamomile, and he remembered their turpentine taste when he put them in his mouth and chewed them. He had been happy that day, as happy as he was fated to be, at home in his rigorous solitude, the prairie in every direction carpeted with plants that were unknown and undescribed, a world that seemed as deliriously new to him as to an infant.

He held the notebook open, turning a few of the pages slowly, lingering among the images of that former life. Then he closed its battered leather cover, and turned to His Excellency Santa Anna.

"I wish to return to the Alamo," he said.

Santa Anna's reply was immediate and unexpectedly reasonable. "Your loyalty is a commendable thing, Señor McGowan. But you must not make the mistake of thinking that in helping us you are hurting your comrades. I assure you they will all die in any case. By providing us with the information we need, you will affect the outcome of the battle only in one particular: you will be saving the lives of Mexican soldiers who will otherwise be killed."

"It is still treachery," Edmund said, doing his best to cut through Santa Anna's web of logic. "I will not help you. And as I came here under a flag of truce, I expect you to allow me to return to the fort immediately."

"Where you will be killed," Santa Anna said, his voice now sharp and malicious, "and your body burned in a pile with your fellow ridiculous adventurers. And perhaps I will have your precious papers burnt along with you."

He turned sharply and left, his boots pounding on the wood floor. Edmund and Almonte were left together in the dark room, the glow of the lamp between them.

"I will take you back now, Edmund," Almonte said in a quiet voice. "I am sorry you could not help us. It is a very great misfortune."

Almonte walked forward and pulled the protective canvas back over Edmund's notes and specimens.

"Do not worry," he said, dropping his voice. "None of this will be harmed. You have my word."

Almonte turned into the front room and swept it with the lamp to make sure that the guard who had been with them had left with Santa Anna. Then he spoke to Edmund in a barely audible voice.

"Tell Mrs. Mott to stay with the other women and children during the battle. They will not be deliberately harmed, though I cannot guarantee against the hazards of chance. I will look for her and try to guide her personally to safety. As for you, my friend: try to find an officer to whom you may surrender. The standing orders are that no prisoners are to be taken, but many officers are uncomfortable with this, and if you assert in a loud voice that you are a spy for Colonel Almonte you might gain yourself enough time for me to come to your aid. There is little more that I can do, I am afraid."

They rode back down Potrero Street in the same carriage, stopping at the Navarro house to retrieve Juana Alsbury, who walked outside with a grim, set face and sat in silence during the short journey back to the bridge. Evidently the interview with her centralist father had not gone well, and she had returned from him with even more defiance than before.

At the bridge Edmund was handed the white flag. Just before Almonte gave him a burning torch to illuminate it, he offered his hand in friendship.

"May God watch over you, Edmund," he said.

"And over you as well."

Then he took the torch and led Señora Alsbury past cornfields and burnt-out jacales to the fort of the Alamo. As they walked, he called out in a loud voice to the pickets that friends were approaching.

CHAPTER THIRTY-TWO

✵

IT WAS after midnight when the Tolucas were finally given the word to march, in absolute silence, from their camp to the attacking positions far on the other side of the river. The cazadores set out in column behind the line companies, Captain Loera marching for once beside them, with hardly a sound but the creaking of the winter branches overhead.

They crossed near an old battery the rebels had built and then abandoned when they took Béxar. There was a natural ford here and the water was only ankle-deep, but the men still moved carefully one by one over a chain of rocks that formed a kind of bridge. Blas had warned them to avoid getting their feet wet at all costs, since it was very cold and the attack was not scheduled until four in the morning. He hoped that when they got to the entrenchments they would at least be out of the wind, and not exposed for hours with chattering teeth and fraying nerves as they waited to attack. The orders that Loera had given him—orders originating with the president-general himself—stipulated that no man was to wear a blanket or overcoat or anything else that might impede him in the assault. Blas had seen to it that every man in his company wore shoes, as the orders required, though several had only sandals and there had been a flurry of last-minute bargaining with one of the grenadier companies that had not been ordered into the attack.

Blas was proud of the way his men had complied uncomplainingly and enthusiastically with every order, from the sharpening of their bayonets and checking of their flints to the tightening of the chin straps of their shakos. Every man who had set out with him from Saltillo was here, even Alquisira, whose arrow wound had healed in splendid fashion and who marched without a trace of a limp.

They were to be part of Colonel Duque's column. Their objective was the north wall of the Alamo. Another column would attack from the east, another from the west, and still another from the south. As they marched beside the river, heading toward the entrenchments four hundred yards to the north, Blas looked back at the Alamo over his shoulder. It was dead quiet, and he could see no one moving on the walls. Smoke from unseen fires within the enclosure rose up and drifted away across the screen of stars. All day long the Mexican artillery had been deliberately silent, in order to coax the exhausted defenders into sleep, and perhaps the stratagem had worked. But even if the nortes within the Alamo were asleep, others might be on patrol outside the walls, and could be encountered at any moment. And there were doubtless pickets stationed at listening posts in every direction.

Every man in the company took the admonition to be silent as seriously as a vow, because Blas had told them what the consequences would be if the plan for a surprise attack failed and the nortes had the leisure to fire volley after volley of canister at them as they ran across the open ground toward the murderous walls. When they reached the entrenchments they were directed, to their bitter disappointment, to a patch of open ground on the far side of a water ditch where the north wind swept pitilessly down upon them from the hills to their rear. Captain Loera turned to Blas and ordered him to see to it that the men lay flat on the ground and make no unnecessary movements until the trumpet sounded for the attack. Then he quickly disappeared into the shelter of the entrenchments.

The men arranged themselves upon the cold earth, their

hands already growing numb and their bodies quaking within their woolen tunics.

"If we have to stay here like this," Hurtado whispered to Blas, "we'll die from the cold before the fight even starts."

"Be quiet," Blas told him. "We have been ordered to wait here and that is what we will do."

"Have you noticed that the captain has gotten himself out of the wind?" Alquisira said.

"What the captain does is of no concern to you."

The men joined him in staring at the dark, distant fort, and their grumbling subsided as their fear of attacking that evil-looking place overrode the discomfort of their present circumstances. The cazadores' orders were succinct: to advance on either side of the line companies, crossing the dangerous open ground as swiftly as possible, to pick off the defenders with their rifles as they showed themselves above the wall, and to join in the storming of the fort by whatever means presented itself. Only ten of the men in the column carried ladders, and only three or four were equipped with axes and crowbars to break out the windows of the rooms that lined the walls. There were no other such implements that Blas knew about, and he worried that the congestion at the ladders and battered-down openings would be so extreme that they would be slaughtered beneath the defenders' guns.

Everything depended on getting over the walls, or through them, and into the fort as quickly as possible. He prayed that the men in the Alamo were indeed sleeping, that the attack would take place more or less on time, before the sun rose and the nortes with their accurate long-barrelled rifles would be able to pick out clear targets.

Blas walked up and down behind his line of shivering men, now and then stopping to inspect a flint or the edge of a bayonet. By and large the men were in an anxious good humor, but he knew that the longer they lay here in discomfort the sooner their mood would fade to dread. Standing, he could see the troops stretched out along this ditch for hundreds of yards. The moon was waning but nearly full, and its light shone on the reclining men, softly illuminating their white crossbelts and trousers and bringing an evil glimmer to the long steel hedge of bayonets. Someone started to sing under his breath, and Sargento Reyna ordered him to hush. One man was saying the rosary through chattering teeth.

"Sargento!" Hurtado hissed, and pointed to the darkness behind them, where Blas saw a half-dozen black forms moving from side to side fifty yards away with fluid urgency, a sight that made the hair rise on the back of his skull.

"What are they?" Hurtado said. By this time seven or eight of the men were staring at the shapes.

"Wolves," Blas said, hoping his voice was calm and his answer carried no taint of foreboding. But no one's thoughts were eased, least of all his. The dark, agitated forms continued to shift back and forth at the edge of vision, never revealing themselves, never entirely withdrawing, but simply observing Blas and his men with an unearthly curiosity.

"Do not look at them," Blas ordered Hurtado and the rest of his men. "Keep your eyes ahead, on the Alamo."

They complied like frightened children, and he stood behind them, listening to the distant scrabble of wolf paws on the dry husks of the cornfield in which they were positioned. He was afraid, but there was no mortal terror in his soul, and he thanked Isabella for that. Before dark that night, when his men were eating, she had come to him with two candles she had scavenged somewhere and drawn him aside into the trees and in the dimming sunlight had performed some kind of blessing on him, chanting incomprehensible prayers as she passed the candles in arcs about his body, touching the bases of the candles to his shoulders and to the crown of his head. He closed his eyes for most of this activity, as seemed proper, but from time to time he would allow his eyelids to part, and he peered at her in the waving candlelight, her face aflame and intent, the globes of her eyes shining.

Finally she had kissed his face, though whether this was part of the inscrutable ritual or a simple human gesture of comfort and affection he could not decide.

"Who are you?" he had asked her, and she had answered with a complex word in her language that she saw told him nothing, and which she then tried to translate into her poor Spanish.

"Mother-father," she said.

It seemed no stranger to him than anything else about her. She was his mother-father. She came from, or was in search of, the place between the worlds.

Where was she now? Back with the women in the chusma on the other side of the river, making bandages, getting ready for the carnage to come. There were no doctors, there were no proper facilities for the wounded. Everyone in the army knew this. What help they could expect would come from the women, from the powers of healing they might or might not possess.

Pacing along in the cold behind his men, Blas tried to train his mind away from the horrors of what lay ahead and to remember Isabella's face in its circle of candlelight. In this suspended moment, as the spectral wolf shapes trotted along the margins of his awareness, as the cold numbed his body, as the Alamo loomed ahead in his sight like a dark range of rock, he felt himself entering once again the place between the worlds. For just a moment his whole being was tranquil, he was exquisitely aware but unconcerned, and he felt how this new confidence spoke to the souls of his men and seemed to quiet them as well, to persuade them that they would all pass through the fire together, and would survive.

———

TRAVIS WAS WAITING at the gate when Edmund returned to the Alamo with Señora Alsbury. He led them immediately to his quarters, where Edmund told him of Santa Anna's rejection of his offer to surrender.

"Very well," Travis said in a level voice. "Our backs are against the wall now, and the Mexicans will find that there will be hell to pay. I did not expect you back, Mr. McGowan. What did Santa Anna want with you?"

"He was interested in learning more about our defensive works. I was unwilling to accommodate him, and so here I am."

"And we are privileged to have you. When do you suppose he will attack?"

"As soon as he can. Perhaps even tonight."

"Captain Baugh," Travis said, turning to his adjutant, "will you please inform the company officers that I want to speak to the entire garrison immediately in the churchyard?"

The garrison, most of them, had to be roused from a stupefying sleep. For twelve days they had endured a more or less constant bombardment, and now that it had been so craftily suspended they were unable to stay awake despite their best intentions. They staggered into the courtyard swathed in blankets, in the pale light cast by the moon, so that they looked to Edmund like the shades of the dead drawn forth from their crypts for some sort of supernatural convocation.

Travis stood in front of the church, waiting on them, staring down at the dirt with his chin cradled on his hand like an actor. Baugh stood next to him, and Crockett sat near the palisade on a chair that someone had left there by the guns. He was wearing his enviable greatcoat, and he smiled at the other men as they came forward. Some of them sat on the cold ground, though the majority remained standing.

Edmund placed himself near Captain Baker and the rest of the men of his adopted company.

"By God, he's called us out here for another speech," Roth said.

"If Bowie was in charge of this place like he ought've been we wouldn't be out here in the cold just to hear some sonofabitch talk," Sparks said. "We wouldn't have been sittin' around for two weeks cuttin' the patchin' neither. We should go get Jim and haul his bed out here. If anybody's gonna talk to us it ought to be him."

Baker hissed at them both to be quiet and reminded them that Bowie was far too sick to be brought outdoors. The churchyard by now was almost full, not just with the men of the garrison but with the women and children, who rarely ventured outside of the safe rooms. Edmund looked for Mary and saw her standing in shadow alongside Dr. Pollard at the corner of the convent building. She was standing on her toes and though he could not make out the features of her face in the darkness he could see her head sweeping slowly across the assembled crowd—looking for him, he thought. He was about to hoist his heavy musket and walk toward her when Travis began to address the men in a raspy voice.

"Gentlemen of the Alamo," he said, "our decisive hour is near."

"He's going to talk like a politician," Roth said in a low, angry voice, and Baker threatened to strike him down with his sword if he did not shut up.

"The intelligence I have received in the last few hours," Travis went on, unmindful of Roth's grumbling, "leads me to believe that we may expect an attack against our position in a very short time. This will be an assault in force, whose aim will be to destroy us to the last man. But neither I nor any man in this post should give up hope. I believe that the fight, when it comes, will be savage; we will face a gothic enemy with no notion of mercy or chivalry or right conduct. But we have repulsed them before and will do so again. And at any moment—perhaps tonight!—help may reach us. The men who failed to make it into the Alamo two nights ago with Congressman Crockett are without doubt positioning themselves for another try."

He reminded them of Major Williamson's letter—its pleas to the Alamo garrison to hold out at any cost, its promises of help from every quarter. All those promises seemed empty now, in this cold, windswept night, with the moon hanging in the sky above the church like a spying, malevolent face. But the men were quiet and still as they listened to this frighteningly young, ceaselessly verbose officer who like all of them was so starved for sleep his mind hovered half the time on the edge of raving lunacy. But his rallying voice brought comfort even to the most skeptical of them, even to Sparks. And Travis had an ear for cadence, so that there was a strange detached musical pleasure in listening to him as he urged them to fight until the last ball and the last grain of powder had been expended, and even then to fight with sword and knife, with club and tomahawk, with bare fists and teeth, because if they could keep the Mexicans out of the fort, if they could hold them away just a while longer, then relief would be certain . . .

Edmund closed his eyes and listened more to those throbbing cadences than to the largely counterfeit hope they expressed. Travis's words had no more meaning for him than the call of a bird, and in fact his mind was now so gauzy with the need for sleep that he envisioned with unnatural clarity the young colonel standing alone on a vast tidal flat, calling out to the wilderness with the creaking voice of a heron. When he opened his eyes again he was looking at Mary, and in the midst of the speech he found himself drifting away from the rest of men and walking up to her in the shadow of the convent. They grazed one another's eyes for an instant; neither spoke a word. Pollard did not see him; he was staring blearily at Travis as he continued his address.

But neither Edmund nor Mary gave any further notice to the speech. She stepped out of the shadow into the moonlight with her eyes on his face, her arm deliberately brushing his as she walked past him and slipped out of sight around the corner of the convent. He followed and stood with her. There were still a few sentinels on the walls, vigilantly scanning the open ground in front of them for any sign of a Mexican attack, but the rest of the population of the fort was gathered behind them in the churchyard listening to Travis. Only Edmund and Mary stood in the vast vacant compound of the Alamo, though Professor found them quickly enough and sat down moodily on his hindquarters with his flank touching Edmund's leg.

"Tell your dog to stay," Mary whispered to him. Edmund did so, and Professor looked at him crossly but complied. Mary began strolling toward the north end of the compound. Edmund fell into step beside her. They walked along the length of the old convent building that now served as the Alamo barracks, and Mary trailed her hand across its stone face as she walked, as if she were an idling girl with nothing on her mind. The exterior of the building was as soft and white in the falling moonlight as the face of the moon itself, and Edmund could see many places where the stone had been deeply pitted in the shelling, though as yet its structure had not been undermined by a direct hit from solid shot. His heart surged wildly in his chest, perhaps from dread at his approaching death, perhaps from the nearness of some other frightful threshold he did not dare to name.

To the north of the barracks was the mission's old granary building, long in disuse, most of its roof having fallen in decades earlier and further damaged in the bombing. Edmund followed Mary as she slipped through the granary's open door and walked back into a corner and took the blanket she wore around her shoulders and set it down. Through the remaining slats of the exposed roof, a patterned moonlight leaked into the room, illuminating Mary's face as she sat down on the blanket and reached out her arms to him.

Edmund joined her there and clasped her body to his. Her head rested beneath his chin and he could feel her cold lips against his neck, and then the warmth of her breath on his face when she lifted her head to kiss him.

"Open your mouth a little," she said, and when he did as she asked he felt her tongue alarmingly touching his own, and then felt it tracing the outline of his cracked lips. He did not think to close his eyes, and so he saw her face as she kissed him. Her own eyes were shut but when she felt his scrutiny she opened them and stared back at him but did not take her lips from his. Travis was still speaking in the church courtyard beyond the convent, his words resounding but indistinct.

It seemed to Edmund that she was kissing him angrily; he was aware of her tears on his cheeks. He felt startled by this unthinkable thing that was happening. It was as if he were suddenly living another man's life, an ordinary man who had not chosen a high untrodden path but walked untroubled along the broad avenue of common creation.

With a sudden urgent motion she pulled away from him and rose to her feet and began unfastening her dress with trembling hands. She let the dress fall to the ground and then with the same compelling haste pulled off her undergarments so that she was entirely naked and violently shivering and exposed to him as no human creature had ever been.

"Will you touch me, Edmund?" she said.

And he did, but he was not prepared; not prepared for the enormous gulf that stood between this new existence and the one he still inhabited; not prepared to forsake his lifetime's lonely grandeur; no more prepared to touch this luminous bare flesh than to hold his hand within a bed of coals. He tore his eyes from her breasts, from the blinding nakedness of her flanks, and stood up and looked into her eyes again, as if for safety, as if they marked some negotiable channel in a limitless ocean of desire. And she must have seen the helpless look in his eyes because her own expression grew stern and frightened in response and when she spoke to him she had to fight her chattering teeth to form the words.

"Will you please take off your clothes as well?" she asked him.

And though he meant to, though his hands went to the buttons of his jacket, all she could notice, all she could feel, was his tortured deliberation. That was what she meant to him, she understood; she was the defeat of who he was, the emblem of his failure to establish himself high above ordinary human endeavor, above lust, above real caring, above death. This realization cracked her heart and enraged her, and to the surprise of them both she lifted her arms in the air and with her naked breasts swaying she struck him on the chest with her fists.

"No . . . no, of course you won't, Edmund! If you did so, you would have to become one of us!"

She reached down and picked up her dress, and when he tried to reach out to her again she backed away from him, out of the slatted moonlight and into the dark corner of the granary, violently shivering and weeping.

"Is something wrong in here?" someone said. Edmund turned and saw a man's form filling the doorway, a long rifle in his arms, the crescent shape of a powder horn swaying in front of his leaning body. He could not make out the man's features but thought he recognized the voice as Captain Carey's. In the darkness behind him other men were walking across the yard and taking up their positions on the walls. Travis's remarks were evidently finished and the assembly breaking up.

"It is a conversation of a personal nature," Edmund said to Carey with as much authority as he could command in his shaken condition.

"Is that Mr. McGowan?"

"It is, sir. Will you leave us alone, please?"

"I will allow you a moment, sir, since you have requested it," Carey said testily, "though as I understand matters you are a private in this army and I am a captain, and your tone of superiority is offensive to good order."

Edmund was in no temper to offer a reply, and Carey turned abruptly and walked out of the granary. In a short moment Mary was dressed again. He spoke her name in a confused, pleading voice but she would not look at him. When she tried to walk past him he took her arm, desperate to find words to say to her, but he knew that even if he could find them she was past listening.

"Mary . . ." he began again.

"Don't speak to me. Don't say my name. I gave myself to you on what may be our last night on this earth, and in your pride and your appalling selfishness you looked away. And so I no longer wish to be in your company."

She tried to pull away from him but he gripped her tighter, and held her there for just an instant more, knowing it was too late to repair the awful breach between them but perhaps not too late to save her life.

"Try to find Almonte at any cost," he said in a choking voice. "He has promised me he will help you if he can."

She inclined her head in affirmation, but she would not look at him, and when he let go of his grip on her arm she left the room in a bitter stride, leaving him alone to contemplate the intolerable empty waste of his life.

CHAPTER THIRTY-THREE

✯

"**D**O NOT let me fall asleep, Joe."

Travis sat upright in his chair, a sheet of paper under his pen. It was a letter he had begun in the early afternoon and returned to time and again during the course of the day, striking out its imperfect phrases with angry swipes of his pen. From the way Travis fretted over the letter Joe decided it was to young Charlie. He remembered the day last spring when they had ridden down from San Felipe to fetch the boy from Travis's wife, and how Charlie had seemed afraid at first of his father, of his expansive, theatrical nature and of his booming voice as they rode back across the empty prairies and through the endless dark canebrakes.

The boy had warmed to Travis soon enough. He was a man who naturally seemed to know where he was going, who always had a destination in his head, and Charlie no less than Joe himself had taken comfort in this—you wanted the man who controlled your life to have confidence in his own. Even Bowie's men, Joe had noticed, wanted to trust in Travis now. When he had addressed the garrison tonight some of them had been mocking at first, but by the end of the speech he had them believing that help might really come, that Williamson and the others were really out there somewhere beyond the ring of Mexican troops, trying to find a way into the Alamo.

What bothered Joe was that he didn't think Travis believed it himself. He was usually a quick and furious letter writer, but now he was wrestling with every word in a way that made Joe think he was trying to set down his final testament. It had been three or four hours since he made his speech to the men, and for most of that time Travis had been on the walls, and Joe with him, staring out into the winter blackness for any sign of movement, either Texian or Mexican. He had doubled the watches, but in the ominous silence of the suspended cannonades the men on the parapets were having trouble staying awake. Even the fierce cold could not keep them from drifting off, and Travis and the other officers, barely conscious themselves, had to repeatedly shake them back to life.

"It would set a poor example if I were to go to sleep," Travis was saying now, putting down his pen at last in weariness and frustration. "You will not let it happen?"

"No," Joe said.

"Good." Travis looked at him with distant, glassy eyes. "Your service to me during this difficult time has been commendable."

"Thank you, sir," Joe replied, irritated at Travis's compliment and at the decorous response it required. He had no ill feeling toward Travis and no particular disrespect either, but he found himself desiring to shoot a pistol ball through his master's chest, and then to go shoot that Private Herndon and grab his colored woman from his dead grasp and walk with her into the Mexican camp. It was a mischievous thought and it passed through his mind with the speed of a blink. He wondered: if something like that appeared in your imagination, was it present in your nature as well? He had lived his slave's life with a neutral, unquestioning mien, but he was starting to think that there was something loud and vigorous and bitter within him as well, something that told him that the destination in Travis's head and the one in his own might be two different places.

"Soy nay-gro," he kept saying now over and over in his thoughts. He was fairly sure that was the right phrase in Spanish. Early in the siege he had heard Crockett jokingly ask Travis how to say "Don't shoot me," and Travis had laughed and said, "Just throw up your hands, Congressman, and say 'No me mate.'" Joe had secretly held the words in his mind, and now he put them together and practiced them: "Soy negro. No me mate." I am a black man. Do not kill me.

Travis went to sleep, his body upright against the chair back, his two arms resting on the desk like weights. His mouth dropped open against his chest.

"Colonel Travis," Joe said, gently at first and then sharply, and Travis jerked awake and said, "Thank you, Joe." But then he fell asleep again, and before he could wake him Joe fell asleep as well.

HIS EXCELLENCY WAS LATE, and thus the attack was late as well. The senior officers were waiting for him in the tent that had been erected behind the protective parapets of the northeastern battery. Cos and Castrillón were holding forth with the strange, heightened casualness of men on the verge of action, Cos describing the elephant he had seen exhibited in Vera Cruz in '32, its great tattered ears and its forlorn intelligence; and Castrillón recalling his study of the Punic Wars, and how the Romans had learned to hack off the trunks of Hannibal's war elephants and drive the maddened beasts back toward the Carthaginian line to trample their own troops.

As they talked, Almonte paced back and forth in silence, studying the face of his watch. Telesforo judged it to be almost five in the morning. The troops were all said to be in place, and many of them had been out in the freezing dark for hours on end. It was reasonably warm in the pavilion;

there was a snapping fire outside that brought in the smell of burning oak to mingle with the aroma of coffee, several pots of which were warming on the spirit-lamps. Telesforo had unwisely drunk one cup of coffee too many, and that combined with the cold and his excited nerves had required him to urinate three times in the last hour, an embarrassing debility, and an unwieldy one for a person with only one entirely functional arm. Now he sat on a camp stool, studying the flames outside through the fabric of the tent, nibbling at a bolillo he had taken from a tray, wishing acutely that Santa Anna would arrive and order the attack made before dawn.

And so he did. "Good morning, gentlemen," he said as he swept into the spacious tent and accepted a cup of coffee from a steward. "You have all had your breakfast? Then let us briefly reacquaint ourselves with the plan of battle."

Telesforo's maps were called for again, and the officers clustered around them, listening as His Excellency described the movements of the four columns, the profound necessity of surprise and of breaching the walls in one powerful wave of motion so that the troops would not suffer from continual fire and the enemy would not have time to spike their own cannon during their retreat. Were the artillery crews prepared to rush in and take control of those cannon? Were the signal rockets ready? Was General Sesma's cavalry saddled up and in position, ready to contain any breakouts to the east and south?

"As you know, gentlemen," Santa Anna said when all was reported to his satisfaction, "and as I now repeat: in this war there are no prisoners. You will make every effort of course to spare the obvious noncombatants, together with any negro slaves who may apply to you for mercy, but the rest of these lawless adventurers will die fighting or pleading, as each sees fit. Now if there are no other urgent matters to take up I will ask you to withdraw to your positions and wait for the signal rockets. Move your men forward with all speed, do not let them waver or lose heart. I have every confidence that this will be a day of glory and gratification to our country. God bless you, my friends, in our endeavor."

He shook their hands in turn. When he came to Telesforo, he gripped his hand hard and drew him forward, so that he could speak into his ear.

"It gives me great comfort," he whispered, "to have officers such as you around—men who I know will not forsake their duty."

Telesforo went out into the cold and hurried to take his place with the Zapadores, who were positioned some fifty yards to the east of Santa Anna's pavilion.

"The men are suffering in this cold," Robert Talon told him. The pompon on his shako was lying almost flat in the wind, and his hands were buried in his sash for warmth.

"The attack will come soon," Telesforo assured. "Before daylight, certainly."

"And will we be in it?"

"I don't know, but if there is significant resistance I think it is almost a certainty."

The two men stared at the Alamo in the distance. Telesforo could barely make out the members of Duque's and Cos's columns spread out along the ground a few hundred yards in front of them. The men were admirably silent but restless and uncomfortable, and he could see them shifting in the cold. It was almost five-thirty, Telesforo reckoned. In less than an hour the sun would start to rise and the army would be exposed to view. Therefore the moment of battle was surely near to hand.

EDMUND SAT at his firing position on the west wall, peering out through his makeshift barricade into the darkness. His recent encounter with Mary had shocked him into a sustained wakefulness, though most of the men near him on this section of the wall—even Captain Baker himself—appeared to have subsided into sleep. Professor, curled up tight against Edmund, slept as well, his body now and then twitching in alarm at some incident in his dreams.

Edmund listened to the two men standing on the battery of the north wall. They spoke in murmuring tones, the rhythms not conversational but formal, and it was not until one of them slipped down onto his knees that he realized they were praying. The act of prayer seemed to calm their spirits, whereas his remained tortured. He had lived his life on a high and austere plane, and it had come to nothing, nothing. He had built up a wall of grandeur, he had scaled himself away from vital human companionship, for reasons he could not now, in these numb, terrible hours before dawn, even remember. His life's work had disappeared as surely and completely as if he had never embarked upon it, and the one person who might have broken through the wall he had constructed now rightly despised him as a coward.

A figure climbed up onto the roof of the building where he sat and walked toward him at a crouch, carrying a Kentucky rifle comfortably in one hand. The man passed Captain Baker, gently shook him awake and exchanged a few words with him—Edmund recognized the voice as Crockett's—then continued down the line, speaking to each man in turn.

When he came to Edmund he bade him good morning and began scratching Professor's ears. The dog opened his mucus-sealed eyes and stared up at Crockett, who was smiling down at him with a fond, amused look.

"I've always enjoyed a particular success with dogs," Crockett said to Edmund. "They find me to be tolerable company. Don't pay me any mind. I'm just restless and took it upon myself to go on a scout. You seen anything moving out there, Edmund?"

"No."

"Colonel Travis gave us a pretty speech tonight."

Edmund nodded his head vacantly. He was not in a listening or talking mood and had a powerful craving to ponder his dark thoughts in solitude.

"You got a discouraged look about you," Crockett said after a reflective pause. He took out a whetstone and began scraping a knife blade across it, taking Edmund's silence as an incentive to keep talking.

"How old are you?" he asked.

"Forty-five," Edmund said.

"Well, I'm a few months shy of the half-century. Never thought I'd get this old, but by God here I am. You think we can keep those Mexicans out of the fort when they come?"

"No."

"I don't either. And I'm uneasy about the matter. This is an unlikely damn thing, ain't it? I never expected to be sitting in a fort in Texas waiting to fight the Mexican army. Hell, a few years ago I didn't even know there *was* a Mexican army. I worry about that dog of yours. I hope he has the good sense to run and hide when this commotion starts and not get too excited about fighting for the liberation of Texas."

Still sharpening his knife, Crockett turned his head to smile at Edmund. Edmund smiled politely in response. Crockett put the whetstone back into his shooting pouch and his knife into a fancy beaded scabbard.

"Well, I believe I will go on to the next man," Crockett said, "since you are doing damn little to improve my spirits. Will you shake hands with me?"

"I will," Edmund said.

It was a leave-taking handshake, charged and lingering.

"Good luck to you, Edmund," Crockett said.

"And to you."

"If you are a friend to me, you will speak my name."

"Good luck to you, David," Edmund said.

Crockett grinned and picked up his rifle and continued down the wall with the same brisk, shuffling pace, on his way to speak to the gun crew manning the eighteen-pounder. Edmund almost blurted out Crockett's name again and asked him to return, so great was the loneliness that now enveloped him.

"I HAVE to go too," Alquisira said, when Salas returned after moving his bowels.

"Go ahead," Blas told him. "But hurry."

Alquisira slipped away from the line of frozen men and retreated a few varas into the darkness, unbuttoning his trousers as he went, and crouched down in the vicinity of several other men from the line companies who were there on the same nervous errand and whose gaseous, expulsive noises disrupted the enforced silence. The wolves had disappeared, but the men felt vulnerable away from the line and did not linger. Alquisira was back in hardly more than a minute, taking up his position again and staring out at the Alamo, his shoulders quaking uncontrollably from the cold.

Blas felt his own bowels stirring, but not severely, and so he remained where he was. Experience had taught him that it was a mistake to fret about minor bodily distractions. They would be quickly forgotten in any case once the action began.

He stood up and walked behind the men once again, inspecting their weapons, making sure the laces of their shoes were securely tied—a continual concern among men who had worn only sandals since boyhood.

"It will be daylight in another hour," Reyna whispered to him as they stood behind the line.

Blas nodded somberly. Daylight, both of them knew, meant slaughter. But just when Blas was about to despair that the attack would be launched soon, he saw Loera running toward them from the entrenchments, his sword already drawn.

"Prepare to attack," the captain told him. "Five minutes."

Blas saw to it that the word was passed up and down the line, and then he lay down once again on the cold earth next to Alquisira and Hurtado and trained his eyes on the objective. The Alamo still seemed silent and unaware to him, but there was a good deal of open ground to cover before they reached the walls.

Loera stood in front of the Tolucas. The moonlight shone on his sword. He said nothing, just stood there as if posing for a portrait.

They heard a hollow crump behind and then a muted hissing sound as the first signal rocket vaulted over their position and then, a few seconds later, exploded in a white burst of light over the courtyard of the enemy fort. Another followed, and then another, and then a bugle sounded attack and Loera stood before them and, pointing his sword ahead, led them at a brisk pace—though not yet a run— toward the walls of the Alamo.

MARY WAS in the hospital when the rockets erupted over the courtyard. Accustomed to the frightening noise and destruction of artillery shells, she was perplexed, and even momentarily heartened, by the softness of the explosion, by the sudden white light that leaked through the seams below the steerhide curtains and bathed the room in an eerie luminescence.

"What's that?" Dick Perry said, jerking upright on his pallet.

Pollard woke up and in one swift motion had left his own pallet and was standing at the window with his rifle in his hands.

"I believe they're coming after us," he said quietly and

turned to the patients in the room. "Any of you men who think you can fight, get to the walls."

Dick Perry, his shattered face still wrapped in bandages, took up his rifle and was out the door without a word to anybody. Lieutenant Main, though weak and as wickedly pale as the white light from the rockets, stood up in his nightshirt, grabbed a loaded musket from the hospital's emergency arsenal, and stumbled outside like a sleepwalker. Frazier and several of the other patients who were cognizant but still too frail to venture outside took up firing positions with Pollard and Reynolds at the windows.

Petrasweiz, who had lost his leg to a cannonball two days earlier, pulled himself out of his cot, only to collapse immediately onto his bandaged stump. His screams startled Mary out of her panic, and she crossed the room to try to help him back onto his cot.

"For the love of God, don't move me!" Petrasweiz cried. "Just get me my rifle and my outfit. It's over there against the wall."

She followed his excited gestures and located his rifle and shooting pouch and brought them back to him, checking first to see that the rifle was loaded and primed.

"You're going to have to move me after all, ma'am, if you don't mind," he said, still breathless with pain. "I'm pointed the wrong way to shoot down any Mexicans."

She helped him turn his body around so that he was facing the door. He screamed piteously during the process but did not give it up. His stump began to bleed again, and he held the rifle with trembling hands.

"Well, are they coming or not?" he said.

Mary peered out onto the courtyard from the bottom of one of the windows. Men were racing to the walls under the unnatural light of the rockets, but as yet there was no gunfire nor any sounds of battle, just a sustained deadly quiet that she sensed would rip apart at any moment.

Mary looked toward the far end of the west wall, knowing that was where Edmund might be. She thought she saw him rise from sleep and stand looking out with the other men toward the north as another burst of light from a signal rocket silhouetted their forms against the darkness.

She ran to the door and called out to him, for what purpose she did not know. "Edmund!" she screamed, but his name had not left her mouth before one of the cannon on the northwest corner exploded with an astonishing roar and that entire end of the fort disappeared in its smoke.

IT WAS the report of the cannon that finally woke Joe and Travis in the Alamo headquarters. They were both sitting in their chairs, and they leapt to their feet at the same moment. Both of Joe's legs were asleep, and he fell down to the floor like a thrashing fish.

"Are you hit, Joe?" Travis said with strikingly real concern as he reached for his sword and his shotgun. He had not lost a moment between sleep and wakefulness.

"I don't think so," Joe said as he tried to regain his footing on his numb, heavy legs.

"Take up your weapon and follow me!"

Travis disappeared outside. Joe could hear him yelling— "Come on, men! The Mexicans are upon us and we will give them hell!"—and he wanted desperately to pull himself off the floor but could not. He was in a panic of helplessness until he started to feel the blood coursing back into his tingling, aching limbs. Then he pulled himself up and half-staggered to the door and out into the brilliant courtyard.

THEY HAD started out at the walk and advanced for perhaps fifty varas through the darkness in obedient silence.

The only noise was the treading of the column's feet upon the ground and the sound of their breathing and the occasional flattened note of a nervous fart. Blas saw the movement all around him in the darkness and felt part of a great swarm. They had been subjected to inhuman cold and tedium for hours now, but at least the attack was truly coming before dawn. Blas had tied the chin strap of his shako uncomfortably tight, and as he walked he worked his jaw up and down to try to stretch it a little. The sweat-stained leather was rank in his nostrils, and he was aware of the coarse wool of his tunic scratching him through his cotton shirt. The Alamo was beautifully illuminated ahead in the light of the signal rockets, and the paths of their journeys could still be traced in the dissipating arcs of gunpowder overhead.

They moved closer, their pace growing naturally quicker, Loera holding aloft his sword. The moon cast a silvery light on the sword and on the endless hedge of bayonets. The men in the Alamo still had not fired on them. They had been caught sleeping after all—just a few more varas.

Someone in the line company could not contain himself anymore and yelled out "Viva Santa Anna!" and the men next to him took up the cry, and suddenly the measured pacing of the advance disappeared and the men rushed forward in a wild heedless run, baring their teeth as they screamed out their war cry. There was nothing to do but follow the momentum that had suddenly been discharged, and Loera waved his sword in a circle and shouted with the rest of them and led them forward on an oblique sweep toward the north wall.

The signal rockets kept streaking over their heads, and the old mission shone in Blas's sight with unworldly vividness. He could see the first men in Cos's column approaching the northwest corner. They were almost under the wall when the battery's two guns fired, setting forth a long jet of flame scything down several ranks of men near the head of the column.

The discharge of the cannon was followed by sputtering rifle fire from the enemy positions. Colonel Duque, the leader of Blas's column, was calling out "To the walls! To the walls, men!" and Loera picked up the exhortation, still waving his sword in the air until a discharge of canister from the convent yard took off his head and the sword arm along with it, and his one-armed, headless body lurched forward a few steps and fell twitching to the ground. Blas ran past it, and past the four or five other soldiers who had fallen with Loera, one of whom had been split almost in half by the blast and now lay in the cornfield bleating in shock and looking like a ruptured sack of grain.

"Hurry!" he shouted to the men around him. "Get to the walls!" They were running directly at the north wall now, completely exposed to the fire of the batteries, and every man knew that his only salvation lay in vaulting over the defenses as soon as he could. Rifle fire spattered through the ranks. The throat of the man next to Blas opened up in a torrent of dark blood, and he dropped his rifle and stood there gurgling. Duque himself was down, shot in the thigh near the edge of the water ditch, waving the men forward though he was voiceless with pain.

The Alamo itself was already completely shrouded in gunpowder smoke, but Blas knew it was in reach. He and the rest of the company were only ten varas from the wall when the two eight-pound guns of the north battery fired almost at the same moment, sending twin pulses of flame through the smoke and a blast of scorching, jagged metal into the ranks of the cazadores.

JOE DIDN'T KNOW where the attack was coming from; he suspected nobody did. It seemed the greater part of the commotion was to the north, but there was rifle and artillery fire to the south as well, so probably they were coming from every direction at once. The blood had returned to his legs now, but they were still a bit numb and the bottoms of his feet were prickly as he ran through the broken earth of the courtyard toward the north wall. Smoke blanketed the compound and that combined with the darkness made him able to see hardly anything at all. Mr. McGowan's dog raced past him on its way to the safety of the barracks, but everyone else was running along with Joe to take up firing positions on the wall.

He started to run up the artillery ramp just as the two cannon at the top roared in sequence, a blast so savage that it shook the ramp and knocked Joe off his feet. The shot had been a hasty one, and the recoil caught one of the gunners and sent him pitching off the battery with his broken arm waving at a crazy angle. Joe got back up on his feet and ran up the ramp into the dingy smoke. He could hear musket balls slapping the outside of the ramparts and feel their passage through the thick air around his head. One of the gunners was already shot dead, and Captain Carey was on his hands and knees vomiting up great waves of blood.

He crawled through the smoke until he found Travis. The colonel was crouched behind a ramshackle wooden barricade, yelling something at the top of his voice to Crockett. Both of the men's faces were black with powder, and Joe could not have seen them if it had not been for the strange muzzy light of the rockets penetrating through the smoke.

Crockett nodded his head in answer to some directive, leapt down off the rampart into the interior of the fort, and started running across the courtyard toward the church.

"There you are, Joe!" Travis shouted at him when he shuffled over to the place where Crockett had been. The colonel gave a quick, wincing grin and leaned over the wall to discharge his shotgun and then he was dead. Joe saw the

back of Travis's skull hinge open and a jet of bloody tissue fly
out and then watched in continued amazement as the commander's body fell backward onto the packed dirt without
bouncing or stirring, its bright white eyes staring up at the
sky with a look of sudden and horrifying contentment.

"He's dead!" Joe shouted to the men around him, but
none of them could hear him against the furious snapping
of musket and rifle fire, and none had time to notice.

THE CANISTER from the cannon blast on the north wall
had ripped through the heart of Blas's rifle company. The
detached head of a man nearby on his flank had struck Blas
on the side of the face, knocking him to the ground. When
he had scrabbled back to consciousness and opened his
eyes he saw the head with its broad pitted face and its
eyes peering straight at him and recognized Hurtado. The
ragged parts of seven or eight other soldados were scattered along the ground, and the survivors were smeared
with their gore. Blas tried to stand, but the earth had turned
into a slick wet pulsing surface that would give his feet no
purchase. Finally he pulled himself upright, smelling the
unbearably pungent odors of blood and shit and rancid
gunpowder.

Petralia was trying to stand too, but his leg had been shot
away. Blas heaved him up by his crossbelt and put an arm
under his shoulder to try to drag him forward, but as he did
so a musket ball burst through Petralia's chest, and he leapt
forward out of Blas's grasp and landed face-down in the
water ditch that paralleled the Alamo wall.

The shot had come from behind, from their own men.
The fusiliers in the line companies, caught in the furnace of
artillery, were firing their muskets in blind panic.

"Forward! Forward!" Blas commanded to anyone within
the range of his voice. "Over the wall!"

With Alquisira and Salas and a half-dozen others he

leapt over the water ditch and ran to the base of the wall, just as the two cannon in the battery overhead roared again. He had his back to the wall and the stone shook violently with the percussion. Other men were crowding around him. They were directly beneath the defenders now, and the enemy artillerists could not train their barrels on them at such a steep angle. Neither could the riflemen above them fire directly into their ranks without dangerously exposing themselves, but this they seemed willing to do. Balls pattered viciously through the ranks, and burning wadding from the rifle barrels above them drifted down and scorched their faces and necks.

Blas groped along the base of the wall through the smoke and the flashing muzzle fire, searching for a point of ingress. But there were no windows or doors on the north side, and the breaches made by the cannonades were heavily defended with enfiladed fire. The only way into the fort was over the top.

"Ladders! Here!" he called out to two badly frightened fusiliers who were carrying a ladder between them with their muskets slung over their shoulders. They heard him and veered in his direction, but before they reached the wall they and the ladder were blasted into shreds by another round of canister.

The attack was failing. All was confusion. Through the intermittently clearing smoke, Blas could see the men of Cos's column milling about in panic at the northwest corner of the wall. None of their ladders were planted either.

"What do we do?" Salas yelled at him. The crowd at the base of the wall was growing denser, the men fighting each other for the merest scrap of shelter from the rain of bullets overhead. Few of the men were even firing back now, fewer still appeared to have any conviction that the position could be taken.

"Move forward and take a shot!" Blas commanded Salas. "We have to clear those men off the walls."

Blas stepped forward a few feet, pivoted onto his knee, and fired at one of the rebels taking aim with a long rifle over the parapet. Blas had the impression that the ball splintered the man's arm and his gunstock, but he did not linger to study the damage. He leapt back against the wall to reload.

"Fire! Step forward and fire!" he shouted to his men, and they obeyed him. Salas's rifle misfired and when he peered quizzically into the pan someone on the wall shot him through the gut. The ball tore out his back as well, and Blas could see a jagged, glistening piece of his spine exposed to the air. He and Alquisira ran out and dragged him back to the wall. His legs lay flat and dead on the ground and as he screamed he belched up so much blood that it made a thick sheen on his face. There was nothing for Blas to do except to keep firing, but as he stepped out from the wall his leg snagged on something and he almost tripped. He turned his head to look and saw that Salas was holding on to the cuff of his trousers and screeching like a baby at the top of his lungs, begging Blas not to leave him.

IT WAS PLAIN to Telesforo Villasenor, observing the battle with Robert Talon from the Zapadores' position near Santa Anna's headquarters tent, that the attack had foundered. The signal rockets had stopped firing and the fortress of the Alamo was illuminated now only by bursts of cannon fire and the staccato twinkling of muzzle flashes. When the light pulsed across the frantic tableau in the distance, Telesforo could still see the silhouettes of men on the walls, firing their rifles at the huddled invaders below. Those men should have been gone by now, engulfed in an unstoppable wave of Mexican infantry. Instead, a quarter-hour had passed in apparent slaughter and confusion.

Telesforo had seen General Castrillón rushing forward

to take charge of Duque's column, after Duque himself had been carried off the field in agony by two ashen-faced soldados. Perhaps Castrillón could make something out of the aimless melee at the base of the Alamo walls, where the two northern attack columns had merged into one cringing mass. But anyone watching knew that unless a second wave of seasoned troops was sent in immediately the attack would end in disaster.

"Good luck to you, my friend," Robert said to him with an outstretched hand when the order to advance finally came. "May you be covered in glory at the end of this affair."

And then the bugle sounded advance and the Zapadores set off with confidence in their hearts toward the Alamo.

"Viva Santa Anna!" Telesforo yelled with the rest as they broke into a dead run. Ahead of him the enemy fortress continued to sputter in and out of sight, glowing beautifully for an instant and then collapsing into darkness, as if it were some sort of willful creature striving to conceal from him its terrible form.

JACOB ROTH was dead, shot through the back of the head and lying facedown with his arms trailing neatly at his sides and a hatchet in one hand. A piece of rock had struck Sparks in the eye. The pain of it had made him uncharacteristically energetic, and he was loading and firing his long rifle with heedless rage. Captain Baker was as yet unharmed, though he continually exposed himself as he ran from one position to the next and Edmund thought he would surely be cut down soon. A Mexican sharpshooter had shattered Patrick Herndon's arm, and he was lying on the ground below them howling in pain while his slave woman tried desperately to stop the pulsing gouts of blood. This was all of the battle that Edmund could see as he hunched behind his parapet, firing as methodically as he could manage into the ranks of Mexican soldiers who were surging now around the northwest battery and trying to gain entrance into the buildings along the west wall. He could hear them yelling to each other in shrill voices, and beneath the continuous rattle of musket fire he could hear the pounding of their axes against the barricaded doors and windows.

Only moments ago the men on the north wall had been cheering as the Mexican attack seemed to founder and retreat, but now the assault was surging forward again, backed up by reserve troops whose ferocious "Vivas" Edmund could now hear travelling toward them across the dark expanse.

The top of a ladder suddenly appeared behind him, with a Mexican officer bounding up its rungs. Fear had contorted the officer's face into an hysteric's grin. Edmund had a fresh charge in his musket but when he shot he missed entirely, and the officer would have cleaved him in half with his sword if a rifleman shooting from the roof of the barracks across the plaza had not shot him in the leg and sent him skittering to the ground. The officer pulled himself up and started coming toward Edmund anyway, and Edmund threw his musket at him and then reached down for the hatchet lying next to Roth's body and threw that at him too. The hatchet sailed clear, but the Mexican collapsed as he tried to put weight on his shattered leg and toppled into Edmund's arms. Edmund grabbed the man's sword arm and fought to keep it from swinging free while with his other hand he tried to pry away his clinging assailant. The officer bellowed in his face and Edmund responded in the same mad tenor by biting him on the left cheek and tearing a chunk of flesh away, with no more deliberation given to the act than if he had been a wolf. Then he kicked and kicked at the man's broken leg until he could feel the blood from

the wound spilling over the top of his own shoes. The officer shrieked in pain and fell to the ground and Edmund finally managed to claw and kick himself free and left the
man lying there in bloodied exhaustion while he groped for
the musket he had thrown away.

He found it just in time to swing it by its burning barrel
at the face of another Mexican soldier vaulting over the
ladder. The butt of the musket cracked him squarely in the
jaw and sent a tremor through Edmund's arms, but the soldier only staggered for a moment before recovering. The
Mexican's own weapon was slung over his shoulder and
while he fumbled with it at the top of the ladder Edmund
swung his musket again and in ducking the blow the man
lost his balance and toppled backward off the ladder.

Edmund took advantage of the confusion to grab the top
rungs of the ladder and pull it up, but before he could get it
over the wall the Mexicans below him grabbed the opposite
end and would have pulled it out of his grasp if Baker and
Sparks had not rushed in to help him. Together they seized
the ladder from the enemy and flung it into the courtyard.

Edmund sank back down behind his parapet and tried to
still his quaking hands enough to load his rifle again. During the interval in which he had been fighting for the ladder, somebody had cut the throat of the wounded Mexican
officer who had attacked him. The officer was sitting upright now with blood spurting out of his wound, slowly
blinking his eyes as if he had just been born into the world
and everything he saw was new and wondrous to him.

SALAS WAS still screaming. To Blas's ears his piteous
voice soared high above the sound of gunfire, the screams
of other wounded men, and the "Vivas" of the reserves
now rushing toward the wall. But all he could do was pry
Salas's fingers off his trouser cuff and falsely promise the

terrified man that all would soon be well. Then he ordered one of his men to get down on his hands and knees at the base of the wall, and another to do the same on his comrade's back, then turned to Alquisira and said, "Follow me!"

Blas slung his rifle over his shoulder and climbed up the shifting, collapsing platform his men had made until he was able to grab a reinforcing timber at the top of the wall and heave himself over. A towering norte shot at him with a pistol to no effect and then attacked him with a vicious knife, and Blas—who had not yet had a chance to rise—had to parry the knife with his rifle and kick at his assailant with his feet until he could maneuver himself upright and find room enough to thrust his bayonet into the clenched muscle of the norte's abdomen. The man shouted in alarm and thrashed about hysterically, and the bayonet was so deeply encumbered in his ribs and spine that Blas had to plant his foot upon the squirming man and push hard before he could release it.

Alquisira and several others were over the wall now, and small as their number was they knew themselves to be the forward edge of an unstoppable assault. Following Blas's example, heartened by the arrival of the reserves, men had forgotten about the ladders and were scrambling over the walls in any fashion they could, or finally breaking through the bricked-over doorways and windows that led directly into the courtyard.

Only a few rebels were left defending the wall. Dead men were scattered about the gun carriages, and those who were not dead or grievously wounded were starting to flee for the safety of the barracks. Loading his rifle, Blas saw Alquisira, in the act of bayonetting a gunner who was trying to spike one of the cannon, topple backward as he was struck by a sharpshooter on the roof of the convent. Blas turned in the direction from which the shot had originated. The faintest wash of dawn was now seeping up out of the

east, making the enemy rifleman visible in silhouette as he
threw away a paper cartridge and began pumping his ramrod down the barrel of his Kentucky rifle. Blas shot him
through the chest, and he hopped backward and disappeared.

Blas ran to Alquisira and helped him to his feet.

"The same spot!" he was crying. "The very same!" He
pointed to the backside of his calf where the bullet had
penetrated, and where less than two months earlier he had
been struck by a Comanche arrow. As the balls from desperate norte riflemen singed the air around them, Alquisira
laughed as if nothing could ever again amuse him half so
much. Then—too maniacally delighted to feel the pain of
his wound—he followed Blas as he jumped down into the
courtyard.

A RIFLE BALL had grazed the back of Joe's hand, and
when he swung his musket by its barrel at a Mexican soldier who was climbing over the wall the blood made his
grip so slick that the gun went flying out of his hand and
struck a nearby Texian in the face. Joe yelled "Negro! Negro!" at the Mexican, but the man was a diminutive Indian,
no bigger than a bird, who didn't seem to understand or
care about Joe's pleading. Despite his size he came on fear-
lessly in a crouching run, intent on impaling Joe with his
bayonet. Joe leapt backward off the parapet to evade him,
landing hard on the small of his back, and the Indian in his
momentum sailed over as well and landed even harder, and
in the confusion of the moment Joe seized the man's musket where he had dropped it and sprang to his feet. This
sudden movement, after his fall off the ramparts, made his
head swirl and caused him to vomit. He heard somebody
shout "To the barracks!" and started running.

But in his confused state he ran in the wrong direction,
toward the west wall. He could see Edmund McGowan and

Captain Baker and several other men fighting off the Mexicans at the top of the wall, and down below in the courtyard more Mexicans were now bursting out of the houses, having broken their way through the barricaded doors and windows with axes and crowbars. They stuck their bayonets into Patrick Herndon, and to Joe's greater horror they did not stop to spare the negro woman who was wailing for mercy by his side, but ran her through as well and braced their feet against her twitching body to pull out their blades and then came after Joe.

Joe ran across the churned-up dirt, across the litter of paper cartridges, toward the other end of the plaza. He ran through the very ranks of the Mexicans who were now jumping down from the north wall and advancing through thick veils of poisonous smoke into the Alamo compound. By some miracle they did not react swiftly enough to kill him, and he broke free from the front of their line and joined the Texians who were withdrawing toward the barracks.

Some of the rebels—Major Jameson prominent among them—were retreating with cool precision, pausing every few steps to fire and reload. Few of the Mexicans who had gained the interior of the fort had a charge in their muskets, and few found the courage to rush with their bayonets into such disciplined fire, and so there was a long, hanging moment as the Texians made their way to the barracks during which it seemed to Joe that the battle was suspended and that it might be possible to surrender. But the moment passed, the enemy began to surge boldly forward as an officer with a bad arm rallied them and waved his sword, and the defenders of the Alamo turned and ran into the dark cells of the old mission convent where monks had once passed this venerable hour before dawn in murmuring prayer.

———

"FALL BACK!" Baker was yelling to the men on the west who were still alive. "Fall back to the barracks!"

"They've got the guns!" Edmund called out to him, pointing toward the northwest battery where Mexican soldiers were already attempting to wheel the cannon around so that they were pointing into the fort. Other soldiers were doing the same with the guns on the northern battery. The crews that were supposed to spike the cannon were either lying dead or joining the evacuation into the barracks.

Baker instantly factored out the situation. Working artillery in Mexican hands would make the barracks a slaughterhouse.

"This way, then!" he said, pointing toward the southern end of the fort. "Hurry!"

Baker, Edmund, Sparks, and eight or ten other men jumped down onto the dirt and began running toward the south gate. Up ahead, the thatch roof of one of the houses against the wall was on fire, and Mexican soldiers were just breaking through the doors into the courtyard. One of them stood uncertainly in Edmund's path, his musket and bayonet levelled. Edmund called out to him in Spanish to get out of his way, and to his astonishment the man did as he was told.

As Edmund and the others ran, they could see another Mexican column launching itself over the southwest battery, driving the men there down from the walls and across the compound to shelter behind the low wall in front of the churchyard. Those who were not taking refuge in the churchyard were fleeing through the south gate. It was clear to Edmund that, with the Mexicans now in control of the Alamo's artillery, the only possible hope for survival lay outside the walls. But they were cut off now by the enemy soldiers streaming into the fort and could not reach the other Texians fleeing through the gate.

They could make a hopeless stand where they were or

climb over the middle portion of the west wall—where the Mexican troops were not so concentrated—and try to reach the river. Edmund did not consult with Captain Baker about it. He veered to his right, where an abandoned twelve-pounder guarded a low spot in the wall, planted his feet on the overheated barrel, and vaulted over into the open darkness of the fields. He crouched there a moment by the water ditch, hardly able to believe that he had not landed on the bayonets of the advancing Mexicans. The enemy was very close at hand, yelling and cursing each other as they continued to clamber over the walls on either end of the fort, but the ground in front of Edmund seemed to be clear. He waited with his heart throbbing for Baker and Sparks and seven or eight other men to join him, and then they set off running for the river.

"MRS. MOTT," Dr. Pollard said from the window. "The Mexicans are overtaking the fort. Will you and Mrs. Losoya please withdraw to the church?"

He meant his voice to sound calm, but it did not.

Mary anxiously scanned the room. Reynolds was with Pollard at the window. Petrasweiz was still lying on the floor with his rifle pointed toward the doorway, and most of the other patients were gripping weapons as well. The exception was a man named Darst, who had come in with the Gonzales reinforcement and promptly fallen ill with a restless fever and for two days had not known where he was or what was happening. Mary went to him and grabbed his arm and began to pull him up from his pallet.

"Let me go!" Darst bellowed in his confusion, but Mary was determined to save somebody if she could and she tightened her hold, and Señora Losoya hurried over and grabbed the sick man's other arm, and together they dragged him down the stairs and out into the churchyard.

"Get down! Get down!" Crockett called to them from the darkness. He was crouched behind the wall in front of the church, firing at the Mexican troops who were advancing across the courtyard. Mary and Señora Losoya dropped to the ground, bringing Darst with them, who groaned and cursed and demanded to know what was going on.

"Can you load a musket, Mrs. Mott?" Crockett asked, passing her a Brown Bess and a handful of cartridges. She pressed her back against the wall and wiped the fouling out of the pan with her thumb, then tore open the cartridge with her teeth. The taste of the horrible grainy powder in her mouth was like the taste of death itself. While she loaded the musket she heard the balls of the Mexicans tapping like little hammers against the other side of the stone wall, and she saw one slap into Crockett's greatcoat and heard him groan.

"Are you hurt?" she called out to him.

"Not in the slightest," he said, but he sat back wearily and began to wheeze.

"If you cut the toes off them chickens they won't scratch your garden all to hell like that," Darst yelled in frightened delirium at the top of his voice.

There was a froth of blood on Crockett's lips, but he pulled himself back into position on the wall and asked for the musket Mary had loaded as he in turn handed her his expensive rifle and the fine beaded shooting pouch that went with it. She began to load the rifle as Crockett took aim and fired the musket with shaking arms. There were twenty or thirty other defenders lined up along the churchyard wall, but their fire was growing erratic, and Mary could hear a Mexican bugle on the other end of the compound calling the men together for a charge.

"No! No! Siéntese!" Señora Losoya called to Darst, who had broken away from her grasp and was standing upright now berating her for bending the teeth on his alfalfa rake.

Mary and Señora Losoya tried to pull him back down to safety but he turned and ran insensibly in the direction of the wooden palisade. Mary heard a sudden tattoo of rifle fire from the Mexican lines, but the darkness was still oppressive and she did not see him fall.

The bugle sounded again and there was a roar from the Mexicans as they made their charge toward the churchyard wall. The Texians met them with all the fire they could manage and then started to fall back, and Mary and Señora Losoya fell back with them. From the edge of her sight she saw Crockett collapse as his foot was torn half off by a musket ball. She did not have the courage to stop and help him. She kept running for the archway of the church door, which was so much darker and denser than the night surrounding it, a gaping darkness like a cavern opening.

Behind her, she heard a strange feral cry and turned her head to see Crockett on the ground with his foot dangling on the end of his leg. He had planted his hunting knife in the abdomen of one Mexican soldado, but there were four others surrounding him, and they were sticking him with their bayonets as he tried helplessly to scuttle away from them, screaming like a panther in rage and defiance.

Muzzle flashes appeared at the door and windows of the church—there were defenders inside covering the retreat across the yard.

"In here, if you please," Captain Dickinson called to her as she passed through the door, and shoved her into the sacristy, where his wife and child and most of the other women and children were gathered. Señora Losoya followed after her. Everyone in the room was screaming. The mothers sheltered their children against the walls. The younger Wolfe boy ran to Mary and shouted that he could not find his father or his brother. His face was so pale with fear that it seemed to glow softly in the darkness like the face of the moon. She squeezed him hard against her skirts but did not have the words to reassure him. A boy no older than Terrell burst into the room and started mumbling incoherently at Susannah Dickinson through a shattered jaw.

"I can't understand you!" she shouted back at him. "What do you want?"

The boy took his jaw in his hands and tried to hold it in place while he talked, but still no intelligible sound came out. Tears ran down his face in sheets as he kept trying to communicate, but finally he just whipped his body around in anger and frustration and returned to the fight. As Mary watched him leave through the sacristy door, she saw the first probing light of dawn begin to spill into the roofless church.

EDMUND AND HIS GROUP were crouched in the ruins of one of the burned-out houses to the west of the Alamo, their eyes fixed on a half-dozen lancers only a hundred yards away, on the near bank of the river. No one spoke. Behind them in the fort, the sounds of battle had tempered in pitch but risen in savagery. The rifle and musket fire was more sporadic now; the cannon were silent, though Edmund and every man with him knew that they would roar again as soon as Santa Anna's artillery crews had finished training them on the defenders who had retreated to the barracks. What they heard instead were the grunts and shrieks of individual combat, men hooting like apes as the Mexican bayonets entered their bodies.

Edmund heard renewed firing and turned to see sporadic muzzle flashes originating from the southeast. Those were the men who had fled out of the south gate—seventy or eighty of them, he judged. No doubt they had been cut off trying to make their way to the Gonzales road and were now making a last stand in the direction of the Alameda.

The sun was starting to rise, a bold seepage of light on the horizon. The sunlight flared off the tips of the horsemen's lances as they patrolled the river. Then a messenger rode up to them, and they spurred their horses toward the new killing ground where the other escapees were now trapped.

Edmund regarded the men around him—Baker, Sparks, David Cummings, someone named Crossman, a half-dozen others he did not know. They were all looking at each other with a piercing intensity, dread, and wonderment on their faces as they realized this was where they were to die and these were the souls with whom theirs would take passage.

"Boys," Baker said, I believe we had best run for it now, as it's as clear a path as we're going to have. We'll cross the river and reconvene on the other side if the Lord has it in His plan."

"I can't swim," Sparks said.

"I have no time to instruct you. Just do the best you can, and we'll see what comes of things."

David Cummings, the polite young man from Pennsylvania who had escorted him and Mary from Castleman's place to Béxar, suddenly thrust out his hand to Edmund and said, "Good-bye."

"Good-bye," Edmund replied, and they were off across the lightening landscape to the river. A voice from their rear called out in a shrill, excited voice, "Enemigos! Enemigos allá! Fuego!" and a moment later there was a ripple of accurate rifle fire. Baker, running ahead of Edmund, suddenly jerked sideways like a roped steer. Edmund felt someone's brains slap him in the back of the neck, he heard Sparks cry out "Well, goddammit!" as a ball hit him, and saw another man on his flank seemingly take flight and soar for an instant before crashing back to the earth with utter finality.

The ball that struck Edmund caught him aslant the ribs and spun him around somewhat, but he kept his footing. Another ball, spent and deflected by its passage through the body of another man, struck him high in the back, burrowing into the muscle there with scalding force.

He kept running, with the three or four other men—

Crossman and Cummings included—who had survived the fusillade. Edmund heard the sound of hoofbeats and turned to see the cavalry patrol they had spotted earlier galloping toward them with their lances down, the riders and horses as sharp as paper silhouettes against the rising sun. The lancers were on them sooner than seemed imaginable. He did not turn to look as men behind him were run through and trampled. He leapt too soon for the river and tore his knee on a tree root and then had to flounder his way forward into the icy water as Cummings and Crossman and several others sailed clear.

Behind him the lancers reined up. The bank was steep and treacherous here and they did not care to follow. One of them took out his cavalry pistol and managed to shoot Cummings through the skull as he was flailing forward toward the far bank.

The water was ten feet deep and Edmund sought out every inch of it, fighting his way to the bottom, where the thick grasses rippled in the current and startled fish scattered away from him in explosive bursts. He let the current carry him and remained underwater for as long as he could sustain himself, and then pushed himself off the bottom for a violently quick gulp of air. In that instant he looked back and saw Crossman upstream, standing on the near bank, his hands in the air, begging a lancer to accept his surrender. Two of the men who had jumped into the river with him had made it across and were trying to pull themselves up the opposite bank, but riflemen were arriving now to shoot them down. All of this was happening twenty yards behind him. Only one lancer was nearby. He rode silently along the bank, keeping pace with Edmund and his progress through the water. The lancer seemed at first to be peering straight at him as he rode, but Edmund realized from the slow, sweeping movements of his pursuer's head that he had not yet been spotted in the dark water.

He took his breath and slipped back underwater. When

he came up again the lancer was still there, and the current
was sweeping him under the bridge across Potrero Street.
But there were soldiers on the bridge, and they cried out
when they saw Edmund's head appear above the waterline.
He clawed his way back down to the bottom again, handing
himself over to the velocity of the deep current. The day
was growing lighter and lighter. Through his open eyes he
saw a gauzy half-lit world whose properties were unthink-
ably strange. He exerted himself furiously to keep from
bobbing to the surface, at the same time feeling the calm,
guiding hand of the river, the same effortless thrust a hawk
must feel riding a warm current of air. He felt as if he were
just now emerging from a beautiful dream into a terror of
wakefulness. As he passed under the bridge, balls from the
muskets of the soldiers overhead streaked through the water all around him, though to his smothered perceptions
they seemed as harmless as raindrops. A turtle flailed up
out of the grass in front of him—an unsuitable water
denizen, Edmund thought, with its awkward, heavy body
and its clawed feet. The turtle passed inches in front of his
face and then exploded as one of the balls struck it in the
center of its shell, and then it sank back down into the grass
like a broken piece of crockery.

He broke the surface again on the other side of the
bridge, roaring for breath, and then felt the river gather and
tighten and turn white with froth. The water was too shallow here to conceal him, but in compensation it was fast,
and he let the rapids take him as they would, beating him
against subsurface rocks and squeezing his torn body
through limestone flues.

The rapids ended in a calm stretch of waist-deep water
in which he felt frightfully exposed. He was somewhere below La Villita, his old neighborhood. Dogs were barking at
him. The battle for the Alamo continued in the distance,
sounds of artillery tearing through the air again, men
screaming for mercy as the lancers ran them down. Mary

was in there. Mary was probably dead now, but perhaps she was not, perhaps she would live; and as he struggled now to save himself he was guided by the speck of a possibility that he might perhaps see her again. There was no other thing he could imagine wanting.

Just before he came to a shallow dam he saw a deep irrigation ditch entering the river from the left, and he swam up its narrow channel for a few yards before emerging into a vegetable garden in La Villita. A man and his daughter stood watching him from the doorway of their house. It was almost dawn. The sun's probing light was violently orange through the thick battle smoke drifting through the neighborhood.

"Por favor," he said to the man. "Tengo que—" But the man drew his child inside and shut the door. Edmund heard the blowing of a horse and the clinking of tack and spurs and turned to see the solitary rider who had been following him along the river charging him now along the edge of the acequia, his lance low and its tip flaring in the sun and his body so high in the stirrups he seemed to hover like a spirit above his horse. Edmund made a move but not swiftly enough, and the lance point cut a deep gouge through the outside of his hip and then tangled itself in the tail of his jacket. As the rider fought to withdraw the lance, Edmund grabbed the shaft and began to wrestle him for it. The horse was experienced and well trained and kept its feet solidly planted in the furrowed earth at the edge of the acequia as the two men struggled for the weapon.

It was the lancer who finally pulled it free. The point ripped through the fabric of Edmund's jacket and, caught off-balance, he fell backward into the acequia and stood up in the thigh-deep water to face his enemy as he rested his lance in its socket and withdrew his carbine to shoot Edmund down.

"Take me at once to Colonel Almonte!" Edmund called out to him in forceful Spanish.

The lancer peered at him along the barrel of the carbine. "Who are you?"

"My name is McGowan. I am a spy for Colonel Almonte and have urgent information for him about a rebel force now on its way to Béxar. You must take me to him immediately."

"Come out of the water," the lancer said. The sun was bright on his helmet, though the predawn gloom still enveloped them, and the man's face was hidden in shadow. Edmund walked out of the acequia with difficulty. The bank was soft mud that would have pulled off his shoes had he not already lost them in the river. He was bleeding badly from the wound in his hip and from his torn knee, and each step he took left him with a shattering pain in his ribs. He could still hear the fury of the fighting in the Alamo. He could hear a mourning dove in the trees lining the river.

Edmund made a point of not advancing further. The man studied him and spurred his horse a few steps closer, until Edmund could see the flaring sunrise in the animal's eyes.

"I will take you to my captain," the lancer said, "and then if he decides that—"

Edmund reached out with both hands and grabbed the bridle on either side of the horse's head, pulling down with all his strength so that the snaffle bit dug hard into the roof of his mouth and made his eyes go white in alarm and pain. The horse danced at the edge of the slippery bank as Edmund clung to the reins on his off-side and the rider tried to frame a shot with his carbine. But the shot came just as he was toppling backward. The ball went wild and the recoil caused the carbine to strike the lancer in the nose as he fell to the ground. Edmund wrapped the offside reins around his wrist so that he could stay attached to the hysterical horse. Somehow he managed to climb into the saddle and to force the horse to carry him into the still-dark calles of La Villita. The lancer got off a shot from his carbine, the ball slapping the outer fabric of Edmund's jacket and passing harmlessly on. The saddle he rode on was already bathed in blood, and each footfall made by his resentful horse sent wild tremors of pain through his shattered body.

"COME IN HERE and get us, you fucking sonsofbitches!" Joe did not know the man who was screaming next to him, or if he knew him did not recognize him, since his face was covered with greasy gunsmoke and his voice was at a madman's thrilling pitch. His eyes were white and the cords in his neck were taut, and he had a sharp piece of metal sticking out of his collarbone. He waved a butcher's knife in front of his face and stood at a gap in the barracks wall that had just been opened by a cannon blast and as he stood there a Mexican sharpshooter shot him neatly in the eye.

Joe could not tell how many men were left alive in the barracks—maybe fifty or sixty. It was hellishly dark. The rooms were thick with dust and gunsmoke that the creeping daylight could not penetrate. In this fouled atmosphere Joe could scarcely breathe, and every surface his hands touched was slick with steaming blood or covered by an unthinkable slime of human remains. Some of the men had lost control of themselves and were sitting there empty-handed and weeping, some like Captain Baugh were still industriously loading and firing their rifles at the Mexican gun crews who were now reloading the eighteen-pounder and the other cannon.

"To cover!" Baugh called out, just before the cannon discharged again and blew him apart. Joe was huddled with several other men in the trench they had dug in the floor of the barracks, but the canister, spalling endlessly off the stone walls, seemed to find the men wherever they were hiding. A man next to Joe named Danny Cloud screamed as a piece of burning metal drilled into his back, and Joe felt the shallow furrow of the trench slowly filling up with blood. There was a ringing in his ears that eclipsed all other sounds, and he felt blood pouring out of his nose and out of the rims of his eyes.

"Here they come!" someone yelled, but the voice sounded faint and far away to him, as if it belonged to a man calling to him from across the ocean. "Here they come!"

And through the black smoke the Mexicans rushed into the rooms with their bayonets. Those Texians who were able to stand met them with knives and tried to fight them off with their broken rifles. Joe no longer had a weapon, and all he could think to do was scramble down the length of the trench shouting "Negro! Negro!" as the Mexicans stepped forward into the darkness thrusting with their bayonets.

One of them stuck Joe in the leg and Joe kept screaming "Negro! Negro!" until an officer appeared and put a restraining hand on the soldier's musket and peered down at him and said, "Es usted un negro? Es usted un esclavo?"

Joe didn't know exactly what he was saying, but he nodded his head wildly and when the officer held out his hand to pull him up off the bloody ground Joe took it without deliberation.

As the Mexican gun crews blasted apart the stronghold of the convent, Blas and a half-dozen surviving members of his company were cleaning out the rooms at the south end of the compound where isolated groups of defenders had sought refuge. They were working their way toward the church, from whose doorway and windows the *nortes* were still putting forth a lively and dangerous fire. But the men were in a killing rake now, and they behaved as if this resistance were trivial. Blas saw men fall as they plunged their bayonets again and again into the bodies of defenders who were already dead, or bent down to strip them of their watches and bloody clothes.

He and Alquisira burst open a door hanging by a leather hinge and led the way into a dark room where a man was lying on a cot holding a vicious-looking knife. Blas at first thought the man was dead, but then he slowly opened his eyes and lifted a trembling hand and held out the blade and spoke to Blas in Spanish.

"Come on," he said.

Alquisira looked at Blas for direction and Blas just stood there not knowing what to do, knowing only that he did not care to stick a bayonet into a dying man. The four fusiliers who entered the room behind him had no such hesitation, and they stabbed the man with a concerted thrust that knocked him off the cot and then they drove their bayonets into his writhing body again and again and then almost turned their weapons on each other as they fought over who was to possess his peculiar knife.

Blas turned and walked outside. Now that the sun was rising he could see dead men everywhere, in the courtyards, on the parapets, in the blood-streaked rubble of blasted-out houses. Fire was still coming from the direction of the church, and Mexican troops were crouched behind the low wall in front of the churchyard, gathering their will for another assault. Blas and Alquisira ran to join them, but before they had gone more than a few varas Alquisira turned pale and stumbled forward in a faint. Blas caught him awkwardly in his arms and leaned him up against the facade of one of the shattered buildings.

"Stay here," he said to Alquisira, as he bound his leg wound again to stanch the blood. "You should not be moving around at all."

Alquisira smiled at him and opened his mouth to reply

but at that moment a well-aimed rifle ball from the upper room of the convent burst into his heart. Blas picked up his rifle and left the dead man where he was and ran across the plaza and climbed the blasted stone stairs leading to the place where the shot had come from. He entered the room in a heedless unbroken motion and saw a man standing at the window desperately ramming a charge into his rifle. The man turned and Blas shot him and then rushed forward to pierce him with his bayonet, and the man writhed on the floor and cursed him in his language until he grew still enough to die. Blas withdrew his bayonet and looked around the room. It was filled with dead men, some of them still lying on cots and pallets, some twisted on the floor, the walls coated with blood and viscera that glowed in the light of the beginning day. This had been the hospital, and the man who had killed Alquisira, and whom Blas had killed in turn, had an intelligent, composed look on his face even in death that made Blas think he was a doctor. He looked out the window. The troops behind the low wall were rushing the church now, tripping on the forms of dead men who had already tried to take the position and been repulsed. A bugle call—Attack!—pierced the morning air with frightening primacy, as sharp as the cry of an eagle. Over by the gatehouse, a Mexican soldado—drunk on killing—was holding a yellow cat aloft on his bayonet.

THERE WERE few men left to defend the church, and it took only a few moments for them to be overwhelmed and to die under the Mexican bayonets. In the sacristy, Mary and the other women heard their death screams and their final savage oaths. One of the defenders ran into the room to try to hide among them, but he was run through with bayonets and driven up against the wall twisting and squealing. The Mexicans grabbed the Wolfe boy from Mary's grasp, and though she shrieked at them that he was only a child and tried to fight them off with her flailing hands, they killed him anyway and dragged him outside on the tips of their bayonets to toss him in a heap beside his brother.

Mary waited numbly for her own death, but the killing of the boy seemed to sober the soldiers, and they withdrew. There was gunfire from the top of the ramp and from within the other rooms of the church, and then there was a sudden vast silence.

A Mexican officer entered the room briefly and told them in Spanish to stay where they were. It seemed they waited there a long time, listening to each other's sobs and to the unbroken wailing of the children. Mary found herself caught in a spasm of hiccoughing, and when another officer entered the room and said, in elegant English, "Is there a Mrs. Mott here?" she could not at first reply.

"I am Colonel Almonte," he said when she'd identified herself. "Are you in need of medical services?"

She replied in a hollow voice that she was not, and he drew her out into the church, away from the hearing of the others. The sun was up now, and through the open door she could see that the churchyard was filled with dead men, among them David Crockett, whose wonderful greatcoat two Mexican soldiers were stripping from his body.

"Our mutual friend Edmund McGowan asked me to look out for you," Almonte said. "And I will do what I can, but we must act quickly, before the president arrives."

"Edmund . . . ," she said. It was a heartbroken question.

"I am afraid he must be dead. Everyone is dead. Here is what you must decide. Santa Anna knows of your involvement in the death of Don Osbaldo Espinosa. He may be generous, or he may not. My personal opinion is that he will certainly not put you to death, but he has made up his mind to be harsh and it is likely he will restrict your freedom in ways that will not be pleasant for you. It is up to you to choose whether to remain here and explain yourself to him, or to take this opportunity to flee. He will be here very shortly, in a matter of minutes. If you decide to leave I have a well-mannered mule at your disposal, and I have written a letter which will serve as your passport among the Mexican forces."

"Thank you," Mary said. "I accept your kind offer of help."

"Then let us hurry."

He led her out past the tangled bodies in the churchyard and through the south gate. She passed the door to Jim Bowie's room but kept herself from looking inside. She kept herself from looking anywhere. The dawn was freezing. The Mexican soldiers who were not still hacking at the bodies or stripping off their clothes were standing about looking bewildered and shivering.

Almonte gave her his passport. He explained that it would surely be honored by any Mexican soldier who could read it, but that it was no guarantee against senseless ambush. He advised her to be boldly conspicuous, to stay to the main roads, not to travel at night.

She thanked him again and kicked the mule forward and rode in the direction of the Alameda. There were dead Texians out here too, scattered all up and down the acequias, lying together in tight groups where they had tried to make a stand. She found herself looking at them, searching for Edmund's body among them, as if even to see him in death might be a comfort. She passed the battery in the Alameda. The soldiers there looked at her curiously, her face covered in battle smoke, her dress drenched in the blood of the boy she had not been able to save. But no one challenged her, and she urged the mule onto the Gonzales road and made her brazen way toward the hills in the distance, her mind clenched tight around the thought that her son might still be alive.

———

BLAS CAME DOWN the stairs from the ruins of the hospital and encountered a soldado attempting to bayonet a small dog. Blas kicked the man hard in the ribs and sent him sprawling against a pile of rocks.

Blas walked on and the dog, sensing a degree of security in his presence, followed along close at his heels. There was a winding scar on top of the dog's head that somebody had stitched together, but otherwise it was unharmed. It was a perceptive animal, and it did not stray from Blas's footsteps as he assembled what was left of his company to await the arrival of Santa Anna.

CHAPTER THIRTY-FOUR

✯

TELESFORO'S MERE PRESENCE at the negro's side was not sufficient to guarantee the man's safety. Several times after rescuing him from the rubble of the convent he found it necessary to rescue him again, fending off his fellow Mexican soldiers at swordpoint as they rushed at the prisoner with their bayonets. The men's eyes were battle-mad and unseeing. They were hungry for some last living thing to kill.

Telesforo told the negro repeatedly not to be afraid as they made their way across the Alamo courtyard, which was filled with men so recently dead that their exposed entrails steamed in the cold dawn. Some of the nortes stirred in agony, but not for long, as the slightest movement attracted a swarm of soldados who had not yet had a chance to plunge their bayonets into enemy flesh.

Telesforo had killed men that morning, but in the honorable heat of combat, and the unmanly slaughter and desecration going on all around him made him ashamed. Once he barked at an hysterical soldado who was cutting off the scrotum of a dead rebel, ordering him to stop, but the soldado simply looked in his direction with glazed eyes, hefted the gruesome prize in his palm, and walked away.

Telesforo would have followed and struck the man down had it not been for the negro, whose security was in his hands. Amidst all this squalid and pointless violence, he felt proud and fine within himself that he had not only saved a life, but in the process had released a downtrodden soul from bondage.

He stood with the negro in the shadow of one of the houses on the west wall of the compound. He spoke to him in reassuring tones, and the man seemed to understand at least a word or two of Spanish, because he nodded his head vigorously from time to time as he gazed with horror at the ongoing mutilation of his former masters. As he stood there as the negro's self-appointed guardian, Telesforo heard the screams and imploring groans of wounded Mexicans both within and without the walls, and he worried for his friend Robert Talon, whom he had not seen since they had climbed onto the ramparts together and been separated in the fierce fighting for an artillery position.

The wounded were receiving haphazard attention from their friends, but the army as a whole was still preoccupied with desecrating the enemy dead and searching through the buildings, hoping to discover some last pathetic pocket of resistance. Only the arrival of Santa Anna, Telesforo knew, could impose proper order, and he was heartened when the president-general walked into the compound through the south gate, wearing not an exquisite uniform but plain campaigning clothes and taking in the destruction with cool professional interest.

"Come with me," Telesforo said to the negro, leading him across the courtyard to where Santa Anna was conferring with Almonte and some of his other senior officers who had survived the fighting.

Telesforo brought the negro up to the group and followed along patiently as Santa Anna strolled through the devastation, waiting for a turn to speak. General Cos was urging Santa Anna to withdraw inside to one of the buildings, as there was still a possibility that enemy snipers were alive. Colonel Almonte begged His Excellency to send out an order to the citizenry of Béxar requisitioning carts for the wounded so that they could be removed to the locations in the town that had been designated as hospitals.

Santa Anna issued a few orders along these lines and

then finally turned to notice Telesforo. There was an unset-
tlingly mild look on the president's face. His was the only
face in the Alamo not smeared by smoke or blood.

"I am very glad to see you have survived, Teniente," he
said. "Who is this you have brought me?"

"A negro, Your Excellency. I believe him to be a slave."

Santa Anna smiled at the negro and held out his hand.
The negro shook it, but lightly and uncertainly, as if it were
the first time in his life he had ever encountered the gesture.

"Welcome to freedom, my friend," Santa Anna said to
the uncomprehending negro, and then turned to Almonte
and ordered him to interrogate the man in his own language.

"Well done, Villasenor," Santa Anna said. "I am happy to
have a chance to liberate this unfortunate man. You have
helped to—"

"Your Excellency!" General Castrillón called from
across the courtyard. He was striding urgently toward him,
and behind him, under guard, came five quavering and
bloodstained norte survivors, one of them still waving a pathetic strip of cloth whose color was meant to be taken for
white but was gray and grimy from battle smoke.

"Who are these men?" Santa Anna said sharply to Castrillón.

"They were found hiding, and wished to surrender. I offered them my protection."

"There are to be no prisoners in this war, General. Have
I not made that point repeatedly?"

"But surely they are of greater value to us as prisoners
than as—"

"Kill them."

"They are under my protection!"

"Villasenor!" Santa Anna said suddenly to Telesforo in a
tone of murderous impatience. "Please kill these men at
once."

Here was the decision of his life. He recognized it completely—to follow the course of honor or the course of flat-tery. And so it astonished him how quickly the choice was made, how in fact he did not choose at all.

"You," he said, pointing to a dozen men from the San Luis battalion who were standing about idly next to the rebel battery inside the gate, "come with me."

The men eagerly obeyed, aware of being under the eyes of the supreme commander. Santa Anna himself took the negro by the elbow and walked off without another word toward the other end of the fort.

Castrillón gave Telesforo a harsh look and walked away as well. Telesforo ignored the look; he ignored the bilious disgust seeping through his body. He ordered the fusiliers to shove the prisoners up against the wall of the gatehouse and to begin loading their muskets. The prisoners stood there compliantly. Several of them were weeping and pleading, a few were on their knees and stalwartly praying, but there was a lively, formidable man who shouted infantile Spanish curses at Telesforo, telling him in a furious, sputtering voice to fuck his mother.

Telesforo wanted the executions to be orderly and efficient, but before the soldados had a chance to fire, this man tried to lead a hopeless break, and the task degenerated into a haphazard, running slaughter, with most of the suffering prisoners having to be finished off with bayonet thrusts. Telesforo himself caught one of the fleeing men with his sword. The norte fell to the ground, looked up to Telesforo in stupefaction with his guts pulsing out of his body, and died with a thunderous emission of wind.

JOE HEARD the cursing and pleading of the condemned men as he walked across the compound in the company of Santa Anna, but he did not look back, especially when the firing began. But one of the prisoners—a little man named

Warner—broke away from the others and was chased down not twenty feet away, and Joe could not avoid seeing the Mexicans converge upon him with their bayonets

While this was going on, Santa Anna's face held no more expression than a rock. Before Warner's screams had even died away he turned to Joe and said something to him in Spanish.

"He wants to know if you will show him the bodies of Travis and Bowie," said an officer who spoke English, "and also that of the American politician named Crockett."

Joe said he would, and Santa Anna smiled and touched him on the shoulder and said, "Thank you, my friend," in English.

Joe led him to the north wall and up the ramp to the battery where he had seen Travis fall. He was still there, though his body had been punctured by bayonets and turned over onto its face. Somebody had stripped off his coat and his boots and his red waistcoat.

"That's Colonel Travis," Joe said to the English-speaking officer, and the man leaned down and pulled the body over so that Santa Anna could look at him. When he did so, Travis's dead staring eyes seemed to train themselves on Joe, but looking past him much as they had done in life.

Santa Anna said something to the officer, who then turned to Joe.

"He wonders if you know his age. He finds him to be very young."

"Mr. Travis was twenty-six years old."

Santa Anna nodded when this was translated, and then followed Joe across the length of the fort to the room where Bowie had been. His body was in there lying on the floor. Somebody had beat in his head with a musket butt and splattered his brains against the wall. Joe had some difficulty finding Crockett, since he did not know where he had been during the battle, but finally located somebody in front of the church who looked like him, and when they wiped the grime off his face Joe saw a tight and perverse version of the easy smile he had worn in life, and that had drawn men to him in the dark times of the siege.

"He asks me to thank you," the officer said after Santa Anna had finished contemplating the body of Crockett, "and to remind you that you have nothing to fear from us. His Excellency looks forward to interviewing you about the situation in Texas when you have recovered a little from the stress of the battle."

Santa Anna took off his hat and lifted his face to the rising sun and looked around at the horrible sights within the Alamo compound as if they gave him satisfaction. Then he smiled at Joe again and said something in Spanish as he stared at the blood-streaked face of the church and the tangled bodies still littering the yard. Joe thought Santa Anna was still talking to him, and he asked the officer what he had said.

"He said it was but a small affair," the man replied.

A FEW MOMENTS LATER, the men who had fought for the Alamo were formed into their crippled ranks in the center of the compound, where Santa Anna addressed them amidst the obscene display of the enemy dead. He had to speak above the cries of his own wounded men as they were loaded onto carts and stretchers and carried out of the fort into the town. He praised his soldiers for their valorous devotion, he lamented those who had fallen, he grieved for the pain of the wounded, though in the years to come those very wounds would be regarded with respect and wonder by their fellow Mexicans. Many great sacrifices had been made today, each of which had engraved itself upon the president-general's heart. Texas had been saved, and these were the men who had saved it.

Blas listened to the words of this oration, but they had no more effect upon his shattered spirit than did the flowering daylight. From where he stood, with the dog patiently stationed beside him, he could see the body of Alquisira still slumped against the wall of the house where he had fallen, his eyes open as if attentive to Santa Anna's remarks, his hands clenched and still. The surviving members of the company stood with Blas in ranks. Half of them were missing. He could not yet know the fate of all the others, but many were dead. Epigenio Reyna had survived, but not Alquisira, or Salas, or Petralia, or Hurtado, or Captain Loera. He had kept all of these men so improbably alive throughout that long, hideous march that it never occurred to him that he was guiding them not to safety but to slaughter.

The work of saving the wounded, of locating and removing the bodies of dead friends, of hauling and burning the corpses of the slain enemy, went on all day. Those who had taken part in the assault were exempt from these hideous and exhausting tasks, but Blas stayed and saw to it that the wounded men of his company were made as comfortable as possible as the carts hauled them away, and then he stood with the dead so that he could help fend off the carrion birds that had already appeared and wheeled in the sky above the Alamo like great swirling clouds of ash.

In the afternoon after most of the dead had been collected he took up his rifle and walked away from the fort toward the bridge that spanned the river. The dog followed him, though he had made no comment to it all day. Blas had had nothing to eat since his midnight breakfast in the long hours before the attack, but even as he stumbled along in weakness the thought of food sickened him. He stepped behind one of the charred walls of the houses the rebels had burned and vomited. As he bent over, the jaguar shooting pouch swayed from its strap in front of his eyes, and the blurry black splotches upon its yellow surface made his disorientation greater and his nausea more intense. He pulled it off and would have left it lying there if he had not

remembered that Isabella had given it to him, and that perhaps it carried some power that was dangerous to forsake.

So he slung it back over his shoulder and continued
walking. There were already two great piles of dead rebels
on either side of the Alameda. The army had spent all afternoon gathering and counting them—two hundred and
fifty-four, someone had said—and now the corpses were
arranged with architectural precision within alternating
stacks of wood and tallow, waiting with the strange compliance of the dead to be set afire.

He and the dog walked across the bridge and down the
main street. They had not gone far when Blas heard the
screams of wounded men emanating from the building on
the plaza that had been designated as the hospital. But it
was not a hospital, he saw as soon as he entered it, it was a
mere warehouse. There were no beds, no cots, no pallets.
The men made a squirming mat upon the floor; they
howled in agony and trained their eyes on Blas when he entered as if he had some hope to bring them. There were no
doctors, no doctors anywhere. A few women of the town
wandered among the wounded men, tearing their linen into
bandages, and those soldados who were not so grievously
hurt tried helplessly to attend to their comrades. The stench
of blood, of vomit, of shit, the sight of jagged exposed
bones and shining bowels, the cries of pain that were so
piercing and inhuman they seemed like the cries of some
taunting unseen beast deep in the jungle—all of this Blas
had seen before, but never in such confused and commingled quantity. He found three of the men from his company:
one with a shattered arm that must come off, one gasping
from a knife wound in the chest, one shot in three or four
places, all of the wounds dangerous but none necessarily
fatal.

He left the building and walked out into the plaza, where
the dog waited for him out of sight beneath a broken cart.
Blas meant to hurry to the battalion's campsite and find Is-

abella, but she was already there, standing at the steps of
the church, tranquilly waiting for him as if she had been
there since the dawning of the world. Her arms were filled
with cloths for making bandages.

When he saw her something broke loose in him, and he
began weeping as a group of dragoons rode by trailing bun
dles of brush for use in the funeral pyres. She did not try to
comfort him. Her look was as placid and unsurprised as
ever, as if everything that could ever happen was known to
her, had been known to her forever, and she existed for no
purpose other than to observe it.

"Help them," he said, when he could speak, gesturing
back to the hospital.

Isabella touched his hand; she looked down at the dog
that had followed him.

"I saved him," Blas said. "I couldn't save my men, but
saved him."

She blinked in understanding, and then let go of his
hand and calmly walked past him to do what she could for
the unfortunate men in the hospital.

AFTER HIS EXECUTION of the rebel prisoners, Telesforo
searched for Robert Talon, but could find him nowhere
among the living or the dead. Finally he was told by a
sargento of the Zapadores that Teniente Talon had been
wounded in the fighting and carried away in a cart to the
hospital.

Telesforo took one look at the so-called hospital and re
solved to get his friend away from this place of obvious and
inevitable death. Though Robert begged not to be moved
again, Telesforo had some men from his unit construct a
comfortable stretcher and convey the wounded man to the
storekeeper's house. The knee of Robert's right leg had
been shattered by a shotgun blast, and it was obvious to

Telesforo from a single look at the mangled bone that the limb must be taken off as soon as possible.

Though there were no proper surgeons attached to the army, Telesforo had heard that there were at least one or two individuals in Béxar who, through long experience in Indian fighting, had developed the skill to remove a limb. He left Robert in the care of the woman who cooked for them and hurried to the headquarters building on the plaza to apply for the services of these men.

Santa Anna was not there—he had gone to the hospital to revive the spirits of the wounded—but he found Almonte and Castrillón and several other members of the staff engaged in dealing with the emergency of caring for the wounded and properly disposing of the dead.

"What is it that you want, Villasenor?" Almonte said to him in a flat, cold voice as he consulted with the alcalde of Béxar about the capacity of the campo santo. "As you can see, we have desperate matters requiring our attention."

"My friend, a teniente in the Zapadores, requires the removal of his leg."

"As do others, I'm afraid. Where is your friend?"

Telesforo gave him the location. Almonte nodded brusquely and said he would send around the best of his makeshift surgeons as soon as it could be managed. But he said nothing else, no genial words of any sort, merely turned back to the beleaguered alcalde. And when Telesforo passed Castrillón on his way out, the general gave him a look of purposeful contempt.

Back in the storekeeper's house, he waited all afternoon with Robert for the surgeon to arrive.

"The prospect of losing the leg does not trouble me," Robert said, taking careful breaths between surges of pain. "It was honorably lost in a cause that has merit. But I will admit to you, my friend, I cannot conceive how I will bear the pain of having it cut off."

"The surgeon will do it swiftly."

"I will certainly cry out. I used to imagine that I could endure pain like a Spartan, but now I find that even the prospect turns me into a weeping coward. Forgive me: I have not asked you of your experience of the battle."

"I am disgraced, Robert."

"Disgraced?"

"I was ordered by Santa Anna to execute five men who had attempted to surrender. It was a dishonorable assignment and the whole army saw how eagerly I carried it out."

"You could not have disobeyed an order, Telesforo."

But even in Robert's healing words Telesforo could hear a tentative note that he could not distinguish from contempt. It was true he was bound to obey the orders of his commander in chief, no matter how disagreeable, no matter—he even supposed—how cold-blooded. But what had caused Santa Anna to turn to him in the first place, and not to Castrillón or any of the other officers in the vicinity whose rank and bearing were greater? Surely the answer could only be that Santa Anna knew that Telesforo could be counted on to carry out this inhuman task without a murmur, that he would not hesitate to sacrifice his honor for His Excellency's continued favor, and that at the bottom of his character there was nothing firmer than obsequious ambition.

The man who came at last to perform the operation was an old ranchero in a cross mood whose apron was already soaked with blood. He brought his son along as an assistant, a boy of no more than twelve, who set out the cutting tools upon a table without a word as his father glanced cursorily at Robert's wound. Robert tried to meet his eyes, but the ranchero was tired and unsentimental and in any case clearly had no solace to offer.

"You will have to help me," he said to Telesforo. "My son can't hold back the flap and compress the arteries at the same time."

"I will help, of course," Telesforo said.

"Good," the ranchero replied. "Then let us go to work at once, so that the poor man's suffering can be behind him as quickly as possible."

Unschooled though he was, the man was fast and sure with his knife and saw, and his son proved to be an unshakable assistant. Nor did Telesforo look away as he held a great flap of Robert's muscle and skin in his hands, as the blood spurted wildly in the instant before each vessel was tied, as the screams of his friend reverberated through the room. He would have taken Robert's place if it would have meant his honor could be restored to him. But there was no healing his wound, no pain great enough to cauterize the shame he felt in his soul.

JOE'S SLIGHT LEG WOUND was bandaged, and he was given clothes that the Mexicans had liberated from one of the Texian stores in Béxar. They were ready-made, and though they did not fit, they were an improvement over the greasy and blood-soaked homespun he currently wore. A Mexican officer took those clothes away and did not return them. Before he was given the clothes he was shown to a room where there was a basin and a looking glass, and he stared at his pinched and aged face and the dark beard that had grown in below his eyes.

Everyone kept talking about the fact that he was a free man, but there was a guard outside his door, and near dark this guard walked into his room as if he owned it and barked something to Joe in Spanish and was angry and exasperated when Joe could not understand or respond. Finally the guard just gestured for him to follow, and he led Joe outside and across the plaza and into a room where Santa Anna was drinking brandy with his officers.

Santa Anna stood and patted him on the back like a dog and the same officer who had translated before—he introduced himself now as Colonel Almonte—asked Joe if he would mind taking a seat and answering a few questions to satisfy His Excellency's curiosity about the rebellion.

Joe sat down on a hard Spanish chair and listened as the questions were put to him—how many men were under arms in Texas? How many were colonists, and how many were volunteers from the United States? What was the disposition of the common rebel to the so-called Texas government? Did he know if independence had been declared, and if so had this declaration helped resolve the disputes among the factions or only intensified them? How many slaves were in Texas? Could they be counted on to take up arms in support of their own liberty? Where did the Indian tribes stand in the conflict, particularly the Comanches? Had he ever seen the Colorado or Brazos River in flood? What about the Neches? The Angelina? Where were the most active ferry crossings? Did he know of permanent bridges? Had he seen any military men in the uniform of the United States? Was President Jackson often spoken of in the Alamo? General Gaines? What had been the defenders' attitude toward Samuel Houston?

Joe did the best he could in answering these questions. He had no reason that he could see to keep any such information to himself. Though he felt a certain grim sadness for the men who had died in the Alamo, he felt just as distant from their affairs as he had when they were alive.

But in truth he could answer very few of the questions, and finally Santa Anna stopped asking them. The men talked among themselves in Spanish for quite some time, ignoring him just as Travis and the others had ignored him, and then finally Almonte bade him stand and Santa Anna walked over to him and pressed some Mexican coins into his hand.

"His Excellency is eager to provide for you," Almonte translated. "But first he asks that you travel to Gonzales and convey to the rebel leader there—we think it may be

Houston—how quickly and decisively the garrison at the Alamo was defeated.

"Then we would like you to become our ambassador to the negroes of Texas—to reassure them of our government's benevolent feelings toward them and our outrage at their unjust servitude. They must know that in the eyes of the Mexican Republic they are free men and women, and that the sooner their masters are defeated, the sooner is the day of their liberation."

Joe walked back out into the plaza, wondering who they were and who they thought he was. They were as full of talk, as much in love with their own flowery speech, as the men in the Alamo had been. He was not a slave among these men, but he still felt like one, the way they took no real notice of him, the way they used him as a sounding board for their high-blown sentiments.

He walked down the street with his guard—a guard he would not require if he were truly free. His new canvas jacket was oversized and stiff. The air of San Antonio de Béxar was filled with the screams of the hurt and dying men in the hospital, and even in the dark, burial details were still busily conveying cartloads of dead soldiers. There was a powerful smell of greasy, burning meat. When he looked down the long main street and out past the bridge he could see two great smoldering fires aglow in the darkness.

"What are they burning over there?" he said in English to the guard, though before he had even formed the words the answer was obvious to him.

CHAPTER THIRTY-FIVE

✦

HAD THE ALAMO FALLEN? Had reinforcements arrived and the Mexicans been repulsed? Terrell knew something had happened, but could not clear his head sufficiently to puzzle out what it might be. The prolonged cannonade he had heard all day yesterday had ceased at nightfall, and there had been no more firing until an hour before dawn, at which time he had heard only brief, erratic bursts, and then silence for the rest of the day.

He was sure there had probably been some sort of battle, but he could no more guess its outcome than he could be sure of his own location. It was night now. He had found a stream that he believed to be the Cibolo and was following it north toward the crossing. In the two days since he had been injured he had eaten nothing except for a handful of pecans. The night was savagely cold, with an unabating north wind. His feet and hands were freezing, the tips of his ears felt brittle as ice. And always the pain coursing through his broken wrist and shattered hand, a pain so shrill and constant that it infected his sleepless mind with despairing reveries. The pain became a demonic animal shrieking in his ear, a cocoon of fire, an endless dark thicket of mesquite from which there was no escape.

Was his mother dead? He could not flee from the thought—it followed along with him, matching its numb footsteps with his own. The night lasted forever. Time lingered heavily, it took on the form of his pain, mocking and tormenting him with its inexhaustible patience. At the end of the night the sun studied him from its fiery lair below the horizon. Then it rose in its imagined glory. Gray clouds swept across the sun's face, muting its color. It hovered there in the winter sky like a white moth, still observing him, disapproving of everything it perceived.

In his left hand, the hand that still functioned, he held his madstone. Whatever powers he had once imagined this stone to have, they were not as important to him now as its simple familiar feel; it was the one fixed point in this wilderness of pain and cold and hollow fatigue. He sat down and burrowed into a declivity beneath a shelf of rock. He seemed to sleep, but sleep was only a feverish and incoherent intensification of the scrabbling pain in his arm. When he emerged from this state he saw that the stream he had been following—the stream he had thought was the Cibolo—was no longer there. Sometime during the long night he had wandered away from it.

He backtracked for five or six unendurable miles and found the stream again, and saw that he had lost it when it veered away sharply behind a screen of cypress. When he followed this turning it led him not just steadily east but south, and after a time the painful realization settled upon him that this could not be the Cibolo after all. The Cibolo, according to the map that he tried now to assemble in his imagination, ran more or less true in the opposite direction. It would not accommodate a detour of this magnitude.

All he could know for sure was that he was somewhere between the San Antonio River and the Gonzales road, in the vicinity of the Seguín ranch. He decided to forget about the watercourses and to strike out to the northwest across open land—eventually, he knew, he must intersect the Gonzales road. He had pledged to travel only at night to avoid Mexican patrols, but his anxiety to reach some source of shelter or food was greater than his fear of being lanced or shot.

He walked all day, across the open prairie, under the mossy limbs of live oaks. It grew warmer in the afternoon,

and his mood and clarity of mind improved with the rising
temperature, but each time a cloud coasted across the sun
he was cast back into hopeless confusion. Blisters grew on
his heels and on the soles of his feet, and once or twice he
blundered like a sleepwalker into stands of prickly pear.

In the late afternoon he found himself in wild, rocky
pastureland littered with flattened mounds of cow dung.
Longhorn cattle stared at him from a careful distance,
slowly sweeping their unwieldy horns from side to side.
Javelinas trotted through the wooded gulleys on surprisingly dainty legs. Hawks perched on the bare limbs of the
trees, warm in their plumage, sated, indifferent.

Before nightfall he found a vaquero's vacant camp: a
holding pen, a jacal, an horno, a brush shed for tack. Terrell
saw no one around, no recent hoofprints or droppings. Inside the shed he found the broken handle of a branding
iron, and with his left hand he used it to pry out the hasp
that secured the door of the jacal against intruding animals.
Inside there was a straw sleeping pallet with a mouldy
blanket, a carved statue of a saint, a tight-lidded crib in
which Terrell found, within a mound of chinaberry leaves
placed there to discourage insects, five or six rolls of peach
leather, a bottle of pickled hog's feet, and a bottle of pic-
calilli.

He ate half of the hog's feet and then the yellow pickles,
breaking open the bottles with the branding iron handle
when he could not remove the wax with his one good hand.
He ate most of the peach leather as well, and with this in-
digestible combination of ingredients warring in his empty
stomach he passed that night in bloated agony.

By morning, the cramps had subsided, and he began to
notice that the heavy, pulsing pain in his right arm was
growing more bearable as well—perhaps he had merely accepted it as a constant presence. But the blisters on his feet
were oozing and inflamed, and his legs were still bristly
with cactus needles that would have to be removed before

they became septic. Lying on the vaquero's sleeping mat, Terrell pulled off his trousers and set to work. It seemed to take him hours to pull out all the needles, and when he was through he lay back in quivering exhaustion and experienced at last a state that he recognized as sleep.

CHAPTER THIRTY-SIX

✦

"ARE YOU in distress, madam?" a tall man with a thinning shock of hair said when Mary rode up unannounced to the gallery of Turner's Hotel in Gonzales.

It was past dark. The man was one of a group standing around a picnic table, their features sharp in the lantern light, as they studied a map weighted down with horseshoes. When he saw Mary he bounded down the steps, chivalrous as a knight, the rowels of his fancy Mexican spurs spinning, and offered his hand to help her down from her mule.

"Are you in distress?" he said again.

"No. Can you get me something to eat?"

"Of course I can. Please come with me."

He led her up past the gallery into the public room of the hotel. There was a fire in the hearth, and until she felt its warmth she did not realize how cold she was. She shivered as someone brought her a cup of tea.

"I am Sam Houston," the tall man said. "Will you tell me who you are and where you are from?"

"My name is Mrs. Andrew Mott," she said, meeting Houston's keen gray eyes. He could not have been much over forty, but his long, heroic face was already a blowsy ruin, a drinker's face with a tracery of florid veins. "And I have lately been in the Alamo. Has word reached you about what happened there?"

"Yes. Several days ago two Mexicans appeared, spreading the rumor that the fort had fallen and the garrison massacred. I had them arrested, not wanting to alarm the populace.

But tonight Captain Dickinson's widow and Travis's slave arrived to confirm their report, and now I suppose you will confirm it further."

Mary simply nodded her head and took a sip of the tea. A platter of cornbread was set in front of her, a bowl of some kind of soup. Houston sat down, sweeping his sabre into his lap, and questioned her relentlessly as she ate. His voice was unfailingly soft and considerate, but she was quite aware that she was under interrogation. Houston wanted to know if she was the same Mrs. Mott who kept a highly regarded inn in Refugio. What had brought her to Béxar? Were all the men at the Alamo indeed lost? Were the Mexican casualties severe as well? Why had she not been detained like Mrs. Dickinson? And since she had not been detained, why had it taken her almost a week to reach Gonzales?

She held nothing back in her answers, even showing Houston the passport letter from Almonte, which he handed to an aide who could read Spanish to verify its contents, and then considerately returned to her. She had been late in arriving, she explained, because she had encountered at the Cibolo Crossing a man whose horse was dead and who was himself grievously wounded—shot through the abdomen during the reinforcement attempt that had taken place two days before the battle. The man had been separated from his comrades, and Mary had cared for him as best she could, hoisting him onto her mule and taking him to Castleman's cabin, now abandoned by the family, where after three days he died.

She did not describe those three days: the poor man's unyielding agony, the putrescent stink of his exposed bowels, the bloody clots he passed instead of urine, the sweaty grip of his arms around her neck while he screamed for relief and begged her to reassure him that his soul would find passage to heaven. Watching him die, it occurred to her that the hideous killing frenzy of the Mexicans at the Alamo,

the ceaseless bayonetting of the wounded, had been an un
intended act of mercy.

She had buried him on Castleman's property, she tol
Houston—not buried him, precisely, as the soil was rocky
there and she was weak and had no implements, but she ha
secured the body as best she could beneath a shelf of roc
and sealed the opening with a tarp she had found in th
barn and then weighted down with stones. She hande
Houston a paper with the man's name on it—Richar
Starr—along with the names of his wife and parents and
map showing where he was interred should they care to re
move him.

The day the man died, she told Houston, she had bee
down at the creek trying to wash the death smell out of he
own clothes when she heard voices at the top of the hill. A
first she had leapt into the frigid water and hidden hersel
below a mossy bank, but when she realized the men wer
speaking English she ran shivering up the hill toward th
cabin. By that time they were already riding hard towar
the Gonzales road, and when she called out to them agains
the wind they could not hear her.

"Yes," Houston said. "Those were my scouts, the one
who found Mrs. Dickinson. I'm sorry you didn't encounte
them as well. They would have done their best to make yo
comfortable and you would have gotten to safety all th
sooner."

Mary continued to answer Houston's questions whil
the room filled up with grim onlookers. The men in the ho
tel were inspecting their weapons and tying their packs an
blankets, and she noticed for the first time that there wa
great agitation on the streets as well, officers collectin
men, families hurriedly packing, the widows and childre
of the men from Gonzales who had died in the Alam
openly wailing and clutching one another in grief.

"What is happening?" she asked Houston.

"We are evacuating the town, Mrs. Mott. The Mexicans are said to be close by. You have time to finish your meal, but I am afraid I cannot offer you the warm hearth you so obviously deserve. We must be on the march by midnight."

"I want to find my son," she said. "He was sent out as a messenger from the Alamo, and I think he may be here. His name is Terrell Mott."

Houston repeated the name to the men in the room, but no one knew it.

"I will endeavor to find him for you, Mrs. Mott. But you must consider that I have only recently arrived in Gonzales from the town of Washington and that what we have here is a thrown-together aggregate of an army whose individual parts are not yet known to me, and which—furthermore—is in an urgent state of flight. At the moment I feel rather like Caesar facing the armies of Achillas, though Gonzales is a poor substitute for the Alexandria of the Ptolemies!"

Houston emitted a brusque, distracted laugh. "Now if you will excuse me I must attend to the retreat. In the meantime I give you into the keeping of Colonel Hockley, who will see to it that you will be made as comfortable as circumstances allow."

Colonel Hockley was amiable and earnest. He observed that her clothes had seen hard use—would she permit him to inquire from some of the ladies of the town if there were a dress or two that she could borrow? He had her write down the name of her son so that he could take it to the various company commanders at the first chance to do so, and said that he would see that her mule was looked after until it was time for the army to set off on the retreat.

In an hour she had new clothes. They gave her a room of the hotel in which to change, and when she came out the rude log building was empty, with only Colonel Hockley standing at the door waiting for her. Everyone else was already out on the dark streets, the army formed up in its ranks, waiting for the order to march. Great fires were burning in the plaza across from the hotel, and down along the Guadalupe River where the men had camped.

"We have given all our wagons over to the families of Gonzales," Hockley explained. "And so are burning up what we cannot carry on our backs. We must be fleet if we're to outrun the Mexicans.

"Here is your mule," he said, as one of the soldiers delivered the animal, along with Hockley's horse. "Perhaps you would care to ride with General Houston and myself."

Except for Houston and a few members of his staff, and a contingent of cavalry, the whole army was on foot. As she and Hockley rode to the head of the column, she saw that Houston's army had no more claim to real military substance than had the Alamo garrison. Like the men in the Alamo, they had no coherent uniforms. Their weapons were haphazard as well—rifles for some, shotguns and muskets for others, sashes and belts crowded with pistols and knives and hatchets. She studied each face as she rode past; the night was dark and she knew the chances of spotting Terrell in this crowd were dim, but perhaps he might see her riding by and call out to her from the ranks.

But no one called, and she found herself cast into a state of disappointment that seemed to rule every aspect of her being. Her exhaustion, briefly forgotten in the hope that she might soon see Terrell, returned with crushing conviction. She was sleepy and dirty and drained of morale and her legs were chafed from long riding. She knew a remedy for this—a few grains of salt dissolved in brandy—but if there was any brandy in this army she was sure that General Houston had long since drunk it up.

The army's wagons, loaded with the possessions of the Gonzales citizens, were already advancing out of the town, and some of the refugees flocked along beside them, carrying their children, driving their oxen and milch cows, trying to pull their dogs out of snarling fights with the dogs of their neighbors. Mary saw Susannah Dickinson riding in the bed of one of the wagons, holding her infant daughter, staring out into the night with dazed indifference.

"Hello, Susannah," Mary said. "Are you and the baby well?"

"Yes, thank you," she replied distantly, looking up at Mary as if she were someone she vaguely remembered from years ago.

There were still lights burning in many of the houses in the town, and through the windows Mary could see families hurriedly packing. No one was staying. They were aroused with the conviction that the Mexicans would torture and kill every living thing in their path.

"Are we ready to embark?" Houston asked Hockley as they sat on horseback looking behind them at the rows of men assembled on the street.

"I believe we are, General."

Houston smiled at Mary. "You have come at an historical time, Mrs. Mott. We have never yet attempted the trick of moving all of our army at the same time. It is rather like trying to train a millipede to waltz."

He stood up in his stirrups and called out in a roaring voice.

"Gentlemen, if you please—Forward! March!"

Those townspeople who were not already on the road came flying out of their houses as the army began to leave Gonzales, anxious not to be left unprotected in a town soon to be engulfed by the Mexican forces. They were in such a rush they did not extinguish the tapers burning in their rooms, and the light from the windows illuminated the column until the last house had been passed.

There was a strange silence as they passed from the town onto the dark prairie beyond; all these hundreds of people joined in fright and confusion and none apparently saying a word, just looking back at the lighted windows until they could no longer be seen.

Mary had seldom known a night so utterly black. The mule Almonte had given her was independent-minded, and on another occasion might have defiantly insisted on a slower pace, but tonight it seemed to concern itself with not being left behind in the darkness by Houston's and Hockley's well-rested horses.

They rode for an hour in the same silence, broken only by the riders who kept coming up to Houston to report some problem or detail with the march.

"Where are we going, General?" Mary asked him at last, in part because the darkness and silence seemed so oppressive.

"East, ma'am," he said, after a pensive silence, as if he seemed to just now be thinking about the matter. "We are presently not in any situation to fight the Mexicans. We have not four hundred men with us, and are encumbered by civilians besides. Colonel Fannin has a sizable force in Goliad, holed up in their so-called Fort Defiance, and I have ordered their withdrawal. I don't want my men forted up, you see, Mrs. Mott. That was our mistake at the Alamo, and by thunder I predicted it. No, we must extend Santa Anna's line of supply, fight him like leatherstockings from the forests and the canebrakes."

"Are Fannin's men to join us, then?"

"Eventually. Don't worry, Mrs. Mott. Your son is either with us, or with Fannin, or with one of the ranging companies. In any case he will turn up soon. All the forces of Texas are rallying to Houston."

The way he spoke his own name in the third person irritated her, as did the feather he had pinned to his hat. She disliked him as well for his hollow gallantry. Where were you? she wanted to ask him. Where were you when we were in the Alamo, counting on you to raise an army to save us? He had wanted the war to go his way, she guessed. He had wanted to take it east, all the way to the Sabine, to the American border, where he could provoke an even greater war between Mexico and the United States. That was what all these grandiloquent men wanted: a bigger stage, a more telling chance to reclaim the reputations they had thrown away to scandal. In order to help the "forted up" men in the Alamo, Houston would have had to abandon his own plans and subvert his own ambition, and men such as he did not do such things, no matter the cost in lives.

Edmund died because of this man, she realized. He had had his own massive ambitions, his own grandiloquence. He would not willingly have sacrificed the lives of others to his purpose, in the manner of Houston, but he had been capable of sacrificing his own earthly happiness, of denying it to himself so thoroughly that it seemed to her a transgression of nature. To live and die without love! Was that not in its way a greater sin, a more heart-breaking crime, than to murder or destroy in the pursuit of love?

They marched all night. Mary slept briefly on her mule, and once woke to the touch of a hand on her shoulder—Houston's hand holding her upright in the saddle as she dozed. Twice she rode up and down the line of marching, weary men, calling out Terrell's name, but no one ever answered, and the procession moved silently on through the darkness. For much of the night they moved through a scattered forest of post oak, across an endless reach of soft sand that made each step a burden. The men staggered and cursed and hopped about on one foot as they poured the sand out of their shoes. There were already carts abandoned on the road, and every hour or so Houston ordered a stop so the straggling families behind the army could catch up.

But he would not stop long. He drove his army and his civilian train forward through the sandy soil and did not stop until an hour before daylight. The men did not even bother to fall out of ranks. They dropped down on the road, on the bare earth, too tired even to spread their blankets.

Mary dismounted. Hockley said he would see to her

mule. She gave him the reins and sat down on the side of
the road, her chafed legs burning, She looked back in the
direction they had come and saw a strange glow on the
horizon.

"They are burning Gonzales," she heard a woman scream.
"The Mexicans are burning our town!"

The sleeping soldiers leapt to their feet and stared at
the conflagration on the horizon. The women of Gonzales,
those who had already lost their husbands and sons and
brothers to the fires of the Alamo, now began to wail with
a shuddering biblical intensity as their homes were burned
as well.

"If the Mexicans are already in Gonzales," Mary said to
Hockley, who stood there watching the flames with a look
of wonderment, "if they are so close, is it wise for us to
stop?"

"The Mexicans are not in Gonzales," Hockley replied.
"It was Houston who ordered the town burned, to deny the
enemy the use of it. We are on a dark course, I am afraid,
Mrs. Mott. But that is the nature of war, you see.

She did not bother to remind him that she already knew
war. And so familiar was she with its horrors that she was
able to lie on the ground now and fall to sleep with the lamen-
tations of women and children still vivid in her hearing.

JOE WATCHED the burning of the town along with
everyone else until the sun came up and the flames were no
longer visible. He fell asleep on top of the baggage wagon
in which he was riding and jerked awake three hours later
when the fight in the Alamo once more poisoned his
dreams.

He sat up. Most of the men were still asleep on the road,
but Mr. Tumlinson was sitting next to him eating his breakfast from a tin plate.

"You want something to eat there, Joe?" Tumlinson said, handing him a cold biscuit with molasses.

Joe said his thank-you and took the biscuit. Tumlinson nodded his head as if Joe's appetite gave him satisfaction. Joe's impression was that he had been given over to this man's keeping until it could be decided what to do with him. Travis was dead, and exactly whom Joe belonged to now was apparently a cloudy issue that the lawyers would get to when there was time for it.

Tumlinson was fifty or so. He had lost a son in the Alamo and was melancholy about it, and kept pestering Joe for information. Joe remembered a man named Tumlinson in Carey's artillery company, but had never spoken to or formed an impression of him and had nothing for certain to tell his father about him except that he was dead along with all the rest of them.

"By God, I will see every last one of those Mexicans in hell," Tumlinson said as he ate a biscuit in one bite and kept his eyes fixed to the west, where the whole town of Gonzales, Joe reckoned, must now be lying in ashes.

His own emotions were as guarded as Tumlinson's were raw. When Sam Houston and the other men of the army questioned him about the Alamo he had answered them with strict honesty and compliance, but each word of recollection he spoke seemed to threaten him with madness. They wanted to know if Travis had died "gallantly," and he said he had, and he even made up a story about Travis drawing his sword after he'd been shot and running it through a Mexican officer. He did not know why he told that story, only that they seemed to want to hear something like it, and in the act of substituting this scene for the horrible true moment in which Travis's brains had flown out of the back of his head he felt as if he had managed to place a plaster over a wound of memory that might otherwise never heal.

Joe turned to Tumlinson and said he had to urinate. Tumlinson told him to go ahead and get it done with, but not to wander out of sight, as the army would be moving out again within the hour.

Why had he asked permission? Joe wondered to himself as he stepped a few paces off the road and unbuttoned his pants. No one had told him that Tumlinson was now his master, he had just guessed that it might be the case. He was angry with himself for so thoughtlessly falling back on the habit of subservience, though his thinking mind told him it made sense to do so. Houston and the others had been as friendly to him as white men could be, but it was clear to Joe that he was not trusted. Tumlinson's eyes were on him at every moment. Maybe they guessed that Santa Anna had made him an "ambassador" to the negroes of Texas, maybe they thought he would run off and start a bloody uprising among the slaves to support the liberating Mexican troops. There were negroes among the families fleeing Gonzales, but Joe had been careful not to approach them. He did not want to make Houston suspicious and end up wearing shackles.

And anyway, the kind of incitement Santa Anna wanted him to perform as an "ambassador" was not in Joe's nature. He did not take easily to walking up to strangers, white or negro; he could no more persuade another man to run away and take up arms against the Texians than he could persuade himself. His strength was in something else—he was as watchful and patient as a lizard. It was watchfulness that had saved him from death at the Alamo, where all those other clamoring men had perished. All he had to do was take notice of everything that occurred around him, not be too quick to act; wait to see if the freedom that Santa Anna promised was real or just more excitable talk of the kind Joe had heard all his life.

"Do you know me?" said a woman standing by the

wagon when he returned. "I am Mrs. Mott. I was in the Alamo."

"Yes, ma'am," Joe said. "I saw you there."

"You are Travis's man."

"Yes, ma'am. I'm Joe."

"Are you all right Joe?"

Joe nodded his head. He looked over at Tumlinson, who was pretending not to notice Joe as he pulled up the hoof of one of the horses on the wagon team and inspected its shoe.

"May I talk to you?" Mrs. Mott said.

Joe shot another glance at Tumlinson and allowed Mrs. Mott to draw him over to the side of the road. There were hundreds of people all around them—soldiers chewing their breakfasts, women wandering off to the trees together to evacuate their bowels, settlers tending to their bewildered stock, children staring forlornly at the ground—but it seemed to Joe that he and Mrs. Mott stood in their own pocket of stillness, bound to one another by their experience in the Alamo just as tightly as a husband was bound to his wife or a mother to her child.

"There is something I want to know," she said, after they had spoken for a few moments about the siege and the final assault and how each had escaped death. "Do you remember Mr. McGowan? Edmund McGowan?"

"Yes, ma'am," Joe said.

"Do you know how he died, Joe? Did you see it happen?"

"I believe I saw him fightin', ma'am. On the west wall. But it was dark and there was lots of smoke, and I was too scared to notice much."

"Do you remember if there were men around him?"

"There was Captain Baker and some others. I don't recall him bein' up there by himself."

Mrs. Mott looked down at the grass and then raised her head again, and Joe thought he had never seen a more sorrowful expression. Something had broken her nose and the bridge of it was flattened and pushed a bit to one side, but otherwise she was handsome for her age, and the gruesome hardships of the last three weeks had not erased the fortitude in her face.

"Thank you," she said. She touched Joe's arm above the elbow in an absent, caressing way and might have even embraced him if Joe, in his watchfulness, had not turned himself to stone. "Thank you. I was concerned that Mr. McGowan did not die alone."

CHAPTER THIRTY-SEVEN

✯

EDMUND HEARD the sound of a horse shearing grass with its great teeth, the bells on the necks of goats, the solemn voices of children as they walked past the jacal where he lay bound in an iron cage of pain. The world was suddenly vibrant with sound. When had the ringing in his ears—the rebounding shriek of battle—finally subsided?

A woman peered in the door, shuffled inside and busied herself with a series of tasks that included changing the nopal poultices on his wounds. He cried out when she moved him to inspect the bullet wound on the back of his shoulder.

"The ball will have to come out," he told her in Spanish. She was sixty, perhaps older. He thought she looked familiar, but his memories of where he was, what people these were, and how he had come to be among them were fragmentary and inexact.

"It is already out," she said. "I took it out two days ago. Don't you remember?"

"Yes," he said. "I do now."

She reached up on a shelf and handed him a flattened lead disk.

"I had to pry it out of the bone of your shoulder with the tip of a knife."

"I think there's another ball in my side."

"No. It went in and out on its own. See?"

She removed an immense poultice from his right side to reveal a massive bruise as bright as a rainbow, and the collapsed tunnel of flesh the ball had made. The ball must have cracked his ribs as well, because it was when he took in breath that the iron cage squeezed the hardest.

The last poultice the woman removed covered a deep, sharp gouge on the edge of his hip, the edges of the wound sewed together with gut thread. Clear pus ran out of the wound, along with nopal sap, when she squeezed it. Edmund cried out despite his best intentions, and when she put the blanket back over him he closed his eyes and gave himself over to strenuous thought, testing himself on whether what he remembered was real. There had been a desperate fight for the Alamo, but if the fight had been as savage and as hopeless as he recalled it, it was wildly unlikely that he could still be alive. But he was, and fragment by fragment the memory of how he had survived began to accumulate and to assume an incontrovertible force: his sense of mad helplessness as the Mexicans poured into the fort; his frantic breath visible in the cold dawn as he raced with Baker and the others toward the river; the odd sensation, as the balls hit him, of being struck from behind and in the ribs by a stout walking stick; the Mexican who had stabbed him with his lance.

"I hear a horse outside," Edmund said to the woman. But time must have passed. He must have slept. She was gone.

But soon she was back with a bowl of broth. A little girl was with her. She sat on a mat on the other side of the jacal, gripping a corn husk doll as if it were a weapon, and stared at Edmund as the woman spooned the broth into his mouth.

"Whose horse is that?" he asked her.

"Yours. That horse is how you came here."

"A roan mare?"

"Yes. With a Mexican army saddle."

He remembered the sodden, blood-soaked weight of his clothes as he forced the horse through the suburbs of Béxar and out onto the Goliad road, with no one to challenge him once he had broken through the net of lancers guarding against escape from the Alamo. The hair of the horse thick

with his blood as well, the creature's hatred of him, its defiant confusion as Edmund kicked it mercilessly ahead. All
day he had fought to stay in the saddle, aware that if the
horse threw him or he otherwise slipped to the ground he
would not have the strength to climb back on board. Wolves
trotted along beside them in broad daylight, maddened by
the torrential scent of blood, and for once Edmund and the
horse had been of the same mind, pounding down the road
with the wolves in pursuit.

He turned his eyes to the little girl, recognizing her now
as the child he had liberated last year from Bull Pizzle's Comanches. So that was where he was: in the old Spanish presidial barracks at the Carvajal crossing.

"The Mexicans will look for me here!" he said to the
woman. "They know this place."

"Calm yourself, señor," she said. "We are in a sheep-
herder's house. It is a mile away from the barracks and cannot be seen from there. We think you are safe for now. The
army is very busy in Béxar. Many soldiers are wounded,
and there is much confusion there."

He slept again, and when he woke the girl was still there
on the other side of the jacal, still clutching her doll. The
woman was gone.

"Do you remember me?" he said to the girl. She nodded
her head.

"Will you bring me some water?"

She picked up an earthen jug and carried it to him. After
he drank she took up her station again on the other side of
the room and continued to stare at him. He wondered what
she saw: the ravaged and defeated man he knew himself to
be, or the mysterious agent of God who had rescued her
from the Comanches?

He could think of nothing to say to her, and she was still
as mute as she had been the day he encountered her. Edmund stretched out his arm and opened his hand and she
shuffled across the dirt floor and laid her own tiny hand in

his palm. He fell asleep and when he woke again her hand
was still there, though it was dark and a shrill night wind
rustled the thatching of the roof. Flores, the man whom
Bowie had almost hanged, was tending a careful fire in the
center of the jacal.

"Good evening, señor," Flores rasped.

"Your voice has improved."

"Do you think so? I hope that is true. Lupita, go with
your grandmother."

The curandera emerged again from the shadows of the
jacal and took the girl's hand and walked out with her into
the night back to the barracks where the rest of the family
was living.

"Tell me what you know about the Alamo," Edmund said
to Señor Flores.

"My nephew was in Béxar two days ago. The cavalry
came here and ordered him to load up our cart with corn and
take it into the town for the soldiers. They demanded almost all our goats as well. The Bexareños told my nephew
that every one of the men in the Alamo had been killed in
the battle. Every one except you, it seems. They burned the
bodies in the Alameda. For a long time we smelled something on the wind—perhaps that was what it was."

"What about the women and children?"

"My nephew says that most were spared, though some
might have died by accident in the fighting."

"There was a woman named Mrs. Mott."

"Yes. We remember her. My nephew tried to find out
something about her fate, but the Bexareños he talked to
knew nothing, and he was afraid to approach the soldiers.
Perhaps she survived. I think there is a good chance of it. If
so, she was probably sent on to Gonzales."

"I have to go there," Edmund said.

Flores shook his head. "We have heard that the rebel
army has burned down Gonzales. They are fleeing in panic
to the United States border. And besides, you are far from

being well enough to travel anywhere. You have lost much blood and my wife is still worried about your wounds. No, my friend—you have to stay here with us for a time."

"Thank you," Edmund said.

"It is we who owe you thanks that can never be repaid."

Flores slept that night in the jacal on the other side of the fire. He had slept there every night, Edmund now began to remember, and every morning his wife came to inspect his injuries and to bring him food, and in the afternoons there had always been the little girl, staring at him with the intensity of someone trying to puzzle out the mystery of her own fate and her own place in the world.

Flores's snore was as thin and ragged as his voice, though the surging wind soon drowned it out. Edmund fell asleep and began to scream as the wind grew more intense and the terror of his memory invaded his dreams.

"Do not be afraid, señor," Flores said when he shook him awake. "God is with you, and you are among friends."

Flores soon was snoring again. But Edmund resisted sleep with all the force of his mind. He lay there listening to the lancer's horse as it danced and fretted at the end of its picket rope, so far from its familiar world.

CHAPTER THIRTY-EIGHT

✴

MARY STAYED with the army, joining in its march across the prairies to Burnham's Ferry on the Colorado, where Houston had announced he would make a stand against the Mexican forces in pursuit. But then he changed his mind and led the army downriver and made camp in a forest on the other side of Beason's Crossing. Rain had come and it was constant, a cold, swirling rain that turned the road into an endless mud pit that sucked the shoes off the men's feet and trapped the cart wheels up to their axles. The civilian refugees that accompanied the army were hungry and exhausted and ill from every sort of affliction from pinkeye to consumption. They did not conceal their lack of confidence in Houston's army to protect them, and the more Mary saw of its slovenly, demoralized aspect the more she thought the panicky settlers were right.

It seemed to Mary that Houston made a show of being whimsical and hard to predict in his maneuverings, as if he were some exalted figure from ancient times who set his course not by the counsel of his colleagues but by the shifting moods of the gods.

At least he did not appear to be drunk as he stood with his officers at the crossing, observing with satisfaction the rising waters of the river that effectively put a barrier between his army and the Mexicans. Day by day, the men grew to like him less. He was more politician than soldier, it was clear, and vacillation and deliberation came more naturally to him than a steadfast commitment to a fight. A number of the men deserted, but far more found their way to the army. The defeat of the Alamo had brought the crisis home to the colonists who had so far stayed out of the war, and every day more of them joined Houston's army, along with more arrivals from the States, until the population at Beason's had increased to fourteen hundred men.

Mary met the bands of newcomers as they churned their way up the muddy roads or crossed the swollen Colorado on dangerous makeshift ferries. She studied the face of each man and questioned the officers but never found anyone who had seen her son or knew his whereabouts. Finally it became obvious to her that he must either be dead, shot down on the roads by a Mexican patrol, or with Fannin's men somewhere along the route of their march from Goliad. If he was alive, all she had to do was stay with Houston's army until Fannin arrived to join them.

They had been at Beason's for two days when the Mexican army marched into view on the opposite side of the river and began building its entrenchments in the rain. Mary stood with Colonel Hockley and a crowd of men on the summit of a steep cutbank well out of musket range and watched the soldados in the distance. The rain pounded down on them where they stood, but Mary was already so soaked through she had ceased to notice it. She wore a borrowed mackinac and a broad-brimmed man's hat that funnelled the water into a cascade in front of her face. The brown water of the river swept by dangerously fast, dipping into frothy shallows where the crossing had been.

"By God, we should attack them now, before they've had a chance to dig in!" a young Kentucky hotspur named Sherman shouted to Hockley through the noise of the rain.

"General Houston won't allow it," Hockley shouted back.

"General Houston has no more spirit than a rabbit! All he cares to do is run!"

Hockley warned Sherman to stop his seditious talk or he would by God have him arrested. Sherman clenched his

jaw and stood there letting the rain soak the fancy blue uniform tunic he had brought from Kentucky. Mary liked him
even less than Houston. The idea of attacking the Mexicans
across a flooded river—when they did not yet even have an
accurate assessment of the number of troops on the other
side—seemed to her preposterous.

Nevertheless, as the days drew on, Houston showed
himself to be in a martial spirit. He rode up and down the
length of the river, inspecting possible sites for a crossing
when the water receded. He was determined to attack at the
first opportunity, Hockley told Mary. He was quite aware of
the men's desire to quit running and make a stand. It was a
desire he shared. But for the moment, while the water was
high, prudence must stay his hand.

The stalemate continued for almost a week—the Mexicans digging in beyond the river bottom on the other side,
the Texians standing on the banks shouting curses at them
and now and then trying a shot with a long rifle, the rains
unabating so that the river, instead of falling, continued to
rise. The army had burned most of its tents in the retreat
from Gonzales, saving only Houston's command tent and
those for storing powder and provisions. But some of the
new arrivals had brought tarps, which they sewed together
to make extensive canvas pavilions under the trees where
the men could crowd together out of the rain. Other such
pavilions were erected for the refugees, and it was while
she was sitting beneath one of these imperfect shelters, trying to coax poor dispirited Susannah Dickinson into eating
at least a soggy corncake, that she heard an eruption of angry curses coming from the army camp.

Mary pulled on her mackinac and strode out into the rain
and across the wet, springy earth to where the soldiers were
standing about stamping their feet and shouting their sono-
fabitches and fucks and goddammits to the unrelenting sky.

"What has happened?" she asked one of them.

"General Urrea has caught Fannin, ma'am."

"Fannin and his *men*?"

"I believe so. Every last one."

She walked over to Houston's tent. The flaps were closed, but she could hear heated voices from within— Sherman demanding an immediate attack, Houston telling him that goddammit he was the commander in chief and did not listen to demands from his subordinates and if Sherman was not willing to follow orders then he should get himself and his fucking popinjay uniform out of his goddam tent and out of the goddam army.

Sherman stalked out of the tent, and Mary rushed inside to take his place before the guards could stop her. Houston was standing in the center of the tent with his arms above his head and his hands resting on the ridgepole as if he were contemplating pulling the structure down.

The guards followed Mary inside, but Houston dismissed them with the barest look and stared at the mildewed canvas in front of him with the concentration of someone looking at a painting.

I am not easily depressed, Mrs. Mott," he said, "but this is a dark hour. Fannin had four hundred men that we desperately needed. He let himself be caught out in the open, on the broad prairie in daylight. He is an ill-fated man, and if events do not soon take a happy turn Houston may become one as well."

"Where are the men now?"

"They were taken back to the fort at Goliad."

"Santa Anna will kill them," Mary said.

"As far as we know, Santa Anna has not yet left Béxar. It was Urrea who captured them. He is said to be an honorable man."

"He is under Santa Anna's orders."

Houston let his gallant mask drop, and he gave her a look of annoyance.

"I'm sure you will forgive me, Mrs. Mott, if I ask you to leave so I can convene a proper council of war."

She left and went back to the tarp and asked to borrow Mrs. Dickinson's canvas sack. Then she went to the army's commissary tent and told the dim-witted boy on duty that she required a quantity of crackers and dried beef, and her manner was so forcefully maternal that he complied without question.

Her mule was picketed with the army horses, and her saddle and bridle were in the stable tent. When she walked into the tent to retrieve them a guard appeared and smiled at her uneasily and asked if he could help her with anything.

"I am taking my mule and leaving," she said.

"I ain't sure you can do that, ma'am," the guard replied in an uneasy voice.

"Well, if it troubles you, you may shoot me," she said.

She saddled the mule while the other men guarding the horse herd looked at one another in confusion. One of them walked off to consult with an officer, but by then she had already kicked the mule into a trot and was following the river south toward the Atascocita road.

The rain lifted as she rode and the sun came out, shining off the wet prairie and on the glistening leaves overhead. She rode hard all day and came to the road and the crossing there before nightfall. She had to cross over to the west, but the water was still too high and there was a Mexican patrol camped on the other side. The sight of the soldiers made her heart throb with fear, but she forced herself to step up to the bank and wave to them as if their presence did not concern her.

She spent a miserable night alone staring at the Mexican campfire on the other side of the river, but in the morning the water was substantially lower, and the crossing was almost exposed. The mule surprised her by its willingness to convey her across the river. It proceeded as deliberately and conscientiously as she could have wished, and delivered her to the Mexican patrol.

"No soy enemiga," she said.

The officer in charge of the patrol looked at her and laughed and said "De veras" and invited her down off her mule. He handed her a battered tin cup filled with hot chocolate and spoke to her in genial but rapid Spanish that she could not understand. From a pocket of her mackinac she produced the passport letter that Almonte had written for her. During the retreat from Gonzales she had stolen a scrap of oilskin from one of the baggage wagons and had wrapped the precious document inside it, but even so the paper was damp and in places the ink had started to run.

The officer read the paper with great concentration and then handed it back to her and invited her for breakfast. He tried to make conversation and asked her what her business was in Goliad, but she pretended that her Spanish was even worse than it really was. She did not want him to have an opportunity to guess that she was travelling to Goliad to somehow try to rescue her son from execution.

They gave her food to supplement her sparse rations, and she thanked them and was on her way again before midmorning. The Atascocita road led straight west to Goliad, but it was a hundred hard miles away, and almost three days had passed by the time she saw the town in the distance and the presidio like a medieval fortress on its bluff above the river.

No one challenged her as she rode into the town, though lancers galloped past her on the road and on two occasions she heard bursts of faraway gunfire. Someone was burning something in the distant fields, or trying to. The dark smoke rose thinly above the treetops and dissipated in the windless sky.

She had been told that Fannin and his men had fought a disastrous battle on Coleto Creek and then been marched back as prisoners to Goliad. Now no doubt they were being held in their former stronghold, the presidio they had confidently renamed Fort Defiance.

She rode toward the presidio determined to see her son, to rescue him if she could and to die with him if she could not. There was no room in her weary shattered mind for any other thought.

The town itself was still. There were no citizens in view but she could hear a woman wailing in one of the houses, crying out "pobrecitos, pobrecitos" over and over again. Before she reached the presidio she heard singing from the direction of the river, and she led the mule down the road to the ford below the hill. There she saw, lined up on both banks of the river, hundreds of Mexican soldiers washing their clothes in the water. A few of the men looked up and stared at her, but no one said anything as they beat their wet laundry against the rocks. She found it curious that so many men—all still wearing their ragged uniforms—would be washing their clothes at the same time; curious as well that these threadbare Mexican conscripts would have any extra garments at all.

Then she noticed that the rocks on which they were beating the clothes were stained with blood, and that the water of the river itself had turned red from the laundering. These were not Mexican uniforms they were washing—the blue woolen tunics, the white cotton fatigues. These were hickory shirts and round jackets and butternut trousers.

A dreadful buzzing came into her head. The skin on her shoulders and on the back of her neck prickled tight in anticipation of the horrible thing she knew she must now discover. She kicked the mule savagely and drove up the road to the crest of the hill, to the gates of the presidio, and somehow argued her way past the guards and into the compound. She saw wagons loaded with bodies that were naked and ghastly pale. The outside wall of the chapel was coated with blood and brains.

"Señora! Señora!" the soldiers called out to her as she ran frantically from one room of the compound to the next, screaming out Terrell's name. When she pulled open the door of the barracks building, she encountered a stench so profound it almost knocked her onto the dirt. The room was filled with wounded Mexican soldiers, groaning and twisting on their cots as maggots pulsed in their flyblown wounds. There were several Americans in the room as well—a man in a faded red jacket probing for a bullet with a bistoury, another sitting in a chair at the front of the room wearing a bloodstained apron and a vacant, disbelieving look.

"Yes?" he said simply to Mary when he saw her.

"I think my son is here," Mary told him.

"No, ma'am. These are all Mexicans, wounded in the battle on the Coleto."

"My son's name is Terrell. Terrell Mott. Please help me."

He looked up at her. His face, with all the pain residing in it, was exquisitely kind.

"I am sorry, but they are all dead. The Mexicans marched the prisoners out this morning; they were told they were being taken to Matamoros. They shot them all on the roadside. Some few may have gotten away, but the lancers are chasing them down. The men who were wounded and could not march were shot in the churchyard."

He gestured with his head toward the man in the red jacket. "Only Dr. Shackleford and myself and the other doctors were spared. They need us to look after the Mexican casualties. All the others are gone."

"My son . . . ," Mary said.

The man gripped her hand. "I am sorry," he said. "I lost two sons today myself."

A Mexican officer entered the room, gagged, went outside for air and then returned and spoke in English to the man in the chair.

"Dr. Kenner, who is this woman?"

"I don't know, Colonel. She is a woman whose son you murdered."

His name was Colonel Portilla. He was young and awk-

wardly shaped, and—as he told Mary when he brought her
to his office in one of the houses outside the compound—
tortured by the vile but necessary task he had carried out. A
soldier's solemn duty, as solemn, it could be argued, as his
duty to God Himself, was to obey without question the orders of his superior officers. He recited this in imperfect
English as he read Almonte's letter.

"Please, where did you receive this letter?" he asked,
passing the paper back to her.

"At the Alamo."

"You were there?"

"Yes."

"And your husband—was he in the garrison?"

"No. Did you kill my son? I have to know if he's dead."

Portilla looked away uncomfortably. He stood and walked
to a desk and withdrew a stack of papers from a drawer,
then sat down again.

"I cannot tell you with definiteness, Señora Mott. But I
have here the lists of men—the muster lists, I think you call
it. It is possible on these is the name of your son."

They were the rolls kept by the company commanders.
She moved from each line, each name, waiting to see the
letters that would seal her heart closed and finally allow her
to leave this unbearable wilderness of hope. As she read,
one of Portilla's men brought them each a cup of chocolate.
He sipped his, watching her face. She did not pick up the
cup and felt it growing cold at her elbow. She came to the
last name of the last muster roll and looked up at him. She
could not allow herself to feel relief, not yet, when so much
cruel mischance was in the air.

"He is not there?" Portilla said.

"No."

"Is good. I hope he is alive. But I must tell you, Señora,
I think there were many men here who were not on these
lists."

She was certain this was true. If Terrell had come to Goliad, he would have arrived late, in the confused and hectic days after the fall of the Alamo. Had he even been formally assigned to a company, it was likely no one had taken the time to enter him on its rolls.

Portilla sipped the last of his chocolate and set it on the desk and stared at the empty cup. She lifted her eyes from the muster sheets and looked at his grave face and made herself form the words, "Where are the bodies of the men who were shot?"

THE BODIES, most of them, still lay where they fell. Some had been dragged onto the funerary pyres whose smoke Mary had seen when riding into Goliad, but this effort at burning had been scattered and short-lived. By and large, the Mexicans had just taken the clothes off the bodies and then left them to the wolves.

In the morning Portilla let her and Dr. Kenner go out under guard to the killing ground to look for their sons. First they visited the pyres. The soldiers had not bothered to gather enough fuel to adequately burn the bodies, and the fires had gone out after only a few hours. When they got there, wolves were pulling half-burned bodies out of the piles. The guards shot at them, but there were too many to shoot effectively and their manner was heedless. Mary and Dr. Kenner ignored the wolves and inspected the awful tangle of limbs, staring at each dead and astonished face. Some of the bodies were charred by the fire and split open, with the fat that had boiled out of them congealed around the base of the pyre. The wolves crept in and licked it off the grass.

She did not find Terrell there, and Kenner did not find either of his sons. In the afternoon they inspected the bloating pink bodies that lay in the fields and on the sides of the roads. Their faces were so swollen it was difficult to discern one man's features from another's. Mary held her breath against the smell but moved through the fields of dead men with staunch purpose. Buzzards settled on the bodies and spiraled as thick as ash in the air.

In midafternoon she heard Kenner gasp and sink to his knees, and she ran to him and put her arms on his shoulders as he stared at the body of a young man with the side of his skull blown off.

"That was Miles," he said when he could speak. "I don't know where Toby is."

The guards were moved by Kenner's suffering, and they told him to stand back while they themselves wrapped the body in a blanket and transferred its putrid, sagging weight to a cart.

They searched for Terrell and for Kenner's other son, not just among the communal heaps of dead but along the riverbanks where men had been shot down or lanced in their scattered attempts to escape. By sunset there were no more bodies left to inspect, and they walked back to the presidio. Behind them, the buzzards descended, and the wolves trotted forward out of the trees.

Mary stayed in Goliad for a week, helping Kenner and Shackleford and the other doctors in the hospital care for the Mexican wounded. Every day she received permission from Portilla to search again for her son's body, and she rode her mule up and down both sides of the riverbank and for a considerable distance onto the prairies beyond. She found a half-dozen more bodies, but none of them were Terrell's.

"Señora Mott," Portilla finally told her, "please will you go home?"

CHAPTER THIRTY-NINE

✦

TERRELL SPENT two days in the vaquero's shack. The provisions he found there were gone by the second day, but he managed to kill a large rattlesnake that had slipped out of its winter den to sun itself on a flat rock. He had thrown his shirt over the coiled snake and then leapt on it and stomped it to death with his feet. He had no knife and no fire kit, so he had merely gouged the meat off the snake with the broken tip of the branding iron and eaten it raw.

The next day he set off walking again across open country and by nightfall had found the Gonzales road. He followed it east to the crossing, never venturing upon the road itself, but stumbling along warily in its shadow. The road was vacant, and the smooth footing it offered seemed to his blistered feet like a greater luxury than food, but he would not let himself surrender to its temptations.

He followed beside the road for two days, with nothing to eat but more wild onions that he managed to locate and grub from the ground with his good hand. He grew hollow-headed again, and though the pain from his ruined arm and hand had lessened somewhat, it still throbbed with every footstep, and as the grievous injury began to heal itself it caused his fingers to clench tighter and tighter into his palm.

On the night of the second day he came to Forty-Mile Hole. There was a fire burning on the margins of the spring and Terrell studied the man who sat beside it for a long time before he decided to call out from the trees for help. The man was a Mexican, dressed in little but rags, and when he heard Terrell's voice in the darkness he gestured heartily with his arm for him to come to the fire. He had shot a snapping turtle through the water with his pistol and now he was roasting strips of turtle meat on sticks.

"Siéntate, joven," he commanded.

He pulled up one of the sticks and with his knife slid the turtle meat onto, of all things, a china plate. Terrell set the plate in the dirt and with his good hand brought the meat to his mouth. The man had made tortillas too, and while Terrell ate he crumbled chocolate into a pot of water, all the while rattling on about something in Spanish.

He said his name was Encarnación, but his name and the fact that he was a metatero were all that Terrell could comprehend. The man was unconcerned about the war, and maybe even unaware of it. He appeared so deeply contented with his present circumstances, so completely attentive to the indecipherable opinions that he could not stop expressing, that Terrell decided he was a lunatic. But he knew that the man had saved his life, and the metatero's crazy insouciance somehow settled his mind when Terrell lay down that night by the fire, and he slept a normal sleep for the first time in what seemed like many weeks.

In the morning, the metatero gave him food enough for a week, if he was parsimonious, and a sack to carry it in. He also gave him an old carving knife that he had sharpened so many times half the blade was missing. The man insisted on sharpening it one last time, shaving a patch of hair off his forearm and inspecting the bare place with a deep, satisfied scrutiny.

Terrell calculated he would make it to Gonzales in two and a half days, and he did, but the town was no longer there. All the buildings were burned, every one, and there were only charred timbers standing. But farther down the road he found farms whose fields had been spared from burning and whose houses still stood, evacuated by their inhabitants in such a hurry that the larders and cribs were still laden with food and starving livestock bleated in the pens.

In one of these houses he even found clothes to wear, a calico shirt and a pair of good trousers that fit him more or less. There were no shoes but he found ointments for his blisters and clean domestic to bind them.

He was walking away from the house when he was caught out in the middle of a field by a group of five riders. He knew it was hopeless to run, and so he just stood there and waited for their arrival and whatever fate they might bring to him. He could see from a distance that they did not wear uniforms, and therefore were not lancers or dragoons, but they could be vaqueros working for one of the centralist landowners loyal to Santa Anna and therefore just as lethal.

But the men belonged to one of Houston's mounted spy companies. They had ridden down the Mill road from the Guadalupe, probing for the Mexican columns, and were now on their way to Mina to shadow the forces of General Gaona, who was said to be leading one of the three enemy armies advancing into the colonies from Béxar.

It was from these men that Terrell learned that the Alamo had fallen, and that every man that he had known there— Mr. McGowan and Travis and Crockett and Bowie and Sparks and Roth and Robert Crossman, who had so kindly saved him from embarrassment when he had soiled his trousers in fear—all had been killed, and all their bodies thrown into the flames and burned so that only ash and human suet and charred bones remained.

The men of the spy company had heard that the women and children had been spared, but they could tell Terrell nothing specific about the fate of his mother. If she was not dead, they speculated, she might be with the refugee columns fleeing to the Sabine. Terrell did not tell them about her involvement in the killing of the ranchero, about the strong possibility that if she survived the Alamo she

might be on her way to some Mexican prison. In the following weeks, as he rode with the spy company all up and
down the Goucher Trace, following Gaona's army from San
Felipe toward Brazoria, he practiced the discipline of never
allowing his anxiety for his mother to become the foremost
thought in his mind. Béxar was now a Mexican stronghold.
If she was there, or on her way deep into Mexico on the
Camino Real, there was nothing for the present that he
could do. All he could do was join with his fellow Texians
and fight along with them for a victory that each day
seemed more improbable.

When the company found him, they had been trailing
extra horses, and it was one of these, a deep-chested bay
gelding named Button, that he rode up and down the trace,
and that time and again carried him to safety as they
harassed Gaona's baggage train or skirmished with his
lancers. For the first week he had to ride with his broken
hand and wrist bound to his body, or the surging pain
would have caused him to black out in the saddle. They
gave him a horse pistol and he learned to load it by squeezing its stock between his knees and ramming home the
powder and shot with his good left hand. But he could not
load the pistol on horseback, and so as soon as he discharged it his ability to harass the enemy was at an end.
Some of the men had sabres, all of them had bowie knives,
or what they claimed were bowie knives, and they argued
incessantly about whose most resembled the knife the dead
hero had used in the Alamo. Terrell had only the skinny,
filed-away blade the metatero had given him, and in a
horseback battle or any engagement at all it would have
been next to useless, especially with his fighting hand crippled and drawn up like a bird's foot.

One April day they sat on their horses on a swelling rise
of prairie, looking down at Gaona's column as it marched
south along the trace between the San Bernard and the Brazos. The rains had brought the land to flower, and great

fields of poppies and bluebonnets stretched away on every hand and seemed to pool and deepen in the contoured pockets of the open prairie. Gaona's army marched knee-deep in wildflowers, crushing the petals beneath their sandals, intensifying the aroma that already hung in the air as heavy as a curtain.

"Well, he ain't headed to Nacogdoches no more, that's for damn sure," the leader of the spy company said. His name was McGehee. He was sipping from a bottle of wine they had recently found left behind in one of the abandoned farms, along with a smokehouse full of hams and a barn laden with cotton that had already been ginned and carded. "Either the sonofabitch is lost or he's decided to head down toward the coast and pitch in with that other column."

McGehee decided that this information was of sufficient interest to send word about it to Houston. He handed Terrell one of the hams and a bottle of wine and told him to ride up the Brazos to Groce's plantation, where the Texas army had located itself after Houston had once again decided not to pitch a fight on the Colorado.

Terrell expected to find almost two thousand men bivouacked at Groce's, but the pickets who met him outside the camp and passed him off to Houston's adjutant told him that almost half the army had deserted because their leader had turned out to be an arrogant and cowardly bastard who did not care to make a stand even when he took a piss. They told him about the slaughter of the men in Goliad, and how a few of the men who had escaped the Mexican guns had wandered into their camp weeks later with all the meat starved off of them and their bodies covered with cactus needles and their eyes wild with what they had seen.

When Terrell was shown into Houston's tent he found the general sitting cross-legged on the ground with his boots and socks off and scratching equations in the dirt with a stick. His feet were immense and shockingly pale—they looked like some kind of gigantic root vegetable. There

was a boy sitting beside him, younger than Terrell but as
gaunt and winnowed as an old man.

"I'm trying to teach this boy the double rule of three,"
Houston said companionably. "He doesn't remember his
name, so we call him Tad. Who are you?"

Terrell told him his name was Private Mott and that he
had news of Gaona's movements. He described how Gaona
seemed to be heading south toward Brazoria, and how it
was likely he would probably encounter Urrea's forces if he
kept in that direction.

"Well, he won't run into the archfiend himself," Houston
said, cheerfully animated by this news. With the stick, he
erased the numbers in the dirt and began drawing lines of
military movement. "Santa Anna's already pretty far east of
there," he muttered to Terrell as he scratched his map, "on
his way to Harrisburg, my scouts tell me. And Sesma's
here, and Urrea's down here somewhere, and now you tell
me that Gaona's heading south along the Brazos. I swear
Santa Anna's got his army scattered like snot in a sneeze.
Mott, you say?"

"Yes, sir."

"Would I have met your mother? Would she have been
Mrs. Mott, from the Alamo?"

Terrell felt his scalp draw up. "Is she dead?"

"No, I'm pleased to say she's not. She was with my army
for a time, and then she disappeared right after we got news
that Fannin's men had been captured. Hockley and I speculated that she went to Goliad, since she had convinced herself that you were with Fannin and that all his army was
about to be shot, which turned out to be perspicacious
thinking."

Houston turned to the unspeaking boy. "Tad here was in
Goliad, weren't you, son? He managed to get clear somehow and wandered in the wilderness like a prophet from the
Bible. What happened to your hand, Private Mott? We have
a doctor who should take a look at it."

The doctor's name was Labadie. He told Terrell that the bones were set and the tendons drawn up and the best he could do was to break his hand into pieces with a sledge-hammer and start all over again. He laughed when he said it, and Terrell, to his own amazement, laughed with him.

McGehee had told him not to return to the spy company, since they would be coming in soon themselves. Terrell asked Houston's adjutant whom he should report to, and he was given the name of a company commander who was short on men because of the recent spate of desertions.

Terrell received directions to the company's camp from the adjutant, but before he reported there he took himself away into the woods for a few hundred yards. He sat down beneath an oak and watched the robins in the underbrush and listened to the cries of the cranes overhead. His face tightened and his chest began to contort and heave with such force that a stranger coming upon him might have thought he was having a seizure, rather than just a bout of weeping. When he was through his ribs were sore and his nose was running, but he still could not draw his thoughts away from those funeral fires at the Alamo.

As he walked back through the camp he passed a group of men who had gathered in a circle around an officer, listening to him read aloud something from the *Telegraph*. The newspaper was somehow still extant, even though Texas itself was in such abject disarray that it could hardly be said to still exist.

"Spirits of the mighty, though fallen!" the officer orated as he read from the paper. "Honors and rests are with ye: the spark of immortality which animated your forms, shall brighten into a flame, and Texas, the whole world, shall hail ye like the demi-gods of old . . ."

It was not until the officer read out the names of Travis, Crockett, and Bowie that Terrell realized he was declaiming about the Alamo.

CHAPTER FORTY

✳

FOR THE FIRST WEEK of Edmund's stay in the make-shift village on the Carvajal, Lupita came every day to sit with him while her grandmother brought him meals and inspected his wounds and Flores passed on the latest rumors he had heard from his nephew about the course of the war. The girl was not eager to speak to him, but after some days he coaxed her into singing a song, and she droned on in a flat voice about a coyote named Nano Coyotito and then about a mourning dove begging a shepherd to feed her berries from the chaparral. And that night, when he had eaten his first substantive meal, eggs and nopalitos, and felt strong enough to stand, she had accompanied him on his first expedition outside the jacal.

When he saw Edmund, the lancer's horse snorted indignantly and pulled at his picket rope. The girl asked him what the horse's name was, and Edmund told her it was Enemigo. Then he asked her if she could name the stars overhead, but all she knew was that the flowing white band that traversed the sky was called the Caminito de Santo Santiago, and that it was a road that God had made so that dead children could find their way to him in the night.

After a few more days, though, the girl grew bored with him, and this fact in its own way gave Edmund pleasure, since he felt how burdensome it was for her to go on believing that he was somehow the signal character in her life—the almost supernatural figure who had saved her from bondage with the Comanches. He much preferred that she took no heightened notice of him, just counted him as another human presence with whom she felt safe.

His cracked ribs were mending, and his scars had mostly knitted, except for the lance wound on his hip, which tended to pull apart when he stood to leave the jacal or thrashed about in his sleep. With every day he felt stronger and more feverishly impatient, and before the lance wound had quite healed he hobbled all the way up from the jacal to the barracks to tell Flores that he had decided to leave the next day.

"You are not as well as you think you are," Flores told him. "Another week more."

"No. I must go tomorrow."

"You will tear open your wounds. Why are you in such a hurry?"

Edmund did not try to form a reply. He did not know the answer himself, only that as his life had returned to him an intolerable yearning had returned with it, and he felt now as he imagined a migrating bird might feel as it beat sense-lessly onward across the sky.

Flores argued that the roads were crowded now with Mexican patrols and belligerent vaqueros, but from his years of botanizing Edmund knew he could find his way to Refugio without the benefit of roads. The country was gen-erally open and easy to follow. He could travel at night, hid-ing himself in the forests and oak mottes during the day, and he was aware of many fords along the rivers, some un-known even to the local vaqueros, that could still be crossed even in high water.

Flores gave up and saddled Enemigo for him. The horse huffed and put his ears back as Edmund approached but then calmed somewhat when he chucked at him in a soft voice and stroked his neck with his hand. He stood on the top of an horno to climb into the saddle, in order to spare his stitched-together body. Even so, he gasped at the pain in his cracked ribs and he felt the edges of the lance wound on his hip straining against their ligatures.

He did not allow enough of a pause when he got on top of the horse for any formal leave-taking. He merely thanked them all and said goodbye to the girl and goaded the horse forward with his heels.

It took him six days. Even at his careful and evasive pace it should have taken him considerably less, but the recent rains had made the creeks higher than even he had anticipated and on several occasions he had to camp and wait for the waters to subside before he thought it safe to proceed with such an untried and unwilling horse. His body hurt constantly, and he slept without fires in the brooding darkness. And yet he was happy, ranging about the country in a sudden spring, with every plant that he saw in leaf or in flower, the lichens glowing with an intense green on the rocks beside the springs, a sky populous with every sort of bird. Somehow, improbably, he had survived the conflagration of the Alamo, and he was beginning to think he might survive the ruin of his career as well. The war would be over, one way or another; and whether Santa Anna was victorious or not, the logic of Mexican politics decreed that he would be supplanted sooner or later. There would be another regime, and if Almonte was true to his word and safeguarded Edmund's notes and collections, there would be another chance to retrieve them and to continue with his *Flora Texana*.

The thought heartened him but, strangely, not enough. Not enough to counter the crushing anxiety he felt about Mary's welfare. If she was dead, so was his one chance. He would resume being what he had been, a man believing in his own presumptive greatness and nothing else. And even if he acquired this greatness, even if the exemplary trials of his life merited its bestowal, what would it really be? Dried plants in an archive, mouldering notes, the brittle pages of a forgotten book.

On the third day he encountered a nameless, meandering creek, hardly more than an arroyo but filled to the banks with water and impossible to cross. For hours he backtracked and scouted until he located a network of boggy tributaries that he crossed one by one, hauling the horse by its reins across waterlogged brush piles and slickrock creek bottoms. The last of these tributaries was shallow and almost dry, the water already turning stagnant in isolated pools. Edmund was weary and wracked with pain from the many occasions that day that he had already dismounted and led the balky horse, and he decided that for this last crossing he would stay in the saddle.

Enemigo went forward willingly enough, but the mud between the pools was deeper than Edmund thought, and with the first few steps the horse sunk up to the hocks and panicked as if he were trapped in quicksand. Enemigo churned his legs and slewed down hard onto his side, launching Edmund into the standing water on the other side of the mud pit. He stood up promptly enough despite the pain in the ribs and managed to grab the horse's reins and coax it forward onto solid footing. From his rib cage to his feet Edmund was covered in slimy mud. He used the edge of a knife to shear the mud off his clothes and then sat down for an hour to test his breathing. When he was sure he had not broken another rib and that his lungs were not in danger of being punctured, he pulled himself back up onto the horse and rode across the twilit prairie where silent herds of deer purled at the edges of the trees.

The next day the wound in his hip felt increasingly tender and when he slipped off the horse and pulled down his trousers he saw that the deep gash the lancer had made was now raw and red again, and starting to discharge a greenish pus. He felt as well the beginnings of a fever, burning up the bright hopes of the previous day.

He located the Mission River and followed it for a day through the tangled timber on its banks, steering around cy-

press knees and ducking his head out of the way of bearded
moss and looping vines. By following the river in this fashion he was able to slip past Refugio itself, which he suspected was invested with Urrea's men, and to approach the
grounds of Mrs. Mott's tavern from the opposite bank.

For a long time he sat there on his horse studying the
dwelling house and the outbuildings to determine if any
Mexican forces had inhabited them. He did not see Mary,
or Terrell, though Teresa was out in the yard hanging linen
on a line.

Closer by, he heard the sound of bare feet splashing in
the river and looked downstream to see Fresada wading out
to check the contents of a weir he had built in a shallow
eddy on the far bank.

Fresada must have detected the hoofbeats above the
sound of the rippling water, because by the time Edmund
came into view the Indian was staring squarely at him. He
stepped out of the river and walked up to him and took the
reins of the horse from his hands.

"Is she living?" Edmund said. And then the fever he had
been trying to outrun all day caught up with him and
blinded him, searing through the channels of his brain.

CHAPTER FORTY-ONE

✦

"**G**ENTLEMEN! Gentlemen! Gentlemen!"
Sam Houston's voice was powerful enough for Terrell to hear above the sputtering gunfire and the screams of the wounded Mexicans as the Texians pounded their heads with the butts of their guns or hacked at their bodies with their carving knives. Houston was begging the men to stop killing, but the killing had hardly begun and everyone knew it.

"Damn your manners!" he was shouting as he rode his horse back and forth behind the overrun Mexican breastworks. "Damn your manners!" Beneath its oily sheen of gunpowder, his face was blanched in pain and outrage. Someone had shot him in the ankle. His bloody foot would not bear weight in its stirrup, and so he was grasping the saddle horn in both hands to keep himself from toppling off the horse.

"Do not kill that Mexican, sir!" Houston said to a man who was holding a pistol in the face of a wounded drummer boy no older than twelve. The man called out to Houston to go fuck a partridge and discharged his pistol inches away from the boy's astonished eyes. The ball punched a hole in his face big enough to blow all of his features out the back of his head.

Houston could do nothing but look down in disgust and allow his frightened horse to bear him away across the line of battle. He had lost control of his army, had been losing control for weeks to his fractious subordinates and the near-mutinous men they commanded. Today, at long last, the army had goaded him into fighting. They had advanced across the prairie toward the Mexican camp as a thrown-together band played a love song called "Come to the Bower." They allowed Houston to direct them in one well-ordered volley, but when he tried to get them to reload and fire again they simply unleashed themselves and ran toward the breastworks with their uncharged weapons, content to club and stab the enemy without any further consultation with their commander in chief.

Santa Anna had screened his army behind a long, piled-up barricade of crates and brush and bits and pieces of cavalry tack and camp furniture, but he had apparently given up expecting Houston to attack and the barricade was thinly guarded, and most of his exhausted men were asleep.

Terrell had expected to be cut down in the first Mexican volley by the canister thrown by the gun tube he could see peering out at them from the breastworks. But the cannon was unmanned, and no organized volley ever came, and when they began running across the prairie he knew with certainty that he would survive and that the Mexicans would be driven back to the marshy lake upon whose shores they had improvidently pitched their camp.

"Remember the Alamo!" his fellow Texians were crying, and Terrell screamed it aloud as murderously as the rest, and "Remember Goliad!" along with it. He was borne along on a rampaging flood. He was deliriously confident, and the more metal there was in the air around him the more invulnerable he felt. When they scrabbled over the breastworks, there was hardly anyone to oppose them. The Mexicans were already fleeing, most of them with no weapons in their hands. Those who had been shot in the first Texian volley were lying in the grass, either dead already or crawling backward on their hands, pleading for mercy. They knew no English. Terrell heard one of them screaming "Goddam, goddam" to a man in a U.S. Army forage cap

who was attacking him with a hatchet. The Mexican seemed
to think that the words had something to do with mercy.

"Goddam yourself, mister," his attacker said, and planted
the hatchet blade in the bone beneath the Mexican's eye and
then began kicking his squirming body when he could not
pull it out.

With his bad hand Terrell could not yet hold and fire a
musket, and so he had advanced with his pistol, firing once
at a face that had peered over the barricade and then just
surging forward with no active weapon and no plan of how
to fight. Now he made himself pause and sit down against
the inside of the breastworks and load the pistol again.
There was a wounded Mexican officer lying only a few feet
away from him. He had been disemboweled by canister
from one of the Texians' two little cannon, and now he just
seemed to be watching Terrell's one-handed loading operation as if it was a thing of great interest to him.

"Señor," he said, as Terrell was ramming down the
patching. "Máteme. Póngame un tiro en la cabeza, por favor."

Terrell knew perfectly well what the man was asking,
but he pretended he could not understand. He told the officer he was sorry for his misfortune but had no way to help
him and then took off running again, following along with
the Texians as they chased Santa Anna's men through the
camp and through the live oak glade behind it. A dense
shroud of gunsmoke hung in the branches, and Terrell
breathed in its fumes as he ran and emerged on the other
side of the cloud with his lungs burning and his throat
parched and not a drop of spit left in his mouth.

He was not fighting; he was just chasing along with all
the rest of them out past the trees toward the marshy ground
where the footing grew spongy under his feet. His shoes
came off but he kept running, his eyes on the white fatigue
jackets of the fleeing Mexicans as they splashed into the
shallow, boggy lake a hundred yards ahead.

Terrell lunged forward through the marsh grass, the water of the slough cool on his bare feet, his toes sinking into mud and scraping against buried shells. Ahead of him, at the edge of the lake, a Mexican soldier, a skirmisher with one of the good Baker rifles, was on his knees vomiting up blood. Another skirmisher was standing by the fallen man as the other men around them fled. He was fighting for his comrade's life with the savagery of a mother lion. A man ahead of Terrell ran straight at him with a knife in each hand but before he even got close the Mexican struck him across the face with his rifle with such force that the weapon broke in two. The butt half of the rifle was attached to the Texian's face as he fell—the blunt end of the cock driven into his eye. When the skirmisher saw Terrell coming he threw the barrel end of the rifle at him but it sailed past, and Terrell cocked his pistol and aimed it on the run and fired with his shaking and unreliable left hand at the center of the Mexican's crossbelt. The shot vaulted him over the kneeling comrade he had been trying to protect.

Terrell was now at the edge of the lake. The water was only a hundred yards across, and it was filled with Mexican soldiers flailing and clawing themselves forward in their attempts to reach the marsh on the other side. The shore of the lake was lined now with Texians, who were taking their time loading and firing their accurate long rifles, shooting the Mexicans in the water. The Mexicans called out to God as the balls hit them, they screamed as they drowned in the deepening water. The lake turned red with their blood. They thrashed wildly on the surface, some of them caught up in the coils of their own exposed viscera.

"Are you animals?" a Texian officer called out in a hoarse voice to the men shooting the Mexicans. "Will you not stop shooting those men?"

They would not, and if it had not been so cumbersome for Terrell to load his pistol one-handedly, perhaps he would have continued firing as well. As it was, stalled at the edge of the slaughter lake, he fell into sickening reflection.

He turned and walked back the way he had come, searching in the marsh grass for his shoes and trying not to listen to the crackle of gunfire behind him, to the undiminishing screams of the Mexicans and the righteous exhortations of the Texian officers.

He came to the body of the man he had shot. He lay on his back with his eyes open to the sky, staring with the unsettling intensity of the dead, as if he perceived something there in the thin clouds. Half of one ear was missing, though it was an old wound. His legs were draped over the body of the man he had tried to save, and whose brains had been beaten out by someone's rifle butt.

"Are you gonna take that, son?" someone said to him. Terrell turned to see a grinning man in a blood-smeared buckskin jacket.

"What?" Terrell said.

"That pouch he's got. If you don't want it, by God I'll take it."

Terrell looked down and saw the shooting pouch made of jaguar skin that was suspended by a strap across the dead man's chest.

"No," Terrell told the man. "I want it."

He bent down and freed the pouch from the body. He squeezed it down into the soggy marsh grass to get it wet and then wiped it with his hand, following the grain of the fur, until the blood came off. Then he folded it up and put it in his haversack and walked off the field as the killing in the lake continued.

CHAPTER FORTY-TWO

✦

"TEXAS IS WON! Texas is won, Mrs. Mott! On the Plain of Saint Hyacinth!"

Edmund felt Mary's cooling hand leave his skin, he heard her whisper urgently in his ear that she would be back immediately, and then she was gone, and he was alone in the dwelling house. The horrible, congested dreams began to creep into his mind again. He had lost the power to keep them at bay; only Mary could do that.

He heard John Dunn's voice speaking to her from the dogtrot. The Mexicans defeated by Houston, Santa Anna captured after fleeing the field and hiding in cowardly fashion in the wilderness, independence, Filisola leading a retreat of all the Mexican armies in Texas.

"Did you hear, Edmund?" It was her voice again. She had come back. Her hand was on his check, on his neck.

"And your son?" he managed to ask.

"I still know nothing. But at least the war is over."

Texas is won! Edmund heard the words again in his roiling mind. For just an instant they filled him with happiness. The silken prairies, the forests and escarpments, the buffalo plains and the seacoast—all under his eye at once. Everything in glorious profusion—flower and vine, grass and shrub, trees magnificent in their texture and solidity, trees as old as the thoughts of God—and none of it described, none of it known, but all of it won! All of it within the compass of his heart, all of it within the reach of his breath. Mary's hand was on his burning brow.

"Shall we go riding after supper?" he said.

"Of course."

"Or we could walk if you prefer."

"A walk would be fine, Edmund."

He nodded in contentment, and then his mood changed in an instant to concern. He wanted to know where Professor was. Mary didn't know what had happened to the dog but she said he was outside, gnawing on a bone she had given him. This calmed Edmund long enough for him to fall asleep again. She sat on the edge of the bed watching him sleep, still touching his face to gauge the progress of the fever.

It was unabating. She knew that; she was scared. She had purged him with calomel, tried to break the fever with nitrous powders, but it had a firmer hold today than it had two days ago, when she had seen Fresada walking up from the creek, half-dragging Edmund, a horse with a Mexican dragoon saddle trailing suspiciously behind.

She had run to him immediately and helped Fresada carry him into the house, but even as she did so, even as she stripped off his clothes and made a poultice for the angry wound on his hip, she felt she was in a cruel dreaming state.

He was lucid for much of that first day and night, and they talked a great deal. They talked of how they had each escaped from the Alamo, and Mary told him of her fruitless efforts to find Terrell, how she had searched for him among the living and in the fields of the dead. It was during this time, when she believed she had Edmund's fever under control, that there arose in her heart a happiness she was almost ashamed to feel. Her son was lost and probably dead, and she had reached the point where hope was more punishing than despair.

"He may very well be alive," Edmund kept reassuring her.

"I'm afraid to think that. I'm no longer strong enough to think that."

"It's not a question of you thinking about it one way or another."

She took his hand as she wiped his sweat-drenched hair.

"You'll soon be well," she said.

"Will I?"

"Of course."

"And then will you cast me out?" He had smiled when he said it, meaning it as a joke. But then he lifted his head feebly off his pillow and touched her arm. His eyes were uncertain and blazing with intent, and she understood that he wanted to kiss her. She pushed him gently back down onto the bed and moved forward to set her lips against his and allowed herself to believe, for just that moment, that the terrors of the Alamo had no further claim upon them.

But that had been two days ago, and in the time since, his fever had taken firmer hold with each passing hour. Now he was awake again, agitated, calling out her name.

"I'm here, Edmund. I'm here beside you."

"Take me outside!" he demanded.

She knew it was his delirium speaking. She did not want to move him. The infected wound in his hip was searingly painful to the slightest touch; and moving him from the bed to a cot narrow enough to fit through the door would only heighten his discomfort. She held his face in both her hands and peered into his manic eyes.

"It is best if I keep you where you are, Edmund."

"Is it still daylight?"

"Yes."

"Then take me out."

It was midday. The spring air was warm. His fever tended to rage its worst in the mornings and late in the afternoons, followed by drenching night sweats. She had hardly slept for days, and the more the fever grew, the more difficult he became, thrashing on the cot as she and Fresada tried to force another emetic into his mouth or change his poultice. She knew that his condition was hopeless, had known it for at least a day. Perhaps if his constitution had not been so weakened by the ague he could have fought off this new marauder. Perhaps if the wound itself had not been so high on his hip she could have removed his leg and stopped the march of the infection. Now all she could do was to try to calm him in his delirium and to speak with him in those brief afternoon hours when his mind was reasonably clear.

He was so much concerned to be outside that she decided it was cruel not to follow his wishes, deranged as they might be. And so she and Fresada and Teresa transferred him to a cot and carried him out into the yard. The place they set him down was within hearing of the river and beneath the shadows of the mossy limbs that grew along its banks. The sky was a startling blue.

"Thank you," he said in a calm voice when they set him down. Fresada and Teresa withdrew. Mary sat down on a chair next to his cot. She pulled the quilts tight on his quaking body. He did not speak. She held his hand.

"Do you see?" he said at last.

She followed his eyes to the roofline of the house, where four owl chicks had perched themselves, staring outward with great and peculiar absorption. The spring breeze ruffled their infant plumage. Their bodies were comically squat and their wings stubby. Though their eyes shone like gems, their expressions were blank, as contentedly blank as the sky itself.

"Owl medicine," he said, as if she would understand what he meant. But like so many other things he had said in the last few days it was meaningless to her, just random words boiling up out of the feverish slurry that had taken hold of his mind.

He was lucid, however, for a good part of the afternoon, and whenever the fever did not have him he seemed content, just lying there and listening to the sounds of the birds in the sky and the wind swaying through the moss.

But then his chills grew too strong, and she ordered him

back into the house and gave him tea to drink and built up the fire in the hearth. He complained of pain in his head, and she swabbed his forehead with cold vinegar and water that seemed to bring him much relief, though he was still pale and nauseated and his skin fiery to the touch.

She gently pulled off his clothes and swabbed him all over with the vinegar and water mixture, washing even his most private parts as if she were his wife of long duration. And then she removed her own clothes and lay under the quilts with him and held him as he shook.

"This is how it would have been," he said. His voice had the timbre of discovery.

"Yes," she answered. "We would have slept every night in our bed like this, without clothes. It would not have diminished you, Edmund, to have this. It would not have diminished you to need me."

"I am sorry, Mary."

She shook her head so energetically that the tears flew from her eyes. She instructed him not to apologize. She told him that they were both yet living, and that what he had sought in coming back to her he had found, and that it did not matter how long their life together lasted, so long as it was truly a life together.

She kissed him as he sank back into his delirious dreams, calling out for his lost dog, screaming that the Mexicans were over the walls and the guns were not spiked. Could she not see that this rainstorm had soaked his drying papers, and that a week's worth of specimens were in danger of spoiling? Did he consider this plant, as he did, to be a new genus of *Asclepiadora*? Did she notice that Cabezon was favoring her left foreleg?

He bolted upright and cried out her name. She whispered in his ear that she was with him, and finally his burning body went slack enough for her to guide him back down onto the bed, and she cooled him again with another vinegar bath and slept with him for an hour or two until he woke and turned to her and said, "Remember me."

He spoke this with clarity, and he meant it, she believed, as the simplest of aspirations. He had once confidently expected his memory to be emblazoned upon history itself, but she understood him now to mean that it was enough that it be recorded on a single human heart. And so she willingly told him that she would remember him until the end of her own life.

MARY HAD NEVER KNOWN where her husband was buried, and over the years this lack of finality, this unclosing door, had caused her much distress. In her youth she had always considered herself unsentimental about graveyards, and rather scornful of the old women who put such value in visiting and tending the resting places of their loved ones. But when put to the test over Andrew, and over little Susie, buried all alone in the wilderness, she had almost fallen apart.

So it gave her an unanticipated satisfaction to work beside Fresada hewing Edmund's grave out of the soil. The site was only a hundred yards or so away from the dwelling house, on a vague rise of land looking out over the river and the coastal prairie that led down to the bayshore. Even so, it began to feel distant to her as she lay alone at night in the dwelling house, and so after a week she began building a path to it. She dug a shallow bed and then sent Fresada down to the shore with the oxcart to gather a load of oyster shell. The two of them worked for days pulverizing the shell and then laying it into the bed. There was a certain stretch of river that was rich in fossiliferous rocks, and after only a few days' searching she had gathered several dozen of these whose shapes and textures and mysterious imprints pleased her. She began lining the path with them, working her way from the grave to the house, burying each rock sufficiently deep in the earth so that it felt mortared in place, and helped give an air of solidity and permanence to this path, which in her grief she thought of as an avenue between the world of the living and that of the dead.

She had counted Terrell among the dead. His was one of those unmarked graves that haunted her. She did not believe he had fallen at Goliad, but thought that he had probably been ambushed along the roads or killed in some engagement so minor it had not yet come to light. His bones were scattered in some field somewhere, or consumed in one of Santa Anna's funeral pyres. Her husband was dead, her children were dead, and Edmund McGowan, in the act of rising to his life, had died as well. The loneliness that Mary felt was the sharpest, most unwavering, most remorseless sensation she had ever known, and it was a marvel to her that she had chosen to endure it.

She had finished the first half of the path when she realized that there were not nearly enough stones after all, and that she would have to make another trip to the river. She sat down on the crushed oyster shell and cursed her lack of foresight and wept in frustration.

She heard Fresada running up the path to her, calling out her name in a tone of voice that she found annoyingly fretful.

"There is nothing very much wrong with me, Fresada," she said to him in a testy, lecturing tone. "You should expect me to break down in tears every now and then, and I will be responsible for pulling myself back together. If you have nothing else to do but attend to my emotions you can borrow Mr. Dunn's wagon again and—"

"It is Terrell coming," Fresada said.

She turned and looked and from her little graveyard summit saw the rider coming from town at a deliberate pace. He had not yet seen them. Even from this distance she could see that one hand was hurt and drawn up, but he held the reins with such assurance in his good hand it was evident he had grown well accustomed to his injury. She watched him for a moment as she used to watch him as a child, observing him secretly, fascinated by the dawning separateness of his life apart from her. Then she rose to her feet and ran toward him down the path she had made, trying to call out his name but producing only a confused gasp in her throat that for all the sense it made might have been the call of a bird.

CHAPTER FORTY-THREE

✣

IT WAS the seventh week of the retreat from Texas, a retreat distinguished by shameful disorder and shattered morale. Telesforo Villasenor marched with his Zapador battalion in the vanguard, but the way the men staggered thirst-crazed across the southern Texas brasada could hardly be termed marching, and to an observer this vanguard would have seemed less like the advancing front of an army than its straggling remnants. Many of the men were barefoot by now, their feet burning on the sandy soil or tortured by pebbles and broken shell. Some had drunk bad water and lay in the line of march groaning piteously and holding their swollen abdomens.

This afternoon some of Telesforo's men had seen a shimmering in the distance they had taken to be a lake and raced across miles of thorny and trackless vegetation to reach it, contemptibly disobeying his order for them to remain where they were until the lake could be properly scouted. It had been nightfall before they managed to make their way back. They had found the water too brackish to drink and had succeeded only in adding more miserable leagues to their endless journey.

Telesforo had been proven right in ordering the men to remain in ranks, but this fact only served to further undermine their regard for him. He was known throughout the army now as Santa Anna's henchman, the craven officer who had executed the prisoners who had honorably surrendered to General Castrillón. It was one of Santa Anna's tellingly remorseless acts, and as such it had helped the norte rebels forge the mad vengeance that carried away Santa Anna's army at San Jacinto.

The noble Castrillón had died there, fighting to rally his men as they fled in terror from the barbarian hordes. His heroism was in blatant contrast to the conduct of Santa Anna himself, who had fled into the countryside and tried to disguise himself as a simple soldado. And when he had been captured, he had been so afraid for his life that he had capitulated to Houston on the spot and agreed to order all his forces in Texas back across the Rio Grande.

Telesforo had not been at San Jacinto. The president seemed to perceive that his ambitious young subordinate had been morally damaged after carrying out his hideous orders at the Alamo and therefore could be of no further use to him. Telesforo was informed through his battalion commander that his assignment to His Excellency's staff had come to an end, and that he should rejoin his unit as it marched east toward the colonies under the command of General Filisola.

Filisola's army had been paused at the Colorado, readying for a push east to join Santa Anna's forces and vanquish the fleeing rebels, when word came of the disaster at San Jacinto. Eight hundred dead, six hundred taken prisoner, the fallen Mexican troops left unburied on the plain or sunk into the mud at the bottom of a lagoon where the rebels had shot them like geese.

That was when the calumnies against Santa Anna began in earnest. The men saw him now not as a leader who gravely bore the interests of Mexico at heart, but as an arrogant and pitiless tyrant who had used the army as a tool of his own vanity and ambition, who drove it into a hostile and unknown land and was content to let it undergo every form of suffering. When at last, due to his overconfidence and inattention, the army was overrun, he had abandoned it; and out of his own trembling fear for his life he had sold Texas—the land that so many Mexican soldados had shed their blood to rescue—to the norteamericano pirates.

"The faithful hound of Santa Anna," Telesforo heard men describing him behind his back. It was said that somebody named Crockett, a politician that the nortes revered, had been one of the men Telesforo had killed in cold blood as they begged for their lives, and that this fact had greatly increased the rebels' rage at San Jacinto. "Remember the Alamo!" they had cried. And when they remembered, they were remembering the disgraceful deeds that Telesforo had performed.

Telesforo had no idea if he had killed this Crockett. All he knew was that he had killed the animating spirit within himself. He stumbled on day after day through this endless desert of thorny brush, with no shade to break the force of the sun and no companion to whom he could unburden his ravaged heart. He saw men die of thirst, clawing madly at the ground. He himself grew so delirious on occasion that he imagined he saw the Rio Grande shimmering in the distance, and the rooftops of Matamoros beyond. Once he would have welcomed this suffering, as he had welcomed the musket ball that had half-destroyed his arm, as he had welcomed the mortal danger as he ran toward the walls of the Alamo with his sword raised, believing against all doubt that here was where his fate resided, here was where he would win the Legion of Honor and the acclaim of his countrymen, and the respect of his own demanding conscience.

But now he suffered with no fine purpose, with no expectation of glory or reward. All he wanted was for the pain to end, for a few drops of water to ease his swollen throat, for his miserable life not to end quite so miserably.

Only one thing brought him interest and nudged his attention away from his own despair. It was the sight of a woman who walked barefoot alongside the column with a small dog trailing beside her. The woman was young— really no more than a girl—but her face betrayed so much self-possession and inner knowledge that she seemed ageless. She was an Indian, Telesforo had heard, from deep in the jungles of Yucatán. The soldados said that she had marched into Texas with a sargento from the cazadores who had been killed at San Jacinto, and that somehow she had escaped being captured by the Texians and had set her own solitary course home, crossing the swollen rivers and boggy roads and joining up with Filisola as he began his retreat.

Telesforo watched her every day. Sometimes she stopped to help a fallen soldado, or disappeared to visit the women and dying children of the chusma, but for the most part she just walked along on her bare feet at an unslacking, eternally consistent pace. Alone of all the refugees in the vanguard, she seemed to know precisely where she was going and when she would arrive. Some of this knowledge seemed to have even seeped into the dog, who appeared sagacious and untroubled as he walked along beside her.

They marched for another week. The campsites where they flung themselves down at night had names—Chiltipiquín, El Carrisito, Rancho Viejo—but they were not places. There were no buildings or obvious features to differentiate them from the wilderness surrounding them. There was only one place, Telesforo thought, and they were in it and would never leave it.

At sundown one day he was walking behind the Indian woman and her dog, watching her as a musician might watch a metronome, or as a child might stare at a haphazard pattern in a plaster ceiling, as if it were the world's pattern displayed there. All at once the girl stopped and just stood there, staring into the distance. Then she turned to him, as if all this time—during this entire hellish march out of Texas—she had been waiting for him to walk up to her. She smiled at Telesforo. The dog sat at her feet. She lifted her arm and pointed forward, across the brasada.

"Matamoros," she said.

He could not see it at first; then, as if he were using her eyes instead of his own, he could at last perceive the thread of river, and the buildings that rose beyond it.

THE BATTLE OF FLOWERS

APRIL 21, 1911

"**M**AY WE HELP you up now, Mr. Mott?"

It was the governor of Texas speaking. He stood with Parthenia and the other alarmed onlookers, extending a hopeful hand. Not a hair of the governor's head was unbarbered, and his exquisitely shaved jowls shone pink in the April sunlight.

Terrell put out his hand and let the governor clasp it, then Parthenia and the others took his elbows and carefully levered him upward to his feet. They withdrew their hands but kept them hovering inches away from his body, ready to catch him should he topple again. He did not. To his own surprise, he found himself standing still plumb to the earth, secure in his oversize boots. The scrape behind his ear stung considerably, however, and he could feel blood leaking onto his collar.

But Parthenia had already pulled Terrell's own handkerchief out of his coat pocket and was applying it to the wound with more painful pressure. She had something of her great-grandmother's nursing interests but, unfortunately, very little patience and a rather harsh touch. When it came to medical matters, she was more of a busybody than a healer.

"I will take you home right now and telephone for Dr. Lindley," she announced. "You might have a concussion. You might even have broken a bone."

She went on to enumerate several other things that might be wrong with him, but Terrell did not listen. The Battle of Flowers had ended, and children had surged forth in front

of the Alamo to gather up the fallen petals and fling them
once more into the air. He saw the man in the jaguar suit,
the man whom he had taken to be the very visage of death,
approaching again. The man climbed up the reviewing
stand one careful step at a time and stood before Terrell.

"I am a doctor," he said. "Dr. Ramírez, from Laredo. Perhaps there is some way I can assist you."

"Why are you wearing that suit?" Terrell said.

The doctor laughed. His strange rictus of a smile turned
into a broad grin, and his glassy eyes were suddenly full of
human depth. He explained that he was a member of the
Order of the Jaguar Knights, a fraternal organization inspired by the ancient Aztec military society of the same
name. It was a relatively new group, made up mostly of
Spanish-speaking doctors in Laredo, Corpus Christi, and
San Antonio, whose purpose was to raise money to build
hospitals for crippled children. As president of the Laredo
chapter, he was entitled to wear a suit made of jaguar skin
at public occasions, and though this had appealed to his
vanity at first, it now only served to make him feel alarmingly conspicuous.

"Why were you staring at me like that?" Terrell demanded.

"Excuse me?"

"Why were you staring at me?"

"Well, if I was—and I apologize for doing so—it was
for a simple reason: you were there, you were in the Alamo.
And so I wanted to look upon you."

HE ALLOWED this Dr. Ramírez to peer into his eyes and
to take his pulse and pronounce him to be sound, with the
caveat that he should be examined as soon as possible by
his customary doctor.

"And now may I shake your hand, Mr. Mott, so that I can

tell my grandchildren that I shook the hand of a man who fought at the Alamo?"

Terrell allowed it, but he liked the man no better and was glad to see him go. He said good-bye to the governor as well, when a young aide hurried up to pull him away to his next appointment.

Parthenia and the young man from the Buick dealership ushered him back into the car, and then Julia hurried up to him and kissed him anxiously, having just heard about his fall from one of the other duchesses. There was a tea at the Menger and after that an all-night dance, but she insisted—trying her best not to make her declaration sound as hollow as Terrell knew it to be—that she did not want to go to either. She would much prefer to come home immediately and tend to her great-grandfather.

"Nonsense," Parthenia snapped, before Terrell had the opportunity to revere himself to Julia by talking her out of this plan himself. "There is nothing wrong with Opa, nothing at all, and you have a very serious obligation to the Order of the Alamo."

They drove away from the Alamo, crushing the flower petals under their tires, Terrell still holding his bloody handkerchief to the back of his neck. Parthenia talked on, lecturing him about something or another, but Terrell took advantage of an old man's drifting awareness and did not listen. At the Commerce Street bridge there was a sign—erected during his administration—warning citizens in English, Spanish, and German to walk their horses over the bridge or they would be fined. They passed a German bakery and a "Spanish" restaurant—the Anglo victors of long ago had succeeded in giving the word "Mexican" a distasteful turn—and a complexion parlor. And there were the Alamo Butter Depot, the Alamo Cornice Works, the Alamo Savings and Loan, the Alamo Poultry Yard.

Alamo—it was hard to remember when that word had

just been a word, when the place it described was not the
Texas holy of holies, but just an old broken-down assem-
blage of buildings on the edge of Béxar, where long ago an
event that was far more ghastly than glorious had occurred.
No wonder that doctor in the jaguar suit had wanted to meet
him. He was a Mexican himself, or at least of Mexican her-
itage, his people cast out and displaced by the marauding
nortes; yet even he could not turn away from the stirring
myth that the Alamo embodied, a myth as carefully culti-
vated as a hothouse plant: Travis drawing his line in the dirt
with his sword, calling on his men to give their lives for liberty. The men answering his call, crossing the line, their
eyes raised to heaven, God Himself smiling down approv-
ingly upon their sacrifice.

As far as he knew, Terrell was the only man alive who
could dispute that myth if he chose to, who could point out
that the Alamo garrison had indeed given their lives—but
oh, not willingly, not exaltedly. Even the children who had
been in the Alamo were dead now, he supposed, at least
most of them. Even the infant girl of Susannah Dickinson,
who had died decades ago after a career as a prostitute in
Austin.

But it amused him to think there might be one adult defender of the Alamo who could, at least in theory, still be
registered among the living. Back in the fifties, when Terrell and Hannah had taken their honeymoon trip to Mexico
City, they had stayed in an old Spanish monastery along
what had once been the Tacuba Causeway. As they sat in
the garden having their desayuno one morning, Terrell
droning on to Hannah in a way he now recognized as
pedantic about how Cortés had once fought his way out of
the Aztec city on this very road, he noticed that one of the
mozos looked electrically familiar to him. He was a negro
in his forties, rather fleshy but not at all inelegant as he carried his tray of orange juice and bolillos and mango slices
to the table he was serving. Was he Joe, the slave Travis had

brought to the Alamo? Terrell was well aware that Joe had survived the battle and had even testified before the new government of the Republic of Texas about his experiences. Unlike Terrell and the other veterans of the war, however, upon whom the government had bestowed bountiful sections of free land that formed the basis of their fortunes, Joe had been remanded as property to the executor of Travis's estate. Only a year after the battle, Terrell had read an ad in the *Telegraph* by this same executor, offering forty dollars for the return of Travis's negro, who had escaped on a fine bay horse belonging to his new master. Joe had been caught in only a few days, but a year or two after that Terrell heard that he had escaped again.

That morning at that inn he had set down his copy of Prescott's *Conquest of Mexico* onto the table and without a word of explanation leapt up from his chair and strode over to the negro waiter. He heard him speaking in perfect Spanish to the travellers upon whom he was waiting, explaining to them what was worth seeing in the old plaza, offering his opinion as to whether a trip out to the volcanoes or to the outlying ruins was worth the aggravation.

"Excuse me, are you —" Terrell had said, but when the man turned and saw him, he had the same alarmed look on his face that that—Terrell realized now—he himself had probably been wearing when he saw the jaguar man in front of the Alamo.

Instead of finishing his question, Terrell had made a flustered, hurried request for pan dulce. The negro had given him a quick smile, told him he would be happy to bring it, and would he and the señora like more coffee or chocolate as well? And then he disappeared into the kitchen bearing aloft his empty tray.

THE YOUNG MAN drove them to Terrell's house in King William, and Parthenia insisted on coming inside and sitting with him until she was quite sure he had not done himself any damage in the fall. She instructed Javier, Terrell's almost equally ancient houseman, to bring her ointment and gauze and tape from the medical drawer, and when these ingredients arrived she applied a bandage to her grandfather's wound with her singular lack of finesse. The power of her will filled the house. She ordered Hortensia, Terrell's cook and Javier's daughter, to set about making a fortifying supper: machacado con huevo, perhaps, though it must be blandified so as not to upset her grandfather's delicate digestion.

"You must have some meetings to go to," Terrell told her with unmistakable bite. This was still his house, and to have his granddaughter trooping around in it like this made him irritable.

"There are no meetings as important as your welfare, Opa," she said, putting up the medical supplies. "Did that man really scare you so badly?"

"I thought he was Death himself, Parthenia."

"Did you? Why?" Another woman might have asked this with a sense of keen fascination, but Parthenia's tone was stern and mildly disapproving.

"Tell Javier to go up into the attic and bring down that old cedar chest."

"Javier is too old to be hauling furniture out of the attic. What do you want it for?"

"Just tell him to bring it."

She would not. The poor man would fall down the stairs with the chest and break his back. Instead she went up and got it herself, wrestling it down step by step and shooing Javier away when he tried to help her.

She then brought it into the parlor and placed it in front of her grandfather's commodious cow-horn chair.

"Thank you," Terrell said to her. He bent down and opened the lid and began sifting through the chest's contents. It was correspondence from his political days, mostly, proclamations for this and that, awards he had received for his efforts on the part of the West End Female Sanitarium and the San Antonio and Arkansas Pass Railway. There were his letters from Hannah, as well; not many, though, since they had lived in intimate proximity during almost all of their marriage, and she had occasion to write only on his rare extended trips.

Parthenia watched as he sorted through these objects. She had seen them before, of course, and now as she saw them again her brusque demeanor softened. Like all club-women, she was a genealogical sentimentalist, finely atten-tive to the various currents of history that had produced her noble line.

"Here are some letters from your great-grandmother," he said, handing her a stack of neatly folded correspondence sheets, fine stationery that had not turned brittle with age, but was still as fresh as today's newspaper. His mother's powerful handwriting coasted across the surface of the pa-per. These were her final letters, written to him after she had married her second husband, a member of the Repub-lic of Texas Cabinet who had turned out to be a bitter en-emy of President Houston. His name was Felix Fulshear, a widower from the DeWitt Colony who, like Terrell, was a San Jacinto veteran. Just before the War Between the States broke out Mary Mott and her new husband had travelled to Kentucky so that Fulshear could sell off some of his hold-ings there to buy more cattle to run on his headright land that had been carved out of one of the big mission ranchos on the San Antonio River.

The letters his mother had written to Terrell from Ken-tucky—her old homeland, though she had no family left living there—were to him the distilled embodiment of her strong and plaintive character. They were filled with ob-servations about everything she saw, the parties they went to, the plays they attended—including one about David Crockett's death at the Alamo—the changing vegetation as glimpsed from steamboat or train window. She died on that trip, carried away by pneumonia, and when Felix Fulshear came home and shook Terrell's hand at the train station he told him that he was now a broken man, because he had grown accustomed to a forceful and abiding love that he knew he could never find again in this world.

Her death had shaken Terrell too, of course, but he knew Fulshear to be wrong in the forecast of his own dismal future, and in fact within a few years he had remarried and was as happy again as could be expected. In Terrell's opinion, his mother had a strengthening effect on men, and it would have been somehow unnatural for her to die and leave her husband weakened and overly vulnerable to the normal disappointments of life.

In none of these letters did she mention the Alamo. It was a topic she avoided all her life, out of sadness and an inborn sense of discretion, and Terrell himself was under strict orders not to trumpet his mother's presence at Texas's mightiest and holiest of struggles. Neither did she mention Edmund McGowan, whose relationship with his mother Terrell had found complex and inconclusive. But it was among the great connections of her life, Terrell believed. He did not quite understand why, but perhaps neither could he have explained his own deep connection to his dead Hannah, or for that matter to his difficult and domineering granddaughter.

As far as he knew, Edmund McGowan left no legacy, nor any mark of the sort that he had once intended. Once a college professor researching a book on pioneer Texas naturalists had contacted Terrell, having heard the name McGowan from several sources but unable to find any material relating to him. Terrell went through his mother's effects and found only one letter, written from Mexico in '35 announcing the botanist's grudging acceptance of a commission from Santa Anna to study the chicle tree in the jungles of Yucatán. Terrell suggested to the professor that he journey to Mexico City and search among the government archives there, since it was likely that at least some traces of Edmund McGowan's remarkable collection still existed. He even offered to cover the professor's travel expenses, since he had his own curiosity about the matter. But the man turned him down—Mexico was known to be hazardous to travellers, with bandits at every turning in the road, and he had six children to support—and when his book came out there was nothing about Edmund McGowan in it.

Indeed, McGowan's entire botanical career, so far as the world knew, amounted only to the discovery of a single flower. Terrell had found it enclosed with the letter to his mother, an almost colorless dried specimen with a label attached giving its Latin name—*Chrysopsis marymottiae*. Not trusting the timid professor with it, Terrell had taken it himself to the man in charge of the botanical garden, who had studied it with a degree of excitement and then sent it on to a colleague in St. Louis who was compiling a new edition of a plant guide to the southern states. Two years later Terrell was sent a copy of the book as a courtesy, and in it was a plate showing the pale yellow aster that Edmund McGowan had named for his mother.

Four or five years after his mother's death Terrell had travelled to New York to meet with a group of investors who wanted to query the mayor of San Antonio about the prospects of opening a manufactory there for the production of horse collars and harnesses. These leather barons were a gregarious and hospitable group, and they put him and Hannah up at one of the city's finest hotels. He was having an early breakfast one day in the hotel dining room as Hannah slept in their suite when he noticed a one-legged old man sitting alone several tables over. The man was paunchy and disappointed-looking, and his thinning hair had been dyed black and pulled across from one side of his otherwise bald head to the other, so that it lay there glistening and lank. Terrell had never seen him in person, but had seen woodcuts and photographs and knew who he was right away. He watched him for a long time. The man was not eating, he was just sipping coffee and glaring impatiently at a newspaper.

Terrell walked over to him and said, "Excuse me, do you speak English?"

"I do, my friend," he replied, with a disarming smile, "though I wish I spoke it better."

"I was at the Alamo."

"In truth? Then please sit down and share breakfast with me."

Terrell had been in a restless and confronting mood, and Santa Anna's invitation caught him off guard. But they were civilized men in civilized surroundings, and so he sat down and fell into conversation with the old tyrant with unsettling ease. Santa Anna talked freely about the Alamo, and about the fighting spirit of the Texians within it, and how remarkable it was—something that could never have been predicted—that these men would grow to become not just heroes but veritable gods.

"You hate me, I think, my friend," Santa Anna said, with a curiously disarming shrug. "You are right to hate me, and I applaud you for it. In those days I was young and cruel and determined not to lose Texas at all costs. And yet I did lose it, and with it went half of Mexico. Now I am not so cruel. I am just an old philosopher drinking my coffee and reading my paper."

He caught Terrell looking at his leg. It was a hideous thing, a botched amputation with the bone sticking out a good two inches and swathed in cotton. Santa Anna told him how he had lost it in fighting the French invasion of Mexico. He had sprung back from his disgrace over the loss of Texas and driven the French from Vera Cruz, and his countrymen had been so joyful they had given his leg a state funeral. But then the villainous forces that had always been jealous of his success had deposed him and dug up the leg from the cenotaph where it was buried and dragged it through the streets. He had no idea where it was now. It was a terrible thing, he said, to still be alive on the earth and not know the whereabouts of all the pieces of your body.

He talked for the better part of the hour, forgetting about Terrell and the charged background the two of them shared, just viewing his presence as another excuse to air bitter complaints: the cruelties that had been inflicted upon him after his capture by the Texians, as opposed to the unfailingly courteous reception he received from President Jackson; his unfair exile in Havana; the rapacity of the United States as evidenced by its invasion of Mexico; the slaughter of thousands of innocent civilians by the so-called Texas Rangers; his renewed exile in Jamaica; his magnanimous gesture, when he rose to power once again, in refusing the title of emperor, and how even this had not appeased his enemies; more exile throughout the Caribbean; the relentless French, ensconced now in Mexico after all, and how he had come to New York to raise an army for one last great crusade, one last grito, to dislodge them.

"But what do I find?" he said. "I find that the emperor of Mexico must sit here in this dining room for an hour waiting on a man I do not even know, and do not now think I care to know."

The man came, with elaborate apologies: a secretary who had written down the wrong hotel, a hopeless traffic tangle as he was racing here after the mistake was discovered. Santa Anna pretended not to be outraged. He introduced the man to Terrell. His name was Adams.

"I'm sorry," Santa Anna said. "Your name again was?"

"Terrell Mott."

He left them and went back to his table. His eggs were
cold. His body was shaking with some emotion he could
not locate. He asked the waiter for more coffee and listened
from across the room to the talk between Santa Anna and
Mr. Adams. In its earnest entrepreneurial timbre it was not
unlike the talk between himself and the horse collar ty-
coons. And in fact, as Terrell eavesdropped with more care,
he realized they were talking not about a crusade to drive
the French out of Mexico, but about the manufacture of
chewing gum.

"WHAT IS IT you are looking for?" Parthenia asked as
Terrell withdrew another layer of papers and documents
and set them on the floor. He did not reply; he was old
enough that he no longer needed to respond to pestering
questions. He came to the filed-down knife that the old
metatero had given him at Forty-Mile Hole, and then the
madstone he had carried in his pocket throughout the early
part of his life, and had only put away after Hannah died,
and after their only daughter—Parthenia's mother—had
perished one summer with tetanus. Finally he pulled out a
cobwebby bundle of old newspapers lying on the bottom of
the chest. He unwrapped the newspapers to reveal an old
canvas haversack that was as stiff and brittle as Egyptian
papyrus.

He pried open the mouth of the haversack and withdrew
the jaguar shooting pouch that had been resting within it
since April 21, 1836.

"What is that, Opa?" Parthenia asked.

"It's something I stole off a dead Mexican soldier and
now wish I hadn't."

He stood up out of the cow-horn chair and walked over
to the fireplace. If he were honest with himself he would

have to admit he was light-headed and queasy from that fall on the reviewing stand, and he suspected that if he bothered to look tonight he would find a sizable bruise on his shoulder blade, as well as the cut behind his ear.

He stuffed the pouch with the newspaper that had surrounded the haversack and set it in the fireplace.

"What are you doing?"

"I'm gonna burn the son of a bitch."

He struck a match to the brittle newspaper and it flared up instantly, and then ignited the ancient residue of gunpowder in the jaguar pouch, so that he heard a sound that he remembered from long ago, the sound of a misfire in the pan. He told Parthenia to bring him more newspaper, and he wadded up the sheets and with his good hand stuffed them inside the pouch with a poker, and when the fire grew hot enough he put some kindling wood on top. The pouch burned like the flesh it was. He could smell the singed fur and within the flames the black splotches and the faded yellowish fur pulsed queasily in his sight. Yellow and black, the cholera colors, the colors of insatiable death.

PARTHENIA WAS sufficiently outdone with him to finally leave, though not before she had moved the cedar chest back up into the attic, where it would be safe from any more of his rampages. Terrell had Javier drive her home in the motor, and when she was gone he walked out onto the porch with a plate of Hortensia's denatured machacado.

He ate his dinner in an old man's contemplative silence and set the plate down next to his chair. Though it was April, and just barely evening, he felt a chill and called out to Hortensia to bring him his sweater. Warblers were streaming through the trees, and above the rooftops of the houses the sky still held a pale wash of blue. Hundreds of great white birds were flying there, coasting in their ragged squadrons from one dying thermal to the next. Pelicans, he realized, late in their summer migrations from the southern seacoasts to the shores of the Great Salt Lake.

He watched the pelicans with a sudden keen intensity, thinking of them as emissaries, though whether they were creatures from the world to come or from the world already past he could not discern. Indeed, he felt suspended now between those two realms, between life and death, and blessedly at home. But like all blessed moments, this one passed swiftly, and he found himself on the porch again, an ancient man recalling a primeval Texas, his mind vibrant with a thousand things—like the sight of those flowers to-day falling across the face of the Alamo—that were not in his power to forget.

AUTHOR'S NOTE

READERS FAMILIAR with the better-known narrative histories of the Alamo and the Texas Revolution—Lon Tinkle's *13 Days to Glory,* Walter Lord's *A Time to Stand,* Jeff Long's *Duel of Eagles,* Stephen L. Hardin's *Texian Iliad*—many find themselves surprised by some of the details in this book and assume that they are errors of fact or simply the careless filigree of a novelist's imagination. None of the above books, for instance, contains an account of David Crockett leaving the Alamo late in the siege to meet up with reinforcements and guide them back to the fort. But in the last few years, Thomas Ricks Lindley, the most dogged and enterprising of Alamo historians, has made a convincing case in the pages of the *Alamo Journal* that such an incident did occur, and that as a result the number of defenders should be amended from the traditional 183 or so to upwards of 250. And it was not until William C. Davis, researching his important book *Three Roads to the Alamo,* came across the battle report of General Ramírez y Sesma in the Mexican Military Archives that it became clear that in the final stages of the battle many Alamo defenders abandoned the overrun fort in a forlorn escape attempt.

These are only two examples among many. I mention them to emphasize that in the writing of this book I have not been whimsical with the facts. Historical novelists are not restricted to the truth, of course; generally speaking, they should probably be accorded as much factual leeway as they can command. But as a reader my own preference is for historical novels that are historically trustworthy, and when I began *The Gates of the Alamo* I made a pledge of absolute fidelity to the truth of the events.

That is a naïve pledge, though, as any historian will tell you. Historical truth is an elusive and subjective thing, and never more so than in the story of the Alamo, which is buried in so many layers of myth and counter-myth as to be nearly irretrievable. Nevertheless, I have done my best. During the years it took to research and write this book I developed what I consider to be an appropriately skeptical attitude toward much of the available source material—from William Zuber's patently fictional account of Travis drawing a line in the sand to the more problematical "diary" of the Mexican lieutenant José Enrique de la Peña. Lindley, Bill Groneman, and other authors believe strongly that the de la Peña manuscript—which recounts the surrender and subsequent execution of Crockett—is an out-and-out forgery. Others, championed by the indefatigable James E. Crisp, are equally convinced it is not. The debate over the authenticity of this famous manuscript is abstruse and sometimes peculiarly heated—it *matters* to people how Davy Crockett died—but in my own relatively dispassionate assessment I have come to the conclusion that de la Peña, forgery or not, is a document of dubious historical veracity. For me, it becomes less impressive with every reading, whereas certain other sources—Travis's letters from the Alamo, Ramírez y Sesma's report, Colonel Juan Almonte's daily field diary of the siege—only grow more convincing.

So the historical context in which my fictional characters are placed was constructed with some care. Edmund, Mary, Terrell, Blas, and Telesforo are all imaginary, though their backgrounds may include a stray fact or two from the biography of an actual personage. Many of the other characters—including Joe, Travis's slave—really existed, and are depicted as they seem to me to have been.

The list of people I am eager to thank for their crucial efforts in support of *The Gates of the Alamo* begins with Esther Newberg and John Sterling, both of whom believed in the book when it was no more than a notion, and extends to Ann Close, who edited the actual manuscript with a judicious and unerring instinct. In between are the following indispensable friends and colleagues: Elizabeth Crook, to whom I must have read every page of the manuscript over the phone, and whose clarity of judgment was unfailing; Jeff Long, who like Elizabeth is a fellow novelist of the Texas Revolution, and who was generous with shoptalk and tips on historical sources; Lawrence Wright, who championed this book at critical moments, and who, together with William Broyles Jr. and Gregory Curtis, during our regular Monday-morning breakfasts, finally shamed me into finishing it; and James Magnuson, another valued friend and trusted reader.

Stephen L. Hardin, the author of the classic *Texian Iliad,* patiently took me through the world of this novel again and again, until I finally began to perceive it on my own.

Kevin R. Young, a leading expert on the Mexican army of 1835–1836, not only helped me with Telesforo and Blas and the other Mexican characters, but was generous as well with his encyclopedic knowledge of all other aspects of the period, especially in terms of material detail.

Alan C. Huffines, whose recent book *Blood of Noble Men* I recommend as a comprehensive guide to the Alamo siege, shared his understanding of military tactics and the reality of combat.

Jesús F. de la Teja did his patient best to educate me on the complex political situation in Mexico during the period in which this book is set.

Patty Leslie Pasztor greatly amplified my understanding of historical botany and gave me a much-needed remedial course in the commonplace flora of Texas.

No one contributed more to *The Gates of the Alamo* than

Tom Lindley, who selflessly shared his groundbreaking research, his amazing recall of obscure historical data, and his own considerable talents as a storyteller to help me shape the novel and to rescue me from countless narrative dead ends.

I am grateful as well to Ricardo Ainslie, Peter Applebome, Daniel Barton, Don E. Carleton, Bill Chemerka, James E. Crisp, William C. Davis, Arthur Drooker, Victo Emanuel, Dan Flores, Jerry Goodale, David Hamrick, Pau Heath, Paul Hutton, Jack Jackson, Tim Lowry, Timothy M Matovina, Joe Musso, George Nelson, David Rickman David Riskind, Robert H. Thonhoff, Ron Tyler, Ton Wendt, Sherry Whitmore, Peg Wilson, and Gary Zaboly And as always to my wife, Sue Ellen, and to our children Marjorie, Dorothy, and Charlotte, all of whom have been hostages to this book for years, and are now lovingly released.